THE SOUND OF WAVES

'Kalki' R. Krishnamurthy (1899–1954) was an iconic writer, and a pioneer of modern Tamil literature and journalism. His induction into journalism was facilitated by his involvement with the freedom struggle. Beginning his career in the scholarly journal *Navasakthi* and the anti-liquor manifesto *Vimochanam*, he served as the editor for *Ananda Vikatan*, before launching *Kalki*, the eponymous nationalist weekly. A prolific writer, along with novels and short stories, he wrote political essays, reformist propaganda, travelogues, music and dance critiques, film reviews, biographies, scathing satire, humorous essays, songs, poems, a film script or two, and translations, including Mahatma Gandhi's *The Story of My Experiments with Truth*.

Revelling in controversial debates on political, aesthetic and ideological issues, Kalki used his writing talent to crusade for several causes. He had chosen the name of Lord Vishnu's final avatar for the destruction of the world as his pseudonym because he was resolved to work towards a new and better world. Today, Kalki is best known for his historical fiction, a genre in which he remains unsurpassed. He is the author of *Sivagamiyin Sapatham*, *Parthiban Kanavu* and the mammoth *Ponniyin Selvan*. *Alai Osai*, which the author deemed his best work, documents the turbulent decades of the freedom struggle between 1934–49, seen through the eyes of ordinary people who were inevitably affected by the socio-political changes.

Gowri Ramnarayan is the inhouse playwright and artistic director of JustUs Repertory. Formerly deputy editor, *The Hindu* and vocal accompanist to renowned Carnatic musician M.S. Subbulakshmi, Ramnarayan has authored original plays, children's books, and a biography of M.S. Subbulakshmi. She has translated the plays of Marathi playwright Vijay Tendulkar, the short stories and biography of Tamil writer 'Kalki' R. Krishnamurthy, and served on the International Federation of Film Critics (FIPRESCI) jury in international film festivals. Currently, she is chairperson, Rukmini Devi Arundale Trust, a senior associate editor for *Sruti Magazine*, adjunct faculty at the Asian College of Journalism, and a freelance journalist.

MISSION STATEMENT

This is an initiative of the Tamil Nadu Textbook and Educational Services Corporation (TNTB & ESC) under the aegis of one of the announcements for the year 2021–22, by Honourable Minister for School Education Thiru. Anbil Mahesh Poyyamozhi to identify and translate into English, Tamil literary works, that they might enhance the reach of Tamil antiquity, tradition and contemporaneity and enrich World literature and to also translate significant literary voices from other Dravidian languages into Tamil. Both ventures are to be undertaken as either independent or joint publications with collaborating publishers.

Members, Academic Advising Committee (Translation)

Dr R. Balakrishnan, IAS, Researcher and Writer
Thiru. S. Ramakrishnan, Writer
Thiru. S. Madasamy, Educationist

Project Execution Team

Thiru. Dindigul I. Leoni, Chairperson, TNTB & ESC
Tmt. R. Gajalakshmi, IAS, Managing Director, TNTB & ESC
Dr S. Kannappan, Member Secretary, TNTB & ESC
Thiru. R. Dhayalan, Financial Advisor, TNTB & ESC
Dr T.S. Saravanan, Joint Director (Translation), TNTB & ESC
Thiru. P.A. Arumugam, Deputy Director (Publications), TNTB & ESC
Dr P. Saravanan, Assistant Director (Publications), TNTB & ESC
Thiru. M. Appanasamy, Consultant, TNTB & ESC
Tmt. Mini Krishnan, Co-ordinating Editor, TNTB & ESC

THE SOUND OF WAVES

Originally published in Tamil as *Alai Osai*

'KALKI' R. KRISHNAMURTHY

TRANSLATED BY
GOWRI RAMNARAYAN

hachette INDIA

TAMIL NADU TEXTBOOK AND EDUCATIONAL SERVICES CORPORATION
LEARN THOROUGHLY

First published in 2022 by Hachette India
(Registered name: Hachette Book Publishing India Pvt. Ltd)
An Hachette UK company
www.hachetteindia.com

SRD

Certain place names, such as Bombay, Calcutta and Madras, among others, as well as the names of certain provinces and presidencies have been used to retain the historicity of the text.

Subsequent edition/reprint specifications may be subject to change, including but not limited to title, subtitle cover or inside finishes, paper, text colour and/or colour sections.

ISBN 978-93-93701-35-0 (Paperback)
ISBN 978-93-93701-58-9 (Limited edition hardback)

Hachette Book Publishing India Pvt. Ltd
4th & 5th Floors, Corporate Centre,
Plot No. 94, Sector 44, Gurugram 122003, India

Typeset in Dante MT Std 10.5/13
by R. Ajith Kumar, New Delhi

Printed and bound in India
by Manipal Technologies Limited, Manipal

MIX
Paper | Supporting responsible forestry
FSC™ C043100
www.fsc.org

CONTENTS

TRANSLATOR'S NOTE

'Why do you spend so much time translating others?' I asked Alastair Reid, whose writings were as brilliant as his translations of Pablo Neruda and Jorge Luis Borges. Reid laughed. 'Would you say they are entirely different pursuits? Neruda had once told me, *"Don't translate my poems, Alastair! Make them better!"* He knew, as I do, that translation is a process of making something your own.'

I was to understand what he meant only during the pandemic in 2020. That year, through the first lockdown, I read aloud Kalki R. Krishnamurthy's *Alai Osai*, published in 1948 (literally, the sound of the waves) in daily Zoom sessions with my daughter Akhila Ramnarayan and sister Rukmini Ramachandran. After each session, we found ourselves discussing not only the novel's literary features, but also arguing about politics, philosophy, ethics, the problems of society, colonialism, gender, protest movements, cultural revisionism and ideas that shape the world. We visited the historical landmarks of the Indian independence movement to which the novel took us; we witnessed extranational events that continue to impact us globally today. With *satyagraha* and *ahimsa* forming the axis of the novel, Kalki's prose compelled us to ponder the values that Mohandas Karamchand Gandhi had resurrected as the force of truth and non-violence.

We asked ourselves, do these Gandhian principles have any meaning now, not as political weapons, but as values in personal and public life? Can violence really be overcome by non-violence? Can compassion conquer aggression? Can faith in peace and truth put an end to injustice and persecution? Most of all, we thought about what the word freedom means – in differing times, places, contexts.

Surely, 'Kalki' R. Krishnamurthy (1899–1954) wanted his novel to ignite such debates. Surely, the same questions ricocheted in his mind when he wrote it.

Kalki had planned to write *Alai Osai* against the panoramic backdrop of India's struggle for independence, a paean to the glory of the Mahatma. It was to end with the waves of freedom resounding in triumphant bliss. But Partition brought with it shrieks of terror and wails of anguish. On 30 January 1948, free India reeled under the shock and grief of Gandhi's assassination. Days later, Kalki's obituary in his eponymous magazine overflowed with the angst, despair and fear for the future that he felt along with his countrymen everywhere. Through all that despondency, he did see a glimmer of hope, too.

> O eyes! Shed tears! Shed tears until not a single drop remains. You will never see the Mahatma's face, full of grace and compassion, ever again! You will never see the copper glow of his form!
>
> O heart! Why do you tremble? Why do you ache? Have you forgotten that there is no death for the soul? If there is no death for the soul, can the Mahatma die?
>
> O hands! Why do you tremble? A thousand times have you inscribed his name! Why do you falter now? Why do you shudder…?
>
> Truth! Are you dead? Dharma! Have you perished? God! Where are you? Are you watching everything as a mere witness…?
>
> We inflicted unbearable pain on his noble heart. We watched as he fasted for our wrongdoings. Finally, we continue to live on even after learning that he slumped to the ground, shot dead by a savage demon…
>
> After the loss of the Mahatma, our life is plunged into a miasma of darkness. And yet, it is not as if there is no light to show the way. The Mahatma has left us an inextinguishable light, the immortal light of truth, to be sustained and fuelled by *ahimsa* and *tyaga*, non-violence and sacrifice. Let us venerate that light of truth. Let us ensure that whirlwinds and storms do not extinguish it.

In March 1948, as Kalki began to write the initial chapters of *Alai Osai* to be serialized in *Kalki* magazine, he must have known that with all the *himsa* the nation had witnessed, the novel could not celebrate the unmitigated triumph of *ahimsa*.

The act of writing became a scrutiny of both actions and the trends of thought during the crucial period when history was being rewritten in the subcontinent. It is as if Kalki directed a searchlight on the human mind through the novel in order to reveal the good and bad, villainy and saintliness, courage and cowardice, hypocrisy and integrity, blindness and foresight. He wrote, too, of temptations and snares, faults venial and unforgivable, disasters natural and manmade, passions channelled and unbridled, the lessons of history learnt and ignored. He claims that it was certainly him who started the novel, but his characters soon took over and began to tell their own stories.

The storyline follows the fortunes of Sita, raised in a poor Tamil family in Bombay, married to an arrogant 'hero' holding an enviable government job in Delhi, an enthusiastic supporter of British rule in India. In contrast, Surya, Sita's cousin and well-wisher, remains a doughty revolutionary and radical reformist, committed to socialism, championing freedom for the nation and equal rights for every citizen.

The Sound of Waves roams through a wide geographical terrain. From rural Tamil Nadu, it traverses Madras, Bombay, Karachi, Delhi, Agra, Lahore, Panipat, Haripura, the fictional southern town Devapattinam, and a royal state in Rajasthan designated as Rajnipur. Kalki had travelled to most of these places himself, first as a young volunteer in the national sessions of the Congress, then as a journalist covering political events.

After writing the initial chapters, he extended his trip to the capital to see his life-long mentor C. Rajagopalachari (Rajaji) installed as the governor-general of free India, to include scouting out the novel's locations in Old and New Delhi, accompanied by magazine illustrator Chandira, and photographer Ellis R. Dungan (an American director of Tamil/Telugu films in the 1940s). He went to refugee camps in Panipat and Kurukshetra and heard first-hand accounts of genocides. Earlier, he had toured through the areas affected by the 1946 communal riots in Calcutta. These *live* experiences gave his novel a national sweep and historic dimensions.

Other happenings in his personal life, too, left their mark on the writer. Once, as a child, Krishnamurthy got nearly drowned in the village pond. His biographer 'Sunda' (M.R.M. Sundaram) suggests that this ordeal might have made the image of getting submerged under the waves a recurrent motif in Kalki's fiction. *Alai Osai* is dominated by the visual, aural and tactile image of the billowing waves. Noting how it becomes an asphyxiating experience for the reader, writer/critic Ki. Va. Jagannathan cites the paragraph where Sita sinks into the River Chenab as one of the most powerful passages in modern Tamil fiction.

By the time Kalki started writing *Alai Osai*, he had become a cult figure in the Tamil realm as journalist, political analyst, social reformist, magazine editor, critic of the arts, custodian of culture, proponent of Tamil music, commentator on current affairs, and ace fictionist. He had even penned a film script and a few poems. A fellow journalist called him 'a film star among writers'. He had written the first historical novel in Tamil, a genre in which he remains unsurpassed. *Parthiban Kanavu* (serialized 1941–43) allegorizes the thirst for freedom in a Chola prince. *Sivagamiyin Sapatham* (1944–46) recreates the glorious era of the Pallavas with their magnificent traditions of art, culture and literary achievements, which were brought to bear on contemporary Tamil self-fashioning. This process was to gain greater power with *Ponniyin Selvan* (1950–54), which immediately followed *Alai Osai* (1948). This mammoth saga of the imperial Cholas was to break records as the single most-read Tamil work of fiction, then and now. By the time it appeared, the Audit Bureau of Circulations had certified that each *Kalki* issue had a print order of 71,366. In the 1950s, *Kalki*'s circulation was higher than that of any newspaper or magazine in any language in India.

In every town and village across the state, on the day the weekly issue of *Kalki* arrived, readers queued at railway stations, bus stops and newsstands, to grab their copies. To avoid tussles among family members, some households subscribed to two issues, in others the whole family gathered to hear the chapters read aloud.

Kalki was not only a prolific writer, but also a sought-after public speaker. He was a proponent of social reforms who ran political and cultural campaigns through speech and writing. He helped organize literary events and poetry festivals, and promoted fundraising for multiple causes. He masterminded mega projects like the building of memorials to Subramania Bharati in the poet's native town, and to Gandhi in Madras.

Kalki's career began when he quit school in response to Gandhi's non-cooperation movement, enlisting in the freedom struggle as a writer of pamphlets for the Congress party. His training in journalism was at *Navasakthi*, Madras, edited by Tamil scholar, trade unionist and independence activist T.V. Kalyanasundara Mudaliar. Further honing came from Rajaji when Kalki assisted his leader in editing and publishing the anti-liquor magazine *Vimochanam*. When Rajaji and other Congress leaders were imprisoned by the British Raj, Kalki went underground to write and distribute subversive tracts. He was also to be charged with sedition and jailed multiple times.

It was when he joined the magazine *Ananda Vikatan* that Kalki came into his own as editor and writer. His political writings provoked strong responses, and his art critiques launched debates. He revelled in polemical disputes with political adversaries and fellow scribes who attacked him. In no time at all, he found himself turning into a beloved author for thousands of readers.

Kalki used his trademark humour – ranging from saucy slapstick to biting satire – to deadly effect in responding to the antagonism engendered by his success. But he did not forget the French philosopher Voltaire's injunction, a favourite, 'I may not agree with what you have to say, but I will defend to the death your right to say it.' He bore no malice or rancour. He was also quick to praise merits in his opponents. In his obituary on Kalki, Dravidian Party leader C.N. Annadurai noted, 'Many had been vexed and angered by the renaissance brought into the field of writing by our movement. But Kalki welcomed it. He never hesitated to applaud the good qualities in his opponents, nor was he afraid to praise them!' Another declared, 'Kalki could appreciate the fragrance of a flower even when it bloomed in his adversary's garden.'

As in the writings of many of his contemporaries, Kalki's essays burned with nationalistic fervour and reformist zeal. A believer in gender equality, he denounced child marriage and campaigned for women's education and widow remarriage, often through the medium of his memorable stories. His women were not always victims. They could be strong, sagacious, possessing keen intellects. They could be free-spirited, dauntless, insisting on their rights in a patriarchal world. In *Sarathaiyin Thanthiram*, his first book of short fiction, a woman uses her wits to solve a tricky problem. In *Ponniyin Selvan,* young Princess Kundavai is deemed the wisest of all. In the controversial novel *Tyagabhumi*, when her father urges Savitri (named after the ideal wife of Hindu legends) to sacrifice her pride and return to her husband, the daughter says, 'I will make any sacrifice for freedom, but not for slavery.' Such a statement could not but provoke indignant protests in the 1930s.

He wrote under no fewer than thirteen pen names, in diverse genres, all progressing towards a single goal. 'Kalki', his best-known pseudonym, makes that purpose crystal clear. A Sri Lankan newspaper quoted him explaining his choice of this apocalyptic figure.

> It is natural for every young writer to believe that he will banish old epochs and create a new epoch. Imagining myself to be a mighty warrior ushering in a new age, I named myself after Lord Vishnu's tenth avatar that heralds a new yuga… (impelled by) the urge to express new ideas, launch readers into new directions, and shape a new age.

Kalki realized that helping overcome the mental stupor engendered by colonization was the first step in creating that new age. Every word he wrote as crusader, reformist, analyst, or fictionist, sought to promote self-confidence and cultural pride in his compatriots, replacing self-distrust and the sense of inferiority. When a critique in 1933 accused him of aiming at propaganda instead of literary worth, Kalki responded by parodying a purple passage about the beauties of spring, somehow turning it into an exhortation to wear khadi in all seasons. He concluded, 'Expect writings of lasting literary value from the hundreds and thousands of Tamil writers who will appear hereafter. Let me be what I am, a propagandist!'

Many works of Kalki have stood the test of time. The historical novel *Sivagamiyin Sapatham* highlights the renaissance of the arts that accompanied the rise of Indian nationalism. But it also underscores how religion can be a manipulative tool in the hands of the state, while championing peaceful co-existence among the followers of different faiths as vital for prosperity. He dwells on how civilian lives as well as art, learning, ethics and culture become the casualties of war.

In his epilogue to *Ponniyin Selvan*, Kalki unequivocally declares that his mammoth five-volume saga reaches its climax where Prince Arulmozhi rejects the throne offered to him and crowns his uncle because he recognizes his claim to kingship as greater than his own. This is the author's exaltation of *satya* (truth), *dharma* (righteousness) and *tyaga* (sacrifice) as the highest human values. However, his legion of readers through generations have rejoiced far more in the swashbuckling adventures and convoluted political machinations foregrounding the novel, not to mention the grandeur of their Tamil heritage that it glorifies.

Kalki remained steeped in Tamil culture, devoted to the Tamil language, and proud of his Tamil identity. But he was a stranger to provincialism. His outlook had a global perspective. This inclusive vision drives *The Sound of Waves*.

Every writer is influenced by other writers. We know that while Walter Scott and Alexandre Dumas triggered his taking up historical fiction, the writers who stirred his soul were the bard Kamban, bhakti songsters, mystic poets, Rabindranath Tagore and Subramania Bharati. *The Sound of Waves* also discloses that Kalki knew his Karl Marx. Utterly condemning violence as a Gandhian, Kalki shapes the character Surya with empathy for the radical revolutionaries of the Socialist Party. As the novel progresses, we also see why Victor Hugo and Leo Tolstoy were so dear to the author. He was won over by their humanitarian vision.

Like all literary works worth their salt, *Alai Osai* brings different experiences to the reader at different times. As an adolescent, I saw it as the story of my parents' generation, moving from village to town, expanding their horizon through education, progressing with reform and modernization. Later, I saw it as a major literary document recording a highly significant time in India's history through the lives of ordinary people. When I became a journalist, I recognized that *Alai Osai* had absorbed a news reporter's documentary techniques in a work of fiction. Now I see how it foreshadowed things to come. It anticipates some of the realities I witness today. I suppose I took on the time-consuming task of translating this novel because I believe that this novel has a resonance beyond the Tamil realm.

Not for nothing did A.K. Ramanujan say that 'translation is repossession'. During the 'Covid years', I was lucky enough to translate Kalki's Tamil biography *Ponniyin Pudalvar* by M.R.M. Sundaram, as *Kalki Krishnamurthy: His Life and Times,* which maps the socio-political, reformist-renaissance movements in India during the first half of the twentieth century, of which Kalki had been witness, participant and documenter. Then, I translated *Alai Osai*, where Kalki himself chronicles the same era through fiction. A work that the author believed to be the 'best offering he could make with pride and humility, to the people of his land.'

I am at an advantage when it comes to translating Kalki's works for a simple reason – I am at home in Kalki's world, and with his words. As his granddaughter, I grew up reading his fiction and non-fiction in the bound volumes of *Kalki* magazine from its first issue. I have sung his songs. In my avatar as a dramatist, I have written and directed two plays based on his work.

Theatrical adaptation brings its own challenges, as, equally, has translation. Kalki's style has been branded as *Kalkitamizh*. It has zest, verve, lilt, pace. It thrives on images – visual, aural, olfactory, even tactile. He uses synaesthesia all the time. Onomatopoetic phrases streak past with carefree abandon. Allusive lines from writers past and present, from Sangam poetry to Subramania Bharati, twinkle in and out, adding context, texture, and charm. Humour brightens understanding. And yet, the writing flows on, with no stops, no breaks!

Kalki was churning out so much every week, and on such diverse subjects, that the handwritten pages were veritably rushed to the press before the ink dried on them, leaving scarcely any time for revision or deliberate craft. What an adventure to try to capture that spontaneity in English!

We know that the cultural milieu of any region is so wedded to its language that it is always difficult to transpose it into another language, especially into the Anglo-Saxon tongue (ironically, the language of the very colonizer against whom the novel militates) which registers a different temperature altogether.

With Kalki, the real problem is to convey the import of his descriptions of nature and landscape, and other external locations and settings. Every descriptive detail has its own resonance, adding nuances in the situations, characters, actions and states of mind. I had to 'shrink' some of them in translation. Elsewhere too, I have abridged passages which glide along in the Indian tongue, but turn redundant in English.

In boyhood, Kalki regularly performed *harikatha*, a form of storytelling with songs and a little dancing in between. This oral tradition informs his writing style. Without being overtly colloquial, it carries the ease, chattiness, digressions and even the repetitions of raconteuring, stopping now and then to address the reader directly. Like a friend talking as he strolls with you, arm around your shoulder and, as Rajaji put it, 'never looking back'. As a translator, I found this tone extremely challenging.

Kalki, too, had faced the challenges of translation with his first published book *Sathya Sothanai*, Mahatma Gandhi's *The Story of My Experiments with Truth*. A newcomer to writing then, he must have crafted his own methods to translate the serialized chapters, working in the same dusty library where he had located them in the issues of *Young India*.

Like Kalki, I had to find my own tools for this new job. My long years in journalism helped me. Writing for an English daily meant that I had to translate much of my source material from the vernacular – oral or written, in first person or third. A Hindustani musician spoke in Urdu, a forest guard in Hindi, a Madurai historian in Tamil, an actor from Trichur in Malayalam. Interviewees from many regions communicated in a language in which English played a minimal role. In translating *The Sound of Waves,* I decided to go with my instinct, relying on careful reading to find my way during the long trek.

Alai Osai follows the old Indian literary tradition of ending on an auspicious note with overt optimism. But Kalki could not shut out the nightmares that freedom brought, nor the echo of the gunshot ending the life of the man who represented the values and paradoxes underpinning that newly won freedom.

He had not read Faiz Ahmad Faiz, but Kalki surely knew what the poet across the border had seen on 15 August 1947:

These tarnished rays, this night-smudged light –
This is not that Dawn for which, ravished with freedom,
we had set out in sheer longing,
so sure that somewhere in its desert the sky harboured
a final haven for the stars, and we would find it.

He also knew that the struggle to maintain freedom is as difficult as the struggle to attain freedom. In the most passionate expression of his dreams and hopes for independent India, Kalki transmutes *The Sound of Waves* into the rallying cry of *satyagraha*, urging us to strive ceaselessly, and with conviction, to better ourselves, the nation, and the world.

PART ONE

EARTHQUAKE

1

THE POST OFFICE

A veritable forest of banyan trees had spread on both sides of the road. It was a dense tangle of aerial roots and branches. As with any attempt to find the supreme being, it was impossible to discover where the road began and where it ended.

The post office of Rajampettai village stood at the corner where the road running from east to west turned towards the north. The door was locked. The postbox, hanging from an iron chain on the pillar, looked as forlorn as an abandoned orphan.

A little ahead, a bullock cart rolled by in slow motion, creaking and swaying to an unhurried rhythm, the cartman's cries goading the animals on.

Facing the post office on the other side of the road was a mithai kadai, with no one in sight outside its precincts. However, from within came sounds of sizzling and sputtering. Along with the aroma of sauteed onions, they announced that the stall keeper was frying masal vadai.

Nesting without a care on the banyan trees were birds who screeched merrily.

There! The tap-tap of footwear announces the arrival of Mr K.P. Bangaru Naidu BPM. Don't miss the 'BPM'! It stands for 'Branch Post Master'!

A village postmaster may earn a small salary but he wields considerable authority, while his official responsibilities are even greater. 'The District Collector or His Excellency the Governor himself has no power inside this post office!' Naidu garu proudly declared. 'Even if the governor asks me to hand over to him a letter addressed to someone else, I have the authority to say *NO*!'

Here he comes, Postmaster Bangaru Naidu. He inserts the key into the lock. The door opens at once.

Bangaru Naidu enters his kingdom. As soon as he crosses the threshold, he stands transfixed, unable to take a single step forward.

Seated inside, Postman Balakrishnan is nonchalantly sorting the mail.

Seeing the postmaster frozen in astonishment, Balakrishnan asks, 'Sir! Why are you staring at me? Do I look like a ghost…?'

'You… you… how… how... how did you get in?' Bangaru Naidu stuttered.

'Witchcraft, sir! For a few years I was a disciple of the great sorcerer Pitambara Iyer. I can glide through walls in the blink of an eye.'

'Tell me the truth, boy! Don't play silly games.'

'Play, sir? Am I a little child to be playing games?'

'Tell me how you got into the post office through the locked door?'

'Was the door locked? Did you check?'

'Of course! I unlocked it just now, with this key!'

'You may have unlocked the lock but did you open the door?'

'Tambi! To unlock the door is to open the door. Why do you speak in riddles?'

'No, sir! Not at all. Maybe you were in a jolly mood last evening. You turned the key in the lock all right but without bolting the latch.'

The postmaster looked up at the ceiling and spoke with folded hands, 'Balakrishna! God has saved us! What a misfortune it would have been if a burglar had got in as you did?'

'What *misfortune?* It would have been the poor burglar's misfortune. What do we have here to attract burglars? Never mind sir, hand me the key to the post box.'

Balakrishnan took the key, opened the post box, brought the mail in, and started postmarking the postage stamps affixed to them.

The postmaster, who was counting the postage stamps that were stored in a little tin box, looked up suddenly and asked, 'Balakrishna, did you change the date?'

Balakrishnan stopped punching to ask, 'What did you say, sir?'

'Did you change the date on the seal?'

'Isn't today the fifteenth?'

'Sixteenth, my boy, sixteenth!'

'Please look at the wall in front of you.'

Balakrishnan pointed to a calendar hanging on the wall. The date it showed was 15 January 1933.

'Oh my God! Have you marked the year too, according to this calendar?'

'Shouldn't I follow the year and month shown on the calendar?'

'Good God! This is last year's calendar. Date and year are both wrong!'

Bangaru Naidu got up and changed the date and the year on the calendar. Now it showed 16 January 1934.

A cart with a covered top, drawn by two stout bullocks, went briskly past.

'Pattamaniam Kitta Iyer sir,' said Balakrishnan.

'Well, it is 16 January after all. Time for the revenue collector to start his rounds,' said Bangaru Naidu.

'Sir? When is Kitta Iyer's daughter getting married? Do you know?'

'Balakrishna! Why should you worry about that?'

'I do worry. If that child gets married, she will go off to her husband's house.'

'That is none of your business.'

'She is the lone visitor to this sleepy little post office, bringing in a bit of life. If Lalita goes to her husband's house, we won't even get a crow to visit us. You and I will have to sit facing each other and swat flies.' Balakrishnan said and added, 'When I worked in the Devapattinam post office, at least a hundred money orders poured in before the seventh of every month.'

'For you?'

'Me? Money orders are meant for those born lucky!'

'How does it help you if others receive money orders?'

'For every money order disbursed, I earned a commission of an eighth of a rupee, which makes it a hundred times that, or half of 25 rupees for every hundred money orders.'

'Why, you are a Maths wizard!'

'I don't get even a fraction of that in this cursed place.'

'Stop it now! Get on with your work. Balakrishna, see, Thangavelu is here.'

Runner Thangavelu arrived at the entrance of the post office, shaking his spear, and making the bells tinkle.

2

A MOTHER'S HEART

More than half the houses in the agraharam street of the brahmins in Rajampettai were in a dilapidated condition. Among those that were still intact, Kitta Iyer's house, with its twin living rooms, stood out in stately grandeur.

In the central hall with its brick and cement flooring, sat Sarasvati Ammal, braiding her daughter, Lalita's hair. The braid was almost done when the distant sounds of runner Thangavelu's bells could be heard in the house.

'Amma! How long will you take to braid my hair? Hurry!'

'What's the hurry? You want to run to the post office in this blazing heat! If there is any mail, Balakrishnan will deliver it right here!' With these words, Sarasvati Ammal almost finished the braid. Lalita sprang up, snatching the braid just as its ends were being tied.

'I will do it, Amma,' she said and started running out.

'Lalita, *Lalita*! Come back at once. If you dare to run out now… I'll see how you get back into the house when you return!'

Kitta Iyer heard Sarasvati Ammal shouting as he stepped into the house.

Seeing her father, the young girl hesitated and stopped. Her face registered both shyness and the trustful confidence of someone who is indulged.

Sarasvati Ammal stood up when she saw her husband. Kitta Iyer asked sternly, 'Sarasu, why are you shouting? Don't you have anything to do other than scolding your daughter?'

'Yes! My only job is to scold your darling daughter. You have spoilt her so much that...'

'Yes! I have spoilt her thoroughly and turned her into an idiot. Never mind. Be satisfied that she was brilliant when you gave birth to her. Now what has Lalita done?'

'She insists on running to the post office. Will the mail remain undelivered if she doesn't go? Here we are in the month of Tai. We must get the child married somehow.'

'Enough! Stop! What is the connection between this and her marriage?'

'Will anyone send a girl who is old enough to get married out and alone?'

'Why not? Will the earth start quaking if we do? The post office is not even two furlongs away. The days of locking up girls inside the house are over. Lalita, go and if there's any mail for me, bring it back as well.'

With a single, sidelong glance at her mother, Lalita was off, running like a doe.

'I have seen a lot of things in my time. But never have I seen anyone spoiling a girl to bits like this. The Bombay trip has totally transformed father and daughter. Who knows where it will all end?' Sarasvati Ammal muttered.

'All's well that ends well. Just keep your mouth shut. You want a highly educated son-in-law! Shouldn't the girl be raised accordingly? If you keep her locked up inside the house...'

From the threshold came sounds of footsteps, and of someone clearing his throat. Sarasvati Ammal moved away and stood by the pillar.

The man who entered was Kitta Iyer's close friend and kinsman, Seemachu Iyer. Their conversation had its own distinct flavour.

'Oy!'

'Oy!'

'Oy! Do you know?'

'Oy! What do you mean?'

'This morning our cousin Kalyanasundaram came from the city. He brought a newspaper with him. Sensational news!'

'Sensational news?'

'An earthquake in Bihar.'

'What? What? What?'

'A stupendous earthquake! It is feared that there has been colossal destruction of life and property.'

'Seemachu, how amazing!'

'What's amazing?'

'Just five minutes ago, I was talking about an earthquake.'

'What did you say?'

'I was telling Sarasu, *will the earth start quaking if the child goes to the post office?* And here you are, with the news of an earthquake in Bihar.'

'How can a brahmin's word not come true? And you are no ordinary man. Yours is a lineage of vedic scholars. You know the *Atharva veda* backwards... Oy! It seems you are being called,' Seemachu Iyer said, as he noticed that Sarasvati Ammal, who had been partially hidden by the pillar, had now stepped forward, and was trying to attract Kitta Iyer's attention.

'Sarasu, come forward and say what you want to say openly! No need to shrink away from Seemachu.'

Sarasvati Ammal said anxiously, 'He mentioned an earthquake. The child has gone to the post office all by herself! Please go and bring her back at once. Or send someone to fetch her.'

3

LETTER FROM BOMBAY

Kitta Iyer wanted to introduce the city's lifestyle to the village. As an initial step he began to call his wife by name and talk to her unreservedly in the presence of other people.

Smiling at his wife's naivete in connecting Lalita's trip to the post office with the earthquake in Bihar, Kitta Iyer said, 'Sarasu! Don't make a fuss! How will an earthquake in Bihar affect us here?'

'How can you say that? How long will it take for the earthquake to reach us here?'

'Nonsense! There are one thousand five hundred miles between our village and Bihar. Don't panic.'

Seemachu Iyer tried to appease them. 'Oy! Don't you know that a mother's heart is obsessed with her child? Not hard-bitten like ours.'

'True! Absolutely true! No one in the world has ever given birth to a child. She produced one miraculously. She wants us to be scared to death of an earthquake in Bihar. See how important it is to educate women!'

'Oy! Shall we play a game after lunch?' Seemachu Iyer tried to change the subject.

'Certainly! Why don't you eat lunch here?' Kitta Iyer asked.

'No thank you. If I do… at home…' Seemachu Iyer said as he left.

Kitta Iyer went to the well in the backyard to bathe.

Sarasvati Ammal stood waiting on the threshold, hoping that young Lalita escapes from the Bihar earthquake and reaches home safely.

Runner Thangavelu had just dumped the big mailbag on the post master's table when Lalita entered the post office. The four-feet long, three-feet wide table was splotched with four thousand ink stains. It seemed as if it was the postmaster's habit to start writing only after testing his pen by splattering ink on the table.

Postman Balakrishnan asked runner Thangavelu, 'Why so late? Did you take a nap along the way?'

'Every single day you ask the same question. Try to run five miles every day and you will know!'

'Stop it! Kitta Iyer's child is here!' said Bangaru Naidu and buried himself in the notebook in his hands.

Lalita came in and panted, 'Any letter for me, postmaster?'

The postmaster looked up as if he had only then noticed her arrival, 'Oh, is it you, child? Take a seat. Let me break the seal, open the mailbag and check.'

'Oh sir! Haven't you opened it yet?'

'Not yet.'

'Open it, sir! Quickly!'

'What's the urgency, Amma?'

'I am expecting a letter from Bombay today.'

'From Bombay? Is that all? Is that so urgent? I thought perhaps it was a letter from Singapore!'

'Is your Singapore so great? In our Bombay…'

'Is your Bombay so great? In our Singapore…'

'Our Bombay has the Victoria Terminus.'

'Your Victoria Terminus is nothing compared to our Singapore railway station!'

'Our Bombay has houses eight storeys high!'

'Our Singapore has houses twenty-four storeys high!'

'Our Bombay has buses with two levels.'

'Our Singapore has rickshaws with two levels!'

'Our Bombay has tar roads smooth as silk.'

'Our Singapore has roads made of rubber!'

'Hmm… hmm… Bombay has my cousin, my athanga!'

'Ho! Singapore has my friend Aiyangar!'

'I cannot argue with you! Please open the mail bag!'

'See, it is open!' said the postmaster as he opened the bag and started looking at the addresses on each envelope. 'Child, here it is, your Bombay letter. But it is addressed to your father.'

'Give it to me, sir. Let me see, oh yes, it is for Appa. My uncle has written to him. Look again, Sir. There must be a letter for me.'

'Uh huh, yes, there's another. But this is also for your father.'

'I will hand it over to Appa. Please see if there is anything for me,' Lalita said in a voice full of disappointment.

Bangaru Naidu came to the last letter and handed it to Lalita saying, 'Here, it was hiding right at the bottom!'

Eagerly grasping the letter, Lalita skipped out, tore open the envelope outside the post office, took the letter out, and started reading.

Dadar, Bombay
14/1/1934

To my dear Lalita, dearer to me than my life, from your cousin Sita:

You must have received the letter I wrote last Sunday. I was so happy when I wrote it. I went on and on for four pages.

Amma saw me writing and asked, 'What do you have to say that takes four long pages?'

I replied, 'Amma, four pages are not enough. I am going to continue this next week like a serial story.'

Amma kissed my cheek and said, 'My darling! I hope you and Lalita remain close friends all your lives.' I was surprised to see tears in her eyes.

'Why Amma! Why are you crying?' I asked sadly.

'I have no friends in this world. I am so happy that you have found a good friend. That's all.'

'Amma, do people shed tears because they are happy?' I asked again.

'Sita! You read so many books. Haven't you heard of tears of joy?' she replied.

'Why are you so happy that Lalita and I are friends?' I asked with some curiosity.

'Well, Sita, who knows? If something happens to me, who is there for you? One day, Lalita's friendship may prove very useful to you.' I was puzzled by the way Amma spoke then. But maybe she had a premonition of the peril we were going to face.

Lalita, Amma came down with a fever the day after I wrote my last letter. She said, 'It's nothing, everything will be fine in two days.' On the third day Appa brought the doctor home. The doctor said it was typhoid. I felt a sharp sense of guilt when he said to Appa, 'She is so undernourished; how did you neglect her for so long?' I remembered how Amma fasted and starved for days without Appa taking any notice.

Lalita, Amma is extremely unwell. The doctor told Appa, 'She will survive only if God wills it.'

Lalita, will God have mercy? Or will he take Amma away and leave me an orphan?

Appa has written to my uncle asking him to come at once. Please tell him to do so. If uncle comes here perhaps Amma will recover.

I don't know if I will be writing to you next week. Whether I write or not, I will always be thinking of you.

Your dear friend,
Sita

Lalita was overcome as she read this letter in front of the post office. She began to sob and cry. Postmaster Bangaru Naidu, postman Balakrishnan and runner Thangavelu came running out.

'What? What is it, Amma?' they asked anxiously. Seeing the open letter in her hand they asked, 'Bad news?'

'Yes, my aunt in Bombay has fallen ill.'

'Why should you cry about that? So many people fall sick. Don't they get well again?' said the postmaster and added, 'Balakrishna! Take this child home.'

'Sure, sir. Come, Amma,' said Balakrishnan and got ready to escort her home.

4

TANTRUMS ON THE THRESHOLD

Kitta Iyer's wife stood at the threshold, waiting for Lalita. When her heels started hurting, she seated herself on the pyol in front of the house. If any man came walking down the street, she retired to the corridor beyond the doorway.

Finally, when she saw Lalita returning with tears in her eyes, escorted by the postman, she became so distraught that she ran to hug her. 'Oh, my child! What happened? See, I was right to feel scared. Balakrishna, why is the child crying? Did she stumble and fall?' she shrieked. In her anxiety she failed to note how a few men had come out of the neighbouring houses and stood watching them.

Balakrishnan explained, 'No, Amma! There was a letter from Bombay. The child read it and started crying.'

'Is that all? What does the letter say? In any case, why should you cry, Lalita?' Sarasvati Ammal asked.

When Lalita did not answer, Sarasvati Ammal became angry. 'Has anyone died? If you won't tell me I can see for myself,' she said and snatched the letter from Lalita's hands.

Kitta Iyer had just come into the living room after a leisurely bath near the well in the backyard. Hearing the commotion, he came out of the house.

Thinking that his wife was beating Lalita for having gone to the post office against her wishes, he said, 'Look, Sarasu! If you want to thrash the child, should you do so in public? Come in, lock the door, and thrash her to death.'

'I haven't beaten your child! She came crying from the post office. When she didn't answer my questions, I tried to take the letter and check for myself. And you accuse me of thrashing and killing her! You and your daughter may do what you like,' hollered Sarasvati Ammal and stomped into the house, sounding like a hailstorm in summer.

Paying no heed to his wife's rage Kitta Iyer said calmly, 'Balakrishna! What's the matter? Why is the child crying?'

Balakrishnan explained, took his leave, and went back to the post office. He had come prepared to enjoy coffee at Iyer's house. But the altercation made him leave at once.

As soon as he reached the post office Balakrishnan said, 'Sir! Kitta Iyer is such a mild-mannered man but what a shrew he has for a wife!'

'What are you saying? Kitta Iyer's wife is so self-effacing. You don't even notice her presence. I have been to their house many, many times. I've never even heard her voice,' said Naidu.

'That's your misfortune, sir,' said Balakrishnan. 'You should have seen her today. O my goodness! The demons Tataka and Surpanakha are nothing compared to her. On the whole, I guess getting along with women is a tough proposition.'

'Balakrishna, listen to me. You are a bachelor. That is why you don't understand this. Every woman has a Tataka and a Surpanakha within. In the same way the goddesses Lakshmi and Sarasvati, the virtuous Sita and Arundhati, are also a part of her being. A husband must invoke the woman he wants to see. If he calls for Surpanakha, Surpanakha will emerge. If he calls Sita, then Sita will appear. Don't get crazy ideas about not getting married. How else will you manage to get proper food?'

'So, it boils down to this. Marriage is all about getting someone to cook and serve meals. Well, if I do get married it will be a "l-o-vvve marriage,"' said Balakrishnan and began to whistle a popular film song.

Back in Kitta Iyer's house the father stroked his daughter lovingly and asked, 'Lalita! Why are you crying? What does the letter say, Amma?' Making an effort to control her sobs, Lalita gave him his letters and said, 'Sita says that Athai is extremely ill. There's a letter for you too.'

Kitta Iyer opened the first letter and began to read. Tears started flowing from his eyes. He went in and sat down on the easy chair.

Soon, Sarasvati Ammal said in a gentle voice, 'Please come and eat.'

Kitta Iyer remained silent.

'Why are you so upset? What does the letter say?' she asked.

'Rajam seems to be unwell,' he said.

'So? She will get well soon. Should you stop eating because she has fallen ill? Come, the children are ready to eat.'

'No, Sarasu. Let the children eat. I don't feel like eating now. Rajam is extremely ill. She has typhoid. She may not…'

'…she may not survive! Last year's letter had brought the same news. We went there and found nothing wrong. Looks like they enjoy making you waste 400–500 rupees!'

Kitta Iyer sprang up from the easy chair in anger. The other, unopened letter on his lap, slid to the floor.

5

KITTA IYER'S FAMILY

Kitta Iyer of Rajampettai was his father's only son. He inherited many acres of fertile nansei land, and the right to succeed to the post of munsif in the village. The land was so fecund that it could yield gold – if indeed gold was sown! But it grew what was far more precious – chamba rice, banana, betel leaf and sugarcane.

Both of his sisters got married when his father was alive. Therefore, he faced no great expenditure after becoming the head of the family. But since he spent money generously on charity, in assisting friends, and on his children's education, there was no augmentation of the family's property after his father's death. His daughter Lalita was getting older by the year. His wife Sarasvati Ammal was convinced that Lalita should have been married a year ago, and her remaining unmarried for another year would bring nothing short of a cataclysmic disaster upon the family.

The reason for Kitta Iyer's lack of interest in arranging Lalita's marriage the previous year was the family's trip to Bombay. Abhayam, Kitta Iyer's older sister, had married into an orthodox family in a village close by. But his younger sister lived in Bombay. When she was young, Rajam had been Kitta Iyer's favourite. There was no end to the pride and delight he had felt at her wedding. Repeatedly did he congratulate the bridegroom for being a lucky man. Almost immediately after the marriage, her husband Duraisami Iyer obtained a good job in the railways in Bombay. Rajam followed him.

It came to be known fairly soon that Rajam's wedded life was not quite so pleasant. The details remained blurred. Rajam, who had more than her share of self-respect, did not want to make her sorrows public. There could hardly be frequent comings and goings between Bombay and Rajampettai. In time all correspondence stopped. Now and then, Kitta Iyer would remember his sister and wonder wistfully about how she may be faring.

A year ago, he received a letter from Rajam. A moving letter. Rajam said that though she had borne her pain with fortitude, it had not gone away. Her health too was deteriorating day by day. She begged her brother to come and see her just once, and soon. She added, 'Please bring my sister-in-law and Lalita with you. Sita is eager to meet her cousin.'

Kitta Iyer was not keen on taking his wife to Bombay. But Sarasvati Ammal was in a completely different state of mind. Except for the pilgrimage to Tirupati to get her son's head tonsured, she had hardly travelled anywhere. Nor did she wish to do so. But now she was desperate to go to Bombay. She said to herself, 'If we remain stuck in these backwoods and not get around a bit, how can we find the right groom for Lalita?'

Finally, Kitta Iyer did go to Bombay with his wife, Lalita, and her younger brother Sundu.

In the new city, Lalita and Sundu were over the moon. Sita was just a year older than Lalita and the girls became soulmates. Gripping each other's hands, they vowed never to forget each other.

Sita was enormously proud to show off her city to her cousins. Whether zoo, museum, railway station, Tajmahal Hotel, eight storeyed houses, roof garden on Malabar Hill – Lalita would simply stand transfixed before each one of them. Sita scolded her repeatedly. 'Come on, move on! Don't be a dunce! Don't stare like a country bumpkin!' Sometimes she gave Lalita a push or dragged her along. Lalita remained tractable, she did not mind being bossed by Sita. After all, it was because of dear Sita that she was getting to see the sights of Bombay. Lalita was on a high throughout the Bombay visit. Never in her life had she been so happy.

Kitta Iyer realized that Rajam's life was full of disappointment and pain. The cause remained unclear. He saw that Duraisami rarely came home. Whenever he did, he spoke pleasantly enough and with respect. 'Duty' kept him away most nights.

Kitta Iyer tried to understand Rajam's difficulties. Lack of money was obvious. Rajam wore nothing round her neck except her mangalyam strung on a yellow thread.

Nor was Rajam bedridden as Kitta Iyer had expected. She moved around briskly.

When Kitta Iyer enquired about her health Rajam replied, 'There's nothing wrong with me Anna! I invited you because I wanted to see you all.'

Kitta Iyer was not deceived. He asked more and more questions to arrive at the truth. 'Rajam, does your husband have any bad habits? Drink maybe…?'

'Drink, horse race, everything…?', she said and began to weep. Kitta Iyer consoled her, and little by little, he learnt the details. From what Rajam said Kitta Iyer guessed that Duraisami was involved not only in gambling but with other women as well. A sense of decorum made him desist from prodding his sister for more information.

Seeing Kitta Iyer's affection for Rajam and sympathy for her sufferings, Sarasvati Ammal began to burn with jealousy. Whenever Kitta Iyer talked to Rajam alone, Sarasvati Ammal invariably interrupted their tête-à-tête. If Kitta Iyer asked his wife to leave them, Sarasvati Ammal hissed scornfully, 'Sharing secrets! Shameful!' She went on muttering, 'That man is as good as gold. This blighted creature has ruined the household.'

She was enraged by the fact that Sita was fairer and better looking than her daughter Lalita. Sita's exuberance infuriated her. She hated seeing Lalita yielding to Sita's authority. Sensing this, Rajam tried to placate her sister-in-law. She frequently warned Sita not to boss Lalita.

But Sarasvati Ammal was not mollified. She was continually comparing Sita's and Lalita's looks. Lalita had a dusky complexion. Sita had a silky, sandalwood sheen. Those who knew the textbook criteria of perfect beauty may have deemed Lalita more beautiful. But general opinion would decide in Sita's favour. Lalita's eyes were shaped like a lotus petal, reflecting serenity. Sita's eyes were wide and round like a lily flower, darting here and there, riveting everyone's attention even as they betrayed her restless temper.

Sita was raised in a metropolis. Lalita in a rustic village. Their apparel, appearance and deportment matched their background. The little curls hanging beside her ears were enough to establish Sita's allure. She chattered with confidence and fluency. Sita scattered ten words before Lalita came around to uttering one. As she was studying in a convent, Sita would astonish Lalita by suddenly bursting into an English song. Moreover, Sita was a year older than Lalita and this made her youthful glow more radiant.

Sarasvati Ammal was unable to arrive at such measured assessments. But in her heart, she knew that her sister-in-law's daughter was better looking than her own. And this knowledge transformed her whole personality.

Until a year ago, the opinion that postmaster Bangaru Naidu had expressed about Sarasvati Ammal had been true. But after returning from Bombay, her temper became more and more volatile. She began to spend more time and effort in adorning her daughter and making her look attractive. This process made Lalita endure countless slaps and reprimands. If Lalita ever mentioned Sita, the house broke into a furor. But all the knocks on the head she received could not teach poor Lalita her lesson. She could not sleep at night if she did not brag about her athanga Sita to someone or the other. And if she did , it was only to dream of chattering about Sita to the girls in the agraharam.

6

THE CONSULTATION

Kitta Iyer picked up the letter that had fallen from his lap when he got up from his easy chair and started reading it. Midway through the perusal he exclaimed, 'Chee! Chee! People who learn English lose all their wits. And if they happen to move to Madras, they go round the bend! Unmitigated arrogance!'

Sarasvati Ammal wanted to say, 'If you don't know English, why curse those who do?' but the word 'Madras' shifted her thoughts to a different direction. Curbing her tongue in her eagerness to know more, she asked, 'Who sent the letter? What does it say?'

Kitta Iyer's momentary anger towards his wife was now directed at the 'Madras people'. So, he replied, 'It is a letter from that moron in Old Mambalam. Dumb ass!'

'Oh, is it your uncle, the younger one? What does he say?' asked Sarasvati Ammal in a voice throbbing with excitement.

'Hadn't Seemachu mentioned a fine prospective groom in Padmapuram? I asked uncle to find out more. It seems he went and saw the family and they told him to bring the girl to Madras, and "show" her to them! Madras people seem to be brainless wonders. They want to us to bring the girl to them, like a cow to the fair. And after all the fuss, do they at least pay money to "buy" the girl? No! It is we who must gift the girl, and her dowry as well. Even if *they* talk nonsense, why should *he* lose his sense? "It may be well to bring Lalita here," says he! Well, well, well!' Kitta Iyer shot his words like arrows.

'You should not get so angry! Don't you often tell me that anger is a sin, a curse? Your uncle is not someone who will write without giving the matter some thought. And even if we *do* take the child, we will be staying with your uncle. We can ask *them* to come to uncle's house. Why should you lose your temper over this?' said Sarasvati Ammal, preaching composure to Kitta Iyer! Her anxiety about finding a good husband for Lalita made Sarasvati Ammal a termagant and a saint by turns.

'Impossible!' declared Kitta Iyer. 'What? Exhibit Lalita before some rank idiot? How gross to have a boy looking at a girl and deciding whether he likes her or not. Obscene, no less!'

Sarasvati Ammal interrupted to ask him, 'Why are you so cross? We don't have to arrive at any decision without consulting the person in the house around the corner.' As she knew only too well, her reference to Seemachu Iyer, cooled his anger at once. Kitta Iyer lunched quickly and went out.

On the pyol of the house around the corner, three men were already waiting for him. Seemachu Iyer was seated with a pack of playing cards in his hands. Panchu Iyer and Appadurai Sastri were reading *Swadesamittiran*, each with a different page spread before him.

As soon as Kitta Iyer arrived, Sastri lifted his head above the paper to ask him, 'Do you know? A huge earthquake in Bihar!'

Panchu Iyer interposed, 'What do you mean *do you know*? It was he who generated that earthquake! Just as he was asking his wife whether a quake would hit us if Lalita goes to the post office, Seemachu entered their house announcing an earthquake in Bihar. The prophecy of the great sage instantly came true.'

'There was a time when a brahmin's word did instantly come true. Now everything has turned upside down. Let me ask you, will the world come to an end if that girl does *not* go to the post office? Doesn't Kitta have servants in the house?'

Seemachu Iyer broke in to say, 'Stop it! Tell us how the world will come to an end if Lalita goes to the post office. Do you know how the world is making progress on all fronts?'

'Such loose talk about progress makes the earth explode in quakes,' Sastri said.

'Why should our talk here bring an earthquake in Bihar?' Panchu Iyer asked.

'How long will it take for the earthquake to get here?'

'Don't know about earthquakes, but the Mahatma is visiting our province!' Panchu Iyer announced as he pointed to the newspaper headline.

'Do you know why he is coming here? To open all the temples to the outcastes. Why stop with earthquake? Earthquake, hurricane, downpour, floods, the great deluge, they will all be upon us.'

'Never mind this nonsense, Seemachu. I came to consult you about something,' Kitta Iyer said.

'Why didn't you say so? Come, let us go in,' said Seemachu Iyer and led him into the hall. Kitta Iyer disclosed the contents of the letters from Bombay and Madras and asked for his friend's advice. Seemachu Iyer gave it to him.

7

PADMAPURAM

Who doesn't know Padmapuram, the new residential colony in Madras city? No reader of the 'City Events' section of the Saturday editions of the city's dailies can miss the announcement of a meeting unfailingly held on every Sunday, at the Sarvagna Sangam in Padmapuram, where some political dignitary, social activist or literary scholar delivered his address. On Monday, reports of those lectures are published across two columns in every daily, pushing all other news aside.

No less than fifteen journalists lived in Padmapuram, in their own or rented homes. They played twin roles – as journalists, and as members of the audience. And therein lay the secret, the reason why, no one, not even the most august celebrities, refused an invitation to address the Sangam. It was a truth universally acknowledged that speaking for 30 members in Padmapuram was more than equal to addressing thirty thousand elsewhere. Justices of the High Court, political savants, intrepid scholars, renowned rhetoricians, award-winning artists, and just about everybody else were delighted and proud to accept an invitation to the Padmapuram association.

Readers may ask: why describe Padmapuram at such length?

Because the hero of our story resides in Padmapuram. In the light of this fact, would any description of the location seem too detailed?

Padmapuram has twelve streets filled with two-storyed bungalows.

Among them, one bungalow stood out prominently. On its two entrance pillars, black marble slabs were inlaid, the first with the inscription 'Devi Sadanam', the other with the name 'Rao Bahadur Padmalochana Sastri, BA, BL, Sub-Judge Rtd.'

Padmalochana Sastri was a pre-eminent resident of Padmapuram. In newspapers, his name appeared regularly in the 'Letters to the Editor' column where the world-famous polemical disputes between Rao Bahadur Padmalochana Sastri and Professor Parivrajaka Sharma were featured. Any mention of the Bhagavad Gita by Mahatma Gandhi, Pandit Madan Mohan Malaviya or Dr Radhakrishnan, became the danger signal, firing Padmalochana Sastri to place his walking stick in a corner, pick up his fat vintage fountain pen, and start writing relentlessly.

When he finished, he tucked the letter into his coat pocket, picked up his walking stick, went straight to the newspaper office, met the editor in person, and placed his letter in his hands. The letter always began with this question: what qualifications did Gandhi, Malaviya or Radhakrishnan possess to talk about the Bhagavad Gita? Next, Sastri proceeded to give the correct explanation of the verse they cited, even as he trounced their erroneous interpretations. He ended by issuing a warning to those luminaries to leave the Bhagavad Gita alone in any disquisition they may deliver in the future.

Two days after the publication of Sastri's letter, readers expected to see Professor Parivrajaka Sharma's rejoinder. Nor were they disappointed.

He began by agreeing unequivocally with Sastri. He declared that the leaders knew nothing about the Bhagavad Gita, nothing at all; they did not even know that they knew nothing about the Bhagavad Gita. Then, deploying the conjunction 'but' to preface his question, he asked, '*But* – what does Padmalochana Sastri know about the Bhagavad Gita? Has he learnt it from a guru through direct oral instruction? Has he at least glanced at the book with his own eyes? If he had done so, why did he mention the 28th verse in the 11th chapter of the Bhagavad Gita when he clearly meant the 27th verse? Then again, did he get his reference right? How ludicrous is it to quote the Lord as saying "Arjuna! Look at me!" Did the Lord indeed say, "Look at me?" O venerable Sastri! Wipe your eyes, *and* your glasses, before taking a careful look at the Bhagavad Gita! Did God say, "*Look at me!*" If He had, would He be the Lord God Himself? Verily, didn't the Lord say, "*You may look at me!*" Even a child who has just begun learning the alphabets of Sanskrit, the language of the Gods, would know that there is a difference of epic proportions between "Look at me!" and "You may look at me!" – as there is between a mountain and a gorge, an elephant and a cat, a buffalo and an ant. But how can Padmalochana Sastri, whose age equals the combined age of two tumbled-down-walls in archaeological ruins, be expected to know that the two phrases are as far apart, as are two different galaxies in the universe?'

Sastri was not someone to be worsted by such tirades. Picking up his pen again he tore Parivrajaka Sharma and his arguments to shreds, and once again made the trip to the newspaper office to hand his letter to the editor personally. After six months of such wars of words, a note from the editor announced that the discussion was closed.

In the year 1934, January had seen twenty-nine days pass by, without sparking any fresh debate between the two men. The reason was simply this: Sastri was deeply concerned about his second son, Saundara Raghavan.

He had been somewhat disappointed by his first son, Sankara Narayanan. True, the boy was intelligent, securing high marks with a first rank, through all his years in school and college. He completed his BA, MA and BL with distinction. After dithering for a while with no more examinations to pass, he became a registered lawyer, beginning his practice under the aegis of his father-in-law, the famous advocate Vyaghram Iyer. The advocate totally appropriated the apprentice. The son-in-law became a part of his father-in-law's household. His orthodox lifestyle took a turn for the ultra-modern. Like his wife, he began to scorn his parents for their hidebound ways. Things came to head when he began to criticize Sastri's newspaper disputes. One day, when he called them ridiculous, Sastri decided that he could no longer put up with his impertinence. With great firmness he declared, 'Yes, my dear boy! I am ridiculous, your mother is Mrs Ridiculous. You, on the other hand, are a brainbox! I will consider you – not as a son born to us – but as having come into the world as Vyaghram Iyer's son-in-law! Go! *Go*! Don't show your face again!'

Sastri's younger son, Saundara Raghavan was as brilliant as his elder brother. University examinations were child's play to him. He had come first with a state rank in the MA course. At that time there was a debate in the newspapers over the government's economic policy as to whether the exchange rate should be fixed at 18 pence or 16 pence to the rupee. With writing skills inherited from his father, Raghavan wrote a letter to the editor on the issue. When published, it drew the attention of noted economists in the country, including officials of the government's Treasury Department. The chief of the department invited Raghavan for an interview. As a result, Raghavan was soon appointed in the revenue department of the British government in India. His starting salary was ₹750 with no limits on upward mobility.

Surely, there was every reason for Sastri to be proud of his son. So, why should he worry? The reason was simple: the son's marriage.

In general, parents worry about getting their daughters married. Padmalochana Sastri's concern was just the opposite, he was worried about his son's marriage. He was afraid that the younger son may make the elder son's behaviour more acceptable. Kamakshi Ammal, his life partner, was even more perturbed.

Let us leave the couple to their worries and go up the stairs to meet our hero.

8

SAUNDARA RAGHAVAN

Five feet nine inches tall, with a well-built figure, chiseled features, hair perfectly cropped and nattily attired, seated on a chair beside the table – there is the hero of our tale: Saundara Raghavan.

On the table before him lay a letter. Beside it was the reply that he had just begun to write. Also on the table were an anthology of the Swedish playwright Ibsen with a newspaper tucked below, and an elegantly framed photograph.

Raghavan held a fine blue-coloured fountain pen in his hand. His attractive, handsome face displayed anger, streaked with disappointment and sadness. His sighs were frequent. The eyes shining with intelligence now had a lost, faraway look.

Let us look at the photograph on the table. A north Indian girl! An extremely beautiful girl. She looks young. And yet, her enchanting face shows the maturity of a reflective mind and knowledge of the world.

Who is she? Why is her photograph on Rao Bahadur Padmalochana Sastri's son's table? Why does he gaze at it and heave sighs? Well, let's take a look at the letters lying open, and see if we can deduce more details.

First, let us see the letter Raghavan has received, written in English, in a woman's handwriting.

GIP EN ROUTE
21/1/1934

Dear Mr Saundara Raghavan,
Namaste.

I got the letter you sent to Bombay just before boarding the train. Therefore, I am writing this on the moving train. I plan to post my letter at the Nagpur railway station.

Your letter clearly spells out your state of mind after I left you. It saddens me. All I can do is to beg you to forget me as soon as you can.

There are many things for you to achieve in the world. If you focus on them, your mind will change and quickly. There is another way to make that change. If you don't know what it is, please ask your estimable mother.

I felt a deep respect for your mother. Unfortunately, I am not fated to become her daughter-in-law. But in no way does it lessen my regard for her. The lady who personifies all the traditional virtues of ancient Hinduism in my eyes, prostrated before me! She pleaded, 'I beg of you! Please grant my request!' I promised that I would do so. I will definitely keep my vow. That promise will give me the strength of mind to bear the burden of my life on earth.

My dear… I think it may not be wrong to address you in this manner. Even if it is, this will be the last time I commit that mistake. May God forgive me.

I burnt all your letters. What is the use of saving them? I request you to do the same. Please throw this letter into the fire, along with all my other letters, and the photograph of me which you have. Why should you hold on to them? It is good for those about to begin their climb to the lofty peaks to get rid of useless baggage. Both of us are journeying into new paths. We may even say that we have been born again, in order to start a new life. See how God sends the newborn infant into the world without any baggage! If the infant had to bear all the accumulated burdens from previous lives, could it begin its new life with ease? Let us consign our old burdens to the flames.

I have been writing this little by little whenever the train halted in stations. To my embarrassment, fellow travelers have been asking me, repeatedly, 'What are you writing so intensely? For the newspapers?'

I...? Write for newspapers? There are others born to... Sorry! Old memories recur. Let me end by telling you the reason for my having undertaken this trip.

You must have read about the ghastly earthquake in Bihar. You will know how the people of Bihar have been afflicted by this terrible catastrophe. Babu Rajendra Prasad has called for volunteers to help those subjected to unimaginable sufferings due to Nature's unaccountable rage. Many groups have set out from Bombay to answer that call. I have joined the first group of volunteers.

As a human being, the only means of finding peace of mind would be for me to seize the opportunity to be of some help to others. Nothing can give me greater satisfaction than for God to take my life as I serve the victims of this disaster.

Most sincerely do I beg your pardon for all the troubles I have brought upon you.

Once again, I beg you to forget me, soon.
Dharini

Readers will not be surprised that a letter like this should make Saundara Raghavan sigh heavily. Again, no surprise that the prodigy who effortlessly answered the most complex questions in university examinations should be so stumped by this letter as to not know how to reply.

Padmapuram, Madras
24/1/1934

Dear Dharini Devi,

The letter that you were good enough to write on the train has reached me. If only you could know how each and every word of yours slashed my heart... the excruciating agony they brought...! But what is the use of writing this to you? How can a heart as hard as iron and flint, as inflexible as the tenets of hidebound faith, know my anguish?

Raghavan's letter stopped here. Unable to proceed, he had simply crossed out line after line.

At this juncture, a most unpropitious interruption occurred in the form of a voice calling from outside the house, 'Sir!'

Irritated, Raghavan got up and looked down from the corner of the balcony. He saw two dyed-in-the-wool brahmins standing at the threshold.

The two men looked up when they heard Raghavan's call, 'Who is there?' One of them was our friend, Kitta Iyer, the munsif of Rajampettai village. The other was his uncle, Subbu Iyer from Old Mambalam.

Recognising Subbu Iyer as his father's old friend, Raghavan said, 'Oh, you have come to see father! I will ask them to open the door.'

The moment his face disappeared from view Subbu Iyer touched Kitta Iyer's hand and whispered, 'Did you see him? That's the bridegroom!'

'Time enough to look at him if he turns out to be the bridegroom,' Kitta Iyer replied.

9

THE DOOR OPENS

Once it was verified that the men at the door had not come to beg, ask for charity, or sell subscriptions, the doors of Devi Sadanam were opened.

'Welcome, sir, welcome! So, it is you! These days it is impossible to keep the front door open. If you do, you are lost! Wastrels saunter in through the open door like dogs,' Padmalochana Sastri said as he led the visitors in.

'Please take a seat. Why should you remain standing? Subbu Iyer, please feel free to seat yourself comfortably on the sofa. Will the sofa wear out if you do? I hate finicky people who have such notions. They cover the floor with a carpet costing a thousand rupees. And when people walk on it, they get distressed. They buy a sofa for two thousand rupees and hide it under a stained and dirty cover. Do you know, when I was in Ramanathapuram district, I happened to visit a wealthy man. Each pillar in his house cost five thousand rupees! Such ornately carved pillars – built only to be hidden under wraps! Now, don't you worry about taking your seat! Please sit!' Padmalochana Sastri chattered without a break. Subbu Iyer and Kitta Iyer found their seats and sat down gingerly.

When Sastri paused to take a breath, Subbu Iyer seized the opportunity to say, 'Do you know what was the most interesting part of last week's lecture at Sarvagna Sangam? Your commendation of the speaker! Brilliant! That is the way to speak. Those who cannot speak as well as you do, had best keep their mouths shut.'

Subbu Iyer was an insurance agent. It was his belief that saying something nice whenever he could, to anyone and everyone, would come in useful at some time or the other.

But Sastri was no fool. Nor susceptible to flattery.

'Yes sir! Yes, ninety other people have laid it on thick like you and issued certificates to my brilliance. But has the import of what I said registered in anyone's brain? Not at all!'

Subbu Iyer asked, 'Why do you say that?'

'What do you mean why? What I am saying is absolutely right. Did anyone think of honouring the venerable scholar who had been invited to come all the way from the banks of the Kaveri to give a discourse on the Bhagavatam? If they hadn't thought of this on their own, did they at least consider it at my suggestion? No, till today no one has offered even a quarter of an anna for him. Life in the city has spoilt and ruined people's hearts. Dharma manages to survive only in the rural landscape. It is utterly destroyed in the metros. Listen, I will tell you something. Don't you know Sundaram Iyengar the high court judge? Subbu Iyer, I am asking you.'

'Of course, I do. How can anyone not know Sundaram Iyengar?' Subbu Iyer said vehemently.

'Oy Subbu Iyer, your secret is out! At no time has there ever been a high court judge named Sundaram Iyengar. The judge I am referring to has a name altogether different. And you got fooled! Well, the point is that Sundaram Iyengar agreed to donate ₹5000 to a charity school. He signed the deed. His name appeared in the newspapers. Then, do you know what he did? O Subbu Iyer, I will tell you! The man who does not contribute to good works is a rogue. But even a rogue may be forgiven when compared to the blackguard who signs his name as a donor and gives the slip when it comes to payment. He too may be forgiven. But the man who signs his name as a donor, gets acclaimed for the deed and dies without paying up – he is the scoundrel of scoundrels. He is trying to cheat this world and the world above. That is what High Court Judge Sundaram Iyengar did. After a while we went to talk to his son. The father had left him a legacy of more than twenty lakh rupees. Shouldn't the son honour his father's word? "Impossible!" he announced implacably. Those of us who had gone to see him got furious. "Lakshmana, dear boy! If you persist in your refusal, we will arrange to raise the promised sum by launching the 'High Court Judge Sundaram Iyengar Fund'. We have great respect for your father. We must do what we can to make sure that his promise is fulfilled." Can you guess the son's response? He said, "Great! Go ahead! I give you my permission, but if the collection exceeds five thousand rupees, the excess amount must be given to me. I am my father's only son. He has no other heir." We returned, hanging our heads. Let me tell you this. Subbu Iyer, the government must demand high death duties from those who amass wealth without contributing to charity. The government must take away in taxes not less than three fourths of any property worth more than a lakh-and-a-half rupees,' Sastri stopped momentarily to catch his breath.

Subbu Iyer cast a meaningful glance at Kitta Iyer as Sastri's last statement confirmed his being in possession of property worth one and a half lakh rupees.

Noting that glance, Sastri quickly said, 'Never mind all these matters. Subbu Iyer! You have brought someone with you. He looks like an important man. His appearance is enough to proclaim that he belongs to the region nourished by the Kaveri. Am I right?'

'This is Kitta Iyer, the pattamaniam of Rajampettai. I had spoken to you about him earlier. I sent a letter asking him to visit, and here he is.'

'Subbu Iyer, why did you not introduce him at once? Having brought someone to discuss important matters, you have wasted all this time in useless gossip. All right. So, this is the revenue official from Rajampettai. Didn't I say his face has the glow of a man who lives beside the Kaveri? So, this is Kitta Iyer. I am very happy to meet him. Does he do anything other than the pattamaniam's job? Any other lands, properties, means, businesses?'

'He has everything! He has sixty acres of nansei land, all yielding two annual harvests.'

'Very well. Has he come to Madras on any business? Or just to see the city?'

'He has seen the city before. He has even seen Bombay. This time he is here to see if he can find a bridegroom.'

'Ohoho! Here for a bridegroom, is he? *Bale!* Bale! Have you taken up this job in addition to your work in insurance? How many houses have you taken him to, so far? How many bridegrooms have you shown him?'

'No, sir. The only place I know is this one. I brought him straight here. Last time when I mentioned this matter, you and your lady said that it would be good for the girl to be brought here. Do you remember?'

'That's right. But don't raise your voice. The boy is upstairs and may hear us...! This is my opinion. You may say that I am somewhat modern in this matter. The boy must like the girl. The girl must like the boy. There must be no room later for either boy or girl to complain about their lives being spoilt. All this is according to what the scriptures say. These days people talk about "dowry". Absolute nonsense! It is totally against the scriptures. If I were to ask for a dowry, I may demand thirty thousand and fifty thousand, as even ne'er-do-wells do these days. For me righteousness is omnipotent. Not money. If it were not so, would I still be in debt despite so many years in office? People who held similar posts have rented out four or five houses they have built with the bribes they have grabbed with both hands. I have built just this single house. And I had to borrow money to do that. Fifteen thousand rupees have still to be paid to the housing co-operative society. If anyone who offers a daughter also pays off this debt, well, their daughter and son-in-law will have a fine house for themselves. But it is up to them.'

Subbu Iyer interposed to say, 'Sir, you don't have to talk about these matters. Kitta Iyer has kept aside thirty thousand rupees for his daughter's marriage. There will be no shortcomings in the customary transactions, all arrangements will be wholly satisfactory.'

'Forget customs! Forget transactions! A wedding is a sacred event.

But the time has gone by when a marriage could be arranged without the consent of the boy and the girl. The boy must like the girl. The girl must like the boy. Has Iyer brought his daughter with him?'

Kitta Iyer, who had been forced to remain silent all this time, now pulled himself together and said, 'I did want to bring her, but at this time, it was not convenient to do so. I am going to Bombay to see my sister. If you agree, once I return from Bombay, I will go back to the village and bring my daughter here.'

'That's all right. Do it at your convenience! But the boy must be married before his leave gets over. Not much time for delay. The boy's mother too is in a great hurry. She has thirty horoscopes on hand. For the last two months her only job has been calling the astrologer home and matching horoscopes. Kamakshi! Come here!' Sastri called out loudly.

10

KAMAKSHI AMMAL

A woman's voice came from the back of the house, 'Coming!'

Sastri shouted, 'Come! Come! Things will get settled only if you come.'

Then, looking again at Subbu Iyer, he said, 'I have entrusted the marriage department to my wife. You cannot find anyone more forbearing than Kamakshi in the whole country. Hasn't she put up with me through all these years?'

'Please! Why talk about our affairs before guests?' Kamakshi Ammal said. To see her in person was to feel that she had been perfectly portrayed in Dharini's letter. The big red kumkumam dot on her forehead, serene face, bright eyes, her speech and deportment, everything proclaimed her to be well born, devout and a fine representative of ancient Hindu faith and culture.

Subbu Iyer greeted her and said, 'Amma! It is me! And I have brought Kitta Iyer, the village munsif of Rajampettai whom I had mentioned to you.'

'Very well. Has he brought the girl with him?' Kamakshi Ammal asked.

'Not this time as he is on his way to Bombay to visit his sister. He says he will bring his daughter after his return. He has brought her horoscope. If the horoscopes match and all other customary matters are discussed and resolved, there will be no difficulty in fetching the girl. If we can finalize all other matters…'

'What other matters are there to finalize? Do what you find

suitable in whatever way you find suitable. If you can bring the girl and show her to the boy, and if he likes her, there is nothing more to discuss. All we have to do is to fix the auspicious hour for the wedding.' Before she finished speaking, footsteps were heard coming down the staircase.

The man who came down was none other than our hero, Raghavan. The talk about the wedding had brought a slight smile to his face, which had earlier registered sorrow and perplexity.

The four persons below turned to look in the direction of the approaching footsteps. Seeing Raghavan, his parents became apprehensive. Had they said anything wrong? Had they done anything that would upset their plan?

Kitta Iyer gazed at the man coming down the stairs with rapt eyes. He was charmed by his distinguished appearance, handsome face and aura of intelligence. 'We would be fortunate to get this young man as our son-in-law. Lalita will be lucky!' he thought.

Looking at the silent company Raghavan remarked, 'It seems you were fixing a marriage?'

'*A* marriage? We were talking about *your* marriage!' Sastri announced boldly. He knew only too well that Raghavan would remain polite before strangers.

'Oho! Is that so! Are you planning to get me married without asking me?'

'What do you mean? Fix your marriage without asking you? What kind of people do you take us for?' Sastri said.

'Our intention is to proceed after consulting you and with your approval. Son! Is marriage a simple matter? Can you marry today and break it tomorrow? Are you a child that we should think of taking such decisions without asking you?' Kamakshi Ammal said.

'These days you can't compel even children to do anything. A ten-year-old girl simply declares, "I don't want this husband!"' Subbu Iyer said.

Everyone laughed. Even Raghavan's face brightened a little.

Seizing the light-hearted moment Sastri said, 'Why beat around the bush? Best to say what we think. Raghava! Our Subbu Iyer had already talked about Rajampettai Kitta Iyer. This is the man himself. He has come looking for a bridegroom for his daughter. You came down just as we were thinking of calling you. Tell us what you want. If everything gets settled, he says he will bring his daughter here for you to see. Fine background, fine family. Your mother and I are very happy about this match. But what is the use of our being satisfied? It is you who will be getting married. Shall we tell him to bring the girl? Tell us what you want. No point in making these people run around for no reason. We have to give them a firm yes or no.'

The smile vanished from Raghavan's face. He scowled and said, 'Appa! If I decide to get married, I will go and see the girl. No need to bring her here.'

11

IF YOU ASK ME

Raghavan's words left everyone silent. No one dared to respond as he strode away without waiting for an answer.

When he disappeared from view, Kamakshi Ammal said to Kitta Iyer. 'Don't worry. I will keep Raghavan in line. But do come back soon from Bombay.'

Kitta Iyer detested the idea of bringing the girl to the city to display her before the prospective groom. He thought it was beneath his dignity. Moreover, the prospect of taking his beloved daughter like a cow to the market, for a strange boy to inspect and say 'Yes' or 'No' was painful to him. Therefore, he was delighted when Raghavan declared that he would go and 'see' the girl in her hometown.

It was with enthusiasm that he said to Kamakshi Ammal, 'Certainly. I will go to Bombay and return as soon as I can. If it is convenient for him, mapillai can come soon after. In fact, I can take him with me.'

'Kitta! Are you claiming him as your son-in-law already? Ohoho!' Subbu Iyer laughed.

'Why not? By Sri Rama's grace, it may happen. When I was called to join you, I was decorating the pictures in the puja room with flowers. Just as I heard the call, "Kamakshi!" a champa flower dropped from the picture of Sri Rama's coronation. I thought it was a good omen,' Kamakshi Ammal said.

'Subbu Iyer, do you know how many people have come searching for us, offering Raghavan their daughters in marriage? At least a thousand! It was this good lady who dodged them all! Now that she herself says that this marriage will take place, this wedding is a done deal!' said Sastri.

'Everything happens for the best. When it was decreed that this wonderful connection should happen, how could the marriage have been fixed elsewhere? Kitta too went through a hundred possibilities last year. He abandoned all of them because in his heart, he was not satisfied. The moment he stepped into this house, he felt very good. There must be some power in you, Sir. Similarly, the lady has something divine about her.'

'Oy! Subbu Iyer, you are a smart man! What do you hope to accomplish with all this flattery? Are you trying to get my wife to consider taking insurance?' As Sastri began to expand on the theme, a flustered Subbu Iyer cut in with, 'Sorry! I am late for work. Please let us take your leave. After all, we are going to be meeting frequently from now on.'

As Sastri got up to accompany them to the front door, four men in Gandhi caps came briskly into the house.

Sastri was startled. 'Who are you?' he asked.

One of the volunteers answered, 'Sir, we are collecting donations for the Bihar Earthquake Relief Fund. Please donate what you can.'

Sastri's face reddened in rage. 'You will get nothing here,' he said decisively.

'Don't be so hardhearted, sir! Lakhs of people have lost their homes, lost their land, lost their property…'

'…Lost their lives! Yes, I know. Do you think I am an ignoramus? The day after the earthquake I sent my contribution through money order to Babu Rajendra Prasad. Go and see other people! Don't waste time!'

'Do *you* have to instruct us to go and see other people?' the volunteers muttered as they left.

'Keep the door open for a second, and somebody or other barges in and asks for donations in the name of earthquake, volcano, hurricane, Congress conference! Or it is a festival there and hymn-singing here! I have made so many donations that I am fed up. Besides, am I a landowner? A zamindar? Do I reap gold from my nansei lands? Thanks to the white man's government I get my pension every month. I may have to bid goodbye to that pension if these "virtuous" men manage to win independence! Do you know that the Karachi Congress session has passed a resolution to the effect that no one should get a salary of more than ₹500 per month! And let us say we give a donation to these volunteers. What is the guarantee that it will go directly into the Bihar Fund? If you ask me, I will say that men should not interfere in happenings like an earthquake. What can mere mortals do against what God himself has decreed?'

Jabbering in this manner Padmalochana Sastri took Kitta Iyer and Subbu Iyer to the front door. The moment they left the house, he shut the door and locked it firmly.

12

IT HAPPENED IN KARACHI

The spacious hall at the back of the house was flanked on either side by the kitchen and Kamakshi Ammal's puja room. Sitting on the swing in the centre of the hall, Raghavan awaited his mother's arrival. The swing moved in slow motion, and his heart swayed with it.

When a man drowns in the sea, they say he sees his entire life pass before his mind's eye like moving scenes on the silver screen. So did certain incidents from his life hurtle past Raghavan's mind.

After meeting the chief of the Department of Treasury in Delhi, Raghavan thought he would visit Karachi before returning home. The national session of the Congress was scheduled to meet that year in Karachi. Like other young Indians, Raghavan too had been passionate about India's freedom and social reform, convinced that India could achieve liberation only if distinctions of caste and creed were erased.

Raghavan did go to Karachi and register himself to attend the Congress sessions. What he observed did not engender in him any respect for the national leaders. 'The world is making tremendous progress. The Ford motor car company is turning out 300 cars per minute. And here we are, stuck with leaders hanging their hopes on the spinning wheel! In our age of industrialization, their goal is to spin 300 yards of yarn per hour. Good grief! With such leaders, how on earth can India make any progress?'

Then Raghavan went to see the symbol of the industrial age: the aeroplane. Karachi had just built a new aerodrome. Planes could be hired for flights of five minutes at a fee of five rupees. The plane would rise 2000 feet high, circle Karachi and make its descent.

Raghavan did not go to the aerodrome with any thought of trying out this offer. But he was forced to abandon the idea of remaining a mere onlooker. In the milling crowd of sightseers, he found himself standing beside three north Indian women. One was older, the second short and stodgy. The third...? Ah...! It was impossible to describe her. It seemed as if the sandalwood glow of the full moon in winter had been spellbound to shape her form. Her eyes sparkled like dew drops under the winter sun. Her voice had the sweetness of little bells tied around an infant's waist, tinkling as he moved.

'Are you from Madras?' asked the young girl. To Raghavan, her voice sounded more intoxicating than the poems of Keats and Shelley that he loved. Taking a moment to ascertain that she was actually addressing him, he managed to reply.

'Are you going to get into that aeroplane?' she asked him. 'Yes,' was Raghavan's ready reply. 'What about you?'

'We'll decide after you tell us what it's like.'

The other girl whispered something into her ear. Both laughed merrily. Raghavan heard only the laughter of the girl who had spoken to him. He learnt that her name was Dharini, the other was Nirupama. He also learnt that they had come to serve as volunteers in the Congress session. Now that it was over, they were sightseeing, like him.

Raghavan climbed into the plane, which took him circling in the air above but his mind hovered on earth. To be accurate, his mind revolved around Dharini. As soon as he got out of the plane, his world was plunged into darkness when he could not find those three women. However, the sun shone again when he located them in another spot. Raghavan made a beeline for the trio. Dharini looked up eagerly to ask, 'How was it?' Hiding the fact that his mind had been earthbound during the flight, Raghavan described the experience as something spectacular. 'Aren't you going to try it?' he asked her. Dharini said ruefully, 'No. My friends are afraid. They refuse to let me go.'

'It is perfectly safe. If the plane had more seats, I would have been happy to take you. But this little plane seats only a single passenger.'

'Right! Can we leave?' asked the other girl. Dharini looked at Raghavan and said, 'We have to go.' As they got into a taxi, Raghavan fancied that Dharini turned to look in his direction.

Why call it fancy? Could it not have been true?

After the flight experience, Raghavan wanted to undergo the experience of sailing on a ship. Some of the attendees of the Karachi Congress returned to Bombay by sea. Raghavan got himself a ticket from the Scindia Company for one of their ships and boarded it. It was a small vessel that sailed close to the shore, crammed high with bags, bundles, trunks, beddings, baskets of food, teeming with a tumultuous crowd of north Indian passengers, all dusty clothes and messy ways. Raghavan thought, 'Good God! How can I endure 38 hours here!' But his attitude underwent a sea change when he saw the three women arrive by boat at the last minute, climb the ladder and get into the ship. The filthy, squalid, ramshackle ship turned into a celestial haven. When she saw Raghavan on board, Dharini's face registered surprise. Raghavan's eye could not miss the joy mingled in that surprise.

This was the first time Raghavan had travelled in the north. There were many things about north India that Raghavan could learn from Dharini, who lived in Bombay. Dharini too wanted to know more about the Madras Presidency. They had much to talk about.

However, speech was perhaps not a real necessity. They were both in that state when proximity and exchange of glances were enough to satisfy. They had to practise dissimulation though, and appear to be no more than chance acquaintances, to avoid drawing the attention of the other passengers. During those make-believe conversations, Raghavan was surprised and thrilled to discover that Dharini could speak Tamil.

There were other young party workers like Dharini and Nirupama on that ship, intent on serving the nation. Nirupama may not have had physical beauty – in fact, her appearance served to heighten Dharini's loveliness – but she had a sweet voice. She led the group in singing nationalist songs in Hindi. They sang the popular song of the Indian flag, 'Jhanda ooncha rahe hamaara' as also Sir Mohammed

Iqbal's famous Urdu poem, 'Saare jahaan se acchaa Hindostan hamaara'. Raghavan saw the women as celestial maidens singing in stellar realms. When he learnt from Dharini that the opening verse in the second song meant 'Our Hindustan is the best among all the nations of the world', Raghavan exclaimed, 'How can any country in the world equal ours when it has given birth to girls as beautiful as you!' The expression on Dharini's face when she heard these words, and the smile dimpling her cheeks, were imprinted in his heart like an Ajanta fresco painted in indelible colours.

All this was some three years ago. During that time their correspondence grew, with letters so lyrical as to make Kalidasa, Kamban, Tagore and Bharati proud. Nor did they stop with letter writing. When Raghavan made a trip to Bombay, Dharini took him to see the fabulous sculptures in the Elephanta caves. Then Dharini went to Delhi. Raghavan, employed in New Delhi, took Dharini around to see the ancient city's old forts, imposing mosques, and the magnificent marble palaces of the Mughal emperors. As they roamed together, they floated in an ocean of bliss.

They considered going to Agra to see the Taj Mahal, but decided to postpone the visit. They resolved to see Shah Jahan's peerless dream of love, holding hands as man and wife, without any fear of unsavoury gossip.

In short, those three years had been an idyll in Raghavan's life. In his career, he was making rapid progress. The big chief of his department had promised to take him to England with him. In personal life, he was soaring in a dream world of romance. He saw streaks of gold everywhere. His ears constantly heard the honeyed music of divine lutes. Walking on the narrow lanes of old Delhi filled with filth and stench, he inhaled the fragrance of the exquisite attar used by Mughal royals, and the rose water in which their women bathed.

What happened to that idyll? How did it end? Why did it end?

When the visitors left, Kamakshi Ammal made for the hall at the back of the house where she saw Raghavan swinging languidly. She sat down on the chair facing the swing. She knew only too well that her son had been waiting for her.

13

WHEN THE SKY CRASHED

Raghavan took his time to speak. Nor could he come to the point at once. He took a roundabout route.

'Amma! Who was it? Some other visitor? I heard a new voice.'

'Four men in Gandhi caps arrived with a donation box to talk about the earthquake in Bihar. You know your father. He refused to contribute anything and drove them away.'

Kamakshi Ammal noted that her words brought a frown to Raghavan's face, but she could not guess why.

Raghavan kept his head lowered. Afraid to open her mouth, Kamakshi Ammal too remained silent. Instinct warned her that he was going question her about some matter of importance.

When he did, he asked in an irate voice, 'Amma! Have you and Appa decided to ruin my life? Don't you want me to be happy? Has Appa's selfishness infected you as well?'

Kamakshi Ammal had been expecting something like this. So, she answered calmly. 'Raghava! I cannot speak for your father. I can only tell you what I feel. From the day you were born, I have thought of nothing but your happiness. Tell me what I should do to make you happy. Do you want me to jump into a well? I will. Do you want me to drink poison? I will. But my dear son, don't ever say that I want my wishes to prevail at the cost of your happiness.' She wiped the tears streaming from her eyes.

Raghavan was immersed in thoughtful silence. She spoke again. 'Raghava! Why do you say I am motivated by self-interest?'

'You are trying to thrust upon me a girl I don't care for. What do you call that?' Raghavan growled.

'Raghava! You have great understanding. The whole country knows that you have no equal in intelligence. And yet you accuse me wrongly! Will I ever say that you should marry a girl you dislike? Your father may; he is relying on your dowry to pay off the house loan. Son, if you like a beggar on the street and want to marry her, I will welcome her with more affection than any daughter of a rich man.' said Kamakshi Ammal in a rush of tears.

'I am not willing to talk to you if you are going to cry. I will go away. I will jump into the sea, lie down on a train track.'

'Please! Don't say such dreadful things! I will stop crying. Ask me what you want.' Kamakshi Ammal said and dried her tears resolutely.

'If you want me to be happy, why did you drive Dharini away?' Raghavan asked in exasperation.

'*Ayyayo*! This is a baseless accusation! Was it I who drove that girl away? Tell me honestly, is she the kind of girl who would allow me to drive her away?'

'Why should she leave in such haste? Surely you must have said something to frighten her into running away!'

'Raghava, I swear on my life that I never spoke a single harsh word. If I had done that, wouldn't she have stayed until you came back and complained to you? Is she a country bumpkin? A scared mouse? If she had really loved you, would she have left just because I happened to say something wrong?'

Raghavan thought for a few moments and said, 'Then tell me just what happened in my absence.'

'Ayyayo! My tongue will never be able to repeat the things she said. She said that she had come here with many expectations. But your father and I were too hidebound for her. You were a complete idiot, running after anyone in a saree. She had come to Madras only to tell me that I should keep you under control. She said many more dreadful, hurtful, intolerable things about you,' Kamakshi Ammal said, covering her face with the end of her saree as she sobbed.

Raghavan was overcome by wrath. He didn't know whether this wrath was directed towards Dharini or his mother.

Suddenly, he remembered something that Dharini had mentioned in her letter. 'Amma! Did you ever touch Dharini's feet? And ask her to do anything for you?'

'I see! So, she has written about it to you! I don't know what lies and falsehoods she has added, but I can tell you exactly what happened. I was alarmed to hear her talk about you with contempt. I told her, "Despite the differences in caste, creed and customs, I am happy that you speak our language. I make a humble request to you. Don't separate me from my son. I live only for him. I fall at your feet and beg you to grant me this boon!" And then I touched her feet.

She shouted "Damn! Nonsense!" and cursed me in English with the words your father uses when he scolds me. "I have no caste or creed. How can I get on with an old stick-in-the-mud like you? Tell your son to behave, teach him discipline and control!" she said, and strode brusquely away. Raghava, I know it must be difficult for you to believe me. But a man came, knocked on the door and asked for her. She got up and went quickly to take a letter from him. Her face changed as she read it. "I'm going. Don't worry, I won't ruin your son," she said, and rushed to the car waiting outside. In her haste she forgot to take the letter with her. I have kept it. You may see it if you like,' Kamakshi Ammal said as she went to get the letter.

Taking the letter from her with trembling hands and beating heart Raghavan began to read it. It had a few brief lines.

> *My darling! My work got over sooner than I expected. I must leave for Bombay today by the evening mail. If you cannot come to the hotel at once, join me at the railway station. I will get a ticket for you as well. How is the spree with Raghavan going? The two thousand rupees he has doled out should be enough. Don't impose any more penalties. It may end in disaster.*

When Raghavan finished reading, the sky and the earth and everything in the universe exploded into chaos. Darkness swooped down in the middle of the day. The planets and the stars shattered to shards.

Raghavan sat immobilized by these emotions. Then, with a sudden bound, he got up and prostrated himself flat on the ground before his mother. 'Dharini was right. I am an idiot. I created a situation where you had to touch her feet. From this instant, you are my god. I will do whatever you say. I will marry whomever you ask me to marry.'

After making this speech, letter in hand, Raghavan went quickly up the stairs. He picked up Dharini's letter and his unfinished reply, tore them to shreds and flung them into the wastepaper basket.

Kamakshi Ammal went into the puja room, prostrated before the portrait of Sri Rama. She got up and tapped her cheeks in thanksgiving.

14

THE COACH ARRIVES

The time has come to take our readers to Bombay again. In fact, readers may have to be taken not just to Bombay, but to places as far away as Calcutta, Karachi, Delhi and Lahore, to observe different events as they develop on the same day, and at the same time.

We are in Dadar, a part of Bombay city, on an unidentifiable street, in an unidentifiable building, part of a topographical network where every street and every building appears to be like every other street and building. This particular building has five storeys and looks just like the other buildings on both sides of the street, as if they had all been cast in a single identical mould.

Kitta Iyer's sister Rajam had lived for twenty years on the fourth floor of this building, in a flat comprising three rooms and a bathroom. All the joys and sorrows of her life were experienced within those three rooms. It was there that she knew the thrills and raptures of conjugal bliss. Her children were raised there. It was there that she shrieked and sobbed when she lost her child. It was there that her heart broke in grief as she wept over the strange behaviour of her husband.

Rajam had been bedridden for over twenty days with little hope of recovery. Her husband Duraisami had tried hard to convince her that she should be hospitalized. But Rajam stubbornly refused. 'I will die where I have lived for twenty years.'

It had been a year since Sita dropped out of school. With much forethought Rajam had trained her daughter in housework. (Who knew what kind of family she would be married into?) That training proved useful now.

There! Who stands beside the balustrade on the narrow balcony, gazing down at the street? Why! Her large round eyes widened in anticipation are enough to make us recognize the girl as none other than Lalita's dearest cousin Sita.

Any remaining doubts are immediately dispelled when a weak voice calls out from within, 'Sita!' Sita's musical voice answers, 'Coming!' as she runs to her mother reclining in bed.

'Sita! I heard a car,' says Rajam, her haggard face brightening in anticipation.

Sita chatters rapidly. 'No Amma. It was some other car. It is still too early. The train would have arrived only by now. No point in getting anxious!'

Hearing a car draw up, Sita runs back to the verandah and looks down into the street. A car has stopped in front of the building. 'Amma! Uncle is here. I will go down and bring him up,' Sita calls out shrilly and rushes down the stairs, three steps at a time.

After descending two storeys, Sita stopped when she saw the doctor. 'Was it you? I thought my uncle had arrived from the village,' she said.

'I see! So, your uncle is coming today! Let us hope his arrival helps your mother's recovery,' the doctor said.

Sita took the leather bag from him. They went up in silence.

When they reached the fourth floor, Sita's eagerness made her look down at the street again. Sita saw her father and uncle getting down from the coach. She screamed with excitement, 'Amma! Amma! Uncle is here! He is really here! It was not uncle who came when I went down, it was the doctor. When I came up and looked down, I saw uncle and father getting down from the coach. That's why they are so late. Couldn't they have taken a taxi?'

'Doesn't matter. Sita, don't go down again. Stay here and help the doctor,' Rajam said.

Sita stayed back with an air of dissatisfaction. The doctor checked the temperature as usual. He placed the stethoscope on Rajam's back.

He shone the torch into her throat. Duraisami and Kitta Iyer came in just as he was writing the prescription after examining the patient thoroughly.

Kitta Iyer was stunned when he saw Rajam.

Kitta Iyer had been somewhat despondent when he left the village. But after seeing Saundara Raghavan, he regained his enthusiasm. Subbu Iyer assured him that the matter was fait accompli. So, it was with high spirits that he started his journey to Bombay. He began to believe that Sarasu was right, the letter must have exaggerated Rajam's condition. Nor did Duraisami say anything to prepare him when he received him at the station.

Kitta Iyer's loving heart was deeply pained when he saw Rajam looking gaunt and emaciated after many days of fever. Not only her physical appearance, but something in her expression made Kitta Iyer feel that she had not long to live. He looked at the doctor with moist eyes and asked, 'How is she, doctor?'

'Now that you are here, she may get well soon. Your sister's illness is only partly due to physical causes, it is mostly psychological. She is convinced that she is not going to get well. Try to make your sister gain some mental strength. Then she will become all right,' said the doctor as he left, with Duraisami accompanying him.

Kitta Iyer sat next to his beloved sister and said, 'Rajam, you heard what the doctor said. You must be brave, Amma! You must not lose heart!'

'Anna! Do you believe the doctor? Do you think I will survive?' Kitta Iyer was unable to answer Rajam's direct query. Wiping his eyes with his angavastram, he said, 'I am making you feel more downhearted. I am sorry for having neglected you for so long.'

'Anna, it is not your fault. What can you do? I was only afraid that you might not come now. I prayed to God to keep me alive till you arrived. Once I unburden my heart to you, I can close my eyes in peace.'

Suppressing his sobs, Kitta Iyer said, 'Don't be silly! Why are you so pessimistic? Nothing will happen to you. You will live to see Sita get married and play with your grandchildren.'

Rajam's sad smile revealed her doubts.

Seeing Sita standing near the door, Rajam made a sign for her to approach.

'Sita! Uncle has come all the way from the village! Shouldn't we give him some coffee?' she asked. 'I will get it at once,' Sita said, running into the kitchen.

15
RAJAM'S SECRET

As soon as Sita left, Rajam said, 'Anna! I don't know how things will turn out. Will I get the chance later to say what I want to say? No, I must do it right now. You'd have brought a trunk with you. Please fetch it.' Unable to guess the reason for her disquiet, Kitta Iyer answered, 'What's the hurry Rajam? It is a heavy trunk. It can be brought here at leisure.'

'Just bring the trunk! First go out and check if my husband gets into the car with the doctor. It is likely that he will go out to buy medicines.'

Realizing that it was useless to reason further with Rajam, Kitta Iyer looked out from the corner of the balcony, saw Duraisami getting into the car, and returned to the room with his trunk.

'Anna, shut the door. Bring the trunk to my bedside. Quick!'

Kitta Iyer obeyed her and watched Rajam's actions in surprise. She sat up and took one of the pillows, removed the pillow cover and unpicked the stitches from one side. She thrust her hand into the cotton stuffing and pulled out two wads of currency notes and an exquisitely crafted necklace of rubies. Diamonds glittered on its pendant. Encircled by diamonds, a topaz dazzled the eye.

'Anna! Please put these bundles of notes and the necklace inside your trunk. Quickly!'

Kitta Iyer hesitated.

Rajam said, 'I haven't stolen anything! Anna, first put them away safely in your trunk. And then I will tell you all about it. I must.'

Feeling that he was part of a strange dream, Kitta Iyer placed the rupee notes and ruby necklace in his trunk. He locked the trunk, raised his head and looked at Rajam.

Rajam remained silent until she regained her breath and overcame her fatigue. Then she said, 'The two thousand rupees I gave you are for Sita's marriage. The ruby necklace must be given to her to wear on her wedding day. Anna, it is you who must get Sita married. Take her with you and get her married to some good man in our native place. Say yes! Only then can I find some relief. As the doctor said, I may even get well.'

'Rajam? Do you have to ask me to do this? I have always considered Sita to be as much my child as Lalita. I will certainly find a good bridegroom for her. You are going to be with her on that joyous occasion. But Rajam, did you have to hoard money for Sita's wedding without your husband's knowledge? I have heard that village women hoard money by selling household utensils and practising thrift. I expected better from you. What will your husband think if he comes to know? And what will he think of me? I don't like this at all!'

'Wait Anna. I am not the kind of person who will do something so wrong. I have not taken even a quarter of an anna from his money. When he faced difficulties, I gave him the jewels you made for me, and those he gave me in the early years of our marriage. How can I save from household expenses? If you lived in Bombay, you will know how impossible that would be. This money and necklace are God's wedding gifts to Sita. You know how I loved story books from childhood. But something happened in my life which is far more incredible than all the incredible happenings in the thousand stories I have read. I am going to tell you about it. Nobody else knows this. Not even Sita.'

Sita appeared with coffee.

Taking the coffee from Sita's hands Kitta Iyer asked Rajam, 'Will you have some?'

'Yes, a little,' said Rajam. 'It is coffee, not the doctor's medicines, which has kept me alive.' Then she said to Sita, 'Child, see if Appa is back. There is no medicine left, not even a single dose. Come and tell me as soon as you see Appa return.' Sita got the hint at once, ran out and down the staircase.

Rajam looked at Kitta Iyer and said, 'Anna, you must never let Sita's father know what I am going to tell you now. Nor anyone else. Not even your wife. I know that you will keep your word. You will, won't you?'

'No, I won't tell anyone. But it would be best if you don't tell me anything. You get breathless when you speak. Did I come to Bombay to make you get worse?'

'I am not getting worse. Listen! It has been twenty days since I fell ill this time. I remember very well that I got sick on a Friday. I had just lit a lamp before the picture of the Goddess. "Mother, you have supreme power!" I prayed, "You must protect my daughter Sita. You must bless her so that she may make a good marriage." Suddenly, I felt strange, I trembled, my head began to spin. I came to lie down on this bed. Sita had gone to meet her friend. My husband had not come back from work. As I told you, sometimes he comes late, there are days when he does not come home at all. As I wondered whether he would come that evening, sleep overcame me. For a while I did not know what was happening.

An hour must have gone by. When I opened my eyes, I saw that the door that had been left shut, was opening. A women entered. She must have been more or less my own age. She looked as if she belonged to the north. She had covered her head. She carried a small leather box. Coming nearer she enquired in Hindi, "Are you Rajam?" Having lived here for twenty years I know Hindi very well. Yet I hesitated and did not answer, not knowing who she was.

She said in agitated tones, "Look, I am here on a matter of importance. No time to waste. Are you Rajam from Rajampettai? Duraisami Iyer's wife?"

"Yes," I said in a faint voice.

"How can I believe you?" she asked and looked around. The photographs on the wall caught her eyes. Anna, you can see that one of them is a photograph taken soon after our marriage. Another is of the two of us with Sita, taken three years ago. Looking intently at the second photograph she asked, "Is this your daughter?" "Yes," I replied. Turning suddenly towards me, she stared at my face. "Yes, you are Rajam," she muttered.

I gazed at her. I cannot describe the glow on her face and the magnetic power of her eyes. I wondered, can there be a woman as beautiful as this in the world? And yet I was frightened when the woman placed her box on the table and went quickly to lock the door. I could not move. I was spellbound like a serpent charmed by a mantra. The woman stood with her back to me, opened her box, picked up some things and came to me.

"Rajam, you will be surprised by what I am going to say," she said. "But first take this money and the necklace. There are 2000 thousand rupees here. The necklace is extremely valuable. I am giving them both to your daughter for her marriage. Don't hesitate. Take them."

I was torn by awe, joy and fear. I was thrilled at Sita's good fortune. I wondered who she was, and why she was giving me these gifts. "Keep them safe!" she said. "I will lock them up later," I said and thrust them under the pillow.

"Rajam!" she said again. "You must be astonished that a total stranger is giving you this money and necklace. Yes, you don't know me. But I have known you awhile. A long time ago, I did something to hurt you. Not deliberately. It was an accident. I give you these gifts in reparation. Keep them carefully and give them to your daughter when she gets married. But you must not let anyone know that I gave them to you, not even your husband! Understand?" she said. I was too stupefied to reply. She asked me again harshly, "Do you understand what I'm saying?"

"Yes…" I murmured. "Will you keep your word?" she asked. I was silent. The woman's face changed. She turned into a flaming virago. Her eyes shone like live coals. She drew something out of her box. It glittered. Can you guess what it was?' asked Rajam and paused.

Kitta Iyer was dumbfounded by Rajam's account. He wondered if she knew what she was saying. But the money and the necklace that he had put away in his trunk were real enough. Could the story also be true?

'How do I know, Amma? Nor do I need to know. You have talked enough. Rajam, don't you remember what the doctor said?'

'Never mind the doctor. Please listen to me. What the woman grabbed from the box was a small, sharp, curved dagger. She held it before my eyes and said, "Do you see this, Rajam? Look again. I am good to good people. I am bad to the wicked. You must do exactly as I say. You must never say a single word about me even to your husband. If I come to know that you did, one day I will strike you with this dagger and yank your intestines out. Be warned!"

I blanked out completely. I stared at the dagger glistening under electric lights. "Don't be afraid, Rajam, don't be afraid. Nothing will happen to you if you do as I say."

As she was talking, we heard footsteps coming up the stairs. "Your husband?" she whispered. "No, my daughter," I said. Her fears vanished. Sita stood outside the bedroom door and knocked. "Amma, are you busy?" she asked.

I called out, "Sita! See if the lamp is burning near the picture of the goddess. Today is Friday. Wash your face, put a fresh dot on your forehead and chant the *Lalita Sahasranamam.*"

The woman locked her leather box hastily. I heard her open the door and go down the staircase. Only then did my breath return. So did my confidence. I slid my hand under the pillow. The money and the necklace were still there. No, I hadn't dreamt it, what had happened was real. Sita came in asking, "Amma, has anyone been here? I heard sounds. Amma, why are you lying in bed at this hour?" She stopped short, transfixed by what she saw on the table. A glittering dagger lay there. In her haste the woman had unwittingly left it behind.

"Amma! Where did this knife come from? It has a strange handle!" she said and was about to pick it up when I said in a palpitating voice, "No, no! Don't touch it!" Sensing my distress, Sita left the dagger alone and stared at me.

Once again, there were sounds of footsteps on the staircase. The woman rushed in like a hurricane, went straight to the table, grabbed the dagger, and thrust it into her leather box. Then she looked at Sita. "Rajam, is this your daughter?" she asked. "Yes," I replied. At once she hugged Sita and kissed her on the forehead. "May God keep you safe. May he protect you from the barbarities of menfolk," she said and left the room.

When the sounds of her footsteps died, Sita came to me and asked, "Amma, who is this mad creature?"

"Sita! She is not mad. She is a very good woman. We are old friends."

"Old friends? But I have never seen her!" Sita said.

"We were great friends before you were born. Then she moved to Parel. She couldn't visit us here," I explained. Yes, I lied. Somehow, I felt I should lie…'

Kitta Iyer, who had been listening to Rajam's story, thought to himself, 'Is this the only lie? Everything she has been telling me is a lie. Poor thing! Having saved money for Sita without her husband's knowledge, she is making up stories now.'

16

GODDESS SUPREME

Rajam's account left Kitta Iyer wondering whether it was a story she had read or made up. It was not over yet… Kitta Iyer learnt that Duraisami arrived a few minutes after the woman had gone. He asked Rajam, 'Did anyone come here? As I came up the stairs a "zenana" woman wearing a burqa went thudding past me.'

Giving Sita a meaningful glance, Rajam said, 'No.'

'Never mind. But why are you lying in bed at this time of the day? Are you feeling unwell?'

'Not at all. Just felt a bit shaky. That's why I decided to lie down.'

Duraisami approached Rajam and touched her cheek. Rajam wondered why his hand was so cold. 'Silly woman! You have high fever. Let me fetch the thermometer,' he said. As he left the room, Sita too touched her mother and exclaimed, 'Yes, Appa is right. You are burning up.'

Rajam realized they were right. And the realization brought doubt. Had high fever made her hallucinate everything that had happened moments ago? It was a painful thought. In the thirty-five years of her life, this was the first time that reality had morphed into fiction. How could she not be disappointed if that fantastic incident turned out to be a mirage!

Rajam thrust her hand under the pillow and touched the notes and the necklace to confirm that they were real. She called Sita, put an arm around her and whispered, 'Don't say anything to Appa. I will explain later.' Sita understood and said, 'Yes, Amma.' Duraisami came with the thermometer. Rajam's temperature read 104 degrees.

'I was wondering why you didn't fall sick this year. And here you are, sick again,' Duraisami said and went to bring the doctor home.

For twenty days after that, Rajam could not leave her bed. At first the doctor diagnosed her illness as influenza. After five days he suspected typhoid. Ten days later he said, 'It could be the new fever – kala hazar.' Finally, he concluded that it was no physical ailment; Rajam had some mental stress. And yet he did not stop prescribing medicines day after day.

Listening to Rajam with some disbelief Kitta Iyer said, 'Enough Rajam! Stop it. You can tell me the rest tomorrow.'

Sita entered the room to announce that Duraisami had returned with the medicines.

Seeing his wife and brother-in-law together, Duraisami said, 'So, now that her brother is here on a rare visit, Rajam has been going yackety-yak. The doctor has said that she must not talk too much. You must make sure she doesn't. She never listens to me.'

Kitta Iyer thought, 'What a task he has given me. Might as well ask me to dam the Kaveri running in full spate.'

The next day the doctor came as usual. He examined Rajam with his habitual attitude of believing that the patient had fallen sick just to give him trouble. 'The brother's arrival has made the sister slightly better!' he said but did not desist from taking pen and paper to write out ten different medicines.

That day, when Duraisami left in the doctor's car to get the medicines, Kitta Iyer sat down again beside his sister and said, 'Rajam, I am not happy with your account of how the money and jewel came to you. Let me give them away to a temple or to some charity. I will get Sita married. Why should we hang on to something given by a strange woman? Who is she? How did she get these things? The fact that she left a dagger here and returned to take it raises all kinds of suspicions.'

'I have thought deeply about this. Like you, I too wondered if I should give it away to some charity. I even thought of donating this to the Bihar Earthquake Relief Fund. But I didn't have the heart to do it. I felt that this is Sita's property, Anna. Did you donate anything towards earthquake relief?'

'Those are all huge problems, Amma. Are they going to be solved by our donations?'

'I don't agree. Shouldn't we show that we also belong to the human race? We can do what we can do.'

'All right. We will. Let us now finish talking about Sita. This money and jewellery…'

'…Anna, this is no ordinary gift, it is blessed with divine grace.'

'How can you be so certain? We don't know anything about the woman.'

For some time, Rajam remained lost in thought. Then, she opened her eyes to say, 'I know who she is.'

'Who is she?'

'She is Devi Parasakti, Anna. The goddess supreme. My prayers of twenty years did not go in vain!' Rajam said, tears of joy rising in her eyes.

Kitta Iyer became even more bewildered. He told himself, 'The doctor seems to be right. There's something mentally wrong with her.' He prayed to the family deity to make Rajam sound of body and mind.

The doctor came again the day after. He examined the patient as usual. 'She's better today,' he said. Then, struck by a sudden thought, he added,

'What your wife needs is a change of scene. She has been in Bombay for twenty years. Let her go somewhere on a holiday. Your brother-in-law lives in the village, doesn't he? Let her go with him on a visit.'

'I have no objections. If Kitta Iyer is ready to take her…'

'What do you mean ready to take her? Of course, I am delighted to take her with me.' Kitta Iyer said.

'Doctor, I have lived here for twenty years. I want to be here for the rest of my days,' Rajam said.

17

DURAISAMI'S HOUSEHOLD

Everyone liked the doctor's suggestion. Except Rajam. Over and over again did Kitta Iyer urge her to come to the village. Duraisami joined him. Sita begged her mother more insistently than the other two, 'Let's go to Rajampettai, Amma. I want to see Lalita.' But Rajam would not agree.

After two or three days there was a change in Duraisami's behaviour. He who had appeared to be calm and generally pleasant, now acted like one possessed. He spent little time at home, didn't talk to anyone and didn't show any concern for Rajam's health. He railed at Sita. He flung pots and pans around tempestuously.

One night there was a big rumpus in Rajam's bedroom. At first Duraisami and Rajam spoke calmly. Kitta Iyer and Sita were in the other room, but they had not fallen asleep yet. They could hear the conversation between Rajam and Duraisami somewhat faintly.

Soon the talk gained in volume. The words became sharp and cruel.

'You will be happy if I die!'

'Why don't you make up your mind and die once and for all? Why do you stay alive to torture me?'

Kitta Iyer recalled the recent change in his wife's nature. He had been saddened by it. But now he felt gratified as he realized that compared to this couple, him and his wife were better off.

Suddenly, they heard the sound of slaps. 'Ayo, don't! Please don't!' Rajam cried. Kitta Iyer thought that Duraisami was beating Rajam to death. Things had gone beyond control, and he could not remain an onlooker anymore. He ran headlong through the door which had been left merely shut.

But what he saw was contrary to what he had surmised. Duraisami was not beating Rajam. He was repeatedly slapping his own head in frustration. Rajam was shouting to make him stop.

In that instant, just as a vast landscape of fields, trees and the distant cloud-capped mountains can be seen through a small window, Kitta Iyer perceived the true nature of the couple's twenty-years' experience of married life. Until then, he had felt sorry for Rajam because he believed that Duraisami was tormenting her. Now he felt sorry for Duraisami because he knew that Rajam was the tyrant.

As soon as he saw Kitta Iyer, Duraisami stopped hitting himself and Rajam stopped shouting.

Kitta Iyer sat down next to Duraisami and asked in a calm voice, 'Should you be doing this?'

'You can interrogate me about what I should do and not do, but can you stop her from being foolish and obstinate? The doctor insists that only a change of place can cure her. But she says she wants to die at my feet. It seems that is the only way she can find salvation. See how her mind works? She doesn't want to live to see our child, Sita, married. And if she were to die, how can I manage with a motherless child? At the very least, can't she die after getting Sita married?'

Kitta Iyer stood transfixed before this torrential downpour. Rajam came to his rescue, saying, 'Anna! I will come to the village with you. I am ready to leave tomorrow. He doesn't want me to live in peace in this house and die at his feet. He wants me to be tormented to death by my sister-in-law and see my remains burning on the banks of the Kaveri.'

'Rajam, why do you talk nonsense? Have you lost it? If you don't want to stay in Rajampettai, you can stay with your sister in the next village! Are we all your enemies? Isn't the doctor's suggestion the only reason for our trying to persuade you? Calm yourself and think about it,' Kitta Iyer said.

'I say this only after calm reflection. Forgive me if I have said anything wrong. I will come with you. I mean it.' Rajam said.

'Do you know why she is defiant? She thinks that it is she who is saving me by staying here. She thinks I will drink myself to death. If I decide to do it, can she stop me just by staying here?'

'Haven't I agreed to go? Why waste more words? Anna, go and get some sleep. Sita, Sita!' Rajam called out.

'Amma,' Sita answered from outside.

'Still awake? Come here.'

Sita came skipping. Her face had brightened. She was used to her parents' squabbles. And now, she was thrilled that their fight had ended with the decision that Rajam would leave for Rajampettai.

'Sita, your prayers have been answered. You were constantly saying that we must go and see Lalita. Finally, we have decided to do just that. Happy?' Rajam asked.

'Very happy,' Sita said.

From that night Rajam's health took a turn for the better.

On the eighth day of Kitta Iyer's visit, Rajam, Sita and he boarded the Madras Mail at the Victoria Terminus. Duraisami came to the station and bought their tickets.

Pandemonium reigned in the station. The tumult of trains simultaneously arriving and departing from twelve different platforms, the clangour of coaches being linked, the babel of thousands of passengers chattering in multiple languages, the cries of *chaiwalas*, *paniwalas*, porters, newspaper vendors – everything mingled to create a deafening uproar. White sahebs and their memsahebs, Gujaratis and Maharashtrians, Parsis and Madrasis, men and women, the young and the old, crashed and collided into each other as they ran in different directions.

None of these scenes caught Rajam's attention. None of the sounds registered in her ears.

Both her eyes were singularly focused on Duraisami. She heard nothing but his words.

As he stood near the door chatting with Duraisami, Kitta Iyer's attention was drawn to the slogans shrieked out by the paperboys. 'Attempt to Kill Rajnipur Maharaja' 'A Woman's Audacity!' 'Arrested, Dagger in Hand' shouted the boys who were selling newspapers in English and Hindustani. With the little English he knew, Kitta Iyer grasped the gist of the matter and asked Duraisami, 'What's this "Maharaja murder"?' He noticed how Duraisami flinched and scowled as he answered, 'Things like this happen all the time in Bombay. None of our business!'

As the train began to move, Duraisami said in loud and emotional tones, 'Rajam, I will come as soon as I can and bring you back. Don't worry! I will be all right. Sita, take good care of Amma. Kitta Iyer, take care! Lock the compartment from inside. Rajam, take care of your health.'

Duraisami spoke with genuine feeling. He fully meant it when he said, 'I will come soon and bring you back.' However, in this world, we see only too often that man proposes and God disposes.

18

THE THREE FRIENDS

Two houses stood facing each other on a main road in Devapattinam, each two storeys high. Both houses had grilled verandahs in front. Both had boards hanging at the entrance – 'Atmanatha Iyer, BA, BL, Advocate' and 'N. Damodaram Pillai, BA, BL, Advocate'.

Atmanatha Iyer and Damodaram Pillai were long standing friends and well-known lawyers in Devapattinam. Both had large households and large earnings, but both had incurred some debts in building large houses.

Two years ago, there was a change in their status. Both tried to get appointed as public prosecutors. They made their attempts openly. 'If by some chance, Damodaram Pillai is not offered this post, it may be offered to me,' said Atmanatha Iyer. Damodaram Pillai declared, 'If Atmanatha Iyer is not given this post, it may be given to me.' Many other lawyers entered the fray. Finally, Damodaram Pillai became the public prosecutor. An overjoyed Atmanatha Iyer was the first to throw a celebratory party.

However, Atmanatha Iyer's mind was irked by the thought, 'Such a good friend! And yet he did not yield to me in this matter.'

'Such a good friend but he did not hesitate to compete with me.' thought Damodaram Pillai.

Hiding these reflections, they continued to be friends.

On the third-floor terrace in Damodaram Pillai's house sat three young men, engaged in carefree banter.

One of them was Damodaram Pillai's eldest son Amarnath.

Another was Atmanatha Iyer's firstborn Pattabhiraman. The third was our Rajampettai Kitta Iyer's son Surya Narayanan.

The first two were both twenty years old, undergraduates studying for their examinations. Surya was two years younger. But he was still working for his SSLC examination as Kitta Iyer had sent him to high school rather late.

Atmanatha Iyer was Kitta Iyer's lawyer and old friend. Therefore, Kitta Iyer had requested him to keep an eye on his son. Surya had his meals in a hotel but stayed in Atmanatha Iyer's house.

'Amarnath, you know that Surya is leaving for his village tomorrow, don't you?'

'Is that so? Why now, with his exams round the corner?' Amarnath asked.

'Someone is coming from Madras to "see" a girl. Appa wants me to be there,' Surya explained.

'How does it matter to you if someone is coming to see a girl? Are you that someone? Or are you the girl?' Amarnath asked.

'Should he not be there if his sister were to get engaged to be married?' Pattabhiraman retorted.

'What? Is Surya's sister Lalita to be married? And someone is coming from Madras to see *her*? Pattabhi, why, I thought *you* were going to marry Surya's sister.'

'Chee! Chee! What nonsense! How can you say this when Surya is here with us?'

'Is it nonsense to speak the truth? I will ask Surya himself. Surya, here is our Pattabhiraman, dreaming of Lalita day and night. Why should someone from Madras come to see Lalita?'

'How do I know? Do they make these arrangements after consulting me? Perhaps Pattabhi's horoscope was not a good match for my sister!'

Amarnath gave a mini lecture. 'Our country is going to the dogs because we still hang on to horoscopes. Every marriage takes place after matching horoscopes. And yet, ninety couples out of a hundred live in hell. Moreover, within a year of getting married, any number of girls become widows. Best to collect all the horoscopes in the country and consign them to flames.'

'All talk and no action. Your father too goes on like this. But when your sister got married last year, did he not call a brahmin priest to conduct the wedding? And though he repeatedly announced his lack of faith in astrology, didn't he consult fortune tellers when he was unsure about securing the public prosecutor's post?'

'Pattabhi, what kind of an argument is this? Am I responsible for my father's actions?'

'Very well. In the same way there is no connection between Surya's sister's marriage and any hurdles in my horoscope. My horoscope was not asked for, nor matched with hers. Don't you know my views on marriage? Haven't I stated over and over again that I will not marry until I pass my exams and find a job with monthly earnings of at least ₹200?'

'Who are you trying to bluff? As if I don't know how agitated you were when Kitta Iyer and his daughter came to stay with you for a week last year. You were scurrying up and down the house, like a cat with newborn kittens. Do you think I have forgotten?'

'Amarnath, I am sorry I talked about this matter. I take it all back.'

'Not possible my dear fellow, not possible. Once the case is brought to court, the defendant cannot withdraw it as and when he likes. He can do it only if the opposing counsel and the court permit him to do so. Pattabhi, do you think I don't remember how you raved about Lalita in those days? Your descriptions would have put Kamban and Kalidasa to shame. I remember how you even made up a verse and sang it. Didn't it go like this? "One day Lalita walked by a pool filled with lilies. The buds bloomed as if they were bursting into smiles, mistaking Lalita's beautiful face to be the full moon!"'

'Amarnath! Enough! Stop it! Don't embarrass me. Surya may take offence at your facetious humour,' Pattabhiraman said, greatly disconcerted.

'Let him. What can he do? Behead me? Surya, what your father is doing is just not right. With Pattabhiraman around, why should he look for another groom? What's wrong with Pattabhi?'

Surya who had been listening with a frown on his face now said, 'May I say what I think? I want Lalita to marry Pattabhi. It will make

Lalita happy too. I don't know why they are trying to get some unknown fellow to tie the knot round her neck. I don't like it at all.'

'Both of you are jabbering without trying to understand what *I* want! I do not have such thoughts about Lalita. But I will say this. It is completely wrong to invite some stranger, showcase the girl before him, allow him to pronounce his judgement on her looks, and then declare that he doesn't like the girl. It may be far less objectionable if the girl too has the right to say yes or no, but the girl never has the guts even to raise her head and look at the fellow.'

Amarnath said, 'How can you say that? Many weddings have been cancelled because the girl rejected the man.'

Pattabhiraman retorted, 'In fiction perhaps, not in real life.'

'Surya, listen to me. Tell your sister to reject the boy who comes to see her,' Amarnath said.

'Surya, don't! Amarnath misunderstands my intentions towards Lalita. A lovely flower blooms on a tree. A man says, "It is beautiful." Does it mean that he should own the flower? I can enjoy looking at the flower, even if somebody else plucks and wears it.'

'Humbug! Only a very rare human being can leave the flower on the tree unplucked. In any case, the flower will look lovely only if it is plucked and worn by someone worthy of it. How can we enjoy seeing the flower worn by an ugly donkey? Nor will the donkey enjoy it. It will mistake the flower for a ball of paper and try to eat it.'

'I cannot argue with you. And yet I know I am right.'

'Surya? What do you say?' Amarnath asked.

'I agree with you,' Surya said.

'See, Pattabhi! The majority is against you.'

'Don't you know that Swami Vivekananda said, *what you call majority is mainly composed of fools*?'

'My dear fellow, Swami Vivekananda may have said it but you and I cannot! He who disdains the majority can never make any progress. If he cannot follow the majority, he must learn to survive by duping the majority,' Amarnath said.

19
THE ACCIDENT

On a pleasant evening in February, a covered cart drawn by two bullocks, their bells jingling, was moving along at a spanking pace on the road to Rajampettai. The cart, the bullocks, and the cloth wound around the driver's head, all proclaimed that the vehicle belonged to Pattamaniam Kitta Iyer. Kitta Iyer's eldest son Surya was ensconced within, trunk and bed roll beside him. His mind was racing ahead worrying about his sister and the 'wise guy' coming all the way from Madras to 'see' her. He was rather angry with that 'wise guy' for no reason. 'Big shot comes to see the girl, passes judgement with a "yes" or a "no". Disgraceful!' This persistent thought troubled him. The conversation on Damodaram Pillai's terrace kept playing in his mind.

Surya looked out, to check the distance yet to be covered to reach Rajampettai.

A milestone came up showing the figure 5 painted in black. 'Three more milestones to cross. Muruga! Can we get home before it gets dark?' Surya asked. 'Easily,' the driver answered. 'If only you hadn't stopped me from whipping the beasts, we would have been there by now. Amma told me to bring you home in time for coffee.'

As Murugan was speaking, Surya noticed another wooden cart moving half a furlong ahead, with some women seated within. That cart also seemed to be on its way to Rajampettai. As Surya wondered who could be in it, a motor car appeared, honking raucously.

'Getting into a motor car simply goes to some people's head. They want everyone to make way for them. Why not lay a separate road for cars alone?' Murugan grumbled as he moved the cart to the side of the road. The motor car overtook them and disappeared in a big cloud of dust.

As soon as it went past them, Murugan said, 'Chinnayya must finish his studies, get a big job and buy a motor car.'

'Then people will curse me just as you cursed those motorists,' Surya replied. At that moment something that happened before their eyes, putting a stop to their chatter.

Overtaking the closed cart preceding Surya's vehicle, the motor car honked to force it out of the way, but the cartman tried to move to the left instead of the right. The car tried to get past the cart on the right side. Finding it impossible, the car swiveled and overtook the cart from the left side, moving so close as to almost graze the bullocks in the process. The terrified bullocks stumbled into the ditch beside the road. When their reins slipped from his hands the cartman jumped down in a panic. The cart toppled, with its topside pointing upward and the rear sloping to touch the ground. The passengers came slithering down as on a slide. Their belongings tumbled down and landed on them.

The car vanished within seconds, hidden behind a thick curtain of dust.

Since the scene was obscured by dust, Surya's imagination exaggerated the extent of the damage. He shouted in alarm, 'Muruga, Go, go! Go faster!'

Murugan drove as fast as he could and stopped the cart near the spot where the accident had taken place.

'Chinnayya! Looks like your aunt, with the Bombay Amma and her daughter! Saami, save them from harm.' Surya did not hear the driver's words. In a flash he jumped down and ran to the toppled cart.

Rajam was still inside, gripping the vehicle's rear latch to keep herself from sliding down the slope. Bundles were scattered beside her. A tin box lay at the edge, threatening to crash any moment. Rajam was afraid that she might get hit on the head if she let go of the latch. Wasted by illness, her emaciated face had turned pale, for her darling daughter Sita was screaming, 'Amma, Amma! I am drowning. Save me, someone!'

Another woman who had fallen four or five feet away from Rajam was moaning, 'Ayyo Appa!' as she cautiously scrambled up to a sitting posture. 'As soon as I heard the motor car, I told the cartman to move aside. Who listens to me?' said she and rained a string of 'blessings' on him. Then she enquired anxiously, 'Rajam, are you hurt?'

Surya had rushed at full tilt, fearing that a terrible disaster had occurred. Now he surveyed the scene and realized that the woman trying to get up was his aunt, Abhayam. The woman inside the cart must be his aunt from Bombay. His concern for them was but momentary, as his eyes and attention switched to the girl who had fallen into the rill beside the road, thrashing her legs and arms in the water shrieking, 'Amma, Amma! I am drowning.' In two strides he was by the stream, to save the girl.

The girl who was shouting and splashing in the water looked at the young man who stood by the stream panting in agitation. At once she stopped shouting, stared at Surya's face as if it were a rare and wondrous sight and broke into tinkling laughter. Surya felt as if the nectar-soaked song of a kuyil had morphed into the many-splendoured blossoms raining on him.

20

INTRODUCING A COUSIN

Once he got over his surprise at her breaking into laughter, Surya realized his mistake. Clearly, she had cried out in fun. Since the stream had no more than knee-deep water the girl had been in no danger at all.

A ditch had formed where water had collected until it became a rill. Red and white lilies bloomed in the waters, among the clustering leaves.

The branches of the roadside banyan trees arched over the stream. The golden rays of the sun beamed through their vernal branches, making magic on the blue waters of the rill.

Beside the stream lay golden sheaves of paddy, bent with the weight of ripened grain. Beyond the fields stood emerald green groves of coconut trees.

These polychromatic scenes of nature imprinted themselves on Surya's mind only to make him perceive them as fake visuals of beauty, serving to highlight the genuine beauty of the water nymph in the stream. A sudden thought flashed through his mind. Through his entire life – as long as there was breath in his body, and as long as his mind remained capable of thinking – he would never be able to forget the scene that he was beholding at that moment.

Surya came down to earth from the world of dreams when the water nymph stopped laughing and asked, 'Periamma! Who is this boy?'

'This is your cousin Surya. Can't you make out just by looking at him?' said Abhayam.

'Oh Periamma, so this is Lalita's elder brother?'

'Yes. Lalita's elder brother. Come out of the water and change into dry clothes,' said Abhayam and then turned to Surya to say, 'From where did you come? This is your aunt Rajam from Bombay, and this is her daughter. You haven't met them before, have you?'

'Athai, I am coming from Devapattinam,' said Surya as he walked away from the stream. 'Lucky that no one got hurt. Let us pay this cartman and send him away. We can all go in our vehicle.'

Sita had come out of the stream by now. 'Periamma! What a perfect spot to get introduced to my cousin! What a pity that the stream did not have more water in it!' she said with a mischievous glance at Surya. Then she went to her mother and asked, 'Amma, you didn't get hurt, did you?'

'I am all right. But Sita, why did you scream that you were drowning? I was frightened out of my wits,' Rajam said.

'Amma, with cousin Surya around, why should you worry? Did you see how he hotfooted to the rescue, to save me from knee deep water?' Sita said as she turned to look at Surya and began to laugh again.

'This girl laughs all the time. She laughs at everything,' Abhayam complained.

By that time both drivers had raised the capsized cart, pushed it back into the street, and somehow got the bullocks in place. At Rajam's insistence, Surya got into the hired vehicle with her. Sita and her aunt into the other. Both vehicles began to move towards Rajampettai.

'Periamma, Surya looks like a carbon copy of Lalita. If he wears a saree, people will think he is Lalita. Are they twins?' Sita asked.

'Chee! Chee! Silly girl. What are you saying? Surya is three years older than Lalita. You know what I want, in my heart of hearts?'

'Tell me.'

Lowering her voice, Abhayam said, 'To get you married to Surya. Kitta will agree at once. He will not refuse to do what I say. But there is that demoness…'

'Who is that demoness, periamma?'

'Who else? Your aunt, Sarasvati. Getting her consent is doubtful. She wants a big alliance, with a dowry and gifts to fill the house.'

'Periamma, you are wrong. Sarasvati Mami is right. People who see Surya and me together will take us to be brother and sister. Will anyone arrange such a marriage? There must be a difference of at least five years between the groom and the bride.'

'Why five years? Two years are more than enough. Your grandfather – I mean my father – was married when he was fourteen years old. Amma was only thirteen then. Do you know how many children she had? Seventeen!'

'That was all right in those days. Today, no boy who is less than twenty will agree to get married. And if he does, the couple will not be happy.'

'Why won't they be happy? They will be extremely happy. If only your Mami agrees the marriage will certainly take place. But why would she agree! She is extremely greedy. But the children are pure gold. They have inherited their father's qualities.'

'Periamma, we should not talk ill of others when they are not present. Why do you say such things about Mami? Sarasvati Mami is a very good woman. Do you know how affectionate she is towards me?'

'Silly girl! You are exactly like your mother. You trust everyone. You will learn about your Mami's nature by and by,' Abhayam said.

At first Surya was disappointed that he did not get into the cart with Sita. But it did not last for more than an instant. Next to Sita, he was eager to get to know his aunt from Bombay.

'Athai, where are you coming from? I thought you were in Rajampettai. Appa wrote and asked me to come because people were coming to see Lalita with the idea of marriage. But I came because I also wanted to see you. Since Lalita returned from Bombay last year, it has become her habit to praise you and Sita constantly. It made me eager to see you!' In his enthusiasm, Surya talked more than he usually did.

'We were here for a week. Abhayam Akka held a sumangali prarthanai in her house and insisted that I should come. This accident happened on our way back. You came at the right time.'

'What did I do? Nothing at all.'

'Don't say that. I was terrified when the cart toppled. It became worse when this silly girl shouted that she was drowning. I got my confidence back only after I saw you. Isn't it true that having our own people with us in times of danger gives us courage?'

'Athai, surely you didn't know that I am one of "your own people" when you first saw me. Why, you have never seen me before.'

'Can you deny the strength of blood ties? I knew you the moment I saw you. Surya, at your age, your father looked exactly like you. You have cropped your hair. Your father had a tuft. Otherwise, you are his mirror image. When I saw you so suddenly, I thought it was Anna who was racing towards us after seeing the cart overturn. I was married when my brother was your age. It seems like yesterday. But twenty years have passed since then,' Rajam said, her vision turning blurry with tears.

'Athai, why did you never visit us after you got married?'

'I was married when I was two years younger than Sita. I left then, to return only now. And yet, I remember this street and rill, field and hedge, grove and wood, temple and pond. Do you know how many times I have travelled to festivals and weddings on a cart like this, and on the same street? When I think about those things, I feel both sad and happy.'

Surya too found himself in a state of wistful joy. He wanted to offer some words of comfort to his aunt, but could not think of any.

21

SITA'S BELOVED

The next day saw the agraharam in Rajampettai bristling with excitement. Though everyone knew that the people from Madras were going to arrive only in the evening to 'see' the girl, no one was able to stay put indoors. More than half the people were standing in front of their own homes. Those who had work indoors kept popping out to look left and right before they retreated within. If the village was in such a state of high expectancy, is there any need to dwell on the height of tension within Kitta Iyer's house?

Seemachu Iyer came early enough to have his morning coffee in Kitta Iyer's house. Scattering his cries of 'Oy oy!', he bustled around, involving himself in the preparations to welcome the guests. Many others kept walking in and out of Kitta Iyer's house for no reason at all. A thousand times did Kitta Iyer have to answer the same query, 'They will be here only in the evening, right?'

Sarasvati Ammal got up at 4.30 a.m. to get started on all the tasks of the day. Long before daybreak, the house was mopped, the front yard swept and adorned with a kolam. After that she engaged herself in scurrying from storeroom to kitchen, kitchen to hall, ordering anyone she saw anywhere, to put away things from the floor into the attic and bring down things from the attic to the living room.

'With everything already going so out of hand, how will I manage when the wedding day comes around?' she moaned repeatedly.

Whenever she saw Abhayam and Rajam, Sarasvati Ammal expressed her satisfaction at their arrival, while strewing double entendres and sly insinuations with all the skills of the great poets. 'You have lightened my load by taking the trouble to come. Would it have mattered if you had not been in such a hurry to get here? Well, don't they say we need people? What can I do all by myself? My mother too is no longer spry. She is not able to handle all the work as before. I am not saying that nothing could have been done if you had not been here. Not at all. And yet, the fact that you made it for the occasion makes me happy.'

Immediately after this she scuttled to her mother to say in a voice loud enough to be heard by everyone, 'Amma! I am unable to get any work done because I see my sisters-in-law standing in my way. And the girl, Sita! She is always buzzing around Lalita, doesn't let Lalita alone for a second! Who would have missed these two women if they had not turned up in such a hurry? Over and above all the work I need to get done, I must also make time to play host to them. Otherwise, I will have to face unnecessary blame. Thank God you managed to get here. I would have been lost without you.'

Sarasvati Ammal was right in saying that Sita and Lalita were inseparable. Lalita welcomed Sita with an eager hug as soon as her cousin got down from the cart the previous evening. After that, not even for a moment did the two girls leave each other's side. At night they even slept on the same mat, sharing the same pillow. No amount of chiding by her mother could make Lalita change her behaviour. From dawn to dusk, the two girls went on huddling and jabbering nineteen to the dozen. Everyone wondered what on earth they had to talk about.

Surya's behaviour was even more surprising. Earlier, whenever he came home, he hardly stayed indoors. Or, he would be found in a corner, reading a book. Seldom did he respond when his mother spoke. He never entered the kitchen, or the inner room frequented by women.

The same Surya was now striding from entrance to kitchen, and kitchen to the room inside. He kept on appearing wherever Lalita and Sita were found together. 'Look at you! It seems you cannot bear to be apart from each other even for an instant! What will you do when you get married and go off to your husbands' homes?' he teased.

It was always Lalita who answered, 'What we do is our business. What's it to you?' Sometimes she said, 'What does a boy have to do with girls' talk? Go and do your own thing.'

'I have nothing to do now, but to look after you,' Surya assured her.

'Get lost!' Lalita told him.

'Why are you driving him away? After all, he is coming to see you out of affection!' was Sita's interpolation.

At this point Lalita's youngest brother Sundu spilled the beans, 'Anna! Why are you lying? Aren't you haunting the house to see cousin Sita?'

'Chee! You donkey! Shut up!' Surya rebuked him.

Sundu said cheekily, 'Well, if I'm a donkey, aren't you the donkey's brother?' Surya ran to grab Sundu's tuft, only to return, in no time at all, to the girls.

It was to escape Surya's hounding that Lalita and Sita went to the poolside bungalow as soon as lunch was over.

When she arrived from Bombay, Sita had stayed in Rajampettai for a week. During that week, the girls often went to the poolside bungalow. With no one to bother them there they talked ad nauseam about their daydreams, all day long. And, instead of going home after sunset, they sat on the steps of the pool and chattered on. The goddess of the sky gazed at them with her million eyes, wondering what endless secrets the two young girls had to discuss!

During one of those enchanting moments at nightfall, Lalita asked, 'Athanga! You have not answered the question I've asked you so many times. Whom are you going to marry? When will you get married?'

Sita looked up at the sky, pensively. Then she glanced at Lalita and said, 'All right. I will open my heart to you. I will not marry to please my father or my mother. I will agree only if my heart is in it. But, will I say "Yes!" the moment someone declares that he will marry me? Of course not! Lalita, didn't I tell you the story of Laila and Majnu? What did Laila demand from Majnu? "Bring me a parrot with five colours from India!" she said. I will not ask for anything so paltry. I will ask my suitor to look at the starry night sky, point to the twelve stars I like, and tell him that I will marry him only if he gets those stars for me. If another takes his place, I will say to him, "Can you bring a champa flower with the fragrance of jasmine from a thornless rosebush?" If yet another man comes along, I will say, "Make me a magnificent painting where the colours of the peacock are merged with the hues of the rainbow…"'

Lalita exclaimed, 'Athanga, what is this! Who can satisfy your demands? People will think you are mad. You will never get married.'

'Not at all! Lalita, the fools will go away saying they cannot bring what I crave. Finally, a man with brains will turn up. "Look here! I have come to offer myself to you. Why do you need anything more?" Without a second thought, I will agree to marry him.'

'Ammammaa! How can you be so callous, and… deceitful?'

'Where is the deceit, Lalita? See what happened when Majnu returned with the Indian parrot! Not finding Laila, he went mad and wandered from place to place. Do you want me to make the man who truly loves me go insane?'

Lalita could not follow Sita's logic. She contented herself with saying, 'All right! Do what you please. Is it possible to beat you in an argument?'

On the day when the visitors from Madras were to arrive, even after the girls reached the bungalow, their conversation did not pick up energy.

'Lalita, we should not have come here today. Mami would have started looking for us by now. She may even think I dragged you here and then scold me.'

'Why should she scold you? If she has to scold someone, let it be me. I know how to handle it.'

'It will take at least an hour to braid your hair with screwpine flowers. It seems the guests will be here as early as at five o'clock. Should we remain here?'

'Are you not a year older than me? Shouldn't any talk of my marriage begin only after your marriage is fixed? I am surprised that father has taken this step. See what's happening today! I don't know why there has to be so much fuss and fanfare. I want to object but I'm afraid that my mother will start a fight if I do…'

At that moment Surya entered the bungalow saying, 'Who is afraid? No need to be afraid of anything as long as I am around.'

22

A SLAP ON THE CHEEK

A few years earlier, wanting to introduce some style and luxury into his life, Kitta Iyer had constructed a bungalow on his own land. He roofed it with palm leaves and sedge grass, fenced it with bamboo poles, planted crotons in front, jasmine and other flowers in the backyard. It became the bungalow by the pond, and the village munsif's chavukkandi, where Kitta Iyer conducted office work and entertained friends. In the summer season, the bungalow was a very pleasant place with cool breezes blowing around it, a congenial spot for a game of cards with a few friends.

After a few years the bungalow started getting dilapidated. But Kitta Iyer had recently renovated it, as Lalita was getting married that year.

Irritated by Surya's sudden entry into the bungalow, Lalita growled, 'No one is afraid! No need for any help from Surya the Super Hero. Can't you leave us alone? Why does a boy have to butt in where women are engaged in their own business?'

'*Women*, are you? Great big *women* indeed! Look at that cheek. Athanga, you tell me. Is this how a sister should talk to her brother? Who is going to come searching for her when she gets married and goes away to her husband's house? Until then, can't she show some affection for the people of her own household?'

Lalita spoke in a hard voice. 'Yes. You are a great big man. You know all about the nature of women. Shut up!'

Sita interrupted, 'Lalita, why do you pounce on your brother like this? No one seems to understand the nature of their own good fortune. Even if they do, they do not appreciate it. Here I am, yearning for a brother like Surya. But you? You are so harsh to him.'

'Well, is that so! Have you joined Surya's side?'

Surya chuckled in delight. 'Why? Should she always be on *your* side? Sita is as much my cousin as she is yours.'

'I am not taking any sides. I spoke only of what is fair. Please, don't get into a quarrel now,' Sita advised them.

'Who is quarrelling? Not I! All I asked was why has he come here. That's all.'

'Lalita, I am here because Athai is searching for Sita. There is a letter from our uncle in Bombay. Since it is addressed to Sita, Athai is waiting for her to come and open the letter. This is the difference between rustics and the well-bred. Here, the first thing they will do is to open any letter, even if it is addressed to others.'

'Why didn't you give Athai's message at once instead of going on and on? Come, Sita. Let us go,' Lalita said.

'Why do you have to go now? Let us stay and chat. Sita will go and return soon.'

'Yes, Lalita. I will come back in five minutes,' Sita said as she left.

There were two reasons for Surya's asking Lalita to stay back. First, aunt and Sita would like to read the letter from uncle by themselves. If Lalita went, she would not allow mother and daughter to have a quiet moment by themselves. Second, Surya wanted to say a few things about Lalita's marriage. He thought that if he missed the moment on hand, he may not get another opportunity to do so.

It was not that Lalita was not attached to Surya. But she had wanted to have a private conversation with Sita and seek her advice on how she should conduct herself when 'they' came that evening. She was infuriated by Surya's arrival, which prevented her from doing so. If she returned home now, she would not be able to have her tête-à-tête with Sita. So, she agreed to stay back.

Surya wondered how he should start. However, thinking about it only made him begin on the wrong note.

'Lalita, you said all kinds of things about your athanga. All lies!'

'What lies?' asked Lalita.

'You said, "Athanga is simply beautiful! She is a goddess no less!"'

'Why, is she not a beauty?'

'Not at all. She is ugly. Wonder which blind man is going to marry her...'

Before Surya could continue, Lalita cried out, 'What? Ugly?' and gave him a tight slap.

Earlier, Surya would have returned Lalita's slap with six knocks on her head. But now he did not. It appeared as if the slap added to his zest. With a beaming face he said, '*Adey* Amma! Such concern for your cousin. An ideal friendship indeed! Lalita, I was simply joking. Your athanga is good looking, all right. But what is the use of having just good looks and brains? Nowadays isn't it money that is needed for girls to make good marriages?'

Lalita's anger bubbled over. 'Money! Money! Money! Yes. For our people money is everything! They will die for money! It seems it is different in the country of the English people! Over there, people get married when they like each other! They don't care how rich or poor you are! Just look at the boys here in our country! You don't have the sense to pick up anything worthwhile from the English people! All you learn from them is to crop your hair, wear pants and shirt, huff and puff in the English language! But when it comes to marriage, you say, "Give me sixteen thousand! Twenty thousand!"'

'Lalita, it used to be a herculean task to get you to speak a single word! When did you become such a chatterbox? God knows what the rascal who marries you will have to endure!'

'Anna! Why curse somebody else if you are angry with me?'

'*Appappaa!* Look at you, rushing to support your future husband. Never mind! Lalita, I came here to tell you something important.'

'Why don't you say whatever it is that you want to say? Why make it such a hush-hush affair?'

'Nothing hush-hush about it. Lalita, I am going to tell you something for your own good. This evening, someone is coming from Madras to see you. If you like the boy, well and good. But if you don't, say so without fear. Don't keep your mouth shut thinking about what

Father and Mother have told you, or out of diffidence. Marriage is no ordinary matter. Once it takes place, you cannot change it, can you?'

'Yes, Anna! I had decided on my own to do just that. In case I don't like the match, you will be on my side, won't you?'

'Of course! You need not have any doubts on that score!'

As she was leaving, Sita had wondered, 'Why come back? Why not take Lalita with me?' She turned back and had taken just four steps towards the bungalow when she heard what brother and sister were saying to each other. She was incensed to hear Surya call her ugly. She also heard the loud slap Lalita gave him in reply. Sita changed her mind and went home.

The shortcut from the poolside bungalow to Kitta Iyer's house was just about half a furlong in distance. During that short walk Sita's mind seethed with inconceivable thoughts. Like a child she prayed in rage, 'The blighter calls me ugly. So! Only a blind man will marry me? O mother goddess! Won't a great man holding a high post fall in love with me and marry me out of hand, to make fellows like Surya hang their heads in shame?' That morning, the hullabaloo in the house had filled her with yearning – would such grand efforts ever be made for her? Surya's words spoken in fun, poured oil on the fire raging in her heart.

At the same time, Sita reminded herself of Lalita's great attachment to her. Why, unable to bear his abuse of her friend, Lalita had slapped her brother on the cheek! What could she do in return for such affection and friendship? Nothing at present. But surely a time would come when she would be able to do so!

Soon, little Sundu came running to the bungalow. 'Lalloo, Amma asked me to bring you back. It seems they must start on your braid. It is three o'clock now and you are still here! Is this the time for talking secrets with your brother?' he shouted in his shrill voice.

23

WHAT IS THIS NOISE?

Sarasvati Ammal had indeed sent for Lalita. As soon as she came home, they began to get her dressed for the occasion. Sita showed great enthusiasm for the task. 'This is how the parting must be done in front, this is how the hair must be plaited, this is how two little curls must be made to hang beside the ears, this is the blouse most suitable for the saree of this colour, bangles on the wrists and flowers on the braid must be of the same colour.' As she lectured on and on, Sita's hands were busily at work executing those very details she gabbled about. Sita's wholehearted zeal in getting Lalita ready melted even Sarasvati Ammal's hardened heart towards the girl.

'After this we must find a mapillai for Sita and get her engaged. It may even be good to have both weddings at the same time, though we don't know if the sastras allow it. It will make economic sense, too, won't it? It will be perfect if the wedding could be held in the month of Chittirai.' Sarasvati Ammal muttered to herself, but loudly enough to be heard by the others.

'Amma, you are talking as if my wedding has been fixed already,' Lalita exclaimed.

'Any doubt about that?' asked Sarasvati Ammal.

Sarasvati Ammal was elated to hear Sita say, 'That's exactly what I am saying. Will those who are coming all the way from Madras undertake this trip just to faff around? And will anyone be able to say "No" after looking at our Lalita?'

'Never mind what the visitors say. What if *I* say no?' asked Lalita.

'Stupid girl! Keep your mouth shut. Don't listen to Surya and talk nonsense,' Sarasvati Ammal growled.

'I have been telling her the same thing, Mami. Why should she imagine she won't like him, even before she has seen him? Mama, who has seen the boy, says that he is as handsome as a god. This time, I think Lalita is being foolish. She has received bad advice from her brother.'

'Lalita, did you hear what your athanga said? Just turn a deaf ear to Surya's babblings. What does he know about these matters? Sita is right. Listen to her advice,' Sarasvati Ammal said.

As Lalita was getting ready, Rajam sent for Surya and said, 'I would like to go around and see the place where I was born and raised. I believe Anna has built a bungalow by the pond? Shall we go there and enjoy the breeze for a while?'

'All right, Athai. Let's go,' said Surya.

They reached the bungalow. Rajammal sat staring at the pond through the window for a very long time. 'I loved getting into this pool and bathing in it. But from the time I reached Bombay, tap water became my Ganga and Kaveri,' said Rajammal with a sigh.

'Athai, I believe you can swim? Abhayam Athai told me,' Surya said.

'Yes, Surya! My father taught me swimming. When I was a child, some woman got carried away on the Kaveri's currents. Saying that women must certainly learn to swim, my father, that is, your grandfather, taught me to swim. I could swim from one end of this pool to the other. Sometimes I have also swum in the river Kaveri. On auspicious times and festival days, we would all take the cart and go to bathe in the Kaveri. I was the youngest in the house. Everyone was extremely fond of me...'

Rajam wiped her eyes and added, 'I've been jabbering nonsense. Well, Surya, I hear that you are studying for the matriculation exam this year. Is that right?'

Seeing the tears in Rajam's eyes, Surya too wanted to change the subject.

'Yes, Athai. It used to be matriculation before. Now they call it SSLC. My mother will understand me only if I say tenth class.'

'Surya, it seems you are staying at an advocate's house and the man has a son who is studying for his BA degree. Is it so?'

'Yes, Athai. Why do you ask?' As Surya asked this question, he realized that his aunt was enquiring about the boy with the idea of getting Sita married to him. The thought pierced him like a sharp needle.

'Surya, you would have heard that my husband is a strange one. I too am not at all in good health. I am anxious to get my daughter married somehow. I have told Anna about it, but he is so busy. Surya, if you can find a good alliance, please let me know! It is for this reason that I said I wanted to talk to you alone.'

'Athai, what's so difficult about this? Sita is good looking and intelligent. Boys will come flocking to compete for her hand. You don't need to worry about finding her a groom!' said Surya. At the same time, he thought, 'Why go looking for others when I'm right here!' He even thought of sharing his thought openly with his aunt, but bashfulness sealed his lips.

'Do you think Sita is smart? Why do you say that? She has turned sixteen, but she hasn't gotten over her playfulness. You saw how she shrieked when she fell into the stream, didn't you?'

'So what? Athai, it is good to see young girls laugh and play! Who likes a crybaby? Lalita's behaviour too has changed after her Bombay visit. Before that she was always morose, fighting with her mother and crying all the time. Only in the last year has she been laughing and playing happily.'

'This silly girl seems to have made your sister laugh endlessly like herself!'

'Why do you call Sita silly when smartness is written all over her face?'

'Surya! Sita is indeed smart in her studies, always a topper in school. She can reproduce any song she hears just once, down to the last note. She has studied up to what they call eighth form in these parts. Her English is good. Ask her to tell a story, and you can listen to her all day. But she knows nothing about the world. I would be at peace if Sita's marriage could be performed this year along with Lalita's.'

As they were talking Surya had a sudden thought. 'Surely Aunt wants to give Sita to me in marriage.' But to yield too easily would lower his dignity. He decided that when his aunt asked him about it openly, he would remain on his high horse and appear to give a half-hearted consent.

So, with assumed indifference, he said, 'What great alliance will you find here that you can't find in Bombay?'

'There may be good alliances to be found in Bombay, but I want to get Sita married to someone here. I feel it is enough for me to have made my life in Bombay. When you return to Devapattinam, will you get me that advocate's son's horoscope? What is his name?'

'His name is Pattabhiraman. The boy is certainly smart. He is studying for the BA degree, but he doesn't own a great deal of property. He has a house, but it is mortgaged. Because of that, his parents are looking for a huge dowry. But there are better options. I will look out for them and let you know. Don't be in a hurry.'

'There may be any number of great options, but must we not settle for what suits us? Surya, these days, those who have given birth to boys demand huge dowries. Let us say you are to get married tomorrow. Will your parents accept anything less than ten thousand rupees?'

Surya wanted to give an impressive lecture denouncing the dowry system. He had just decided to express his confirmed views on marriage when he saw the expression on his aunt's face change. Her face showed signs of fear as she asked 'Surya? What is that sound?'

'Sound? What sound? I don't hear any sound,' Surya said.

'Listen carefully. Surya, doesn't it sound like the waves of the sea?'

Then Surya too heard it. He looked outside the bungalow. His eyes caught sight of the spreading grove of casuarina trees. The soughing of the gentle breezes of spring, wafting through the intertwining branches of the casuarina trees in the grove, created the illusion of the sound of waves on the sea.

Realizing this, Surya said, 'Athai, the leaves in the casuarina grove are rustling and that is sounding like sea waves.'

Rajam's face cleared a little when she saw that it was true.

'Athai, what if it *had* been the sound of the waves? Why did you get so scared?' Surya asked.

'I will tell you some other time,' Rajam replied.

From the distance came the honking of a motor car's horn.

24

THE HEART MISSED A BEAT

When they heard the sounds of the motor car's arrival, Surya said, 'Athai, looks like the people from Madras are here. They said they would be coming only at 5 p.m. But here they are at 4.30 p.m.!'

'Yes, my son. When the time is right, everything happens quickly. Come, let's go!' said Rajam.

'What are we going to do there? Let the others do as they will. I don't care for any of this!' Surya grumbled.

'Is this the way to speak! A wedding is going to take place in the family after twenty years. You are the bride's elder brother! Should you not be in charge of everything? Though my presence is of no consequence, people will misunderstand it if I am not there for the occasion. Come, let us get going!' Rajam said.

On the way back Surya asked, 'Athai, you had a letter from Bombay. Was it from Athimber? Anything of importance? Won't he be joining us here this time?'

'It seems there is a town called Patna in the north. He says that he may have to go there. On the return journey he says he may come here. By chance if Sita's marriage gets fixed by then…'

'Athai, why are you harping on marriage like the women from the village!'

'Surya, it is something to worry about.'

As they walked into the agraharam, they saw the motor car standing in front of Seemachu Iyer's house.

In Kitta Iyer's house, Lalita was at the last stage of getting dressed. Sita's agitation had reached a fever pitch. She was engaged in shifting one bangle from Lalita's wrist to the other, taking off a ring from one of her fingers and sliding it over another, removing the flowers from her hair and adjusting them as she tucked them back again, beautifying Lalita by combing her hair in front on both sides, and changing the pottu on her forehead ten times.

As soon as she saw Surya, Sarasvati Ammal demanded, 'Where were you all this while? "They" arrived half an hour early. You were missing when we looked for you to take their tiffin to them. Seemachu Mama is jumping up and down, driving us to make haste. Finally, I sent it across with the cook and asked Sundu to go along. Go! Go and serve mapillai his tiffin and coffee. I have sent the rava kesari I made. The cook may forget to serve it. Go! Go quickly!'

'I'm not going. How many people do you want to send? I don't know why you are making such a fuss so soon, and for no reason,' Surya said.

'Very clever. Like father like son! With people like them, I don't know how I am going to manage to get the wedding organized.'

Sita intervened, 'Surya? Why can't you listen to your mother? Who is to take care of the bridegroom, if not you?'

'All of you have already decided that he is the mapillai. But he has not come to see Lalita yet,' Surya remarked.

Sita said to Surya, 'Cousin, if you are going to be so recalcitrant, I will go in your place and serve tiffin to our visitors. What are you doing here instead of making your way there as a smart, debonair male member of the family, and saying "Welcome sir!" with a handshake?'

'All of you show so much concern for those who have just arrived. Who bothers about anyone belonging to this household? I too am hungry. Does anyone ask me to have tiffin? Nobody cares. Bad!' grumbled Surya as he left.

When Surya reached Seemachu Iyer's house, the visitors from Madras – the prospective bridegroom, his father, mother and Subbu Iyer – were eating their tiffin. Surya stood in the verandah, holding a pillar. Seeing him, Sastri, the former sub-judge enquired, 'Who is this boy?'

'He is the girl's elder brother, Surya Narayanan. He is studying for the SSLC.'

Saundara Raghavan MA, raised his head and declared, 'Why should studying for the SSLC make him so angry?'

Surya did not enjoy Raghavan's humour. He said, 'Why should I be angry? It looks as if you people were angry even before you came here. That is why you are refusing everything that is being served.'

'Bale! Bale!' said Padmalochana Sastri. 'Kamakshi, did you hear the boy speak? At least now do you agree that I was right when I said that there was something special about the waters of the Kaveri?'

'All boys are smart these days!' said Kamakshi Ammal.

'Do girls lag behind in any way? You will know the answer when you talk to his sister. Oy! Subbu Iyer, don't you agree with me?' Seemachu Iyer said, calling Subbu Iyer to the witness box.

'We will know everything in quarter of an hour,' replied Subbu Iyer non-committally.

Lalita's beautification process was finally complete.

'Sita, now go wash your face and get ready,' Lalita said.

'Why should I get all dressed up? Look! It will look good if this curl hangs by the ear, just so!' said Sita, and began to attend to Lalita once again.

'Enough!' said Lalita. 'Will you, or won't you, get going now? If you don't wash your face and wear a nice saree, I will go into the room inside and lock myself in. Those who have come to see the girl will have to go back without seeing her.'

'Sita, why don't you listen to her? Why should you be so obstinate? It looks like Lalita wants you to accompany her as her friend. How will it be if you stand beside her, all shabby clothes and oily face?' Abhayam said.

Sarasvati Ammal agreed. 'Your aunt is right. Sita, do what she says.'

'All right! What can I do if everyone insists?' Saying so Sita began to start getting herself ready.

That was the moment when Sarasvati Ammal's mother called her daughter, hustled her to the backyard and whispered something to her.

'You always come up with something strange! Keep quiet. The water in the well will not be taken away by the river in spate!' Sarasvati Ammal's response was heard by everyone with the utmost clarity.

The moment Sita changed her saree and came out refreshed in appearance, Sarasvati Ammal said, 'Sita! Sita! See! Your uncle is standing at the threshold! Ask him to come in for a minute. He has not told us about what the child should do when they come.'

Abhayam interposed. 'Why should he tell us? Don't we know? The child must enter the room with a tray with betel leaves and areca nuts. She must put the tray down and prostrate once before everyone. If anyone asks her any question, she must answer loudly and clearly.'

'That is as it may be! But call your uncle for a minute,' said Sarasvati Ammal.

Sita went to the threshold and looked out. Mama and a few others in the village were standing under the thatched canopy in front of the house.

As Sita hesitated, wondering if it would be all right to call her uncle, the motor car arrived and stood in front of the house. Her eagerness to catch a glimpse of the mapillai made Sita tarry on the steps.

First, an elderly man got down from the car. After him a young man stepped out. He must be the bridegroom. Adadaa! How handsome he is! Lalita is lucky. No doubt about it.

Sita's heart rose and blocked her throat. Tears were about to fill her eyes. Her head began to spin. She pulled herself together, quickly. And as she did, she saw that the young man was looking at her. She was overwhelmed by bashfulness to think that he might mistake her for the bride. In two leaps she was inside the house to say, 'They are here!' Then she went to Lalita, hugged her, and said, 'I saw the mapillai. He is extremely handsome! As Mama said, he looks like a god.'

'Chee! Stop it!' said Lalita.

25

SPEAKING GLANCES

Hearing the bustle of people entering the house, the women rushed to hide themselves in the inner room and kitchen.

Sarasvati Ammal alone emerged shortly, and went to greet and welcome Kamakshi Ammal, the prospective mother-in-law.

The men sat on the chairs placed in readiness. Silence reigned for a while.

'Oy! Why don't you ask the girl to join us?' Seemachu Iyer suggested.

'Oy! Why don't *you* do that?' Kitta Iyer replied.

Seemachu Iyer strode to the inner room and said, 'Ask the child to come. The auspicious time falls between 5.30 p.m. and 6 p.m. It is already quarter to six. She must make haste!'

Sounds of argument could be heard from within. Seemachu Iyer said again, 'So what? Let Sita come too. Anyway, the bride and the groom are not going to start talking secrets today, are they? There's time enough for all that later.'

Lalita and Sita came out of the room. Tray in hand, Lalita walked with her head bent low. Sita held her by the hand and seemed to be propelling her forward.

Sita did not lower her head. She looked up at everyone confidently. That sweeping glance took in the groom-to-be as well. She saw that he was not looking at Lalita as she had expected, but at her. Sita got gooseflesh.

Walking as if in a dream, Lalita placed the tray on a three-legged stool beside the seated company. Then she prostrated before all of them.

Sita checked to see what the mapillai was doing when Lalita prostrated before them. He was looking at her, not at Lalita. And not merely looking either, he actually smiled! The stars rained down from the sky and filled the world with their luminescence.

When Lalita rose from the floor, she felt an uncontrollable desire to see the man who was to be her husband. With difficulty did she raise her lowered eyelids. It was Padmalochana Sastri whom she happened to see. She felt an instant's terror, 'Ayo! Not this man!' Then she collected herself with, 'Chee! It cannot be. He must be the mapillai's father.' Then she saw Saundara Raghavan. But he was looking above her shoulder with a smile on his lips. Lalita cast her head down again.

'Which child have we come to see now? Is it the child whose braid is ornamented with jewels?' asked Padmalochana Sastri in a strong and hoarse voice. It fell upon Lalita's ears like the voice of the god of death. In the play she had seen, the god had spoken in the same voice!

His wife Kamakshi Ammal said, 'What an absurd question! Can't you recognize the girl by just looking at her? Not even by the fact that she prostrated before us?'

'I do know it! Still, I want to be sure of making absolutely no mistake. Never mind. Can the girl read? How much schooling has she had?'

Seemachu Iyer answered, 'What a question! *Can* she read and write? Why, she does half her father's work as the revenue officer! There is no storybook or novel she has left unread. Her English is excellent. The bridegroom will know how good it is when he talks to her later.'

Hearing this, Saundara Raghavan, the groom-elect himself chipped in. 'Why later? Why not now?'

'Mapillai, you said it! How right you are! But after all, you see, we are all country cousins here! That kind of modishness has not penetrated to these places. After the wedding is over, when you take the girl to your home, in ten days she will master all the trendiness you want. Oy! Kitta Iyer! Am I right?'

Sub-judge Sastri cut in to say, 'Why ask Kitta Iyer? I can answer you. I am not very much in favour of these modern trends. My wife is even more orthodox. We don't want our daughter-in-law to pass examinations in English and take up a job. And yet, we must take note of the fact that the boy belongs to these times. It is natural for him to want an educated girl. Never mind. Does the child sing? Has she been taught music?'

'Oy! Kitta Iyer, why are you silent? Do I have to give all the answers?' said Seemachu Iyer.

Kitta Iyer said at once, 'The child has not had formal lessons in music. There are no facilities for that in these rural regions. But she sings well. I myself have taught her. I have some knowledge of music.'

'Ohohoho! You have taught her yourself? Does she know any Muthuswami Dikshitar's compositions?'

'Of course! Lalita! Sing "Mamava pattabhirama"!'

All this while Lalita had kept her head down. Now she raised it to look piteously in her father's direction and looked down again.

'No matter if she doesn't know any composition by Dikshitar. Let her sing a composition by Syama Sastri.'

'Oh yes, the child knows Syama Sastri's songs as well. Sing "Saroja dalanetri", Amma!'

'How about Tyagaraja's "Marugelara"?' Seemachu Iyer prompted her.

Lalita remained silent.

Saundara Raghavan interposed with a taunt. 'If she doesn't know any of them, she can sing stanza one from Tyagaraja, stanza two from Dikshitar and round it off with a Syama Sastri finale.'

There was some muffled laughter among the menfolk, whispers among the women. Sparks flew from Surya's eyes.

It did not at all look as if Lalita was going to give in. Speaking in a soft undertone, Sita urged her, 'Why are you keeping quiet? Sing!'

When Sita's urgings proved useless, she glanced at the groom elect. An exchange of glances was enough to make them grasp what they felt. Saundara Raghavan's eyes said, 'How can life go on if I marry this timid mouse, this country bumpkin?' Sita's eyes expressed concern, 'My heartfelt sympathies!'

'Sita, why don't you sing with Lalita? The child is too shy to sing alone,' Subbu Iyer said.

Sarasvati Ammal came up close to Sita and added, 'Yes, Sita! Sing with her.'

'Let me think now... Why, Lalita! Don't you know "Nagumomu"? Let us sing it together! Don't you dare let me down by remaining silent!' said Sita, and began to sing in a voice bright and loud. Lalita joined in part way through the song, but her voice could not make any impression. It was Sita's voice that dominated. When Sita essayed the second part of the composition and rendered the high notes with flair, Lalita tried to do the same, but her voice shrilled out a discordant note. Stopping abruptly, she pulled her hand away from Sita and rushed towards the inner room.

Everyone felt awkward. Kitta Iyer raised an angry voice, 'What is this, Lalita!'

Sarasvati Ammal grabbed Lalita's hand and asked, 'Silly girl! Every day you sing for three hours as if you were giving a concert! What happened to you today?'

Lalita pushed her mother's hands away and went in.

Poor Sita was left stranded and stunned. Then, rolling her eye once and throwing a glance at the groom elect, she too went inside.

Kitta Iyer got up, but Padmalochana Sastri asked him to take his seat again.

'Never mind! Do not trouble the child anymore. We heard her voice. It is very sweet. We can listen to her another day at leisure.'

'The girl is not dumb. That much is clear. That is more than enough,' was Raghavan's snarky comment.

'Don't say such things,' Kamakshi Ammal chided him, and went inside.

The men and the women talked among themselves for a little while. Then the visitors from Madras went back to where they had been put up.

26

RAIN OF FLOWERS

That night, when the cook returned after taking their dinner to the visitors from Madras, Sarasvati Ammal asked him, 'Sankara! What were they talking about? Did your deaf ears happen to catch anything?'

'No, Amma! Nothing of interest whatsoever!' he replied.

'You first say that you heard nothing and then say that it was of no interest. What does that mean?'

'I half-heard a few words. The talk was about money. In tens of thousands. If educated people, people of status are so commercial...'

'What's wrong with that? Those who bear sons will certainly talk like that. If there is to be a wedding tomorrow for our sons, will we get it done without hard cash? It is rumoured that the boy's father is money-minded. The mother must have been telling the son that they must not be shameless and demand far too much. If you ask me, I will say that it is best to discuss everything that must be discussed straightaway and firm it all up. See, there should be no room for complaint later.'

Though Sarasvati Ammal talked non-stop in this manner, she could not quieten her nerves. She called Sita and said, 'Child! Can you go to their house and enquire if they have everything they need? Also, tell Seemachu Mama to come here at once.'

On the way Sita saw Seemachu Iyer heading towards Kitta Iyer's house, but she did not turn back. She went on. Saundara Raghavan was seated on an easy chair in the front hall. When he saw Sita, he sat up and asked, 'You came alone? Or did you bring your friend with you?' Sita hesitated and then answered, 'I came alone. Did you not alarm my friend?'

'Is she still crying? Or has she stopped?' Raghavan asked.

'Why should she cry?'

'She did not sing when she was asked. So, I thought perhaps she had started crying. Never mind. At least you open your mouth in speech. What a problem if you too had been a dumb damsel!'

'If someone had come to "see" me, I too would have been just as dumb,' said Sita and went in, feeling that she should tarry no more. For some reason her heart was beating fast.

In the inner courtyard, Kamakshi Ammal and Padmalochana Sastri broke off their conversation when they saw her.

'Child, why are you here?'

'Mami asked me to check if the food and everything else was to your satisfaction,' Sita replied.

'Tell her that everything was just fine. Is that all?'

'That's all. Mami! I also came to say something about Lalita. Please don't come to the wrong conclusions because she did not open her mouth today. There is no one in the whole world who is as smart as our Lalita. She talks vivaciously, always. She sings far better than I do. Her voice is as sweet as a *kuyil*'s call. Somehow, she got a little scared because newcomers had come to see her with marriage in mind. Please do not misunderstand this!'

'Isn't this girl really smart?' Padmalochana Sastri said.

'No wonder you mistook her for the bride-to-be!' said Kamakshi Ammal.

'Why not? She too will have to get married one day. Child, what does your father do in Bombay?'

'He is in the railways, Mama!'

'His salary?'

'Three hundred rupees a month, but what does it matter how much it is? It is just about enough to make ends meet. You can tell just by looking at me.'

'Are you saying this because you are not wearing jewels like Lalita? By Lord Rama's grace, you too will wear as many jewels one day,' Kamakshi Ammal said.

'Do we need the Lord's grace for something as paltry as jewellery?' Sastri asked.

'Yes. For jewellery, and for everything else, not even an atom moves without him,' replied Kamakshi Ammal and added, 'Never mind! Sita! Hasn't your father made any arrangements for your marriage? Hasn't he done his homework on any mapillai for you?'

'Mami! My father is against an early marriage. And I am on my father's side. Amma keeps on talking about it, though. Tomorrow, she may say something about it to you as well. Don't pay any attention to her!'

'Why do you say that? Should you not be married at the proper time?' asked Kamakshi Ammal.

'Yes. But people ask for five thousand and ten thousand! Where will my father find the money? That is why I have decided that I will not get married.'

Sastri remarked, 'Boy or girl, this is the kind of regard and respect that children must show their parents.'

'Lalita is just the same. Never crosses her parents. Mama, if she gets married to your son tomorrow, she will behave in the same way towards you. Do you know what I told her after you left yesterday? I said, "Lalita, once you are married, your mother-in-law and father-in-law are everything to you, your parents will take second place." And Lalita replied, "Is there any doubt about that?" Mami, did you hear that? Lalita will not behave like these modern girls, showing no respect to others, throwing her weight around. I know I am only a young girl. Please don't get me wrong. Your son will be lucky to marry a girl like our Lalita. And yes, certainly Lalita is also lucky to marry your son!'

'What an amazingly good girl she is!' Sastri exclaimed.

Sita was elated to hear this. She realized that to stay any longer would be inappropriate. 'Mami, I'm leaving now. If I have said anything wrong, please forgive me.'

As she made her way out, Raghavan said, 'I heard everything you said about your friend to my mother. Even if a lawyer had been hired for ten thousand rupees, he would not have spoken as you did on behalf of your friend. Your friend must be very lucky to have you for *her* friend.'

'Thanks,' said Sita.

'Why thank me? It is I, who should thank you.'

'I will not accept your thanks now. I will accept it when you leave tomorrow after getting the wedding fixed.'

'The wedding must indeed be fixed. But for that, isn't it necessary to have the consent of both parties?' asked Raghavan and smiled. Sita returned the smile and left. Her mind could not grasp what Raghavan's smile and words had meant. Perhaps they made sense to her soul deep within.

One thing was certain. As Sita walked towards Kitta Iyer's house, the celestial beings – deva, gandharva, kinnara – all showered flowers full of fragrance on her. Playing on instruments from the heavens, immortal maidens sang honeyed songs. Sita moved along dancing blissfully to those songs. She did not ponder what had happened to her, nor probe into the source of the ecstasy that overwhelmed her, an ecstasy she had never experienced before.

When she reached home, she recovered somewhat from the illusion. Going straight to Sarasvati Ammal she said, 'Mami! You don't have to worry. Our in-laws to be were mesmerized by the way I showered praise on Lalita. Their son too was listening to this. Tomorrow, they will not leave without fixing the wedding, I'm sure.'

Her heart brimming with gratitude, Sarasvati Ammal said, 'Can't the people older than you have at least a fraction of your intelligence! See, no one has even bothered to go and greet the guests. None of them will budge from here. Do you know what Seemachu Mama says? He says that he has a feeling that this alliance will not go through. Who asked for his opinion? It is his habit to always say something negative.'

27

LIGHTNING STRIKES

The great outdoor council of Rajampettai had assembled under the thatched summer awning in front of Kitta Iyer's house.

Seeing Kitta Iyer emerging from the house, Panchu Iyer said, 'Your son Surya is dropping bombshells. He says it is all wrong to lavish money on a wedding that goes on for four days. Taking or asking for dowry is immoral, he says.'

'What is so surprising about it? These days everybody is saying that it is not fair to waste money on needless ostentation when the poor people continue to suffer,' Kitta Iyer said, supporting his son.

'It would be all right if they stopped there. Let them say that money must not be wasted, we must be frugal. We can let it go as a matter between father and son. But Surya talks like a confirmed socialist! "The workers are sweating it out on the fields. And we are spending the money raised from the sweat of their brows on extravagances," says he. On top of that, he warns us that things cannot go on like this forever.'

Seemachu Iyer commented, 'What else do you expect, man? Do you think things will roll along like this for a million years? You live like frogs in the well! You are ignorant of the way the world is moving now. "The land belongs to the man who ploughs" is the maxim of the time.'

'Appa! Seemachu! So you too have gone over to his side! Today they say, "The land is for the tiller!" Tomorrow it will be, "Paddy for the harvester!", "House for the mason!", "Clothes for the washerman!",

"Car for the driver!", "Medicine for the doctor!", "Train for the porter!" They may even say "Food for the cook!" *Vinaashakaale vipareeta buddhi!*' declared Appadurai Sastri.

'It will be very convenient for me if all revenues belong to the revenue collector.' Kitta Iyer quipped. 'But what is the use of getting incensed? It is inevitable that what has to happen, will indeed happen at the appointed hour. Should we not change ourselves according to the needs of the time?'

'We will change, sir, we will change! If the matter is reasonable, we must change with the times. Earlier the death anniversary rituals used to get over at 3 p.m. Now they say that the brahmins must be fed by 10 a.m. We have to accept these changes as we move on, but are we ready to accept the concept that the land belongs only to the ploughman?' Sastri asked.

'Right or wrong, if the world accepts change, what is the use of our remonstrations?' Kitta Iyer said.

'Let the world accept it. Let the Creator of the cosmos himself accept it. But how can *we* accept something that is not right? After all, doesn't Mahatma Gandhi say again and again, "Do what you think is right, even if you have to stand alone." But what do *you* say? "Don't use your own own brain, blindly accept what some greenhorn says."'

'Who is asking you to accept it?'

'What do you mean "who says"? Surya said it just now! Wasn't he lecturing us?'

'He will say all these things now. When push comes to shove, he will say something different. Let's see! Ask Surya if he will give away his share of the family's land holdings to the field workers?'

'Seemachu Mama, I may even do that! Or I will get into the fields and start ploughing. Then the land will be mine.'

'Well said, young man, well said! Do you think you will be the only one? If indeed such times come to pass, won't we all tuck up our veshtis and plunge into the fields?' said Panchu Iyer.

'What I say is – why wait until then? Why not improve our lifestyle right away? If the ploughing and planting are done by us, will it be possible to lavish money on four-day wedding celebrations?' asked Surya.

'Well, now we know what Surya's point really is. He is advising his father not to spend too much money on Lalita's wedding. That's all! Right, Surya?' Seemachu Iyer said.

'Not at all! I will never talk to my father with such effrontery.'

'Even if Surya says such a thing, I won't listen to him. Aren't they saying nowadays that girls must get an equal share of the property along with boys? I am going to spend on the wedding only what belongs to Lalita as her share,' Kitta Iyer clarified.

'Just one thing, Appa. I agree that Lalita has a share in the property. But what right do we have to spend her share the way we want? I object only to its being spent on the dowry and other wasteful extravagances,' Surya explained.

'Well, you have to go on objecting! When the entire world moves in a certain direction, can we take a different route?'

Velayuda Mudaliar, who had joined them from the adjacent street of the *Vellala* community where he lived, broke in to say, 'I have a question. Granted the land is for the ploughman. But who does the actual ploughing? Is it not the bullock that drags the plough across the field? So doesn't it mean that the land belongs to the bullock?'

'Mudaliar! You have certainly delivered the knockout punch! Hey, Surya? What do you say to that?'

Surya was rather startled. 'This is a joke! The land cannot belong to the bullock. It can only belong to the ploughman who drives the animal.'

'Let us say you are right. It seems some countries use a new machine called the "tractor" to plough farm land. You can plough five hundred acres with a single tractor. Does this mean that the man who drives the tractor owns all those five hundred acres? If that is so, I will somehow purchase a tractor. I will even learn to drive it!' said Velayuda Mudaliar.

Surya thought for a minute and said, 'It is not wholly right to say that the land belongs to the ploughman. The land really belongs to the government.'

'Bhesh! Are you saying that all the land belongs to the white man? We are already staggering under the weight of his taxes.'

Surya replied, 'You say this because right now what we have is the white man's government. It is inevitable that our own government will be established in India sooner rather than later. Then, if all the land becomes public property, it will also become the common property of all the citizens of the nation. Then, just like a clerk in an office and a teacher in a school, field workers will be paid salaries, whether they plough the field by yoking cattle to the ploughshare, or with a tractor.'

Panchu Iyer asked with some heat, 'And then, what do landowners like us do? Stand around sucking our thumbs.'

Velayuda Mudaliar commented, 'It is not so bad for you brahmin folk. You will go and find a job somewhere and survive somehow. If nothing works out, you will at least start a café, but *our* plight will be disastrous.'

As this debate was going on in the outdoor parliament assembly, Annam, Seemachu Iyer's better half, walked past them and vanished into the house. Presently, a fearsome earthquake seemed to explode within. Shrieks of rage accompanied the sounds of someone weeping and sobbing. In the midst of all this clamour, Sarasvati Ammal's mother unleashed a thunderous diatribe. 'Didn't I tell you not to invite these saboteurs? Did you listen to me? Did you listen to me when I took you aside before they came to see the girl and warned you? Didn't you tell me that floods could not wash away the water from the well? And what happened? Everything has been washed away! Everyone thinks I am stupid, mad. It is *you* who are a brainless moron! You have fed a viper.'

Sarasvati Ammal's reply was heard by everyone with the utmost clarity. 'Amma! Who knew that such a disaster would overtake us? Dei Sundu, call your father, immediately. The house is burning here. And there he is chatting away. Call him at once!'

Kitta Iyer got up hurriedly and stomped into the house.

'What's all this rumpus? Who has been struck by lightning?'

Sarasvati Ammal shouted, 'Yes, lightning has struck us! It has struck you, me, and our child Lalita. Hear what Seemachu Mama's wife has to say. See what those wonderful people you brought from Madras have done! See the result of your bringing your darling sister from Bombay and treating her like a queen!' Sarasvati Ammal shouted.

'All right. I will listen. Please lower your voice! Don't scream as if someone has lost his life,' Kitta Iyer said.

28

THE ENGAGEMENT

Kitta Iyer's admonition had some effect. The commotion within the house simmered down, and the matter came to light.

Seemachu Iyer's wife Annam had overheard what was being discussed by the visitors from Madras. She became aware that the young man did not want to marry Lalita, he wanted to marry Sita. At first, his father and mother tried to make him change his mind. As he refused to budge, they willy-nilly agreed with him. Still, they hesitated to broach the subject with Kitta Iyer. They asked Subbu Iyer of the insurance company for suggestions. They were debating whether to explain the matter here and now and get a 'yes' or 'no' right away, or go back to Madras and write about it.

When he heard this, even gentle Kitta Iyer's ire was aroused. But not knowing whom to pounce on he said to Seemachu Iyer, 'Did you hear this? Oy! Didn't I say so way back then? Now do you know the calibre of the Madras people?'

'Oy! How can I not know it? And yet we must not come to any decision on the basis of what this numskull says. This halfwit is a habitual troublemaker intent on making some mischief or other. Her deaf ears could have misunderstood their utterances completely. In any case I will go and find out what the matter may be.' Turning to his wife, he said, 'Aei! You moron! Get yourself here! As if I don't have troubles enough, I must put up with you as well! Aei! Blight of Saturn! Will you or won't you follow me?'

Seemachu Iyer's cry of love made his soulmate murmur, 'Why

are you pouncing on me?' as she followed him. The husband's fond endearments could be heard as they went down the street.

The import of Seemachu Iyer's harsh words for his wife cleared the minds of the family somewhat.

'Why is this brahmin shouting at his wife? What can she do?' Sarasvati Ammal said.

'What can anyone do? Everything happens as fate decrees,' said Kitta Iyer.

'Will Lalita never get married because these people said no? Give me leave and I will bring a thousand proposals by tomorrow,' said Appadurai Sastri.

'Enough! Enough! No need to talk about my daughter's marriage this year. First, let all our visitors go back to their own places,' Sarasvati Ammal said.

Just then, Rajam interposed to say, 'Anna! It is all my fault. I am the unlucky one. Wherever I go, misfortune trails me.'

'Don't talk nonsense! Who said anything to you now?'

'That girl is sobbing away inside,' Abhayam said. 'What can she do? Sita did say that she would stay away from the visitors. It was Lalita who insisted on Sita accompanying her. Did your wife stop her? No!'

'I am an idiot. My daughter is a bigger idiot. Everyone knows this. You people who know everything were there too! Why didn't you remonstrate then?' Sarasvati Ammal snarled.

'Enough! Stop this argument. Go and console the child who is crying away,' Kitta Iyer said.

'What should anyone cry now? Why this sham after the deed is done?' Sarasvati Ammal said.

Inside, Lalita who was trying to console Sita, heard it all. Her mother's last words made her rush out in a fit of rage and grief and say, 'Appa! Please listen to me! I will never marry the boy who came here today, not even if you cut me to pieces! Right from the beginning I have been saying that I am not happy with any of these arrangements. None of you listened to me. Amma is scolding Sita without cause. Even the gods will not put up with it! Sita did not want to come with me. I forced her to accompany me. What is the use of getting angry with her? If you go on unjustly blaming Sita, I will leave this house. I will jump into the well and die!'

Lalita's concern for her friend moved everyone, but it stoked Sarasvati Ammal's rage. 'Go! Go and jump into the well! Do it right away! I will tell myself that I never gave birth to a daughter!'

'Adadaa! What's all this! Nothing has been decided yet. Hasn't Seemachu gone to find out how things stand? Let him return and we will see,' said Appadurai Sastri.

'Let Seema Mama find out whatever he wants. Even if that boy says he will marry me, I swear that I will not marry him!' Lalita vowed.

'Lalita! Is this *you* saying such things!' Kitta Iyer said.

'Is she speaking her own mind? She is only spouting what she has been taught,' said Sarasvati Ammal.

'Do you mean me?' asked Rajam. 'I have done no wrong. I have not spent even half a moment with Lalita!'

'I'm not saying anything about you! I am talking about my own son. Surya's bad advice has turned Lalita mad. Someone has poisoned his mind.'

Surya who had remained silent all this while now broke in. 'Nothing is wrong with *my* mind. I did say that there was no need for all this foolishness. No one listened to me. Amma! Your whole generation is now suffering the consequences of getting married. Leave us free to do as we like. Lalita will marry if she wants to. If she doesn't, she will not marry. What is true for Lalita applies to Sita as well. If Sita doesn't like the great big genius from Madras, she can openly say so. No need for her to sob and cry!'

Surya's blood was boiling. He had not liked the brainbox from Madras anyway. The news that the man wanted to marry Sita instead of Lalita added insult to injury.

Sita was lying face down and sobbing away in the room inside. Lalita tried to console her and help her regain her composure. Poor, guileless Lalita hardly knew Sita's state of mind. Sita was weeping to hide her joy. Her world had turned into a garden of bliss, filled with trees and shrubs and rainbow flowers. Birds sang, peacocks danced, deer pranced, leaped and ran, parrots lisped, pigeons kissed, and the gentle breezes blew, laden with the fragrance of sandalwood trees. However, somewhere in the far distance she could hear the seas where mountainous waves rose high and crashed down.

Presently, Seemachu Iyer sent for Kitta Iyer. Sub-judge Sastri and his wife explained the matter clearly to him. 'There is nothing wrong with your daughter. She is lovely. But youngsters of today have their own quirks. Raghavan says it was Sita he saw first. "I liked her at first sight. If I marry at all, I will marry no one but Sita," he says! We tried our best to talk him out of it. He will not listen. If you agree, we can do the engagement ceremony even tomorrow, but please tell us frankly if the girl or her mother does not like the idea. Feel no pressure.'

Kitta Iyer was dumbfounded. He could not think of anything to say in reply. 'Well, I will go and ask the girl's mother and let you know,' he said and left. But he did not go straight home. He took Seemachu Iyer and Subbu Iyer to the poolside bungalow for consultation. Both said unanimously, 'This is nothing short of serendipity! We can find a hundred matches for Lalita, while securing an alliance for the girl from Bombay may be a difficult task. These people are ready to take her without a dowry. Why should we refuse? The best thing is to accept this offer and have the engagement performed by tomorrow.'

Since Kitta Iyer's initial anger had cooled down by then, he too felt that it was a fair decision. He returned home around 1 a.m., wondering how on earth he was going to convey the decision to his wife and get her to accept it. His son Surya showed him the way.

Unable to sleep, Surya had been tossing and turning in bed. By the time his father returned, his mind had cleared. Who knows? Perhaps this was God's will! Was there any doubt that Saundara Raghavan, with a job in Delhi and a salary of ₹750, was a far better match for Sita than he could ever be? Maybe his cousin's luck had brought the man down here! What right did he have to stand between Sita and her happiness?

Surya recalled what his friend Pattabhiraman had said during a conversation on the terrace of Damodaram Pillai's house. Didn't he say, 'I will be happy to look at a flower blooming on a shrub, even from a distance? I don't have the desire to pluck it, crush it and smell it!' 'What a generous heart Pattabhiraman had! Why couldn't he, Surya, follow his example?'

When Kitta Iyer returned well past midnight, Surya asked him, 'Appa, what did they say?'

'You are still up, Surya! On my way back, I was thinking of asking you for your opinion. What Seemachu Iyer's wife said was true. The boy insists he wants to marry Sita. His parents have agreed. They say that they don't expect dowry or other customary wedding gifts. I respect your views in such matters. Please tell me what you think.'

'Appa, since it has come to this, I will now tell you that our advocate Atmanatha Iyer's son Pattabhiraman wishes to marry Lalita. Didn't you go to Devapattinam last year and spend a few days in the advocate's house? Pattabhiraman had seen Lalita then. He likes her. He was disappointed when we looked for some other bridegroom. His father too was a little unhappy. He hinted at it by saying, "We don't count for your father. He will look for someone with a higher status."'

'Advocate Atmanatha Iyer's son is a good choice. It was not that I did not remember him, but your mother demanded that we should look for someone with a higher status. As for me, I am perfectly content to give Lalita in marriage to Pattabhi. Let us reflect a little more on it and take a decision. But what do you say about this matter concerning Sita?'

'I am all right with it so long as Athai and Sita are happy. Should we not be pleased to gain such a good alliance without involving high expenditure? We, too, will earn a good name out of this.'

'Surya! In that case, *you* must convince your mother and persuade her to agree to this arrangement. She has transformed herself into the terrifying Bhadrakali. Anything I say will infuriate her even more. She will think I am taking my sister's side and supporting her daughter.'

'Yes, Appa, I'll do it. I will make Amma agree.'

What Surya had undertaken was not easy. But he succeeded in the end. What changed Sarasvati Ammal's mind was Surya's reminding her that if Lalita married the boy from Madras, she would go away to far off places like Delhi or Lahore. To marry Pattabhiraman would mean she would be settled at easy visiting distance.

The next evening, with everyone's consent, Madras Padmapuram Sub-judge Padmalochana Sastri's son Saundara Raghavan was formally engaged to be married to Bombay Duraisami Iyer's daughter Sita. The engagement was conducted upon the assurance given by Rajam to the prospective in-laws that her husband Duraisami would have no objections to the marriage. It was Lalita who was most ecstatic during the event. She even addressed Raghavan as 'mapillai' and began to talk to him.

29

LETTERS FROM BIHAR

Raghavan was in a state of exuberance when he returned to Madras after getting engaged to be married. He believed that a new and joyous chapter was beginning in his life. He tried to forget Dharini, and almost succeeded, but two letters he received two days after he returned to Madras reminded him of that connection. The moment he saw the first letter, Raghavan knew who had written it. The beautiful writing with rounded letters was in Dharini's hand. He was agitated by both his eagerness to open the letter and his apprehensions about its contents.

Muzzafarpur, Bihar
9/2/1934

My dear,

You may have received my letter written on the train. I thought that would be my last letter to you. But after coming here, however much I try, I am unable to forget you. Everyone has gone to sleep in this earthquake relief camp. Sitting beside a dim kerosene lantern, I am writing to you because I want to involve you in the work that I am now engaged in.

It has been ten days since I came to Bihar. The scenes I have witnessed in these ten days cannot be forgotten even if I were to live for a thousand years. They cannot be forgotten in this birth or the next, and in all the births to come. What I see in the daytime, I see again in nightmares. My strength of mind enables me to suppress my feelings during the day, but not at night. Sometimes I wake up shaking and screaming in terror, at other times sobbing in pity.

You will know what I feel if I relate some incidents here.

Babu Lakshminarayan Prasad heads the khadi service centre in Bihar. A month ago, after completing his supervisory rounds, he left for his native town to see his wife and children. On the way, he was startled by a feeling that the whole world was turning upside down. He realized that it was an earthquake. He reached home in a state of trepidation, not without cause. A mound of earth and stone and pieces of wood lay where his house had once stood. 'My wife! My children!' he shrieked as he began to push the earth and the stones away. Many volunteers rushed to help him. His wife and children were found under the debris, their bodies crushed beyond recognition! Reduced to insanity, Babu Lakshminarayan Prasad is now wandering in that area screaming, 'Where is my wife? Daughter? Son?'

Prabhavati was a woman who lived in Mangir town. She was a widow, but was bravely raising her children as a single mother, with the little that her husband had left them. Her infant was sleeping in the cradle. Another child was playing in the yard. Prabhavati was cooking in the kitchen. There was a sudden bump. The house was shaken violently. The cooking vessels got scattered. A loud series of noises in the backyard made her remember the calf there. Prabhavati ran to the yard. The roof had fallen to bury the shed where the calf had been tied. Hearing the same sound in the front part of the house, she ran towards it. The house had fallen on both children, covering them completely. Shouting and screaming, Prabhavati made her way out of the house. 'I have lost my children! Won't the earth open up and swallow me?' she screamed. The good woman's wish came true, instantaneously. The earth cracked up where she was standing. Prabhavati fell in and disappeared. You must know that Mithila, the birthplace of the legendary Sita devi, is the Bihar of today. Mother Earth, who once took Sita into herself, has swallowed so many good wives today.

My dear! I stood near one of those cracks and gazed into the earth beneath. I couldn't stop myself though others tried to stop me. I went as close as I could and bent down to look at the yawning abyss. The cavity plunges down into the incalculable depths of the farthest underworld. A little below the surface there is nothing but the blackest and measureless darkness. Gazing for too long into the abyss makes the head spin.

The earthquake has brought about countless and bizarre changes. High lands have suddenly plunged down to become huge lakes filled with water. Lakes have turned into hard and parched earth without a drop of water.

Huts, houses and mansions, company buildings and railway stations, are all reduced to debris, broken, fallen and burnt.

It is estimated that 25,000 lives were lost in the earthquake. Lucky are they who died! The lakhs of people who have escaped and survived, are now struggling without food to eat, clothes to wear, or a roof over their heads, and no place to go.

My dear! If you come here and see these horrors, you too will begin to wonder if there can be anything more important in life than serving the people who have been struck by such colossal misfortunes.

Volunteers have arrived from all parts of India for earthquake relief work. Everyone is serving under Babu Rajendra Prasad's leadership. Babu Rajendra Prasad is an amazing man! His composure, humility, love and eagerness to serve remain incomparable.

Pandit Jawaharlal Nehru was here a month ago. I saw him at the Congress session in Karachi, where you and I met for the first time. I had not known that he was a man of outstanding nobility. He works shoulder-to-shoulder with the other volunteers, totally unconscious of his pre-eminence as a leader. Ah, what zeal! What fervour! What speed! What briskness! He never walks but runs all the time!

Something unusual happened yesterday. Nehruji was going down the street where everything had been reduced to rubble. Suddenly, a piteous sound was heard. It sounded like the barking of a puppy. Nehruji stopped there and then, listening intently. Then he began to clear away the earth and stones which had formed a little mound. Many volunteers followed suit and worked briskly. After half an hour's labour they found what they were searching for. Wooden frames had fallen one on top of the other, roofing a hollow space below. A little boy lay dead in the hollow, guarded by a living puppy. Who can guess how it had managed to stay alive for so many days? The dog should have run out the moment the blockage was cleared. But no! It remained where it was, sniffing at the boy.

Oh my God! After witnessing so many of these hideous scenes, how can any mind engage with our impermanent life on earth! What can the goal of human life be but the service of suffering humanity? If you come and see how things are here, you too will come to think as I do. We shared similar thoughts on so many issues. How can any comfort be found in a government job, a huge salary, a luxurious lifestyle, motor cars, tea parties...

Yours,

Dharini

30

IS THIS YOUR FATE?

When Raghavan began to read Dharini's letter, his heart brimmed with the old love and fervour. Reading about the horrors caused by the earthquake moved him deeply. But the final part of the letter hardened his heart once again.

Raghavan harboured the conviction that no one with his brilliance had ever been born in India until then. Dharini's love for him had fostered that belief. And now, he was infuriated when she started lecturing him on the purpose of human life. How presumptuous! 'Who is she to give me advice?' he thought. 'Thank goodness! I escaped from such an insolent chit! The elders certainly knew what they were saying when they declared, "The words of elders are like nectar!" What a good thing to have listened to Amma in the matter of marriage! What Appa says is also true. Women must remain within the house. Who can say where it will all end if women start going out in the name of public service working for the nation! I have allowed myself to be blinded by Dharini. Her attractive face and superficial glamour deluded me. As a matter of fact, can it be said that Dharini is really more beautiful than Sita? No. Or is Sita less smart? Not at all. How sharp-witted she was when she spoke to Amma and Appa the other day? In addition to beauty and smartness, Sita possesses the great quality of modesty. Her behaviour will be a perfect fit for family life. She will show respect to elders and win their approval. Why, she has made even Appa, who thinks of money all the time, change his mind! God's grace is wholly with me. That is why I have been able to escape from all the problems of linking myself to Dharini for life. What about when I went to "see" Lalita? Was it not God who made Sita appear first? I must thank Amma. If she had not been so tenacious, I would have found myself trapped, and forced to suffer all my life.'

As he was absorbed in these reflections, Raghavan's attention fell upon the other unopened envelope. He picked it up and opened it.

What it contained startled and stunned him. It was a letter from the earthquake relief workers' camp in Muzaffarpur.

Muzaffarpur
12/2/1934

Dear Sir,

We are giving you the sad news. A volunteer from Bombay by the name Dharini was staying in this camp and serving the victims of the earthquake. Her noble qualities had earned her accolades from everyone. Leaving after lunch yesterday, she did not return at night. Unfortunately, she had a single bad habit. She frequented the places where the earth had cracked open and stood peering into the abyss. She did not heed our repeated warnings. Yesterday, those who saw her last in the afternoon, say that she had been standing near one of those yawning cracks and gazing into it. Our relentless search for her since then has yielded no results. Dharini used to often say, 'I want to go into the earth as Janaka's daughter did.' We are forced to conclude sadly that her desire must have been fulfilled. We have no information about Dharini's family or friends. We are writing to you because we found your address noted in her diary. We request you to pass on this information to Dharini's family if you happen to know them. We will instantly notify you, should Dharini return to the camp, having merely lost her way.

Yours,
Sarala Devi

As he read the first few lines of this letter, all the anger Raghavan had felt towards Dharini evaporated. His heart was filled with love and pity. Tears stood in his eyes when he finished the letter. He got up, went to the wardrobe, unlocked it and took Dharini's photograph out of it. He went on gazing at the photograph intently, for a long time. Dharini's words, the expressions on her face, the way she walked and moved, everything unfolded in succession before his mind's eye. 'Oh my God! Is this your fate?' thought Raghavan. His tears rolled down and fell on Dharini's photograph, drop by drop. At the same time, a strange sense of peace pervaded his heart.

During the following week, Raghavan went on anticipating the arrival of more news, even good news, from Muzaffarpur. In vain.

31

FIGHT BY THE SLUICE GATE

The calendar on the wall of the post office at Rajampettai showed the date as 1 April.

Mr Bangaru Naidu BPM was sitting on his throne and checking the accounts for the stamps.

Postman Balakrishnan was postmarking the envelopes.

'Stamps are missing,' said the postmaster.

'How many? What denomination?' asked Balakrishnan.

'Two stamps, three fourths of an anna each.'

'Is that all? Write it off as masal vadai expenses!'

'What's the use of asking you for suggestions? Never mind. Are you still postmarking mail?'

'This wedding business in the pattamaniam's house makes my hand ache dreadfully with all the postmarking it demands.'

'Not one, but *two* weddings are going to take place. A thousand invitations were printed. Still they're running short!'

'Do you think both weddings will take place, sir?'

'Why not? Everything has been confirmed and they have dispatched the invitations.'

'Is it enough to print invitations? I consulted an astrologer. He told me that one of the weddings was a doubtful starter.'

'Why did you go around consulting an astrologer in this matter?'

'Just like that!'

'So, this is what you are busy with! That is why you have kept three letters undelivered. All letters for the pattamaniam's household must be delivered at once. They may contain important information.'

'What important information? What will happen if they are delivered two days late? Will heads be cut off?'

'I am not talking about cutting off heads. Kitta Iyer is a good man. He has invited us too to the wedding. We may get a sumptuous wedding feast. You will attend, won't you?'

'No, I won't. They will feed us in a sequestered space. That's the brahmin community for you!'

'Appa, don't talk ill of brahmins! The scriptures say that in times of antiquity, God made the brahmins emerge from his face, the kshatriyas from his shoulders…'

'Stop, sir! Who wants all these old stories? Aren't they all lies written by the brahmins themselves? In today's world, there is no brahmin, no shudra. All are human beings.

'Any scripture that differentiates between one human being and another must be thrown into the flames!' Balakrishnan declared.

'Do you attend the meetings of the Self Respect movement?'

'I go to the meetings of the Self Respect Movement as well as the Congress.'

'In that case, there is no hope for you. Anyway, go at once and deliver the letters addressed to Kitta Iyer's house. There are letters for that lady from Bombay and her daughter as well.'

'That girl from Bombay is a gabbler. I was in their house the day before yesterday. She spoke to me rudely, without any courtesy. I told her, "Look, lady! You keep all your rudeness for Bombay. Won't do here."'

'She cannot have the good nature of Kitta Iyer's child, certainly. But when she first came here, she seemed all right. She must have become swollen headed after getting engaged to a man with an eight-hundred-rupee salary.'

'What does it matter whether he earns eight hundred rupees or eight thousand rupees? Everyone is equal. Duty is duty. Friendship is friendship! Mind you, it is not as if it is certain that the girl from Bombay will get married. It may break off.'

'How can you mouth such words, such thoughts?'

'Can I speak with my hand then?' said Balakrishnan and left with the mailbag.

Surya came to the post office soon after Balakrishnan left it. He asked postmaster Bangaru Naidu, 'Any mail for our house, sir?'

'Oh yes! For you, your father, the lady from Bombay and her daughter. Balakrishnan has taken them for delivery. Did you not see him on the way?'

'No! I didn't see him,' said Surya as he walked away.

Surya was in a state of great enthusiasm. All the wedding arrangements had been made according to his wishes. It was his effort that had brought about the engagement between Lalita and Pattabhiraman. People on both sides were delighted by it. Rajam suggested that Sita's marriage could be performed at some temple somewhere. It looked as if others would agree, but Surya insisted otherwise, and planned for both weddings to take place under the same canopy.

Enthused by all these happenings, Surya took a great interest in the wedding preparations and assisted his father by taking several preparatory tasks upon himself. Luckily, the SSLC examinations got over soon enough for Surya to reach the village ten days ahead of the weddings.

Surya had written to Pattabhiraman concerning the clothes to be purchased for the formal ceremony of inviting the bridegroom. Going to the post office expecting Pattabhi's reply, he returned disappointed. On the way home, he looked at both sides of the street to see if Balakrishnan was smoking a furtive *beedi*, behind a tree.

His guess proved to be right. Balakrishnan was sitting under the bridge near the sluice gate and engaged in reading a letter attentively.

So attentively that he remained unaware of Surya coming close enough to stand just behind him. Surya felt a strange suspicion. He stopped himself from calling out, 'Balakrishna!' and stared at the envelope lying beside the postman. It was addressed to his aunt from Bombay.

Surya became angry. 'Dei idiot! What are you doing?' he roared. Taken aback, Balakrishnan turned and shouted, 'Whom are you calling idiot? I am not an idiot. You are an idiot! Your father is an idiot! Your grandfather is an idiot!'

Surya's rage became uncontrollable. 'Dei! You commit a crime and dare to talk back to me!' he roared again and placed his hand on Balakrishnan's neck. Balakrishnan responded with a punch. The two men began to engage in fisticuffs.

As they were slamming into each other, a closed bullock cart came down the street. Sita, Lalita and Rajam were in it.

'Ayo! What's this! Surya and postman Balakrishnan are fighting!' Lalita cried out.

'That's right! How shameful!' Sita exclaimed.

With deepfelt dismay Rajammal shouted, 'Surya! Surya! What's all this in the middle of the street! Stop it at once!'

When they heard Rajam's voice, both men stopped fighting and stood shamefaced.

'Come, Surya! Get into the cart. Let's go home,' Rajam said.

'Athai! This is only a mock fight. You carry on. I will follow you.'

'Is that true? Balakrishna, is Surya telling the truth?' Rajam asked.

'Yes, Amma! We were just fighting for fun,' Balakrishnan said.

The vehicle rolled on.

Sita looked at Lalita and said, 'You are so bright. Why is your brother such a fool?'

'Don't say that, Sita. Surya is not a fool! He is a very good boy. There must be some reason behind the fight.' Rajam said.

The cartman joined in to say, 'Yes, Amma! Our young master is a very good boy. He has been somewhat different only over the last few days.'

When the vehicle rolled away into the distance, Surya said, 'Balakrishna, it was wrong of me to have fought with you. I am sorry about that. But what you did was wrong too, wasn't it? Should you have opened a letter addressed to someone else? And that too, should you have done it when you are yourself the postman?'

'It was wrong. I know. But I did it in good faith. If you read this letter, you will know why I did so,' Balakrishnan said and placed the letter in Surya's hands.

Surya's face became flushed as he read the first few lines.

'How did you know that it was this kind of letter?' Surya asked Balakrishnan.

'A postcard came yesterday. By chance I happened to glance at it. It had some nonsense scribbled on it. I became rather suspicious when I saw this envelope. I thought it best to open it and read the letter. It was as I feared. No matter. If you have no objections to it, I will seal it up again and deliver it to the lady. I will hand over all the letters that arrive in the same manner. But don't think you can threaten me or assault me. I am good to those who are good to me. A rogue to the rogues! Do you understand?'

'Haven't I already admitted that I was in the wrong? I say it again. Now forget it. You must do me a favour. Until this wedding gets over, hand me all the letters addressed to my house. I will take a look at them, and then deliver them as I think fit.'

'This is against the rules. Letters must be handed over to the persons to whom they are addressed. However, I will do this because you have asked me. But remember, I am a big rowdy. I am not afraid of anyone.'

32

THE WORLD OF LOVERS

From the day their weddings were fixed, Sita and Lalita were in a dream world. They wandered at will like butterflies fluttering their iridescent wings in the realm divine. They buzzed like honeybees through the coral lily trees of paradise and drank honey from the flowers mingled with the nectar of the gods.

One day Sita's mother spoke of the pleasure of bathing in the crystal-clear waters of the vast Kaveri river in summer. Sita pestered her uncle and persuaded him to let them go to bathe in the river. They took the closed cart. Rajam accompanied them.

Bathing in the Kaveri, Sita and Lalita experienced the pleasure of the gopis sporting with their adored Krishna in the river Yamuna. It was on their way back from the Kaveri that they saw Surya and Balakrishnan engaged in fisticuffs. But very quickly, they forgot all about the incident. After lunch, they went to the poolside bungalow, seeking its seclusion to continue their intimate exchanges.

Since it had rained heavily in the month of December, the pool was full even though it was the beginning of summer. It was still midday, but the cool and gentle breezes that wafted across the pool swept the girls away into a dreamworld.

Their conversation began with some teasing.

'Lalita! They will ask you to sing at the nalangu ceremony. You absolutely must sing "Mamava Pattabhi Rama"! If you don't, I will never speak to you again,' Sita began.

'You sing "Marugelara, O Raghava"! And that will give me the courage to sing what you want. You are brave, Sita! I simply don't have it in me, what can I do?' Lalita replied.

'You are a fraud! Are you claiming that you are not brave enough? Why? A year ago, didn't you and Mr Pattabhiraman get yourselves engaged without anyone's knowledge? Did you do it because you don't have the guts?'

'Sita! It is not like that! We didn't exchange a single word!'

'Didn't you? How can that be? Lalita, don't lie! Is speech confined to the spoken word? Don't the eyes speak? Didn't you tell me all about your Devapattinam trip of last year? What is the need for any verbal talk? What did Rama and Sita do? Rama was walking down the street of Mithila city. Sita was standing on the balcony above. They did nothing more than look at each other with their eyes. Was it not enough to inspire eternal love between them?'

'I am not saying that it is not enough. But is there any harm in talking if one has the guts to do so? Didn't you answer him when he called you and spoke to you after you got engaged? Tell me all about it again, one more time.'

'I will be happy to repeat it even if you ask me ten times. After the engagement ceremony was over, my parents-in-law-to-be sent for me. The lady hugged me, kissed my forehead and blessed me. She talked on and on, "You will be the goddesses Lakshmi and Sarasvati in our household. Our clan will flourish through you," and so on and so forth. All I understood was her saying that they were letting me marry their son without dowry and wedding gifts for the sake of my goodness and beauty. All the while, my mind was with the mapillai. Then the couple left us by ourselves.

I was ready to leave when he looked at me and said, "Don't be in such a hurry. I am going to ask you a question."

I bowed my head and remained silent. He spoke again. "After talking nineteen to the dozen yesterday, if you decide to remain dumb today, I will not let you go. You will have to answer my question. Why did you want to marry me?"

I looked up at him. I wanted to laugh as I thought of the answer I was going to give. "Should it not be *me* asking this question?

It was *you* who came to see my friend and said that you wanted to marry *me*!"

At this, he burst into laughter. But stiffening himself, he said, "Does it mean that you are not in favour of this marriage? Even now, it is not too late. We can stop it. If your heart is not in it, tell me so at once."

"My heart is not with me anymore. Didn't you take it away the moment you stepped out of the motor car?" I said. Lalita, you should have seen his face then. It was suffused with joy! He said, "I have seen and moved with so many girls with BA and MA degrees. But never have I seen a girl as smart as you! I don't feel like leaving you now!" But my conceit made me say, "That is what you say now. But tomorrow, who knows? You may forget me. There will be so many girls with BAs and MAs!"

He said, "Complaining already? Forget BA and MA! Nothing but dust at your feet. I will not be able to think of anyone but you!" I was overwhelmed. But I said somewhat perversely, "That is what King Dushyantan told Sakuntalai. He forgot her the moment he went back to his city." Calling me lovingly by name, he said, "Sita, Dushyantan was a king. He could do anything. But am I not an ordinary man?"

"You are my king!" I said. He replied, "Dushyantan was the king of a whole country. I am king only to you. Come here! I will give you a token." I went closer thinking that he was going to give me a ring or a fountain pen. But he took my left hand with both his hands and kissed it. Lalita, even now when I think of it, my whole body feels the thrill of that touch!"'

As she listened to the dialogue between Sita and Saundara Raghavan for the fifth time, Lalita's heart felt all the turbulence of the storm-tossed seas. She yearned to know if her partner Pattabhiraman would indulge in this kind of love talk. Quickly pushing the thought aside, she said, 'Sita, Dushyantan was the monarch of a vast empire. Is it not surprising that he fell in love with an orphan girl raised in a hermitage?'

'True,' said Sita. 'But there are many stories like that. Do you know the story of Anarkali?'

'No, I don't. Tell me.'

'Salim, the son of Emperor Akbar, fell in love with the daughter of his nurse. He swore that he would marry her and no other. From behind the rose bushes in the palace garden, Emperor Akbar overheard their conversation. He was enraged by the thought of the son who was going to ascend the throne after him marrying the daughter of a nurse. Instantly he issued the order to arrest and imprison Anarkali. I believe Anarkali means pomegranate bud in the Persian language. It was Salim's special name for her. In prison, Anarkali yearned for Salim and believed that he would find her and marry her. But a long time elapsed before Akbar died. The moment he became king the first thing that Salim did was to go to release Anarkali from the prison house. But by then Anarkali had turned mad. She could not recognize Salim. "Who asked you to come here? Who are you to free me? Salim will come and release me. I'm staying here until then," she told him. Salim's heart was broken. Anarkali died soon after this.'

Tears poured down from Lalita's eyes.

'Silly girl! Why are you crying?' asked Sita.

'I don't know. Why should their true love end in tragedy?' Lalita sighed.

'Most love stories end like that. Look at Romeo and Juliet! There was no love like theirs in the whole world. But both died in the end.'

'It is not so bad if both die. But how painful is it if one dies and the other lives! Look at Salim! Wasn't it he who became Emperor Jahangir and married Nurjahan? So what if Nurjahan was a famed beauty? How could he forget Anarkali?'

'Some men are like that, but not all. Lalita! Look at Jahangir's son Shah Jahan! He married Mumtaz Mahal. He did not forget her even after her death. He built the Taj Mahal in her memory. He kept gazing at the Taj Mahal from his palace until he died.'

'The story I like most is about Satyavan and Savitri. Savitri loved Satyavan who had lost his kingdom and was tending his blind parents in the forest. Her determination did not give way even when she knew that he had only a year to live. She argued with the God of Death and brought her husband's life back to the earth.'

'You can also argue that there is nothing greater than the love between the god Subramania and Valli. Valli was from the gypsy tribe. Subramania was the son of a god, the general of the heavenly hosts. And yet, he married Valli! Is it not a miracle? Lalita! Don't you sing a song about Subramania? Why don't you sing it now?' she said.

As the song came to an end, Surya entered with his aunt Rajam and exclaimed, 'Bale! Bhesh! Lalita, you sing so well. Why did you refuse to sing on the day the visitors from Madras came?'

Sita answered Surya, 'On that day, she was in no mood to sing.'

Then the two girls left the bungalow to find a spot where they could talk all by themselves.

When Lalita and Sita left, Rajam looked at Surya and asked, 'Child, why were you fighting on the street with the postman? Tell me the truth.'

'Athai, I refrained from telling you about it because you are preyed by so many worries already. Why add to them?'

Rajam said, 'Surya, having faced innumerable sorrows and problems, I have become numb to them. However unpleasant the matter may be, it will not affect me. So don't hesitate to share it with me.'

33

AUNT AND NEPHEW

Surya went on gazing at the lily pond and the casuarina grove. Then he said, 'Really speaking, it is no big deal. Have you heard of anonymous letters? Letters left unsigned? Some people write such letters out of jealousy and spite. Such a letter was addressed to you. Postman Balakrishnan had opened it and was reading it. He's a rascal! That is why I fought with him.'

'I have seen that boy here several times. He seemed to be a good boy. Forget him for now. Tell me what was written in that letter!'

'Do I *have* to tell you?'

'Anything about your uncle? Or about me?'

'Not about you two.'

'Then, was it about Sita? What did the scoundrel say about Sita?' This time Rajam's voice shook with uncontrollable fury.

'No, no, not about Sita. What is there to say about Sita? Athai, it is your good fortune to have had a daughter like Sita.'

Rajam's face shone again. 'Not even about Sita? Then what did it say, and about whom?'

'I find it difficult to spell it out, Athai! Yet, it is something you should know anyway. It seems Raghavan had a relationship with a girl in Bombay. One day, she came to Padmapuram, fought with him and created a racket. It became a standing joke for the whole city. There was a whole lot more about him, ending with – should the girl be given to such a man?'

Rajam heaved a big sigh. She remained lost in thought for a while. Then she asked, 'Is that all? Or is there more?'

'There were disparaging remarks about the money-mindedness of the groom's father and his wife's nasty treatment of her first daughter-in-law which drove the girl back to her own parents' home. The letter asked, do you really want such an alliance?'

Again, Rajam spent some time in reflection. Then she asked, 'Is that all? Anything else?'

'Nothing except some drivel about "better to throw the girl into a well than to hand her over to a family of this kind". Athai, I have instructed Balakrishnan to deliver all your letters to me. What do you say?'

'Surya, though you are not old in years, you are mature and have a sense of responsibility. Your mother often talks about this with pride. She is absolutely right. I am going to ask you for your advice. What do you think about this letter, Surya? Do you think what it says may be true?'

'No. I don't think so. Athai, I think someone has been prompted by jealousy to write this. I think that it would not be right to cry halt to this wedding because of this letter. But I don't know what you think! And if uncle gets to know about this, whatever will he say? He is not here, yet.'

'I had a letter from your uncle four days ago. He says he will be here the day before the wedding. It seems he made enquiries about the boy in Delhi. What he learnt was highly satisfactory. They said that mapillai had earned a reputation for his brilliance, he was a favourite with his superiors in the office and that his salary could rise to ₹2000.'

'Athai, now, don't you think I'm right? Envious people must have sent this letter.'

'It is so difficult to get a good alliance these days. Many people must have wanted to give their daughters to a man like him. Their failure to secure the alliance may have prompted them to write in this manner.'

'That must be it. No doubt at all!'

Rajam said, 'I did enquire about the mother-in-law and father-in-law. It is clear that Kamakshi Ammal is blameless, it is the girl who is a nasty creature. Don't we know that it must be so from the fact of her refusing to stay in her husband's house and going back to her parents? Perhaps it was she who got this letter written through someone else to make mischief.'

'Highly possible!'

'So, on the whole, you too think that this marriage *should* be performed!'

'Certainly! We should not back out after getting all these preparations done.'

'What can we do even should there be some truth in that letter! If God wants this wedding to take place, no one can stop it. Sita will lead a happy and comfortable life if it is the wish of the Mother Goddess.'

'No question about it, Athai. Didn't it become obvious that it was God's will when the man who came to see my sister said that he wanted to marry Sita?'

'Surya, do you know how confused I was during those two or three days? I couldn't sleep at all thinking about the pain that my sister-in-law must have felt. It was you who somehow managed to pacify your mother. Even your father was angry. It was you who at once brought up the name of the advocate's son and calmed your father down. What would have happened if you had not been here? As I think more and more about it, I have become convinced that everything is taking place according to God's will.'

'Should we obstruct God's will because some jealous people have sent an anonymous letter? Never!'

'I feel the same way, Surya! The arrangement you have made with postman Balakrishnan is a good one. Take all the letters addressed to me and Sita. Read them. Hand them to us or tear them up at your discretion. It may be good if you do that with letters addressed to your father as well. Someone may write to him as they did to me.'

'Yes, Athai. That is what I'm going to do.'

'Surya what can I do in return for your assistance? I will pray to God for your well-being at all times and for you to get a high-ranking job.'

'A high-ranking job? For me? I don't wish for one. I want to work for the land where I was born, serve the poor and the destitute. I have no desire to acquire a high post or earn a great deal of money. Athai, I seek your blessings to develop the will and strength of mind to serve others!'

'Surya, so young and so altruistic. When you grow older you will do a great deal to help others. But we must also take care of ourselves, a little.'

'That won't work, Athai. If you think about your own work, you cannot work for others.'

For a while, silence reigned in the poolside bungalow. In that silence, the wind blowing through the casuarina grove resounded like the waves of the sea.

'Athai, once before you were scared by these winds sounding like the sea. You said that you would tell me why,' Surya said.

A cloud passed over Rajam's face.

'Surya, at just this moment, I too wished to tell you about it... Was I not sick and bedridden in Bombay before coming here? I had all kinds of feverish hallucinations. Some pleasant, others terrifying. Sita and I are standing on the seashore. Sita walks into the sea. "Don't go! Don't go!" I scream at her. But she cannot hear me above the sound of the waves. She keeps going farther into the ocean. Suddenly, a huge wave rolls and crashes over her. I rush headlong into the ocean to save her. I can swim, and so I manage to battle the waves and keep going. But as far as my eyes can see, there is nothing but waves and ocean. Sita is not visible at all. "Sita! Sita!" I keep on shrieking through the roaring waves. My arms are exhausted. But just then, I touch something. It is Sita's hand. I grip her hand. The bangle breaks. The hand seems to slip. But I don't let go. I grip it even more firmly. Many, many times did I have the same dream. Each time, I awoke just as I grabbed her hand. I would feel as if what had happened was real. Even now, I tremble when I remember it. When I hear the wind blowing in the casuarina grove, I remember that dream.'

Surya remained silent. Then he said, 'Did you share this dream with Sita at any time?'

'Yes, I did. I have asked her to be careful.'

'Athai, you should not have told her!' said Surya.

34

TEARS AT THE WEDDING

Rajampettai was the scene of great tumult and clamour. Could any wedding at Kitta Iyer's household be an ordinary event?

The piping and drumming had begun to resound a week in advance. After that, no stove was lit in any of the households in the agraharam. Every meal was at Kitta Iyer's house. Children frolicked all day long under the wedding canopy which covered the whole length of the street. Cattle bells rang constantly. Not even for a moment could any of the carts remain idle.

The families of both bridegrooms arrived a day before the wedding. The village turned into a fairground. Crowds gathered, as massive as those at chariot processions in temple festivals. Pipes and drums and firecrackers made for a spectacular *jaanavaasa* procession of the mapillais down the street.

Amidst all the exuberance and enthusiasm, what made everyone entertain some misgivings was the fact that Sita's father Duraisami Iyer had not arrived as yet.

There was no suggestion of cancelling Sita's wedding for that reason. Rajam's anguish may be guessed, though she did not give the slightest outward sign of her feelings. She declared that the wedding must go on even if her husband did not turn up on time. Duraisami Iyer's letter, which had expressed his heartfelt satisfaction with the alliance, was of immense help to her in this matter. After reading that letter, the in-laws overcame even the slight hesitation that they may have felt. After that, everyone began to crack jokes about working for the railways.

The old gag about the station master asking for leave to perform his seemantam ceremony during his wife's pregnancy, and being told by his white superior to get it done by proxy, was repeated over and over again with innumerable variations.

Kitta Iyer consulted his sister when Duraisami failed to arrive by the last train at 10.30 p.m. It was decided that Rajam's elder sister Abhayam and her husband would give the bride away.

'Sita is lucky. That is why she has an old devout couple who unfailingly perform the traditional rituals to give her away in marriage,' Rajam consoled herself.

There was no end to Abhayam's pride. Complaining about Duraisami's absence, she tore around performing multifarious tasks with great speed. 'From dawn tomorrow, I will have to remain seated on the silken mat! I won't be able to do a single thing then. Everything must get done today.'

In every arrangement he made for the wedding for which he was personally responsible, Kitta Iyer made no distinctions between Lalita and Sita. Whether sarees for the brides or veshtis for the grooms, he made sure that they were equal in quality. This was not the case when it came to the preparations and gifts of which the women of the house were in charge. Sarasvati Ammal did everything to discriminate between Lalita and Sita. Sarasvati Ammal's mother was particularly keen to highlight these differences. Rajam's elder sister Abhayam was equally keen to change things round. She frequently sought Rajam to bemoan, 'Look at this injustice! Does one eye get cosseted and the other abandoned? How can our sister-in-law be so partial? And her mother makes things three times worse! You and I were also born in this very household. Does Lalita have rights that Sita does not?'

Mollifying Abhayam became Rajam's chief responsibility. 'Akka! Don't say a word! I am keeping my spirits up because things are moving along though my husband has let me down by not arriving on time. Anna's good nature is responsible for that. What will my situation be without his kindness? By God's grace, the bridegroom and his parents are not the kind of people who find fault. So, why are you making an unnecessary fuss?'

Sita was deeply chagrined. She was infuriated by her father's absence. Anguish welled up in her heart when she thought of being denied all the splendid attention Lalita was receiving. She felt a rush of anger when she saw the difference between the way Lalita's in-laws and hers were treated. Sita suppressed all these feelings with the thought that made her exult, 'Let it be! Let Lalita enjoy all the fanfare, but does she have my good fortune? Can her husband compare with mine?'

Surya was miserable, because of a telegram that had arrived the night before, addressed to Rajam. When he went as usual to the post office to collect the mail, he also took delivery of a telegram that the runner had brought in separately. When he opened and read it, he was not only startled, but plunged into a state of stupefaction. The telegram said, 'Stop the wedding. I will come in person and explain. Duraisami.'

Surya could not easily make up his mind as to how he should act in response to the message. It was possible that the mischief makers who had sent the anonymous letter had sent the telegram as well. What pandemonium would ensue if he showed the telegram to the others or revealed its contents! It would be difficult for them to believe that it was a fake telegram. What a disgrace it would be to stop the wedding after the in-laws had arrived and all the arrangements made? How grief-stricken Sita and her mother would be! What would the mapillai's family think? People in villages for miles around would laugh and indulge in mockery! Should a fake telegram be allowed to cause such havoc?

Surya decided that in any case, for the present, chaos and confusion should not be unleashed by publicising the telegram. Duraisami Iyer may arrive before night fell. Let him stop the wedding if it was necessary. Even then it would be his duty to demand the reasons and argue with him against the move.

After taking this decision, Surya was plunged into greater

befuddlement by Duraisami Iyer's not arriving by the night mail. 'Let God show the way. Let things happen as they will. The right thing to do is to bury this telegram,' Surya decided. But the suppressed telegram made it impossible for him to get even a wink of sleep.

The next day, preparations for the marriage ceremony began well before dawn. Ten o'clock was the appointed hour, but everything happened in a rush. There were continual cries of 'The hour has come! Hurry! Hurry!'. The two bridegrooms had barely taken a few steps in the kasi yatra ritual when people started yelling, 'Enough! Enough! No need to go all the way to Kasi!' Their uncles carried the brides on their shoulders as the couples exchanged garlands – all in record time.

The sacred hour for the marriage ceremony arrived. With the ear-splitting wails of two nagasvaram pipes, tavil drums banging away to make the houses shake, mantra chants filling the sky, and the women of the household singing a medley of a hundred discordant notes, Saundara Raghavan tied the auspicious thread around Sita's neck. At the same moment, Pattabhiraman made three knots in the marriage thread he tied around Lalita's neck.

After this, there was some depletion of the noise and the stress. Those who had been sweating in their seats in the closely packed crowd, stood up with a sense of fait accompli and walked out to take in the air.

Surya, who had been pacing in and out of the house a thousand times since morning, came out of the house. Now his mind found some of its tranquility restored. 'The wedding is over. Nothing can be changed now.' The thought calmed him.

That was when the tinkling sounds of the bells round the bullock's neck announced the arrival of the cart. Kitta Iyer's closed cart came rolling down the street. It was the cart that had gone to the railway station the previous night and had waited there all this while. It was not empty. The person seated inside must be the uncle from Bombay. Surya hastened to welcome him.

The cart came to a stop. Before the man inside could get down Surya said, 'Athimber! Why so late?'

The man inside was indeed Duraisami Iyer. He looked Surya up and down.

Surya introduced himself. 'My name is Surya. I am Sita's cousin.'

'I see! Kitta Iyer's second son?'

'Yes. Athimber! Why did you arrive so late? It is fifteen minutes since the wedding thread was tied. Abhayam Athai and her husband gave the bride away.'

'What! What! Marriage performed? For whom? When?'

'Why? For both Sita and Lalita!'

'Sita! For Sita too? Who is the bridegroom?'

'Why! Saundara Raghavan! Why, Athimber! Didn't you receive the wedding invitation? But you knew all about it! Hadn't you written from Delhi?'

'I had sent a telegram...' Duraisami stammered.

'Telegram? What telegram?' asked Surya with great daring.

'I had sent a telegram asking for Sita's wedding to be stopped. Didn't you get it?'

Managing to quell his confusion, Surya said, 'O! I remember now! A telegram did arrive a few minutes ago. It was impossible to open it in the melee. Nor was it possible to hand it to Athai at that time. Is this the telegram you sent?'

Taking the telegram Surya drew out from his shirt pocket, Duraisami Iyer opened it and said, 'Yes. This is it. Why did it not arrive yesterday? Must have been delayed because this is a remote village. Well, everything is God's doing. What can we do? Surya! Don't mention this telegram to anyone.'

'All right. Anyway, what is the use of talking about it now? What has happened has happened.'

'Yes. What has happened has happened. It is God's will!' Saying so, Duraisami Iyer tore the telegram to shreds and threw the bits down.

Until then, Sita had been rejoicing as she cast sidelong glances at Raghavan. Suddenly, she saw her father coming in through the front door. All the tears she had suppressed burst out in floods. They cascaded down from her eyes like a waterfall.

Rajam was so overwhelmed by emotions that she stood holding

the pillar, transfixed. She could not comfort her daughter. Abhayam, who had just given Sita away in marriage, took up the mother's responsibility. 'Silly girl! Why are you crying now? Your father is here. Be happy that he was able to be here, at least now.'

Sita's mother-in-law too came close to her and comforted her. Little Sundu, who had been engaged in knotting the ends of Sita's saree with the mapillai's upper cloth, also tried to console her, 'Don't cry, cousin! If you do, all the black *mai* in your eyes will drip down your cheeks!'

Duraisami Iyer came and sat down beside Sita. 'Don't cry, my dear! The train let me down. Otherwise, would I have stayed away?' he said and gently patted her on the back.

When the crying didn't stop even then, Saundara Raghavan touched his wife's hand lightly and said, 'Sita!'

At once, the tears ceased to flow. Just once did Sita look at Saundara Raghavan with her large round eyes swimming in tears. So much was conveyed by that glance. So many mysterious secrets of the heart, quite beyond speech, were imprinted on it. With the lexicon of love, Raghavan recognized them all.

PART TWO
HURRICANE

1

THE JOURNEY TO DELHI

The Grand Trunk Express huffed and puffed on its track exhaling a miasma of grit-filled smoke, emitting shrill screams now and then. It was bursting with passengers, fatigue-ridden by the journey of forty-eight hours.

To them, the single hour that remained before reaching their destination seemed to stretch to eternity. Sita was travelling on that train with her mother-in-law in a second-class compartment. She was so keyed up that the hour seemed like an endless epic age to her.

But who is the VIP enthroned on Kamakshi Ammal's lap? Why is Kamakshi Ammal putting up with being repeatedly slapped on her cheeks and shoulders by that august personage?

What follows is droller still. Sita places her forefinger over her nose, glares at the VIP and threatens her. 'Vasanti, don't you dare slap Patti!' At once Vasanti slaps Sita on both her cheeks. Mother-in-law and daughter-in-law laugh loudly together. For Vasanti is none other than Kamakshi Ammal's darling granddaughter, Sita's and Raghavan's first child. She is now two years and six months old.

Vasanti's actions were prompted by her grandmother's shutting the window to prevent the child from sticking her head out of it. Vasanti's demand was that it should be opened at once, for what was the use of train travel if you cannot see out of the windows on both sides? Since Kamakshi Ammal was unable to furnish a satisfactory answer, she was soon forced to open the window.

As soon as the window was opened, pointing her chubby little finger outside Vasanti asked, 'Amma! Whath is thath? Patti! Whath is thath?'

'It is an old fort,' Sita replied.

'Whath is a fff-or-th?' Vasanti lisped.

'A fort is a fort. Surya Mama will have to be here to answer all your questions.'

'Call Sooorrryaa maa maa…'

'Keep quiet! He won't hear me above the din of the train. He will come when the train stops.'

'Amma…!' Vasanti grumbled and began to look out of the window.

Kamakshi Ammal now exclaimed, 'There's a fort! And here's another! Wherever I look there are forts. Wonder who built them!'

'Must have been built by many different kings. Delhi has been a capital city for over a thousand years. Such ruined forts abound between Agra and Delhi,' Sita replied.

'We see innumerable temples on both sides when we travel in the south. But there seems to be no temple in these parts!'

'Only in Mathura-Vrindavan. The Vrindavan temple was built by Vaishnavas who came from the south. If you go to Kasi, they say you can see a number of temples.'

'Are there no temples in Delhi?'

'No, Amma! Muslim kings ruled Delhi for a very long time. That is why you can see mosques everywhere. If not a mosque, a tomb where some Muslim king is buried. But they say that a very rich man called Birla is now building a temple in the city.'

'You keep chanting "Taj Mahal! Taj Mahal!" Is it also a tomb of some Muslim king?'

At that moment, Sita was not thinking about the Taj Mahal. Her mind was chanting 'Delhi Junction! Saundara Raghavan!', in alignment with the drone and beat of the train's wheels. She knew that her husband would be waiting on the platform to receive her.

Though her mind was elsewhere, her sense of duty made her respond to her mother-in-law's questions.

'No, Amma! Taj Mahal is not the tomb of a king. A queen is buried there. An emperor called Shah Jahan who ruled in Delhi was besotted by his queen, Mumtaz Mahal. When she died, he did not marry again. He built a resplendent tomb of white marble over the place where she was buried and had it ornamented with flowers of multi-coloured gems. It seems nothing on earth is more beautiful!'

'You haven't seen it?'

'Not yet. Last time I came to Delhi, I didn't spend even three whole months here. Your son insisted that we should go to the Taj Mahal. But before we could, he had orders to go abroad.'

'What does it matter, Sita! You are going to be in Delhi now. Go and see it whenever you like.'

'What do you mean, "Go and see it!" You must come with us.'

'Why should I? Going to a temple would have some meaning. What's the use of going to the Taj Mahal?'

'Don't say that! You will be absolutely astounded when you see it! The palace built by Shah Jahan is in Delhi. It has two great halls – Diwan-i-Khas and Diwan-i-Aam. We can gaze at them all day! One can never tire of the sight even if we had ten thousand eyes! The palace harem has pools and rills and marble fountains where the queens bathed. Adadaa! Unless you see it with your own eyes, you cannot know their splendour!'

'Splendid they may be, but I don't care for them. I will see in this darling child all the temples, shrines and sacred pools combined! But Sita, was Delhi always ruled by Muslim kings? Never any Hindu raja?'

'There were Hindu kings in Delhi over a thousand years ago. Have you heard of Prithviraj?'

'I may have heard the name. But I remember nothing more. Go on, Sita! Storytelling may help us to pass the time!'

'There was a king called Prithviraj in Delhi. The neighbouring kingdom was ruled by a king called Jayachandra who nourished a lifelong enmity towards Prithviraj. But his daughter Samyukta fell in love with Prithviraj and was determined to marry him.'

'How did she fall in love with Prithviraj? Had they ever met?'

'No, Amma. Samyukta had heard tales of Prithviraj's valour and handsome appearance and lost her heart to him.'

'Some love! And then?'

'Jayachandra organized a swayamvara ceremony for Samyukta to choose her bridegroom. He invited the kings of the fifty-four kingdoms. All except Prithviraj. He also had a statue of Prithviraj placed at the entrance of the swayamvara hall as a common guard!'

'Chee! Chee! What a cheap trick!'

'It was his misfortune, what else? It was a time of misfortune for our whole country. Do you know what Samyukta did? Walking down the hall with the wedding garland in her hands, she passed every suitor until she reached the entrance where she knew Prithviraj's statue had been installed. Swiftly, she threw the garland around the neck of the sculpted figure!'

'What a silly girl! What is the use of garlanding a statue?'

'The moment the garland touched the statue, it came to life!'

'A statue? Coming to life? I see you are making it up!'

'No, Amma! It is a true story. The real Prithviraj was hidden behind that sculpture, waiting to carry her off at the opportune moment. In an instant he lifted her up, placed her on his steed, and flew away. Don't ask me if he really flew away! He galloped so fast that it seemed as if he was flying. Jayachandra and his henchmen followed, but they could not catch up. Prithviraj's soldiers arrived to stop them.'

'So! Prithviraj and Samyukta married and lived happily ever after, like the god and goddess of love!'

'It would have been a great ending. But no. At that time Muhammad Ghori invaded India from the north. Prithviraj routed his army and made him retreat. After two or three such failed encounters, Samyukta's father Jayachandra sent a missive to Muhammad Ghori offering his help. That was how Muhammad Ghori and Jayachandra joined forces and fought against Prithviraj, who fought valiantly until he dropped dead on the battlefield.'

'Ayo! Poor man! What was Samyukta's fate?'

'She jumped into the fire and gave up her life.'

'What a calamity! That is why they say that everything must be done according to the advice of elders. Things would not have taken this turn if Samyukta had listened to her father!'

'How can you put the blame on Samyukta! How can what

Jayachandra did be just or right? Why couldn't he have let his daughter marry as she wished? Moreover, his hatred for his own son-in-law made him join forces with a foreigner! What a great betrayal that was! If you ask me, I will say that it is extremely wrong for parents to interfere in the matter of their children's marriage. Those who do so must be thrown into the lime pits!'

These words triggered an old memory in Kamakshi Ammal. She winced. Sita saw it and asked, 'Amma! Do you have a headache?'

'No!' replied Kamakshi Ammal, and added, 'What you say is not entirely true. Sita! Parents are not always wrong! After all, what every parent wants is the happiness and well-being of their children! Not everyone is like Jayachandra. Parents reflect on what is good for their children before advising them.'

'You are right, Amma! Not everyone will be a Jayachandra. Take my own wedding. It happened only because you let your son do as he wished. How could it have taken place otherwise?'

Once again Kamakshi Ammal felt an arrow pierce her heart. She decided to change the subject.

'Sita! Why is Surya not yet married? Any flaw or problem in his horoscope?'

'No. Besides, Surya is not all that old. He must be only twenty or twenty-one. But he says that he will never marry.'

'All boys say that. Only when push comes to shove will they say "Yes!". What about Surya's education?'

'He was studying for his BA. Now he has quit his studies.'

'Why? Was he poor at studies? Surya doesn't look too bright.'

'He may not look bright. But Surya is extremely intelligent. It was entirely due to him that my marriage took place! My uncle and aunt were furious when your son said, "I like Sita, not Lalita!" It was Surya who calmed them down.'

'Could the anger of your uncle and aunt have stopped the marriage? It is God's will that makes things happen… Sita! Why did Surya give up his studies?'

'He says he doesn't like "English" education! If he passes his BA, his parents will pester him to take up a job. Someone or the other will trouble him with offers of marriage.'

'How can you say that an offer of marriage is troublesome? I am asking for all these details about Surya with my brother's daughter in mind. What is he going to do if not take up a job?'

'There is a Congress session happening somewhere here. He has come to attend it. He is not going back, he says. Wants to stay in Delhi and write for the newspapers.'

'Oh! Does he write for the newspapers? Is he that clever? That's not bad at all! Sita! Don't you know that Raghavan got this prestigious job because he wrote in the newspapers?'

'Please don't talk as if Surya and your son are equals! Does he have your son's education? Or his brilliance? All he can do is scribble pedestrian stuff for some Tamil paper.'

The train gave a loud shriek and slowed down. The din made by the crowds could be heard in the distance. Sita looked out of the train.

'Amma, Amma, there! I can see the station. Your son will be here.'

Sita patted Vasanti and said, 'Vasanti, Vasanti, we are in Delhi. Your father will be at the platform. Wake up! Wake up!'

Amidst the ear-splitting groans of the machine and the cries of human beings, the Grand Trunk Express entered the Delhi railway station.

2

MEETING AT THE RAILWAY STATION

As the Grand Trunk Express entered the railway station in Delhi, the faces of hundreds of people appeared and disappeared before Sita's eyes. But neither her eye nor her mind paid the slightest attention to any one of them. Her eyes were searching for a single handsome face, a face imprinted in her heart and merged with her soul. When that face became visible Sita's shriek rose above all the noises in the railway station, 'Vasanti! There! Appa!'

Raghavan was picking his way fussily through the crowds and advancing towards their compartment. Suddenly, he came to a halt.

On the track opposite the Grand Trunk Express, another train gave a screech as it was about to pull away. Saundara Raghavan glanced at that train. He hesitated for an instant. Then, instead of coming towards Sita, he hurried to the train moving in the opposite direction. This time he did not mind the jostling crowd but crashed and banged into others as he ran. Two women were seated by the window in that train. Raghavan said something to one of them. She replied. He spoke again. Meanwhile the train began to move. Raghavan stood stock still, looking at the girls, until the last compartment went by with the guards. Then he turned and came to Sita's compartment.

Sita watched the scene with unblinking interest. She felt some disappointment at Raghavan's going to the opposite train even after catching sight of her and the child. She did not know the women on the other train. And yet, Raghavan's going to talk to them, considering them to be more important than herself, made her feel a sharp pain.

All this was but an instant's experience. As he approached, Sita was overcome by euphoria and held Vasanti out of the window. 'Vasanti, go to Appa!' The child leapt into the father's arms. Raghavan took her joyfully. And yet, his face showed that his mind was not wholly focused on the child.

Kamakshi Ammal knew nothing about this fleeting drama. She was busy checking their luggage and getting the pieces down.

'Sita, get down. I will follow after all the luggage has been taken down,' she told her.

Sita went to stand beside Raghavan who was giving instructions to the porters. She expected him to say something. But he did not look as if he was going to open his mouth.

'Amma and I were placing bets about whether or not you would come to the station.'

Raghavan did not hear her. His mind was elsewhere.

'Two days before we left Vasanti became ill. We were afraid that we may not be able to undertake the journey.'

This caught Raghavan's attention. He asked, 'What was the matter?'

'It looked like indigestion.'

'Children should never get indigestion. If they do, it is entirely due to the carelessness of those who raise them,' Raghavan said in a flinty tone.

Realizing that she had struck the wrong note, Sita lapsed into silence.

Kamakshi Ammal got down after checking under the seats. Approaching Raghavan she said, 'Why, son! You have lost a great deal of weight!'

'Yes, my anxiety at not seeing all of you for so long has made me lose weight,' he said.

Surya, who had been travelling on the same train in another compartment, came up to them.

Raghavan looked him up and down but did not say anything. He looked at the porters and said, 'Pick up the luggage!'

Sita was crestfallen to see Raghavan ignoring Surya. She looked at Surya from the corner of her eye. Surya had a smile on his face.

Then, gathering courage she said, 'You do know Surya, don't you?'

'Surya, who?' asked Raghavan.

'Surya? Why, Lalita's elder brother Surya!'

'Mapillai! You seem to have completely forgotten me.' Surya said.

'O! The boy who was angry throughout the wedding! Why is he here?'

Kamakshi Ammal made a welcome interpolation. 'Surya took care of us all along the way. We would have found it very difficult to manage without him.'

'Was he on the same train? I did not see him!' Raghavan said.

Surya said, 'Mapillai, sir! I came by third class. Nor was I of any extraordinary help to them.'

'Doesn't matter. It will be good if I am not addressed as Mapillai Sir. It sounds rather uncivilized.'

By then the porters had loaded themselves. Kamakshi Ammal took the child from Raghavan's arms. Everyone started following Raghavan.

'Is this our motor car?' asked Sita. Her voice was bubbling with excitement.

Raghavan gave no answer. Once the luggage was loaded, he made Kamakshi Ammal and Sita sit at the back with the child. He took the driver's seat in front.

There was an empty seat beside him. Sita thought that he would ask Surya to take it. But Raghavan did not.

Sita looked at Surya disconsolately. Surya's face expressed empathy.

The car was about to start. Sita said, 'Amma, Surya seems to be taking leave of you!'

Kamakshi Ammal said, 'Surya, you must visit us before you go back!'

Sita felt grateful to her mother-in-law.

'Righto! I will certainly make it. Mapillai, what is your address?'

Surya was already aware of Raghavan's nature. But he did not intend to give up his claim on his athanga. He had decided that he would go and look them up even if the mapillai did not invite him to do so.

'Number 8, Nadir Shah Road,' growled Raghavan and started the car.

Sita regained her zest when the car began to move. 'Vasanti, see! Appa is driving the car.'

'I thoo will thrive the car!' Vasanti lisped.

Sita laughed loudly. 'Did you hear that, Amma! Your granddaughter says she too will drive the car!'

'She might, at that!' said Kamakshi Ammal. 'Who knows what miracles are in store for the world by the time she grows up!'

Raghavan interposed, 'Amma! Women driving cars is not a miracle of the future! There are many women drivers filling the streets with hazards. When a woman is seen driving, the street gets emptied in no time at all! Terrified citizens run and hide themselves!'

Sita laughed in enjoyment of Raghavan's sally. Past experience had taught her that he got angry if she did not understand his jokes and laugh at them. Raghavan did not explain what she did not comprehend. He put a full stop to the exchange with 'Why am I wasting my time on you!' So, Sita developed the habit of laughing at his jokes whether or not they made sense to her.

The car gave a lurch and ground to a halt before Sita could stop laughing. Raghavan had applied the brakes with a sudden jerk. An old Muslim woman escaped with her life. If the car had moved half an inch forward, it would have hit her.

At first Kamakshi Ammal and Sita did not know what had happened. When they saw what it was, they felt a sharp sensation at the pit of the stomach.

'Why car sthop?' asked Vasanti.

When the car began to move again, Kamakshi Ammal asked, 'Son! Why haven't you engaged a driver?'

'If I engage a driver, I will have to pay him! Where will I get the money? Drivers are expensive in this city,' Raghavan said.

Both his wife and mother knew that Raghavan's salary at that time was two thousand two hundred rupees. They assumed that he was joking when he said that he could not afford a driver. Sita laughed.

'Why are you laughing? You think I'm joking?'

'Yes,' Sita said.

'Why do you think I'm joking?'

'Who will believe that you cannot afford a driver? Even your darling daughter will not believe it!'

'So! You are raising your daughter to be just like yourself!'

Sita continued to laugh as she answered, 'How else can I raise her?'

At that moment Raghavan's car proved that it made no discrimination between Hindus and Muslims. It tried to run over a Hindu woman. Fortunately, it stopped short of the deed.

'Son! Raghava! It looks like you have not yet learnt to drive properly. Can't you engage a driver until you learn to drive well?'

'Amma! I know how to drive a car. But my mind is somewhat unsettled today. That is why…'

'Why should it be unsettled today?'

'What if someone presumed dead suddenly reappears and swears that she is not who we thought she was…'

'What are you saying, Raghava? I was not as unwell as all that. I had influenza for four days. That's all. *Ei*, Sita! Did you exaggerate my condition in your letter to him?'

'I did not write about your illness at all!' Sita said.

'I didn't mean you, Amma! I didn't even know that you had fever until now. I mean someone else…'

'Who was it who died and came back to life?'

'Did you not see at the railway station?'

'No! Which railway station?'

'The railway station in Delhi. A train began to move on the opposite track just as your train came to a halt. Didn't you see…?'

'I saw nothing. Who was on that train?'

'I'll tell you later,' Raghavan said.

Kamakshi Ammal had not seen the train on the opposite side. But Sita had. Sita had seen and imprinted on her heart the scene of

Raghavan running towards that train, the train leaving as he tried to talk to a woman inside, and the curious expression on his face as he turned away and made his way towards them.

She urged her mother-in-law to pursue the matter by saying, 'Amma, ask him who was on that train!'

The car had stopped for the third time. Since it stopped with a lurch, mother-in-law and daughter-in-law were thrown into a panic once again.

'What! What is it?' they asked.

'We are home,' Raghavan announced.

Sita looked at the house. A lovely little bungalow. There were flowers and saplings in front and at the sides. Pleasure rose and overflowed in Sita's heart. 'Vasanti, look at your house! How beautiful it is!' she exulted.

'Appa builth thith houth? For uth?' Vasanti asked.

3

THE SEED OF SORROW

As soon as they were married, Raghavan took Sita with him to New Delhi. As a temporary measure, they had stayed in an 'English' hotel for a month. During that time, they floated in the celestial spheres!

They wandered hand in hand through New Delhi's beautiful roads and squares, in Old Delhi's ruined forts and its fine palaces and mosques. Now and then, Raghavan recalled having roamed in the same places a few years ago, hand in hand with another girl. But he gripped his wife's hand all the more firmly as he dismissed those thoughts.

Then it became necessary for Raghavan to make a trip to England. He took Sita to Madras and left her with his parents. He consoled her in a thousand ways. He explained that going abroad at that time would be of immense value in his profession, an opportunity that may not come again, and that it would be foolish to let it slip through his fingers. Was he not unhappy at having to leave the wife he had chosen with all his heart and married with so much love? Should Sita stand between him and his chance to make progress in life? He also swore that he would take her with him the next time he went abroad.

On the one hand Sita was terribly unhappy at having to part so soon from her heart's beloved. But she was proud that her husband was going abroad. She laughed through her tears and wept as she laughed. She begged him not to go. The very next instant she insisted that he should. Finally, she bid him goodbye.

It was fifteen months before Raghavan returned. During that

time some important incidents occurred in Sita's life. Her mother Rajam died with the satisfaction of having given her only daughter away into a good family. She was fortunate enough to breathe her last with her head on the lap of her husband, Duraisami Iyer. In addition, she had the good fortune of being cremated by the shore of the river Kaveri.

For many days after her mother's death, Sita was lost in sobs and tears. She could not get over her grief despite all the consolations offered by her mother-in-law. None of the explanations given by her father-in-law from the Bhagavad Gita could bring her solace. Her husband's absence when the tragedy occurred served to heighten her sorrow.

Saundara Raghavan was not beside her to share her great affliction. Therefore, Sita's woe was prolonged. Her sorrow was dispelled only after another important and joyful incident took place in her life.

Everything was forgotten when, by God's grace, Sita survived a life endangering ordeal and saw the precious child she had delivered. After this, where would she find the time to mourn her mother? Moreover, Kamakshi Ammal and other older women in the neighbourhood repeatedly remarked, 'Your mother has returned as your child!' Sita began to believe it. The elation she felt in looking at her child made her forget the face of the mother who bore her. She bloomed in body and mind, thinking about her husband's astonishment when she showed him their child.

Before he went abroad, Raghavan had arranged with his parents for Sita to attend a convent school. He wrote a furious letter upon learning that she had not done so. His father sent this reply, 'The date for your seemantam ceremony has been fixed for next month. Come at once.' Then Raghavan knew why Sita did not go to the convent school. Whether he was happy or irked remained unclear. His sardonic reply was a six-months' postponement of the ceremony. 'If not possible, get a substitute to stand in for me.' Sita, who treasured Raghavan's lctters, was so enraged by this one that she tore that letter to shreds. She even complained to her mother-in-law about it.

During this time, mother-in-law and daughter-in-law achieved great closeness and unity. Sita once said to her mother-in-law, 'Amma! It seems my sister-in-law went off to her parents' home saying she could not live in the same house with you! What an unconscionable demoness she must be!' She also told the neighbours about how well her mother-in-law treated her. Kamakshi Ammal's dream came true. She began to walk on the streets of Padmapuram with her head held high.

Saundara Raghavan returned from England. His face shone with heartfelt delight when he saw the child. He even forgot his anger over Sita not attending the convent school. He left, promising to take his wife and child to New Delhi as soon as he could find a house there. It had taken all this while to find a good house.

A week had passed since Sita came to New Delhi. It was spent in setting up the new house. Everyone was continuously engaged in shifting chairs, cupboards and beds from one room to another, making arrangements for cooking, finding a mortar, pestle and grinding stone, or in setting up the radio and the gramophone in the right place. Every evening Sita wanted to go for a walk with Raghavan as they were wont to do as newlyweds. But household chores made her suppress that desire.

A week later, Sita said to Raghavan in the morning, 'Please come home early enough to take me out somewhere.'

'Why should I "take" you out? Why don't you go wherever you like, whenever you like?' Raghavan said.

'Should I go alone, all by myself?'

'Why not? Will someone abduct you on the way? We have the British Raj still. The Congress has not taken over.'

'True, no one will carry me away. But if I have to go alone, I won't go at all.'

'Don't go alone. Take your mother-in-law with you!'

'As if I need your permission to take my mother-in-law out!' Sita said, pretending to be put out.

'All right! All right! Don't get angry! I will come soon and take you out for an evening walk,' Raghavan said as he left the house.

Raghavan did return early. 'Shall we go walking in the motor car or by foot?' he asked.

Laughing at Raghavan's wisecrack as usual, Sita said, 'How can we go walking in the motor car? Let us go by foot.'

Kamakshi Ammal said that she would not join them but take care of the child at home. That was exactly what Sita wanted. She started her walk with Raghavan blithely. They went round the Connaught Circle once and made their way to India Gate.

They sat down on the lawn beside one of the little streams there. The sun had set. Dusk was falling. Competing with the stars in the sky, the electric lamps in India's capital began to shine everywhere.

'Can the celestial world that people talk about be more beautiful than this,' Sita exclaimed.

'Can't say. Haven't been to the celestial realms,' Raghavan replied.

Sita chuckled and said, 'Nor have I. But you have been to London and Paris. Aenna! London and Paris must be more beautiful than New Delhi?'

'I will answer your question if you swear that you will never address me as Aenna,' declared Raghavan.

'All right. I will not call you Aenna anymore. I will say, "What Sir!" Is London more beautiful than Delhi? What Sir?'

'London is beautiful in its own way. Delhi in another way,' Raghavan said.

As he talked to Sita, Raghavan's eyes had been roving everywhere. When two girls walked together on the street, Raghavan, who had been reclining on the lawn, sprang up to stare intently at them. Then he sank back on the grass once again.

Sita recalled the incident at the Delhi railway station.

'What Sir! You talked to a woman at the railway station the other day. Who is she?' Sita asked.

'How does it matter to you?' Raghavan's voice registered harshness.

'Why not say who she is?'

'Won't.'

'Why not?'

'I know so many people in this city. Can I be telling you about each and every one of them?'

'I should know the people you know.'

'It is enough if you know what you have to know. You don't need to know everyone in the city.'

Sita controlled the anger welling up within her.

For a while both remained silent.

'Why Sir! You won't tell me who she is?'

Silence.

'Is she a woman from our part of the world? Or is she from here?'

Silence.

'Is this why you brought me on a walk?' Tears trembled in Sita's eyes.

"This is why I didn't want to bring you. You have started displaying all the vicious traits of women, you hellcat!' Saying so, Raghavan got up from the lawn.

'I am no hellcat,' Sita said and continued muttering.

The seed of sorrow had been planted in Sita's young and innocent heart. Who knows when it will sprout and grow and become a tree? The fruits it would yield?

4

AT THE STREET CORNER

That night, Sita could not go to sleep for a long time. She went on ruminating over the fact that on the first day after settling in their new house in Delhi, when her beloved husband took her out walking, she had irritated him by her stupid behaviour. And yet, the thought that he refused to reveal the identity of the woman continued to hurt her like the pricking of a needle. When she was staying in her father-in-law's house in Padmapuram, a few women had started telling tales about Raghavan's old love. Sita had cut them short and dismissed those rumours as springing from jealousy. Now she remembered the gossipmongering. 'Perhaps it was the same girl he saw on the train. Perhaps he sees her everyday instead of going to the office as he claims he does!' Then she chided herself. 'What folly is this! She went away to some other place! Moreover, from his obvious surprise when he saw her on the train, it didn't seem as if he knew her all that well. Why am I hurting myself unnecessarily? They are right to say a woman has a callow mind! He came to see Lalita, refused to marry her, chose to fall in love with me and marry me instead! How wrong it is for me to unnecessarily suspect the noble man who came to make me his own!'

She vowed that she would never allow what happened that evening to recur, never make the kind of enquiries he disliked. However, after arriving at so firm a decision, she continued to feel the sting. 'Even if I had spoken out of turn, why could he have not told me who she was? Why should he refuse?'

But when she got up at daybreak on the next day, all the smarting began to dissolve, like a nightmare fading away. It disappeared without a trace when Raghavan smiled at her when she handed him his morning coffee. As usual, Sita brought Vasanti as Raghavan was leaving for the office. Raghavan took the child in his arms and fondled her. He put her against his shoulder and patted her. He pinched her cheek lightly. 'Vasanti? Will you come to the office with me?' he asked. 'Yeth Appa, now,' Vasanti replied. 'Great! I can imagine how much work will get done if I take you with me,' he chuckled.

Kamakshi Ammal who happened to come out of the kitchen, said, 'Just you wait. When Vasanti grows up she will overtake you! She will hold a job far higher than yours!'

'Any doubt about that? Can Sita's daughter ever lag behind?' Raghavan quipped.

Sita could not contain her pride. 'Am I so brilliant? Vasanti takes after my mother-in-law. That is why she is so smart. See how they resemble each other!' said Sita and put Vasanti's face next to her grandmother's. Kamakshi Ammal's delight knew no bounds.

'So! No credit to me! You have appropriated all of it for yourselves!' said Raghavan as he handed the child to his mother and left for the office.

Another week passed. Sita kept expecting Raghavan to invite her to take a walk with him. She was forced to bring it up when it didn't seem like he was going to do so.

'It has been some time since we went out. Shall we go today?' she asked.

'Yes. But you must not ask silly questions as you did the last time. If you agree, we can go,' Raghavan said.

'I won't. But if I do, please answer me without getting angry.'

'No. If you say something stupid, I *will* get angry. Better we stay at home.'

'I will not ask you anything. If you like I will remain dumb,' Sita said.

'See, you have begun it right here! I'm not coming,' Raghavan said.

Sita got scared. 'I didn't mean it! Come on, let us go somewhere!' she said.

That day, they walked in a different direction. There was hardly any conversation during the walk. Sita was extra careful to avoid anything that might sound wrong. Raghavan too did not look around. It was Sita who cast intent looks at every woman who passed them.

They reached a little park with flowering shrubs between. 'We've walked enough. Let us sit here for a little while before we go back,' Sita said.

There were some garden seats around the circular lawn. There were people seated on some of them. Raghavan and Sita sat next to a flowering plant. On one of the benches sat a Parsi gentleman and his lady. They were enjoying themselves as they watched their two children at play.

'We could have brought Vasanti to play here,' Sita said.

'Can she walk so far? Is it possible to carry her all the way? We will have to take the car,' said Raghavan.

'Yes,' Sita agreed. After a pause she added, 'Should we not take Amma and Vasanti and show them the wonders of Delhi?'

'We should. But they will make little sense to Vasanti at her age. Amma is not interested in sightseeing. But still, tomorrow being Sunday, I am thinking of taking all of you to the Red Fort and to the Qutub Minar,' Raghavan said.

Sita's listlessness when they began their walk changed to elation. 'Yes! When are we going to see the Taj Mahal? You said that you would take me there on my first visit to this city. But the foreign trip came up. Do you remember?'

'I have also been thinking about that. If we go to the Taj Mahal, we must make it on the day of the full moon. Only then can we truly appreciate its beauty.'

'You once told me that seeing the Taj Mahal under the moonlight is to see the palace of a celestial nymph. What, Sir! Can't we make it for next month on the day of the full moon? What do you say?'

'Let us see.'

'Should we not take Amma and Vasanti?'

Raghavan did not answer. His mind had wandered elsewhere.

The sun had set. It was getting dark. Thousands of lights began to glow, adding splendour to the city. The lamp posts shining all around them between the lush green trees made a lovely show.

Winter was ending. Little drops of dew began to fall. Sita felt cool and pleasant within and without.

They got up and started walking. As they reached the point where they had to turn into their street, Sita became alarmed and halted for a second. She took a step back. A woman, knife in hand, was standing before her under a big tree. Gossamer mist covered her form like a thin curtain. The light from the lantern post at the corner of the road beamed through the mist and made her face dimly visible. The woman looked like a phantom in a stage play, covered by a thin transparent cloth.

Sita drew back, while at the same time feeling that she had seen the woman somewhere, long ago. An almost inaudible gasp of fear came out of her mouth. Raghavan who was following her, supported her with his arms as he asked, 'What is it?' There! Sita gestured with an outstretched arm. The woman started moving away when Raghavan saw her. In no time at all, she vanished into the dark mists.

The incident did not affect Raghavan at all. 'Silly girl! Many people come and go on the streets of Delhi. Why are you afraid?' he asked Sita.

'I am not afraid,' Sita said. But an inexplicable fear entered and ensconced itself within her being. She could not speak anymore. She decided to tell Raghavan more about that woman at leisure, when they went to bed that night.

5

HARIPURA CONGRESS

When Raghavan and Sita reached home, they could hear the child's tinkling laughter. They went in and saw Surya playing with the child and making her laugh.

'Oho, Cousin! When did you come?' asked Sita in delight.

'About half an hour ago. Athanga, I was just wondering if it would take a long time before you returned. Mapillai, sir! Vasanti is complaining that you two have left her patti alone and got lost somewhere! She has stayed behind to take care of her patti. How's that?'

Raghavan let out a crack of laughter. Lifting up Vasanti he asked with mock anger, 'You bad girl! Did you say that?' 'Yes. I thith. Why thith you leave me and go away?'

'Cousin? How did things go at the Congress?' asked Sita.

'Fantastic!' Surya replied.

'With your cousin attending it how could it have been anything but fantastic?' said Raghavan.

'Surya has been telling me story after story about the Congress. But please, sit down and have your dinner first. The food is getting cold. After that you can listen to him at leisure,' Kamakshi Ammal told them.

When they went back to the living room after dinner, Surya described the grand events at the Haripura Congress held under the leadership of Subhash Chandra Bose. Raghavan too listened with interest, without his usual hauteur.

Surya finished recounting and said, 'Everything went off well. But we were not particularly satisfied.'

'What do you mean by "we were not happy"? Who is *we*?' Raghavan enquired.

'I am talking about the Socialist Party. I belong to it.'

'What does "Socialist Party" mean?' asked Sita.

Raghavan rushed in before Surya could answer, 'Socialist Party means flattening everyone down to the same level – rich and poor, intellectuals and idiots, good and bad, man and mouse – and drowning them all in the ocean.'

'Athanga, don't be scared. Mapillai is joking.'

'Never mind! What about the Mahatma's influence on the Congress?' Raghavan asked.

'Nothing can diminish his influence. It was his influence that made for such a splendid session of the Congress in a remote village where it was held this year.'

'If we let things go the Gandhi way, India will have no one left but paupers and mendicants. Everyone will have to take up the begging bowl – with no one to give alms. So long as Gandhi's influence lasts, India will never amount to anything,' Raghavan spoke with heat.

'Raghava, don't say such things about Gandhi! People say that Gandhi is a great soul, an avatar,' Kamakshi Ammal said.

'People? Why, the people will say anything blindly! What is your opinion about the Mahatma's influence?' Raghavan asked Surya.

'I don't see the Mahatma as you do! He is a great soul. India has benefited enormously by his presence. But on certain issues, we differ from him. For example, the Mahatma has regressive ideas about the rulers of the principalities. He says that they must not even be mentioned in the Congress meetings. We, on the other hand, say that all these royals must be gotten rid of!'

'Please! Don't either of you say anything negative about Mahatma Gandhi. My mother told me that the Mahatma is God. I will not put up with anyone saying anything different,' Sita declared.

'So, you too have started discussing politics!' Raghavan remarked.

'Athanga, let us agree that the Mahatma is divine. But don't we ask the gods to give us boons? We make our petitions to Gandhiji in the same spirit.'

'Once you accept someone as God, why ask for anything? Doesn't God know when to grant boons? Does he have to grant them only when we ask for them?' Sita asked.

Raghavan was surprised by Sita's argument. 'Surya, your athanga is the right person to quiz you. Let me see how you answer her!'

'We have known about athanga's smartness from way back when. No wonder Lalita is ready to give her life for her athanga! She babbles about athanga even in her sleep,' Surya said.

The conversation shifted to Rajampettai, Devapattinam and the kinsfolk there.

'Surya, you could have gone to Haripura via Bombay. To go via Delhi seems like the most roundabout route,' Raghavan said.

'I told your mother that I was going to the north. She asked me to escort her to Delhi and then go where I must. That is why I took this route.'

'What do I know? I thought "north" meant somewhere near Delhi!' said Kamakshi Ammal.

'People have the same mindset here. They see a man from Madras and ask him about Rameshwaram. They think that the whole Madras Presidency is situated within ten miles of Rameshwaram.' Raghavan said.

'Appa, Raghava! When are you going to take me to Kasi?' Kamakshi Ammal asked.

'Yes… yes… But let us take it slowly, one by one. First let us take a look at Delhi. Tomorrow I am thinking of taking all of you to see the sights of Delhi.'

'Surya! Have you done any sightseeing in Delhi?' Sita asked.

'Not yet. I am thinking of doing that tomorrow,' Surya answered her.

'Excellent! Why don't you join us? At least the conversation will be interesting,' Raghavan said.

That night, Sita was in a state of ebullience. She was delighted to recall that Raghavan had talked to Surya pleasantly, without scorn or distaste, and had even invited him to join them for the sightseeing trip.

She resolved to talk to Raghavan about the woman at the street corner before they went to sleep. She began with, 'The woman we saw today…'

'Are you launching your "woman saga" all over again!' Raghavan snarled.

The woman that Sita had in mind was different from the one in Raghavan's thoughts. Raghavan's snapping made her hesitate and then let it go. 'Why invite trouble by talking about unsavoury subjects when we are happy?' And yet, she was unable to erase from her mind the image of the woman with the knife standing at the street corner.

6

HALF THE MARRIAGE

'And I had been thinking all along that the white man was very clever. Now I see that he has his share of silliness. Why else would he have shifted his capital to this city filled with ruined forts, graveyards and mosques. He could have stayed in Calcutta,' Kamakshi Ammal expressed her opinion when she came home after seeing the sights of Delhi.

'Amma, how can you say that? Wasn't Shah Jahan's palace in the Red Fort amazing, splendid! When the Delhi palace is such a thing of beauty, I wonder what the Agra Palace and Taj Mahal would be like,' Sita mused.

'I donth wanth mothor car! I wanth thonga. Surya mama! Will you thake me on a thonga yetherday?' Yesterday and today were the same in Vasanti's lingo.

'All right, Vasanti! I will take you on a tonga yesterday as well as tomorrow.' Surya assured her.

Everyone entered the house and sat on the sofas in the living room.

'So, the white man has come to Delhi by mistake. But Surya, who wants to drive the white man away, has also landed up in this same city. What a joke!' Raghavan said.

'Where else can we go to drive the Englishman away? Don't we have to come to where he has settled!' Surya retorted.

'Is that why you have come to Delhi? Is it then dead certain that the Englishman is going to be driven away!' Raghavan scoffed.

'Didn't we see it all today? How many kingdoms have been established in this city from Mohammad Ghori's time? Is the Englishman going to be an eternal presence here? The British Raj will have to go the same way as they did!' asked Surya.

'Who knows! What if it were the fate of the Englishman to live in this ruined city,' Kamakshi Ammal exclaimed.

'Amma! Why do you find so many faults with this city? How beautiful was the place where Prithviraj's temple and palace once stood? I didn't have the heart to walk away!' said Sita.

'Siva, Siva! A mosque built after breaking a temple down! And you took me to see the sight! The sins incurred in seeing this city can be washed away only after going to Kasi and bathing in the Ganga,' said Kamakshi Ammal.

'Mami, the Yamuna runs through this city! Won't our sins get washed away by bathing in the Yamuna?' Surya asked.

'Somehow I cannot believe that this is the Yamuna mentioned in the Bhagavatam.'

'What did you expect? Did you imagine that Lord Krishna would be standing under the kadamba tree by the Yamuna river and playing the flute? That was the dwapara yuga of truth and virtue! This is the kali yuga of evil and dissolution! A different age altogether!' Raghavan jeered.

'Your father would read from the tenth canto of the Bhagavatam and expatiate on the verses. *Adadaa!* It was as if Krishna and his gopika maidens were standing before you by the Yamuna river... Raghava! When are you going to take me to Kasi?'

'You will complain even more if you go to Kasi. Don't imagine that the Ganga will be like our Kaveri with lush groves on either side!'

'Never mind Kasi. What, Sir? When are we going to Agra?' Sita asked.

'Let us go on the coming full moon day. Surya, you will join us, won't you?' Raghavan said.

'Certainly! Here I was, worried that you might leave me out!' Surya said.

To Raghavan, taking Surya along proved to be highly convenient.

Instead of addressing all her questions to him, Sita alternated between Raghavan and Surya. Surya answered with enthusiasm. This was a great advantage to Raghavan.

When they went to an old palace or fort, Raghavan found a place to sit and told the others to go ahead and see the sights and remained lost in a reverie. And yes, there was something to mull over all by himself. It was the thought of the girl he had once roamed with in those very places. Was the girl he saw at the railway station really Dharini? If not, how could she look exactly like Dharini? Could there be such a striking personal resemblance between two women? If it was indeed Dharini, the news of her death must be false!

Dharini herself or her clone, Raghavan felt that he could never have peace of mind unless he met that woman and spoke to her again, just once…

But how could he meet her? Where could he seek her? Raghavan remembered that she had taken a passenger train that went towards Agra. She might still be in Agra! Or he may perhaps be able to meet her on the way to Agra. Who knows! Stranger things have happened in the world.

It was with these kinds of thoughts that Raghavan planned to go to Agra on the next full moon day.

When Surya said he would accompany them Raghavan asked his mother, 'Will you come too?'

She replied. 'What I saw today was more than enough for seven lives to come! I'm not coming to see ruined forts and tumbledown mosques. I will stay at home and take care of the child.'

'Excellent! Just what I thought. We will make a trip to Agra now. After that, I will send you on a pilgrimage with Surya. Surya, what do you say? Will you take Amma on such a trip?'

'What objections can I have? I too have wished to see the sacred sites of India. I should be lucky to escort someone so devout as Mami!' said Surya and took his leave.

After Surya left, Kamakshi Ammal said, 'Raghava! Surya is a wonderful boy. I like him very much. For two years they have been looking for a boy for my sister's daughter, Ambujam. Why not our Surya?'

'Why not! Certainly! With your decision, half the marriage is over. If Surya agrees, the other half can be finalized.'

'Of course, he will agree. What is wrong with Ambujam? Bit dark, but good looking all the same. Also, Surya belongs to the Congress. He will create no difficulties about that.'

'If Surya agrees, I have no objections. You are free to get Ambujam married to Surya.'

'If our Sita joins me in persuading Surya, he will agree.'

'Amma, somehow, I feel that Surya doesn't like any talk about marriage. Surya's mother had found a girl for him. It is rumoured that it was the proposal which made him fight with his family and leave home. If you ask me, I will say that it is best to leave matters of marriage to the person concerned. Those who wish to marry must not be prevented from doing so. Those who do not wish to marry must not be compelled to do so. Parents who do that must be thrown into the lime pits!' Sita spoke heatedly.

Sita was saying this for the second time. Raghavan noticed how it made Kamakshi Ammal flinch.

7

LALITA'S LETTER

To my friend as dear to me as my life,

I was enormously pleased with the letter you wrote on reaching Delhi. After having gone so far away you have still not forgotten to write to me! I pray that for as long as we live, our friendship may remain the way it is today.

You must be busy with having to set up a new house in a new city. I think that is why your letter is so short. I counted the words. Thirty-six in all. Never have you written so short a letter. Once you settle down in the new house, you must write to me in detail as usual. Not less than seven or eight pages!

You may be surprised that I am writing to you from Rajampettai. Surely, you will be surprised if you know why I am here. I will give you a clue. I am wearing bangles on both arms, from wrist to elbow!

Now do you know why I am here? Sita! It is four days since the valaikappu ceremony was performed for me. The seemantam ritual takes place next month. I will have to go back to Devapattinam for that. I don't know if you know that the seemantam must take place in the in-laws' house.

Only now has my mother found true happiness. All this while she had been finding fault with me. 'Other women are holding two children in their arms! Why not you?' she nagged. It was impossible to explain that such things were in the hands of God. But now she has overcome her feelings of injury and is happy. She has stopped scolding me. Instead, she laments, 'Ayo! This girl must survive the ordeal of childbirth! Will they send her here for the delivery?' Endless though it is, it is a happy lament!

Sita! I remember that no valaikappu or seemantam was performed for you. You had written that your husband could not make it home from abroad for those ceremonies. In a way, it turned out to be a good thing for me. Until then my mother had been angry that the man who had come to see me, married you. But her anger vanished when she heard that seemantam was not performed for you.

Don't ever imagine that I hold such thoughts! What do rituals matter? Is there anything to equal the boundless love your husband has for you? Surya once said, 'Do the white people and the Christians perform valaikappu and seemantam? Aren't their children doing just fine?' I agree with him. In my opinion there is nothing in life greater than a husband's love. In this, you are lucky. I, not so much.

Don't think that I am complaining about my husband! There is no limit to his love and affection for me.

My dearest friend, I am now telling you what I had not mentioned all this while. Though my husband is extremely fond of me, in many ways he remains his mother's son. He never crosses the line she draws for him. I don't object to his devotion for his mother. But should he put her first even in matters concerning his wife? He takes me out only when his mother gives him permission to do so. If I complain, he advises me, 'Don't you know my heartfelt love for you? If we don't do what mother wants, it will simply lead to unnecessary squabbles. Patience wins in the end!'

I had already hinted at my mother-in-law's nature. Sita! How gentle she seemed at the wedding! But soon, she revealed her true self. She put off the consummation of our marriage for two years. She gave her consent only after my father fell at her feet and agreed to all her demands. But was she happy when all her demands were met before the consummation rites? No! I am telling you what I have never told anyone before. My mother-in-law is a very nasty woman, a demoness in fact! There is no end to the ways in which she mistreats me. Whatever I do appears to be wrong. If I don't perform a particular task she asks, 'Can't you think for yourself? Must you do everything only when you are told?' If I do follow that advice she says, 'Should you not consult me?' My sister-in-law is not happy at her marital home. My mother-in-law is upset about her daughter being treated badly by her in-laws. She takes it out on me.

About my husband... Honestly, I don't know what to say. Doubtless he has great affection for me. But is affection alone sufficient? In his concern for his mother's likes and dislikes, he never spares a thought for my very human feelings. I don't think he has ever thought about me as someone who has left her parents, brothers, house, hamlet, and all her kin, to come to him as her only refuge and shelter. Never on a single day did he take me out, not even to the cinema. Never on an evening walk to see the garden in his town. Not even to a temple or a shrine as the old-fashioned do. Some time ago, Pandit Jawaharlal Nehru came to Devapattinam. The entire town went to hear his speech. I begged to go. 'Amma will be angry,' he said and left me at home. It is 'Amma! Amma! Amma!' all the time. One day I lost it. I asked, 'How long are you going to keep me in prison?' He gave his usual smile and said, 'Wait. We will set up our own household. After that all the rules will be made by you. We will hold hands and walk down the street every day!'

Did he mean it or was he making fun of me? I don't think he will set up his own household. At times I wish he didn't have this advocate's job. Can he not get a job in some place faraway – Bombay, Delhi, Calcutta! I am waiting for the right time to make the suggestion.

Sita, you are lucky! Your situation is exactly the opposite of mine. Your mother-in-law and father-in-law adore you. Your husband has a job in India's capital. He took you to Delhi as soon as you were married. I don't have to ask how things are going for you now. He must be taking you everywhere. You must be going to the cinemas every day. I find my happiness in thinking about your great happiness.

From the moment I came to Rajampettai I have been thinking of you. Each day, when I hear the postal runner's jingling bells, I remember how I used to run to the post office for your letters from Bombay. I remember all the fantasies we span sitting on the steps of the poolside bungalow. I remember all the stories you told me – Laila Majnu, Anarkali, Romeo Juliet, Sakuntala, Samyukta – those characters stand before me! Sita! The love that people talk about, do you find it only in stories? Is it to be found in real life as well? It seems Edward the eighth, the king who ruled

India all this while, has given up his kingdom for the love of a woman! Is this true? Sounds incredible!

Yesterday I thought of you when Amma, Sundu and I took the cart and went to bathe in the Kaveri. Surya's fight with postman Balakrishnan near the sluice gate seemed to be happening before my eyes.

Sita! I was very happy to learn from your letter that Surya was of help to you on your journey to Delhi. You say that Surya may settle in Delhi. I will be happy if he does. Because I know that you will take care of him.

You had asked why Surya gave up his studies and talks as if he hates the world. I didn't know the reason then. But now, after coming to Rajampettai, I do.

You don't know my eldest brother, Gangadharan. You must have seen him just once during our wedding. I never liked him. He is a ruffian. It seems Gangadharan thrashed a field worker because he did not obey him at once. The workers were about to launch a protest. Surya went to the field workers' street and apologized on behalf of his brother. The workers were satisfied with this.

The next summer when they were both in Rajampettai during the holidays, Gangadharan quarrelled with Surya. 'Who asked you to apologize on my behalf?' he asked and thrashed him. Surya bore it patiently.

Their misunderstandings increased. Last year when both brothers were here, Surya spoke up for the field workers over some land issue. Gangadharan thrashed Surya again. Everyone in the agraharam was on Gangadharan's side. Embittered, Surya declared, 'I don't want any part of my inheritance. Keep it all!' and left home. He gave up his studies because he didn't want to take money from the family. Appa and Amma are constantly talking about it and feeling miserable. Sometimes they accuse each other of being the cause of this unfortunate turn of events.

Sita! I feel more and more miserable when I think of Surya. He is a very good boy. Do you know how fond he is of me? He has great affection for you too! Please take care of him as long as he is in Delhi.

This letter has become far too long. I have been writing it for three days, pouring out things that I had kept hidden for a long time. Where will I have the time in my husband's house to write such a long letter? Moreover, I would be afraid that someone might see it. Forgive me if I have written anything foolish. You are my dear and only friend. To whom else can I unburden my heart? Please write soon and in detail.

From your dear friend who is always thinking of you,

Lalita

8

SITA'S REPLY

Lalita's letter generated diverse feelings in Sita's heart. She felt pity for Lalita's life in her husband's home. At the same time, when she compared Lalita's life with her own, she felt a certain kind of gladness deep within her heart. She mused, 'Whatever it may be, she should not lament so much!' Then she thought, 'Poor thing! To whom can she talk? Her mother is wholly mad! Ammammaa! What a long letter! Nine words to say what can be said in one!'

When she finished reading the letter Sita wrote this reply:

My dear friend Lalita,

I received your letter. I felt somewhat unhappy when I read it. I also felt angry with you. You had kept so many things from me for so long. Is this true friendship? Never mind. From now on, whether sorrow or joy, good or bad, you must write at once and in detail. If not, what is the use of being friends? Isn't friendship all about sharing joys and sorrows?

Love is not just confined to fiction. My life proves that it exists in this world. Lalita, I must admit that I am truly fortunate. But never will I forget that in a way, this good fortune came to me because of you. I am overcome by an inexplicable feeling when I think that you may have been here in this lovely bungalow in New Delhi instead of me. How can I express my gratitude to you?

I was sad to hear about your life with your in-laws. It amazes me that when the world has made so much progress and modern ways have come to stay, there are still people like your in-laws! This makes me furious.

But don't think that your husband doesn't love you because he does not take you to the movies! This is the way the rustics talk. Menfolk have many concerns. It is we who must understand. We must not think that the world has come to an end because one's husband has talked to another woman! Only uncivilized and illiterate women entertain such suspicions.

Nor can I fully accept what you have said about your mother-in-law. Everything depends on how we conduct ourselves. Once we leave home and go to our husband's home, we must accept the mother-in-law and father-in-law as our parents and treat them as such. My sister-in-law went back to her parents, taking her husband with her. But look at the way I have conducted myself! My mother-in-law has endless regard for me. She often says, 'Even a daughter cannot be so affectionate to me as you are.' You too must forget your father and mother and treat your in-laws as your parents! And when you do, see how they change!

Surya has returned from the Congress. Lalita, happy news! My husband has come to like Surya a lot. They have become close friends. They talk tirelessly about the Congress and the British government.

Last Sunday we went to see the the Red Fort, Jantar Mantar and other sights in Delhi. Surya's joining us made it so pleasant!

Tomorrow, we go to Agra. Surya is coming with us. But not my mother-in-law. She says she will stay at home minding the child.

The Taj Mahal, one of the wonders of the world, is in Agra. You have read about it in history, haven't you? The Taj Mahal is the magnificent monument that emperor Shah Jahan built to memorialize his queen consort Mumtaz Mahal. We are making this trip to see it.

It is an overnight train journey from Agra to the princely state of Rajnipur. It has a vast lake with a mansion on it. My husband says that from Agra, we should go there as well. Yesterday he was fighting with Surya because Surya said that he would skip Rajnipur as he had to attend a meeting in Delhi.

I will take good care of Surya. Lalita, you need not worry about him at all. I am thinking of telling my husband to secure a job for Surya at the right time. My mother-in-law wants her sister's daughter to marry Surya. How wonderful would it be if Surya settles here with his family! Then you too will come to visit Delhi now and then.

I remember taking you to see the sights of Bombay. Do you know how happy I would be to take you around Delhi?

There! My husband is asking me to join him for a walk. I will write again after returning from Agra.

Your dear friend,

Sita

NOTE: A small incident took place at the railway station the day I reached Delhi. I got hugely perturbed about that. But now it is clear that there is no reason for any anxiety. I will tell you about my stupid suspicion when I see you next in person. You will split your sides laughing!

9

THE JASMINE TOWER

As the train approached Agra, the argument between Raghavan and Surya had become so heated that their voices could be heard above the clangour of the rolling wheels.

'More and more, moderation is afflicting the Congress. What changes did we see after the Congress ministries were established in the states? None! From governor to village munsif, everyone is as autocratic as ever. Police control remains just the same as before,' Surya complained.

'Is that all? Why, it looks as if you will complain about trains running as before, posts delivered as before, magistrates punishing burglars as before! What kind of a socialist are you? Are you demanding that all rules and regulations, and all those who exercise authority – from the governor to the village munsif – must be struck down? How will the government function without them? Are you saying that there is no need for any kind of governance?' Raghavan asked.

'Your idea of governance is the Indian Civil Service (ICS) government established by the British. Was there no government before the arrival of the Englishman?'

'Why, of course there was! Before the British, India had fifty-six kingdoms – Anga, Vanga, Kalinga, Kukkuta, Karnataka, Maratha and so on. There were kings, badshahs and sultans too. They ruled according to their personal whims. Do you want to go back to that kind of royal governance? But then, you also want to abolish the princely states!'

'Yes. We must abolish the royal principalities altogether. I am not saying that we must return to some ancient set up or to the Peshwa rule. Does the rejection of the old forms of governance in favour of the new mean only the ICS government of the British Raj? Are there no other nations in the world? And don't they have their own forms of government?'

'Yes, my friend, yes. There is Hitler's rule in Germany. Mussolini's in Italy. On the way back from England, I went to Germany and Italy. If you see the kinds of governments operating in Europe, famous as it is for its education and civilization, you will acknowledge the superiority of the British Raj.'

'However diabolical they may be, Hitler and Mussolini operate within their own countries! They don't want to conquer the whole world like the Englishmen! They have not brought other countries under their lethal sovereignty!'

'How would you know? They will surely reveal their true selves when the opportunity presents itself. They will be many times worse than the Englishmen. Look at the atrocities being committed by Japan in China.'

'Japan is the only Asian country that can bring the English to heel. Anyway, all that is touted about the atrocities perpetrated by Japan in China is nothing but British propaganda! How do we know what is true? If you ask me, I will say that any other regime will be better than the British regime which destroys the soul of the nation. It creates division and bad blood between the people of that nation.'

'Has British rule created more division and discord than what our nation has already experienced?'

'If the Englishman had not interfered, all our divisions and discord would have ended by now.'

Sita intervened now to say, 'Enough, stop fighting! We have reached Agra station.'

The Mughal emperor Akbar elevated the status of Agra by shifting his capital from Delhi to that city. Akbar's grandson, the emperor Shah Jahan, made the city renowned in world history by building the dreamlike Taj Mahal there, and other palatial mansions of marble as well.

Visitors to Agra usually go to see the old fort, which has palaces within the complex. Next, they make their way to the Taj Mahal in a dazed state of mind, wondering if there could be anything more marvellous than what they had already seen. Then when they see the Taj Mahal, they become too dumbstruck even to feel astonishment.

Sita, Raghavan and Surya too went to see the old fort first. They were amazed by the high walls of the fort and the palaces within, which appeared to have been built but yesterday. They were astounded by the majesty of the fort's doorways. Pulling themselves together, they made their way to the general audience hall called the Diwan-i-Aam. On the way, Sita saw the rose garden and ran in to take a closer look. She exclaimed, 'What, Sir! Anarkali must have sold flowers here. Salim must have met her right here. Wonder which secret passage led them to the banks of the river Yamuna!'

'You have still not forgotten Anarkali!' Raghavan laughed.

'How can I forget Anarkali! I came here principally to see the spot where she sold flowers!'

'Who is Anarkali?' asked Surya.

'Don't you know? You mean you've never heard of Anarkali?' asked Sita.

'No, athanga! I don't care much for stories and novels.'

'Where does our Surya have the time to read stories and novels? When he does not even have the time to struggle with Karl Marx!' Raghavan scoffed.

'Cousin! I will tell you. Anarkali means pomegranate bud. It was the name Prince Salim gave her.'

'Who is Salim?' asked Surya.

'You don't know even this much? It was the name of emperor Jahangir before he ascended the throne.'

'Surya! Don't you underestimate your athanga. She is an expert in Mughal history. When in doubt, Jadunath Sarkar and Vincent Smith usually come to consult Sita.'

'He always makes fun of me! Cousin, you listen to me. When he was young, Jahangir had a nurse. The nurse had a daughter. Seeing her beauty, he named her after the pomegranate bud and called her Anarkali. He swore to marry her...'

The storytelling went on as they reached the marble hall called the Diwan-i-Khas where their astonished gaze took in the beautiful pillars and ceiling covered with a host of designs inlaid and painted with floral designs.

Then they went to the women's quarters in the palace. They saw the apartments of Shah Jahan's daughters, Jahanara and Roshanara. They saw the hall of mirrors and marble pools where the queens and their maids-in-waiting played games in the waters. They saw the marble brooks where the water flowed crystal clear, with tinkling sounds reminiscent of the anklets of the queens of yore.

'Adadaa! How this palace must have looked when those queens and princesses lived here!' Sita sighed.

'Why, it must have been sheer hell for those who lived here. A prison house! What does a parrot think when it looks at the cage where it is confined? Even if it were made of gold and studded with rubies, to the parrot the cage is nothing but a prison,' Surya replied.

'Bale! Surya! You and Sita are perfectly matched.' Raghavan said.

'You are both trying to make me out to be an idiot! Will describing this marble palace as a prison make it so? And who will refuse to live in a prison like this? I for one will be happy to stay here!'

'Sita! Don't be so entranced! No woman in this country was safe when the rajas and badshahs who built these palaces were alive. If the ruler's eye fell upon any girl, she had to lose her life, or her honour! Somehow, by the grace of God, the British Raj was established in India!' Raghavan remarked.

'I will never accept this. What has changed because of the British Raj? Even today, in the royal principalities under British sovereignty, the maharajas perpetrate horrendous atrocities!'

'Please do not start your fight all over again! You are wrong. I too have read a bit of history. When they brought a jagirdar's daughter before him, didn't Maharaj Shivaji say, "If I'd had a mother as beautiful as you are, I too would have been handsome!" Didn't he return her to her father with every courtesy observed? Look at Shah Jahan who built this palace. Did he so much as glance at any other woman after marrying Mumtaz Begum? Why, he did not forget her even after she died! How many crores of rupees he lavished to build the Taj Mahal for her! Look!' Sita pointed ahead.

By then they were walking on the upper balcony through the famous part of the palace called the Jasmine Tower. From there, on the other side of the Yamuna, the Taj Mahal could be seen in all its splendour.

For some time, all three stood still, lost in the beauty of the scene.

Sita said, 'You are both trying to drive me insane! Can't we know the kind of person Emperor Shah Jahan was by simply looking at the Taj Mahal? What travails, efforts and expenses must have gone into the creation of the Taj Mahal! How much love and adoration he must have felt for Mumtaz Mahal! Did it all end with the building of the Taj Mahal? Once it was built, he went on gazing at the Taj from this Jasmine Tower, until he died at last!'

'Yes, Sita! You have guessed right. It was from here that Shah Jahan kept looking at the Taj Mahal until he died,' said Raghavan.

'Do you know why? Athanga! I will tell you the history I know. His son Aurangzeb did not approve of the royal coffers being emptied in this manner. He imprisoned his father in this fortress, saying, "You may go on gazing at the monument you have built in the memory of your precious wife!" Shah Jahan stayed here and kept gaping at the Taj Mahal, and died with a sigh.' 'It is exactly what I would have done had I been Aurangzeb,' Raghavan remarked.

'Please don't say such things! How can you talk like this after seeing these wondrous sights!

'Where have your eyes gone?' Sita exclaimed.

At that moment, both Raghavan's and Surya's eyes were focused on the three persons who were approaching from the opposite side. Two women and a man. The same girls Raghavan had met at the Karachi aerodrome. One was Dharini. The other was her friend. Raghavan stood stock still. His eyes refused to move away from Dharini's face. He was unable to take in anything or anyone else. He forgot where he was and with whom. A single thought had taken root in his mind. Dharini was coming.

10

DAYDREAM

For a whole moment, not only the earth, but all the fourteen mythical worlds were rendered motionless. In the cosmos filled with multitudinal reverberations, not even the rustle of a tiny leaf was audible. It was as though the god of the winds had lost the power of movement.

Raghavan's voice rose from the nadir of the underworld. 'Am I seeing something real? Or am I dreaming?'

'Yes! The poets have described the Taj Mahal as the "dream of love" and the "marbled illusion". However, from here it appears to be a solid building, not an insubstantial dream,' Dharini replied.

Dharini's friend, Nirupama broke in to say, 'Mr Raghavan...? What a serendipitous meeting!'

'Yes, I am that unfortunate being,' Raghavan said to Nirupama.

'Since when did you develop such humility? Who is the woman standing behind you?'

Nirupama's question made Raghavan recoil.

'Why should you ask him? Can't you guess? It must be his wife,' Dharini said.

'Is this true?' Nirupama asked insistently.

'Yes,' said Raghavan, swallowing hard.

'Ha! What a beautiful girl! Call yourself unfortunate after marrying a girl like this? That's funny!' said Nirupama and continued, 'Who is the young man coming up behind you?'

'My wife's relative,' Raghavan muttered.

'His face seems familiar, I have seen him somewhere recently,' Dharini said.

'How could you have seen this boy? You are mistaking him for someone else,' Raghavan said dismissively.

Surya came forward to say, 'She is not wrong. I saw her at the Haripura Congress.' Then, looking at Dharini, he added, 'Weren't you at the Praja Socialist Party's meeting?'

The reference to the Haripura Congress made Raghavan think about the Karachi Congress which had taken place eight years ago. As he recalled his meeting Dharini at the Karachi aerodrome for the very first time, Dharini was saying in her pleasant voice, 'Yes. I had come to the socialists' gathering. You gave a marvellous speech. How can I forget it?' These words fell on Raghavan's ears as if in a dream.

Steadying himself, Raghavan realized that she was talking about Surya. He remembered how Dharini had once praised his writing skills.

'I see! I didn't know that Surya was such a loudmouth!'

'There was nothing loudmouthed about his speech. It was brief but wonderful,' said Dharini.

'He must have thundered about leveling the differences between the rich and the poor, cutting bureaucrats' salaries, getting rid of the princely states. No big deal. Anyone can do it spectacularly!' Raghavan said.

Nirupama intervened again. 'Please stop your argument for a moment. I will introduce my husband to you, Mr Veni Prasad BA LLB. The famous advocate in the city. Only, as he has no practice, his main job at the moment is to welcome his wife's friends and host them. Dharini is staying with us. He will be very happy if you will all join us. We will provide all the facilities we can. How long are you planning to stay in Agra?' Nirupama asked Saundara Raghavan.

'Only until tomorrow. Thank you for your kind invitation. We will avail of it at some other time. I don't want to stay in the same house with those who lie.'

'What's that? Who lied?' Nirupama asked.

'Your friend. Ask her if she did not send me a letter saying that she was dead.'

Dharini smiled and asked, 'How could I have written a letter saying I was dead?'

'If you didn't write it, you got someone else to do it!'

'But my death was a fact.'

'In that case, how can you be here right now?'

'I was resurrected.'

'What for?' Raghavan asked harshly.

'After dying I remembered the two thousand rupees I owed you. I came back to life because I knew that you would be spending sleepless nights over it.'

'Even lies must have some credibility. But your lies are beyond belief. When I saw you at the Delhi railway station, did you not say, "I am not Dharini"? Why did you lie then?'

"That's not what I said. All I said was, "I am not the old Dharini". The train moved on before I could say anything more.'

'Ah! As before, you manage to cop out with some explanation or the other!'

'In every way I am what I was before. There would be no need for such talk if others too remain unchanged. Never mind! Where can we meet you again? Shouldn't the money be returned?'

'No hurry! I can take it at any time. But I must see you again. Have you seen the Taj Mahal?'

'The idea is to see it in the yellow light of the evening and under the full moon at night.'

'We are also planning to be there at that time. We can finish our talk then.'

They had by then reached the spot where they had to go in different directions. The two groups took leave of each other and parted ways.

When Dharini and the others left, Sita, who had not spoken until then broke her silence. 'Who is that woman?' she asked Raghavan.

'Ask your cousin!' Raghavan said.

'Why should I ask my cousin? Why don't you tell me? Don't you know her?'

'Certainly, I do. She is a woman, just like you!'

'That much I can see for myself. Feminine in form but masculine in behaviour. Looks like she was born a woman by mistake.'

'What you say is absolutely right. Therefore, you will not be bothered if I talk to a woman who should have been a man, will you?'

'How does it matter even if you were to talk to an honest-to-goodness woman? Do you think I am a country bumpkin? I was born and raised in Bombay!'

'I forgot that monumental fact. Please forgive me!'

'But I don't like it when things are hidden from me. Isn't she the girl you ran to meet at the Delhi railway station? Why would you hide that?'

'Surya! Did you see how clever your athanga is? She thinks I hid something from her out of fear! This is the problem with our women. They have jaundiced eyes!'

'I don't have jaundiced eyes. Why did you become cagey when I asked you about the woman you met at the railway station?'

'Cagey? Certainly not. I went to talk to her thinking that she was someone I knew. She denied it. You went on pestering me about her. What could I say? Didn't you realize how it was when you heard us talking just now?'

'You were talking in English. How can I know what you were saying? I don't know that much English.'

'If you don't, keep your mouth shut.'

'All you know is to fly at me... you never say anything amiable.'

Surya heard these exchanges as he walked behind them. He remembered the lines of the poet Bharati saying, 'Once a drop of poison is added, will the honey remain what it had been before?' Ruefully he wondered if a drop of poison had entered the couple's happy life.

He gave a little lecture. 'Athanga! What you said about that girl is totally wrong. She is a dedicated patriot. You would have known the nobility of her character if you had seen the way she hastened to serve the people at the Haripura Congress. The sweetness in her voice as she enquired *pani chahiye*, do you want water, was enough to assuage thirst. Don't have wrong thoughts about her!'

'Dharini was right! You *are* a windbag! How you do run on!' Raghavan said.

They continued with their sightseeing in the Agra Fort. But their earlier enthusiasm was gone.

'I'm tired of plodding on. Shall we go back to the hotel?' Sita asked.

'Yes. Since all the edifices are built of marble, they look the same. We must go back. Moreover, we must see the Taj Mahal in the evening.' Raghavan said.

'You may say the same thing about the Taj Mahal. After all, it is also made of marble,' Surya said.

Raghavan released a flood of words. 'Ah! That's a different story altogether! The Taj Mahal is not a building. It is a divine form of sculpture imbued with life. The living symbol of the renaissance of the Mughal era. A flying craft of white flowers bearing the god and goddess of love. A live visual painted with moonbeams, the gentle zephyrs, the colours of the rainbow and the pleasures of love. A beautiful enchantress haunting the hearts of those who have glimpsed her but once. A life spent without seeing the Taj Mahal is no life at all!'

All three returned to their hotel for lunch followed by a siesta.

Sita was dressed in the iridescent colours of butterflies' wings. Her head was partially covered by a veil as light and transparent as a web. She was adorned with invaluable pearls and rubies. Her feet and fingernails were dyed crimson.

She was strolling through the halls and terraces of marble manors inlaid with designs of rainbow gems. She rejoiced as she saw the little rills here and there, babbling sweetly over the marble channels. Some of those streams made little pools where lilies and lotuses bloomed in a profusion of leaves and creepers. Some pools were covered with roses that had bloomed on that very day. Mingling with the fragrance of flowers were scents of incense, and the attar of roses that queen Nurjahan had discovered and gifted to the world.

Sita stood at the edge of the pools gazing at the floating flowers. Her whole body quivered in delight on seeing the beauty of her luminous form reflected on the crystal-clear waters.

Suddenly she was surrounded by several serving maids. Who knows where they came from? All had the eerie beauty of a cobra raising its hood and hissing at will. Like a snake showing its tongue, each pointed her forefinger at Sita. Their eyes sparkled like flames. 'It is she!' 'It is she!' they hissed in unison.

'Come! Come with us!' they called out to Sita. Unable to refuse, Sita followed them.

In a vast marbled hall, the Mughal empress sat on a throne with a backrest shaped like a peacock. Such arrogance in her posture! She did not greet Sita. She did not ask her to take a seat.

'Who is this demented halfwit? Why have you brought her here?' the empress asked the maids.

One of the girls answered, 'Your majesty! This is the evil creature who has stolen the heart of our prince. Sita, the Rajput maiden.'

'Is that so? Let her remain alive until midnight!' was the royal command.

At twilight, Sita wandered everywhere in the palace garden. She plucked roses and jasmines and inhaled their scent. Though her heart was filled with anxiety, she also believed that the prince would come and save her. When she thought of the prince, Sita saw in her mind's eye Saundara Raghavan in Mughal attire.

Fear broke in as light faded into darkness. Midnight came all too soon. The lights that had made the palace glitter were now being put out – one by one. Sita was left with nothing but herself, solitude and darkness. Through the lattice window carved on the marble wall, a single moon beam entered to touch Sita's cheek with deep sympathy.

Suddenly voices were heard outside the room.

'Looks like she has fallen asleep.'

'Well, in a little while she is going to sleep forever.'

'I for one am not happy with killing her in one go. If she can be imprisoned like Anarkali, she will go mad with her own laments and die all alone.'

'Come! In any case, let us go and consult the empress.'

The voices yielded to silence. Trembling all over, Sita stood up. It would be dangerous to tarry there even for a moment more.

Somehow, she must escape from the harem prison. It would be lunacy to expect the prince to come and save her. How could he save her when he didn't even know she was here? Why did she come here against the prince's counsel to remain in Delhi?

Slipping and stumbling through the dark verandas of the palace, Sita walked on. She tried to find the door by sliding her hands against the wall. The gleams of light streaming in now and then through the latticed windows, showed the way. Many a times did she mistake walls for doors. And when she did find a door, it would not open. After wandering for what seemed like ages – though it was but an hour – a door opened at her touch. When she crossed the threshold with pounding heartbeats, she was transfixed by the huge demonic figure looming before her. She knew who it was. It was neither man nor woman. A eunuch who was deaf and dumb, but with a piercing eyesight. He knew his duty very well. His first duty was to stop anyone from getting out of the harem. He had a sword to cut anyone who tried to break free to pieces. He had a spear to throw at anyone who escaped the sword.

Sita was shaken by terror. The eunuch spoke no word but glared at her and rolled his eyes.

Sita forgot herself in her fear and shrieked, 'Surya! Surya!' She knew that her cousin, Surya, had hidden himself somewhere close by to save her.

Sita's shriek was answered. 'Surya is not here. But I am!' a voice announced. Even as Sita wondered whose voice it could be, beyond the courtyard where the moon shone bright, a form emerged from a chamber shrouded in darkness. As it advanced, Sita knew who it was. It was the same woman who had come to see her sick mother and had given her money and jewelry. The same woman who had been standing on a street in New Delhi, knife in hand. The woman held a knife even now. In the moonlight the rim of that knife shone like a streak of fire.

Who was this woman? Why was she appearing now? Was she coming to kill the eunuch and save her? Or was she going to kill her for the crime of having tried to escape from the harem?

'Athanga! Athanga! What's this? Why are you talking in your sleep? Get up!' Surya said.

Sita opened her eyes. She was embarrassed to realize that not only had she fallen asleep at midday but also babbled through her dream. To cover up she said, 'I was not talking, Surya! Where has he gone?'

'He went to get a tonga. Get up! Quick! Shouldn't we be leaving for the Taj Mahal? It is four o'clock already!'

11

TAJ MAHAL

Under the golden moon, the Taj Mahal looked like a newly-wed maiden whose desire mingles with bashfulness as her lover approaches. The mesmerising enchantress seemed to be lost in thought, her form partly hidden by a Dhaka muslin veil as soft and white as a tumbai flower. Four tall minarets stood at the four corners, like maids guarding her on all four sides.

The moon tried to embrace her with his countless arms of gold. But they fell away, unable to touch her chaste form. Wondering if she evaded him from bashfulness, he called upon the dark shadows to assist him. But the shadows turned into an armour to protect her from his lecherous advances.

Unable to bear the angst of love, the despairing moon decided to end his life and fell headlong into the stream before her. Filled with pity, the white lady too leapt into the waters! Until, at last, in the crystalline waters of that marble-floored stream, the golden moon and the Taj Mahal embraced each other.

Sita forgot herself as she wandered into the world of the lovers. Ah! How long had she nurtured the desire to see the Taj Mahal! How many times had she travelled to this spot in her imagination! Today, all those dreams had come true. It was beyond doubt a most significant and wonderful day in Sita's life.

Sita, Raghavan, Surya, Dharini, Nirupama and her husband Veni Prasad were seated under the light of the golden moon, on the white marble floor, beside the blue stream.

They had spent the whole evening roaming around the Taj Mahal. They went in to see the tombs of Shah Jahan and Mumtaz Mahal. Around the tombs, they marveled at the intricate designs inlaid on marble. They saw the gems and floral patterns from many faraway lands. They competed with one another to climb the four tall minarets surrounding the Taj Mahal to enjoy the view on all sides. They plunged into the Yamuna to splash and play in the waters. They laughed merrily as they skipped and ran and tried to catch one another. They even exchanged playful slaps.

Tired after frolicking through the whole evening, they sank down beside the stream. It was around 9 in the night. Silence reigned. But peace did not rein in every heart. Sita, Raghavan, Dharini and Surya found their hearts in a state of turbulence.

Sita began by saying, 'What is the use of living without seeing the Taj Mahal at least once? Can such a life be called a life at all?'

'To see it during the day is one thing, but viewing it at night, under the full moon, like this, is quite another!' Raghavan said.

'You must see the Taj Mahal and die. Why should you hang on to life after that?' said Surya.

Sensing his derision, Sita responded, 'You are right, cousin! No need to live on after seeing the Taj Mahal.'

'That's what the moth believes when it sees the flame!' Surya said.

'If an edifice like this is to be constructed over my grave, I am ready to die right now, this very minute,' Nirupama said.

'Don't say such things! Nowadays it is hard enough to construct buildings for people to live in. How can we put up buildings for the dead?' Veni Prasad remonstrated.

'Mr Veni Prasad! It is not just your wife, but any number of women have said the same thing, including white memsahebs. Brainless! Once dead, how does it matter whether the corpse is burnt in a yard or buried under a Taj Mahal? It makes no difference!'

'Absolutely right! This mausoleum is of no use at all to the dead Shah Jahan and Mumtaz Mahal. But so many people like us who are still alive, get to enjoy this wonder of the world. Omar Khayyam's verse is a perfect fit for a place like this. "Taj Mahal to dwell in; a jug

of wine; a book of verse; you beside me; is there a greater paradise?"'
Raghavan said, his gaze fixed on Dharini.

'This kind of fantasy may come true for you and Mr Veni Prasad. But what can people like Dharini and Surya do?' Nirupama asked.

'They too will marry one day. In Surya's case, there is nothing to worry about. The bride is ready and waiting.' Sita said.

'Athanga! You think of love and marriage all the time. Is there nothing else in the world?' Surya scoffed.

'In this world, there is nothing greater than love. Poems and epics are inspired by love. Without love can there be a Ramayana by Valmiki? Or Kalidasa's *Sakuntalam*? Or the plays of Shakespeare? Can the writers of today create their modern works of fiction without love?'

'Ah! Throw your novels into the dustbin! Those who have nothing to say write love stories! Wastrels with nothing to do write love poems!' Surya said. His frenzy and fury were mounting with every passing minute.

'Do you want everyone to write like Karl Marx?' Raghavan mocked him.

'Everyone need not write like Karl Marx. They can write like Tolstoy! Like Mahatma Gandhi! Jawaharlal Nehru! Bernard Shaw!'

'Cousin! Can one write like Subramania Bharati? Remember what Bharati said about love?' Sita asked him.

'When Bharati was in his right mind, he wrote about freedom. When he was besotted, he sang of love!' Surya said.

'Surya seems to have been disappointed in love,' Dharini said and smiled, her teeth sparkling like pearls in the moonlight. Her face reflected her sympathy.

'Not at all!' said Surya, somewhat bashfully.

'Surya is an oddball. Always contradicts himself. Sita! What has Bharati said about love?' Raghavan asked.

Softly, Sita crooned a verse which said, 'We will dance of love in peace, we will applaud love with both hands.'

'Please sing the whole song. All of us want to hear it,' said Dharini.

Nirupama agreed. 'This is the right place for music. We have wasted all this time in useless chatter. Don't be shy, give us a full-throated song!'

Sita looked at Raghavan. 'If you can sing without going offkey, go ahead!' Raghavan said to her.

Sita was angered by Raghavan's remark. But she pulled herself together to say, 'Offkey or in tune, I can only sing what I know!'

'We know nothing about "on key" and "off key". All the notes are the same to us. Please sing!' Nirupama said and added to Raghavan, 'Plug your ears if you don't like it!'

Sita sang verses ending with 'Let us dance celebrating womanhood, let us hail the victory of womanhood.'

Penmai vaazhgenru kootiduvomadaa
Penmai velgendru kootiduvomadaa

Everyone looked at Sita as she sang. Raghavan looked at Dharini.

When the song ended, Nirupama and Dharini expressed their delight. Dharini explained the meaning of the song to Nirupama and her husband.

Raghavan said, 'What kind of a song is this with all these harsh *daa-doo* sounds! I don't like it.'

Surya cut in, 'The song has many sound ideas. But why panegyrize love to such an extent? "Soar with the winds and fight with the skies at a sidelong glance from the lover!" Rubbish! India has become enslaved and emasculated by people who behave like this! Like Prithviraj Chauhan! Athanga! Sing a national song by Bharati!'

'I don't know any national song. If I do sing one, it will be nothing but cacophony and discordance!' Sita said.

'Dharini! You know a national song in Hindustani! Please sing it.' said Raghavan.

'Yes, Dharini! How about "Sare jahan se accha"? Haven't heard it since our trip from Karachi to Bombay,' Nirupama urged.

Dharini sang. The birds fell silent. The nocturnal insects ceased their humming. The breezes were stilled. The full moon was overwhelmed by Dharini's song. The stars stopped twinkling in their eagerness to listen. An Englishman who was trying to take photographs in the moonlight shut his camera to listen to the song with his memsaheb.

When the singing was over Nirupama and her husband exclaimed, *'Accha! Bahut accha!'*

'Bale! Bhesh!' said Surya.

'If you can't sing like this, you are better off keeping your mouth shut,' said Raghavan.

Surya noticed that Sita was hurt. He said to her, 'Athanga! You too can learn this song. Do you know what it means? The first line says, "India is the best among all the nations in the world."'

'Undoubtedly! The Taj Mahal is proof enough!'

'You are wrong. India's glory does not stem from the Taj Mahal. India attained its glory from the Himalayan mountains, the river Ganga, from Buddha, Asoka, Shivaji, Jhansi Rani!' said Surya.

Raghavan said, 'There are mountains like the Himalayas and rivers like the Ganga in other countries. But nothing like the Taj Mahal. Therefore, India acquires its glory from the Taj Mahal.'

'I think India doesn't need this glory,' Surya said.

'The seventh wonder of the world is no wonder to you?' Raghavan asked.

'Well, the world will not come to an end if Mr Surya doesn't find it wonderful. India's glory shines because of this edifice. It also testifies to unchanging love,' said Veni Prasad.

'Ah! You too have started eulogizing love!' exclaimed Surya in a voice full of disgust.

'Why do you give love such a drubbing? Wasn't the divinely beautiful Taj Mahal born out of love?' Nirupama asked.

'Madam, please listen to me. This building was not born out of Shah Jahan's love! It was born out of his despotism. His despotism was such that his own son Aurangzeb had to imprison him.'

'History has established that Aurangzeb was a tyrant and entirely devoid of aesthetic sensibility. How did Shah Jahan become a tyrant? History declares that he was a very good man!'

'Yes. He was a very good man. But do you know how many people had to suffer because of that good man's hubris? Do you know that it took twenty years to finish constructing the Taj Mahal? Do you know that twenty thousand workers had to shed their sweat and blood, day in and day out? Do you know that crores of rupees squeezed and extracted from the people as taxes were lavished on this building? Should twenty thousand people have killed themselves labouring for twenty years for the sake of a single individual's conceit, or his extraordinary love, for that matter? No way can I accept it as being justified. You know what I would do if I had the authority?' Surya ranted and paused for breath.

'What will you do if you have the authority?' Dharini asked with a smile.

At a toy shop near the entrance of the Taj Mahal, Sita had bought a small marble model of the monument as a souvenir. It happened to be lying beside Surya. Now he picked it up. 'If I had the authority, at this very moment I would smash down and shatter to shards this monument built by an imbecile king to display his personal vanity!' he shrieked as he threw the model away. The miniature model went straight to Dharini. Everyone shouted in apprehension, fearing that it may hit her head or face. Fortunately, it landed near Dharini, not on her. The speed of its fall shattered it to bits. One of the shards popped up to hit Dharini on the forehead. It pierced her just below the hairline. Touched by a moonbeam the drop of blood oozing from Dharini's ivory-hued face shone like the mythical ruby on the serpent's hood.

Those who had been relieved to see the souvenir falling on the ground were now startled by this unexpected turn. Everyone except Surya cried out and surrounded her. It was Raghavan who reached her first and tried to stanch the blood by pressing the wound with his hand. Nirupama forcibly pushed him aside and bound up the scratch with her handkerchief.

Raghavan's action made Sita, who had gone up close to Dharini like the others, feel the stab of a searing pain.

For some time, commotion reigned around Dharini. But calm was soon restored. Everyone went back to sit down in their places once again.

Veni Prasad looked at Raghavan and remarked, 'Your friend seems to be a hooligan!'

'Dumbo! See how he is sitting mumchance without bothering to apologize!' Raghavan said.

'Why are you making such a huge fuss over a trifle?' Dharini asked.

'Thank God it hit the forehead. What would have happened if it had hit the eye?' Raghavan said.

'Well, it didn't! So why talk about it? It will be of great help to me if all of you stop making a fuss,' Dharini said.

Sita remained silent. Her heart was filled with turmoil. She wondered why such a fuss was being made over a trifle. Then she thought, 'Good that she got hurt. Why didn't she get a bigger wound?' She also wished she had been hurt instead. Then everyone would have surrounded her and made a fuss over her. She sympathized with Surya. 'Poor boy! What can he do? Why are they berating him for a shard hitting her by mistake?' She felt remorseful as she remembered, 'The only person who has true affection for me in this world is Surya and I humiliated him!' She went on glancing at Surya, hoping to convey her empathy.

But he was looking at the sky, lost in thought.

All conversation petered out.

'We have seen enough. Let's return to the hotel,' Sita said.

Everyone got up to go.

As soon as they reached the hotel, Surya picked up his things and left for the railway station saying that he needed to be in Delhi urgently.

12

THE HISTORIAN

To Dharini Devi,

I regret causing the mishap you suffered this evening at the Taj Mahal. I had absolutely no intention of hurting you or making you bleed. You too will not entertain such a doubt. I threw the toy because I became emotional. I was not sorry about its shattering to pieces. Nor would I be in the least sorry if the real Taj Mahal were to be reduced to rubble. This vast nation was trapped in the hands of an old moron. In his old age, in the grip of a stupid hallucination called love, the king made a big toy. Believing that it would bring satisfaction to his beloved's soul, he spent crores and crores of rupees on that toy. This is what mindless herds gape at as one of the wonders of the world! They chatter about it in astonishment! Such is my firm opinion.

But what have you to do with a long dead old man's Taj Mahal? I have no anger towards you. I did not aim that toy at you in deliberate anger. Not in the least did I expect that its shard would hurt your forehead and draw blood. Once again, I ask your forgiveness for this unexpected mishap.

But before ending this letter there is something that I must say. Did I not say that I did not want to hurt you? But I did want to slap all those who surrounded you, making a mountain out of a molehill. If I had had a cane, I would have whipped them and dragged them away.

Brainless imbeciles! What shrieks and commotion and panic over a trifling scratch!

The people of this land will have to bear innumerable sufferings before Mother India can become free. Lakhs of people must sacrifice their lives, jump into the fire with their eyes open. Look at other nations in the world that have attained their independence! How many people have lost their arms and legs and eyes and are crippled for life in fighting to save their nation! How many live on with scars all over their faces! In our country, we make such a hullabaloo over a drop of blood from a small scratch on the forehead! God knows how our nation is going to achieve independence when so many poltroons and hysteria patients abound!

Our ancestors had certainly been different! Tomorrow, you are going to the land of the brave Rajputs. What such valiant men and women dwelt there once! Is it not the realm where thousands of women jumped into the blazing fire as soon as they got the news that their fort had been breached, their enemies had entered! It seems Rana Sangram Singh bore the scars of ninety-six battle wounds! The great warrior considered those scars to be more precious than golden ornaments studded with pearls and gems. Today, in our land of valour, a small abrasion makes us lose our wits! Not in women alone, it induces hysteria in the menfolk as well.

I will stop here. Our poet Bharati has written a song about what the heart cannot endure. Sita knows it. Ask her to sing it for you.

Yours,
Surya

Dharini was reading this letter on the train from Agra to Rajnipur. She read it once, then reread it, before locking it in her briefcase.

Raghavan asked, 'Why! You are locking it up with such care! Is it a love letter?'

'Gibberish!' said Dharini, in response to Raghavan's remark. But Raghavan pretended not to have understood and asked, 'Why safeguard "gibberish" in a suitcase?'

That morning, when Dharini and her friend got into the train, they saw that Sita and Raghavan had already boarded it. With misgivings Dharini asked. 'Where is Surya?'

'He did not join us. He has gone off to Delhi,' Raghavan replied.

'Did you fight with him about last night's incident and drive him away?' Dharini asked.

'No. He must have felt embarrassed. He insisted on leaving,' Raghavan explained.

To save her cousin's face, Sita said, 'He had some urgent work. Even earlier, he had said that he would come only to Agra. He has left a letter of apology for you.' Turning to her husband she added, 'Why don't you give it to her?'

'Let the train start. What is the hurry?' Raghavan said.

Dharini said, 'Apology? Letter! You have fought with him and driven him away over a trifling matter. I am very unhappy about it.'

Sita felt good about this remark. But Raghavan retorted angrily, 'Trifling? What would have happened if the eye had been injured instead? Under no circumstance should human beings behave like beasts!'

'Yes, that boy behaved like an uncivilized yokel,' Nirupama said in Raghavan's support.

'So, you think that people who live in the cities are highly civilized! You don't know how they can turn into lions and tigers, ghosts and ghouls!' Dharini said.

After a pause, she asked, 'Where is that letter?'

'Why! Looks like you will not be satisfied unless you see it!' Raghavan said and handed the letter to her.

When Raghavan sneered about its being a love letter, Dharini thought she should read it aloud to everyone. But she changed her mind at once. These people would never understand what the letter meant, she thought. They would simply ridicule it all the more. So, she turned to Sita and said, 'When you see your cousin next, please tell him that there was no need at all for such a long letter of apology.'

Their train entered the land of the Rajputs, sanctified for over a thousand years by the blood shed by its valiant heroes and the tears of noble women. As far as the eye could see the land appeared to be dry and parched, scattered with bare rocks, ruined forts, broken towers, dilapidated mosques. No greenery. No dense forests. No paddy fields stretching like green carpets. Not even golden crops of wheat. Only thorny bushes growing here and there at will.

'Is the entire landscape like this?' Sita asked.

'No. It will be different when we reach Rajnipur. But until then this is it!' Raghavan answered. 'Everywhere people are shouting slogans of "Independence!" "Independence!" Well, this is the result of the Rajput warriors fighting for their independence. Most of Rajasthan has turned into a desert.'

'Rajasthan did not become a desert because the Rajputs fought for freedom. This is the result of their fraternal fights. If the elder brother fought for freedom, the younger joined his enemy. How many Rajputs turned into slaves and spent their lives in serving the Mughals! As a country, India too has fallen only because of these fraternal brangles. The funny thing is, though we have studied all this in history, we have still not learnt our lesson. We continue to fight with our brothers.'

'Madam! You talk like a great historian!' Raghavan scoffed.

'What did you say?' asked Nirupama and burst into loud laughter.

Raghavan blinked, not knowing the cause of her mirth. 'Why are you laughing?' he asked.

'I laughed because you said "like" a great historian,' Nirupama clarified.

'I don't understand! What is there to laugh about in that statement?'

'You are thinking of the old Dharini engaged in the nation's service. After the Bihar earthquake she joined college, got her bachelor's degree and is now engaged in historical research with a university fellowship. I thought you knew this. Why else do you think she is roaming from place to place, dragging me along? Right now, the research is focused on Rajasthan.'

Nirupama's explanation triggered all kinds of speculations in Raghavan's mind. He was astonished. Ah! It was her passion for learning that made Dharini reject marriage. Could she not have disclosed this truth? If she had, would he have hindered her in her educational pursuits?

After this, Nirupama went to sleep. Raghavan questioned Dharini about her college life. She answered desultorily. In a while Raghavan fell asleep as well.

Then Dharini moved close to Sita and asked, 'Please tell me about your cousin Surya. Is he always so excitable?'

Sita's anger had been mounting step by step. She had learnt several things from the time she met Dharini the day before, from what Nirupama and Dharini had let fall, and from her own guesswork. It was obvious that Dharini and Raghavan were old friends. There must be some truth in what the neighbours in Padmapuram had gossiped about. It was crystal clear that even now, Raghavan felt attachment for Dharini. Her heart boiled at the thought of their having hidden these things from her. Chee! Chee! What a shameless creature she is! Why is she following us? Why can't she get lost somewhere else? Without Surya and Nirupama's husband, all bonhomie was lost. If only she had known that things were going to take this turn, she could have refused to accompany them. Even now... why couldn't she just say, 'I will not come if she does. Take her with you. I will go back to Delhi.' Again and again, Sita's lips trembled in the effort to spill her thoughts. But the words would not come. Partly because she was afraid of the consequences of speaking out.

Sita was in this state of mind when Dharini moved close to her and asked her to tell her about Surya. Sita was infuriated. She snapped, 'Why this interrogation about Surya now? Like me, he is an idiot. Like me, he has no one.'

'Why do you speak with such bitterness? Surya has expressed heartfelt sorrow for having hurt my head. A man with upstanding traits but seems to be somewhat excitable in nature. All I wanted to do was to send word to him that my bruise has healed and that he should not worry about me. But it's all right if you don't want to talk about him.'

Sita changed her mind. 'No, no! I am not at all bitter. Surya is a very good boy. Nor does he get excited easily. In my uncle's family, it is Surya who is known for his steadiness and forbearance. I was really surprised when he spoke so passionately and threw that toy. Poor thing! Who knows how stressed he has been! On the whole, he is unlucky! Why else would he have to come here and endure sufferings? He could have finished his studies and found a good job.'

Upon Dharini's enquiring, 'Why do you call him unlucky?' Sita told her all about Surya. Little by little, she told her about his parents and siblings, his quarrels with his brother and the people of the village. But she said nothing about her own family or marriage.

13

RAJNIPUR

Sir Adivarahachari, Divan of Rajnipur, had a fondness for intelligent young men. Raghavan had met him on board as a fellow passenger and made friends with him on his voyage to England. Adivarahachari had been greatly impressed by Raghavan's sharp brain and savvy conversation. He also believed that the more acquaintances he had among those employed in New Delhi's secretariat, the greater the advantages he could count on.

Adivarahachari had invited Raghavan to visit Rajnipur with his wife after his return from England. It was in response to that invitation that Raghavan had now gone to the divan's mansion. Dharini and her friend went to seek other quarters.

Unfortunately, Adivarahachari was out of town on official work. However, seeing Raghavan's telegram, he bid his wife and daughters to take care of him and his wife. They welcomed the couple.

Adivarahachari's daughters, Bhama and Dhama had visited England. They were steeped in 'English' etiquette. One was thin and tall, the other short and plump. Both had bobbed hair. They never stepped out without lipstick. They spoke only in English. And that too, in the lingo of the characters of the English writer, Wodehouse. They had trained themselves to become adept at playing the piano and in ball room dancing.

With them, Sita was completely at a loss. At first, they spoke to her in English. Seeing her bewilderment, they tried to repeat what they had said in their faltering Tamil. The little English Sita knew proved useless now because the girls pronounced the words as Englishwomen did. Sita struggled like a fish out of water.

They were far more at ease with Raghavan who chatted enthusiastically with them. They guffawed loudly at his puns and sallies. Though Sita found this somewhat repugnant, she was neither irked nor angered by it. We don't know whether it was because the girls were not particularly good looking, or because she knew in her heart of hearts that Raghavan did not have any respect for them.

Raghavan had remarked about the girls' lack of good looks and odd ways. 'And yet there is a great deal you can learn from them,' he told Sita. 'Certain kinds of appearance and behaviour are essential for moving in New Delhi's social circles.'

'What should I learn from them? To wear lipstick?' Sita laughed.

'Yes. What is wrong with lipstick? Don't they chew betel leaves in our country? Why, don't we make a great fuss about poets' comparing the heroine's lips to corals and pomegranate buds!' Raghavan said.

'Such things must be natural,' Sita said.

'Natural? Nonsense! To be natural you must be like the savages in Africa. Combing your hair with a parting, putting a dot on your forehead, applying kohl to the eyes, colouring hands with henna: are they "natural" processes? Is it natural to pierce holes in your ear and nose and hang ornaments on them? Every kind of beautification and ornamentation is an artifice,' Raghavan said forcefully. Sita could not answer him. But for the sake of saying something, she said, 'There must be some limit even to ornamentations. Look at Dharini! She has a college education and a degree. Does she use lipstick?'

'Some people are born beautiful. They will look good even if they do nothing to enhance their appearance. But can everyone be like that? That would be like a cat trying to burn stripes on its skin like a tiger!'

Sita wished she had not mentioned Dharini.

Among the capitals of the royal states of India, Rajnipur stood out for its beauty. Raghavan and Sita spent the following day exploring it. They enjoyed seeing the old and new palaces of the Maharaja of Rajnipur, the marble mansion where the spring festival was celebrated, the gardens, the zoo, an old fort and other ruins at some distance from town.

Wherever they went, Raghavan seemed to be in a tearing hurry to get it over and done with. Sita, who was keen to see all the sights as well as she could, tried to take in everything quickly enough to accommodate Raghavan's restlessness.

As they were returning to the divan's mansion, Sita remarked, 'We haven't seen those two all day!' At once she bit her lips wishing she could unsay it.

'I've also been wondering about that. They said they would call, but they haven't,' said Raghavan and broke off to scream at the divan's driver, '*Thehro!* Stop!' Sita was discommoded by the sudden bump when the driver – who had never in his life been commanded so peremptorily – stopped the car by applying the brakes with a jerk. Looking up, she saw that Dharini and Nirupama were getting down from a tonga before a house on the street.

Raghavan asked Dharini grimly, 'Why did you disappoint us today?'

'Disappoint you? We can see nothing if we go sightseeing with you. There will be time only for debates. That is why we went by ourselves,' Dharini replied.

'Is this the plan for tomorrow as well?'

'If you are going to the lake tomorrow, we will come with you. Can you come here and pick us up?' Dharini asked.

'I can, certainly. But don't take me in again. I will be very angry if you do,' Raghavan said.

Now Sita knew why Raghavan had been so restive all day. She had but a half hour's sleep that night. When she got up in the morning her head felt very heavy, as if it was being pounded on both sides. 'I am not coming to the lake today. It will be better if we can return to Delhi,' she said to Raghavan.

14

RAJNIPUR LAKE

That afternoon, Raghavan looked at Sita and asked, 'Do you really have a headache?'

'Can there be a false headache? What kind of a question is this?' Sita replied.

'All right. Then, I'll go,' said Raghavan and began to leave.

'Where are you going?' Sita asked.

'Don't you know that you must never ask that question when someone is about to go out? Where else will I go but to the lake?'

'Are you going to leave me and go by yourself?'

'Why? Dharini and her friend have said they would come.'

'You will leave me here all by myself and take them with you?'

'What do you mean "all by myself"? This is a house, not a wilderness! Bhama and Dhama will take care of you.'

'I cannot talk to them.'

'Then just stay quietly in bed.'

'Do you have to go?'

'Yes. I must. I cannot change my plan for the sake of your headache.'

'Will you change your plan if I die?'

'Die, and then you will know!'

Sita was so riled that she wanted to cry. But she realized that there was no use arguing with Raghavan.

'If you are a woman, what's the use of complaining about a

headache? Instead of lying alone and dying here, I will come with you and take my last breath there.'

'The last breath can be taken sooner rather than later. Come on, be quick!' Raghavan said.

They did not exchange a single word in the car. Sita wiped her eyes frequently.

The car stopped before the house where Dharini and Nirupama were staying. From the balcony upstairs Nirupama clapped her hands to draw their attention and said, 'Please come in. It will take another ten minutes for Dharini to get ready.'

'I'm not coming. I'll stay in the car. You get terribly annoyed if I am late by a single minute. Now...?' she said.

'Don't talk nonsense! Understand?' Raghavan growled as he got down from the car and went into the house.

Every minute seemed an age to Sita as she waited in the car. After many such minutes, loud laughter was heard from upstairs. The sounds kindled fire in Sita's heart. She looked up. For a while there was nothing but the sounds of talking and laughter. Then, suddenly, the window framed a scene. Raghavan was trying to give an envelope to Dharini. She was refusing to take it. Raghavan grabbed her hands and forcibly tried to thrust the envelope into them. Dharini freed herself and ran away, still refusing to take it. Raghavan ran after her.

The scene which lasted for barely thirty seconds etched itself on Sita's mind like a camera shot. She lost all her powers of thinking. Then, doubts crowded into her mind and began to prey upon it. Surging fury made her body tremble.

Soon, Dharini and Raghavan came down. Making Dharini sit beside Sita at the back, Raghavan took the front seat. Sita expected Nirupama to join them and became alarmed when the car began to move without her. She wanted to enquire about it, but her tongue would not move.

Looking at the expression on her face Dharini asked, 'Sita! Are you not well?'

'I've had a headache since morning.'

'Looks as if you are in great pain. Even your voice sounds different. Should we continue with this outing? We could have gone tomorrow!

Is the lake going to run away?' Dharini's words added fuel to the fire raging in Sita's heart.

'Who listens if I say I will not come!'

After a pause Dharini resumed, 'Nirupama has stayed back because she too is not feeling well. It's not too late. Let's turn back. What do you say, Mr Raghavan?'

Raghavan answered her, 'Her headache is not all that bad. It will go away when we take a boat and go sailing on the lake.'

The Rajnipur lake looked as if a vast portion of the sky had been carved out and placed on the earth.

Two mountain ranges stood on either side of the lake like the guardian walls of paradise.

On the other two sides, trees rose thick and high framing the azure expanse in green.

It was a place where the silence of midnight reigned, the tranquil stillness of dawn prevailed and twilight's enchantment abounded.

Looking at the vast blue waters, a layperson could experience the bliss that mystics achieved when they saw the ultimate reality within themselves. Those who saw their forms reflected on the lake's surface could feel the thrill of the lover seeing himself reflected in the eyes of the beloved. Anyone who saw the waters of the lake knew a mother's joy when she saw her newborn infant smiling for the first time.

Flocks of thousands of birds, each white as a tumbai flower, made an unforgettable sight.

It was beside this lake that Raghavan, Dharini and Sita got down from the car.

Dharini exclaimed, 'I have seen many scenic landscapes. Nothing like this!'

'That is why I insisted on bringing you both here. Even the famous lakes of Switzerland are nothing compared to this! But my efforts have left me half dead!' Raghavan said.

Sita gazed at the lake in silence. Seeing the severe scowl on her face Dharini said, 'The lake is certainly beautiful. But it would have offered a better experience for a twosome, or perhaps four people.' When she said this, Dharini had Raghavan and Sita in mind.

But Sita misinterpreted her and muttered, 'I did say I won't come.

Who listened to me?' Then she made rapid strides towards the lake, sat down under a tree by the shore and continued to stare at the waters. Though her eyes were fixed on the lake, her mind wandered elsewhere. Chilled though they were by wafting over the waters, the breezes inflamed her whole body.

Watching her striding away Dharini told Raghavan, 'Why is your wife behaving like this today? This is no mere headache. She seems to be suffering from some mental trauma as well.'

'Had I known she would behave like this, I would have never brought her here.'

'I can see that you do not have the ability to understand a woman's mind. Your wife wants to have the pleasure of enjoying this scene with you, alone.'

'What can I do if I bring her alone? What can we talk about? We have nothing in common. What she says doesn't interest me. She never understands what I say.'

'And whose fault is that? You should have educated her to your level of thinking. Or, you should not have married someone who was not your equal in understanding. What is the use of complaining after having made that mistake?'

'The fault is not mine, Dharini! It is yours. The result of what you did.'

'Stop it! Let us go to your wife. Come! Otherwise, her problem will get worse.'

'Let it get worse. I don't care!' Raghavan said. And yet, he followed Dharini as she walked towards Sita. Both sat down beside her.

There was no boat on the lake's shore. But some boats were on the lake, sailing to a little island surrounded by thick groves. A big mansion could be seen through the tall trees.

'Who owns that mansion?' Dharini asked.

'Such an expert on history as you are, don't you know this? It looks as if you explore only ancient history. The palace belongs to the ruler of this principality. The late king used to often stay in this mansion. All his fun and frolic took place there! Did you know that some five-six years ago there had been an attempt in Bombay to kill the king of this state? The person who tried to kill him was a woman. The newspapers gave it a great deal of publicity. But the attempt did not succeed. The only result was that the woman was sentenced to two years of hard labour in prison. The king escaped without a scratch. Two years ago, he died from excessive drinking.'

'Who is the present king? What is he like?' Dharini asked.

'He is a young boy, studying in Dehradun. Divan Adivarahachari, our host, is taking care of the kingdom.'

'So, things are going well for the kingdom.'

'Up to a point. But Vinayakrao Madhonkar, the evil minister of the old king, is still alive. In the palace and in the state, his atrocities are legion. The divan too is rather careful where he is concerned. If not, he will start some rumour and make the divan lose his post.'

Sita, who had been distracted in the beginning, began to pay attention when she heard about the attempt to murder the king. When Raghavan finished talking about Madhonkar she asked, 'Who was the woman who tried to kill the king of this state?'

'I see! You have been paying attention! No one knows who she is. Some say she is a Muslim, others say she is a Hindu. A few declare that she belongs to the south. What does it matter? Whoever she may be, she must be a demoness. What guts she must have had to try to commit murder in broad day light?' Raghavan said.

'Men can commit any atrocity. It is wrong only for the women to take revenge,' Sita said.

'What! What! So much sympathy for a murderess! Where did you learn to talk like this?' Raghavan asked.

Dharini interrupted to say, 'Do you know what happened to that woman afterwards?' She had remained silent until then, but now her voice betrayed a curious change in tone. Dharini's voice shook as Sita's had done earlier.

But Raghavan did not notice it. He said, 'Who knows? Who knows where she is wandering about after two years in prison? What do we care?'

Sita remembered the incident where a woman with a knife had come to her flat in Bombay a few days before she had left for

Rajampettai with her mother; the suspicions that rose in her mind when she read the news in the papers as she boarded the train; the woman she saw at the street corner the other day in Delhi. But she kept her mouth shut. Her mind kept going back to the knife that the woman held in her hand. There must have been a sound reason for her attempting to kill the king of this state. Who knows what atrocities he had committed? But do men alone perform atrocious deeds? Women do too. For example, what can one say about a shameless woman like Dharini? There is nothing wrong in killing such women. If only I had a knife with me now!

Becoming suddenly conscious of the monstrous thoughts her mind was harbouring, Sita became startled as she glanced at Dharini's face. She caught sight of the bruise on her forehead. Ah! Surya had done a good thing. 'How wonderful it would be to have him here now!' she thought. 'He would talk to me with zest, and not leave my side even for a moment! If he were here, I wouldn't have to care about these two!'

At this moment, one of boats reached the shore. The passengers got off the boat.

'Shall I engage a boat?' Raghavan asked.

'I am ready. But what does your wife say?' Dharini responded.

'She will join us. If she doesn't want to do that, let her stay on the shore. We can both go,' Raghavan said and went to hire the boat.

When Raghavan went away, Dharini asked Sita, 'Sita! Are you perhaps angry with me? You are not yourself.'

'Not myself? Not *myself*? This is me, "myself", always,' Sita muttered.

'Again, you sound angry! Sita, I want to be your friend.'

'Why? We hardly know each other!' Sita replied.

Dharini was too taken aback to reply.

A little later Dharini asked, 'Sita! You are wearing a ruby necklace. Where did you get it?'

Sita was perturbed. All kinds of vague suspicions rose in her heart. 'This hellcat wants to ruin me, somehow,' she thought. 'Perhaps she may accuse me of theft! Who knows? Ayo! Why is Surya not here, now?'

Dharini asked again. 'Sita! Didn't you hear me? I asked you about the necklace of rubies you are wearing.'

'My mother gave it to me. Why do you ask? Do you think that I have stolen it?'

'Ayo! Why do you speak so harshly? I asked because I wanted to know where you got such a beautiful and intricately designed piece of jewellery. Why does it make you so angry?'

'I am not angry.'

'All right. What is your mother's name, Sita? Where were you born?'

'I'm not in the right state of mind to answer you.'

'That is obvious,' Dharini said.

Raghavan had hired a boat. 'Get in quickly. It is already quite late,' he said.

'Do we have to? Why not just go back?' Dharini asked.

'Don't be silly. I had a tough time convincing this boatman to take us. Don't create more trouble now. Sita! Get up! Get into the boat quickly!'

Sita got up and came to the boat. Raghavan held her hand and guided her into the boat. Dharini tried to get into the boat by herself. It was not possible. The boat kept moving.

'Here, give me your hand,' said Raghavan and helped her in.

Dharini sat next to Sita. Raghavan sat facing them. The boat began to move. No one noticed that by then the sky had darkened, the clouds had gathered and the winds had begun to blow hard.

When they reached the lake, little waves had been gently lapping the shore and merging silently into the waters. But when they got into the boat and started sailing, the waves had begun to resound as they rose one foot high and foamed at the edges.

The boat made its way to the island of groves in the middle of the lake, which was about two furlongs away. But by the time they had covered half a furlong, the winds became powerful. The waves were rising higher and crashing in a swell of foam. Their sound had now become loud and reverberant. The boat rocked in every direction as it went up and down.

The boatman said something in his own language.

Dharini said, 'What's this! The wind has become very strong. Shall we go back?'

'We cannot give up what we planned to do. Should we fear so much for life?' Raghavan asked.

Sita looked around and rolled her eyes. Then she began to shriek and wail, 'Ayo! Amma! I am frightened!'

Raghavan said curtly, 'Sita, what's this! Are you, or are you not, going to stop this boohooing at once!'

Sita's frenzy increased. 'Ayo! Amma! You were right! I am going to fall into the waves and die!'

This unexpected development baffled Raghavan. He looked at Dharini in great perplexity.

'This is the reason why these accursed persons should not be brought along on outings. Please try to calm her down,' he said.

'Mr Raghavan! No point in trying to calm her down. Your wife has become hysterical. Ask the boatman to turn back,' she said.

Raghavan shouted loudly and ordered the boatman to return to the shore.

The boatman replied, '*Kuch dar nahi saheb!* Nothing to worry about.'

'Whatever it may be, turn back at once!' Raghavan bellowed.

'The boatman won't turn back. Someone has coached him,' Sita sobbed even more.

'Don't talk nonsense, Sita! Shut up!' Raghavan berated her and turned to the boatman again. 'Turn back! Turn back at once! Otherwise…'

'*Theek, saheb, theek*!' said the boatman.

The truth was that the boatman *was* trying to turn back. But with the wind and the waves it was no easy task. He rowed with all his might but the boat kept swiveling round and round.

Sita's wails increased in volume. She went on crying out at intervals, 'Amma! You were right!' Her hands were shaking badly.

Seeing this Dharini said, 'Mr Raghavan! Her hysteria is getting worse. Come here, sit beside her and hold her hands.' She took one of Sita's hands in a firm grip.

Sita shook her hand free from Dharini's grip and sprang up to stand on the boat. The boat see-sawed madly.

Sita screeched, 'Oh! So, you want to brand me as hysterical and push me into the waters? I am not hysterical. I will not fall into the lake!'

'Come quick! Hold her!' Dharini screamed.

Raghavan got up and took a step towards Sita. At that very moment a big wave rose and spilled across the boat. The boat rocked as if it would capsize. Raghavan slipped and fell within the boat. Sita emitted a shrill scream as she fell into the waters.

Dharini hollered, 'Ayo! Oh my God!'

The boatman was spouting indistinguishable drivel.

The boat which seemed about to sink, somehow rose and straightened itself.

Sita who had plunged into the waters was now coming up.

The boat was moving away from her.

Sita's head rose above the waters once with the cry, 'Amma!' The scream was heard above the roaring winds and booming waves. The cry for help pierced Dharini's and Raghavan's hearts like a spear thrust.

Dharini squealed, 'Why are you standing and doing nothing! Jump in! Save her!'

Raghavan had just got up after his fall.

'Ayo! I don't know how to swim.' he cried and stood looking at Sita's bobbing head.

A horrific thought arose in the deep recesses of Raghavan's heart. 'May be this is what they call destiny! If Sita were to die...?' But without allowing that thought to proceed Raghavan shouted, 'Boatman! O boatman!'

He wanted to tell the boatman to row up close to where Sita was drowning. But before that Dharini had leapt from the boat into the waters and was swimming masterfully towards Sita.

Varuna, the god of the waters, and Vayu the god of the winds, stood still to watch this miracle.

15

REBIRTH

A stupendously loud reverberation prevailed all around. No other sound could be heard. No other thought could penetrate through that booming noise. Sita wondered what that resonance could be.

After a long spell, memory returned in a flash. It must be the sound of the waves that her mother had so frequently warned her about. A deafening sound. It began when she was asphyxiated under the water… Sita remembered wondering how the sound had been so much louder under the water, how she had thought she would not survive. If only she had listened to her mother!

At that moment of calamity, her hand had felt a touch. A single hand. It had a bangle. It had to be a woman's hand! Who is that woman? Must be her mother who had promised to save her in the time of danger. All these thoughts returned to her. But she could not open her eyes. It was light everywhere and dark everywhere. She could not open her eyes. Despite all her efforts, the lids refused to open.

What is this? A voice… Whose voice? If only this dreadful din of the waves could be quelled! But surely, the sound has decreased in volume. Two persons are talking. What are they saying? Thank God! Though the eye cannot see, the ear can hear.

'Your wife is regaining consciousness… Soon, she will open her eyes.'

'Sita has been reborn today. She has survived because of you. You are her second mother.'

'I heard that Sita is a motherless girl. Is that right?'

'She did not appear from the earth as the legendary Sita did. She was born from her mother's womb. But her mother is not alive. You are her mother now.'

'Let it be as you say. If I am Sita's mother, you will have to be my son-in-law. Mind-boggling! A son-in-law who did not get off the boat when his wife was drowning!'

'It is you who are responsible for that! You forced me to take two thousand rupees from you. How could I suddenly jump into the water with those notes in my pocket? I think you didn't understand what that fool of a boatman said. Nowhere in the entire lake are the waters more than neck deep. Sita couldn't have committed suicide here even had she wanted to.'

'Enough! Stop it! Sita is regaining consciousness. Quick, put her on your lap. When she comes to herself, she will never forgive you if she sees herself lying on my lap and your clothes dry.'

'You don't know, Dharini, you don't know! You don't know the extent to which our women possess the power of forgiveness.'

Sita's mind did not grasp all the details of this conversation. Only a few words made sense to her. But she could piece out what had happened before she began to drown. She realized that it was Dharini who had saved her as she was struggling in the waters of the lake. She sensed that she was lying on Dharini's lap. When her husband was talking about the power to forgive, she felt herself being gently lifted by Dharini and placed on Raghavan's lap.

'Sita! Sita!' Raghavan called out as he touched her eyelids gently. The eyes opened at once. They looked intently at Raghavan's face. We don't know what Sita conveyed through her eyes. Did she say, 'However great a scoundrel you may be, I have the power to forgive you.' Or did she warn him, 'There is a limit even to my powers of forgiveness.'

'Sita, look! Do you know who I am?' Raghavan asked.

Sita responded feebly, 'How can I not know you… Mr Saundara Raghavan, MA.'

'Bale! Bale! Well said! Now let me see if you know the person in front of you?'

'How can I not know my own mother?'

Raghavan was taken aback. Did she hear his conversation with Dharini? Or had she lost her wits?

With a sudden movement, Sita got up from Raghavan's lap. Before the two of them could guess what she was going to do, Sita prostrated before Dharini and then held her hands. 'You saved my life. I have been reborn. You are my mother in this new life.'

Dharini tried to remonstrate, 'Sita! You are wrong. It was not I who saved you. Your husband...' But Sita cut in. 'I know. How can I not know when I see your drenched saree and his dry clothes?'

Raghavan intervened to say, 'Sita, Dharini is lying. You guessed right. It was Dharini who saved you. You know that I cannot swim. If I had brought you alone our fate would have been terrible indeed. I will learn to swim before the next time I take you on a boat.'

'No need to learn swimming for my sake. I am never going anywhere near the waters again,' Sita said.

Sita's heart was bubbling with a joy she had never felt before. That joy suffused every atom in her body. She had returned from death's door. An instant's delay and her life would have been over. This was her second life, a rebirth. She was still alive. The blue lake before her, the lush green trees, the white birds... they were all real. In the distance, the darkening sky was bending to embrace the earth. She was lying on Raghavan's lap. Dharini was sitting in front of her in a drenched saree and a face brimming with compassion. The boat was real. The motor car was real. The darling child she had left in her mother-in-law's care in New Delhi was real. Ah! How full of happiness is the world! How joyful to be alive! Is there anything more idiotic than to make such a life miserable?

When the three of them returned, the divan too had returned from his trip. Hearing about the incident on the lake, he and his daughters became extremely anxious and perturbed. They heartily applauded Dharini's courage. The divan came to like Dharini a great deal. He insisted that she should bring her friend to his house and that everyone should stay for another two days with him. His daughters agreed with him. Sita was emphatic.

Dharini and Nirupama arrived at the divan's house. For the next two days, his house was filled with laughter and joy. In those two days, Sita and Dharini became inseparable friends.

Raghavan was extremely happy to see this. It appeared as if the qualms in Sita's heart had been completely erased.

Before leaving for Delhi, when Sita and Dharini found themselves alone, Dharini asked her, 'Sita, on that day I asked you about your ruby necklace. You did not give me a satisfactory answer. Can you tell me now?'

'Akka! On that day I must have been afflicted with some kind of madness. Everyone I saw aroused my fury. On the boat you too said that I had hysteria. I feel embarrassed to think about it,' Sita said.

'Don't think about it. Sita! Whatever it was, you have dropped it into the lake now. You must forget that old story completely,' Dharini told her.

'All right. I will try. I had wanted to tell you about the ruby necklace. It has been in my thoughts from the time I came to this town.'

'Why? What is the connection between this town and your necklace?'

'No direct connection. But I recall a series of incidents. Listen, I will tell you.'

With this preamble Sita began to narrate the story of how she got the necklace. She told her how, when her mother was sick and bedridden, a veiled woman came stomping up the stairs to give her mother the ruby necklace and two thousand rupees for Sita's marriage. The woman had rushed out leaving her knife behind, but returned to hug and kiss Sita before taking her knife back. Sita also told Dharini about how, when she left for Rajampettai with her mother and uncle Kitta Iyer, she had heard the shouts of the newsboys on the railway station.

'Even back then I had the suspicion that perhaps the woman who gave me the jewel was the same person who tried to kill the Maharaja of Rajnipur. Since I came here, I have been thinking about her. And by chance he too initiated the subject on the lakeshore. Akka, what do you think about all this?'

'There may be some truth in your suspicions. But it is best for you not to mention this to anyone. Have you ever told your husband about it?'

'No. If I do, he will not pay attention.'

'It is best not to mention it. Men have strange ways of thinking. He might simply ignore it. Or he may pick up the necklace and fling it into the lake saying, "Why do we need it?"'

'It was this fear that stopped me from telling him.'

'You must keep your mother's wedding gift carefully. What is your mother's name, Sita?'

Dharini learnt some details about Sita's father and mother. 'Where is your father now? Does he ever come to see you?' she asked.

'It has been a while since he came to see me. Amma is dead. I don't know if my father is alive. No letter from him has come in a long time. Akka, I am an orphan. My uncle's daughter Lalita in Devapattinam is my only friend. Now I have found you.'

After a pause, Dharini asked, 'Did your mother say anything about the woman who brought the ruby necklace?'

'No. Perhaps Amma didn't know her. If she did, she did not tell me.'

'Sita! You did not see that woman again, did you?'

'I did… once.'

'Where? When?'

Sita told her about seeing the woman with the knife at the street corner near her house in New Delhi.

'I have been wanting to see her and have been searching for her for ever so long. But I am unable to catch sight of her.'

'Akka! Is that so? Why should you search for her? Do you know her?'

'I do.'

'How?'

'She is my mother.'

Sita was plunged into astonishment. She stared and stared at Dharini. 'Now I see it! Now I know why I felt so strongly that I had seen you before.'

'Sita, you are wrong. She is not my birth mother; she is the mother who raised me. Till today I don't know my real parents. I am searching for Raziya Begum to find out who they are.'

'Raziya Begum? So, is she a Muslim?'

'Yes. My foster mother is a Muslim. Four years ago, I had gone to Bihar to serve the victims of the earthquake. At that time Raziya Begum was sentenced to two-years' imprisonment for attempting to kill the Maharaja of Rajnipur. Though I've searched high and low I haven't been able to find her after her release. Sita, now you have come to know my misfortune.'

With tears in her eyes Sita said, 'Akka, if I see that woman again, I will definitely let you know.'

'Please tell her that I am desperate to see her. Tell her that I have decided to end my life if I can't meet her.'

'Akka, you cannot take such decisions. I have placed all my trust in you,' Sita said.

16

DEVAPATTINAM ELECTION

My best and dearest friend Sita,

I received your affectionate letter. I was extremely happy to read all about your visit to the Taj Mahal and the wonders you saw in the Agra Fort. When I read it, I felt as if I had accompanied you and was looking at all those scenes with all of you. I also felt sad that I did not have the good fortune to have gone with you to see them in person. I don't know when I may have such luck!

I told 'him' about all of you going to the Taj Mahal and asked if we too might make such a trip someday. He answered in his habitual dismissive style. 'There are so many sights to be seen in our Tamil country, the big temple in Thanjavur, the sculptures in Mahabalipuram. And you regret not being able to see the Taj Mahal!' I wished I had not opened my mouth. My mother-in-law, who had been eavesdropping, began her tirade lasting all day. 'People wish to make pilgrimages to Kasi and Rameswaram. Will anyone want to see tombs built by Muslim kings?'

My situation has become far worse after my return from the valaikappu ceremony. Sita, listen to this.

A gentleman called Damodaram Pillai lives in the house opposite to ours. He is also an advocate. He and my father-in-law are old friends. Damodaram Pillai has a son, Amarnath. Amarnath and my husband are very good friends. When Surya was here, the three of them used to study together.

Amarnath was married two years ago. The girl is from Tirunelveli, the daughter of the deputy collector there. She is more educated than both of us. But this has not made her even the least bit arrogant. We became acquainted at her wedding. And she became my friend since she moved to this town a year ago. Not my dearest friend like you, but a friend with whom I could have companionable chats. Confined as I am almost entirely to the house, Chitra's friendship offered solace. We met every day, at her house or in mine. Our friendship pleased our husbands.

Sita, now all that is gone with the wind! We don't visit each other. We don't talk to each other. We don't even glance at each other. Do you know why? Municipal elections were held here when I was in Rajampettai. Damodaram Pillai stood for elections. My father-in-law worked for another candidate, Rajam Iyer. In a public meeting, my father-in-law accused Damodaram Pillai of fawning over the white man. In retaliation, Damodaram Pillai chastised my father-in-law for displaying his 'brahmin nature'. The quarrel intensified. Now there is no exchange of words between the two families. They, who had been friends for over thirty years, are now ready to strike and stab each other!

Sita, do people lose their minds when they grow old? It seems the municipality is about engaging sweepers to clean the streets! No salary either! I am astounded. Why should they fight over a post for clearing garbage? And because of this I have lost the single friend I had. Even brief visits to the opposite house are forbidden. My house has become a real prison now.

Never mind my story. Sita, you had written briefly about going to Rajnipur. You said that you fell into the waters but got out without any danger. I thought that it was a bit of fun. But I came to know the truth from Surya's letter. It seems you escaped from a great disaster! How on earth could your husband have remained on the boat? It seems some woman called Dharini, who happened to be on the same boat, jumped into the lake and saved you! What would have happened to you if she had not been there! And what would have happened to me? I am still holding on to this dream that some day good times will come for me, I will get to stay with you for a few days, see Delhi and Agra… And you are subjecting yourself to such dangers.

Someday, if ever I see your husband, I have decided to scold him well.

Shouldn't a man know how to swim? Even if he couldn't swim, should he have stayed put on the boat and watched you?

When I told my husband about this, he too was very sorry, he even got angry with your husband. 'What kind of a man is he?' he asked. I have many complaints about 'him'. But it is certain that he would not have held back at a time of danger. Last year, a little girl was about to drown in the Kaveri floods. He jumped into the river, brought her to the shore and revived her. The entire town was talking about this with pride.

I have written to Surya and taken him to task. After coming to Agra with you, why did he have to return without accompanying you to Rajnipur? What did he have to do that was more important? I have told him that he must take excellent care of you.

Sita! Please, you must also take care of Surya, a little. I feel such pity when I think of Surya. He has left his birthplace, land, house, property and gone to Delhi where he is not able to get even proper food to eat. Listen to this. He has asked me to send him some money, that is, if I have any! If not, he says, at least ask your husband to lend me some. He will not write home for money. He will not accept the money that father sends him.

I trust that the child Vasanti is growing well day by day. Is she a good and happy child?

I often wish Vasanti had been a boy and my child had turned out to be a girl. Do I have to explain why? You may solve the riddle by yourself!

Your friend for life,
Lalita

Sita read the letter and looked at the clock. It was 8.30 p.m. Why hasn't he returned yet? Should he come later than usual on a day when she was alone in the house with the child?

17

LALITA! I AM AFRAID...!

In the beginning of June, New Delhi registered a temperature of 110 degrees Fahrenheit.

Those who went out during the day suffered as if they had been thrown into a lime pit. Those who were at home felt as if they were being steamed in a brick kiln. Day or night, the breezes blew fire. Water sprinkled on the cooling reed curtains sizzled as it dripped down.

Fearing that their brains would boil in the heat, the Lord Viceroy who ruled India from Delhi, and most of the governing bureaucrats, had fled to the top of the Shimla hills.

Sita and Raghavan too were scheduled to go to Shimla though Kamakshi Ammal kept on saying that the hills did not agree with her constitution. Receiving a letter about the wedding of her brother's daughter, she left, promising to return after a month.

Work prevented Raghavan from moving to Shimla. He told Sita, 'Will you go with the child? Nothing to be afraid of. Many women do go by themselves.' But Sita was firm. 'Never. I won't go. Why should I go when you cannot come with us?'

Though Raghavan and Sita were willing to give up the hill station, their Nepali servant was not. After continual complaints about not being able to bear the heat, one day he departed without informing them.

On the same day, the maid too went round the bend. She asked for three-days' leave. When Sita refused, she walked out announcing, 'I don't want this job!'

Sita was alone in the house with the child. Vasanti dropped off to sleep after repeatedly asking when her father would come home. Sita began to be preyed by her sense of solitude.

That morning Raghavan had left for work promising that he would somehow locate Surya and bring him home. Perhaps that was the reason for his delay. 'Let Surya come! I will show him,' Sita vowed to herself. 'The things he had written to Lalita! Why should he have written about the incident at the Rajnipur lake? And why should Lalita repeat it to her husband? What will they think about *her* husband?

'Let them think what they like! Who cares about what those country bumpkins think anyway?

And yet… a reply must be sent to Lalita. If I think about it, whom do I have besides Lalita? I was so over the moon about Dharini's friendship! After returning to Delhi, she has not even bothered to peep in! Will Lalita behave in this manner? Nothing like an old friendship. A new friendship is like bonding on a train.'

Coming to this conclusion Sita began to reply to Lalita.

My dearest Lalita,

I was extremely happy to receive a detailed letter from you. What you said about the Devapattinam garbage election was hilarious. I also noticed that you have lost your friend. You deserve it! Lalita, when you have your closest friend in me, how dare you strike up any other friendship? God has punished you for doing that!

However, I wish to let you know that I too have made some new friends here. Hadn't I mentioned the daughters of the Divan of Rajnipur? They returned to Delhi two weeks ago and visited us at home. We went to the viceroy's garden party together. Oh my god! What can I say! It was even more amazing than the marvels we have read about in Arabian Nights, or the wonderful scenes in films. How can I convey the beauty of the viceroy's garden? Do I describe the flowering shrubs and ornamental trees? The unobtrusive glow of lights hidden in shrubs and trees? The clothes and ornaments worn by the dignitaries who were present? Lalita! The white women wore shining black gowns. The women of our country wore traditional sarees in many colours. Each saree had a distinct style as did the jewels they wore. Dazzling! I was awestruck. But to the daughters of the Divan who had often attended such parties, it was all commonplace. They knew most of the attendees and introduced me to many of them. The 'How do you do?' with which the English women respond when we are introduced to them...! Lalita! What is the point of constantly criticizing the English people! There is so much for us to learn from them. For example, we can learn to be courteous in our interactions with each other.

You had written about the elections in Devapattinam. Elections are held in England too. There, it is the loser who first congratulates the winner! But in our country, members of the opposing party treat their rivals like enemies for life!

Earlier, I had written to you about modern make-up with disdain. I have changed my opinion. Only after the party at the viceroy's mansion did I realize that there is beauty in applying lipstick. My husband goes on repeating the English saying, 'When in Rome, do as the Romans do.' I too have decided that when I am in New Delhi, I must do what the people in New Delhi do. Who cares if we insist that our countrified ways are the best? Our grandmothers applied tonnes of turmeric paste on their faces. Tell me, do we follow them...?

It looks as if Surya has written all kinds of rubbish to you. Don't believe them. I am going to have a fight with Surya when he comes here. Why does he write about something that he did not see, but only heard about? I don't know who told him about this. Maybe it was the same Dharini whom he has mentioned. Thinking back, I feel suspicious of her. Everything about her is a mystery. She has not come to see me even once after returning to New Delhi. Instead, she has met Surya and stuffed him with all kinds of falsehood.

Will my husband simply sit and watch me drowning in the lake? That is an out and out lie. The boatman told him that the water was no more than neck deep. That is why he remained in the boat thinking that he could easily pull me into it. But that woman called Dharini jumped into the waters, bent on showing off her swimming skills. All said and done, women should not try to do what has to be done by the menfolk. What to do, such exhibitionists are also a part of the world!

It is true that I fainted and fell into the waters, but the rising waves were only partly responsible, my fears did the rest. When the waves rolled over my head, I concluded that I was dead. Lalita! Nowadays I often feel scared. I am suddenly overcome by fears. In Rajampettai, this would be ascribed to malevolent spirits. Grandmas will make up stories about evil spells. But I don't believe in such things. I wonder if it is some kind of illness.

Even now... see... suddenly my heart has begun to beat fast. My hands tremble. Why should I be afraid if the shrubs rustle beyond the window? What does it matter that there is no one else in the house? There are people in the neighbouring house. They will be here if I call out... No reason for my fears...

Sita stopped writing. Was it true that there was no reason to be afraid? There was absolutely no stirring in the air! How could shrubs rustle when there was no breeze?

Her eyes looked out of the window, breaking her determination to refrain from doing so. Only a brief glance. And yet, in that split second, she thought she had seen a figure in a burqa. Was it just an illusion?

Sita's tongue cleaved to the roof of her mouth in terror. She wanted to scream. But no sound came out. Her arms and legs were trembling. Her teeth were momentarily stuck together. Then they began to rattle.

It took all of five minutes to get out of her state of fear. Chee! What madness? Why this needless fear?

Sita tried to resume writing to Lalita. But she could think of nothing to write. Instead, she started thinking, 'Did I lock the doors in the front and at the back? The maid who left in a huff may not have locked the back door. Why am I scared as never before? In any case, it would be a good thing to lock the front and back doors.'

Sita got up bravely and went to the bungalow's threshold. She looked up and down the silent street. No car appeared. She locked the door and came in. She must check the back door. She took a step... What is that noise? Not the sound of a rifle. Not the crash of thunder.

Not the roar of a tiger. Or the hissing of a snake. It was the mundane sound of water running from a tap.

It was coming from the bathroom. Once again Sita's tongue cleaved to the roof of her mouth. Her feet became rooted to the spot... Someone must have entered the house surreptitiously and gone into the bathroom... opened the tap... Who could it be?

18

WHO'S THERE?

Sita got a grip on herself. Chee! Should she be afraid of an open tap? She herself might have left it running. She could hear it now because she had come out of the office room. Should she be afraid of something so trivial? Sita smiled at her own stupidity. She walked on thinking that she would close the tap and lock the back door.

Before she took four steps, the sound of running water ceased. The sudden and complete silence plunged Sita into a state of terror.

Someone must have closed the tap!

Sita remembered seeing a burqa-clad figure among the bushes through the window. Someone must have entered the house through the back door and gone into the bathroom. Who?

Sita tried to reassure herself. Maybe the maid had second thoughts and has returned. She might have been embarrassed to come through the front door and had taken this back route.

The tap began to flow again. No longer could Sita bear her suspicions and fears. She was determined to see who it was. Steadying herself with an effort, she reached the bathroom. The door was shut but left unlocked. With shaking hands, she knocked softly. The water stopped running. In the silence Sita asked, 'Who is there?' She could not recognize the voice as her own!

Footsteps could be heard within the bathroom. Every step made Sita's heart pound. One, two, three, four, five – the door was opened from the inside. A figure stood at the doorway, knife in hand.

A spectre? A spook? Human? Were those eyes on a face? Or

burning flames? Red coloured electric bulbs?

She had seen this form somewhere! Where? When? Sita began to wonder, 'Why is my head spinning? Can't hold on to anything! Was this what is known as the undoing of the brain? Why is this figure standing still? Why is it staring at me with its flaming eyes? Ayo! I feel faint! No. I am not. My mind is clearing. Eyes too can see. That figure is smiling! It opens its mouth and speaks!'

'Sita? Do you remember me?'

The moment she heard the voice Sita recollected everything. Chee! She is no phantom! This is the woman who had appeared mysteriously when her mother was on her sickbed! But didn't Sita see her somewhere else? Where was that? Two months ago, she had seen the woman, knife in hand, standing behind the tree at the street corner.

Hadn't Sita talked about her to someone? Yes. To Dharini! Dharini was her foster child. Her name was Raziya Begum.

'Sita, why are you staring at me? Don't you know me?'

Opening her mouth with great difficulty Sita whispered, 'I do.'

'Who am I?'

Sita thought for a minute, touched the necklace at her throat and said, 'The woman who gave me this.'

'Good girl! You remember. Are you alone at home? Nobody else?' the woman asked.

Sita did not hear the question. Because her eye and mind were now focused on something else. One half of the handkerchief hanging from the woman's waist was bright red in colour.

Sita rolled her eyes and squealed, 'Ayo! Blood! Blood!' All of a sudden, she was overcome by sobs and tears.

Raziya Begum took two steps and came close to Sita. She grabbed one of her shoulders and growled, 'Look, Sita! I thought you would be a good girl. But you are just as stupid as every other girl. Do you know what I will do if you howl and scream? I will kill you like I killed a mad dog on the street a little while ago!'

Sita's sobs ceased instantly. Still looking at the handkerchief, she asked, 'Is it the dog's blood?'

'Yes. Looks like it is frightening you! Wait. I will wash it,' said the woman as she went to open the tap and wash the handkerchief in water. But the stain could not be washed away. She threw it down saying, 'This has to be burnt.'

Sita's mind had begun to work again. She thought, 'Can what she said about the dog be true? If she had killed a dog, why should she come through the back door? Did she come knowing that I was here? Or by accident? What is to be done if he comes home now, suddenly? Somehow, she must be persuaded with pleasant words to leave before that. Oh God! Why did she land up in this house? Couldn't she have gone somewhere else?'

The woman asked again, 'Are you alone at home?'

'I am alone now. But my husband will be here soon. For some reason, he is late today.'

'Who knows which girl he is chasing in the city? Rascal!'

The words gave Sita a severe jolt. Terrible suspicions sprang up in her mind.

'What are you saying? Do you know something?'

'Silly girl! How can I know anything about your husband? I made that general statement because I think all men are rascals. What do you think? What's your husband like?'

'How can I answer that question? On the whole, he is a good man. But he is somewhat short-tempered. It could end in trouble if he sees you in this condition. Before he comes, you...' Sita hesitated.

'I understand. You are saying that I should go before your husband returns. What a kind soul! You don't have the heart to offer me a morsel of food!'

'Ayo! Don't say that! I have thought so much about how you helped me get married. I was only thinking about how to explain who you are should he come home now. Please do eat something before you go!'

'Sita! I don't want food. After many long years, it is only today that I feel satisfied in my belly and mind. But I cannot go anywhere tonight. I am exhausted. It has been many days since I slept well. I must sleep here tonight before I leave. No need to introduce me to your husband. Nor is there any need for him to know I am here. Does this house have a room upstairs?'

'No. All the houses allotted to government employees in New Delhi are single storeyed.'

The woman looked around. Pointing to the room opposite the bathroom she said, 'What's in there?'

'Firewood, miscellaneous stuff,' Sita replied.

The woman opened the door and checked the room. 'All right. I will sleep here. No one need know. Lock the door from outside.'

'How can you sleep here? It is windless and full of junk!'

'Never mind, Sita! I have slept in places far worse.'

Sita's heart melted when she heard this. She remembered the many things she had imagined about the woman's life. Doubtless she had endured great miseries. It was certain that those miseries had been caused by the king of Rajnipur. But what kind of miseries? Sita wanted to ask the woman about them. But now there was no time for that. At any moment her husband may return. If he did, he would certainly drive out the woman who looked like a mad creature.

'At least let me get you a rug and a pillow,' Sita said as she went in to fetch them quickly, with a niggling feeling of having forgotten something important. She must make herself remember it. Suddenly, she did. It concerned Dharini.

Giving the rug and the pillow to the woman Sita asked, 'Are you sure you don't want any food? I can bring puri and chapatti to you right here. You can eat whenever you feel hungry.'

'No! No! What's today? Tuesday?'

'Yes.'

'I fast on Tuesday nights. What time does your husband get up in the morning?'

'Usually at 7 a.m. I get up at 6 a.m.'

'In that case, please open this door as soon as you get up.'

'You don't have to wait for me. There is another door to this room. It opens into the backyard. In the morning, you can leave whenever you like.'

'Excellent! How many children do you have?'

'Only one. She is going to be three. Her name is Vasanti. She went to sleep just 15 minutes ago.'

'May Vasanti live and prosper! May she not be subjected to the brutality of men.'

'You must have undergone great trials.'

'No time to talk about them now. Get going.'

'I must ask you about something.'

'Be quick. I am exhausted.'

'What is your name?'

'How does it matter what it is!'

'Do you think I won't know it if you don't tell me?'

'Tell me.'

'Raziya Begum.'

The woman looked at Sita with surprise and anger, 'Who told you?' she asked.

'I will tell you later. Is your name Raziya Begum or not?'

'Yes and no. My name is Ramamani. I assumed the name Raziya Begum for a time and for a reason. Someone has told you about it. Who can it be? That silly brahmin?'

Sita did not know which silly brahmin she was referring to, but she said quickly, 'It was none other than your daughter, Dharini.'

As Sita had expected, her answer startled the woman. 'Really? Was it Dharini who told you?' she asked.

'Yes, Dharini.'

'When? Where did you see her?'

'We went to Agra some time ago. That's where we met.'

'Then?'

'From Agra we went to Rajnipur.'

If the woman felt any disconcertment, it was certainly not visible. Her face looked wooden.

Sita went on. 'We talked a lot in Rajnipur. I asked Dharini about her parents. That was when she told me that you had raised her. I guessed that it must be you.'

'Have Dharini and you become close friends?'

'How can we not become friends? I fell into the lake from the boat. It was Dharini who jumped in and saved me.'

Raziya Begum's face brightened. 'My daughter is my daughter indeed!' she rejoiced.

'You have so much love for your daughter. But it has been years since you saw her. She told me to inform her at once if I saw you.'

'Do you know where Dharini is now?'

'She said that she was in this city. She has given me her address. Shall I send word to her tomorrow morning? Why don't you stay here till tomorrow and see Dharini before you leave? It may be good to tell everything to my husband as well.'

Raziya Begum dropped the rug and pillow and said in minatory accents, 'Sita! Place your hand on mine!'

Sita did as she was bid.

'You must never tell Dharini, or your husband, about my coming here tonight. Swear that you will never do so. If not, I will kill you right now just as I killed the mad dog,' said Raziya Begum as she pulled out with her left hand the knife she had stuck into her waist and raised it. Her face which had calmed down a little while ago now reflected murderous frenzy.

Terrified, Sita swore to do what she was asked, thinking why on earth had she let herself talk to that crazy woman.

A horn blared outside, again and again.

'He is here. Get into the room, quick!' Sita said.

'Take care! Don't mention me even by mistake!' warned Raziya Begum as she went into the room.

Sita locked the room securely and heaved a big sigh. Then she went swiftly to open the door.

19

HELLO! POLICE?

Sita opened the front door to a scene that filled her with wonder and astonishment.

The car came to a stop in front of the house. There were three persons on the front seat. They got down, one by one – Saundara Raghavan, Dharini and Surya.

The fact that they had been squeezed together in the front seat imprinted itself on Sita's mind like a photograph.

At once Sita's attention went to the back seat. A longish bundle was lying on it. Was it a bundle? Or…

Sita's troubled mind now began to get agitated. Her body began to tremble.

She remembered her duty to welcome the visitors. They were coming to the steps at the threshold. Sita saw their faces in the light of the dim streetlight. Why do they look like this? Why do they have such an expression on their faces? As if they have lost something… Or… as if they are coming to a house of death…! Why?

Raghavan came first. 'Move aside,' he said. 'Why are you blocking the door?' His voice sounded strange to Sita. It was not the usual angry voice. It was a voice full of disgust and haste. Why is he coming home in such a choleric mood?

Sita moved aside. Dharini came next. Sita wanted to say something to welcome her. But the expression on her face did not seem to be receptive to words of welcome. Moreover, Sita was disconcerted as she was in two minds about Dharini – thinking about Dharini's mother or foster mother who was in the back room right then, and about Dharini having been sitting shamelessly between Raghavan and Surya in the car. Dharini walked past her into the house before Sita could decide on her mode of welcome.

Sita had no problem in talking to Surya. 'Cousin! What's this? Where are you coming from? Why do all of you have such an alarming expression on your faces? You look as if you have committed murder!'

Startled by the word 'murder' Surya looked intently at Sita. In measured tones, he said, 'It is something terrible. Athanga, let us go in first and then I will tell you at leisure.' He continued, 'We may appear to be perturbed, but why are you looking distressed? You are not unwell, are you?'

'Me? Nothing wrong with me. But I do feel disturbed. What can I do if he leaves me alone and gets back so late? Surya, why have you not come by all this while? Where did you find this woman?'

'You mean Dharini? She had come to see me in my room. Raghavan happened to drop in at the same time. Dharini wanted to see you. So, all three of us came together.'

'I saw the wonderful way in which you three arrived! Looks like this wretch will never remember that she was born a woman.'

Surya looked at Sita in surprise. 'Athanga, a terrible incident has taken place. Come in. I will tell you everything.'

When Sita and Surya went into the drawing room, Raghavan was standing there with the telephone receiver in his hand. Dharini was seated on a sofa. Before Sita could think of speaking to her Raghavan asked jumpily, 'Sita? What is the child doing? Has she gone to sleep?'

At that moment the child's voice was heard coming through the office room. 'Appa! Appa!'

'She had been sleeping all this while. Your voice has awakened her. Even when she's asleep the child thinks only of you!' Sita said.

'All right! All right! You can boast about your child later. Go and put her to sleep. Tell her that her father will come soon. She must not come here right now. Understand? Go! Be quick!'

From Raghavan's tone Sita realized that the matter was serious. She followed his injunctions and went in.

'Has Appa come, Amma?' Vasanti asked.

'Yes, Vasanti. He will come and lie down next to you. Go to sleep now!'

'Is Appa angry?' Vasanti asked.

Perplexed as she was, Sita was amused by Vasanti's question.

'Not at all, Vasanti! Some other people have come with him. He is talking to them. Go to sleep.'

Within a moment, the child was asleep.

'All three may not have had their dinner. How to make food for all of them? Both servants have left,' thought Sita as she came back to the drawing room.

Raghavan was talking on the telephone.

'Hello? Police station? Who...? Saundara Raghavan speaking. There has been an accident here. No, not a car accident. Could be murder... Yes, we suspect murder... Please send someone at once. Thank you.'

Standing at the door, Sita heard this exchange and entered the drawing room when the telephone conversation was over. No one seemed ready to talk to her. No one even looked at her face. She walked as if in a dream and sat down next to Dharini. When Sita thought about Dharini's mother in the room at the back, and her arrival with a blood-stained handkerchief, she felt that she would go mad if she didn't say something.

'Akka, what's the matter? Why is he calling the police?' Sita's question sounded shrill and squeaky. Dharini said nothing. She looked as if she was in a daze.

Raghavan interposed, 'Sita! Keep your mouth shut. Don't become hysterical now. If you do, I may end up killing someone.'

Sita began to shake.

Raghavan looked at Surya and said, 'Come, Surya! Let us go and stand outside. The police will be here any minute.'

20
A WEIGHT LIFTED

As soon as the men went outside Sita moved closer to Dharini and asked, 'Akka, what's this? He talked of such dreadful things on the phone! What is the matter? Why has he called the police?'

'Yes. It is a dreadful matter.'

'What is it? Tell me quickly!'

'Why do you want to know, Sita! It is better that you don't know. What is the use of your getting to know about it?'

'You talk just like him! Why shouldn't I know? Why should I not know what all of you know? The more you try to hide it, the more I get stressed out.'

'You are right. It is not as if you will never get to know about it if I don't tell you. I hesitated because I find it loathsome to talk about.'

'Then don't! Let him come in. I will ask him.'

'No! I will tell you. The three of us were coming together. On the way, at the turning near the street corner…' Dharini paused. Her body was trembling like a leaf.

'Akka! You are such a brave woman! Why are you frightened?'

'Yes, Sita! I am frightened. I have never been so frightened before. I have seen indescribable horrors during the Bihar earthquake. They did not frighten me as much... Look…! See how my hand is shaking.'

Only then did Sita look at Dharini's hands. 'Ayo! Looks like blood!' she said in a terrified voice.

'Don't shout! Yes, it is blood. What did you think it was? Did you think I had painted my nails with "cutex"? I heard that you are adopting all those modern styles.'

'Who told you?'

'Dhama and Bhama told me. What does it matter? I am not going to fault you – or them!'

'Thank you! Tell me about what happened today. The three of you were in the car. Then…'

Dharini haltingly narrated all that transpired. The three of them were in the car when Raghavan suddenly applied the brakes at the corner where the street turned to lead to his house. 'What? What?' Dharini and Surya cried out simultaneously. Raghavan got down without replying. The others too got down. Something lay across the street before the car. Going nearer, they saw that it was a man's body.

'Some drunkard is lying here! Blighter!' Raghavan cursed.

Dharini wondered if the car had hit him. She thought that with his mind on their conversation Raghavan had unheedingly run into the man crossing the street.

Surya had the same doubt. He said with some hesitation, 'Perhaps the car hit him.'

'Nonsense! Certainly not!' Raghavan said firmly.

'Even if it had not hit him, it might have run over the body lying on the ground. Let us go and check it out,' Surya said.

'Yes, we must,' Dharini agreed.

'Let us just go around him and drive on. Get into the car,' Raghavan said.

Not heeding him, Surya and Dharini went up close to the man lying on the street.

From the clothes he wore, he appeared to be a person of eminence. Placing a finger on his nose Surya said, 'He is breathing. He is alive.'

Dharini noticed that the front wheels of the car were touching the body. She became convinced that the car had pushed the man to the ground.

'Get in, let's go!' Raghavan urged them.

Dharini objected to this. 'Great! Should we just disappear after hitting a man in the middle of the road and toppling him to the ground? We must take him to the hospital at once.

Surya agreed.

Raghavan said, 'In that case you good samaritans can pick him up and put him on the back seat. I can't.'

'I will, certainly,' Dharini said and raised the man's head. Surya raised him by the waist. When Dharini placed her hand under the man's neck to lift him, it became wet. When he was lifted, a pool of blood could be seen below the head. Dharini did not lose her self-control.

She managed to control her shaking hands. They carried the man and placed him on the back seat. Seeing the puddle of blood Raghavan cried, 'This is a calamity!'

'We are responsible for the calamity. Drive to the hospital,' Dharini said.

'Great! Get in!' Raghavan said.

Quickly, both got into the front seat.

As he started the car Raghavan said, 'Rank idiots, both of you! It was a mistake for me to have sought you!'

'Yes. It was a mistake. Who asked you to come?' Dharini asked.

"I am paying for it. You have entangled me in a murder case. This car did not even touch that man. If it had, there would have been no blood under him. Someone has stabbed him and left him there. Why have you gotten me unnecessarily involved in this case? Not just me, yourselves as well!'

When she heard what Raghavan said, Dharini began to think that it must be true. She wondered if Surya and she had made a mistake.

'Mapillai, if what you say is true, why should we be afraid? It will not be possible to accuse us of this murder,' Surya said.

'That's all we need now! Is it not enough to be forced to bear witness in a murder case? Is it not enough that our names will be bandied about in the newspapers?'

'What has happened has happened. What should we do now? Think!' Dharini tried to calm things down.

'I have lost the ability to think. You must come up with ideas! Where should I take the car now?' Raghavan asked.

'Let us go straight to the hospital. Or to the police station,' Surya suggested. Dharini agreed.

'Can't go to both places at the same time, can we? Where should we go first?' Raghavan asked.

Both remained silent as they did not know what to say.

'My hands are shaking. I will hit a tree if I continue to drive. I will take the car home. Let us make a call from there,' Raghavan said.

At once, Dharini thought of Sita. How bewildered she would be if she came to know about these happenings! She had some inherent hysterical tendencies. What is to be done if they get stimulated? She wanted to beg Raghavan not to go home. But the car had come to a halt. They had reached Raghavan's house.

Sita who had been listening to this account with great eagerness and fear, now said in a trembling voice, 'Akka, what a catastrophe! Will he be in danger? Will the police arrest him?'

'Don't be afraid, Sita! Even the police of New Delhi will not be so stupid. Moreover, your husband has influence, he holds a senior position. He cannot be arrested. He might be asked to go to the police station to give his testimony. Nothing more,' Dharini said.

Sita felt a great weight lift off her mind. She was able to think about other things. She quickly recalled that Dharini's mother was locked in the junk room at the back of the house. But Raziya Begum had placed a gag on her mouth. Could Sita break her promise to her?

Suddenly Sita recalled what she had seen on the car's back seat. 'Akka, that bundle in the car…' she faltered.

'Yes, Sita! It was no bundle. It was the man from the street we placed inside the car. But why should we go on talking about it? Let's talk about something else.'

Now Sita understood the reason for all three being seated on the front seat. Her mind jumped to another thought. 'How did the three of you meet today?'

'I had been to see Surya in his room. Your husband landed up there searching for Surya. All three of us came to see you. This happened on the way,' Dharini explained.

'You went to see Surya? Why, you never came to see me even once! Have you forgotten me?'

'No Sita, I have not forgotten you. I did want to come. But I wondered what your husband would feel about it. Surya too hesitated for the same reason.'

Sita was irritated to hear this. The two seemed to have joined ranks now! She had been left out in the cold. Why should Surya care for Dharini more than for her? Sita said, 'Why should you be afraid of my husband? Will he eat you up? He is always thinking about you! I did not know that Surya was so deceitful.'

Dharini looked hard at Sita and said, 'Why do you say that? I have never seen anyone more straightforward than your cousin.'

'Yes, Surya used to be innocent. But for some time now, he has become deceitful. Is this the first time you saw him since you returned from Agra?'

'No. I went to see Surya as soon as I returned. Hadn't he written to me apologizing for having hurt my forehead? I went to put his mind at rest about it.'

'That's what I thought,'

'What did you think?'

'I thought you would have met Surya. Not only did you see him, you also told him about what happened in Rajnipur. He has written to my people. Akka, you are highly educated. You know a lot. You should not have spoken so reprehensibly about my husband to Surya.'

'Ayo! What is this? What did I say about your husband that was reprehensible?'

'You told Surya that he sat on the boat and watched me drowning in the lake. What could you have said about him that could have been worse?'

Dharini remained silent for a while. Then she said, 'Yes. It is true. We had an argument about the selfishness of men. I told him then about what happened in Rajnipur. Why should the truth be hidden?'

Sita spoke fast. 'That is not what I think. Even if it is true, you must not talk about other people's misdeeds. You must hide them, cover them up. Otherwise, you cannot live in this world.'

Dharini looked at Sita in astonishment. She was surprised that a young woman who had little education and less knowledge of the world had discovered so great a truth. Also, she began to wonder if Sita was conveying some hidden meaning.

Before Dharini could think of saying something conciliatory, a motorcycle arrived outside noisily.

'The police are here,' Dharini said.

Both of them forgot everything else as they anxiously pondered on what was going to happen.

21

THE MAD WOMAN OF RAJNIPUR

After a short initial exchange, Raghavan and the police officer entered the house.

Raghavan pointed to Dharini and said, 'It was this lady.'

'I can guess as much from her face. She has been badly frightened. I am not saying that there is no reason to be afraid. Still… Why, it looks as if she has not washed the blood off her hands!' the police officer said.

'I was not sure whether I should. I was waiting for you to come,' Dharini said.

'See how her voice is trembling! It was because of this lady that I did not drive straight to the police station. It will be good if somehow her name can be avoided,' Raghavan said.

'I will do what I can. You have her address, don't you? In case she is needed to bear witness…?'

'If you inform me, I will bring her whenever you want. It will be good if it can be avoided.'

'Let us see! Don't be afraid, ma'am! Go and wash your hands clean. Women should never intervene in matters like this. Let this be a lesson to you. Don't talk about this incident with anyone. Don't let it be known that you know anything about it!'

Then the police officer turned to Raghavan and said, 'Come, let us go. It may perhaps be too late already.'

'Sita! I will be back soon. Let Dharini stay here tonight!' Raghavan said.

Sita only half heard what the police officer said to Dharini. It appeared to her that her husband was saving Dharini and facing the danger himself.

'Where are you going? I will come with you!' she said shakily.

The police officer realized why she was afraid. 'Is this your wife?' he said. 'Don't worry ma'am! We are not arresting your husband and taking him away. He has to come to the police station and sign an affidavit. That's all. He will be back in half an hour.'

Sita looked at Raghavan to check whether this was true. His face brightened somewhat as he replied, 'Yes, Sita! I am in no danger. Surya and I will return in half an hour.' He added as he followed the police officer, 'Dharini, tell Sita all about it. She is unnecessarily distressed.'

In a few minutes the car and the motor cycle left from the front yard. Sita locked the front door and said, 'I am not going to get into that car ever again. Nor will I let the child get into it! It must be sold, and another purchased.'

'Yes! I will not get into that car even if I am asked to do so. I am surprised that you have been so brave,' Dharini said.

'Had my mother-in-law been here now, there would have been a great big rumpus. She would have needed ministrations. And thank goodness the child had fallen asleep.'

'Sita! I am eager to see your child. Let me wash my hands first. Why just wash hands? It would be good to have a bath. It is not enough to bathe in tap water. I must go to the Ganga and have a holy dip,' she said.

'Bathe in tap water for now. Later we will see about bathing in the Ganga,' Sita said and took her to the bathroom in the front part of the house. She did not dare to step into the rear portion.

When Raghavan and Surya returned, they saw Dharini and Sita preparing rotis in the kitchen. This gave them great satisfaction. 'We are not at all hungry. But we will eat something since you have taken so much trouble,' they said. Seeing that Dharini had bathed, they too went to have a bath.

Surya went to bathe in the bathroom at the back of the house. 'Athanga, what's in the locked room facing the bathroom? I heard some noise there,' he said.

Turning her face away Sita said, 'Must have been a bandicoot.'

'No. It sounded as if someone was knocking on the door from inside.'

'Perhaps it was a cat scratching,' Sita said.

'Dharini! You have left your handkerchief in the bathroom. It was blood stained. I washed it and hung it up to dry,' Surya said.

'No! I did not leave it there!' Dharini said and looked at Sita. Sita looked back at her.

'You have forgotten it!' Surya said.

Wanting to change the subject Sita said, 'This car must be sold at once! I will not get into it again.'

Raghavan said, 'I have made that decision already. I am going to sell the car first thing tomorrow. How times have changed! Stabbing a man walking down the street! And that too in New Delhi...!'

Everyone sat round the circular table to eat.

'Sita! Your cousin is a brave man! As long as he was in the car his hands and knees were knocking together. The moment we got down, he was all bravado!' Raghavan said.

'I admit that I was scared. But unlike you, I will not say, "What's it to me?" and walk away after seeing a man in the throes of death,' Surya responded.

'Enough! Please talk about something else!' Sita begged them.

'What should we talk about? You begin!' said Raghavan.

'Ask these two why they never even thought of dropping in here all these days,' Sita said.

'Sorry Athanga! I was up to my neck in work. From now onwards I will come often, that is, if mapillai has no objections...'

'What objections can I have to your coming here? Are you giving lame excuses?'

'That's the way to corner him!' Sita said and continued, 'Surya, what objections can he have to your coming here? Work did you say? But you could make time to see this Akka!'

'Athanga! We belong to the same party. It was in connection with work that we had to meet often.'

'I know nothing about parties. I will be happy only if both of you start coming here and often.'

'I would have come, Sita! I will tell you the truth, I refrained only because I was afraid of your mother-in-law.'

'Why should you be afraid of my mother-in-law? Even I am not scared of her! Surya must have told you a load of lies about her! You can never find a mother-in-law as good as mine in the whole world! She shows more affection to me than she would to her own daughter!'

At that moment, Raghavan's affection for Sita reached its zenith. Not affection alone. Gratitude as well. He looked at Dharini interrogatively. It was a look that said, 'What do you say now?' Dharini too looked at Raghavan. Sita did not notice their speaking glances. Even if she had, she would not have comprehended the import of the language of their eyes.

After dinner, the ringing of the telephone coincided with their entry into the drawing room. Raghavan picked up the receiver. 'Dead, is he? Adadaa! Has the doctor certified that he died from a knife thrust? Very good… Who…? Vinayakrao Madhonkar…? No loss to the world… But murder is murder… Who can it be? Any guess… the mad woman of Rajnipur…? Never heard of her…! All right, all right. I will take care of it… Thank you very much!'

As soon as Raghavan replaced the telephone receiver, three voices simultaneously cried out in alarm, 'What? What? What?'

'Sita says that we must never talk about that matter!'

Sita said, 'Tell us now. All I said was that we shouldn't talk about it while eating.'

'Then listen! Death occurred half an hour after we left. The doctor has certified that the cause of death was being stabbed by a knife. Vinayakrao Madhonkar is the name of the man who was murdered. Didn't I mention the evil minister of the old Maharaja of Rajnipur? It was he! He had been residing in this city for some time. Many knew him in the club where he drank and often created a racket. It seems the woman who is well known as the madwoman of Rajnipur had been regularly following him for some time. Madhonkar had lodged a police complaint against her. She had once attempted to kill the Maharaja of Rajnipur. They think that she must be the culprit in this case as well. How's that? We have read ever so many whodunnits.

This real-life incident seems to beat them all hollow! Sita, you like detective fiction, don't you?'

Sita and Dharini exchanged looks when 'the madwoman of Rajnipur' was mentioned. Their eyes reflected horror and pity.

Since Raghavan had addressed her directly, Sita said, 'Such things are best left to happen in fiction. Not in reality.'

'Do you know what I think? There should be many more like the madwoman of Rajnipur. Only then will the kings of our princely states and their evil ministers learn their lesson,' Surya declared.

'What makes you rage so much at the rulers of princely states?' Raghavan enquired.

As they were arguing, Sita's mind was wholly focused on the locked room at the back. The madwoman of Rajnipur was in her house right then! Should she inform someone in present company about it? What kind of disaster would be sparked by such a disclosure? What disaster would occur if she did not disclose it? She was Dharini's own or foster mother! How would Dharini react if she knew that her mother was a murderess? Perhaps she knew it already! Dharini had wanted to see her and learn about her parentage. Would she get an opportunity to do that after this? That madwoman must be Dharini's own mother. She would have lied to Dharini about being her foster mother because she had intended to perform this deed.

In a flash, Sita recollected something else. Why did that madwoman show so much affection for her and her mother? Why did she give them the money and the necklace? She felt an irrepressible desire to know the reason for this. It also struck Sita that she should no longer wear the jewel gifted by a murderess.

22

THE DOOR OPENED!

The clock struck midnight. Sita counted 'One, two, three…' At the stroke of twelve, she thought, 'An hour left. Until then, I must not go to sleep.' But what if the others too did not go to sleep? Surya and her husband were still talking in the next room. Dharini too was twisting and turning on the bed next to hers.

Sita pondered, 'We have read about such things in stories. Who ever thought they would happen in real life? The mother is asleep in the back room, not knowing that her daughter is here! The daughter is asleep without knowing that the mother is in the same house. What if the daughter learns that the mother came to hide here with a blood-stained knife…? Is it right for me to say nothing? But how can I? If my husband alone were here, perhaps I could have told him… Anyway, how is it certain that the woman is the murderess? She could have turned up here by some unconnected mischance! Why should her claim of killing a mad dog be untrue…? But why should she have entered surreptitiously? How she frightened me! Adadaa! I forgot the letter I was writing to Lalita and left it on the table in the office room! No one would have seen it. If anyone does, it would have to be my husband. But he never looks at my letters. What a noble trait! Even if he happened to glance at it, he would not read it after seeing that it is addressed to Lalita. How strange to think that Lalita should have been married to him and in charge of this household. I am occupying the place she should have occupied… What's this? My eyes are closing by themselves! Must not sleep... Must not sleep today…

Sita woke up when she heard the clock strike two. Oh God! She had drifted off to sleep! She looked at the clock on the wall. In the dim light of the nightlamp, it showed 2 a.m. Not too late. She could still go that room. But she must make no noise, make sure that Dharini and the men in the next room were fast asleep.

What's that? The sound of opening of a door…? At this time…? No, no. It must be a door in the neighbour's house. Or maybe just a delusion…

Ayo! What was that? A hazy figure…! There…! In the long mirror. Terrifying! A bearded face with a fez on the head! Glowing embers for eyes! The blood froze in Sita's body, her limbs became immobile. The form was no longer visible. But in the darkness, an arm seemed to appear by itself, and guide the figure away. They were gone!

Sita sat up in bed. She looked at the long mirror on the opposite wall. She turned to look out of the window. Nothing! Just a delusion!

No sound in the next room. The men were fast asleep. Dharini too was asleep. This was the right time to see Raziya Begum. It was crucial to warn her. She must not be here at dawn.

Sita slipped her hand under the pillow and took the keys. She got up noiselessly. The door to the left led to the dining room from where she could reach the rear part of the house.

Sita took slow, soft steps, which could not be heard even by herself. Finally, when she came to the junk room, she ran her hands on the door and found the lock. But she could not find the hole to insert the key. She had to switch on the light. So what? It would be good to have some light. If she opened the door in the dark, what if the madwoman of Rajnipur were to jump up with a scream? Moreover, she had a knife!

Sita's searching hand found the light switch and turned it on. What was that noise? Footsteps? Maybe the woman was moving about in the room. That was good too. No need to shake her awake.

Sita knew why she had erred in trying to open the lock in the dark. She had been trying to insert the key at the back of the lock! When she realized this, Sita felt the urge to giggle.

Now the key turned in the lock. The door opened. Placing one foot inside the room, Sita looked in. Why, there was no one there!

She put another foot in and looked around. The room was empty.

Weird! Were the happenings in the early part of the night merely dreams? Had she imagined a woman in the bathroom, who went into the junk room, bidding her to lock it from outside? No! Not at all. They had been real. But how did the woman disappear magically?

Sita saw the door at the back of the room. The latch was undone. The woman had opened the back door and was gone. Raziya Begum must have heard the police arrive. She must have left when things settled down. Sita could not learn what she had wanted to know from her! Never mind! It was more than enough that somehow, the woman had decamped from the house. It would be best if she never returned. Who cared about secrets! It would be more than enough if her husband and child stayed safe and well, and peace prevailed in her life. No need to undergo the kind of horrors experienced on that day.

When Sita came out of the room and felt a sudden pricking of the thumbs… As if two eyes were staring at her. Startled, she turned around. Dharini was standing at the threshold of the dining room.

Sita stared at Dharini with an irrational fear. She stood still, as if she had lost the strength to lock the door again. Dharini approached her with a smile on her face. 'Sita, why are you afraid? I came to see the same person you did. Is it not natural for me to have a greater interest in meeting her than you?'

Looking at Dharini with eyes widened in wonder, Sita asked, 'How did you know?'

'Just guessed. Sita, your words and actions aroused vague suspicions in my mind. Suspicion turned to conviction when Surya mentioned the blood-stained handkerchief. Moreover…' Dharini paused hesitantly.

'Moreover...?'

'I did something that I shouldn't have done. Sita, you must forgive me. When I went to see your child, I happened to notice your half-written letter on the table. Prompted by an unconscious instinct, I read it. At the end of the letter…'

'Akka, is this the way to behave? Even *he* doesn't read my letters!'

'Haven't I already asked you to forgive me?' Dharini asked in remorse.

'Let it go! Did you know that I got up and came here? You weren't asleep?'

'How can I find it in me to sleep Sita, when such terrifying incidents had taken place? You showed great interest in getting me to sleep. So, I pretended to be asleep. I was disappointed when I saw you falling asleep. But the clock struck two. You got up, took the key and walked out. I followed. I was afraid you'd see me when you switched the light on. But you didn't. You opened the door and went into the room. You were disappointed. But I was not…'

'Why not? How did you know that there was no one inside?'

'Before the clock woke you up, I saw someone going through the garden. Sita, was there only one person in this room, or were there two?'

'Only one. The one you called Raziya Begum. Why do you ask?'

'Because I saw two people leaving. Sita! Somebody must have come and taken Raziya Begum away.'

Sita remembered what she had seen on the mirror. She asked in flustered tones, 'Who was the other, Akka?'

'I don't know. I saw someone with a beard and fez, and red eyes. I feel that I have seen that face somewhere, sometime,' Dharini replied.

'I feel the same,' Sita said.

'You do? How? Did you see them?'

'I caught sight of a face appearing on the long mirror before me. It vanished at once. I thought it might be a delusion. From what you say it had been real enough.'

'If I had seen mother alone, I couldn't have borne it. I would have shouted, "Amma!" I stopped myself only because there was someone behind her.'

Sita said, 'Is she really your mother? I cannot believe it… Should we continue here? The child may wake up and cry. The men may be startled into thinking that something has befallen us. Let us go, lie down and continue our talk. I will never be able to sleep now. You must tell me all about yourself.'

23

DHARINI'S STORY

The two women were seated on the bed. At Dharini's request, Sita had told her everything she knew about what had happened earlier in the night. Now it was Dharini's turn.

Dharini heaved a big sigh and said, 'The heroines of old tales always begin by asking, "Should I narrate the story of my birth or the story of how I was raised?" I cannot narrate the story of my birth. It is to learn that story that I have been searching for Raziya Begum. Just when I thought I had succeeded, she slipped through my fingers. Maybe all for the good. What can I ask her when such an appalling incident has occurred? How can she say anything?'

'Is she really a Muslim? Akka! Is Raziya Begum her real name?'

'No. I will come to that later. I had always thought that she was my mother. No mother in the world could have raised her daughter with more love. She protected me as if I were her own life. But from childhood I realized that there was a difference between me and the other girls. My mother did not run a household with my father. I felt that she was hiding and living as if she feared someone. A man came to see my mother frequently. I was used to calling him "Appa". I don't know whether I got into that habit by myself or if someone taught me to do so. I had called him "Appa" as far back as I can remember. Sometimes he and Amma were extremely affectionate towards each other. Sometimes they fought like lions and tigers. I had come to know that they were not a married couple. But I did believe that he was my father. Despite their constant fights, they were united in their love for me. All I had to do was to say that I wanted something, and it would be with me in the blink of an eye. If I fell even slightly ill, they were ready to die for me. They unhesitatingly lavished money on raising and educating me. For all that they did, they did not have a great deal of money. My mother had several valuable jewels when I was young. One by one, she gave them to my father to be sold. Sometimes Appa brought in money. Amma would stubbornly refuse to take it because she knew that he did not have much. Moreover, he had another family to support. Sometimes Appa would bring me new clothes without Amma's knowledge. When she came to know, she would fight with him. My life went on in this manner. In my convent I made a friend, Nirupama. Her friendship raised my spirits whenever I became despondent.'

Sita interposed to ask, 'The woman I met in Agra? I liked her a lot! That's how friendship should be.'

'Yes. We were of the same age. As we grew, we began to think and talk about the future. We exchanged confidences. We decided that we would not marry but dedicate ourselves to the service of the nation. Nirupama changed her mind when someone appeared who cared about the beauty of her soul. She is fortunate.'

Sita saw tears moistening Dharini's eyes. Her heart melted. 'Akka! One day you too will be as fortunate as Nirupama.'

'But there is a difference between us. Sita, will any man marry someone who doesn't know who her parents are? Even if the man agrees, his family must agree! Let it go. I am not interested in marriage. I am sincerely committed to the nation's service. Nirupama and I joined the salt satyagraha in Bombay. We were too young to be sent to prison. But repeatedly, we were taken and left outside the city. Nirupama and I found it great fun because we were together. When that movement ended, we went to the Karachi Congress...'

Dharini paused for a few moments and continued with a sigh. 'Then we had the desire to see this sacred land of India. We roamed everywhere. That was when the shocking news of the earthquake in Bihar shook the entire nation. Nirupama and I joined the group of volunteers from Bombay who went to work for earthquake relief. Important events happened in both our lives when we were serving the earthquake victims. Nirupama met Veni Prasad. After a while she married him.'

'Akka, go on! What was the important incident in your life?' Sita asked eagerly.

'Nirupama got married. I died. That is what I wanted everyone to believe. I left after making everyone who served with me believe that I was dead. The news that made you suspect my mother made me take such a step. I was totally confounded by my mother being accused of murder and thrown into prison. It was my mother who claimed all my love in the world. My love for her triumphed over whatever faults I found in her behaviour. I could not bear the thought of her facing blame and misery. I was preyed by all kinds of suspicions as I wondered why she should have tried to kill a maharaja. That was when I met my father at the Delhi railway station – I mean the man I had thought was my father until then. He shared some information, which he thought would bring me solace. One was that the woman I had believed to be my mother was in fact not my mother. Instead of consolation, this brought me excruciating pain. A single light had been glowing in my dark life. Now it was extinguished. I was preyed by all kinds of suspicions. If she was not my mother, he could not be my father. So, who am I? Who is my mother? Who is my father? Sita, that was when I came to understand the meaning of some of the words my foster mother had let fall in a bout of rage. I began to suspect that I may be the daughter of some maharaja of a princely state. I understood why she kept on shifting her quarters and changed her name from Ramamani to Raziya Begum. My father told me something else. My mother not only changed her name to Raziya Begum, but she would often say, "I am going to become a Muslim, the only way to live without being troubled by menfolk." My foster father said that before she attempted murder, she had really converted to Islam. He left me after trying to put heart into me and giving me the time and place for our next meeting. But I didn't have the heart to meet him again. I was waiting for the day my mother would be released. I was at the gates of the prison-house, but no woman was freed on that appointed day. When I made enquiries, I learnt that Raziya Begum had tried to stab someone in jail and had been shifted to the lunatic asylum. I went to the lunatic asylum and learnt that she had been released after recovering her sanity. From that day I have been searching for Raziya Begum. Sita, I went to Rajnipur for that reason. There I heard that someone called the madwoman of Rajnipur was roaming in Delhi. Therefore, I have been searching for her in Delhi as well. And this disaster took place on the day I could have finally met her…'

Silence prevailed in the room. Sita broke it when she asked, 'Do you think that Raziya Begum is mad?'

'How can I know, Sita? It has been more than four years since I saw her last. Perhaps she has gone mad. I know that there is a great rage burning in her heart. Overpowering rage can turn to frenzy. From frenzy, it is but a step to madness. In a way it would be good if she were adjudged insane. If she is captured, they won't hang her. They will send her to the lunatic asylum.'

Sita thought of how that frenzy and madness could have been directed at her. She had escaped from a great danger that day.

After a while Sita said, 'Just one more question. Akka, did you ask me about the ruby necklace I wore because you thought that Raziya Begum must have given it to me?'

'Yes. I wanted to confirm it. It was the last jewel my foster mother had after selling all the others.'

'Why did she gift that ornament and the two thousand rupees?'

'Sita! Do I have to spell it out? Can't you guess?'

Sita had indeed made her guess already. Now it was confirmed. The man whom Dharini called father must have been her own father. That was the reason why her household had been preyed by poverty in her childhood and her mother grief stricken. The woman must have mysteriously brought the gifts as her reparation.

Sita recalled how her father had gone to Delhi before her wedding.

He must have gone to see Dharini. Where was he now? So many years since she had seen him. Dharini too had not seen him. Who knows whether he was alive? If he were, would he not have come to see the daughter born to him, at least once?

'Akka, whatever it may be, you must always be my elder sister!' Sita said.

The clock struck four.

24

THE GOOD MOTHER-IN-LAW

One day, quite unexpectedly, Dhama and Bhama landed up at Sita's house. Sita was delighted by their visit. The house was filled with chatter, teasing laughter and bonhomie.

After enquiring about each other's well-being and making much of Vasanti, Bhama said, 'Where is Mr Raghavan? We have come to congratulate him.'

'My mother-in-law is coming from Madras today. He has gone to the railway station to pick her up,' Sita replied.

'Ayo! Mother-in-law! Terrifying!' Bhama said.

'Sita, do you know? It is the "mother-in-law phobia" that has made us both vow never to get married!' Dhama said and guffawed loudly. Bhama joined in her laughter.

Sita laughed but said, 'But my mother-in-law is a very good person. I am not afraid of her.'

'So, it is your mother-in-law who is scared of you!' Bhama said and broke into laughter.

'Not at all,' Sita assured her and added, 'Bhama, is it true that among the English people, the sons-in-law are terrified of *their* mothers-in-law?'

'Nothing but light-hearted jests by humourists. People here take them for gospel truth and start criticizing English society!' Dhama explained.

'Why do you want to congratulate my husband?' Sita asked.

'Because Mr Raghavan has shown exemplary courage. The people here would have simply removed themselves from the spot saying, "Why invite trouble?" But Mr Raghavan had been abroad! So, he took the man stabbed and abandoned on the street to the hospital and informed the police as well. Our father commended Mr Raghavan highly for his sense of duty. Sita, we came to convey this to your husband and congratulate him.'

Sita clearly remembered how her 'foreign-travelled' husband had said, 'Why should we invite trouble? Let us go.' It was Surya and Dharini who had insisted that the body should be taken to the authorities. She also recalled how Raghavan had repeatedly chided them, 'Your stubbornness has brought this trouble upon us!' But Sita buttoned her lips. Why should she refuse to accept the distinction conferred upon her husband by Bhama and Dhama?

Then, as if she suddenly recalled the fact, she asked them, 'Poor man! It seems he belongs to your town! Is it true?'

'Yes. He does belong to our town, that is, to Rajnipur. But no need to be sorry for him. A very bad man. When the old maharaja was alive, his actions had been insufferable. Once our father became the divan, he became somewhat scared and quietened down. He stayed in Delhi most of the time. Appa was anxious about the conspiracies he might hatch here and the men whom he would ruin. His death is no loss to the world. But the law is the law. Father is therefore making a great effort to pressurize the police to discover his murderer. Don't you know that the police in New Delhi is corrupt through and through?'

Sita became angry with the divan of Rajnipur. Why should he take an interest in this matter?

'Does it mean that the murderer has not been identified yet?' she asked.

'How will they find him? They will investigate for three years and then declare that the murder never took place. That's the Delhi police for you!' Dhama shrugged.

Sita reflected that it would be good if things turned out that way. She was astonished at her own concern for a murderess.

'No suspects?' she asked.

'Someone called the madwoman of Rajnipur had been trailing

Madhonkar for some time. The police suspect her. But I don't think it is possible. Can a woman perform such a daring deed?'

Dhama retorted, 'Why not? There are a number of demonesses among women. Moreover, who knows what atrocities Madhonkar may have committed! The fury he provoked?'

The telephone rang. Sita picked up the receiver and asked, 'Hello! Who is it?' It was Surya. He was coming to Sita's house with Dharini.

'How delightful! It has been many days since I saw you. Come quickly!' Sita said.

She told Bhama and Dhama about their imminent visit. The sisters were happy and said, 'Since we won't be able to meet your husband, we will wait to see Dharini at least.'

'He should be home soon. You can meet him too,' Sita said.

Sita wanted to see Surya. She also wanted to see Dharini. But she did not like their coming together.

Raghavan's complaint had become imprinted on her mind. 'Surya and Dharini are often together, openly roaming together across the city. This is not right! Why should Surya go astray? How pained his parents will be if they get to know about these goings on?'

Sita too thought that they were doing something wrong. But Raghavan blamed Surya. Sita faulted Dharini. Surya was an innocent from the village. Experienced in the ways of the world, Dharini was leading him astray. She decided to warn Surya about falling into Dharini's trap.

Sita was in two minds about Dharini. Whenever she saw her face-to-face, she felt an involuntary surge of affection for her. She would have been happy had Dharini turned out to be her sister, the child of her stepmother. Sita was disappointed that it was not so.

But when Dharini was not beside her, she felt an unreasonable anger towards her. She thought that Dharini was responsible for the poverty in her childhood home, for her mother's sorrow, why, even for her mother's untimely death. Moreover, she knew her husband and was able to move around with him freely. Now she has driven Surya crazy. Was this the right kind of conduct for an Indian woman? How good Bhama and Dhama seemed in comparison with Dharini!

They might be excessively steeped in European modes. So what? But their conduct was irreproachable!

'Whether I like it or not, he likes the way they comport themselves,' she thought. 'Therefore, I must make friends with them, and learn to conduct myself as they do. They mingled so easily with everyone at the party in the viceroy's mansion! I must learn to do the same. I may not like their ways all that much. But should I not make myself into the kind of person my husband likes? Isn't this the advice that my mother-in-law has been giving me?'

Having reached this decision, Sita told Bhama and Dhama, 'I will be ever so happy if you both remain in this city. I have no friends here. I find it difficult to pass the time.'

'We may shift here sooner than later. Sita! It looks as if father will get a big post in the Indian government. He has received the offer. Father is hesitating though…' Bhama said.

'How do you lack friends, Sita! You have Dharini,' Dhama said.

'It is the same thing to have Dharini for a friend as not to have her for a friend. If she comes here, she goes on and on about socialism, Congress and the revolution,' Sita said.

'I had imagined that you too had a penchant for these causes!'

'Not at all. I have devotion for Mahatma Gandhi. I don't like it if anyone criticizes him. I fight with my husband too if he complains about Gandhi,' Sita explained.

'Gandhi is a great soul, no doubt. But his economic ideologies are completely outdated. If we listen to him, India will have to go two thousand years backwards,' Dhama said.

'Can we do without trains, cars and electricity?' Bhama asked.

'Adadaa! How ravishingly the trees and creepers were lit up at the viceroy's garden party to which you took me the other day! I began to wonder if it was the realm of the gods!'

'That party was nothing! Sita, you should have seen it all when Willingdon was viceroy. Then you wouldn't have wondered whether it was the celestial realm. It *was* the celestial realm! After the arrival of this Bull Keepers' Viceroy, things are nowhere as posh as they used to be. Do you know that Lord Linlithgow has been named the Bull Keepers' Viceroy?'

'Oh yes, everyone is poking fun at him!' Sita said.

'Things are getting from bad to worse. They catch hold of fellows who herd bulls and pigs and send them off to India to be viceroys and governors,' Bhama shrugged. Dhama added, 'If the Labour government takes over in England, they will send their railway porters and postmen to be governors in India. The maharajas and nawabs of our country will have to salute them!'

Bhama said, 'If things go according to the socialists and the Congressmen, the porters and postmen from our own country will become governors and viceroys! What do you prefer, Sita?'

Sita remembered Rajampettai and its post office. She giggled at the thought of postman Balakrishnan in the governor's seat. She felt that the Indian government and its bureaucracy should continue as before.

At this moment, Surya and Dharini entered the house. Dhama and Bhama hugged and shook hands with Dharini, welcoming her with 'Hello! My dear!' Sita took Surya aside and said, 'Cousin! Why do you want this friendship with Dharini? What will your parents think if they hear about it? Don't spoil your name. I will find a good girl and get her married to you soon.'

'Athanga, where did you learn to talk like this? Please don't get any wrong ideas about Dharini. Didn't I already tell you that both of us belong to the same socialist party? That is why we need to meet and talk often. We have decided to go to Lahore soon.'

Dhama screeched, 'What secrets are you sharing with your cousin? Have you decided not to introduce him to us? We won't gobble him up! Bring him here!'

Sita and Surya went to join the others.

25

I WILL SHOOT HIM!

As soon as he was introduced to Bhama and Dhama, Surya asked, 'As we came in, we heard some talk of maharajas, governors, porters and peons. What was that all about?'

Sita explained.

'One day, these things *are* going to happen. Railway porter will turn governor. A mason from a factory will become the governor general. A postman will be prime minister. We must be prepared for these changes. Don't think that high posts will always be occupied by entitled beings with an "English" education. Who was Hitler, the man who is making the whole world tremble before Germany today? A painter of walls. Those who ruled Germany for a thousand years have disappeared without a trace. What about Russia…?' Surya went on and on.

'Oh my goodness! A fire-spewing socialist!' said Bhama.

'Yes. My cousin is a radical. He left home after fighting with his father and brother for taking the side of the agricultural labourers in the village. I believe he declaims passionately in public meetings. But I haven't heard him until now,' Sita said.

'You call me a fire-spewing socialist? True. Our party is going to ignite the fire to scorch, blaze, burn to cinders and dispatch to the other world all the maharajas, divans, zamindars, jagirdars and capitalists who squeeze poor labourers to extract monstrous profits! Wait and see!' Surya thundered.

Dhama said mockingly, 'Do as you please with maharajas and jagirdars. But let the poor divans go!'

Bhama asked, 'Such big talk! Will the lava from your volcano burn down the British government in India?'

'One day the British government will also meet its end. Until now, the British government in India has been escaping by donning an asbestos armour. But it will not last long. The authoritarian regime in India will meet its fate soon enough,' said Surya.

'What is "asbestos armour"?' Sita asked. 'Never heard of it.'

'A new artificial material called asbestos has been discovered. Fire cannot burn it. Do you know the asbestos armour with which the British have covered themselves? The disunity between Hindus and Muslims. The British rule India by dividing Hindus and Muslims.'

'When will that division end?' Dhama asked.

'The only way is through an economic revolution. Among the poor there is no distinction between poor Hindus and poor Muslims. It is the same among the labourers. The poor working classes will awaken if we can convey this truth to them. Then, they will not allow power hungry politicians and British diplomats to exploit them.'

Vasanti, who had been listening eagerly to the adults without understanding anything, now jumped up and ran to the front door shouting, 'Appa is here! Appa is here! With Patti!'

'Yes, it looks as if he is here. Carry on. I will let them in,' Sita said and went quickly to the front door. Carrying the child on her hip, she stood waiting in the front verandah.

The car came to a standstill in front of the house. Raghavan strode in before his mother got down. Going to Sita on the verandah he hissed in rage, 'Sita! Why did you write such nonsense to the people at home? One day I am going to thrash you black and blue. You have gotten above yourself! Bitch!'

'Ayo! What's this? I didn't write anything!' Sita said. She controlled the fury and the sobs that threatened to overcome her. This was the first time Raghavan had cursed Sita so obscenely.

'Don't lie! Didn't you write to your friend Lalita saying that I pushed you into the Rajnipur lake?'

Sita realized that what Surya had written to Lalita had come to her husband's ears with this twist. Someone had mentioned it to her mother-in-law in Madras. Her mother-in-law had detailed it as soon as she got down from the train. For the first time, Sita felt angry with her mother-in-law.

'Why are you staring at me without giving an answer! Did you, or did you not write this?' Raghavan asked.

Sita thought for a second. She could have said that it was not she but Surya who had written what he had heard from Dharini. But if she did, Raghavan would be enraged with Surya. Better to accept the blame.

'I did not write anything like that…' she began propitiatingly.

'You did not write like *that* but like *this*! Your nastiness is becoming obvious now. One day I am really going to shove you into the lake. Wait and see.'

'No! No! Don't shout! The child is frightened out of her wits. There are visitors in the house,' Sita said.

Instantly Raghavan came to himself. 'Who?' he asked.

'Dharini is here…'

'I see!' said Raghavan. There was an immediate change of expression on his face.

'Dhama and Bhama are also here.'

'Those hags! No wonder there's such a commotion! Is that all? Any more…?'

'Surya is also here…'

'Why did that rascal come here? One day I am going to shoot him,' Raghavan muttered.

Sita was deeply anguished. She was astounded by the sudden revelation of Raghavan's demonic nature.

Kamakshi Ammal came up the steps after having got down at leisure and checking to ensure that the servant had brought out all her luggage.

'Raghava! What is this? Fighting even before I step into the house?' she said. 'You think your quarrelling will make me go back? I will not leave my granddaughter and go back so easily! Vasanti, come, darling!'

Vasanti who had been dumbfounded by her parents' fight now jumped into her grandmother's arms.

26

WAR OF WORDS

There was a huge difference between the Raghavan at the threshold and the Raghavan who entered the house. The fiendishness was gone without a trace. His face and words were brimming with geniality. Sita was happy to see the transformation. She was happy that he displayed his spleen and vexation to her alone.

Raghavan first welcomed Dhama and Bhama and spoke buoyantly to them. Then he looked at Dharini and said, 'What's this! To see you is getting to be as rare as catching sight of the crescent moon on its third night!'

'Is it not natural for the full moon to turn into a crescent at times?' Dharini replied.

'The moon is always the same. It is to us that it appears at times full and at other times as a crescent,' Raghavan said, and added before Dharini could respond, 'But one thing is certain. When the moon joins the sun, it will disappear completely!' Then he looked at Surya to ask, 'When did you arrive?'

Surya, whose name meant 'the sun', reddened in anger when he heard Raghavan's pun about the sun and the moon. Without showing his annoyance he said, 'About half an hour ago. Dharini and I came together.'

Dhama and Bhama now intervened to congratulate Raghavan on his having taken the body on the street to the hospital. Raghavan answered, 'What's so great about it? Something that everyone must do as his duty. Let's talk about something else!'

'It doesn't seem great to you. But to us it appears great. Poor thing, on that day your wife must have been completely overcome.'

'Yes. After that I couldn't leave her alone in the house. That is why I wrote to my mother at once and brought her here.'

'We hear that your mother is a very sweet lady. That's what Sita says. Aren't you going to introduce her to us?'

'She has just reached home after two days of train travel. My mother is rather orthodox. She has not eaten anything during the journey. It will take her an hour to bathe and get refreshed,' Raghavan said.

Both Bhama and Dhama chorused, 'We will not go without seeing your mother.'

Sita went in and said to her mother-in-law, 'Amma, they say they won't go unless they meet you.'

'Why girl, why are these witches allowed here? And no remonstrance from you! I have never seen anyone with less sense!' Kamakshi Ammal said.

'Amma, though they look the way they do, they are really very good people.'

'Good people? People like them should never be allowed inside the house! Tell them that I am overcome by fatigue and will meet them another day,' Kamakshi Ammal said.

Sita returned to the drawing room to say, 'Amma has a headache. She says she will meet everyone on some other day.'

The telephone rang. Raghavan picked up the receiver. 'O! It's about Madhonkar. They have found the murderer…? Who is it…? Adadaa! What a daredevil! Very good… I am ready to bear witness to anything I know at any time… No. I'm not going anywhere. I will be in town. Righto!'

Dharini and Sita looked at each other. Their eyes reflected anxiety and fear.

When Raghavan finishing talking everyone cried out simultaneously, 'What? What?'

'It seems the police have identified the man who killed Madhonkar. The murder was committed by a servant who had worked for him for a long time. He himself has admitted to his crime…'

Sita cut in to ask, 'How can that be?'

Dharini's voice was heard calling out, 'Sita!' Sita looked at her face. She recognized the warning in Dharini's eyes.

Dharini said, 'Sita, why do you have to barge in with your opinion? What do we women know about police matters?'

'Sita takes great pleasure in expressing opinions on matters she knows nothing about,' Raghavan said.

Sita pulled herself together to say, 'Yes. What do I know about this? It was just an involuntary remark. But you were talking about testimony and summons. What's that?'

'Testimony means testimony,' Raghavan said.

'But why should you give testimony?'

'I must testify to having taken a body from the street to the hospital…'

'Then shouldn't Surya also give testimony?'

'Yes. He will also be summoned to be present in court.'

'That's why I asked. He is planning to go to Lahore. Tell him not to go.'

'Oh! Going to Lahore? Why should we stop him? Even if we do, he is not going to listen. Moreover, the case will not begin tomorrow! It will take a long time,' Raghavan explained.

Then, impelled by a sudden thought he asked, 'Is Surya going alone?'

'Dharini Akka is going with him,' Sita said.

'Dharini! Is this true? What's happening in Lahore?' Raghavan asked in consternation.

'That is what we have been discussing all this while. Mr Raghavan! You ask him! It seems India must achieve independence! As soon as it does all the kings of the princely states, their queens, divans and divans' daughters must be completely annihilated. All high-ranking bureaucrats must be knocked down… That is why they are going to Lahore. How's that?' Dhama asked and burst into laughter. Bhama joined her.

There were more roars of laughter when Raghavan asked, 'Very good! But why Lahore? Has anyone hidden India's independence in Lahore?'

'You laugh without knowing anything about the matter. Will idle laughter make everything all right?' Surya said.

'Please keep quiet, all of you! No one should laugh. Silence! Let Surya explain. If it doesn't get into our heads even then, let us climb to the top of the Qutub Minar, jump down and give up our lives,' said Bhama.

'If anyone dares to laugh, Surya will toss whatever he can grab and break our heads! Take care!' Dhama said, referring to Surya's having thrown the toy at the Taj Mahal grounds.

Surya suppressed the feeling of humiliation triggered by this remark. He went on, 'Yes! Sometimes, it is impossible not to be angry with those who remain utterly devoid of the ability to think. "English" education has destroyed our brains. How can we retain the capacity to think if we stuff our brains with the dates of Henry II's wedding, Henry VII's divorce, Charles I losing his crown and George III turning insane? Raghavan asked if anyone has hidden India's independence in Lahore. No one has hidden our freedom anywhere. It is shining before us in all its radiance. It is we who have lost our eyesight and turned blind. The first obstacle to India's independence is the division between Hindus and Muslims. Some factions in the Punjab have started demanding a separate nation for the Muslims. This is nothing but a diplomatic conspiracy hatched by the British. The socialist conference is going to take place in Lahore to evolve a strategy to destroy this conspiracy. It is in the Punjab that the seeds of the Hindu-Muslim discord were sown. Since then, campaigns have been launched to prove that Hindus and Muslims belong to different races. That is why we are holding a conference to ponder the issue.'

'O! You are going to start thinking about it only now, are you?' Raghavan scoffed.

'Our strategy is ready. What is left to be done is to formulate an action plan. It is the power-hungry politicians and government officers who foster dissensions between the Hindus and the Muslims…'

'You can't sleep at night if you don't say something nasty about government officers,' Saundara Raghavan said.

'Government officers belong to the most educated and intelligent segment of the Indian society. They are expending their intelligence and education in fostering foreign rule! Who else is to be blamed if not them?' Surya asked.

'Blame them as much as you like. I have no objections. We can handle all your accusations. But tell us what your great strategy is!'

'All communal differences and discord begin with the entitled classes. The masses are misled by their propaganda. This hatred has not spread among the labourers and the poorer agricultural workers in the villages. There is no reason for them to hate one another. The poor Hindu and the poor Muslim belong to the same race. The Muslim labourer and the Hindu labourer belong to the same caste. In the same way, the capitalist Muslim and the capitalist Hindu belong to the same class. We want to run a zealous crusade to bring this home to the impoverished masses.'

'Oh yes, when the sky falls, we shall catch larks. When it comes to any matter of conflict, the poor Muslim and the rich Muslim, the Muslim labourer and the Muslim capitalist, the Muslim servant and the Muslim ICS officer will all get together. Never will the poor Muslim join forces with the poor Hindu. No threat to our jobs as long as you and your comrades depend on this singular strategy to attain independence. Nor is there any danger to your father's post as divan,' said Raghavan, addressing his last words to Dhama and Bhama.

Surya said, 'Let us say you are right. But we do not depend on this single plan alone. These are merely instrumental strategies. In any case, it is absolutely certain that India will achieve its independence. Very soon, we are going to get a great opportunity. We must not cheat ourselves by letting the opportunity slip from us. Fortunately, we have found a leader with foresight to show the way. It is Subhash Chandra Bose who is going to get freedom for India. At the Haripura Congress he called youngsters like us together and gave us a talk. He highlighted what he himself had observed in Germany and Italy. "It is certain that there will be a world war soon. That is India's opportunity. And we must be ready to seize it," he said.'

'There never will be a world war. I too have been to Europe. England is not ready for war. So, there will be no war. Hitler and

Mussolini will achieve what they can through their intimidating tactics alone,' Raghavan stated.

'This war of words is not going to end anytime soon. Sita! I need something from you. Come!' said Dharini as she caught Sita's hand and took her inside.

27

THE REASON FOR THE JOURNEY

As soon as they were alone Dharini asked, 'Sita, did you hear that the culprit has been found?'

'Yes, Akka. Surprising! I was going to make the mistake of referring to Raziya Begum. You stopped me at the right moment.'

'Sister, let this matter be a secret between the two of us. Don't mention it even to your husband! You must know by now that he gets easily put out. If you tell him about it, he may pounce on you with "Why didn't you tell me at once?"'

'That is true. I will be extremely cautious. But what do you think? Akka, can what the police say be true?'

'What do we know, Sita? It may be true. It might have been wrong to suspect Raziya Begum. She did not tell you everything, did she? And all my efforts could not find her. It is best for both of us to forget the incident of that night.'

'Now I am amused to recall the unnecessary fears and trepidations I felt on that night. Never mind. You said you were going to Lahore. It worries me. It will cheer me up if you and Surya come often. My husband will be delighted even if you come by yourself.'

'Sita, it is no longer feasible for me to come here frequently. Your mother-in-law will not like it.'

'You are mistaken about my mother-in-law. When you meet her, you will know that she is a very good woman. She may not like it if you were like Bhama or Dhama. But she will definitely take to you.'

'Then let me meet her right away. Who knows whether there

will be an opportunity to do so later? Why don't you go and join the others? I will talk to her as if I happened to come across her by chance.'

'Perfect! You will win her over in no time at all!' Sita said and went away.

Kamakshi Ammal was sitting in the puja room, her eyes closed in meditation. 'Amma, do you remember me?' Dharini asked as she prostrated before her.

Startled, Kamakshi Ammal opened her eyes. When she saw that it was Dharini, she gave her the traditional blessing, 'May you prosper!' and then asked, 'Do you live in this city?'

'I was here for a while. But I am leaving soon.'

'Is that so?' Kamakshi Ammal's voice reflected her sense of relief.

'Amma! Haven't I kept my promise to you until now? I will continue to do so. You need not worry.'

'I have no worries at all. All I wish is for everyone to prosper in their lives. Every day, all the time, this is my prayer to Lord Rama! My older son has become useless to me. My trust in Raghavan has kept me alive. He must not suffer in any way through you. That's all!'

'Never, Amma! Nothing bad will happen to anyone in your family because of me. There are many reasons for that.'

Two days later, Raghavan went to Dharini's room. Surya happened to be there at that time. Raghavan noticed that both were making preparations for a journey.

'So, you are sure about going to Lahore,' he said.

'Yes, we are leaving by the night train,' Dharini replied.

Raghavan looked at Surya and said, 'Look, Surya! Go to Lahore! Go to Rawalpindi! Or make your way to Kabul. Perhaps it will be best for you to go into the deserts of Central Asia. After all, the desert is the right place to hunt for mirages like socialism and communism! But don't drag Dharini with you. It is not good for you. Nor is it good for her,' he said.

Surya listened to this with a beaming face and said, 'Mapillai, sir! You are making a mistake. I am not taking Dharini with me. It is she who is forcing me to accompany her.'

'Dharini! Is this true?' Raghavan asked.

'Yes. You know that I am doing research in history. I need to go to the Punjab for that.'

'Enough! Enough! Keep your historical research to yourself! Women had safeguarded the purity of this country called Bharat. Now even that virtue is under threat! But there is no time to argue about it now. Dharini, I must have a word with you.'

Seeing how perturbed and agitated he was, Dharini asked him, 'According to your ethical code, can women talk to men in private? Is it not against your dharma?'

After a moment's dismay Raghavan said, 'But *you* don't have any objections to that! Therefore, I too have no objections. Dharini, it is a very important matter.'

Surya left them saying, 'I have some work to finish before we start. I will take my leave, Dharini. Send word at once should there be any change in the travel plan!'

After Surya's exit, silence reigned in the room for a while. Realizing that Raghavan was not going to start talking, Dharini said, 'What is this crucial matter to be discussed in private?'

28

THE SURGING SEA

Raghavan went to the door and looked out. He made sure that Surya was not standing on the staircase. Then he looked out of the window. He saw Surya walking away on the street.

Coming to stand in front of Dharini like a character on the stage, Raghavan asked, 'Dharini, don't you know what I want to tell you when we are alone? Are you truly unaware of the state of my mind? Or are you pretending to be unaware of it?'

'If I know your mind, then you too should know mine! In that case, there is no need to speak, nothing to say or to hear.'

'No. I am not able to know your mind. There was a time when I did. Before any thought appeared in your mind, it was reflected in mine. Similarly, I would think about something, and you would say it aloud. Again, when you had a thought, I put that thought into action. No longer. A curtain of illusion prevents me from knowing your mind. If only I knew the dastardly scoundrel who put up that curtain between us!'

'Sir, you have created it yourself. What is the use of getting angry, imagining it to be the work of another? I have some work to finish before starting on the journey. It will be good if you can say what you want to say, and quickly.'

'I will. I certainly will. I was only waiting for the opportunity. I don't want to beat around the bush. I will be frank in saying what lies in my heart. Dharini, I cannot live without you. Not anymore. My heart is not with me since I saw you at the railway station three months ago. From the time I saw you at the Taj Mahal and spent two or three days in your vicinity, I have gone totally out of my mind. For the last three months, I have not been able to concentrate on anything. I am unable to do my work at the office. Even my boss, an Englishman who has great fondness for me, has been repeatedly finding fault with me. "What has happened to you?" he asks. I cancelled my Shimla trip because of you. How could I be happy in Shimla when you were in Delhi? What does it matter whether it is Shimla or Kashmir? Wherever I may go I am never going to be happy without you. Dharini, do you remember how we had planned to go to Kashmir on our honeymoon?'

'My friend! I beg of you, please don't repeat those old stories now. Forget them as you would forget old dreams,' Dharini said.

'You have done so, Dharini. You are lucky. But those old dreams are constantly eating into my mind. I don't know whether they bring me joy or sorrow. Do you remember how once we strolled on the Chowpatty beach in Bombay, and went up to the hanging gardens on the Malabar Hill? After roaming in the garden, we sat on a wooden bench under a bower of creepers. Those creepers were lush with leaves and flowers of many colours. Myriad butterflies fluttered their wings in perpetual motion as they rose from the creepers and went back to settle on them. One of those butterflies perched on your shoulder. I said, "Dharini! Look at this butterfly! It believes you to be a flowering creeper! I won't say it is mistaken!" You shrugged. The butterfly flew away. I said, "When you moved your shoulders, it was as though a creeper was shaken by the gentle breeze." You answered, "I don't like poets comparing women to creepers. How can women live in freedom if they are so weak?" I replied, "It is true that women cannot be free. But why should they be free? Why should the creeper stand alone when it has a tree to bear it?" That was when you said, "Call me creeper, or even a shrub. But don't call yourself a tree!" I said to you, "If I can be lucky enough to bear a creeper like you, I am ready to morph into a tree, right away." You replied, "Take care! Don't come too close to me. I will cast a spell and turn you into a tree!"

"Let me see your spellbinding power!" said I. You glared at me in feigned anger. We went on gazing at each other. As the minutes passed, our faces came closer and closer. Our eyes began to devour one another. Finally, you lost. Getting up swiftly, you broke into tinkling laughter and said, "This tree is scary! It keeps moving closer."

Then we held hands and walked on. Dusk had fallen by the time we came down the garden on the hill and into the streets of Bombay. A song came from a gramophone in a nearby mansion. A film song by Saigal. *"Prem nagar mein banaongi ghar"* ... I said, "This is our song! Let us build our home in the city of love." Dharini! Do you remember those moments? Or, do you dismiss them as a lunatic's ravings?'

Dharini's mind might have melted as she listened to this long speech without interruption. She was unable to respond at once. She hesitated and stammered as she replied, 'I was listening attentively to all that you have said. And no, I have not forgotten. But now I know that we were mistaken. There is no such thing as *prem nagar*, the city of love is not real. It is a city of illusion. The fantasy of poets. Even if it were real, I do not wish to build my home there anymore. Instead, I want to build a home in *seva nagar*, the city of service. Raghavan, if you had seen all that I have seen, if you had experienced all that I have experienced, you too will come to think as I do. You will not waste time in hallucinations of love and romance. Like me, you too will reflect constantly on whether you can reduce the pain of others, just a little.'

'Dharini, can you and I reduce the sufferings of all the people in the world? Are you and I more powerful than God? People are happy or unhappy according to God's decree. What monumental arrogance to think that we can reform the world, reduce the sufferings of the people in the world, and increase their happiness? Why do you talk like that idiot Surya? Did you learn all this from him?' Raghavan expostulated, too aggravated to retain his self-possession.

But Dharini did not lose her composure. 'Why are you so perturbed? There is no need at all to drag Surya's name into this. I had these experiences long before I met him. I arrived at certain decisions. I have not taken up a life of service because of any arrogant belief in my being able to change the world created by God, or because I think I can change human destiny. I find peace and happiness in serving those who suffer. My mind refuses to go into any other direction in life. You declared that for each individual God has decreed a specific pathway to follow. When I met you, at first, I did not realize that our ways were so diametrically different. My brain was clouded in those days. When the clouds disappeared, I perceived the truth. Forgive me. Let me follow my own path.'

'Never! It is now that illusion is clouding your vision. What you saw in those days is the truth. It is also wrong to say that *your* way is different from mine. In Hindu dharma, the man's path is the woman's path. A woman does not have her own individual path to follow.'

'You have acquired a wife who believes completely in what you say, and worships you as someone who is more than God. It is your good fortune, Raghavan. When you talk to me of love, don't you think of Sita at all? Don't you have any pity for a helpless woman who has entrusted herself to you with complete faith? How can you have the heart to betray her?'

'Ah, who betrayed whom? Dharini, you left Madras without informing me. You abandoned me, who had placed complete trust in you! You left a silly letter, which could be misconstrued. I don't know if that was also a deliberate ploy on your part. Did your betrayal end there? No. You had a letter sent to me which made me believe that you had died in the Bihar earthquake. I was forced to marry Sita because of all those betrayals.'

'Let us admit that I did betray you. I did it for appropriate reasons. But you did not marry Sita in the way in which everyone usually gets married. You saw Sita when you went to see another girl and…'

'Yes! I was intoxicated by her and married her! Is this what Sita boasted about? Isn't it enough to show you what a bumpkin she is! Dharini, sometimes I take Sita to parties at the viceroy's mansion, or at the homes of high-ranking officers. All the time I experience the pains of hell. Who knows what solecism she may commit? Every moment I am terrified that she may break a glass, spill tea over herself or babble some nonsense to god-knows-who. And then, I think of you. If you could accompany me to the parties in New Delhi...'

'You are completely wrong! I will be worse than Sita. I know nothing of modern etiquette.'

'It is different with you, Dharini! In a single day I can teach you how to behave at parties. There will be no shame even should you commit a breach of etiquette. If Sita makes a mistake, people will laugh at her. But if you do, they will think that it is the latest trend. If you wear your earring on your nose, the very next day everyone will follow suit. If you spill tea on your saree, everyone will spill tea on their clothes. This attribute is a gift from God.'

'Raghavan, after all this time, you have not understood my nature. You think we can live together.'

'Dharini, don't think your obstinacy will make me draw back. Ask me to give up my job and go to an ashram with you. I will do so, immediately. You have still not understood the depth of my love. I am ready to make any sacrifice for you. You can test me in any way you want.'

'There is only one test that I have for you. If your feelings for me are genuine, guard your wife with loving care. Don't abandon that helpless girl.'

'Who said anything about abandoning her? Let her also be around.'

'Are you saying that I would be the mistress while she, the wedded wife, remains with you for performing the sacred rituals?'

'Chee! Chee! What are you saying! I am not so base. Dharini, I don't care how much ridicule and humiliation I will have to face. I am willing to marry you as well.'

'What! *What!* Can you please say that again?' asked Dharini in astonishment.

'I will marry you with the sacred fire as my witness! All that you have to do is to say yes. I will make all the preparations for the wedding at once.'

'Raghavan! Have you thought about what your wife's opinion may be in this matter?' Dharini asked. Her voice sounded harsh and inflexible.

'I don't care. Can one give up all the pleasures in life for the sake of someone else? Moreover, I'm not saying I don't want her at all. She can also hang around.'

'I see! That is inordinately generous. But think about it this way. What if Sita loves another man and wishes to marry him?'

'Chee! Chee! How can you say such a thing? It is against Hindu dharma.'

'Has Hindu dharma washed its hands off the menfolk so that they can do whatever they please?'

'Yes! Doesn't Hindu dharma permit men to take several wives? Don't many of the Gods have two wives? Krishna had eight!'

'Raghavan! It is true that Krishna had eight wives. But the same Krishna showed his cosmic form to Duryodhana. He covered the whole sun with his discus. Can you do all those things? Look at the avatar of Rama. A role model for human behaviour. He married none other than Sita. Your name is Raghavan. Your wife's name is Sita. Protect your Sita the way Rama protected his Sita. I will say just one more thing. You have still not understood what kind of person your wife is! You cannot find her equal even if you were to search the whole world. Treat her with loving care. That is your life's dharma. It will prove to be good for you.'

'I don't want a lecture on dharma! Listen. I will divorce Sita and leave her free to find someone to marry. Will you then agree to marry me?'

'You are saying this because you are confident that Sita will never leave you, she will remain at your feet in total surrender. Never mind Sita for now. Once you had great devotion for your mother. Did you think about how she would react to this?'

'My mother wanted a daughter-in-law who would be meek and mild-mannered. She has found such a girl. What more can she want? Yes, I do respect my mother. But I cannot always be her slave. She does not have the right to ruin my life. Dharini, these are my final words. Listen to me. Cancel your trip to Lahore. Think about us and arrive at a decision. If a journey has to be made, let us make it together. I will take you to Kashmir and Dehradun and Darjeeling and Ooty. Then

I will take you to London, Paris, Vienna and Naples. After travelling across Europe, let us go to America. Let us go to San Francisco, New York, Washington, Los Angeles! Dharini, what do you say?'

'I repeat what I said at the beginning. Your goals in life are different from mine. Never can they meet. Take Sita to all the places you have mentioned. That is also what is good for you,' Dharini said.

Raghavan stared at Dharini in astonishment. Then, he laughed angrily as if he had come to a decision.

'Dharini, I know why you say this. I also know who has captivated you and made you reject me. This is the work of that rascal Surya! A few days ago, I obtained a licence for a gun…'

'Raghavan, don't sully your tongue with meaningless abuse! Don't try to frighten me either. After seeing the earthquake in Bihar, I am no longer afraid of death.'

'Again, you misunderstand me! I did not say that I was going to shoot you dead. I wanted to say that I will shoot myself with the revolver and die.'

'I don't care about my death or anybody else's death. What does the Bhagavad Gita say? You can kill the body but not the soul.'

'Dharini, only now have I come to know your true nature. You are not a woman. You are a fiend! Your beauty is like the beauty of the demoness Surpanakha… All right. I will see how Surya and you get into the train tomorrow!'

Raghavan left the room with this vow.

As soon as he left, the tears that had been welling up in Dharini's eyes until then, came rushing down in a deluge.

PART THREE
VOLCANO

1

THE VENDOR OF JOSS STICKS

A horse cart clattered along the main street of Devapattinam town with a young passenger seated inside. His turban of multi-coloured stripes with dangling tassels suggested that he was a vendor from India's central provinces. The tin trunk and bundle of cloth beside him confirmed this assumption.

The cart stopped in front of advocate Atmanatha Iyer's house. The young man paid the cartman before picking up his luggage and dismounting from the vehicle.

'*Seth!* Shall I wait? Will you be coming soon… *jaldi*?' asked the cartman. The young man answered, '*Nahi, tum jao!*'

The vendor stood outside the grilled iron gate. Seeing a young woman inside, the man called out, 'Amma! Will you buy joss sticks? Attar, musk, sandalwood powder? Benares silks?'

The voice of a young woman answered, 'No! Go away!'

'Why are you so determined about turning us all away? Everyone said that there is a sixtieth birthday celebration in this house tomorrow!' said the young man as he opened the grilled gate and entered the house.

Between the gate and the front door were several attractively coloured croton plants, a manoranjitam shrub and a pannir tree.

Two women were standing near the front pyol – one young, the other old. 'Listen to this! The child is going to turn one, and he says we are celebrating his sixtieth birthday!' the young woman said and laughed loudly.

The older woman said, 'Look at him striding in, bold as brass! We must keep the gate locked!'

The young man barged in and exclaimed, 'Arey baap re! Looks like the fragrance of the flowers here would beat my attar, musk and sandalwood hollow!'

Placing his trunk and bundle on the pyol, he opened the box saying, 'Amma! Don't you really want joss sticks, attar, musk and sandalwood powder?' The heady fragrance of incense filled the air.

'Lalita! The joss sticks seem to be very good. Why not buy some?' Lalita's mother, Sarasvati Ammal asked.

'No need!' said Lalita to her mother as she ordered the man, 'Take them away!'

'Don't be so curt, chinnamma! Listen to what periamma says!' the vendor said and turned to ask Sarasvati Ammal. 'Has Kitta Iyer arrived from the village? Has his older son Gangadharan come too?'

'What! You seem to know everyone! Who are you?' Sarasvati Ammal asked.

'Times have changed indeed! What to do? His own mother cannot recognize her son!' remarked the vendor and removed the multi-coloured turban on his head.

'Amma, it is Surya Anna!' Lalita shrieked.

'O my darling boy!' Sarasvati Ammal cried and hugged him.

'Surya! Why this dreadful disguise?' Lalita asked.

'Just thought I'd amuse you!' Surya answered.

Sarasvati Ammal said quickly, 'Amuse us! What nonsense! Lalita's father-in-law will be back from the court anytime now. He will find it strange indeed if he sees you in this garb! Your father and brother are arriving tonight. Go and get out of these clothes at once!'

'All right. But I need to be left alone for half an hour to change. Lalita, isn't your husband's room upstairs free?' Surya asked.

Before Lalita could reply, Sarasvati Ammal said, 'Yes, it is free. But this girl doesn't let anyone enter it. She has put up her husband's photograph on the wall. One of her daily rituals now is stringing a flower garland to adorn that photograph! Even the legendary Savitri would not have done such penance for Satyavan! Surya, you know the news, don't you?'

'You mean mapillai's imprisonment? How can I not know about it? But I was surprised all the same to see it in the newspaper. I never imagined that our Pattabhi would dare to go so far!' said Surya.

'Surya! He did not go to jail for setting fire to the court, derailing train tracks or demolishing bridges. On the second of last October, on Gandhiji's birthday, he addressed a public meeting where he condemned the Mahatma's imprisonment. They arrested him and threw him into prison,' Lalita explained.

'I don't know when these problems are going to end. It is all my misfortune. Surya! Look at you! You are wandering from place to place. I found such a good household to give Lalita in marriage. And this is what is written in her destiny!' Sarasvati Ammal said sadly.

'Amma, why don't we keep our grumblings for later? Let Surya get his business done before everyone turns up,' Lalita said.

'Lalita, can I occupy your husband's room for two days?'

'Of course, you can! Don't I know how close you are to him! Who has a greater right to occupy his room?' Lalita said.

Surya mounted the stairs with his trunk and bundle and entered Pattabhiraman's room. The room was in apple-pie order. The desk with its ink bottle and pen, the bookshelf, the coat stand, everything was spotless. Even the corners of the room were dust free. As Sarasvati Ammal had mentioned, there was a photograph of Pattabhiraman hanging on the wall, and a portrait of Mahatma Gandhi on the opposite side. Both were ornamented with freshly strung garlands of flowers. The room was suffused with the scent of jasmine blossoms.

Looking at Lalita who had come up to show him in, Surya remarked, 'Lalita, you have given your husband a status that is equal to Mahatma Gandhi! Now we will have to call him "Mahatma" Pattabhiraman!'

'Mahatma Gandhi is the greatest living soul in the world. So, I worship him. Your friend is my God. I worship him as well,' Lalita said.

'I applaud your devotion. Lalita, it seems your mother-in-law is no more.'

'It is two years since she passed away. If she had been alive last year, she would have been broken-hearted to see her son go to jail. I have a heart of stone. That is why I am still alive. Anna, I am ashamed to think of having complained about my mother-in-law. Only later did I come to know of her affection for me. I also understood that all the faults she had found in me were for my own good. My mother-in-law died holding my hand. She didn't show as much concern even for her own son!'

'Lalita, that is the way of the world. Those we consider to be amiable, turn out to be nasty. Those who are nasty change into good persons. Who expected Sita's husband Saundara Raghavan to be such an abominable man? Amma talked about your unhappy fate! She would have known what it really means if you had been married to Saundara Raghavan instead of Pattabhi. Ayo! My heart breaks when I think of all the sufferings Sita is undergoing!'

'Yes, Anna! You must tell me all about it. The letters she wrote when she first went to Delhi were so full of euphoria. As time went on, they became less frequent. Her last letters were steeped in sorrow. It seems she has sent her child to Madras with her mother-in-law. Why?'

'I will tell you later. Sita's life has turned into hell. Your situation is far better! How is your father-in-law?'

'My father-in-law treats me as if I am someone to be protected even from the blowing winds. I am the mistress of this household. I have all the keys. I didn't want a birthday celebration for the child tomorrow. Why perform the rites when his father is in jail, I said. My father-in-law declared, "No! This is the first male child of the house! His first birthday *must* be celebrated." My husband too wrote the same thing from prison.'

'What about the misunderstanding between your family and the people in the opposite house? Are you still not on visiting terms?'

'Two days ago, Amarnath and his wife Chitra came from Calcutta. Tomorrow, I am thinking of asking for my father-in-law's permission to go and invite them. How meaningless to have a celebration without inviting neighbours!'

'Do that, Lalita! You must certainly go and invite them. I am thinking of going there tonight. Do you know how many nights your husband, Amarnath and I have spent on the open terrace in the opposite house, in cheerful camaraderie? Can't understand how such close friends can turn into enemies overnight!'

'This is all the work of the old men. My husband kept quiet out of respect for his father.'

At that moment, little Sundu, now a well grown young man – rushed panting up the stairs. Astonished by the sight of Surya he yelled, 'Ayyayo! Is this Surya! Why, he has a moustache!'

'Sundu! Don't you like my moustache? In that case I will remove it before I do anything else,' said Surya. He removed his north Indian garments as well and appeared like the familiar Surya in veshti and jibba.

2

'LET JAPAN COME!'

When Surya went to the opposite house at 8 p.m., Amarnath was standing outside as if he was expecting him.

'Welcome! Welcome! May the freedom fighter Surya's arrival be welcome!' Amarnath joked as he caught Surya by the hand and took him inside.

In the living room, a young woman was sitting on the sofa, embroidering flowers. Amarnath looked at her and said, 'Chitra! May I introduce my dear friend to you. Surya! This is Chitra, the lucky girl who married me. An extremely skilled artist. If she draws a squirrel, it almost resembles a goat.'

Surya asked laughingly, 'And when she draws a goat…?'

'It looks like Amarnath,' Chitra retorted.

'See, Surya! Doesn't this prove that Amarnath resides permanently in this lady's heart? Lucky me!' Amarnath said.

Chitra responded, 'Nowadays it is so difficult to find houses on rent. How convenient it will be if everyone can reside in someone's heart!'

Listening to their merry banter, Surya thought they made an exemplary couple. He said, 'Amarnath, what Lalita said about your wife is absolutely true.'

'Who is Lalita?' Chitra asked.

'What do you mean? My sister Lalita who lives in the opposite house.'

'I see! You mean the daughter-in-law of the enemy? It has been many years since I met her. How could she have described me?' Chitra asked.

'She wrote saying that you were great friends.'

'Not at all. Are we not enemies for life?'

'Surya! Chitra is furious about the misunderstanding between the two houses, which arose during the municipal elections. It makes her rail like this,' Amarnath said.

'I am not angry. I only pity the human beings who behave in this manner. If the people of the Tamil realm want to learn how to live, they must go to Calcutta and live among the Bengalis for at least two years,' Chitra said.

'I don't agree. What is it that the Tamil people must learn from others?' Surya asked.

Amarnath said, 'Listen Surya! I went to Calcutta mainly because I found it impossible to manage her here after the election fracas. Now I wish I hadn't! She has become obsessed with Bengali culture. She has completely lost it after hearing that Netaji Subhash Chandra Bose has established an independent Indian government in the Malay country. If only she can get an aircraft, she will fly away to Netaji, leaving me bereft.'

Hearing footsteps at the entrance Chitra got up and began to go up the stairs saying to Amarnath, 'Your father is here.'

'Lalita will come to invite you for the birthday tomorrow. You must certainly come,' Surya said.

The young men got up when Damodaram Pillai came in. 'Appa, see who is here! Can you recognize him?' Amarnath asked.

'O! Is it our Surya? Perhaps I am wrong. Getting old. Can't see too clearly,' Damodaram Pillai said.

'Yes, Appa. It is Surya. Surya himself,' Amarnath assured him.

'Namaskaram!' Surya said.

Instead of going straight to his office room as the young men expected, Damodaram Pillai sat down on the sofa. When the young men took their seats, he looked intently at Surya.

'Yes, it is Surya indeed! Oy! Surya Narayana Iyer! They said you were somewhere in Afghanistan. Then they said you were sighted in Moscow. Then it was announced that you had reached Saigon. But here you are, in our own town! What is the state of India's independence? Where have you parked it now?'

'Mama, I am happy that I have been in your thoughts, enough for you to have made Inquiries about my whereabouts! But I did not go to any foreign country. India's independence is right here in India. Why go to Afghanistan to find it?' Surya said.

'Oy Surya Narayana Iyer, isn't Netaji Subhash Chandra Bose reputed to have established an independent Indian government in Malaya? They also say that Jayaprakash Narayan has established it in Nepal or Tibet. All lies?'

Amarnath said, 'Honestly speaking, India's independence is being established in Ahmednagar jail by Mahatma Gandhi, Jawaharlal Nehru and the other leaders.'

'Surya Narayana Iyer, do you agree with Amarnath?'

'Mama, I will answer only if you call me Surya.'

'All right, Surya, now tell me. How and in what way will India achieve independence?' Damodaram Pillai asked.

'Cannot say! It may come through in any way, and in every way. But when it does, the people must be ready to seize it. Now our priority is to prepare the people for independence,' Surya said.

'An impossible task! Surya, do you know the only way in which we can prepare our people for independence? The Japanese must invade with an army, conquer India, and rule it for at least ten years. The Japs must grab everyone by their tuft, give them a good shake and wipe out all differences of caste and creed. All those who have been burping away after meals of rice and lentils must be forced to eat fish and meat. Ten years of Japanese rule and India will start deserving independence. What do you say?'

'I don't agree. If we stay under Japanese rule for ten years, we will have to endure another 140 years of the same. But I don't think the Japanese are imbeciles. Instead of trying to conquer India, they will try to establish India's independence by helping Netaji Subhash Chandra Bose. It is more expedient for Japan to have India's friendship than to conquer this country and rule it themselves.'

'You know what is expedient for Japan. But does Japan know it? A man got scared by a barking dog. Another asked him, "Don't you know the saying that a barking dog never bites?" To which the first man replied, "I do. But does the dog know it?" Likewise, will Japan know its advantage in supporting Netaji!'

'Fifty thousand men have joined Netaji's army. It is Japan that has armed them,' Amarnath said.

'Is that such a great number? Can the whole of India be captured by fifty thousand?' Damodaram Pillai asked.

'If Netaji comes with fifty thousand, there will be lakhs of men to join them here!' Surya said.

'In Bengal alone fifty lakh will join. All of Calcutta is talking incessantly about it,' Amarnath said.

'Let fifty lakh, why, let fifty crore join the army. Let Netaji come to New Delhi and crown himself emperor. I have no objections! But anticipating the arrival of Netaji at some unspecified date in the future, some scoundrels are now indulging in acts of sabotage here. A completely asinine thing to do! Why not wait until Japan arrives? Why start derailing trains and destroying bridges? Acts of sabotage are not only crimes against the government, they are crimes against the people. If I were the judge, I would sentence such saboteurs with capital punishment.'

As Damodaram Pillai talked on, Surya's face lost its brightness and became dark. Amarnath noticed this change. Surya knew that Amarnath had noticed it. Whereupon he looked at Amarnath as if he expected some assurance from him. Amarnath's eyes gave him that assurance.

3
BIRTHDAY RAID

Young Balasubramanian's first birthday celebrations began with the resounding music of pipes and drums. Everyone in the house was happy. Surya's unexpected arrival inspired this buoyancy. Kitta Iyer and his wife were thrilled to see their son after such a long time. Lalita's elation was obvious. She almost forgot her husband's incarceration as she bustled about getting things done.

Atmanatha Iyer, Lalita's father-in-law, was extremely happy that due to Surya's arrival, friendly relations had been resumed with Damodaram Pillai.

Surya too was happy as he had never been before. Gone were his doubts about how he may be received by his family. Amarnath had not forgotten his friendship, and Damodaram Pillai had been all bonhomie in chatting with him. This enhanced his glee. That was not all. His elder brother Gangadharan who had fought so fiercely with him, now spoke to Surya with affection. 'Surya, Appa has grown old. He is not able to manage the lands. It is not possible for me to give up my job to go and live in the village. It is enough for you to have wandered for five years. You must settle down in Rajampettai and be of help to father. Do what you will about the labourers. Come home!' These words amazed and delighted Surya. He repeatedly asked himself why everyone was so kind to him.

Seeing him being made much of by everyone, Lalita's first child, Pattu, very quickly became his friend. She sat on Surya's lap and refused to get off.

In the morning, just as Surya was feeling happier than he had been for a long time, the postman arrived. His voice sounded familiar to Surya. Lalita said, 'Anna, do you know? Postman Balakrishnan has been transferred to this town. It is he who delivers the post on this street.' Before she could finish, Surya heard Balakrishnan inquire, 'Is anyone named K.S. Narayanan visiting this house?'

Surya came out and said, 'Balakrishnan, how are you? Do you remember me?'

'So, it's you, sir! That's what I thought. How are things? What's the news? When did you come? Please see if this letter is for you,' said Balakrishnan and held out a letter.

Seeing that it had been addressed in Dharini's hand, Surya took it eagerly and said, 'Yes. It is for me.'

'I see! You have shortened K. Surya Narayana Iyer to K.S. Narayanan. Just what I thought! There is a letter for Lalita Amma too.' Seeing Lalita come up, he handed the mail to her with, 'Here's your letter. Is today your son's first birthday? It seems as if the wedding at Rajampettai took place only yesterday!'

Then he looked at Surya and said, 'Sir! Do you remember how we fought beside the sluice gate? You were angry with me for opening the letter to your aunt!'

'What about it? It happened so long ago,' Surya said.

'I mentioned it only to tell you that I did not open the letter that I just handed to you. Do you understand?'

At once Surya turned the letter over in his hand, looking at it carefully and suspiciously.

With a smile Balakrishnan asked, 'Why, sir? Has it been opened?'

'No,' said Surya.

'That's what I said. I am not responsible for any such thing. Don't let old memories make you doubt me, understand? Lalita Amma! Nor did I tamper with your letter. Mr Surya is suspicious by nature! But he must not suspect me. Shall I take my leave?'

'Postman! Please come for lunch this afternoon!' Lalita invited Balakrishnan.

'Those days are over. Now I too bear the burdens of a family. I will get told off if I don't go home for lunch. Never mind lunch, Amma. A good heart is what we need. That's all. Mr Surya, don't think I opened your letter and read it. Got it? Lalita Amma, know what I'm saying?' Balakrishnan said as he strode away.

When he left, Surya said, 'Why, Balakrishnan seems to be more cracked than before. Still babbling nonsense.'

'That is not babbling, Anna. Nor is he a crackpot. Haven't you understood what he meant?'

'Can there be any meaning in his drivel?' Surya asked.

'Why not? I am surprised that you don't know this. Maybe it is not prevalent in the north. From the time my husband went to prison all the letters I get are opened and read before they are sent to me. They say it is called censoring.'

Surya was disconcerted. He examined the letter on both sides and said confidently, 'No one has opened my letter.'

'How do you know that it has not been opened? Some letters are openly checked and labelled "Censored". Others are opened surreptitiously and sealed without revealing that they have been checked. I get letters of both kinds.'

'They may do that with your husband's letters from prison. Why would they open my letter?'

'They may have opened it because it is addressed to this house. Nor are you beyond suspicion. You are involved in seditious activities, aren't you? We can never make out whether any mail has been opened. But Balakrishnan knows it at once. From what he let fall, I think both our letters have been censored. Anyway, let's read them.'

Lalita broke open the envelope. Her face bloomed when she saw that it was from her husband. 'He has timed it to reach us on the child's first birthday. How wonderful it would have been to have had him here! How happy he would have been to see you!' she said and went in to answer her mother's call.

Surya opened the letter he had received. His perplexities vanished as he read it. It was Dharini's letter. She would not have written anything that would be useful to the CID. Members of the revolutionary group did not mention their names when they wrote to each other. Everyone had a sobriquet. Dharini was 'History'. Surya was 'Messenger'. With so many precautions having been taken, what could the CID glean by censoring his letter?

As Surya had surmised, Dharini's letter held nothing that could be useful to the CID. But there was something in it to arouse Surya's anxiety. 'Athanga's situation has worsened, both physical and mental. She wants to meet you. Come as soon as you can. Things may end in disaster if you don't come at once, History.'

The letter disconcerted Surya. It could not be said that he had accomplished the work for which he had come down south. Now he had to go back hoping to finish it later. Ah, what a problem this was proving to be! Why should he have an athanga to spoil all his endeavours? That brute, her husband; what kind of a man was he? It was impossible to gauge how Sita's life was going to end.

Priests, family members and friends began to arrive for the first birthday ceremony. Surya went into the house.

The vedic rituals began. Women sang auspicious songs. The nadaswaram party played splendidly. Surya became so wholeheartedly involved in the ceremony that he almost forgot his athanga's problems and the work that had brought him down south.

In the opposite house, at 10.30 a.m., Damodaram Pillai sat reading in his office room. The telephone rang. He picked up the receiver and said, 'Hello! Damodaram Pillai here. Police station? What's the matter…? Opposite house? I don't even step into it! You know it very well… No, I didn't see… Don't know… I don't know anything… Come! Come! Please do come! I will watch all the fun from my own house…'

After replacing the receiver Damodaram Pillai looked up and remained pensive for a few minutes. Then he called Amarnath.

Amarnath came into the room.

'Looks as if you are going out,' he said.

'Yes, Appa! Chitra and I were just going to the opposite house. We can go, can't we?'

'Certainly, you can go. I have no objections. But there's this to think about.'

'What's there to think about? Chitra and I are definitely going. In all fairness, you should come too. How long should we feed this rancour in our minds?'

'No! No! Rancour must not be allowed to fester. Honestly, I too was planning to come to the ceremony. But now there is an obstacle…'

'What obstacle, Appa?'

'It looks as though the town police have received some information about your friend Surya…'

Startled, Amarnath exclaimed, 'What! What!'

'Yes. Some information from the CID about Surya. Just now the DSP called and asked me, "Do you know if a boy called Surya has come to the house opposite yours?"'

'What did you say?'

'I said, "Don't you know that there's a lifelong enmity between me and the people in the opposite house!" He asked, "Didn't you see a young newcomer at the entrance of their house?" I retorted, "Do you think I have nothing to do but watch people coming and going on the street?"'

'And then?'

'Then what? The police will be here soon. There will be an uproar in the opposite house. If I am seen there what I said to the DSP will be proven false.'

'Appa! What is to be done now? Shouldn't Surya be warned?'

'That is up to you. I have told you what had to be told. Take the appropriate steps. One thing though. The warning must be given immediately. The police will be here in 15 minutes. If they arrest him and take him away, they will make him spill the truths he doesn't even know… Even in your dreams you cannot imagine how barbaric the police can be. Do you understand?'

'Appa! I get the shivers as you talk about it. But what is the use of a mere warning at this point? You say that the police will be here in 15 minutes. How can he escape before that? Where can he hide?'

'Don't ask me! How can he find a hiding place all of a sudden? Unless some neighbour comes to his aid?'

'Appa, forgive me. Can I shelter Surya in this house?'

'Asking me again? You have as much right in this house as I do. Do what you think best. If you like, lock him up in the back room upstairs and lose the key. But it is all on you, understand?'

In no time at all, Amarnath got out and went to the opposite house. In five minutes, he returned with Surya, took him upstairs and locked him up in the back room as his father had suggested.

A few minutes later, the roar of a motor cycle was heard on the street. With it came a jeep. Policemen came marching from both sides of the street. A police van with a barred cage for transporting criminals accompanied them.

Police jawans surrounded Atmanatha Iyer's house. A few moments passed in shrieks and confusion.

The brahmin priests stopped chanting mantras and came running out. The police walloped them with their lathis and drove them back into the house. An authoritarian voice bellowed, 'Don't let anyone get away.'

The nadaswaram group tried to make its exit. In consequence, the tavil drum was torn on both sides, while the nadaswaram pipes and the cymbals were broken into a hundred pieces.

When the police officers entered the house, Kitta Iyer stood on the threshold. He guessed that they had come to capture his son. But he did not know that the bird had flown. He stood majestically with his hands folded across his chest and declared, 'Vedic rituals are being performed inside. No one must enter. You will have to step on my dead body to do that.' Before he could finish, he was slammed on the head and shoved by the neck.

Atmanatha Iyer came forward to say, 'Why, sir? Why are you creating such a racket? Search calmly and take whomever you want. No one is stopping you. Don't frighten the women unnecessarily.' His pacific remark brought him beatings on the head.

The police clattered into the house. They searched every room, in front and at the back, upstairs and downstairs. They kicked everything, they broke and shattered everything that they laid their hands on. They thrashed everyone on their way. They entered the bedrooms and slashed the beds and pillows. They went into the store room and broke all the pots and pans. They rushed into the kitchen and stirred the boiling sambar with their lathis. But the man they sought could not be found.

The women ran amok crying in bewilderment. The children screamed their heads off.

By this time Kitta Iyer managed to pull himself up, come inside and shout, 'Keep quiet, all of you. Let things happen as they will. There is a God above.'

At first, mistaking Gangadharan to be their prey, the police gave him a few beatings. But they let him go, as the tuft on his head proclaimed that he was not the insurgent they sought.

Having been needlessly lammed, Gangadharan hollered, 'I knew it way back when. Didn't I say don't let that scoundrel into the house? Did you listen to me? You coddled your darling son. He is nothing but the devil himself. Doesn't he always bring trouble with him?'

The police searched the house thoroughly but to no purpose. The man they looked for could not be found in any room or cupboard, sacks of rice, or inside the cooking vessels, or in pillows and beds. Some police jawans tapped the floor to check for an underground passage. After half an hour's tumult, the police were ordered to withdraw.

Damodaram Pillai stood outside his house and watched the pandemonium in the opposite house. His face sparked fire.

He saw the police coming out empty-handed. Going up to his friend, the DSP, he said, 'I am ashamed of what you did today. What satisfaction do you get out of beating these brahmins? Should you not display your valour to the Japanese?'

'Mr Pillai, you don't know what you are talking about. We received information that a saboteur had come to this house. There was a plot to blow up the bridge across the river Kaveri with bombs...'

'Yes, they have demolished the Kaveri bridge. Go, Sir! Should I talk about their brains? Or about your brutality? Is this the way to win loyalty for the British Raj? All right... did you find the boy you wanted?'

'He is not in this house. But he must be in this town. We will catch him somehow,' said the DSP.

Making a spectacular din, the motor cycle, jeep and the policemen armed with lathis left the street.

From Atmanatha Iyer's house came the sound of Lalita's sobs, mingled with the wailing of her two children.

4

THE YOUNG RENUNCIATE

The clock struck ten. The night sky was shrouded by black clouds. It was drizzling continuously. Cold winds were blowing.

All the lights had been switched off in Damodaram Pillai's house. Darkness and silence reigned within.

A motor car glided from the lane nearby and stood in front of Damodaram Pillai's house. A shadowy form emerged from the dark house. In the dim streetlight it appeared to be that of a young ascetic in saffron robes, water jug in hand. The monk stood near the pyol, looked up and down and across the street. Seeing no one, he jumped into the car. The car started moving noiselessly. When it crossed the streets of Devapattinam to reach the road beyond, Amarnath who was driving the car broke the silence, 'Thank God! We have escaped. Nothing to fear now.'

'I will be afraid so long as I am in this car. Once I get down it will be all right. When I think of how you risked danger for my sake…'

'You seem to think that you are the only man in the entire country who has any daring.'

'Amarnath, I am prepared to be arrested at any moment. Someday I will *have* to get arrested. It is different for you. If you suffer because of me…'

'It is not I who suffered for your sake. Those who did were your father, brother and your sister's father-in-law. They got a sound thrashing today. Your mother and sister were anguished beyond measure. Consoling them became an impossible task for me.'

'I am ashamed to think of it. What must they be thinking of me for taking off and leaving them to suffer?'

'They will be happy that you managed to escape. Even now all that they are worried about is your safety.'

'All said and done, what I did today was shameful. My conscience would not have allowed me to hide knowing that they were being beaten. If the letter from Delhi about Sita had not reached me, I would have given myself up to the police.'

'No one would have been happy about that – including my father.'

'I am astounded by the sympathy Damodaram showed towards me!'

'Why do you think he did it?'

'What else but the fact that I am your friend?'

'No, British losses in Singapore have brought about a change in our people. From little kids to old codgers, everyone has come to believe that the British Raj is going to quit India.'

'How is this connected to your father's helping me?'

'If the Englishman leaves India tomorrow, who will gain authority? Perhaps revolutionaries like you? My father came to your help thinking that it would be smart to load half his cargo on *this* ship.'

'What is the use of loading any cargo on a leaking ship like me? But I will never accept your reasoning. He must have done this because I am your friend, and he is fond of me.'

'Let us say you are right. What did you say about your athanga?'

'Didn't the mapillai who came to see my sister Lalita insist that he liked Sita and got married to her? Do you remember how that romance became a nine-days' wonder for us? That marriage has ended in disaster. They are going at each other all the time, hammer and tongs.'

'You exaggerate, Surya. In our country, ninety-nine out of hundred couples fight incessantly. Does it mean that they are not happy? Chitra and I fight at least half a dozen times each day.'

'Amarnath, your quarrels are lovers' quarrels, fun fights. It is different with Sita and Saundara Raghavan. Their life is like a partnership between a cat and a mouse.'

'Saundara Raghavan has travelled abroad. He occupies a high post in the government. He might have wanted his wife to adopt an ultra-modern "English" style. Your athanga may not have been amenable to it. I know many ICS officers who have cast their wives aside for this reason.'

'Sita cannot be faulted here. She might have hesitated at first. But later, if Raghavan took one step forward, Sita took two. I feared that athanga had gone too far in this direction. But this did not change things. Saundara Raghavan is becoming more and more brutal.'

'Now I know the reason. At first, when they are newly married, our young men want their wives to be sociable and modern. Later, they come to dislike it. They begin to think that women must follow Hindu dharma and remain modest, reticent. But by then, the women don't want to go back to the old ways. Listen to me, Surya, don't interfere! In course of time, things between them will automatically get better.'

'Amarnath, my aunt, who had suffered all her life, requested me on her deathbed to take care of her orphaned daughter. I cannot forget it,' Surya said.

When the car drove through the bends on the road, its headlights beamed on a land brimming with water. The Kaveri was flowing at a little distance.

'I have seen many parts of the north, completely parched and dry. Nothing like this. A land so munificently enriched by water,' Surya exclaimed.

'You haven't come to Bengal, Surya! It is more fertile than Tamil Nadu. During the monsoon, it is water, water everywhere.'

'But you say there is a famine in that land!' Surya exclaimed.

'That's what makes it weird. Those who come to Calcutta from the rural regions are dying on the streets.'

'But you are returning to Calcutta when things are in this state?'

'I have my job there! Also, it doesn't mean that the forty lakh people in Calcutta are dying without food just because there is a famine in Bengal.'

'I know! Actually, there is dearth of money, not of rice. A few rascals have hoarded it all. The poor and the powerless are sacrificed on the altar of their greed. Isn't that so, Amarnath?'

'Our country has greedy devils. And you say you want total freedom for this country.'

'On the day the Englishman goes away from India, all these evils will disappear with him. Aren't they but the evil consequences of British rule?'

'Tell me honestly, do you believe that the Englishman will ever leave India?' Amarnath asked.

'Certainly, I do. I have travelled from Kashmir to Kanyakumari. Amarnath! Bengal is the only place I haven't visited. Everywhere I went, I saw how the masses are seething. The country is like a huge volcano. We don't know exactly when this volcano will erupt and spew lava. All that is needed is a catalysing incident to make it explode. Forty crore people will rise up in rage and launch a revolution. The blaze will reduce the British Raj to ashes.'

'Enough, Surya! Enough! It is cold outside but your words have increased the temperature in this car... There! Mylampatti station! And now we must part ways,' said Amarnath.

The lights were twinkling in the distance. A small building, a semaphore and other signs of a railway station could be seen dimly. Amarnath had brought Surya to this out-of-the-way station as it would have been dangerous for him to board the train at the Devapattinam junction.

The car came to a halt under a tree. Luckily, the rain had dwindled to a drizzle. Surya opened the door and got down from the vehicle.

'Surya, you look exactly like Swami Vivekananda right now. People who see you will think that you are an eminent young monk,' Amarnath said.

'I am nothing but a fraud. I feel rueful about having to assume this sacred garment as a disguise.'

'But do you think it is sufficient? Will the CID tigers be fooled by this disguise?' Amarnath asked as he got down from the car.

'Cannot say. South Indians are good at every job, they make clever CIDs as well. I have travelled across great distances in the north! But it was in Devapattinam that they spotted me. What happens afterwards does not matter so long as I can make it to Delhi,' Surya said.

Shaking Surya's hand, Amarnath said, 'I feel bad to leave you here, Surya. Come to Calcutta as soon as your work in Delhi is over. Calcutta is a paradise for rebels! Even if you were to trip over policemen, they would not catch you. Come and stay with me. You have my Calcutta address, don't you?'

'Yes, I will, and I do remember your address,' said Surya. A lightning flashed. The tears in his eyes shone like pearls.

Amarnath said nothing more but reversed the car and drove away.

Surya walked alone in the dark and reached the railway station. The station master, the clerk and the two porters on night duty were astonished by the glow on his face. 'Where is swami coming from? Where is he going?' they asked. But all their questions met with a single response from the holy man, '*Hara hara Mahadeva*!' The southbound train arrived. The swami went to the platform. The porter at the gate wanted to stop him. But the station master said, 'Don't! Don't stop the swami!'

The swami hastened to the train, now standing on the platform. He had the second-class ticket that Amarnath had purchased for him at the Devapattinam station. But he went looking for a third-class compartment. In most of them, the windows had been shut against the rain. The swami got into a compartment which had a few windows open. One of the double seats was occupied by a single passenger. A diary and pencil lay beside him. The swami stood next to the unoccupied seat and intoned, 'Hara hara Mahadeva!' The man looked up and said, 'Please take this seat, swami!'

The swami sat down, pulled out a little pouch tucked at his waist, took a pinch of sacred ash from it, smeared it over the man's forehead and intoned, 'Muruga!'

The man asked, 'Where is Swami going?'

'Returning from Kasi. Want to go to Rameshwaram. Who knows what Murugan's grace will decree?'

'Does swami have a ticket?' the man asked.

'Up to Madurai. A devotee purchased it. Beyond that, it is as Muruga wills!' said the swami and showed his ticket to the man.

'This is a second-class ticket! Swami got into a third-class carriage by mistake.'

Speaking of himself in the third person, the holy man declared, 'We knew what we were doing. Even if a devotee had purchased it, we do not want to travel second-class. When the train stopped at this station, we got down from the second-class and boarded the third-class.'

The man was flummoxed.

'This is what a true renunciate should be! Nowadays so many fake swamis abound,' he said.

'All in God's hands!' the swami replied.

The train chugged on. Outside, the drizzling continued. The passengers were swaying in their sleep.

But neither swami nor his newfound devotee could sleep.

'My son, your mind is full of anxiety,' the swami said.

'Yes, swami. My wife is not well. I have been taking her to the hospital for a month. No improvement. And then I was given this duty.'

The swami pulled out his pouch saying, 'This is sacred ash from the Viswanatha temple in Kasi. Take this and smear it on your wife's forehead. She will get well.'

The man accepted the ash with reverence, tore a page from his diary, placed the ash on it and wrapped it up.

'Is that the only worry you have?'

'Nothing serious. If I succeed in the task I am engaged in, I will get a promotion. Otherwise, it will be a black mark.'

'Aren't you searching for someone?' the swami asked.

'True! True! Does the swami possess foresight?'

'Muruga's blessings!' said the swami.

'Will I find the man I am looking for?'

'How can we know?' asked the swami. Then, tapping his forehead he added, 'It appears that the man is right here on this train.'

'There are five hundred passengers on this train. What can you do if you are asked to find someone without being given any information about his physical appearance? Swami, nothing can be worse than a government job, particularly in the CID force!' said the new disciple.

'True, my son, true! Give up this dreadful job! By Muruga's grace you will find another, a better one.'

The train reached Dindugal junction. The man said to the young renunciate, 'I will get down and search in one or two more compartments. Please stay right here and hold my seat for me. Swami need not worry about the ticket from Madurai to Rameshwaram. I will buy it for you in Madurai.'

'Having or not having a ticket is all the same to one who gets in or out of trains according to God's command,' the holy man replied.

Within ten minutes, CID Keshavan returned with a railway officer. He was surprised to see the seat empty. He ran here and there to check if he had perhaps made a mistake with the compartment. He asked the sleepy passengers if anyone had seen the young monk who had been sitting there. Everyone said, 'No!' The whistle blew. It was time for the train to leave. The officer shouted at Keshavan and departed. Keshavan got into the train and took his old seat. 'Muruga's will!' said he as he extracted from his pocket the little packet with sacred ash from the Viswanatha temple in Kasi. He opened it and smeared some of the ash on his forehead.

5

THE SECRET OF SUCCESS

In the bungalow named Devi Sadanam, situated in Padmapuram colony, the crowning glory of Madras city, Rao Bahadur Padmalochana Sastri appeared to be rage incarnate.

He was pouring onto the page all the diabolic, vicious, monstrous, malevolent fury surging in his heart. The article he was writing for an English magazine was so inflammatory that the paper threatened to burst into flames.

A colossal polemical battle was being fought between Padmalochana Sastri and Professor Parivrajaka Sharma in the columns of the same magazine. The root cause of this war was a lecture delivered by Padmalochana Sastri at the Sarvagna Sangam in Padmapuram.

In that lecture, Sastri had analysed the concept of the varnashrama system in Hindu society, which divides the four stages of human life as those of the student, householder, retiree and renunciate. Pointing out that western countries struggled with horrendous tribulations and wars only because they failed to follow the varnashrama system, Sastri dwelt at great length on the glories of the final stage of sanyasa, renunciation. When a man knew that his life was about to end, it was best for him to turn into a monk.

In general, all these ideas would have been wholly acceptable to Professor Parivrajaka Sharma. But it became his indispensable duty to attack them because they had been delivered by Sastri and widely covered by the press.

Sharma's long letter declared, 'The Hindus of the ancient age did not give any great importance to renunciation. A man without a wife had no right to perform ritual sacrifices. Only after Gautama Buddha did renunciation come to be exalted in India. Those who are afraid that their sons will not perform death rites for them adopt renunciation as an eleventh-hour strategy. Sometimes, sons who want to be free from performing such rites get their fathers' heads tonsured and force them into saffron robes. I hope Rao Bahadur Padmalochana Sastri will not suffer this fate.'

Sastri rained his retaliatory recriminations. 'Which illiterate ignoramus says that renunciation is not exalted by Hindu dharma? Wasn't Adi Sankara – who systematized Hindu dharma – a renunciate? Didn't Swami Vivekananda make the entire world aware of the greatness of Hindu dharma? Who can be such a numskull as to not know the glory of Maharishi Ramana? The poet Valmiki has indubitably established how renunciation was esteemed in the age of the Ramayana. Why else would Sita treat Ravana with such respect when he appears in the guise of a monk? Moreover, the very order in which they are listed proves that renunciation, being the last, is therefore the noblest stage in human life.'

Could Parivrajaka Sharma let Sastri have the last word? 'Rao Bahadur Padmalochana Sastri thinks that Sankara, Swami Vivekananda and Maharishi Ramana lived *before* the Buddha. But history will not reverse itself at Sastri's bidding. I am happy that Sastri mentioned the "Ravana sanyasi". Valmiki has established the fact that even in the age of the Ramayana, renunciation offered the best disguise for fraudsters and fakes.'

Sastri was trying to camouflage the weakness of his arguments when he heard a voice raised outside his bungalow with the call for alms, '*Bhavati bhikshaam dehi*!'

He looked out from the balcony upstairs and saw a young monk standing below. His astonishment knew no bounds. He leapt down the stairs three steps at a time, with the kind of excitement he had never felt before. He yelled to his helpmeet, 'Kamakshi, look, a miracle! A young monk is standing in front of the house. His face is so radiant. I had gooseflesh when he called out, 'Bhikshaam dehi'. Quick, bring the key to the front door! How long should a great soul be made to stand waiting at the threshold? He looks like an avatar of Adi Sankara himself. The good fortunes of our ancestors have made him come seeking this house. Why do you still remain standing here?'

Kamakshi Ammal who had by then looked out and seen the monk said, 'Why are you getting so flustered? The front door is open. What kind of great soul is going to miraculously jump down from the sky? Must be a monk from the Ramakrishna Mission collecting donations.'

Sastri's exuberance came down by several degrees. Perhaps this was a request for donations from the Ramakrishna Mission. Yet, in that case, there would have been no call for *'Bhavati bhikshaam dehi!'* This restored his courage as he went to the front door. Vasanti and Kamakshi Ammal followed.

By this time, the swami had opened the door and entered the house. When they saw him up close both Kamakshi Ammal and Sastri were bemused by the thought that his face looked familiar.

When the monk asked, 'Mami, do you recognize me?' Kamakshi Ammal suddenly realized the truth.

'Our Surya,' she exclaimed.

'*Our* Surya? What nonsense! Who is *our* Surya?' Sastri enquired.

'Rajampettai Kitta Iyer's son.'

'Really? That is why I too feel that I had seen him before,' exclaimed Sastri.

'Yes. In my life before renunciation, I was called Surya. In this stage of life, I am Sutantirananda,' said the monk.

'Is that so? How serendipitous!' said Sastri and took Sutantirananda into the hall and seated him on the sofa.

'Why have you renounced the world at so young an age! It is all right to become a monk in old age after going through everything in life. Did your parents agree to this?' asked Kamakshi Ammal.

Sastri interposed before the swami could reply, 'Bhesh! As though he can become a sanyasi only after taking your permission. Once you renounce the world, who is your father? Who is your mother? Swami! If a thousand young men can renounce the world and propagate

Hindu dharma like you, why, our Hindu dharma will be rejuvenated. When and where did you enter this stage in life? From which great guru did you get your initiation? How long has it been since you became a monk? Where did you go after becoming a monk? How long do you plan to stay in this city? Tell me everything. Kamakshi, go to the kitchen and do the needful. Swami must be offered his bhiksha in the ceremonious manner. Understand?'

'I understand very well,' said Kamakshi Ammal.

When Kamakshi Ammal went to the kitchen with Vasanti, Sastri said, 'How did you enter this state of being? They said that you had joined the Congress and were working for the Quit India movement!'

'Yes, that is also true. I was travelling everywhere for the Quit India movement. I happened to meet a monk in Haridwar. I served him for a year as his disciple. Then I accepted sanyasa from him and have been on a pilgrimage to many sacred places. I am now returning from Rameshwaram.'

'There must have been noble souls among your ancestors who had performed great rites and sacrifices. That is how you have achieved this good fortune in your youth. How many days are you planning to stay in this city?'

'I am planning to leave the day after tomorrow.'

'Never! You must stay here for at least a month. And you must accept our hospitality for bhiksha and puja. I will make arrangements for you to give a series of discourses at the Sarvagna Sangam. You must expatiate on the ancient Hindu dharma, and on varnashrama dharma in particular. Members of our Hindu society have lost their reverence for sanyasa dharma. Even learned fools like Parivrajaka Sharma hold mistaken beliefs in this matter. Your discourses must stun them all into speechless wonder!'

A young woman came in through the front door as they were talking. She wore pure white khadi. Her hair hung free, in the modern 'bobbed' style. But her movements and deportment were modest.

'Namaskaram, Mama! Is Mami in the kitchen?' she said and went to the rear part of the house.

'Who is this lady?' asked the swami.

Sastri answered, 'My elder daughter-in-law. Some of her friends have gone to prison during this August 1942 movement. Another friend has joined Netaji Subhash Chandra Bose's INA forces. This has made her khadi and Congress mad. Overall, it is a good change. She says she will move in with us. It is I who has been urging that we should wait. Will it not endanger my pension if the police came to arrest her here?'

'Even if your pension is endangered now, will it not return when independence is attained?' asked the swami.

'Perhaps! But is India going to attain independence through the attempts of a chit of a girl like her? When it has not been attained despite Mahatma Gandhi, Vallabhbhai Patel and Jawaharlalji going to prison?'

'Do you think India will never achieve independence?'

'Not through these people. By God's will, it is going to come from another direction altogether. The kali purusha, the ruling figure of this last age of Kali, has taken birth in Germany. I mean Hitler, of course. Some nitwits here declare that Hitler's assault on Russia is stupid. They think they are smarter than Hitler. It was with India in mind that Hitler went to war with Russia! As soon as he captures Stalingrad, with a single bound he is going to land in India. Fifty thousand air ships packed with military troops will be here with him. Hitler has explicitly announced that the Aryan race is the highest in the world! Doesn't it follow that the capital of the world empire must be established in India? Do you know the first thing he is going to do when he lands in India? All those geniuses who are babbling about eradicating caste differences will have to cover their faces in shame! Adolf Hitler is going to divide all the people of the world into four castes. Then we will get to know the glories of the varnashrama dharma!' cried Sastri.

Damodaram Pillai in Devapattinam had announced that Japanese invaders were going to erase caste distinctions in India. Here Padmalochana Sastri insisted that Hitler was going to establish the caste system. Controlling the laughter bubbling up inside, the swami asked, 'But some people say that Hitler will eventually lose!'

'Some people? *Some people* spout nonsense! But will their nonsense put a stop the wheel of destiny? Do you know the kind of life Hitler leads? Doesn't eat meat. Doesn't touch liquor. Doesn't even glance at any woman. He has been a celibate from the time of his birth. Swami! Don't imagine that Hitler is an ordinary man! He is a hatha yogi. He is the avatar of the kali age. Don't you know that the masters of the Sanskrit tongue are now in Germany? One day, Hitler called all the German scientists. He told them, "Pack up all your damfool research. Take up the Atharva veda." The result? One by one new weapons appear – V One, V Two, V Three! Englishmen, Americans and Russians are left gaping. They don't know that these are all secrets garnered from the Atharva veda. Are you listening?' said Sastri as paused in his peroration.

'Yes,' said the swami non-commitally.

'Does swami know who it is that Hitler has by his side, to choose the right day and auspicious star for every move? Have you heard of the famous astrologer Mannargudi Panchu Sastri? His own daughter's son Pichu Sastri is the man Hitler now has by his side. Generals and field marshals may say that this is the right time for the army to start marching. But only if Pichu Sastri looks into the panchang treatise and says that the army may leave, does Hitler gives the order to march! That is how he attacked Czechoslovakia and France. Otherwise, could he have captured the land in just ten days where Napoleon was born...? Victory upon victory! The whole world is surrendering at Hitler's feet.'

The swami wondered when Sastri's outpourings would end. When would he get a chance to speak to Kamakshi Ammal about Sita? Alone? Finally, the swami found a way to shut him up. 'What you say may be right. But you are talking so loudly! The CID fellows are everywhere. What if they happen to overhear and report you?'

Sastri's tirade ceased at once.

6

IS MARRIAGE NECESSARY?

As soon as Sastri went upstairs, Kamakshi Ammal burst out, 'Surya, what have you done? Renunciation, and at this age? My husband goes on and on about renouncing the world, but his attachments and bonds are increasing with age. Now the elder daughter-in-law has started showing her fondness! But you have accepted saffron robes at this age! This is not good. I don't even know how to address you. Perhaps I must address you with respect, as Swami!'

Surya replied, 'Mami, you need not worry about that. Call me Surya by all means! I will confess that I have adopted this disguise for a reason. I have not really renounced the world and become a monk.'

'What madness! Why did you adopt *this* disguise among all others? The ways of today's youngsters are strange indeed! Perhaps you have joined the movies?'

'Not at all! Haven't I already joined the freedom movement?'

'Freedom movement? Rubbish! Get rid of this costume before you do anything else! I am looking for a girl for you to marry. Seeing you in this guise gave me a shock.'

'Is getting married so important? Do all those who get married live happily?' asked Surya.

'Many do. Some people are unable to be happy, it is their fate. Think about it! Is there anyone in the world who is always happy? Rama married Sita and went through a great deal of suffering. But can it be argued that Rama should never have married Sita?' Kamakshi Ammal asked.

'Rama and Sita had great love for each other. With that kind of close bonding, a couple can put up with any number of difficulties. But that is not the case with the couples of today!' said Surya.

'Surya, you are saying that my son and daughter-in-law do not have that close bonding. This is the result of disregarding the elders and doing whatever comes to your mind. Why have the elders decreed that a marriage must be fixed after horoscopes are matched? Only to prevent such mishaps. I went on urging that their horoscopes should be matched. No one heeded me. Even this brahmin who always talks about tradition and custom lost his head. Who knows what flaw there may be in your athanga's horoscope? We came to your village to see your sister Lalita. Her horoscope tallied perfectly with Raghavan's. These difficulties would not have arisen if that marriage had taken place,' said Kamakshi Ammal.

'My sister would have undergone the sufferings now endured by my athanga,' said Surya.

Kamakshi Ammal became angry. 'Well said, Surya. You think that your athanga is innocent. It is Raghavan who is tormenting her. When they were newly married, I too thought that your athanga was a naïve ingenue! I was delighted to have a daughter-in-law like her. Only as time went by did I realize what a demon she was! It was wrong to have named her Sita. She should have been called Tataka or Surpanakha.'

'How did an innocent girl turn into a demon? There must have been a reason for it.'

'Reason? What reason? We had believed her to be meek and mild. I have seen a number of obnoxious women in the world. But none like your athanga! Sometimes I get frightened. What if she mixes poison…'

Surya cut in with a shriek, 'Ayyayyo! However vile she may be, she will surely not be such a devil as to poison her husband.'

'Lower your voice. Did I say that she would poison her husband? Your athanga is not such a fool. All I am afraid of is that she may drink poison and blame Raghavan for it. She may leave a note saying, "I am dying because I cannot bear my husband's cruelty." Such thoughts oppress me when I think of her manic frenzy.'

'Mami! How desperate Sita must be to think of taking poison to end her life? There must be a reason for such desperation. If your son is faultless, what other reason can there be?'

Kamakshi Ammal's response came like a rain of arrows.

'Who said my son is faultless? He went to see your sister and then he saw this beauty on the street and insisted he would marry her. That was his fault. Marrying her without even a copper coin as dowry, that was another fault. Raising her from the rubbish heap to such heights was a fault. I warned him again and again, "Don't spoil her!" He didn't listen. He took her on pleasure trips to Agra, Kashmir, Shimla... He didn't have the time to take me to Kasi but he was ready to take Sita to London. He took her to the parties at the viceroy's mansion. He made her study English. He taught her to drive a car, shake hands with other men, sit next to other men! Now he is reaping the fruits of all those mistakes. Any other husband would have beaten such a wife, driven her out and married another!'

Realizing that he was making no headway, Surya changed tack.

'Mami, Sita is a motherless girl. No one knows whether her father is alive. She has no shelter except with you and your son. If she is beaten and driven away, she has nowhere to go except to jump into a well. I was responsible for getting Sita married to your son. It was my insistence that made my parents agree to this match. My athai used to say, "I have spent all my life in misery. Let my daughter get married into a good family and be happy." I feel miserable when I remember these things and see your son and daughter-in-law in this state. That is why the important tasks I have undertaken are getting postponed. I wish to do something that would make Sita and your son happy. That is why I came to you. If I know where Sita is going wrong, I will do my best to advise her to change herself.'

Surya's persuasive words reduced Kamakshi Ammal's anger.

'Don't you know that I have the same wish? I know that in their heart of hearts they have affection for each other, but they quarrel from morning to night. Your athanga's contentiousness is the biggest problem. She is always trying to get above herself. She disagrees with whatever he says. She nags him relentlessly if he talks to any women.

What can a man do if he is always tormented when he comes home from work? Sometimes he gets furious. Does she know how to restrain herself from retaliation, at least when he is angry? No! Ask Dharini! Sita became sick and nearly lost her life. Dharini nursed her day and night and saved her. When Sita became well, there was no end to the way she berated Dharini. Once I made Dharini suffer. It was in this very puja room that she fell at my feet and asked my permission to marry Raghavan. I refused because I did not know to which caste she belonged. My son would have been happy if he had married Dharini. I barred the way. I think it is Dharini's anguish which is now tormenting me and my son.'

Surya became lost in thought. He became angry with Dharini. With this story behind her, he thought that she should never have intervened in Sita's and Raghavan's lives. Was it so certain that deep down, Raghavan and Dharini did not still feel the attraction of their old love? If so, what was so wrong about Sita's jealousy?

Quickly, Surya stopped his thoughts from taking this direction and said, 'Mami, what is the use of thinking about what happened in the past? We must see what can be done to make your son happy. I will bear in mind what you said about Sita's contentiousness and advise her to the best of my ability. Please try to do what you can to persuade her. When are you coming to Delhi?'

'I am waiting for Raghavan's letter. I am afraid to go to Delhi. I am afraid of what may happen to this child caught between husband and wife. Why should I not tell you? Once, Sita made this child tell her father, "Don't scold Amma, don't beat her!" He gave the child a beating. The child got fever...'

'Ayo!' said Surya.

'You feel pity, don't you? But for three days Sita did not disclose the fact that the child had fever. Then Raghavan came to know. He brought the doctor home. See what a devil your athanga can be!'

Surya wondered if Sita did it out of devilishness or because of her well-intentioned desire to shield her husband. Deciding that it was useless to argue about it with Kamakshi Ammal, he said, 'I will go to

Delhi tomorrow. I will talk to Sita and let you know. Let us somehow broker peace between husband and wife.'

'I too have been praying to all the gods. Surya, listen. It is the two of them and this child whom I love most dearly in the whole world. You talk to Sita in your own way. Also, see if you can locate her horoscope and send it to me. Should there be any flaw in it, we can perform the propitiatory rites,' Kamakshi Ammal said.

7

ON THE SILVER STREET

It has become imperative to take the readers back to the historic city of Delhi. In the second half of 1943, the city saw a rapid increase in cash flow and population. As the war was getting closer to the borders of India, wartime preparations were being zealously carried out in the capital. British and American soldiers, Gurkha sepoys, Sikh troopers and south Indian servicemen were seen everywhere. There was a demand for taxi, tonga and rickshaw as never before. Under such circumstances, where was Surya going to get a vehicle to hire?

Surya came out of the railway station and stood thinking for a few minutes. He had to decide whether he should make his way to New Delhi or to Old Delhi. Finally, he decided on Old Delhi. He started walking briskly.

His pace slackened when he reached Chandni Chowk. He began to ruminate on the historic events that had taken place on the 'Silver Street'.

Once, as the richest street in the world, Chandni Chowk showcased ornaments of gold and silver, jewels with the nine gems, rare and miscellaneous wares from across the world, silken garments and Persian carpets sought by kings and emperors. Those who lived on the street and had their shops there were immensely rich. Was it not natural that a place of such accumulated wealth should attract hazards?

Not just once, but many times did the Silver Street face catastrophes.

Five hundred years ago, when Muhammed bin Tughlaq ruled Delhi, a demon named Taimur marched in from Mongolia with a monstrous army. He defeated Tughlaq's army at the entrance of the Delhi Fort and entered the city. He massacred the subjects in their thousands. He looted all the wealth of the Silver Street. He made rivers of blood flow across the rich carpets on which princes and princesses had once walked.

Taimur stayed in Delhi for two weeks and left after plundering and sacking the city. After his departure, Delhi awoke and realized that the nightmare had been the reality. And yet, possessing as it did an amazing life force, the city rose again, in wealth and in splendour. Where rivers of blood had flowed, once again the jingling of gold coins and the tinkling of princesses' anklets could be heard.

Three hundred and forty years rolled by, after which a monster called Nadir Shah came from Persia with his vast troops. Sitting on the top of a mosque near the Chandni Chowk, Nadir Shah enjoyed watching his troops vandalizing and pillaging Delhi. Once again there was a river of blood, forming pools everywhere. This hair-raising blood bath is remembered by the name Khooni Darwaza, the bloody portal, given to the gateway at one of the corners of the street.

Twenty years after Nadir Shah's onslaught came Ahmad Shah Abdali, to plunder whatever Nadir Shah had missed. This time too, it was the Silver Street that underwent the greatest devastation. After Ahmad Shah, the Scindias, Holkars and Rohillas sacked the city.

Finally, Delhi drew the compassion of the British. British troops took revenge on Delhi after the failure of what was named the Sepoy Mutiny in 1957. For a whole week the city saw nothing but raids and slaughter. Then the British authorities brought their troops under control. Halting the indiscriminate butchery, they held 'proper' trials and began to punish the revolutionaries. Gallows were erected by the British Army tribunal on the same Silver Street where Nadir Shah and Ahmad Shah had conducted their genocides. Thousands were hanged.

As Surya walked down the street, these historic events appeared sequentially on his mind and made his flesh creep. But he also felt the thrill of astonishment. Today, how spectacular the sights on the same street where those horrors had taken place! How many shops! What fabulous goods on display! And the people! From so many races, regions, creeds! Hindus, Muslims, Sikhs, Bengalis, Punjabis, south Indians, British Tommies, American businessmen! What crowds! What cash flow! Will the Silver Street face calamities again? Will it see looting and plundering? Rivers of blood? Will the Germans or the Japanese or the Russians come with their armies? Will Chandni Chowk turn into a battleground again?

Though his mind was engaged, Surya's eyes continued to search for something, or someone. The disappointment on his face showed that it was all to no avail.

Surya crossed the Silver Street and reached the Jama Masjid, the largest mosque in India, built by emperor Shah Jahan. He mounted its steps. Along the way, he halted to glance at the surrounding streets below. Then he looked at the fort situated at a little distance. He remembered that the space between the mosque and the fort had once been thickly populated, until the British cannons destroyed them all. Surya's blood boiled when he thought of the atrocities committed in Delhi by the British who called themselves educated and civilized.

Will the time ever come when Hindus and Muslims dismissed their petty dissensions to drive the British out? Will the day dawn when the Indian flag will displace the Union Jack in Old Delhi and New Delhi?

Surya's musings were cut short when his left hand was seized in an iron grip.

8

UNDER THE TREE

Surya saw that the man who had his left hand in his iron grip was a tall and burly policeman. In a split second, a thousand thoughts leapt and raced in Surya's mind. After having travelled so far and for so many days, should he have been trapped by a lazy lump of a Delhi policeman? That too when he had important tasks to complete? Couldn't he have had two more days' respite? Without revealing his perturbation Surya demanded in an admonitory tone, 'Who are you?' His tension mounted when the man replied, 'Inspector saheb asked me to bring you.' Becoming more flustered, he said, 'I won't come. I don't know your Inspector saheb.'

The policeman replied, 'You won't say this if you see the Inspector saheb. Come quickly.'

His tone aroused Surya's suspicions. The policeman's grin and wink confused him further. Moreover, their contretemps began to attract a crowd on the steps leading to the Jama Masjid where they had been standing. Surya decided that it would be better for him to accompany the policeman. 'All right. Where is the Inspector saheb?' he asked. 'Come quietly, follow me at a distance, don't come too close,' the policeman said and started walking.

Surya gained confidence because the policeman walked ahead without looking back, making it feasible for him to escape if he wished to do so. Surya's suspicion became a certainty as he followed the policeman without letting him out of his view. The policeman strode through the noisy crowd around the Jama Masjid and reached the clock tower on Silver Street. Then he entered the compound of the town hall and reached the vast open grounds behind it.

There were a few trees and shrubs in that open space now called the Gandhi Maidan. When they reached the maidan, the policeman pointed to a tree. 'Inspector saheb is behind that tree. Go! It won't be good for me to hang around when you and the Inspector saheb converse. There may be many secrets between you!' he said and smiled again.

With mounting curiosity, Surya approached the tree. He could see a woman sitting behind it, absorbed in a book. Who was she? Before the question could form itself in his mind, the sound of his feet made the woman raise her head and glance at him. Surya was filled with delight when he saw that it was Dharini.

'Welcome! Welcome! May the warrior Surya's arrival bring jubilations!' Dharini said.

'O! So, *you* are the Inspector saheb! I was momentarily confounded when the policeman gripped my hand,' Surya said, as he sat down in front of her. He added, 'I know how savvy you are! But I did not expect you to have caught a policeman in your trap!'

'What would be the plight of lesser mortals if the revolutionary warrior Surya shows himself to be afraid of a policeman?'

'Did I say anything about being afraid? I played so many tricks in so many places to evade capture. I wore several disguises, including that of a monk! After having gone through so much to reach Delhi, how could I not be alarmed at the prospect of being locked up by the police before meeting you?'

'Were you able to accomplish all the tasks you had taken up?' Dharini asked.

'How could I after getting your letter with its emergency call? You will be surprised to know the train of disasters that letter managed to set off! What happened to Sita for you to write so? Really, I get angry when I think of Sita. So many tasks of national importance getting interrupted for the sake of one person...!'

'I don't see it the way you do. We pride ourselves on our singular ability to perform these tasks for the nation. But I think it is more meaningful to save someone we know from misery, than to try to save the nation.'

'You have been indulging in profound philosophic reflections since we last met. Last time we talked, we had decided that the welfare of the nation was more important than the plight of individuals. I don't know the reason for this transformation.'

'Your athanga is the reason! Never mind the fate of the nation, it is enough if Sita is relieved from pain.'

'You have developed boundless compassion for Sita. I can't fathom the reason.'

'Should there be a reason for feeling affection for someone?'

'Not at all. Women fall in love with first-class rogues only because love requires no reason.'

'I don't understand you. Are you saying that women fall in love only with rogues? I don't agree. There are some upright men for women to fall in love with. I know one such upstanding man,' Dharini said and looked away.

'I know that exceptionally upstanding man! Isn't his name Saundara Raghavan?' Surya asked in exasperation.

'I did not have Saundara Raghavan in mind. And yet I will not call him a rogue. He may commit some mistakes. But I know that he has great love for Sita. With her meaningless suspicions, Sita is turning his love into poison,' Dharini said.

'Good. At least, you understand the inmost workings of Raghavan's heart better than Sita!'

'Sometimes, the view from afar is clearer than the one up close. That is why I am able to understand Raghavan's heart better than Sita.'

'Who knows? You may be closer to Raghavan's heart than Sita!'

'Surya, you are being perverse. If you are going to continue in this vein, I don't wish to talk to you. You can leave.'

'Does this maidan belong to you?'

'All right. I will go,' Dharini said and got up.

Surya was flustered. He entreated, 'Dharini, I take back everything I said. I was wrong. Please do sit down! Before you go, tell me what I must do for Sita.'

Dharini sat down again and said, 'I don't know the reason for this sudden change I see in you. Someone must have said something to sour you. Did you see Sita before coming here?'

'No. I came straight from the station. I haven't even gone to my room. How is Sita? What should I do about her?'

'Some kind of poison has entered her mind. Some suspicion has lodged itself there. That is why her family life is getting ruined. You must go at once and try to understand what is eating into her. It may be good to send her to some other place for a while.'

'Where can she go? There is only one way for Sita to gain peace in her life. She must get a divorce. But neither Hindu dharma nor British law allows it. So, she has to die in misery.'

'I too have thought sometimes of how happy Sita can be if she can get a divorce and marry you.'

'Not at all. You are making a huge mistake. The affection I have for my athai has made me take an interest in Sita's welfare. In everything else, Sita's ideals and mine are totally incompatible. Sita belongs to the tribe of butterflies. She loves glitz and razzmatazz. She thinks that attending parties is the highest goal in life.'

'Was Sita born with these attributes? Weren't they acquired later?'

'What does it matter how and when she acquired them! I want to share something with you. I had disguised myself as a monk for a short spell. I was forced to maintain the deception for several days. During that time, I did think of becoming a genuine renunciate. The thought gained in strength after meeting and talking to Kamakshi Ammal in Madras.'

'I acclaim your decision!'

'I am glad that our minds agree in every way.'

'So am I. But how is it that Kamakshi Ammal became your guru?'

'I went to inquire about Sita. She told me about how your devoted nursing saved her from typhoid.'

'Is that all? But how did that influence you to renounce the world?'

'Kamakshi Ammal told me a few other things as well. She told me about Raghavan wanting to marry some other girl when he was young, the girl's eagerness to do so, and her own refusal to give permission to their union due to differences of caste. I commend Raghavan wholeheartedly for fulfilling his mother's wish with such devotion.'

'Now I understand the reason for your strange manner today. But tell me, did Kamakshi Ammal tell you about the girl's opinion at the present time?'

'No. How could she know that? She did say that Raghavan might have been happy if he had married that girl.'

After a few moments' reflection Dharini said, 'What is the connection between this and your renunciation?'

'One day, if I want to marry someone, and learn that she is in love with someone else, what is left for me to do but to renounce the world?'

'You are completely wrong! Today, there is absolutely no place for Raghavan in that girl's heart. If she learns about your becoming a monk, she too will join a convent and become a nun.'

Surya held Dharini's hands and asked eagerly, 'Is that true?'

'Why don't you ask your heart?' Dharini replied.

'Until now, I was afraid to believe what my heart told me. I thought my heart was deceiving me. How could I believe that someone as unfortunate as myself could have such extraordinary luck?'

'The heart did not deceive you. The restless mind did. The same mind is deceiving Sita as well. Go at once and see how she is doing. It has been twenty days since I saw Sita. I am worried about her.'

'All right. Shall we meet in the same place tomorrow?'

'No. Look around and you will know how many people are watching us. Our friends are eager to hear of your experiences. Come to the clock tower tomorrow at the same time. Policeman Indulal will bring you to our quarters. Don't follow me now. Stay under this tree until I join the policeman.'

Dharini got up and walked away. Surya remained seated in the same spot and watched her and the policeman until they disappeared in the distance.

9

THE HEART STOPPED

Surya thought that he would go on his way after Dharini disappeared from his view. However, he saw three strangers, who had been sitting at a little distance until then, coming towards him. He waited for them.

The three men came and sat down around Surya.

'Brother? Where do you come from?' one of them asked.

'Madras,' Surya said.

'Ah! Madras!' all three intoned together.

After a pause one of them asked, 'A girl was sitting here. What is she to you?'

'A friend,' Surya said.

'Ah, friend!' they chorused again.

The conversation stalled. After waiting for a while Surya said, 'Why do you ask? What do you want?'

The first man said, '*Bahut accha!* Right question! We will tell you.'

The other two repeated, 'Bahut accha! Right question! We will tell you.'

Surya had already begun to suspect that they belonged to some royal state. Now, their lead-and-chorus delivery convinced him that it was so.

'Tell me. I am waiting,' he said.

'You don't want that girl's friendship,' one of them said.

The other two repeated it.

'Why? What is wrong with her? What is the harm in making friends with her?' Surya inquired.

'That is a VIP matter!' said one.

'Yes, a VVIP matter,' the others said.

'Then go tell the VVIP! Why tell me?' Surya asked.

The three of them looked at one another.

'It is getting late. I'm leaving,' Surya said.

One among the trio looked at the other two and asked, 'Shall we tell him?'

'Shall we tell him?' they repeated.

The first man looked at Surya and asked, 'Brother! Do you want money?'

'How much?' Surya asked.

The first man looked at the other two and asked, 'He wants to know how much. Shall I tell him?'

'Tell him!' they said.

The first man asked, 'Brother! Do you want a lakh of rupees? One lakh!'

Surya was somewhat staggered. Slowly pulling himself together he asked, 'Counterfeit notes? Or real money?'

'Ah! Counterfeit!' exclaimed all three and laughed.

Then the first man said, 'Not counterfeit. Genuine cash. If you don't want currency notes, we can give you gold.'

'Give me!' said Surya and extended his hand.

'Clever boy! Say "cash" and he holds out his hand,' they laughed.

Finally, one of the men swallowed hard before saying, 'Can a lakh of rupees be obtained for free? You can get it if you help us.'

'What kind of help?' Surya asked.

'We have orders from the VIPs to get the girl you had been talking to a little while ago. If you help us to do that, you can get all of one lakh rupees.'

Surya was expecting something like this. Nevertheless, he was infuriated to hear it.

He somehow managed to suppress his anger. What was the use of getting angry with them? There were three of them. Three hefty roughnecks. Getting into a fight with them would affect his work. Moreover, he wondered what their real intentions were.

Pretending to think it over he said, 'Give me two days. I will think about it and give you an answer.'

'Where and when can we meet?' the first man asked.

'Let us meet here the day after tomorrow,' Surya said.

'Where are you staying?' one of them asked.

'Right now, I don't have a place to stay. I have to look for one,' Surya said and got up. The three men got up too.

Wherever he went, the three men tailed him. It took a very long time for Surya to lose them by wandering through circuitous routes. He was determined to see Sita that night at any cost.

Sita was sitting in one of the rooms in her house, all alone.

Tick-tock, tick-tock, tick-tock... went the wall clock.

Sita's heart was beating to the rhythm of the clock. She knew that every beat was bringing her life closer to its end.

As the hands of the clock moved closer and closer to midnight, the piercing thorn in Sita's heart became more painful.

Eleven thirty. Only half an hour left in her life span. Sita had decided to shoot herself exactly at midnight.

Why should she look ugly in death? Shouldn't those who saw her exclaim, 'Adadaa! Even though he had such a beauty for a wife, Raghavan was not lucky enough to live with her for long!'

With this thought in mind, she had worn fine clothes and ornaments and made herself look beautiful.

She wanted to write to Vasanti. But when she thought of the child, she was overwhelmed by sobs. The thought of dying without seeing her was heartbreaking. What could she write to the child? Should she say, 'Your father has killed me. Take revenge on him!' Chee! Chee! What a crazy notion!

She began to write to Lalita. But she could not go beyond 'My dearest friend Lalita'. Thinking of Lalita brought a flood of old memories. Ah, how happy had the days in Rajampettai been when she shared endless secrets with Lalita! The elation she had felt when Raghavan came to see Lalita and said that he would marry her instead. And now, she was undergoing the torments of hell. Had that betrayal returned to afflict her now?

What should she write to Lalita? Should she say, 'Forgive me'? But it would make no sense to her! Even if Sita poured out her sorrows, Lalita would be unable to comprehend them. Lalita was leading a happy life. Those who were happy could never understand the sorrows of others.

Thinking of writing to her husband made her feel as if her heart would explode. What could she say? 'I have no one in the world but you. But you have come to loathe me.' Or should she say, 'You have been ceaselessly asking me to get lost. Now I am getting permanently lost.'

Tears rained from Sita's eyes. None of the innumerable ways in which Raghavan tormented her affected Sita as much as his frequent cries of 'Get lost! *Get lost*!' It smote her with grief. Where could she get lost? She had no mother. Nor any information about her father. All she could do was to get lost in death.

Ah! Couldn't Mother Earth take her away as she did her daughter, Sita, from the epic? Couldn't her mother Rajam take her away as the legendary Sakuntala's mother took her daughter away?

Such things happen only in stories, not in real life. The only way out was to shoot herself. Luckily, her husband had bought a revolver for which she was thankful. Should she leave a letter expressing her gratitude to him?

Ayo! Why is this clock in such a great hurry? Why is it running so fast? Why was her heart beating so fast?

There! The hand of the clock has come close to midnight! Just a few minutes left!

Sita had decided to shoot herself when the clock struck twelve.

Her husband would return at twelve thirty. The job must be over before that. He may be blamed unnecessarily if she did it when he was at home. Why should she earn the notoriety of being described as someone who ruined him in death as in life? Vasanti would become motherless, but should the child be deprived of her father?

The last two minutes were over. Ding, ding, ding, ding… The clock began to strike twelve.

Sita counted the strokes. She would pick up the gun on the last stroke.

Suddenly, Sita heard footsteps. Her heart stopped beating. Her hand lost its power to move.

Who was it? Her husband? Had he come early? Had the intuitive linking of heart with heart made him realize what was about to happen, and come to save her? When he saw the revolver in her hand, would he guess what she was about to do? Would he understand her anguish? Would he beg her to forgive him?

10

'JUST ONE WAY'

Sita did not turn to look behind her even when the footsteps sounded very close. Let him know what she was about to do. Let him be startled to see the gun. Let him question her.

In a swift movement, the man who had entered snatched the gun from her hand. 'Sita!' he exclaimed.

To her great disappointment, Sita realized that the man was not Raghavan, but Surya. In that instant, her attitude underwent a strange transformation. Sita changed her mind about giving up her life. She decided that she must remain alive for as long as she could and go on causing Raghavan as much vexation as possible. She needed Surya's help to fulfil this newborn ambition. She had to act in a way that would make this happen.

'Cousin! You came at a good time,' she welcomed him.

'Hardly! I arrived in time to prevent you from doing what you planned to do.'

'What do you think I planned to do?'

'Why should anyone be found at midnight holding a gun?'

'To shoot any burglar who may break in.'

'Can burglars break in so easily in New Delhi? That too with a watchman outside?'

'How did the watchman let you in?'

'He was sleeping soundly.'

'Yes. The servants in this city are always half asleep. Do you think I was going to shoot myself?'

'I will be very happy to know that it was not so. But your face and the tears in your eyes tell a different story. A letter I received from here also leads me to think so.'

'Who wrote the letter?'

'What do you care, Sita?'

'What did the letter say?'

'The letter said that you were greatly perturbed in mind. I came in person to learn what it may be. Athanga, are you not perturbed? In that case, I will return to my work at once.'

'Surya! What is the use of hiding the truth from you? I need your help. I *was* about to shoot myself. Surya, before dying I wanted to write a letter to my darling child. But I could think of nothing to write. If I tell you, won't you convey it to her in person? Won't you go to Madras someday?' Sita said in a piteous voice.

'Athanga, I was in Madras and Devapattinam some days ago.'

'Did you see Vasanti?' Sita asked, visibly flustered.

'Yes. I met your father-in-law and mother-in-law as well.'

'How is Vasanti? Did she talk to you?'

'Physically, she is well. But deflated in mind. She yearns to see her parents. I am astonished that you have the heart to shoot yourself, leaving the child behind.'

'Can't you see from this that I am experiencing the torments of hell in my life?'

'Athanga! We create our own heaven and hell. Haven't you heard it being said, "The kingdom of God is within you"?'

'Such philosophies are of no use to me anymore. Nor have I created my own hell. All of you threw me into this hell. Marrying him was a great mistake. Surya, there is absolutely no compatibility between us. He should have married an English memsaheb, or a Parsi lady, or at least someone like your friend Dharini…'

'Why should we mention other people, Sita?'

'I won't, if they leave me alone. But when I was bedridden, Dharini and my mother-in-law tried to kill me by giving me poison. I thought so highly of my mother-in-law. But now I know what a demoness she is!'

'Sita! Have you gone mad? When you were about to die, they nursed you day and night and saved your life. And you talk about them with such venom!'

'How do you know that their nursing saved me? Only from what they told you! I am not so brainless. One night, I saw Dharini and my mother-in-law whispering furtively together. Dharini mixed a white powder with my medicine. She thought I didn't see her. I swallowed it. Sleep overcame me. The dosage must have been insufficient. I woke up in the morning, alive. I became careful. I threw away all the medicine that Dharini gave me, after pretending to take it. If you don't want me to shoot myself, get me some poison from your friend, Dharini.'

'Athanga, you have flipped out! Otherwise, you would not say such outrageous things. When you had fever and were sleep-deprived, they must have consulted each other and given you a sleeping dose.'

'Yes, they gave me a dose to sleep forever. But not enough of it. That is why I survived.'

'You could have shared your suspicions with your husband.'

'He would not have believed me. Why, you yourself don't believe your athanga's words! I am an orphan. I have nowhere to go. No one will believe me. Why did you come? Leave me and go about your business!' Sita said and shed tears.

'If I had been bent only on my own business, I would not have left so many important tasks and travelled a thousand miles to come here. I have dropped not only my business, but the nation's business to be here. I want you to be happy. Tell me about the problems you have with your husband. I will take him to task. I am not afraid of him.'

'*You* are not afraid. But *I* am. He will direct all the anger he feels for you towards me. How can *you* understand my troubles when even other *women* don't? He takes me to a party. And there, before other women, he humiliates me. Whatever I do turns out to be wrong. If I talk convivially, he says I am a loudmouth. "Why do you display your imbecility? Why don't you shut up? I'm so ashamed!" he says. If I keep quiet, he says, "Why did I marry someone who cannot talk pleasantly to other people!" If I don't laugh, he calls me a dumbass without a sense of humour. If I weep, he says, "Why don't you get lost?" I am deeply wounded when he asks me to get lost. Where can I get lost? I have nowhere else to go to except to get lost from this world. Cousin, give me the gun before you go.'

'Athanga, drop this talk of dying. So long as I am around, you are not an orphan. Be patient for a few days. I will think about it and find a solution.'

'I cannot bear it anymore, even for a day. There is only one way for me to go on living. But you will not agree to that.'

'Tell me.'

'Delhi has become hell for me. Take me away from this inferno! This house has become my prison. Free me from this prison-house! I will come to any place that you pick. I am ready to go with you anywhere – Bombay, Calcutta, Lahore, Ceylon, London, America!'

'Athanga, if the time comes, and if it is necessary, I will take you to those places. But this is not the right time. I am involved in the Indian independence movement. I have taken a vow before my comrades that I will not take up any other job until India attains independence. Let India become free. After that…'

'Surya! Is there no part for women to play in India's freedom struggle? Can I not do whatever it is that Dharini does? Like my husband, do you also think that I am useless? Take me with you. And see me perform fantastic feats! You people talk incessantly about freedom, but hide in narrow lanes and blind alleys. You disguise yourselves, change your names and wander about in the night. Take me! I will hold a sword in my hand like Rani of Jhansi and fight on the battlefield. I will travel through the nation and recruit millions of fighters. I will transform cowards into heroes. See if I don't establish India's freedom just as Joan of Arc did in France!'

'This is not the age in which wars are fought as the Rani of Jhansi and Joan of Arc did. This is the age when bombs are dropped from the skies to kill thousands upon thousands. It is not possible to establish independence by fighting openly with the British Raj. Right now, it is not even possible to hold a public meeting in this country. How can a whole army be recruited or march into the battlefield when you cannot even shout *Inquilab zindabad*?'

'In that case, take me to Gandhiji's ashram and leave me there! I understand that there are many poor and orphaned people like me in that ashram, even a white woman who has come from abroad. A Muslim girl too! I will follow Gandhiji's orders as they do.'

'Athanga, the Mahatma is in prison. I don't know who is staying in his ashram now. They will not accept any newcomers at this time.'

'Then why don't you enroll me in a good film company? In none of the many, many films I have seen in Hindi and Tamil does anyone know how to act in sad sequences. I will become famous for my incomparable depictions of tragedy. Surya, what do you say?'

Surya was dumbfounded. The Rani of Jhansi, the Mahatma's ashram, the silver screen! He found it incredible that Sita's mind could simultaneously focus on three wholly dissimilar ideas.

Had she developed a touch of madness? He decided that he would placate her for the moment and take a decision after consulting Dharini.

'Athanga, I know nothing of cinema. Nor do I know anyone from the film world. Therefore, your last notion is an impossibility. But it is not as if there is no place for you to stay for some time. I would ask you to go to Rajampettai. But I know my mother. She doesn't like you. There is no one in the world who loves you as much as Lalita does. I cannot tell you how unhappy she is to know that you are not happy. You know how close I am to Lalita's husband. He is now in prison. You can certainly go to Devapattinam and stay there for some time. You can get Vasanti to join you there.'

'Don't I know that Lalita loves me? There was a time when I felt remorseful for having been disloyal to Lalita in marrying my husband. But now I am happy to know that I have done her an extremely good turn. But I will not go and stay in Lalita's house. You have still not understood my intention. If I go to Devapattinam my husband will come to know about it within two days. I want to go to some faraway place, which cannot be discovered so that he may worry and wander in search of me. Tell me if you can take me to such a place.'

'What will your husband and others think if we take off together without informing anyone? Will it not give room for needless suspicions? Have you thought of that?' asked Surya.

'Let them think what they like. I don't care. Do you know, three months ago, my husband got into a car with some woman? His car crashed into a military truck near Panipat. He was unhurt. The woman was injured. This made him the laughing stock of New Delhi. Which law says that men alone can do whatever they like?'

'Athanga, there is no such law. A wrong deed remains wrong whether done by a man or a woman. But I have an idea. Listen, you know that I have two friends in Devapattinam. One is Lalita's husband Pattabhiraman. The other is Amarnath who lived in the house opposite to his house. He and his wife Chitra are now in Calcutta. Amarnath and his wife are good people. Lalita has told Chitra all about you. I will take you to the nearest station and put you on the train to Calcutta. You can go and stay with Chitra and Amarnath. I will keep an eye on your husband here. If it becomes necessary, I will tell him where you have gone.'

'That's just what you must *not* do. He must never know. I will let him know my whereabouts in my own time. I am ready to go to Calcutta. But you must personally escort me there, today or tomorrow. I cannot go alone. Perhaps your friend, Dharini may not like you taking me.'

'Sita, your head is stuffed with outlandish ideas. I am not afraid of anyone. But we must be convinced that we are doing the right thing! Give me a little time to reflect,' Surya said.

'Certainly! But do all your reflection right here... Why! My cousin has come after such a long time. And I did not even offer him a glass of water. I will make some Ovaltine for you. Go on and reflect,' said Sita as she got up and went to the kitchen.

Surya's mind was plunged into misgivings. 'What's this! I have taken on such a fearsome responsibility! How will it end?' he thought in bewilderment. He wondered if he could extricate himself from the situation.

The telephone rang.

Lost as he was in his own thoughts, Surya did not stop to wonder who could be calling after midnight. He picked up the receiver and said, 'Hello?'

Hearing the telephone ring, Sita hurried out of the kitchen. Her face registered consternation when she saw Surya speaking into the receiver.

11

RAGHAVAN'S ORDEAL

Adivarahachari, the Divan of Rajnipur, had made his permanent home in New Delhi. He had been given the post of counsellor to the rulers of the royal principalities on matters of law. This job spelt little work, but a large income and great influence. His daughters Dhama and Bhama had become well known in New Delhi's social circles and were invariably seen at the viceroy's palace, and at parties thrown by the rulers of the royal states and other high-ranking bureaucrats.

At 11 p.m., they had just returned from a party with their father. Raghavan was with them. All four of them began to play a game of cards.

When the game was all set, Bhama asked, 'Mr Raghavan, why didn't you bring your wife to the party? Does she still remain unwell?'

'Physically she has recovered. But having been bedridden for so long, her mind is out of sorts. I go home to face endless complaints and relentless weeping,' Raghavan answered.

'You should have ensured a change of place for someone who had been so severely ill. It is wrong to keep her here,' Dhama said.

'Don't I know it? I have tried my best, asking her any number of times to go to Madras, to see my mother and her relatives. But it is she who has to agree! My lot is pitiable indeed. Trouble awaits me in the office and at home. I am at my wits' end. Sometimes I wonder if I should simply commit suicide. The only time I feel at peace is when I'm here, chatting with all of you.'

'We know about your troubles at home. What is the problem at the office?' Dhama inquired.

'Ask your father! He will tell you. Divan saheb! I am thinking of becoming a Muslim. What do you say?' Raghavan asked.

Adivarahachari went on looking at his cards without answering.

'Why should you become a Muslim?' Bhama asked in surprise.

'Nowadays, you have to be a Muslim to get a promotion in government jobs. A man who joined four years after me has been promoted to a post higher than mine. He was saying "Yes, Sir!" to me. Now I have to say "Yes, Sir!" to him. Is he a genius? A man with exceptional brains? No! A perfect fool. And I have to work under him! I am unable to endure this humiliation. Divan saheb! Advise me. Shall I convert to Islam? Or should I resign?' Raghavan asked.

Adivarahachari opened his mouth for the first time to say, 'Wait.'

'And if I wait? Do you think there will be a change in this situation?'

'If these Congress leaders become a little rational, the situation will surely change. But they are squatting in prison cells at a time when they should be offering to help in the war effort, and capture all the seats in the districts. If only the Congress leaders had shown intelligence, they would have had more than half the seats in the Viceroy's executive council. The mistakes of the Congressmen have become advantages for the Muslim League. Muslims have come to occupy all the important posts with confidence.'

'Divan saheb! What if the Congressmen change their attitudes? Under the guise of offering justice to the minority they will make the majority suffer. They will give concessions to Muslims. I have now come to appreciate the ideologies of the Hindu Maha Sabha. It is not as important to fight the British as it is to eliminate Muslims. What is the use of India attaining independence with eight crore Muslims still in the country?'

Bhama asked, 'Mr Raghavan, just a while ago you said that you were going to turn Muslim. Now you say that Muslims must be eliminated!'

'What else can I do? Either we must get rid of the Muslims, or become Muslims ourselves. Then there will no longer be any room for partiality in the matter of official postings! I am begging your father to get me a job with some royal state or the other. At the divan saheb's bidding, I am willing to resign from this dreadful post.'

'Appa! Why don't you do something about Mr Raghavan's request?' Bhama asked her father.

'I do have it in mind. But he must not resign from his post. Only if you are employed can you get another job, not if you resign,' said the former divan.

'You have been saying this for a long time. All right, I will wait and see,' Raghavan said.

'Mr Raghavan, is there no other reason for your getting overlooked other than the fact that you are a Hindu and not a Muslim?' Dhama asked.

'That I am a Madrasi is an important reason. When my boss, an Englishman, was the finance minister, he used to choose Madrasis for all the important appointments. But now, to be a Madrasi is to be hated on sight. A Muslim is the first choice. Or a retarded nincompoop. But no Madrasi! The Muhammad bin Tughlaqs who rule India today may even demand excess tax for intelligence.'

Adivarahachari intervened to say, 'Raghavan, that is not what Dhama meant. There is another complaint about you, which has become the talk of the town.'

'What complaint?' Raghavan asked.

'For a whole month you had kept a woman belonging to the revolutionary movement hidden in your house. Is that true?'

'You mean Dharini? It is a pack of lies to say that she belongs to the revolutionary movement. Nor had I hidden her in my house. When Sita was ailing, Dharini stayed with us to nurse her and saved her life. Your daughters know Dharini. What a gentlewoman she is and how intelligent!' Raghavan said.

'One may be gentle and intelligent. That does not mean that such a person cannot be an insurgent,' Bhama remarked.

'Even if it is true, how am I responsible for that? How do I know that she is a rebel? Don't you know how many true-blue revolutionaries were hidden in the homes of top-ranking officials in New Delhi? Where was Karunadevi concealed? In whose house did Chandrakanta Sinha hide for three months? What did they do to those who gave them shelter? Why accuse me alone?'

'They are all people in very high places. No one will dare to accuse them. But that is not the case with you. Raghavan, you are in a position where you expect to be promoted.'

Bhama said, 'That is not all, Appa! He is under suspicion for hiding a revolutionary. His wife Sita is under suspicion for aiding a revolutionary. It seems Sita's name was mentioned in a letter that went to Madras from here. It had been addressed to someone called Surya. Yesterday, a CID officer asked me about Sita and Surya. He wanted to know how they were related. I said that I didn't know.'

'That police officer made some smutty remarks.'

'What! *What*?' Raghavan cried out in agitation.

'He asked me if they were lovers. Since I knew Sita very well, I told him that it was totally false, slanderous, and made him take his words back.'

'What you did was absolutely right,' Raghavan said. 'But it is true that Surya is a scoundrel. It seems he went to see my mother in Madras some time ago, disguised as a monk, and asked her a number of unwarranted questions. If I see him again, I will give him up to the police before I do anything else. Do you know if there is a warrant for his arrest?'

'There is a warrant in his name in three states – Madras, Bombay and the Central Provinces.'

'Good! It is good for the nation if people like Surya are thrown into prison. The independence movement will gain in purity,' Raghavan said and went to the telephone.

'Who are you calling at this hour?' Bhama asked.

'Before I go home, I usually call to find out if my wife is asleep. If I return when she is awake, she stings me like a scorpion.' Raghavan said.

'Ayo, poor man! Your situation is pitiable indeed,' Bhama said.

Saundara Raghavan dialed the number of his house. When he heard the voice on the telephone, Raghavan's face became suffused with astonishment and rage.

12

'SURYA, GO AWAY!'

As soon as he heard Raghavan's voice, Surya looked at Sita's face. He was confused. Had he made a mistake in answering the phone? To Raghavan's query, 'Who? Surya? When did you come?', he had replied, 'Just today.'

'I see! You will wait until I come, won't you?' asked Raghavan. 'O yes,' Surya replied. Then he gave the receiver to Sita saying, 'It is mapillai!'

Surya could not hear what Raghavan said. But he saw Sita's eyes misting and tearing up when she answered, 'No! He just came today.' She replaced the receiver after saying, 'Yes, yes. I will ask him to stay.'

'Athanga! What did mapillai say?' Surya asked.

Sita looked away. Then she broke into sobs and said, 'Surya, go, go away at once!'

'Athanga, why are you asking me to go? Mapillai asked me to stay!' he said.

'That is exactly why I am asking you to leave. He told me to make you stay. But I am afraid. Surya, I believe that something disastrous will happen if you stay here. Go away.'

'It will be disastrous for me to decamp in a hurry. Should I leave when he has particularly asked me to stay? Won't it give rise to needless suspicions?'

'Are those suspicions newfound? Surya, you are naïve like a child! He has untoward suspicions about you and me already. That is why he is tormenting me.'

'Nonsense! Let him come. I will confront him.'

'You cannot dispel his suspicions by confronting him in person. You will only make him angrier and he will take it out on me. There will be murder if you stay here today. Don't make me responsible for it. Please go away! I fall at your feet and beg you.'

Surya noticed that Sita's frenzy was mounting. And yet, he did not have the mind to go. 'Sita! Don't get frazzled. If I go now, will it not confirm his suspicions?'

'He whom I worship as a God, suspects me! That is why I asked you to take me away. But you are a coward. You make a great fanfaronade about women's emancipation, but you will not do anything concrete. Nor have I placed my faith in you. One day I am certainly going to run away from him. Please, don't put me in a difficult position, leave at once.'

Surya feared that if he stayed, Sita would burst a blood vessel and faint. He must go. But he could call her tomorrow. He would decide what was to be done about Sita after consulting Dharini the following day.

'All right, Athanga. I will leave. But when do we meet again? Shall I call you tomorrow?'

'Yes. Call after 11 a.m. I will tell you everything.'

'Athanga, remember this. Should you really want my help, I will not draw back. Make up your mind and tell me. Your welfare is most important to me. Even India's freedom comes after that.'

It cannot be said that Surya truly meant every word he spoke at that moment. He was more intent on raising Sita's spirits and preventing her from acting in haste.

But Sita took them to be completely sincere. 'Thank you, cousin! Amma had told me to ask for your help in times of danger. Her words have not been in vain. Call me tomorrow afternoon. I too will take time to reflect. Let it not be said that I acted in haste.'

Surya got up to leave. He had already tucked into his pocket the revolver that he had taken from Sita, deciding, 'It is dangerous for these two crackpots to have a gun in the house. With me, one day it might come in handy.'

He was leaving when the sound of the horn was heard outside. The motor car rushed into the house and stood at the entrance. Surya and Sita stood transfixed.

Raghavan parked the car in the portico and came striding in.

He stared hard at Sita and Surya alternately. His glance held some of his vindictiveness. But without revealing his inordinate malice he asked, 'Why, Surya! You seem to be ready to leave?'

'Yes, mapillai! I must go. It is already twelve thirty. I was waiting to leave after you came,' Surya said.

'You seem to have become quite the night bird.'

'So have you. You have returned home after twelve thirty in the night!' Surya's pert retort stirred Raghavan's anger.

'I had to go somewhere on an important job.'

'I too have important work. I have told a few friends that I will meet them tonight.'

'Great! Meeting friends at this hour? And after the meeting? Will you go off to rob and steal?'

'Robbers go about in the night. Those who go to catch them will also have to go about during the night. We are engaged in the mission of driving away those who have plundered India. Don't you know this, mapillai?'

'How will I know? Perhaps your athanga might know. Don't you come to see her often?'

'Not often. The last time was three months ago. You were out of town. Your mother was here. I met her.'

'You even went to Madras. I came running to learn all about it from you. And you say you have to go. Can't you stay the night and leave in the morning?'

'No, sir! I must go right away. I saw your mother and child in Madras. Your child wanted to come here. I did not bring her because I had many jobs along the way. I will give you all the details at another time.'

'What does "another time" mean?' Raghavan asked.

'If possible, I will be here tomorrow. If not, the day after. I will tell you all about my travels and experiences.'

'All right. Then you may leave now. If you come tomorrow, will it also be at night?'

'Yes. To escape from the eyes of the police, I have to make it in the night. I don't want to cause any trouble for you with the kind of work I am doing. You hold a post in the government. And not an ordinary one at that.'

'Such concern for me? Never mind. Is this the kind of fate that should have been in store for Rajampettai Kitta Iyer's son?'

'What kind of fate?'

'You hide from the police like a thief and move around stealthily in the night. Well, Surya! Where is your friend Dharini? Do you see her?'

Surya looked at Sita. He saw that her face had turned cruel.

'I think Dharini is in town. I may see her.'

'If you do, tell her that I want to see her about an important matter. Do you know where she stays?'

'I know the old place. But Dharini has moved somewhere else.'

'I know the old place, not the new. One day, when I was near the Jama Masjid in Old Delhi, I saw someone like Dharini walking along. I thought it was she and approached her. She quickly turned into a narrow lane and disappeared into a house. I knocked on the door. It seemed to be a street of Muslim residents. A hundred Muslims surrounded me and wanted to fight with me. It was quite a task to escape from them. The first thing that you people must do is to drive all the Muslims out of this country. If not, this country will never prosper.'

'We don't think so. Muslims were born and raised in this country. They are our brothers. Why should we drive them away? Once we thrash the white men and get rid of them…'

'Then what you say will be the law. The government will be in your hands.'

'I don't know about that, mapillai. We may all have to give up our lives in the freedom struggle. But one thing is certain. The representatives of the people of this country will soon begin to rule India.' Surya said and left.

Raghavan remained seated on the sofa without heeding Surya's departure. But Sita went with him to the front door. As soon as they reached the front steps she said softly, 'Surya, swear that you will call tomorrow?'

'All right, athanga.'

13

'IF YOU ARE A CHASTE WIFE...'

When Sita returned after bidding Surya goodbye at the front door, she saw Raghavan getting up ferociously.

Eyes flaming, Raghavan asked, 'What secrets did you share with him?'

Without realizing what she was saying, Sita blurted out, 'What's it to you?'

'What did you say?' Raghavan said and gave her a hard slap.

Biting her teeth as she bore the pain, Sita said, 'Is that all? There's another cheek too!'

'Have you become the Mahatma's disciple? Take this!' Raghavan said and slapped her other cheek.

Sita stared at him and went to the kitchen.

'Taking off in a hurry? Come here, answer me before you go!' Raghavan bellowed.

Sita brought a glass of Ovaltine from the kitchen and put it on the table.

'Is it Ovaltine or have you mixed poison in it?' Raghavan asked.

'Yes, I have,' Sita answered.

'Then you can drink it... No, you have some work left to do. Don't leave the world so quickly!' Raghavan said as he picked up the glass and flung the Ovaltine out of the window.

'You don't have to put up with a murderess in the house. I will leave tomorrow,' Sita said.

'Where do you mean to go?' Raghavan asked.

'What does it matter to you where I go? Why should you ask?' Sita said.

'I asked you because I am the man who married you. When I asked you to go, you refused, obstinately. Now you say you will leave tomorrow. Where do you mean to go? With whom do you mean to go?'

'With Surya, if he takes me. Otherwise, I'll go alone,' Sita said.

'Where is Surya going to take you? He is hiding from the police! You will have to go alone. Where will you go?'

'I will get lost somewhere. You have been constantly asking me to get lost.'

'Get well and truly lost! But before you do, answer my question.'

'What is there to say when one is about to get lost?'

'You must give an answer. I have doubts about you and Surya.'

'What doubts?'

'I have doubts about your character.'

'Very good.'

'Good did you say?' Raghavan snarled and gave Sita two more powerful slaps.

Sita did not move. She did not shed tears. She did not even wince.

'Very good. Thrash me to death once and for all.'

'Why do you want me to kill you?'

'Then I don't have to run away tomorrow.'

'You are troubled by guilt. That is why you keep talking about running away.'

'I don't feel guilty.'

'Then why are you ranting about running away? Why should you run away from your wedded husband?'

'You have withdrawn from me. How can two people with their minds totally disconnected from one another live together?'

'If I have drawn away from you, it is entirely because of your behaviour. Why should Surya come to see you in my absence? Look here! If you are truly a chaste wife…'

'If I am a chaste wife… Oh my God! What a strange world it is.'

'Never mind philosophical discussions about the illusory world. As a chaste wife, will you obey me?' Raghavan asked.

Sita remained silent.

'Answer me!' Raghavan said menacingly.

'If you tell me what it is, I will tell you if I can or cannot do as you say,' Sita replied.

'I shall not. You must be ready to do whatever I say. Otherwise, you must walk out of this house.'

'I have already told you that I am ready to leave. If you like, I can clear out right now.'

'Is it not the duty of the wife to obey the husband, unquestioningly?'

'It may be so for couples who are of one mind. But you have suspicions about me. I have suspicions about you. In such a situation, how can I agree without knowing what I am supposed to do?'

'*You* have suspicions about *me*? Excellent! But let it be for now. What you must do, is this. You must call the police station right now, this very minute, and tell them about Surya's visit.'

'Never!'

'Why do you care so much for Surya?'

'Surya is my uncle's son. It was he who got us married. Surya is now involved in the freedom struggle. He came here trusting both of us, convinced that we will not betray him. To betray him to the police would be treachery.'

'I may be ruined by your cousin Surya. He is involved in revolutionary activities. It was very wrong of him to visit a government servant's house. It has prevented me from getting promoted. Now, I have to see those who worked under me getting promoted to positions above me. I will lose my job if I don't submit this information today.'

'Let us not betray a friend for the sake of a job. I would rather go begging from house to house to raise money.'

'Bitch! Should I expect your beggar's alms for my livelihood? Do you expect me to give up a job which brings me two thousand rupees a month, for your folly? But for this problem, I would have been speedily promoted, with a monthly income of three to four thousand rupees. Dumbo! Do want me to give it up?'

'I would die rather than inform the police.'

'Don't I know that? I simply wanted to call your bluff. Go, get lost!' Raghavan said and shoved Sita by the neck into the bedroom.

Sita went into the bedroom and lay on the bed. Not a drop of water came from her eyes. The cheeks that her husband had slapped were throbbing in pain. She wondered if all the happenings of the day were real or whether she had dreamed them in her sleep.

She heard Raghavan dial the telephone in the next room. The moment she heard Raghavan say, 'Hello, police station?' she got up and came running to seize Raghavan's hand holding the receiver. 'Who are you calling?' she asked.

With his face turning black in anger, Raghavan glared at her with savage eyes and asked. 'What is it to you?'

'How does it not concern me? You are calling the police about Surya. I will never let you do it. Kill me before you call,' Sita said.

'What will you do if I call from the office tomorrow?' Raghavan asked.

'I don't care so long as I don't hear it!'

'Why are you so concerned about Surya? A little while ago you declared that you had nothing to do with him.'

'I did not say that. Surya is the only person in the whole world who has any concern for me. He will be ready to do anything for me. How can I watch you betray him?'

'Devil! You are crazed with your infatuation for Surya.'

'Very good.'

'Very good? *Very good*?' Raghavan shouted and raised his hand.

'It is very good that your tongue has not fallen off after speaking such heinous words.'

'Are you cursing me?' Raghavan said in a state of uncontrollable fury and hit Sita with the telephone receiver.

In a flash Sita's expression changed. Her eyes welled up. Placing her hand over the ear that had been hit, she wailed in a rush of sobs and tears. Overcome by delirious frenzy she cried, 'Amma, Amma, I hear the waves! Amma, come and take me away with you! Amma.' Raghavan realized that Sita was having an attack of hysteria.

At once Raghavan held her by the shoulders and made her sit on the sofa, gently. 'Don't, Sita. Don't! I was only testing you.' he said in soothing tones as he stroked her back.

Presently, Sita lay face down on the sofa. Her sobs and wails ceased, and sleep overtook her.

Surya, who had gone out of the house earlier, had opened the gate, only to shut it again, before returning to the garden. He stood outside the window unseen, and witnessed the whole scene. He could not hear every word, but his eyes saw everything clearly.

Surya could not bear to hear Sita screaming for her mother as Raghavan hit her on the ear with the telephone receiver. He thought of grabbing the gun and shooting him. But he decided to wait for one more day. Moreover, he had important jobs that were still pending.

As Surya walked towards Old Delhi in the dark hours after midnight, his mind seethed as it had never done before. 'How does the nation matter? What does it matter if freedom slips away? There are many to attend to the nation and its struggle. But Sita is orphaned and helpless. My first duty is to protect her. How can I fulfil that duty? I must decide tomorrow after consulting Dharini. Until then, my poor athanga must stay alive, though trapped in the demon's grip!'

With these reflections, Surya walked on. He spent a sleepless night.

14
THE HIDEAWAY

The next evening, Surya walked down the Silver Street, his mind in a state of fervid agitation. His face revealed his mental trauma and lack of sleep.

Surya had called Sita at 11 a.m. Twice he found the number engaged. The third time he could hear Sita's voice. 'Surya, did you call me a little while ago?' she asked. 'Twice,' Surya replied. 'But I could not reach you.'

'The phone rang half an hour ago. I picked it up thinking that it must be you. A voice said, "I am Surya. When can we meet?" Since I had doubts about it being you, I hung up. What do you think about this?' Sita asked.

'Surprising! Who could it be? Your husband?'

'No. It was not my husband's voice. Let it be. I must see you today. Where? When?'

'I will come to your house after two days,' Surya said.

'No, no, if you don't see me today, you won't see me alive. It will be dangerous for you to come here. I will come to Old Delhi and see you.'

'What an idea, Sita! Won't your husband come to know? Since he is already suspicious…'

'I must absolutely see you this evening. My husband has a party to attend this evening. He will return late. I will meet you and get back by then.'

'In that case, let me come there.'

'Never, you must never come anywhere near this house anymore. I will be in Old Delhi by 6 p.m. Where should I meet you?'

Surya could only think of the maidan behind the town hall. Sita agreed to meet him there.

Surya wrestled with anxieties. 'Why did I ask her to come? Will this make more trouble for Sita?'

Now Surya was in Chandni Chowk because, before meeting Sita, he had to see Dharini and the other comrades as previously arranged.

He recalled how, just the day before, three men had promised him a lakh of rupees if he helped them to capture Dharini. This memory intensified Surya's perturbation.

As soon as he passed the Khooni Darwaza with its bloody history, a burly Muslim League volunteer collided with Surya and said, '*Maaf keejiye. Quaid-e-azam zindabad*!' Surya looked up crossly because he thought that the man had deliberately bumped into him and was offering a satirical apology. When he saw the man wink, Surya knew that it was the same man who had appeared in a policeman's disguise the day before. 'Why this costume today?' asked Surya. 'How can I survive in the same disguise? The leader asked you to be careful. You look just like you did yesterday,' the Muslim League volunteer said.

'So what? No one knows me here,' Surya replied.

'One can't be sure. We have information that the CID is making serious inquiries about you.'

'Is the leader in our quarters?'

'Yes. Follow me, but not too closely,' the man said and walked briskly ahead. Surya followed him as he entered a narrow street branching off crosswise from the road on the left of the Jama Masjid. Twisting and turning into alleys, he reached a narrow lane where the sun may never have entered and stopped in front of a house with a Muslim League flag hanging outside. Surya joined him as they entered the house together. In the front room, a man who appeared to be a Muslim cleric sat reading, moving his fingers over the lines of a book which looked like the Quran Sharif in Arabic script. After raising his head to glance at the new entrants, the maulvi saheb resumed reading.

As Surya wondered who the maulvi could be, and why he seemed familiar, the volunteer took him by the hand and guided him behind an old bookshelf. There was a gap between the shelf and the wall into which a man could squeeze himself through with difficulty. His guide opened a door on the wall, pushed Surya in and shut it behind him.

Surya stumbled in the dark. The next moment a woman's soft hand caught his and Dharini's voice whispered, 'Come with me.'

As Surya walked on, holding Dharini by the hand, he had the eerie feeling of entering an ancient royal palace through a secret tunnel. His mind built incredible castles in the air.

Surya reached a dimly lit old world chamber. Its stone pillars suggested antiquity. A spacious room though the roof was low. When Delhi was frequently ransacked by marauders like Nadir Shah and Ahmad Shah, the rich merchants of Chandni Chowk had hidden their priceless treasures in this dark chamber, which was extremely difficult to find.

That old secret chamber was now one of the principal hideouts of the activists involved in the revolutionary movement.

There were some twenty people in the chamber. Some were lying down and engaged in reading. Others chatted in groups or were smoking cheroot. A few were asleep. Their costumes varied. Surya noticed a policeman's uniform and cap hanging from a nail on the wall. He realized that it had been worn by the man who had taken him to Dharini the day before.

Pointing to a man who was writing, Dharini said, 'The chief.' Surya went up to him and said, 'Inquilab zindabad!'

When they saw the newcomer, everyone gathered around the leader.

'Where did you go? What is the situation in those places?' the leader inquired.

'I have been to the Central Provinces, the Andhra region and Madras. I travelled almost down to Madurai. Wherever I went, I saw that the hearts of the people are rumbling like a volcano. The volcano may explode at any time. Floods of lava are going to reduce the British Raj to ashes.'

'Why? What is the basis of your belief?'

'I happened to meet a sub-judge in Madras, now retired and pensioned. He is anatomizing astrological charts to discover the date on which a victorious Hitler is going to invade India. In Devapattinam, a Divan Bahadur who belonged to the Justice Party for a very long time says, "India can only be saved by the Japanese." Everywhere the masses passionately believe that the Englishman will lose the war and British rule will be forced out of India.'

'What is the use of faith and passion? In what way are the masses ready to act to expel the British, and establish a government of our own? Last year, on 9 August, we expected the revolution to blaze across the entire nation. It did not happen.'

'It is disappointing. Most of the people expect that freedom will be attained with an armed invasion of India by Germany or Japan. Some expect Subhash Babu to gather his army in Malaya and come to India via Burma. Most people do not think that they themselves must do something for freedom. A few volunteers without fame or influence are raising the revolutionary flag here and there. However, the brutal torments they are subjected to by the police terrify the people. I saw an example of such police brutality…' Surya said and detailed the atrocities perpetrated by the police at a child's first birthday celebrations in Devapattinam.

After listening to everything the leader said, 'Those who fought wars of independence in other countries have undergone far greater horrors. Our people have lost their valour. Long term foreign rule has turned them into weaklings. However, there is hope as long some people refuse to yield. The bitterness in people's hearts will not remain quiescent forever, one day it will surely come to a boil. But until the volcano bursts, we must make sure that the fire of the revolution is not extinguished. Surya, we learn that the police in this city are aware of your arrival and are making inquiries about you. It would be good for you leave the city immediately. Will you go to Calcutta? There is an important job to be done there,' the leader asked.

'Yes,' said Surya.

The thought came to him that if Sita continued to be recalcitrant, it would be convenient to take her with him and leave her in Calcutta.

His chief gave Surya detailed instructions about the task in Calcutta.

15

ANOTHER'S SECRET

From the dark chamber, Surya and Dharini emerged into the room where the maulvi saheb was reading the Quran. They went up the narrow staircase in a corner of that room and seated themselves on two old cane chairs.

'When do you intend to leave for Calcutta?' Dharini asked.

'Today. But a decision must be taken about Sita before I go. Are you going to be in Delhi?' Surya asked.

'No. I am going to Bombay. They have completely uprooted the British Raj in the Satara district in Bombay Province. A citizens' republic has replaced it. Not even a paisa is collected as taxes for the British government. I have been ordered to go and see this miracle in person. If a single district in every state can pull off the Satara miracle, we can say goodbye to the British Raj.'

'Are you going alone?'

'What is wrong in going alone? What can anyone do to me?'

'Listen. Yesterday, three men came to me after you left the maidan. They promised me one lakh rupees if I captured you and handed you over to them. At first, I could not believe my ears. Then I realized that they were in earnest.'

'How strange! A lakh of rupees? For *me*? Who can those madcaps be? Not the police! They will not offer more than ₹5000 even for the great leader of the revolutionary movement! Do you think they were ragging you?'

'Not at all. They meant it all right. After that, they followed me.

I think they are palace employees in some royal state. Their master must be a raja or a nawab.'

Dharini laughed outright and said, 'What fun! Surya, I have an idea. We are struggling without funds to run our movement. Now we have found a way! We can earn one lakh in a stroke! Put off going to Calcutta and trace those people. Hand me over to them and take a lakh of rupees.'

'Let India remain enslaved rather than win freedom by conducting a revolution in this manner!' Surya said.

'Why refuse the money that is available? What can they do to me even if they take me with them? Am I a little child? Can they gobble me up?'

'They may very well do that and more! Why not? Dharini, you do not know how many demons roam the world in the guise of humans! I understood this clearly last night when I saw how Sita was persecuted by that demon of a man!'

'What's this! Did you go to Sita's house last night? What did she say? I see that she has complained a great deal about Raghavan.'

'I did not know this from what Sita said. At first, I did not even believe what she said. I thought she had lost her mind and was spouting nonsense. Only when I saw it with my own eyes did I come to know what Sita told me was not even a fraction of the truth.'

Then Surya described everything that had happened from the time he went to Sita's house.

As she listened, Dharini's face became steeped in sorrow and dismay.

'I would have never believed all this if you had not seen it. I never imagined that Raghavan was such a brute.'

'Who did? If I had known that things would take this turn, would I have ever got them married? Would I have hidden the telegram I received from Sita's father and made sure that nothing prevented the wedding from taking place?'

'How wrong it is to interfere in other people's affairs! Would the father of the bride have sent a telegram like that without deep reflection? You should not have interfered in the matter.'

'What's the use of saying this now? By now, Sita might have reached the maidan. What should I tell her? Should I take her to Calcutta with me?'

'Is it not enough for you to have made the mistake of interfering in Sita's life once? Don't do it again. Her life will be finished if you take her to Calcutta. Say something reassuring and take her back to her house. I will take care of her. I will meet Raghavan and talk to him this very night.'

'How will you meet Raghavan tonight?' Surya's voice echoed curiosity and vexation.

'I am thinking of going to the party that he will be attending,' Dharini said.

'What a risk to take! I hear that the Delhi police have registered a complaint against you. How will you go to a party hosted by a government officer?'

'The complaint is registered in my name. But no one knows that the name is mine! The man who throws the party today belongs to the viceroy's executive council. His wife is a close friend of mind. After attending the party, I am going to be staying in their house for two days. I will be travelling to Bombay with a government pass from him.'

'Your ingenuity stuns me! I too have adopted some disguises to escape from the CID. But what you do is simply astounding!'

'Let us postpone patting each other on the back. Please go and take care of Sita. When I think of Sita's physical and mental condition, I get apprehensive about her going to the maidan all by herself. Foreign soldiers and native sepoys are wandering about everywhere in the city.'

'Soldiers and sepoys? What about vultures from the royal states circling above? Dharini, you too must be careful.'

'Don't worry, I can take care of myself. It is Sita who worries me. Please go at once. Meet Sita. Mollify her somehow and take her back to her house. From today, I guarantee there will be a change in Raghavan's behaviour.'

'I don't like it at all that you should be meeting and talking to that blackguard.'

'You think I enjoy meeting Raghavan? I am doing it for Sita's sake.'

'Dharini, can I ask a question? Why are you taking so much interest in Sita's case?'

'Is it not reason enough that she is the revolutionary warrior Surya's cousin?'

'No, you would not have been impelled to nurse her as you did and saved her life for that reason alone. Nor would it have made you ignore her abusing you and think of her welfare. There must be some other reason.'

'What you have surmised is true enough. There is a reason for me to have greater concern for Sita than even you. But please do not ask me about it now. It is someone else's secret. I should not speak without that person's permission,' Dharini said.

'Since you have so much concern for Sita, do make inquiries about her father when you go to Bombay. I will give you his old address. We will have to take on lesser responsibility if we inform him about Sita's condition.'

'Surya, don't be surprised. I know where Sita's father can be found. But right now, he cannot help Sita. Nor will Sita be happy to learn about his present situation.'

Surya had guessed that Sita's father had been sentenced to long term imprisonment for committing a big crime. Dharini's words confirmed his suspicion. Suddenly, a face appeared in his mind. It was the face of the maulvi saheb with the beard.

'Dharini, there is a maulvi saheb seated below and reading the Quran. Who is he? Can you tell me?' he asked.

'Yes, I can. That maulvi saheb is my father... Shall I bring a mattress to cushion your fall as you tumble down in a swoon?' Dharini asked him.

—

16

SITA'S ABDUCTION

After taking him through a maze of unidentifiable but equally narrow and grimy lanes, to reach the spot from where the Jama Masjid could be seen, the Muslim League volunteer said to Surya, 'Will you be able to make your way from here?'

Surya said, 'Thank you' and walked towards Jama Masjid. His legs were wobbling.

The city of Delhi was spinning around him. Dharini's announcement that a Muslim maulvi was her father had shocked him out of his wits. His castles in the air cracked and shattered and came crashing down upon his head. If this was true, his life had to change its direction. To marry a Muslim girl, he would have to become a Muslim. He was not quite ready to give up the ancient Hindu dharma.

'On the one hand, among insurgents, she is a radical revolutionary. She also maintains her friendship with highly placed government officials. Haven't we read about bewitching women working as secret agents during war times? Until the end, it is not possible to discover for whom they gather intelligence. How nonchalantly did she say, "Hand me over and accept the money!" Close as she is to members of the viceroy's executive council, how can she be believed when she says that she is in love with an impoverished man like me? Her influence on Raghavan gives rise to all kinds of suspicions. What is her real attitude towards Sita? Can she have her own agenda for being so concerned about Sita? What *is* that agenda? Together, all these people have turned Sita almost mad. Is it right to trust Dharini and go to Calcutta, leaving that helpless girl bereft of support?' Preyed by these thoughts Surya crossed the Jama Masjid and entered Chandni Chowk. When he reached the town hall, he saw Sita standing alone in a corner. Immediately rushing towards her, he asked, 'Sita, have you been waiting for a long time?'

'Just a quarter of an hour. I don't like being stared at by the people going up and down the street. I was thinking of leaving if you didn't turn up in the next five minutes. Thank goodness you are here.' Sita said.

'Ayo, why didn't I come five minutes later!' was the thought that crossed Surya's mind. But almost at once, Surya felt ashamed of his selfishness. Helpless Sita had no friends. Should he too abandon her?

Both walked on the street behind the town hall and reached Gandhi Maidan. Surya led her to the same tree under which he had conversed with Dharini the day before. They did not speak as they made their way because Surya's mind was busy reflecting on his duty to Sita.

As soon as they sat down under the tree, Sita said in a trembling voice, 'Cousin, leave this city at once. The police is looking for you. It was the police who pretended to be you to get information from me. I made my way here only to tell you this. I was afraid to say it on the phone in case it was tapped. Surya, go away!'

'Athanga, why worry about me? What if the police do capture me? I am ready to be arrested at any moment and thrown into prison. Last night I feigned my exit, only to return to the garden and watch through the window. My blood boiled when I saw Raghavan hitting you. I even thought of shooting him down. I did not believe you when you complained about your husband. But all my doubts were cleared when I saw the way Raghavan treated you. I will not blame you if you want to run away from such a demon. I leave for Calcutta tonight. Come with me. I will leave you at Amarnath's house and go about my own work. Amarnath and his wife Chitra will do anything for me. They will shelter you...'

Sita, who had been listening half-heartedly until then, now interrupted, 'Surya, no need for that. I have taken a decision about what I should do.'

'Athanga, don't take that decision. Why should you give up your life? For a pitiless monster like Raghavan? So long as I have breath in my body, I will take care of you. I will be on your side even if the whole world turns against you. You must give up on the idea of ending your life.'

'Surya, I have given up my thoughts of ending my life and giving up on my husband. I have decided to behave according to his wishes and win his approval. You will wonder how I could take this decision after the happenings of last night. Perhaps you won't even believe me. But this afternoon, I read about Kasturba Gandhi's life. It changed my mind. Do you know the sufferings that Kasturba has undergone? She has even gone to jail in her seventieth year! How noble she is! I too have decided to live according to my husband's wishes.'

Surya felt as if a great weight had been lifted from his mind. His heart empathized with Sita's decision. But his mind objected to it. He said, 'I cannot agree that a woman must put up with her husband even if he mistreats her. Such dogmas were established by men to enslave women. They belong to the past. Today's dharma is that men and women are equal. You mentioned Kasturba Gandhi. Her husband is a noble soul acclaimed by the world. Can others be compared to Gandhi?'

'Surya, was Gandhi a Mahatma when Kasturba began to live as her husband wished her to do? Was he not an ordinary man then? He became a Mahatma because Kasturba saw him as a God. I did think about women's freedom. Surya, my husband never asks me where I go, what I do. It was I who did, and ruined his life. He had given me complete freedom. I did not give him any kind of freedom. The more I think, the more I realize that all the faults are mine. Somehow, my mind had gone astray. Now I have made my decision. It is useless for you to try to change it,' Sita said.

Surya was astounded. 'I will never try to change your mind,' he said. 'It will be good if you can be what Raghavan wants you to be and reform him. I have no greater delight than in seeing you and Raghavan live happily together. Let's go! It has become dark. I will escort you to your house and go about my business.'

'You don't have to come with me. Find me a taxi,' Sita said.

'No. Sita! I will certainly perform my duty. Nowadays, Delhi has become more dangerous. It is not right for women to go alone, certainly not after it gets dark.'

'Surya, why are you so scared?'

'Last evening, Dharini and I were talking under this tree…'

'Talking to Dharini? Here? You never told me!' Sita's voice now revealed spite as it had not done until then.

'There was no need to do so. So what?'

'So, nothing! What did Dharini and you talk about under this tree?'

'Many things. About the revolutionary movement and how to take it forward. We also talked about you.'

'What did you say about me? Why was it necessary for you to talk to Dharini about me?' Sita asked.

'We talked about the frail state of your physical and mental condition. We wondered how we could help you.'

'I don't need any help.'

'When Dharini left, three men came up and offered me one lakh rupees to help them abduct Dharini. How's that?'

'How terrible! Who can they be?'

'They appeared to belong to some royal state. This is the state of Delhi today, in the year 1943, under Viceroy Wavell's regime. How will I have the heart to send you off alone, in the dark?'

'Surya, you don't have to worry about me. Will the men who offered one lakh rupees for a beauty like Dharini even mention me? With my looks, were I to be auctioned, no one will offer even a fraction of that sum! I should be ever so grateful to my husband for rejecting Dharini and marrying me instead!'

'I will take you home today. It is my duty. I will be worried if I don't.'

'Surya, it is for your sake that I am asking you not to come. The police are circling my house, waiting to arrest you.'

'Haven't I already said that I am not bothered about that?'

'You may be longing to be arrested and find your peace in jail. But did you think about the fact that my husband is a government employee? What will happen to him if you are arrested in his house? Won't his position be endangered?'

Surya was transfixed in amazement. Then he said, 'Forgive me. I never thought of that. Right. I will accompany you till we get close to your house. Then you can make your way by yourself.' Surya said. Sita agreed.

The street leading from the maidan to Chandni Chowk was deserted. A big motor car was parked at the end of that street. Its number, 1111 – embedded itself on Surya's mind. There were two men in the car. Two other men were standing near the fence by the street and smoking cigarettes. Surya felt a vague suspicion as he walked past the car with Sita.

Surya and Sita reached Chandni Chowk and stopped a taxi. When they got in, the taxi began to go towards New Delhi.

Surya suspected that their vehicle was being followed by the motor car. But he could not be sure as the roads in Delhi always had many cars going up and down. When they reached Jantar Mantar, Sita said, 'Stop. Our house is nearby.'

'All right,' Surya said and asked the taxi to stop.

'Shall I get off? Will you take this taxi home?' Surya asked.

'No. The servants will wonder about my coming home in a taxi. If I walk home, they will think that I had been out on a stroll as usual,' Sita said.

'All right,' Surya said.

As soon as she got down from the taxi, Sita asked, 'You *will* go to Calcutta tonight, won't you? Please do, Surya.'

'I will,' Surya said.

'I don't know if we will see each other again! I will never forget your affection for me and how you have helped me.'

'I can never forget you, Athanga!'

Sita started walking down the street. Surya stood on the kerb watching her.

The white moon was shining bright. From the gardens of neighbouring houses came the scent of flowers blooming in the night. The breeze blew gently. From a house nearby came a song from the gramophone, *'Soja, rajkumari! Soja!'* Sleep, princess, go to sleep…

In such a setting, walking down the street all by herself, Sita appeared to be part of movie sequence.

Surya stood musing, 'What does the future hold for Sita? Could she have had a real change of heart? Did she mislead me? Will she drink poison and die? If that happens, will I not bear some responsibility for her death?'

The car that had followed them went past Surya. Once again, its number – 1111 – caught his eye.

The car came to a halt when it reached Sita. Two men jumped down. They pushed Sita into the car and got in after her. The door was shut. The car roared and reversed to start moving towards Surya.

All this took less than thirty seconds during which Surya's mind remained frozen. As the car zipped past him, his mind began to work again. He seemed to hear a faint voice from the car shouting, 'Cousin!' Surya pulled out the gun from his pocket and shot at the car. The shots missed the tyres. Jumping quickly into the taxi he shouted, 'Follow that car. I will give you whatever you want. I will shoot you if you don't!'

'There's very little petrol, saheb!' the taxi driver said.

'Never mind. Keep moving as long as it lasts,' Surya said.

Just then, a policeman appeared and asked, 'Was it you who discharged the shot? Hand over your gun!'

Surya gave a hard push to the policeman. The policeman reeled and fell at a little distance. 'Jao! Jao!' shouted Surya. The bewildered taxi driver drove on.

The policeman got up and blew his whistle thrice. Soon, a police jeep arrived with four policemen in it. The policeman on the street got in and said something to the others. The jeep began to move at great speed, following the other two cars.

17

BLOCKED BY THE YAMUNA

Sita found herself being driven at a great speed from New Delhi to Shahjahanpur. Going through Chandni Chowk, crossing Jama Masjid, passing the Red Fort on the right side, the car raced over the train tracks and approached the Yamuna Bridge.

For a few moments, Sita remained immobilized. Then she remembered Surya's warning. The thought that Surya was following her kept her courage up. She believed that Surya's car would catch up with hers. But when the car approached the Yamuna Bridge, she felt a jolt of fear. The bridge was narrow. Vehicles could cross it only from one side at a time. Policemen stood on both sides of the bridge. When vehicles were allowed to cross from one side, the other side was closed. When the stopped cars were allowed to move, the vehicles on the opposite side were ordered to halt. When she thought about this, Sita became apprehensive about what would happen if her car was allowed entry and Surya's vehicle was stopped before it could follow.

Sita's fears came true. As soon as her car entered the bridge, the policeman raised his hand to stop all the vehicles behind it. Sita was overcome by a terrible fear. It rose from the intestines to the chest, and streaked up from the chest to block her throat. A bomb exploded in her head. With an involuntary scream of terror, she tried to jump from the moving car. The man seated next to her hit her on the face, hard. At once Sita's scream stopped. So did her attempt to jump out. Silence reigned in the car. Some of the cars coming from the opposite direction heard the scream and their passengers stared at Sita's car as it passed by. But it was driven at such a speed so as to make it impossible for anyone to discover anything more.

Sita's wits returned when the man hit her. In that split second, her mind regained normalcy. She began to think about her situation calmly.

She recalled her rash dismissal of Surya's warning. Now she was in real danger. Who was abducting her? Why? She recollected what she had heard about brutal crimes against women in north India. Her body trembled from top to toe at the thought that she too might be sold off somewhere.

Or, would they take her to the harem of a lecherous raja or nawab? She had heard about such happenings too, read about them in newspapers and novels. She never thought that such things could happen in her life. But now...?

One thing was certain. Shrieks and physical resistance would not help her get away from these hellhounds.

She began to think about the stratagems of escape devised by women in similar situations in the novels she had read. But unexpected assistance and opportunities had come their way. In her case, God had prevented any assistance from reaching her.

'O river Yamuna! O sacred Yamuna! Why have you made me suffer? Why did you stop Surya at the crucial moment? I don't know what terrors are in store for me...! But why should I lose all hope so quickly? Surya may be delayed by a quarter of an hour. That's all. Will he stop following me for that reason? Never... It would be good to delay the car somewhere. But how? Yes! When we cross a town, I can say I am thirsty and hungry. Somehow, I can beg and plead and get the car to stop. To achieve that I must talk nicely to these men and make friends with them.'

Having made this decision, Sita was wondering how to start a conversation, when the man spoke to her. 'Daughter! If you don't shout and scream and give trouble, nothing bad will happen to you. I am extremely sorry for having had to hit you.'

Sita had noted that the speaker was somewhat elderly in appearance. His voice and manner proclaimed genuine sympathy.

Steeling herself, Sita said, 'Who are you? Where are you taking me?'

'Right! That's the way to talk. I will tell you. We are taking you to your revered mother,' said the man.

Sita felt an uncontrollable urge to burst into laughter. It was many years since her mother died. Such a long time since her body was cremated on the banks of the Kaveri. Now this north Indian fellow was saying that he would take her to her mother! Lunacy!

Was she dreaming, perhaps? Or was she dead? Were these events happening after death? Were these men the messengers of the god of death? Were they really taking her to her mother in the other world? No! Never heard of travelling by car in the other world! Nor did these men appear to be spirits!

Sita pinched herself to clear her doubts. She was alive in flesh and blood.

Then, what did this man's statement mean?

Sita wondered if she had misunderstood him. She asked the man again, 'Where are you taking me?'

'I told you! We are taking you to your mother. Your brother too is eager to meet you,' the man said.

Sita's astonishment increased. A brother! Her brother! Her mother had mentioned the male child who had been born before Sita. Her mother used to lament, 'He looked like a prince! Had he remained alive, I would never have worried about your father being what he is. You and I were unlucky!' That child had died two years before she was born. If only she had had a real brother! Would she have had to face all these troubles…? And now this man was babbling about a brother waiting for her! And yet, why should he lie?

Her thoughts were interrupted by a sudden, shadowy notion, an amazing doubt, an unbelievable desire. 'But why can it not be true? Why should this man imagine such falsehood? Can my random daydream of the mystery about my birth be a fact? I had dispelled those fantasies by telling myself that they were the result of my pouring over novels! What I am experiencing now is beyond fiction! A mystery greater than those found in detective fiction! Who are these men? Why are they carrying me away? What is going to happen to me when I reach the final destination?'

Lights could be seen in the distance, with the din signifying that they were getting near a town.

Sita once again returned to the idea that she must do something to facilitate Surya's attempts to reach her.

'I am hungry! And thirsty! Can I get something to eat and drink?' Sita asked, in her attempt at delaying tactics.

'All right, we will see,' said the man. He had been talking to Sita in Hindi until then. Now he spoke to the men in front in some other language – Sita could not make out whether it was Punjabi or Marwari.

The car drove through the narrow streets of a town. It stopped in front of an eatery with a sweet stall displaying puris, laddus and other sweetmeats. A thousand flies buzzed over them. Milk was thickening as it boiled in a wide-mouthed brass pan. The smell of rancid ghee heating on a pan assaulted the nose, merged with the stench of the sewer.

A man got down from the car and went to the stall.

Sita thought of shouting and creating a racket. But she changed her mind at once. Looking at the people going up and down the street, she felt that attracting their attention would be to exchange one danger for another.

But was that the only reason? Or was it curiosity, buried deep within the subconscious, to learn where the journey was going to end? Who can fully understand the workings of the human mind?

The man returned with a parcel of puri and sweets, and a clay jar filled with scalding hot milk.

Sita's notion of delaying the journey did not get fulfilled as they did not linger there for more than five minutes.

At a little distance from the town, the road showed a deserted landscape on both sides, dotted with short mesquite shrubs and clumps of flame of the forest trees.

After a while the car halted again. The man asked Sita, 'Will you have puri and sweets?'

Sita refused as she remembered the buzzing flies.

'You said you were hungry,' the man said.

'I don't like puri or sweets, only rice.'

The man laughed and said, 'Look at her! She wants rice, she says.'

Then he added, 'Come on, have some milk!'

Sita agreed, thinking that another refusal would give rise to suspicions.

They poured the milk from the earthen jar into a tumbler and gave it to her. The milk was redolent with the aroma of cardamom and saffron. Tasty too...

The car started moving after she had drunk the milk. Soon Sita found that she could not keep her eyes open. Had they added something to the milk? 'Ayo! Why have they given me this sedative? Will they kill me and throw me into the wilderness? Is this my fate? I am departing from this world without seeing my darling child. Good for my husband! Let him rejoice when he learns that I have been murdered!'

For a moment, Sita thought of shrieking. But she could not. Her eyes closed, her head was spinning, her body went limp.

Somewhere along the road, Sita sensed that the car had stopped. A vehicle coming from the opposite direction stood next to her car. Words were exchanged in an unknown language, sounding like voices from a well. An older woman got down from the other vehicle and sat next to Sita. After that Sita lost consciousness.

18

FRACTURED HEAD

After the spectacular dinner hosted by the member of the viceroy's executive council was over, it took the guests about half an hour to find their cars and depart. As usual, the former divan and his daughters got into Raghavan's car. During the drive, Dhama and Bhama chattered about what they had seen and heard at the dinner. But Raghavan remained silent, without joining in their discussion as he usually did. He did not get down with the divan and his daughters when he stopped the car in front of their house.

'Mr Raghavan! Aren't you coming in? We can have a game of cards,' Dhama said.

'No. Today I have to get home soon,' Raghavan replied.

Bhama whispered something to Dhama, which set them both laughing.

Raghavan got down from the car and accompanied them up to the threshold and stopped.

'I know why you laughed,' he said.

'Of course, you would! All I said was that you are mesmerized after seeing Dharini at the party. Isn't it true?' Dhama asked and laughed again.

'Partly true. But have you realized what a huge mistake you made in calling Dharini a revolutionary?' Raghavan asked.

'Mr Raghavan, why do say it is a mistake?'

'Could she have attended this dinner party had she been a freedom fighter? Did you not see the affability with which the executive council member and his wife treated her? Any need for further proof?'

'Mr Raghavan, in some ways, you have remained a little child. It only proves how clever she is.'

'It also proves the cleverness of our CID police!' Raghavan said.

'That is also true. The revolutionaries have a secret hideout in Delhi. The CID have deliberately left Dharini alone in order to discover it,' Dhama said.

'Really? Sounds incredible!'

'Why are you hurrying home today?'

'Sita's condition has been getting worse for the past two days. Her mental state more so. I am thinking of requesting for a month's leave and taking her to Madras.'

'I see. Now we understand. Are you and Sita going by yourselves, or is Dharini accompanying you?' Dhama asked.

'I suppose you will leave Sita in Madras and go to Bombay,' Bhama remarked.

'How do you know? You talk as if you heard all this from close quarters,' Raghavan said in surprise.

'Don't you know the proverb about a snake being able to sniff out another snake?'

The telephone rang inside the bungalow. Adivarahachari who had already gone into the house, picked up the receiver and asked, 'Who is it?' Then he said, 'The call is for Mr Raghavan.'

Raghavan went in, picked up the receiver and heard the news. His face showed alarm and perturbation.

'What? What?' Dhama and Bhama asked.

'The servant says that Sita had gone for a walk in the evening and has still not come home!'

'Go quickly and see what it is. At the dinner they were talking about some rumpus near Jantar Mantar at 8 p.m. Gunshots were heard,' Dhama said.

'What connection can there possibly be between Sita and the gun shots?' Raghavan scoffed.

'Nowadays you cannot say what will happen and when. Go at once and check it out. Don't hesitate to call us if you need any help,' Bhama said.

'Yes, my boy! Go quickly and see what it is. Call if necessary,' Adivarahachari said.

On reaching home Saundara Raghavan could learn nothing more. All that the servants told him was that Sita, who had gone for a walk in the evening as usual, had not returned.

Raghavan asked anxiously, 'Any calls from any friend's house?'

The young cook said, 'None. But the police called four times.'

Somewhat startled, Raghavan asked, 'What did they say?'

'All that they asked was if the master had come home,' the cook said.

Raghavan called the police station. A police officer he knew spoke to him.

'Mr Raghavan? I have been calling you since 9 p.m. You must have just returned from the dinner. It will be good if you can come here at once,' he said.

'What is it about?' Raghavan asked.

'It can only be told in person. Come at once,' the police officer said.

'I have a problem here. My wife Sita who went for a walk in the evening has still not returned.'

'Is that so? It becomes even more imperative for you to come here immediately,' the police officer said.

When Saundara Raghavan reached the police station, the police officer heard all the news about Sita from him.

Having informed the police officer of what the servants had said, Raghavan asked him, 'Have you received any news?'

'Yes. But it is not useful information,' the inspector said.

Then he pulled out a handgun, placed it on the table and asked, 'Do you know to whom this belongs?'

Startled by the sight of the gun, Raghavan said, hesitantly, 'I... don't know...'

'Raghavan, this is great. Are you trying to hide it even from me?' the inspector asked.

'No... Yes... Sorry. I couldn't recognize it at once. It is mine. How did you get it?' Raghavan babbled and floundered.

'From the young insurgent you had informed us about. How could he have accessed it?'

'I swear I don't know!' Raghavan said.

Then the inspector took Raghavan into the lock-up. Surya was lying there, unconscious, with his head and shoulders bandaged.

'Arresting him was no mean feat. He tried to get out of the clutches of four police jawans and escape. As a result, he has been hit on the head and shoulders. His skull has been fractured!' the inspector said.

19

'WHAT KIND OF A WORLD IS THIS?'

When Raghavan came to Adivarahachari's house the next afternoon, his face was shadowed by despondency. His sunken eyes and countenance testified to the fatigue of a sleepless night.

Bhama welcomed Raghavan with a cry, 'What's this? You look like someone who has lost his wife!'

Raghavan winced, as if he received a fresh wound.

'I never thought that you would speak with such lack of sympathy. I'm leaving,' he said.

Dhama got up and stood before Raghavan barring his departure. She said, 'Ignore her! Bhama's tongue is steeped in poison. Her job is to drive everyone away. Please come and sit down. You know that you have no friends in Delhi who care for you as much as we do.'

Giving up his notion of leaving, Raghavan sank down on the sofa. 'Why in Delhi? I don't have friends anywhere. Office colleagues are like people you meet on train journeys. So long as things go well for you, and they can get their work done, everyone will act like your best friend. The moment you are in a bit of a trouble, everyone will forsake you, like rats desert a sinking ship. I believe that you and your father are exceptions to this rule. Good or bad, my mind finds peace in consulting your father about it. Where is he now?'

'You know father's friend Khajanjia, the banker, don't you? He is launching a new insurance company today with a few others. Father has gone there. He is a director in the company,' Dhama explained.

'Some people suddenly strike it lucky! A few years ago, this

Khajanjia was an ordinary man. Now they say he has earned some five or six crores! For all that, the man cannot even sign his name in English! So many have studied economics like me and got degrees only to spend their entire lifetime with nothing but their monthly salaries. And always with the trepidation of being fired at any time by the idiots above them. As it happened to me today,' Saundara Raghavan said.

'What! *What*!' 'They've fired you?' 'You've lost your job?' 'Why?' 'Atrocious!' Bhama and Dhama rained exclamations alternately.

'The job has not been completely lost. They have suspended me during the period of enquiry. But even if they take me back, I have no intention of returning. I have been asking your father for a long time to recommend me for some other job. This is the right time for it. He must absolutely help me. I have nowhere else to go!'

'Father will not find it difficult to do so. He will certainly ask Khajanjia to give you a job in the bank or in the insurance company. You know that father has great concern for you. So, you don't have to worry about a job. But please tell us all about what happened. Why have you been suspended? Why the enquiry?' Dhama asked.

Bhama intervened to say, 'Why are you harassing him with all these questions! Poor man! He has come to lament about his missing wife!

'Keep quiet! Let her be, sir! Go on, tell me all,' Dhama said.

'When I reached the office today, the head of the department sent for me. I went, suspecting that something unpleasant was afoot. He said, "Raghavan! It has become necessary to suspend you. I am sorry. You must know the reason." I said to him, "No. It will be good if you can explain."

"All right. I will tell you. There is a complaint against you for having sheltered insurgents in your house," he said.

"How can that be? It was I who gave information about the insurgent to the police!" I told him.

"The police already knew about that man and were ready to arrest him. What was the use of your disclosure at that time? A last-minute effort to escape blame," he said.

I was flummoxed. Then I remembered what Cardinal Wolsey had said when he was sentenced to death. I repeated Wolsey's words, "If I had served God as diligently as I have done the King, I would not have suffered this fate."

He said, "The complaint against you is that you have *not* served your king well, understand? Government officers, especially those who work in New Delhi, must be like Caesar's wife, above suspicion. You remember that these are war times? We are in a crucial situation now. That is why they have posted an army general as the viceroy of India. Can't you guess the kind of emergency in the war situation which has led to General Wavell being appointed as India's viceroy?"

"Easily! Because he was sure to lose every battle on the warfront," I said.

The officer laughed and said, "You can convey this opinion during the enquiry. You may go now."

I asked, "What is my crime? What are the accusations against me?"

"They will tell you everything in detail at the enquiry. But I can give you a hint. One reason is that your revolver was in the possession of the man who has been arrested."

"Couldn't he have stolen it?" I asked.

"Yes. But where is the proof? Your wife having suddenly disappeared last night is another reason for suspicion." When the officer said this, I was dumbfounded. "What is the connection between my wife's disappearance and what we are talking about?" I asked.

His answer made me forget all my anxieties and afflictions. I burst into laughter. Even now I feel like laughing when I recall it,' said Raghavan and broke into a silly, feeble laugh.

'Are there government officers with a sense of humour?' Bhama asked.

'He has no sense of humour, not at all. I laughed because what he said was so ludicrous. He said that Sita too was a rebel. Surya and she had conspired to perform many acts against the law. They were sending information to enemy countries through the secret radio about the movements of Indian troops. And with my support. I had pretended to inform the police while at the same time warning them to escape. Sita has gone into hiding somewhere all by herself. How's that?'

'A fine tale! One day the police may come to search this house to see if Sita is hiding here.'

'The police in New Delhi will believe anything!'

'Why will they not be convinced if those who lodge the information do it convincingly? True, the police are ready to swallow anything. But what if they get something substantial…?'

'Bhama, you are talking in riddles again. Something substantial? From whom?' Raghavan asked.

'Raghavan, don't you think that someone must have lodged a complaint about your wife and that young man? It must have also been suggested that you are complicit in this matter. Otherwise, they would not have suspected you to this extent and taken action against you.'

'Oh God! Is that possible? Who could have lodged such false information?'

'Could it not be the person you were repeatedly talking to last evening? Who else is privy to intimate details in connection with your household? Who else could have given information with such convincing credibility?'

'You mean *Dharini*? Are you joking? The day before yesterday you called her a revolutionary. Today you say that she could have spied on us! Bizarre!'

'Nothing bizarre about it. There is no contradiction between what we are saying today and what we said the day before yesterday. Among the rebels, Dharini is a rebel. Only by enacting such a role can she discover the secrets of the revolutionary movement and convey them to the government.'

'Are you saying that Dharini is a double agent? A government spy who also lodges false complaints! What kind of a world is this!'

However, even as he voiced these sentiments, Raghavan began to wonder, 'Could this be true? Otherwise, how can she have such influence with high-ranking government officials? How can she move so closely with them?'

Bhama said, 'This is a terrible world. Full of lies, conspiracies, betrayals and stratagems. But in this world, there are also a few innocents like you. Never mind! What happened to your wife? Any news?'

'Nothing. There is something of the tragicomedy about this. I had decided to make a change in my life and start a new and harmonious chapter in my relationship with Sita. I reach home and find that she is not there! How about that!' Saundara Raghavan said.

'The triumph of destiny,' Dhama sighed.

'I will not put the blame on destiny. I will say that the good intentions of an innocent man called Raghavan were overcome by a woman's evil genius,' Bhama declared.

'Keep your mouth shut! Understand?' Dhama admonished her and added, 'Why, sir! Are you saying that there is no news at all about Sita? No information could be extracted from the arrested Surya? After for all, the police inspector is your friend!'

'True, he is a friend! He has helped me once before. This time too I have placed my trust in him. My reputation will be lost if Surya is subjected to a public trial in this town. At my request, the inspector has agreed to send him to Nagpur. He has also promised to speak in my favour during any *in camera* inquiry. But he has not been able to discover anything about Sita. Surya remains unconscious due to his head injury. The inspector interrogated the driver of the taxi that Surya had taken. The information he gave was incredible. A young man and a woman got into his vehicle in Chandni Chowk. The woman got down when they reached Jantar Mantar and walked on. In a few minutes another car came to a halt beside her, pulled the woman in by force and drove on speedily. At Surya's command this driver followed them. When they were at the Yamuna Bridge, his taxi was stopped after the other car was allowed to pass. At that point, the police van arrived to capture him and his passenger. From the identifications he gave, there is room to suppose that Sita was the woman who had been abducted. But when you think about whether such things can happen in New Delhi in the year 1944, they do not at all seem credible. Moreover, why should anyone abduct Sita? My head starts spinning when I think about all these things,' Raghavan said.

'True enough! But haven't the police tried to discover the car that went ahead?' asked Bhama.

'They did. The taxi driver had given them the number of that vehicle. They sent telegrams everywhere to stop the car wherever it appeared. The car was spotted at a distance of a hundred miles from here. The police inspector called me this morning and told me that there is no news of any woman being found in it.'

'So, your wife, Sita, has indeed disappeared. Mr Raghavan, my heartfelt sympathies,' Bhama said.

'I have no sympathy for him,' Dhama declared. 'Though he had eyes, he had turned blind to what has been discussed by the entire city!'

'How did I turn blind? What was the entire city talking about?' Raghavan asked.

'Does it have to be bluntly announced? They said that it was wrong for you to have sheltered Sita for so long. Now she is lost once and for all. It is something to be happy about!'

Raghavan knew what Dhama was referring to. With his head bowed, he remained silent for some time. 'In any case, my life is ruined. I had a job. Now that's gone too! What is left for me in life?'

'What do you mean, what is left? Why, there is a lovely child in Madras. Who can stop you from bringing the child here and leading a happy life?'

Raghavan's eyes welled up. 'If I bring the child here, the first thing she will ask is, "Where is my mother?" How will I answer her? Besides, who will look after her?'

'What's so difficult about that? Before bringing the child, you have to provide a mother for her. Someone to run the household and be the child's mother. No need to worry about your job. If this job is lost, our father will find another for you, with a higher salary.'

Raghavan pondered Dhama's idea of providing another mother. But his mind would not allow him even to think about it.

When he reached home, he could not face the doleful look on

the faces of the servants. Every room, every corner, every picture, reminded him of Sita. He was moved as he recalled the happy days they had spent in that house at first. He also recalled the fights that broke out between them later. When he thought of those fights, he began to feel that it was he who was to blame. But what was the use of repenting now? Would Sita ever return? Would he ever have the heart to replace her with another woman?

Why should it happen on the day he returned home, determined to begin a new chapter in his life, without quarrels and misunderstandings! His good intentions had turned to dust…!

As he thought about it, Raghavan felt certain that Sita must have run away because he had alienated her. She must have left, unable to bear his cruelty. Where could she have gone? Could she have jumped into the Yamuna and killed herself? Or taken the train to see the child in Madras? In that case, he should get information very soon.

Can there really be any connection between Surya's arrest and Sita's disappearance? Never! It must be some odd mischance. Raghavan also reflected on the hints dropped by Dhama and Bhama about the relationship between Sita and Surya. He concluded that it could never be true.

It is true that he too had wounded Sita with snide remarks about Surya. But not because he entertained any base suspicion about Sita's character. Then, what was the real reason for the malice he felt towards Surya? For his descending to the heinous level of informing the police about him? After subjecting his conscience to a thorough scrutiny Raghavan discovered the truth. This disaster had overtaken him because he had directed all the towering rage that the friendship between Dharini and Surya had aroused in him towards Sita.

He recalled how Dharini had pleaded with him at the party on that very night. She asked him to take Sita to Madras and come to Bombay where she would share a secret about her birth with him. What could it be?

The remarks made by Bhama and Dhama about Dharini being a secret agent were absolutely absurd! The sisters could be malicious. Their job was to criticize someone or the other. They could be of no help to him. Dharini alone could console him and help him at this time.

He must meet Dharini and get her advice. She must be immediately informed about Sita's disappearance.

Did she not say she would be staying for two days in the house of the officer who gave that party? Raghavan picked up the telephone and made his inquiry. Dharini was no longer there.

Raghavan saw a desolate future stretching before him.

20

THE PALACE GARDEN

When Sita regained consciousness, she was greeted by birdsongs, the rustle of the dancing leaves and the tinkling of little bells. The clock struck six. Her eyes opened at once. What she saw all around her plunged her into astonishment – marble walls as white as gleaming ivory, marble floor covered with carpets of charming and unusual designs, chandeliers of varying kinds hanging from above. When the pleasant morning breezes stirred now and then, the chandeliers swayed, their glass prisms tinkled.

Sita saw that she was lying on a silken mattress between velvet pillows in an ornate bed. One after another, memory replayed the happenings of the night before. The dull jabs of pain where she had been hit on the face assured her that they had been real. Her abduction by strangers with Surya following her until he was stopped at the Yamuna Bridge, her being drugged, a woman getting into the car at some point – they were all real events. Her journey had ended in this palace.

A winsome garden could be seen through the window where pools of marble had fountains scattering pearly drops of water. Tiered, terraced, colonnaded mansions towered beyond the garden.

Sita had heard a great deal about the atrocities committed in her own times by the rulers of the princely states. Had a maharaja become infatuated with her and had her brought to him? How could she protect her virtue if this indeed proved to be the case? If she failed, she must find a way of committing suicide. But at first, she must behave in a propitiatory manner.

The sound of footsteps made Sita sit up in trepidation. The door of the chamber was gently opened, setting up palpitations in her heart.

The woman who entered was a common attendant. She spoke sweetly and respectfully in Hindi. Sita understood that she was asking her to get freshened up in the adjacent bathroom, as breakfast was ready to be served.

After breakfast, the effects of sedation had still not worn off completely when she heard two or three voices. She feigned to be asleep, wanting to learn what they were talking about. A voice said, 'The sedative seems to be acting still.' Sita knew that it was the voice of the man who had brought her in the motor car. 'Are you sure that this is my sister?' asked a young male voice. 'Yes. No doubt about that. I have fulfilled the queen mother's command to the letter,' replied the first voice. Sita had gooseflesh when a third voice, belonging to an older lady, said, 'This girl should have been raised in the palace just like you. Fate kept her apart all this time.' But she did not have the heart to wake up just yet. Perhaps this too was a dream. Muddled as she was, Sita kept her eyes firmly shut.

A few minutes later the lady said, 'Let us return after some time.' The visitors left. Giving them some time to leave, Sita opened her eyes and looked at them through the window. It was not difficult for her to recognize the prince and the queen mother.

Sita got up and came out. Other palaces stood around the garden. Through the gaps between them, a blue lake could be seen in the distance.

Where was the palace located? Which king owned it? Did she have any claim to these splendid royal possessions? Did some freak of fate decree that she, a princess born in a royal dynasty, should be raised in an impecunious family, lead a simple life, and undergo untold miseries? And now, have all those miseries really come to an end?

Who was that lady? The mother who carried Sita in her womb

for nine months? Perhaps an older, or a younger aunt? Was that handsome prince her own blood brother? A miracle had taken place in her life. It must be true that she was a royal princess. Why else would such great efforts have been made to fetch her there!

What would her husband's reaction be when he came to know about this? Would he feel privileged to have married a princess from a royal clan? Would he feel remorse for having treated her savagely all this while? Would he be glad to know that she continued to see him as her husband and God? Would he stop shaming and scorning her and start loving and cherishing his wife? In all fairness, he should ask her to forgive him. He should repent for the injustice and brutality he had shown. He should also swear never to behave in that manner again. But Sita was not going to insist that he should, she would never have the heart to humiliate him. If he were to begin to apologize, she would cover his mouth with her hand and beg him to stop. After all, he was her beloved husband. Did he not fall in love with Sita and marry her when she was poor and helpless? Did he not refuse to marry someone like Lalita who was born and raised in affluence?

What would Lalita think when she came to know about this? She would certainly be delighted at Sita's good fortune. Still, not wholly free of envy. Would she not feel a little jealous when she knew that destitute Sita, whose marriage was performed as an act of charity, was born in a royal family in a powerful state?

'How should I behave with these people? I must be careful and firm. I must show them that I did not approve of the methods they used to bring me here. I must not accept whatever they say at once. I must figure out their purpose and deal with them accordingly. How good it would have been to have Surya here to advise me in this situation. Poor man! Who knows what state he is in now? Perhaps he is still hunting for me? Or has been captured by the police! Once I know my situation in this palace, I must make inquiries about Surya and help him. Who else has greater concern for me?' Ruminating in this manner, Sita strolled in the beautiful palace garden. Now and then, she stopped by a bunch of blooms, plucked one and inhaled its fragrance. She stood gazing at the many birds singing on the trees.

When she was tired of walking, she seated herself on one of the marble benches. Castles in the air appeared and disappeared with the speed of lightning. Love and desire, joy and sorrow, rancour and elation, surged and subsided like tidal waves.

They came again, the queen mother, the prince, and the attendant.

Sita looked up and stared at them with unblinking interest.

The queen mother's face creased into a smile.

'Daughter, so, you have started strolling in the garden! I am very happy. You have every right to stroll in this garden. And the right to dwell in this palace. Are you surprised to hear this?'

Sita said nothing in reply. She was perplexed by many questions. But she doubted if she knew enough Hindi to be able to speak to the queen mother. Surely, the Hindi she had absorbed in dealing with the servants in her Delhi home would prove adequate for this tremendous occasion.

'Daughter, why are you silent? We are not strangers to you. I am your stepmother. He is your brother. Fate has forced you to dwell elsewhere all this time,' she said.

Sita was dumbfounded. Elation contended with amazement. This is no dream. Poor Sita is truly a princess born in a royal dynasty. What is this but a miracle of miracles! Can there be any good fortune greater than this?

'Daughter! You have still not opened your lips. Perhaps you are angry about the way you were brought here. Despite the many messages I sent, you did not agree to come. Therefore, it became necessary to bring you by force. Please understand! Your brother is going to be crowned soon. He insisted that before his crowning, reparation had to be made for the injustice done to you. What choice had we but to use compulsion to bring you here?' said the queen mother.

The prince joined the conversation and said, 'Sister, Mother speaks the truth. It was my eagerness that dictated the use of force to bring you here. Please forgive me if you experienced any discomfort on the journey. I also know that you are engaged in making great efforts for India's freedom. I didn't want to hinder you in any way. Honestly speaking, I have no desire to crown myself king. I want to drive the white man away and establish India's independence. It would be difficult to find a better time to achieve it than during this time of war. And yet, for the sake of my mother, I am going to accept the responsibility of governing this kingdom. You must stay here and help me. Sister, will you?'

Sita felt as if she had been left blindfolded in the wilderness. What were they talking about? Was her insufficient knowledge of Hindi making her misunderstand what they were saying?

Deciding that it would be wrong to stay silent, Sita said, 'I am a helpless woman. How can I help you? Besides, should I not ask my husband? It was wrong of you to have brought me here without my husband's knowledge.'

Her words staggered the prince and the queen mother as if they were caught under a landslide. They looked at each other. Then they looked at the man who stood a little apart from them.

'You said that she was highly educated. But she speaks broken Hindi,' the queen mother said.

'She talks of a husband! Is she married then?' asked the prince.

The third man asked Sita in astonishment, 'Are you married?'

'Why not? I have been married for a long time. I have a child too,' Sita answered.

The prince asked, 'Madam, who are you? Where do you come from?'

Some inexplicable instinct stoked Sita's anger. 'Did you have me abducted without knowing who I am?' she asked.

'Madam, please tell us. What is your name? Who are your parents?' the prince enquired.

'Certainly! My name is Sita. My father's name is Duraisami Iyer. My mother's name is Rajam. My husband's name is Saundara Raghavan. My respected father-in-law's name is Padmalochana Sastri. What else do you want to know?'

'Enough, madam, enough,' the prince said and pounced on the attendant. 'Gyandas! How absurd! How inopportune! How could you make such a blunder?'

Gyandas took out a photograph from his pocket and compared it with Sita's face two or three times.

'A mistake! O my God, a mistake! This woman looks just like her. But she is not the other! What a terrible mistake! What can be done now?' groaned Gyandas as he joined in the lament.

The queen mother looked at Sita and asked, 'Woman, tell the truth. Isn't your name Dharini?'

That single query was enough to make Sita comprehend every aspect of the situation. All her castles in the air and daydreams of fantasy splintered, cracked, were powdered to dust, floated in the air, fell to the ground, mingled with the earth, and lost forever.

O God! These feckless morons have brought me here, mistaking me for Dharini. And here I was, building castles in the air.

Disappointment, envy and wrath, transformed Sita's mind into a volcano. Her words exploded in a flood of flaming lava.

'I am not Dharini. Nor was I born in your debauched clan. I am no siren to entice nincompoops with tantalizing wiles. I am a poor girl born into a poor family. I have lived honourably with my lawfully wedded husband. You have ruined me with your monstrous folly. What is to be my fate now?' she shrieked.

'Woman, don't rave! What has happened has happened. I will have you taken back to where you were found,' said the queen mother.

'What do you care? You say so easily that you will send me back. But will my husband accept someone who returns after straying in unknown places? You are nothing but depraved sinners. Heartless, self-seeking monsters! Your dynasty will be completely ruined and lost without a trace!'

The queen mother and prince did not wait to hear more. They walked away in haste, showering reproaches on the attendant who tried pleading and appeasing in turns as he followed them.

Sita began to sob and wail as they went out of sight. The grief buried in the inmost recesses of her heart came surging up in tidal waves. Scalding hot water streamed from her eyes and burnt her cheeks. If only she had had the power of the heroines of the epics,

Sita would have instantaneously reduced all three to cinders. If she had been a queen with the authority to punish, she would have issued a command to cast Dharini into the lime pits. Humiliation and disappointment gave rise to diabolical thoughts in Sita's mind. 'Ah! Wherever I go, that harpy turns up as my enemy! Was she born to shatter my hopes and destroy my life! O hideous monster in the guise of a bewitching beauty! Will no man of valour come forward to humiliate you and teach you a lesson? Won't Surya do it if I ask him? If no one comes to take revenge on you, the next time I see you, I will poison you myself!'

21

THE ACCUSATION

Pandemonium reigned at the railway station in Agra, a junction where tracks intersected from many directions. The incessant arrivals and departures of trains created a tremendous clamour. The crowds were unmanageable. Every available space was filled. Half the passengers were British soldiers and Indian sepoys. It was a crucial time during the World War. Lord Wavell, formerly an army general, occupied the viceroy's seat. All the battles he had taken part in until then had seen the British troops retreat. To overcome this opprobrium, Viceroy Wavell was making mega-scale military preparations, determined that come what may, he would not withdraw from India. Therefore, in the second half of 1943, India's trains were packed with soldiers. Huge cannons and their barrels were stacked on the platforms.

Sita was sitting in a corner in the second-class waiting room. Her hand rested on a small trunk on which she leaned. Her mind wandered everywhere.

Five years ago, Sita had come to the same Agra city with Surya and her husband. Thrilled to see the palaces in the Agra fort, and the Taj Mahal, she had woven many pleasant dreams.

Stranger than all those fantasies were the happenings of the day before. For a few hours she had experienced the pride and joy of believing herself to be a princess. In an instant, a single word had shattered all the joy and pride. Those who had been responsible for beguiling her into succumbing to that illusion had disappeared after leaving her at Agra station with a second-class ticket to Delhi. They had also left a small trunk with her, containing gifts to compensate her for the mishap she had undergone, despite her refusal to take it. Sita did not even bother to open the trunk to see what it held.

Sita's mind was engaged in thinking about her future. She had a ticket to Delhi. The Delhi train would be arriving soon. But how could she face her husband? He who had been berating her without cause, may now reject her utterly! He may believe that she was engaged in some nefarious plot with Surya! Would he believe her if she told him what actually transpired? Would he not reject it as a figment of her imagination? Why not carry out her earlier intention of leaving him? But where could she go? Vasanti was in Madras. If she went there, how could she face her in-laws? Better to follow Surya's suggestion and go to Calcutta. So many women take up jobs and live independently. Why not find a job and then write to get Vasanti to join her in Calcutta? Perhaps it was best to go to Delhi first...

As Sita's mind was swinging between Delhi, Madras and Calcutta, her eyes fell upon a face at the doorway. It belonged to a Muslim man of around fifty years of age. His eye was riveted on her. Where had she seen him before? Recollection came in a flash. On that frightful night when Raziya Begum had entered her house with a blood-stained knife, hadn't a face stared at her and Dharini through the window? Perhaps it was the same man! Why was he here? Why was he staring at her?

Sita had heard that Agra was a dangerous city where evil men captured and sold the women who were careless or unprotected. Had she not suffered enough? Were there to be more sufferings in store for her? But she was in a railway station. A public place where thousands of men and women milled around by day and by night. Unlike in the past, women travelled by themselves. Why should she be afraid?

With a monstrous roar, a train rolled into the platform. Several passengers got up and left the waiting room. Trunk in hand, Sita too got up in haste. Determined not to glance at the saheb standing near the door, she walked past him with an averted face. But intuition told her that the red eyes of the saheb were fixed on her in a piercing glare.

When she learnt that the train that had just arrived was bound for

Delhi, Sita looked for a seat in the second-class compartment. But it was already packed with passengers. They refused to let Sita get in. Sita went searching for a less-crowded compartment, without soldiers and sepoys. Finally, she found a rickety old compartment. When she got in, she was startled to find the Muslim saheb seated there. Was there enough time for her to get down and look for another carriage?

As Sita was struggling with her dilemma, two men came to the compartment. One pointed out Sita to the other. The second man looked hard at Sita and asked, 'Madam, does this trunk belong to you?'

'Yes. Why do you ask?' Sita asked. An instinctive apprehension of imminent danger angered and perturbed her.

'Yours? Are you sure?'

'I am sure.'

The man blew a whistle. Two railway policemen appeared at once. 'Go on! Get down!' the man ordered Sita.

Just then, a railway official happened to come by. Sita called him and said, 'Sir, please help me. These men are troubling me.'

He questioned the policemen. One of them replied, 'This lady has stolen this man's trunk. And she insists that it is hers.'

The railway official looked at Sita and said, 'Madam, the railway police station is right here, close by. Go there and tell the truth to the police inspector. No harm will come to you. If their accusation is wrong, the inspector will let you go. I will put you in the very next train.' As he left, he muttered, 'Can't believe anyone these days.'

Realizing that she had no other option, Sita got down from the train. Assuming confidence, she challenged them, 'Come, I will talk to your inspector. I will demand reparation for this injustice.' As she walked to the police station, Sita's heart beat fast, her legs wobbled. But she did feel some satisfaction at having escaped from the burning eyes of the saheb. She looked behind her to make sure of the fact.

O my god! The danger was not past. The saheb too had got down from the train and was following her at a distance. Ayo! Why? What was he going to do to her?

22

THE RELEASE

Sita stood in the witness stand, having been accused of theft. Her mind was disoriented and on the verge of a blackout. Two days earlier, she had been exhilarated to think that she was a princess from an old dynasty. Today she was standing in court, accused of theft.

Three witnesses had testified for the prosecution. One of them declared that the trunk belonged to him. He had been sitting on a bench at the Agra railway station when he felt thirsty and went for a cup of tea. He returned to find his trunk missing. He searched everywhere and saw a woman sitting with his trunk beside her. Even in her terrible situation, Sita could not refrain from smiling when she learnt that this great fibster's name was Lala 'Satyaprakash' Gupta. The light of truth!

The second witness was the policeman who said that on Gupta's complaint, he had made the woman get down from the train with the trunk and took her to the railway police station.

The next to give evidence was the police inspector to whom the charge was made at the police station. 'At first, I did not believe that this lady had stolen the trunk. At Satyaprakash Gupta's insistence I asked her, "What is in the trunk?" The woman stood in stupefied silence. But Gupta gave a list of things which were all found in the trunk. He had the key as well. Moreover, this lady did not give me any satisfactory information about herself. She refused to give even her address. Therefore, I changed my mind and registered the case.'

What the inspector said was true. Sita did not know what was inside the trunk. Nor did she wish to give her address because she did not want her husband to have to put up with more humiliation. But how to prove that she was innocent?

An elderly court attorney agreed to defend Sita. When she told him the truth, he shook his head and said, 'If you have writing skills, you can become a famous novelist. But no one will believe this story in court.' He did his best in cross examining all three witnesses. But to no purpose.

The prosecution had just one more witness to go. But the magistrate favoured haste. 'Why do we need more proof? The case is clear,' he said.

However, the prosecuting police advocate said, 'Please bear with me. The fourth witness saw the theft with his own eyes.'

At once, the evil Muslim saheb came to the witness stand.

Sita's suspicion about why the man had been following her from the previous night was now confirmed. Only to bear false witness and prove her to be a thief. Sita thought, 'What harm did I do to you? You want to hurl the last stone to kill his unfortunate being who has endured so many unexpected, unbearable sufferings!'

The rogue took the oath to speak nothing but the truth in the name of the All Mighty. Then he began to answer the prosecutor's questions.

'You did see this woman stealing the trunk, didn't you?'

'No. I did not see it.'

'How do you know she stole it if you did not see her stealing it? Do you have any other reason to infer that she did so?'

'No. I know that this lady did not steal the trunk.'

Sita wondered if she was hearing right.

Lala Satyaprakash Gupta's face paled.

The policemen looked at each other.

The magistrate began to listen attentively.

The defence counsel's face brightened.

The prosecutor exchanged a few words with the police inspector and declared, 'I conclude my examination because the witness has turned hostile.'

The defence counsel jumped up to request, 'May the court please allow me to ask a few questions.'

The magistrate too had become interested in discovering the truth. He gave his permission.

'Janab! How do you know that this woman did not steal the trunk?'

'Because I know who stole the trunk.'

There was tumult in court. Whispers rose and subsided quickly.

'Who stole the trunk?' asked the defence counsel.

The man hesitated.

'Was it Satyaprakash Gupta?'

'No.'

'Then who?'

'It was I'

'What? Speak clearly. Look at the court and speak the truth.'

'I stole the trunk. I took it and got into a compartment. This lady got into the same compartment after I did, and sat next to the trunk.'

'Did you not give a written testimony to the police last night saying that you saw this lady steal the trunk with your own eyes!'

'Satyaprakash Gupta asked me to do so. He agreed to give me five hundred rupees if I did.'

'Why then have you switched sides to tell the truth now?'

'My heart did not dare to lie after stepping into the witness stand and taking an oath in the name of Allah.'

'But why did this woman insist that the trunk belonged to her?'

'I don't know what she said to the police. She looks as if she is not in her right mind,' the saheb said.

Sita's attorney kept his closing argument brief.

The magistrate dismissed the case and told the defending attorney, 'Something must be done to safeguard this lady. She must be entrusted to her relatives. Until then, it would be good to place her in some suitable institution.'

'I will,' said the attorney.

The old attorney, a good man, realized that Sita was not mad. He took her home for lunch and back to the railway station at night. On the way he einquired, 'Do you know the saheb who bore witness?'

'No. Where is he now? I must see him and thank him,' Sita said.

'Daughter, will you listen to me?'

'Of course. Should I not have that much gratitude for you?'

'Good. Listen! God saved you today. It is true enough that the man's testimony was the reason for your release. But I don't think he is an honest man. He must have had some reason to get you released by claiming that he had stolen the trunk. You may be in greater danger now.'

'God is compassion incarnate. Won't he save me hereafter as he saved me today?'

'He will. But we must also be careful. It is certain that the saheb did not steal the trunk. I believe you when you say that someone gave it to you. Then why does he plead guilty'

'Sir, where is that man now? Will they perhaps arrest him?'

'Yes, they have.'

'Sir, you must help him. God will bless you!'

'I had gone to see him a little while ago. He said nothing about himself. He talked only about you. He insisted that somehow, I should send you safely to Delhi where you will be taken care of. In my opinion, you must not go to Delhi at all. I think there is someone there waiting to harm you. If you insist on going back to Delhi...'

'No. I am thinking of going to Calcutta. But I have no money for the ticket.'

'Don't worry. I will get you a ticket. There may be someone I know who is going to Calcutta on the same train. I will ask them to take care of you. All right?'

'All right. When good days return, I will send the money back to you.'

'Who is asking for money? I will be happy if you reach Calcutta safe and sound,' the attorney said.

23
HAPPY TIMES

The long and winding lake brimming with water, surrounded by grassy banks, lies like an enticing scarf of blue silk bordered in green, fluttering around a woman's neck. On the lake, an island of emerald groves creates an artist's dream, from where medleys of bird songs come floating on the gentle winds. Water birds and jaunty skiffs skim the waters.

In the evenings, men and women dot the lawns on the lakeshore, lying on the grass, spinning daydreams, or engrossed in heated debates. Older couples chat convivially. Young lovers and newlyweds engage in non-verbal communication – eye to eye and heart to heart.

On that day, Amarnath, the son of Damodaram Pillai of Devapattinam, and his wife Chitra, had come to enjoy the cool breezes on the lake shore.

'Nothing can equal the beauty of this lake in Calcutta,' Chitra exclaimed.

'You are unable to shake off your obsession for everything in Bengal. But this scene does not gladden me now as it used to do before. All I see is pathos, as though this lake has been filled with Mother Bengal's tears over the plight of her children,' Amarnath said.

'Didn't you once say that this lake was brimming with the tears shed by Mother Bengal on reading the novels of Bankim Chandra and the poems of Tagore?' Chitra asked.

'After seeing the streets littered with the corpses of those who starved to death in this terrible famine, I feel that stories and novels are nothing but madness! That is why Mahatma Gandhi said, "What is the use of art in a country where the people starve? The song of the spinning wheel is the sweetest of all." Once, when the Mahatma and Tagore debated over this matter, I thought that Tagore was right. But after witnessing the horrors of the last three months, tens of thousands keeling over and dying on the streets without food, I have come to believe that the Mahatma was right!'

Chitra said with commiseration, 'The people of Bengal have such devotion for their land, and for God. I don't know why God is testing them!'

'The Bengalis are good people, but they believe that Bengalis belong to the tribe of gods, and all others to some inferior caste. They may go all the way up to Lahore to find work, but they resent people from other states earning their livelihood here. God has punished them for their narrow provincial outlook,' Amarnath said. 'Why are you turning God into a brute? Will God send such a cruel punishment to the people of the land where Krishna Chaitanya, Ramakrishna Paramahamsa and Vivekananda were born? What does it matter if people belonging to the land where Deshbandhu Chittaranjan Das and Subhash Bose were born, took some pride in their province?'

'Then why are they undergoing this calamity?'

'How can famine be avoided if avaricious devils hoard all the grain?'

'But it was God who created those devils! Therefore, God has to take responsibility for every kind of human action!'

'You have joined the communists and become an atheist! I won't talk to you,' Chitra said.

Amarnath said teasingly, 'At last! My allegiance to communism has enabled me to silence a woman!'

'If it is God who has sent this famine, surely something good will come out of it. This is not the first time that Bengal has been afflicted by drought. Don't you remember how Bankim Chandra described the famine in *Ananda Mutt*? It gave rise to a great revolution, and the great mantra "Vande Mataram". This famine too is going to generate a colossal revolution. The volcano will explode and destroy British sovereignty in its flaming lava. India is going to attain independence.'

'I don't believe famine-stricken masses will turn into revolutionaries. And how can the dead rebel? Five lakhs have died in the famine in Bengal. Chitra, if only a quarter of their number had been ready to give up their lives for freedom, India would have attained its independence by now. But though they may die in street corners, the people won't come forward to sacrifice themselves for the nation.'

'Of course they will! The problem is that there are no leaders to guide the masses. If only Subhash babu were here! What a leader! Innumerable Indian volunteers are joining Subhash babu's army in Malaya, ready to sacrifice their lives.'

'If Subhash babu were to win, instead of British rule, Bengali rule will be established in India!'

'So what? Why not the Bengalis rather than a foreign regime?'

'I only told you like it is! All said and done, the Bengalis are jingoistic. Look at the consequences. Bengal is now under the rule of the ministers of the Muslim League. These leaguers are also Bengalis, but what kind of Bengalis!'

'Dr Tagore is also a Bengali. Why don't you look at him? Did he not say the world is one, all humankind belongs to the same caste? I don't like the way you find fault with Bengalis, not at all. Moreover, should we blame the people of the region where we earn our livelihood? Enough. Let us go. Didn't you say that we must go to Howrah?' Chitra said as she got up.

Amarnath got up saying, 'Chitra, I want to go back to Tamil Nadu.'

'You will have to go alone. I don't like the small mindedness and petty behaviour in your region. The Tamil people do nothing but carp at each other.'

'Do you think the Bengalis are devoid of this trait? That's all you know!'

'I have no wish to dig into other people's faults.'

Arguing endlessly, as only couples with genuine rapport can, they reached the parking lot and got into their car.

Amarnath and Chitra resided in a charming bungalow in Tollygunge, a suburb in Calcutta. Earlier, they used to go to the lake regularly to enjoy the breeze. But these outings became less frequent when the famine victims started arriving in the city. Moreover, Chitra had joined an organization, that provided famine relief, as a volunteer. It had been launched to aid women and children who came as refugees from Burma. Then the famine began and the organization continued to serve orphaned women and children who came to Calcutta, emaciated and half dead.

After three months, when things began improving in the last few days, Amarnath and Chitra had decided to go to the lake and visit friends in Howrah.

Many big trading companies conducted their business in the streets near the Howrah railway station. Those streets were wide but still so congested that every car had to crawl through them in the evenings.

'Lakhs of people died in the drought. And yet, these streets are jam-packed with people,' said Amarnath.

'Please don't perform any heroic deed for population control by running over someone or the other,' Chitra said.

'On this street, anyone the car runs over is bound to be a black-market dealer. Killing such people is a service to the nation,' was Amarnath's rejoinder.

24

THE EXPLODING VOLCANO

Evening was turning into night. The street lamps had been switched on. But since the lamps were covered by air raid protection blinds, they did not shine brightly.

'Calcutta has lost its lustre with the coming of this Japanese war! How dazzling the lights used to be in this place,' Chitra said.

She had just finished speaking when deafening explosions rent the air. At once, an ARP (Air Raid Precautions) siren blared its wailing song, making their flesh quiver. Amarnath and Chitra realized that a Japanese aircraft was dropping bombs, and that the ARP siren was issuing its warning, not before, but after the event. This was a new experience for them. Their bodies began to shake. Their heartbeats accelerated. Chitra gripped Amarnath by the shoulder. Amarnath stopped the car by the kerb. The huge jostling crowds began to scatter and disappear in all directions. The vehicles came to a standstill on both sides of the street.

The explosions ceased. Five minutes passed. The couple concluded, 'It is over, we can go.' The very next instant… God! What a bizarre phenomenon! The light of a million suns sped towards the earth! Followed by a colossal explosion – the monstrous, ear-splitting blast of all the moving bodies in the galaxies detonating and crashing together. Their car rocked and juddered. The glass windows cracked and splintered. Hideous wails echoed all around them.

The horrors were not over. At a little distance, a mammoth

miasma of smoke rose in spurts and spread everywhere. A crimson blaze shot up through the smoke, as if to cover the whole sky above.

Chitra had been holding Amarnath tight all this time. She opened her mouth to say in a trembling voice, 'Ayo! What is this?'

'The TNT depot must have caught fire. That is why the noise was so deafening!'

'The world has come upon evil days. No doubt about it,' Chitra said.

'Evil days had come upon the world long ago! Now they have arrived in Calcutta,' Amarnath said.

'Let us go back to Madras,' Chitra said.

'Let us first go home tonight. We can think about going to Madras tomorrow,' Amarnath said.

'Turn back, let us go home. Let us not go to Howrah today.'

'I am waiting for my hands to stop shaking. We can't go to Howrah today even if we want to.'

His statement was confirmed by the scenes taking place before them and the sounds reverberating around them.

The gigantic blaze was rising with greater force. Mighty flames shot up around the blaze. Smoke rose in clouds and spiralled up to fill the sky. People ran screaming to where the fire was spreading.

Fire engines clanged their bells as they came from all directions.

Horns boomed in a hideous and deafening cacophony as all the vehicles, immobilized until then, started moving simultaneously.

When the winds cleared the smoke now and then, the fire lit up the tops of the multi-storied buildings on either side of the street, where human forms were outlined in silhouettes, like scenes from hell.

Chitra closed her eyes and covered her ears. 'Are you not going to turn around?' she asked.

'I will. Keep an eye on both sides, and at the back,' Amarnath said.

The car started moving and crossed the street to enter another where a big crowd had gathered. As they neared the crowd, they saw that the people were looting a Marwari shop and running away with whatever they could grab.

A few policemen stood watching the looting in silence.

Amarnath hesitated when he reached the edge of the crowd. Should his fear of the rogues make him retreat? But he drove the car through the crowd. Some men banged on the top of the car. Others knocked on the doors. Some others tried to stop the car. There were shouts and shrieks. A voice cried out, 'Maro! Maro!'

Amarnath drove the car in a state of terror and sped away as soon as he cleared the crowd.

'Chitra, how shameful! A bomb explodes, there is an outburst of fire and here, looters break into a shop. Things are in this state and we demand independence for India. Excellent!' Amarnath exclaimed.

A stone was hurled at the car. As it hit the moving car, it resounded like an exploding bomb.

'See how right I am! What would have happened if this stone had fallen on me or on the glass window?' Amarnath said.

'Haven't I admitted that you are right? We have earned enough. Let's leave for our hometown tomorrow. Let us live there with what we have, in peace.'

'And will there be peace in our place? Will the people there be any different! Won't they do what the people here are doing?'

'Our folks will never behave with such bestiality,' Chitra said with conviction.

A little later, they saw that a bus had fallen sideways. It was burning.

'How can a bus catch fire?' asked Chitra.

'Some scoundrels must have set fire to it,' said Amarnath.

'Why?'

'Is there a reason for the actions of scoundrels? They find their happiness in looting, murdering and burning.'

In front of them, they could see a body sprawled on one side of the road. A woman's body. A boy was bending over it.

'Stop! Stop the car,' Chitra shrieked.

The car stopped. When he saw the car, the boy bolted down the street.

'What was that boy doing?' Chitra asked.

'He was removing the bangle from her wrist. He ran away when he saw us. Chitra, you complained about how you missed seeing corpses on the roadside in the last few days. Now your desire is fulfilled,' Amarnath said.

'Don't talk nonsense,' Chitra said and added, 'Maybe she is still alive. Let us go and check.'

They got down and went near the recumbent form.

'Looks like a woman from Madras. A young woman,' Chitra said.

'Will the god of death spare her just because she is from Madras? Come! Let's go!' Amarnath said.

'Why should we assume that she is dead? Check if she is alive.'

'Why don't you check? You have more experience in these matters,' Amarnath said.

Chitra placed her finger on the nose of the woman who was lying on the ground. She was breathing faintly. Then she placed her hand on her chest. The heart was beating.

'She is alive. Quick!' said Chitra as she slid her own hands under the woman's head. 'Why are you standing like a tree? Quick! Hold her by the feet and raise her.'

Amarnath groaned as the couple carried the stranger to the car and placed her on the back seat.

'Drive on! Quickly! Save her life!' Chitra said.

As he started the car Amarnath asked, 'Where should I go?'

'Home!'

'In that case I will stop the car and throw the body out. What if she were to die in our house?'

'I have never seen anyone more pitiless. All right. Drive to the orphanage. Hurry!'

Amarnath drove at super speed. When the woman lying unconscious felt the breeze blowing on her face, she began to revive in body and mind. The first aid given at the orphanage helped her recover fully.

Once they knew that the danger had passed, Chitra and Amarnath went home.

25

LALITA'S LETTER

Chitra's husband Amarnath was getting ready to go to the office.

'Can you come home a little early today? The lake will be very pleasant after the rain, we can go there,' Chitra said.

'All right. All right. Since the other day, the word "lake" has begun to frighten me. What if we are forced to rescue another drought-stricken woman? Far better to go to a movie. *Anna Karenina* is showing now.'

'The ways of men are strange indeed! They melt when they see an abandoned woman spreadeagled on the streets – in a movie! But if they see her in that situation in real life, they carefully avert their eyes!'

'Who denies it? Can a woman lying on the street in a movie be an ordinary woman? She has to be a Greta Garbo or a Norma Shearer or a Kanan Bala! Guaranteed to melt any viewer's heart!'

'Mister, stop! The woman whom you saved is in no way less important than your Greta Garbo or Kanan Bala. Listen to me. Come home early this evening. I have told her that I will take her to see the sights of Calcutta. She has agreed to join us,' Chitra said.

'No, there's a saying in our Tirunelveli regions, "buying trouble on the roadside". I will come back only at 10 p.m.'

'Why are you so vicious about a woman we know nothing about?' Chitra demanded.

'We have to be careful precisely because we know neither her name nor her background. If she were an honest woman, why should she hesitate to mention her name and place of residence? She has still not disclosed them!' Amarnath retorted.

'So what? There can be any number of reasons for that! She seems to have suffered a great deal. I am ready to appear before any court and swear to her integrity. There is no end to the praises showered on her by Madam Saudarini, the head of the orphanage. She bathes fifty orphans per day. She works tirelessly without complaining. Madam Saudarini says that it would be of great help to her if the woman continued to stay there.'

Amarnath demanded drily, 'If she is so wonderful, why should she refuse to disclose her identity?'

'Who knows? Like you, her husband may have a brutal temperament! He might have beaten her and driven her away.'

'All right, all *right!* See if I don't beat you and drive you out of the house tomorrow!' Amarnath said.

'If you do, I will announce to the whole world about how my dear husband thrashed and kicked me out of the house!' Chitra retorted.

The servant boy brought the mail in. As he sorted them, Amarnath handed an envelope to Chitra saying, 'A letter for Madam Chitra, from Madam Lalita.'

Chitra took the letter to her room. She was back in five minutes with a shrill cry, 'Listen to this story.'

Amarnath looked up and remarked, 'Seems to be a story of electrifying mystery and suspense. Who has written it? Lalita?'

'Yes. Lalita herself! But what she has written is no fiction. It is a real-life account, more startling that fiction. Here, read it!'

'No, I won't. Then you will want to read letters addressed to me.'

'I have never seen a more obstinate man! At least listen to what it says. Lalita's brother Surya tried to escape from the police in Delhi. When the police surrounded him, he shot at them before they captured him. He was badly wounded in the scuffle and is in a precarious situation. Lalita and her parents are extremely distressed. They have another mishap to contend with. Sita has disappeared! Vanished without leaving any information as to her whereabouts. Surya's arrest and Sita's disappearance took place on the same day.

Sita's husband has written to Lalita's father, asking to be informed if she turns up in Devapattinam or Rajampettai. Lalita is more distressed by Sita's disappearance than by Surya's plight.'

Amarnath became lost in profound cogitations. Jumping up suddenly he said, 'Chitra, four days ago, there was a report in the newspaper about a mishap in Delhi. Do you remember reading it?' With that he went to the corner where newspapers were stacked and began to rummage through them. In a few minutes, he found the paper he was looking for.

'Here it is. Chitra, listen!' he said and read it aloud. 'Four days ago, the news of the police arresting an insurgent named Surya Narayanan was published in our columns. His resistance at the time of arrest resulted in him being severely hit and wounded. He was hospitalized for treatment under police custody. Information has been received about his escape from the hospital last night. His escape remains a mystery. We learn that the secret police are searching for clues in this matter.

'Meanwhile, it is also learnt that the woman insurgent who disappeared on the day of Surya Narayanan's arrest continues to remain untraced. It has come to be known that she was exceptionally resourceful, lived in Delhi under two different names, and had close affiliations with people in the top echelons in government circles. The secret police are gathering evidence about this woman as well.'

Amarnath finished reading and asked with great excitement, 'Chitra, I didn't think of our Surya when I read this report. What can we say about his ingenuity? It was not such a big deal to have misled the police until now. But to have escaped once again from the hospital, while under their eyes, and after being badly wounded! Chitra! Aren't you amazed by Surya's daredevilry?'

'Never mind boasting about Surya! I am thinking about the mysterious disappearance of Sita! Listen to me. Please take leave from your office today. Let us both go to the famine relief centre, right away,' Chitra said.

'Why?' Amarnath asked.

'Haven't you twigged it? I have my doubts about the woman we admitted at the orphanage.'

'Are you saying that she could be Sita? Bhesh! There would be some sense in her going to Devapattinam or Rajampettai as her husband suggests! Why should she come all the way from Delhi to Calcutta?' Amarnath exclaimed.

'Very clever! You are forgetting that Sita is a rebel. Will it not be like notifying the police if she were to go to Devapattinam or Rajampettai? She has come to Calcutta to go underground. And poor thing, she met with some disaster on her arrival. But you have seen Sita before. Surely you can recognize her?'

'I saw her but once at the wedding. And that was ten years ago.'

'Come and look at her properly. Then tell me if you can identify her as Sita.'

'Sita or not, what do I care? I will drop you at the orphanage and go to my office,' Amarnath said.

Both got into the car and reached the orphanage. Amarnath left Chitra there and went to his office.

26

ANXIETIES OVERCOME

Amarnath returned from the office rather early, wondering if Chitra had returned by then, or whether he would have to go and pick her up from the orphanage. He parked the car in front of the house.

Chitra rushed out as soon as the car arrived. Her face was shining, jubilant.

'So, you have discovered her identity?' Amarnath cried.

'Yes. I was right. You insisted that I could not be!'

'The poet Tiruvalluvar has declared that the woman who truly worships her *husband,* has but to say the word, and hey presto, the thing will happen! So, how can your prediction fail?'

The couple entered the front hall. And there, Amarnath was startled to see a woman seated on the sofa and reading a letter.

When she saw them, the woman got up hurriedly and went up the stairs.

As soon as she disappeared, Amarnath asked, 'Chitra, Is that Sita? Not content with discovering her identity have you brought her here?'

'Yes, would I leave any task I undertake, unfinished?' Chitra said.

'Undoubtedly! Am I not always praying that you may never undertake any task? Now you have brought this devil home!'

'Please keep your big mouth shut.'

'Goddess, forgive me! You have discovered and brought home this maid from the celestial spheres! For what purpose? Please favour me by disclosing your intentions!'

'What do you mean "intention"! She is your dear friend Surya's cousin. Should I leave her at the orphanage?'

'Why not? Besides, how do you know for sure that she is the same Sita?'

'She has admitted it.'

'How did the woman suddenly decide to admit the fact?'

'I employed my own strategy.'

'May I humbly request you to deign to let me know what it was?'

'When you left me at the orphanage, I went straight to Sita and tried to talk to her. As usual, she remained mumchance. She was serving food to the children. I began to talk to Madam Saudarini who was standing by. I gave her the news about Sita. I noticed how startled Sita was when I mentioned Surya's name. In a little while, Sita came searching for me. She asked me what I had told the chief. I repeated it, and then asked her, "Are you not Sita?" She admitted everything. I invited her home. She refused, saying that she liked serving the children in the asylum. I compelled her to come home by saying that she could take her turn to serve there twice a week as all of us did. What do you think of my stratagem?'

'Should you ask? You should really be working in the CID department. Right now, they are struggling to capture UGs because they don't have brilliant strategists like you.'

'Who is a UG?'

'Don't you know? Those who go underground, evade the police, and continue to pursue their revolutionary activities. I saw some policemen and CID agents standing at the corner of the adjacent street. It seems they are hunting UGs.'

'Really...? Perhaps...' began Chitra and stopped quickly.

'Perhaps what?'

'Nothing. Will you talk to her?'

'Why trouble her now?' Amarnath said.

'No trouble,' Chitra said and went leaping up the stairs.

However, Sita told her, 'No, not now... My mind is not at peace today. Didn't you show me Lalita's letter? As I read it, I was overcome by old memories. I will talk to your husband tomorrow.'

As they were talking, they heard men stampeding into the house, their boots making a great noise. As Chitra came down the stairs she saw policemen and CID agents standing below. Her head began to spin. She steadied herself by holding on to the rails on the staircase.

The man who appeared to be the chief of the posse was telling Amarnath, 'This UG woman is extremely clever. She had been deceiving the Delhi police by living under two names – Sita and Dharini. See what happened just now. Knowing that we were going to the orphanage, she has somehow tricked your wife into bringing her here! We had been waiting all this while at the street corner for you to come home.'

'Inspector, you are making a great mistake. This lady is no UG. Nor does she belong to the revolutionary movement,' Amarnath said.

The inspector said, 'Mr Amarnath, how do you know? We have all the necessary proofs. Even a photograph.'

After that, things moved quickly. Amarnath came up to where Chitra was standing on the staircase to tell her about the matter. She groaned a great deal over it. 'Can't you stop this?' she pleaded.

'You don't know anything about the police. When it comes to duty they have no friends, they are strangers to pity. It is a big thing that they are not arresting us as well. We will have to send your friend away. Later, we will see what we can do. We can even appeal with a writ of habeas corpus.'

Chitra was in tears as she ran up to inform Sita.

At first Sita could not take it in. But once she understood what was happening, she felt as if a great weight was removed from her heart. No more worries about where to go and what to do! God had sent her this assistance on his own. Inside the prison house, she could have peace.

True, she could not see Vasanti anytime soon. In a way, that was also a good thing. What could she tell the child if she saw her? What answer could she give if the child asked questions about the father? The grandmother would look after the granddaughter. It was enough if the child had a good life. Good times may return, God may bring them together again...

Without any hesitancy, Sita came down and gave herself up to the police.

Amarnath requested the police inspector to treat Sita with the respect due to a woman of gentle birth. The inspector promised to do so.

As Sita was leaving the house, with tear-streaked eyes Chitra hugged her and said, 'Sita, don't worry! I will make my husband appeal in court with a writ of habeas corpus and get you released. You will be back very soon.'

Sita replied, 'Please don't do anything like that. Chitra, god has sent me this boon on his own. You should stop worrying about me.'

PART FOUR
THE DELUGE

1

A MOTHER'S GRIEVANCE

The planet Jupiter has completed an orbit since we were last in Rajampettai village. Eleven years and ten months to be exact. The old post office looks much the same. But we see a few cinema posters on its walls and pillars. The space between them is filled with the slogans 'Jai Hind!' and 'Victory to Netaji!'

The banyan tree with its spreading branches and hanging roots is to be seen no more, leaving the street bare, and without its old charm. A ration shop has replaced the sweet stall. Four or five women are standing there, baskets in hand, waiting for the shopkeeper to favour them with their quota of rice. There is some activity within the post office. Postmaster, postman and runner are discussing the imminent strike. No one we know, all newcomers.

Let us leave these strangers and go to the agraharam in Rajampettai village, which is still inhabited by the people we know.

There are changes in the agraharam. More houses have become dilapidated. No thatched canopy in front of Kitta Iyer's house, the frontage too no longer appears attractive. But Seemachu Iyer's house looks better than before. He has rebuilt the house on a stronger and larger scale. Having started a textile store in Devapattinam at the right time, he has been blessed by the goddess of wealth.

Kitta Iyer has suffered losses in recent times. Land issues have made for long-drawn disputes between the workers and the landowners. A year ago, the court brought a verdict in favour of the landowners. Kitta Iyer had to bear the brunt of conducting the case. This not only increased his financial losses, but also earned him the animosity of the workers.

The last year saw Kitta Iyer struck by an unforeseen disaster. Robbery and banditry had been rampant in the surrounding regions. In their written testimony, one of the captured bandit gangs mentioned Kitta Iyer's connection with their activities. Kitta Iyer was immediately suspended from his post as pattamaniam. He suffered untold agonies through the legal proceedings, and was ashamed to step outside the house. Moreover, an enormous sum had to be spent on litigation. Finally, both police and official enquiries established his innocence. The false testimony had been motivated by personal rancour. And yet, even though the verdict proved that it had all been much ado about nothing, Kitta Iyer could not but hear rumours about his suppressing the truth with bribes.

Ten days ago, Kitta Iyer was returning from Devapattinam after visiting his son-in-law who had just been released from prison. At 10 in the night, as he was being driven home in a bullock cart from the railway station to Rajampettai, seven or eight masked men surrounded the vehicle, thrashed both the cartman and Kitta Iyer, grabbed his wallet, and ran away.

Kitta Iyer came home with gashes all over his body. That night, he became afflicted with high fever.

When they heard the news, Lalita and Pattabhiraman rushed to Rajampettai with their children. Pattabhiraman left after two days. At the request of Kitta Iyer and Sarasvati Ammal, he left Lalita and the children behind for a longer stay.

Kitta Iyer was lying half asleep in the bedroom. He had recovered somewhat, but did not have the strength to get up and move about as before.

The central hall in the house replays the scene that we had seen twelve years ago. Mother Sarasvati Ammal is braiding Lalita's hair. But Lalita is no longer a young unmarried girl. She is the mother of two children. Those children, Pattu and Balu, are seated nearby, looking at the illustrations in a Tamil magazine.

Lalita's face does not register much joy. Her moist eyes are like the dark monsoon clouds ready to burst into a downpour. Something utterly trivial could trigger them to rain tears.

As always, Sarasvati Ammal is ready to pull the trigger. She is unleashing her grievances now, as she braids Lalita's hair.

'The humidity is unbearable, but the wretched rains don't come! In the fields, all the crops are getting parched under the sun. Don't know when God will show mercy! I think God has lost his power in this age of Kali. Otherwise, would such atrocities take place? There was a time when even the mention of your father's name was enough to set town and countryside trembling. But now, he is accosted by bandits who hit him and steal his purse! He is left with neither power nor authority!'

Lalita interrupted, 'Amma, you did not tremble before father even when the whole world did! You were fighting with him even then.'

'Very clever! Is it not enough for everyone to respect her husband the way I did? This family has been reduced to this sorry state only because I held myself back from fighting with him. Take your wedding, now. If I had been allowed to have my way, would I have gotten you married into that household? Imagine throwing a jewel into the dustbin. That has been your fate.'

'Don't talk nonsense, Amma! The children might hear you.'

'Why not? Let them hear me! Let your son and daughter go and complain to mapillai if they like. I am not afraid of anyone. Gandhi, Congress – that's all they talk about. Your husband is back home after two years in prison. Why should he go to jail? Did he loot or steal? I was scared that this husband of mine might follow his son-in-law to jail. Thanks to my prayers we were spared that humiliation. All right, so your husband spent two years in jail. What did he get out of it? Some people join the Congress and become 'member' or something and earn money. Did he? No!'

'Amma, my husband did not go to jail to become a member of the legislature or to obtain any other official post. He did it for the nation's independence!'

'All right. Let me see, has independence been obtained? You people swore that Hitler would win, and the Englishman would slither away with his tail tucked in. Your brother Surya the know-it-all even suggested that your father should give up his post as pattamaniam. What happened? I don't see any independence-shindependence anywhere...! Forget independence, at least, mapillai can start going to court and earning some cash! What is the use of studying law and sitting at home with folded hands? Can sitting still make ends meet? If he doesn't want to practice law, mapillai should find another job. You are a woman with a family now. Is money overflowing in this house? Am I able to do anything for you by way of cash or in kind? Even if I do, you don't know how to save it and live a good life. You declare nonchalantly that you have sold your gold waist belt at his bidding! What can I say about your wits? Even if he cannot make new jewels for her, will any husband sell his wife's ornaments? Shameful!'

'Amma, if you go on blaming him, I will leave right now, instead of two days later,' Lalita snapped.

'Go, go! Get going this very instant. It is my fate that though I slave for all of you, no one has any pity or concern for me. Whom can I blame but my destiny that my own son and daughter are turning into my enemies! Did I not carry you in my womb for ten months? Doesn't a mother have the right to say a few words?'

'Amma, say whatever you like about me, I will take it. But don't say anything about my husband. You were the one who "discovered" him and got me married to him. What is the use of complaining now?' Lalita remarked.

'I did not go searching everywhere to "discover" this mapillai! Your father arranged it at your brother Surya's urging. I had found a man for you who was earning a salary of a thousand rupees. We were not fortunate enough to secure him. Your wonderful aunt from Bombay turned up at the right time, with daughter in tow. I banged my head against the wall saying that no other girl should be allowed in the house when the boy came to see you. No one paid any attention. Do I have an English education? Do I know the modern ways? I am nothing but a numskull, a country bumpkin. And yet what this numskull and bumpkin suspected came true. Your athanga Sita enticed the man who came to see you. Who knows what alluring charms and intoxicating spells she had! The man who came to see you, followed her like a fatuous zombie. Meanwhile, your fortunes took a nosedive.'

'Not at all! My fortunes were in great shape. What did fate have in store for Sita who married a man with a salary of a thousand rupees? Don't you know all about her sufferings? Last month, Chitra wrote to me about what a scoundrel Sita's husband was! If I had been married to him, wouldn't I have undergone Sita's share of sufferings?' Lalita asked.

'Not at all. That girl Sita had a blighted horoscope. That is why wherever she went, she faced what she had to face. If I had given you to that man, you would have lived like a queen!'

'If my horoscope had predicted good fortune, I should have enjoyed prosperity in the household I did go to! Why hasn't it been so?' Lalita asked.

'I have no answers for insolence. What is lacking in the household you went to? You have everything – house, money, property! What can fortune or horoscopes do if we bring hardships upon ourselves? It is not as though you cannot find food to eat without selling your gold waist belt. Mapillai has gone crazy. And you dance to his tune.'

'All right, Amma! *All right*! Haven't you finished the braiding? Enough. Let me go!' Lalita said.

All this while Sarasvati Ammal had been braiding Lalita's hair. She knew that once she released her, she could not get her daughter to sit down and listen to her grievances. So, without any haste, she had continued to braid her hair in slow motion.

Just as she was tying up the ends, the postman called at the front door. Lalita sprang up at once, tugging the braid free from her mother's grip.

'The years have brought no change in you. Thank goodness you stop at the door and don't go running all the way to the post office!' Sarasvati Ammal cried. Lalita barely heard this tirade as she went to answer the door.

2

'SITA IS COMING!'

The elderly postman at the front door looked at Lalita and asked, 'Are you Lalita Pattabhiraman?'

'Yes,' Lalita said as she extended her hand to receive the letter.

Lalita opened the envelope eagerly. There were two letters inside. One was from her husband. The other appeared to be in Sita's handwriting! Lalita read her husband's letter first.

Dear Lalita,

My blessings.

When I write to you, I want to begin with 'My life!', 'My one true love!', 'Sweet essence of passion!', 'The partner of my life!'. But when I actually start writing, I end up greeting you in the good, old-fashioned, traditional manner.

I reached home safe and sound. No one accosted me or robbed me of my wallet. Even if someone had made the attempt, he would not have found much. Only the train fare to Devapattinam with a bonus of an anna and a half. How disappointing for him!

The cook has taken leave at the perfect time! I am doing the cooking now. Your brother Sundu has issued a certificate for my culinary skills, with a first class.

Your mother had asked you about what I'd gained by being sentenced to prison. What greater gain can there be than the fact that I have learnt to cook? Could I have done this if I had not been behind bars? Not with all of you shouting your heads off if I so much as put my foot into the kitchen.

Hadn't you told Sundu to help me? Yesterday he upset the gravy on the stove. 'Enough, boy, enough!' I told him. 'The greatest assistance you can give me is to stay still!' Even now I am terrified that Sundu may turn up to help me!

Has your mother forgotten the waist belt? Have you told her that it was not made of gold, but polished brass, and that I did not sell it but gave it away? Who knows, she may get more incensed if you do! You know your mother. Do what you think best!

I hope that Mama has recovered completely by now. I feel terrible when I think of his undergoing such a calamity. It would have been far better to have listened to Surya and followed his advice. It would have prevented both loss of money and loss of name. However, it is as God wills!

When are you planning to return? From the enclosed letter you will know the reason why it has become important for you to return as soon as possible.

Your friend Sita has given me a fright by announcing her visit. What if she lands up when you are not here? Madam Sita is used to fashionable lifestyles in metros like New Delhi. I am a hopelessly old-fashioned creature. How will I know how to welcome and host a woman like her?

Therefore, as soon as you see this missive, please take leave of your father and mother, and come home.

Yours,

Pattabhiraman

Though the letter contained several details, the only information that impressed itself on Lalita's mind was, 'Sita is coming.' As she began to read Sita's letter, she heard her father's affectionate call, 'Lalita!' She went to answer him, still reading.

Kitta Iyer asked, 'Lalita! Any letter for me? You seem to be holding two! Are they both for you? Who has written to you?'

'One is from my husband from Devapattinam. The other is from Sita. Appa! She has written from Chitra's house in Calcutta. She is coming to see her daughter in Madras, soon. She says she will come to Devapattinam as well.'

'Is that so? So, Sita has written to you! I wish to see her and give her some advice. Lalita, if she comes to Devapattinam, will you ask her to come and see me? It looks like I will not be able to get about for another month or so,' Kitta Iyer said.

'Yes, Appa. I will ask her to come. May I go home now? He has asked me to come back soon as Sita is to visit us there. I feel bad about leaving you in this condition. And yet...'

'Yes, Lalita! Mapillai has come home just now after spending two years in jail. How long can you leave him alone? Since Sita is also coming there, certainly you must go soon. Sometimes I too feel like settling down in Devapattinam. I cannot be at peace in this village anymore.'

'Why, Appa? Why should you ask anyone's permission to come to Devapattinam? I will leave tomorrow. I will write to my husband immediately.'

Lalita went to write her letter. Her darling daughter Pattu and son Balasubramanian came to sit beside her.

Pattu asked softly, 'Amma, a letter from Appa?'

'Yes. Here, have a look.'

Pattu stumbled over the first line and said, 'Amma, Appa's writing is all crooked. I can't read it. Who has written the other letter?' 'It is from Sita athanga,' Lalita answered her.

'Who is Sita athanga?' Pattu asked.

'Your grandfather had a younger sister. She was my athai. Sita is her daughter. She says that she is coming to see you both very soon. Before she does, you two must become very good. You should not badger anyone with questions.'

'No, I won't. Amma, I have never seen Sita athanga. What is she like?'

Lalita was struck by an idea. She left the letter half-written, opened an old cupboard and rifled through the junk. At last, she located an old photograph. She showed the photograph to her children and said, 'See, Pattu! This is Sita athanga. This is me. When we were young, we were great friends. This photograph was taken just before we got married. We would go to the poolside bungalow and chat all the time. All that seems like a dream now,' she said.

Sarasvati Ammal came to Lalita and asked in a loud voice, 'Lalita! What is this I hear? Is Sita really coming to Devapattinam?'

'Yes, Amma. Sita is coming. Why are you getting into a flap over it?'

'Why is that accursed creature coming at all? Who asked her to come? Lalita, listen to me! Write to her at once. Tell her that it is not convenient, she need not come now.'

'Amma, Sita is not coming to this village. She is coming to see my children and me in Devapattinam. Why are you making such a fuss?'

'Are you and I strangers to each other? Am I not the mother who gave birth to you? Aren't your children, my grandchildren? I don't know why all of you turn abrasive when it comes to me!'

'You never liked Sita athanga.'

'And why should you like the person I dislike? Listen to me, Lalita. She is accursed. Her mind does not harbour good thoughts. Even if you feed milk to a snake, it will produce nothing but poison. Write at once saying there is no need for her to come to Devapattinam at present. Post it today, right now. Understand?'

Just then, they heard a bullock cart pulling up in front of the house.

'As soon as I heard the crow cawing in the courtyard yesterday, I knew some guest or the other would turn up. Pattu, go and see who has come.' Sarasvati Ammal grumbled.

Lalita got up and went to the door with Pattu. Her face shone with surprise and delight when she saw the visitors.

3
DOCTOR'S ORDERS

Sita, Surya and Sundu got down from the cart. Lalita hardly saw Surya and Sundu. After greeting them perfunctorily, she gripped Sita's hands and took her inside.

'I was just thinking about you. Remember the photograph that the two of us took before the wedding? I showed it to Pattu and Balu. Pattu is my daughter. Balu is my son. The postman came just now. My husband had forwarded your letter to me and asked me to return before you came to Devapattinam. It seems he doesn't know how to host you since you had led a fashionable life in Bombay and Delhi. Isn't that funny! I decided to return. Appa said that he wanted to see you. He asked me to send you here for a visit. And here you are!' Lalita's excitement spilled over in a rain of words.

By this time, they had reached the hall. Pattu and Balu looked at Sita with shy wonder. 'Your children?' Sita asked. 'Yes,' Lalita said and added to the children, 'Didn't I say that Sita athanga was very beautiful? You can see for yourselves whether I was right or wrong. Sita, how can you look so beautiful after suffering so much and spending time in jail? Don't know how your husband can bear to be separated from you! Why did he have to go abroad so urgently? Never mind. Why didn't you bring Vasanti with you?'

Sita's face had a drawn look. Now it drooped even more.

'She is attending school. I didn't bring her because I didn't want to interrupt her studies. Lalita, where is mama? Can I see him?'

'Why not? Just a little while ago Appa was saying that he wished to see you. He will be very happy that you have come. Sita, you know about the disaster that overtook Appa, don't you?'

'I heard about it when I reached Devapattinam yesterday. Your husband told Surya. That is why we took the train to come here at once.'

'My husband is rather diffident with women. But he has great respect for you. He has been inquiring about you ever since he heard that you had gone to prison for the sake of the nation. Sita, until your husband returns from abroad, you must stay with me in Devapattinam. You must not go anywhere else, got it?'

'What's the hurry to decide now, Lalita. let us go and see mama now,' Sita said.

Seeing Sarasvati Ammal coming towards them, Lalita said, 'Amma, see, Sita athanga is here.'

'Namaskaram, Mami. I trust you are well,' Sita spoke with deference.

Sarasvati Ammal scowled and said, 'So you are here. Welcome! I have heard all kinds of things. Nothing pleasant. But anyhow, you have made your way here. You know that mama is unwell, don't you? He must not be pestered. Doctor's orders. Lalita, do you understand? Don't allow Appa to talk too much.'

Lalita was pained. She glared at her mother in anger. Sita cut in to say, 'Mami, I won't engage mama in a long conversation. Don't I know we must not overtax those who are unwell?'

'How can you not know it, Amma? You have lived in the big cities – Madras, Bombay, Delhi, Calcutta! I have been confined to these uncouth regions. It falls to my lot to deal with worsening conditions. At my age, am I able to spin around like before and get things done? A couple of guests arrive, and I get the wind up. Do I have help in the house as before? No. Your mama's debts have increased. Can't afford to employ a cook.'

'Enough, Amma! You can keep the whining for later. Sita, come! Let us go and see your mama,' Lalita said and dragged her away.

Surya and Sundu got up when Sita and Lalita entered the room. They were sitting beside Kitta Iyer's bed and talking to him.

'Athanga, Appa is not as happy about my coming home as he is about my having brought you. He wants to hear everything about you,' Surya said as he left the room with Sundu.

Sita prostrated before her uncle. Kitta Iyer sat up, touched Sita's head affectionately and said, 'Be as prosperous as a queen!'

Seeing her uncle so enfeebled, and thinking back to the many memories that flooded her, Sita's eyes began to rain tears.

Kitta Iyer misunderstood the reason for those tears. He too had heard his wife's words to Sita and had been saddened them. Therefore, in a voice trembling with emotion he said, 'Don't be sad, Sita. You know your mami's nature only too well. Many changes have taken place in the world. But your mami remains the same.'

Sita said as she wiped her eyes, 'I was overcome to see you like this! There was nothing wrong in what mami said. It's all due to the time at which I was born.'

'What is wrong with the time of your birth? You were born on an auspicious day and under an auspicious star. The difficulties rising before you like a mountain will vanish like the mists. You will live in happiness and prosperity,' Kitta Iyer consoled her.

'Mama, may your blessings come true! But first, you must get well. I was devastated to hear that you had been attacked. What barbarians they must be to hurt someone like you who has never even thought of hurting a fly.'

Kitta Iyer said, 'Destiny, Amma, destiny! What is the use of cursing them? Sita, listen to this! When the bandits surrounded the vehicle and started hitting me, one of those punches landed on my head. I felt an excruciating pain. I thought I was going to die. Do you know who came into my mind at that moment? Your mother Rajam! I thought she was standing in the sky and beckoning to me with her lean arms outstretched, saying, "Anna, come!" I thought, "O my God! I have not taken leave of my child, Sita. What can I say when Rajam asks me if Sita is doing well?" All this happened in a split second.'

'Mama, this shows how much love you have for my mother and for me. But please don't talk so much. Shouldn't we follow the doctor's orders?'

'Yes. I must not talk too much at one go. I was eager to see you and to tell you a few things. I was afraid that I may not be able to see you at all. Thank God you have come to see me. Let us talk tonight at leisure. Go now, take a bath and have your lunch,' Kitta Iyer said with great affection.

4

THE ILLUSION CALLED LOVE

That evening, Sita and Lalita went to the bungalow by the pool. It could no longer be called a bungalow. Gaps yawned on the roof. The floor was pitted and cracked. On the wall, the paint had faded in patches. The ornamental bamboo fence had broken down in several places, and the sticks were lying on the ground.

Not only the bungalow, but the pool too had lost its charm. Not that there was any lack of water. But the old border of oleander and hibiscus plants was missing. The steps down to the pool were cracked and covered with moss.

Sita and Lalita sat on the broken steps. For a while, Sita kept staring around her. She had the feeling of something being quite different. Then it came to her in a flash.

'Lalita, what happened to the casuarina grove on the other side of the pool?'

'Cut down and sold for firewood,' Lalita replied.

'That is why the entire place looks stark and bare. Without the casuarina grove, this pool has lost all its beauty. This place has become desolate, like my life,' Sita sighed.

'I don't know why you are talking like this. Nor could I make sense of your last letters from Delhi. What is your problem, Sita? Why do you speak as if you are embittered with life? Is it that you and your husband are not able to get on? Didn't you get married in this village after falling in love? The people in this entire region went on talking about your "love marriage" for ages! Was that love false? Why can't you both get on? Does he not have any real love for you?' Lalita asked in disconsolate tones.

'I don't know. I don't know if he has any love for me. Right from the beginning, there was a wall between us. It hid his heart from me. I did not try to break the wall. I did not have the courage to make the attempt. I was afraid of what I might see there... phantoms and specters, wild beasts, or perhaps a siren like the celestial Menaka who enticed the legendary sage Vishwamitra. Therefore, I did not try to know his mind. Had I done so, I might have been murdered, or turned into a murderess myself,' Sita said.

'This sounds mysterious and chilling. Sita, when we were newly married, we sat here on so many days and talked on and on. With what exhilaration did you describe his love for you! I was happy to hear it all. Sometimes, I felt disappointed because my husband did not treat me in the same manner. Now, after listening to you, I wonder if the elders are right after all when they call everything an illusion,' Lalita mused.

'No doubt about it, Lalita. Some people say that love is the only truth in this world of illusion. Novels and plays and movies say so. There are many kinds of delusions in this world of illusion. Love is the biggest of them all. When they grow up, I am going to tell our daughters, "Don't get crazy ideas about love from books and plays and films. You can find lifelong happiness only in a marriage arranged by the elders." Giving them the example of my life, I will prove that love is nothing but delusion.'

'Sita, I can't believe you. I think some great sorrow or ordeal makes you talk like this. Can you say that all the joy you experienced when we were newly married was false? I remember everything you said, seated by this very pond, as if it was but yesterday! How your whole body quivered when you heard his name. Even now, I cannot believe that it was all merely delusional.'

'I too cannot believe it. Lalita, even now I get gooseflesh when I think about it. After our first exchange of glances, when we first expressed our love, the whole world was transformed into paradise. When he spoke of love and surprised me with my first kiss, I did not remain human, I turned into a celestial nymph. All the stars in the sky ornamented my body. All the flowers on earth bloomed on me. Diaphanous moonbeams draped me. The breezes blew only to cool my body. Sandalwood spread its scent only for my pleasure. The silk sarees I wore acquired their sheen from the beauty of my form. I experienced all this with my senses. Lalita, how can I describe the passion he felt for me in those days. I felt that the love Romeo had for Juliet, or Majnu for Laila, could not equal his love for me. I compared the feelings of lovers in fiction with my husband's love for me and was convinced that I was luckier than they were. He and I floated in a golden boat on an endless sea, on a never-ending voyage. We circled the skies in the starry galaxies riding on an ethereal chariot driven by silvery swans. But one day, it did come to an end. A woman like you and me came to intrude in our life of bliss. A blight descended in an instant. My paradise turned into an inferno. Lalita, I heard a song when I was in prison. I used to sing it whenever I felt sad and low. Shall I sing it for you?' Sita asked.

'Please do! Do you have to ask? I have always loved your singing. Is it a Bengali song?'

'The song I heard was in Bengali. But I translated it. Listen,' said Sita and began to sing a tune steeped in sorrow.

Who took me in tenderly,
in a golden boat, on a milky ocean?
Who left me there,
when the wind rose, and the sea swelled?
Who stood by himself,
in the sky above, by the honeyed moon?
Who left me alone,
after sweeping in to enfold me in love?

Sita finished the song and broke into sobs. As Lalita put an arm around her and consoled her as best she could, she thought, 'Ayo, poor thing! Her mind has become unhinged by all the afflictions she has borne!'

5
SEDUCTIVE SIREN

A gentle curtain of dusk was falling on the stage we call the world.

Black clouds had gathered at the northeastern corner of the sky. Flashing in and out, streaks of lightning tore across the clouds from end to end.

Cold breezes blew. The palm fronds swayed and rubbed against each other to give rise to a murmur of sounds. A cow returning to its shed after grazing in the fields, suddenly remembered its calf and let out a resounding 'Moo!' A village musician went by singing a philosophic strain.

Farther away, a fledgeling flautist was trying to play a raga, which tried to morph into another.

In the grove of honey trees close by, a night bird screeched shrilly as it flapped its wings and flew from one tree to another.

One by one, the stars began to peep through the canopy of the night.

Slowly, Sita's sobs subsided.

'Athanga, shall we go home?' Lalita asked.

'Lalita, where is my home?' Sita said.

'As long as I am alive, my home is yours,' Lalita answered.

'Lalita, I know how kind-hearted you are! That is why I came to you. But is that enough? However intimate the friend may be, can anyone be as free in any home other than in one's own?'

'Why not? You have as much freedom in my house in Devapattinam as I do. In fact, even more,' Lalita said.

'You are saying this out of your love for me. What about the master of the house?'

'If he is the master, I am the mistress. I have as many rights in the house as he does. You don't know my husband's nature. Sita, he will show you more affection than I do. He has praised you many times ever since he learnt that you went to prison, and are working for the freedom of the motherland. He will be happy for you to stay in our house as long as it takes,' Lalita told her.

Sita wanted to disclose the fact that she had not been imprisoned as a freedom fighter, but because she had been mistaken for another.

'I did not serve the country as you people seem to think,' she began.

But Lalita cut in, 'I know everything. Surya had written about it to me. People who do nothing swagger around with much fanfare. Why should you say you have done nothing after having done fantastic things? Humility must have its limits.'

Sita thought, 'I see! So, it is Surya who has written to glorify me. Why should I give him away? If people think highly of me, why not let them continue to do so?'

So Sita changed her mind and said, 'It's not like I did something others have not done. Your husband too has been in prison for more than two and a half years!'

'Yes, I feel proud about it,' Lalita said.

For a while, they remained silent.

Suddenly, Lalita broke the silence. 'This is what I cannot understand. You say that you are not happy in your married life. I have preserved all the letters you wrote when you were newly married. I read them often, with all the enjoyment of reading an interesting novel. Don't be angry, I have even showed them to my husband.'

'Ayyayyo, how embarrassing! Had I known this, I would never have written to you,' Sita cried.

'Why are you so agitated? What's wrong? My husband has greatly enjoyed your letters. Sometimes I have felt that because he read your letters, his lukewarmness towards me changed to affection.'

'I am happy if my letters were of some help to you.'

'But when I think of your condition now, I feel extremely unhappy. Athanga, how did your husband's mind change? You mentioned a woman. Who was that wretch? What is her name?'

'Her name is Dharini.'

'Dharini? Surya has written about her. He said that she was very clever, helpful and that she had saved your life.'

'Surya is a noble soul. He has a very good heart. This makes him credulous. That is why he exalts Dharini to the skies. He does not know her real nature.'

'Is she so wicked?' Lalita asked.

Sita took time to reflect before saying, 'How can I say that Dharini is wicked? She is a very good woman in her way. It is true that she saved me from drowning in the lake. That was not all. It was she whose nursing saved me when I had high fever. When we were by ourselves, I felt that she was my own sister. I used to feel a greater love for her than I feel for you. I did not have the heart to leave her for even a single moment. I thought that we should live together and die together. But when I saw her standing beside my husband, my mind underwent a drastic change. My love turned to venom. My whole body began to burn. I felt that either I should kill her, or die…'

'Ayo! Athanga! You sound so cruel! I never experience such sensations. I don't feel angry or unhappy if I see my husband talking to another woman. Why should you have such misguided feelings? I feel that it is *you* who is in the wrong.'

'Lalita, you are lucky! Not even in my dreams would I want you to experience my torments. But don't think that I must take all the blame. There are some strange women in this world. They have a rare and magnetic power. Such women must remain God fearing, and lead lives upholding the moral codes. If not, they can destroy any number of households. Don't get angry when I say this. Surya is such a good boy! But he too has been spellbound by that siren,' Sita said.

'In a way I am happy to hear this. Surya is also getting older. How long can he remain single? Amma is ceaselessly lamenting that Sundu's marriage is getting stalled because Surya refuses to get married. I don't think Surya will marry any girl from our parts anymore. If Surya and Dharini are in love, why should they not get married?' Lalita said eagerly.

'Lalita, love is nothing but deception!'

The sound of footsteps cut through Sita's remark. It was Surya who approached them.

He said, 'When two women get together, they can talk about nothing but love and marriage! Appa is all by himself, looking for you, and perturbed by your absence. He asked me to fetch you both at once.'

6

WATER BUBBLES

Kitta Iyer's voice sounded frail and weak. 'Sita, I have been expecting you for a long time. Should you have lingered beside the pool after dusk? Hadn't I told you that I wanted to talk to you about something important?'

Sita began to mollify him. 'Mama, please forgive me. After all, I am going to be here for a few days.'

'It is true that *you* are going to be here for a few days more. But I should be here too, *alive*,' Kitta Iyer said.

'Ayo, Mama! Why do you say this? I am an orphan. Helpless! If you too start getting angry with me…' Sita began to shed tears.

'Sita, don't be upset! I shouldn't have said that. But why should we be afraid of death? One day all of us will have to leave this world! Haven't the wise men described life as a bubble on the waters?'

'Mama, Mama! You must be angry with me for some reason. That is why you are speaking in this manner. I thought that no one in the world had more love for me than you. But I see that you too detest me. I will leave tomorrow.'

'Sita, be patient. Listen to me. I am not angry with you. I am angry with myself. I have been bedridden for some time. It gave me time to reflect. I am beginning to feel that all that I have done in the last few years is wrong. Our elders have established the varnashrama dharma in our land. We hold on to the varna part of it still. We declare that we observe the codes of our caste. And how? Only as far as the observance remains convenient to us. As people get older, they must take up vanaprastha, they must retire. I have been old for quite some time. My children have established themselves. I have grandchildren too. Why should I still bear the burden of this household? To what purpose? Listening to bad advice made me earn the implacable enmity of the workers' community who had been with this family from my grandfather's time. I drove them away from their dwellings. I won a case against them in court. What was the use? Those who had been wishing this family well for generations are now cursing us. Finally, I met with this disaster. I escaped with my life due to the good karma of my ancestors. Instead of killing me there and then, the bandits let me go. May things go well for them!'

'Mama, the sinners who hit you must be damned. Let their hands rot!'

'Why curse the arrow instead of the bowman? God resides in all living beings – in the man who attacks and the man who is attacked. In getting angry with those who attacked me, am I not getting angry with God himself? In fact, God appeared in the form of those robbers to teach me a lesson. To say, "You are sixty years old. O mindless creature! Are you still going to stay mired in the material world?" Sita, I don't want to stay in this village anymore. Thank God Surya is here! I am going to entrust all my family responsibilities to him and take my leave. I must go to Kasi and bathe in the Ganga. I must see the three sacred rivers meeting in Prayag. Then I must go on a pilgrimage to Haridwar, Rishikesh and Badrinath. I wish to go up to Mount Kailas itself. Some days ago, I read a book about the journey to Kailas. Since then, I have been meditating on the mountain.'

'Mama, if you are planning to go on a pilgrimage, I will come with you. I will take you everywhere,' Sita said. She rejoiced to have found a way to spend her time in seeking salvation.

'Sita, nothing will give me greater joy than to go to all those sacred places in your company. But you must mend your life before you and I can undertake that pilgrimage,' Kitta Iyer said.

Sita did not reply. Head bowed, she continued to sit in silence.

'You are silent because you know what I am talking about. I cannot tell you how anguished I have been ever since I learnt that your husband and you are unable to get on. Your wedding was conducted in this village. The man who came to see Lalita saw you and said he wanted to marry you. Your mami burned in fury. Any number of people felt jealous. But I was overjoyed and got you married along with Lalita under the same canopy. I expressed my gratitude to all the gods for your good fortune. Should it end like this? Your mother spent all her life in misery. Should you suffer the same fate? Tell me, Sita. Can't you be happy with the man you wished to marry?'

'Mama, what can we do when fate is against us? You rejoiced when I got married. So did I. But who expected that my husband's nature would turn out to be like this?'

'You talk about your *husband's* nature. Have you thought about your own? Easy to find faults in others, difficult to recognize our own. However abominable a man may be, in time he may be reformed. It is possible for a good woman to bring about that transformation. Sita, you are educated. You have understanding. Surya praised your service to the nation. I am happy about all these things. Now listen to me. You are all struggling to bring independence to India. But do you know the crowning glory of India? Many countries in the world achieve greatness for a certain period of time, after which they are utterly destroyed. But for thousands of years, our country has neither been destroyed, nor has its glory diminished. Noble souls like Mahatma Gandhi are still born in this country. Do you know why? Only because of the greatness of our women. It is *their* goodness that safeguards this country. You must have read what Gandhiji wrote about his wife Kasturba. How patient and forbearing she remained even when her husband berated her without cause. It made him feel penitent! We don't have to look that far. Take your mami now. It is true that she fights with me relentlessly. But has she ever acted against my wishes? I have scolded her so many times. Has she ever threatened to leave this house?'

'Mama, Kasturba has divinity. Mami is extremely fortunate. She has you for her life partner. But I have been blighted, always. My husband was in Calcutta for a whole year when I was in Alipore jail. He knew that I was in prison. But not even once did he come to see me. Even so, I had decided that as soon I was released from prison, I would go and fall at his feet, beg his forgiveness. But what happened? A month before my release he went abroad. I was soured by what I heard about the life he led in Calcutta. I decided that it was impossible to live with him again.'

'Sita, you must not arrive at any decision based on hearsay. There are reasons for Raghavan to be angry with you. He lost his job because you welcomed Surya to your home and later, you got yourself imprisoned. Was it some ordinary post? How can he not be furious when you made him lose a government job which brought him two thousand rupees a month?' Kitta Iyer asked.

'Losing that job was no deprivation. He has found a job in a bank at a higher salary,' Sita said.

'I am going to see Raghavan as soon as he returns from his foreign trip. You must come with me. I will be at peace only if I clear the misunderstandings between the two of you and see you living happily together once again. Your mother's soul too will find peace in the world above… Tell me, Sita, any news of your father?'

'I have a doubt about him. I hesitate to share it with you. Mama, I suspect that Appa has converted to Islam.'

'*Siva! Siva! Siva!* It is unbearable to even hear this. Why do you have this suspicion?'

'Don't you remember that when Amma and I were in Bombay, a woman came home and gave us a ruby necklace and some money?'

'Yes. What about it?'

'I saw the same woman in Delhi. A bearded saheb was with her. Later, I was charged with theft and taken to the court in Agra. I was dumbstruck, not knowing where to turn, when that saheb came to court and said that it was he who had stolen the trunk. He was sentenced for it too. When I was doing jail time in Calcutta, I wondered who could have made such a sacrifice for me. The more I thought about it, the more I felt convinced that it was my father.'

'O my God! Who can believe that Duraisami would lose his mind like this. Can this be true? Even if he had been weak-minded where a woman was concerned, in time the weakness should have been overcome. To convert from one creed to another for such a reason…? What are your husband's thoughts in matters of religion?'

'He has great faith in the Hindu religion. He dislikes all other religions. Particularly Islam. He was full of rage because when he was employed by the government, Muslims below him in rank were promoted above him.'

'What a reason for abhorring another religion! Well, I suppose it is good that he has faith in his own creed. Just you wait, I will surely succeed in bringing about a change in him. Sita, very soon, your sufferings will be over.'

'Mama, you say that my sufferings will be over. I cannot believe it. I experience fears without any cause. My heart beats loudly, I feel a griping pain at the pit of my stomach. Nightmares prevent me from finding rest or sleep.' Sita trembled as she spoke. Tears came to her eyes.

Kitta Iyer, who had been reclining as he talked, now sat up, touched Sita's head, and said, 'Child, nothing but hallucinations! Your mind is distraught because of the memories of your past sufferings. When you feel afraid, chant Rama's name. All your fears will be dispelled. Moreover, am I not going to be with you? I will see to it that you have no more troubles.'

Lalita walked into the room. Hearing Kitta Iyer's last words she said, 'Appa, what is this? You said that you were going to come to Devapattinam with me. In half an hour you have forgotten all about it and are now making plans to go with Sita! Surely, this Bombay athanga has magnetic powers.'

7

ETERNAL LIFE

Kitta Iyer had given his reasons for India's glory remaining eternally intact.

On the same day, his son propounded a different reason for the same concept at the parliament assembly convened on the pyol in Kitta Iyer's house.

'Hear me out,' Surya began. 'Let us say we clip several mails together. The mail at the top represents the time after the appearance of homo sapiens on planet earth. All the mails below represent the ages before the birth of man, when other living beings inhabited the earth. Among them were gigantic creatures as high as a palm tree. Where are those dinosaurs now? They have disappeared without a trace. Archaeologists discover their skeletal remains, trapped and preserved through the millennia, under sheets of ice. What is the reason for the extinction of those terrifying beasts? Only that they could not adapt themselves to the changing climatic conditions. But creatures who adapted themselves to change, continue to live in increasing numbers, generation after generation.

Take the human race for example. At certain periods, in several countries of the world, men have lived on the pinnacle of glory. However, those ancient civilizations of Babylonia, Assyria, Greece and Egypt have been vanquished and decimated. Our India has a civilization older than any other in the world. What is the reason for its not having been destroyed until now?

Only the fact that our ancestors went on changing their lifestyles according to the changing times. For example, in vedic times, they performed many rituals where they sacrificed horses, cattle and sheep, offered their flesh to the Gods, and consumed it themselves. Gautama Buddha appeared to trounce the sacrifice of animals. The Buddha's ideologies spread across the world. In India, the people of those times assimilated his most important tenets. Sacrifices came to an end. In later times, those who appeared as avatars to establish the Hindu dharma like Sankara and Ramanuja, did not insist on the performance of yagnas. Great devotees like Tulsidas, Tukaram and Tyagaraja did not demand yagnas.

Solely by its frequent adoption of new ideas, and by changing old tenets and habits, Hindu society has sustained its life force down to our times. And in our time, Mahatma Gandhi has taken birth to counsel us about the social reforms we must bring about – without causing harm to Hindu dharma. According to his teachings, we must get rid of untouchability, caste distinctions and child marriage.

If we adapt ourselves to the needs of the times, the people of India can abide in the world with glory intact. However, if we mulishly refuse to change the customs and practices prevalent in our grandparents' times, we too will become extinct, as did many species of animals and communities of human beings in many different lands.'

Panchu Iyer, one of the men listening patiently to Surya's lengthy harangue, interrupted him now. 'Right, my boy. Any number of changes have taken place in our own times. When I was a young boy, people of other castes were not allowed to see a brahmin having his meal. A brahmin was ostracized from his community if he ate with members of other castes. Who follows those customs now?'

'Mama, unimportant changes are taking place. Is it enough? No. It would be a great mistake to think that we can treat the workers on our lands the way our grandfathers did.'

'Panchu Iyer, see. I wondered why the boy was meandering in circles! Finally, he has come to the point – the matter of the field workers. My son! This issue has been taken to court and the verdict has been announced. Stop talking about it,' Appadurai Sastri said.

'Surya, Sastri is right. Leave the kisan agitation alone. We will take care of it. Tell us about the swaraj movement. Mahatma Gandhi and the other leaders made such tremendous efforts! What are the results? When are we going to get independence? Where is Netaji Subhash Chandra Bose now? What does Jayaprakash Narayan say? What has been gained by your shouting "White man! Quit India!" When are the white men going to quit India?' Seemachu Iyer queried.

Panchu Iyer said explosively, 'And just where did these people let loose their mighty shouts of "White Man! Quit India"? In our village market! Is the white man standing in the barren tracts where our donkeys roam for him to be driven out by their howls? Why not holler where the white man can hear them? Then, even if he did not quit India, at least he would be deafened!'

'Mama, just you wait! Now it seems to be a matter for ridicule. But soon, you will see. The white man is going to decamp, bag and baggage,' Surya said.

'Well, my boy, well indeed! They have been saying this for thirty years now. Some time ago they proclaimed that independence was going to arrive within a year. But it slipped away! They promised that it was a done deed during the salt satyagraha. Then they said, "Mahatma Gandhi has gone to London to bring independence to India." After that they declared, "Irwin has surrendered." Even in 1942, they said, "It is here." They followed it up with "Netaji is coming with his army." Nothing but hot air! The Englishman remained nonchalant even when he was being harassed by Hitler on one side and Tojo on the other. Is he going to give freedom to India after winning the war?' Velayuda Mudaliar shook his head.

'Mudaliar, I had the same thoughts! Many others too thought that we should wrest independence for India during the war years. But he who is an avatar, Mahatma Gandhi, he thought otherwise. He said that the British must not be harassed during war time. He said that just as the cobra allows itself to be controlled by the mantra, we too must be controlled by truth. Many like me dismissed his injunctions and became secretly involved in the movement. All to no avail. Finally, we have come to the conclusion that India will obtain its independence only through the Mahatma's action plan,' Surya explained.

'You and your cronies are highly educated intellectuals. That is why it took you so long to decide that Gandhi's modus operandi is the best. All of us are illiterate rustics. Therefore, we came to that conclusion right from the start. Thirty years ago, we became convinced that if India is to attain independence, it must come through the Mahatma. Don't you know that your father and I began to wear khadi way back when? We still do. Though Seemachu sells mill cloth, what he wears is khadi,' Panchu Iyer said.

'Mama, when you have such unshakeable faith in the Mahatma, should you not follow all his teachings?' Surya demanded.

'What are the teachings of the Mahatma that we have not followed?' Appadurai Sastri enquired.

'The Mahatma says that freedom is going to come soon. Before it does, we must remove all our flaws and be ready to receive it,' Surya replied.

'What are these flaws and how must we eradicate them?'

'Most importantly, there must be no misunderstandings between the landowners and the field workers. Everyone must accept the principle that the man who labours has the right to enjoy the fruit of his labours.'

'O Surya Iyer, you may talk about anything except about this workers' business. Your father is already suffering from the consequences of having overly indulged them. They tried to take his life. He was saved by God's grace!'

'I will never believe that the workers tried to kill Appa. Never! Why are you blaming them for what some bandits did?'

'All right, let it go! Why argue? The police enquiry is going on. Truth will out. And once it does, you will be singing a different tune.'

Lalita interrupted the debate. 'Anna, Appa is calling for you.'

'All right! Go to your father,' the pyol parliamentarians said as they dispersed and made their way to their homes.

Surya went to his father and sat down beside his bed. 'Sorry, Appa! Our debate must have given you a headache. I raised my voice unthinkingly.'

'Surya, I heard everything you said. It did not give me a headache.

On the contrary, it made me happy. My reflections have led me to conclude that you are right. Stay in this village and do everything as you will. I give you all the authority to do so. I don't wish to stay here anymore. I feel like undertaking a pilgrimage. Lalita is asking me to come to Devapattinam. Sita says she will take me to places like Kasi, Haridwar and Badrinath.'

'Why should Sita take you Appa? *I* will take you! I lived in Kasi for six months.'

'Surya, it will give me greater satisfaction if you stay here and attend to the fields and do what has to be done.'

Sarasvati Ammal came in at that moment and said, 'Surya, don't let your father talk too much. It is midnight now. Should he not be asleep?'

'Amma is right, Appa! Go to sleep. We can talk at length tomorrow. I will do as you say,' Surya said.

On the next day, Surya did not get the opportunity to speak to his father at length.

Nor did the need arise to decide who would take Kitta Iyer on a pilgrimage.

That night, after laying his heart bare to Surya, Kitta Iyer went to sleep in peace, one he never woke up from.

The next morning, piteous cries and sorrowful laments arose from the house.

It was Kitta Iyer's niece Sita who wept and lamented more than all the others, and with the deepest sorrow.

8

'PRAISE THE GREAT RAINS!'

The train chugged on through wind and rain like a warrior disregarding the shower of arrows as he advances towards the goal.

Sita, Lalita, Lalita's husband Pattabhiraman and their two children were in a second-class compartment. All their attention was focused on the sights outside.

The sky was covered by dark clouds turning day into dusk. It was raining heavily. On one side, the noisy downpour attempted to break the glass windows to shards. But the windows on the other side showed the different scenes flitting by.

The train was moving through lands rich in water and vegetation. The leaves of the coconut trees assaulted the skies as they danced like dervishes in the buffeting winds. The dense, luxuriant clumps of bamboo swirled in circles, spraying fountains of raindrops around them.

It was touch and go for the birds sheltering on the wind-tossed branches of the mango trees. Suddenly, one of the branches cracked and fell to the ground. A crow perched on the falling branch tried to spread its recalcitrant wings and emitted a raucous cry as it managed to fly to another tree.

'Ayo, poor thing!' Sita cried pityingly and looked at Lalita. As Lalita was saying something to her son Balu at that time, she turned to look at Pattabhiraman.

Pattabhiraman was observing Sita. In particular, he saw her pitying the rain-drenched crow.

'The crow is going have a difficult time,' he told her.

Lalita asked, 'Which crow? What are you talking about?'

Sita and Pattabhiraman remained silent.

'Why are you silent? What's the matter? Can't you tell me?' Lalita asked again.

'A branch broke. A crow shrieked as it rose from that branch and flew to another tree. You didn't see it,' Pattabhiraman said.

'Balu asked me something. I was answering him. That is why I didn't see the crow,' Lalita said.

'That is what I said,' Pattabhiraman remarked.

'A crow is not more important to me than the child,' Lalita said.

'Who said that the crow was more important than the child?' Pattabhiraman said.

The train moved on.

Along the way, near a village, a funeral pyre was burning on a bare stretch of land beside the fields. Some people were trying to put up a thatch above the pyre to prevent the fire from going out.

Pattu said, 'Look, Amma!'

Everyone looked in the same direction. 'We burnt Mama on a pyre like this,' Sita said and began sobbing.

There were tears in Lalita's eyes too. She said, 'I am not as affected by Appa's death as in seeing you grieving for him.'

'There is no need for anyone to grieve over Mama's death. He would have undoubtedly reached the highest state in the afterlife,' Pattabhiraman said.

Sita stopped sobbing. She wiped her eyes and said, 'That is true. Having given birth to a son like Surya is enough to have taken him to the highest state in life hereafter.'

'Undoubtedly. Look at the way Surya managed to get the workers on board,' Pattabhiraman said.

'When father died, all the field workers came in a group and burst into wails,' Lalita recalled.

The train went on moving.

There was water, water everywhere.

'What's this? A deluge! Looks like it has rained more heavily here,' Pattabhiraman said.

'It could have rained just as heavily in Rajampettai after we left,' Sita suggested.

'People were complaining about the lack of rain. Now it is pouring down,' Lalita said.

Pattabhiraman displayed his scholarship. 'People realize the value of rains only in its absence. The sages of the vedic age prayed to Varuna, the god of the waters, as much as they worshipped Surya, the sun god. The Tamil epic *Silappadikaram* hails the sun and the moon in this beautiful verse where it says, "Praise the great rains".'

'Still, it is better not to praise the rains over much. What will the poor do if it pours like this? Look!' said Lalita, pointing to a small village. Water was flowing through its street like a flooding river. The rain-battered walls of a hut were being washed away. Two men and a woman were trying to salvage the few pots, pans and other belongings from the hut.

'How many huts must have fallen like this? How the poor people who dwelt in those huts will suffer!' Lalita groaned.

'I wish I could jump down from the train right here. I want to run to the people who have lost their homes and possessions and help them,' Sita said.

The rains became heavier. The winds gained velocity as they buffeted around them.

The train kept moving on, creaking and swaying and struggling to crawl along the tracks.

9

PATTABHI'S REBIRTH

The train reached Devapattinam around 8 p.m. Its rows of lights were reflected on the waters gathered on both sides of the track. Similarly, the streets lights in Devapattinam twinkled in twin rows on the sea of water filling the streets. Against the black clouds shrouding the night sky, and the darkness enveloping the earth, these multiple rows of electric lights and their reflections created the illusion of a magical realm having come down to the terrestrial world from above.

The train came to a halt at the station. The station had a roof but was open on all sides.

As they got down from their compartment, piercing winds and lashing rains attacked Pattabhiraman and the others. Shivering porters came to assist them with their luggage.

Just then, a great mass of people, all dripping wet, came rushing into the station. In a few moments the entire platform was packed. Water dripping from bodies and garments flooded the station.

At first Pattabhiraman was astonished to see so many passengers rushing in to board the train. But the train left the station without anyone getting into it.

'Who are these people?' Pattabhiraman asked the porter.

'Sir, the hurricane has destroyed their homes. These accursed crowds have come here to shelter from the rain,' the porter explained.

'Why do you curse them? Where else can the poor go?' Sita asked him.

'Why not find a choultry or an office building? Anywhere but the railway station? I am tired of driving them away. My throat is hoarse after shouting at them again and again,' the porter grumbled.

With great difficulty, Pattabhiraman managed to hire a vehicle to take them home. As soon as they reached the house, Lalita began to bustle about setting things to rights. Pattabhiraman went to his office room, checked his letters and began to read the newspaper. The children changed into dry clothes, ate their dinner and went to sleep.

Sita sat in a corner all by herself, without changing her clothes.

Lalita came out to the hall to call Sita and Pattabhiraman to dinner.

'What is this, Sita? You haven't even changed your clothes,' she remonstrated.

Pattabhiraman came out of his office room.

'I keep thinking of those poor people. All of them, including the children, are going to spend the whole night in wet clothes. I don't have the heart to change into dry clothes. I feel guilty about not getting drenched out there, and instead, enjoying the comforts of this house,' Sita said.

'Yes, it is something to feel sorry about. But what can we do when those afflicted are not ten or twenty but in their thousands! In the morning, let us see what we can do to help them,' Pattabhiraman said.

'Let us talk about it over dinner. Come,' Lalita said.

'All those people are going hungry tonight. The children must be crying. How can we have the heart to eat?' Sita said.

'Therefore, we must stop thinking about it. We can never have peace if we keep reflecting on the sufferings in the world,' Pattabhiraman said.

'Is it not enough for us to worry about our own problems? Why should we go out of the way to worry about the problems of others?' Lalita said.

'Some people are able to do that, not I,' Sita retorted.

'I keep thinking about Pattu and Balu getting drenched in the rain. I am worried that they may catch a cold,' Lalita said.

'How many children did we see at the railway station! They will be exposed to the wind and the rain all night long. Who will take care of them if they fall sick?' Sita said.

'I too have been thinking about that. In the morning, I will consult my friends and we will make some arrangements. Now change your clothes, come and eat,' Pattabhiraman said.

Sita got up and joined them. After dinner, the three of them talked for some time before going to bed.

As soon as she was in bed, Lalita pulled the blanket over herself and went to sleep peacefully.

Sita could find no sleep at all.

Musing over Sita's kind-heartedness gave Pattabhiraman a sleepless night.

The next morning, as soon as the day broke, Pattabhiraman went out, thinking about fulfilling the promise he had made to Sita. He made inquiries and gathered information about the huts that had been destroyed and the people who were suffering without food and shelter. He returned in the afternoon and told Sita about the arrangements that he and his friends had made to start flood relief measures.

Sita told him, 'I have some experience in this kind of work in Calcutta. Let me join you in doing whatever I can for the women and children.'

Pattabiraman agreed happily. 'There are a few other women who may render such service. I will put you in touch with them.'

From that very afternoon, both Sita and Pattabhiraman began to engage themselves in flood relief work in different parts of the town.

At first, the victims were given a few days' shelter in the local schools. Meals had to be cooked and distributed. Those who had fallen ill had to be treated and given medicines.

Precautions had to be taken to prevent the children from falling sick.

When the rains came to an end and the ground became dry again, facilities had to be provided to build new huts for all the victims.

It took three months for the relief work to get done. Through those three months, Pattabhiraman and Sita worked ceaselessly. They found many collaborators in the town to join them. Sita's zeal, hard work, pleasant nature and affability enthused everyone. She came to be well known all over Devapattinam.

Pattabhiraman's zest for life had waned from the time he returned from prison. Independence was nowhere in sight. There was no sign of any enthusiasm in the entire nation. He didn't like the idea of continuing his practice in court. Moreover, where could he find the clients? Nor did he have any other work to do.

He who had lost heart under these circumstances now appeared to have been reborn. There was a great deal of flood relief work to be done. It was work that he greatly enjoyed. In the evenings, when they returned home, Pattabhiraman and Sita talked enthusiastically about what had been achieved during the day. In general, the ambience in the house became more buoyant. This made Lalita very happy.

Lalita would often say, 'Sita, this house has never been so lively. Nor has my husband been so cheerful. He has come to like you very much. Is there anyone on this earth who will not like you? Please stay in this house, always.'

Sita would reply, 'It looks as if God wills it so. Anyway, where can I go?'

'The only thing I'm not happy about is that you have left Vasanti in Madras. Fetch her. She will be the third child of our house,' Lalita would say.

'I am thinking of bringing Vasanti here as soon as schools shut for the summer vacation,' Sita would answer.

As the days went by, Lalita's authority in the household waned even as Sita's influence increased.

Pattu and Balu began to give more importance to their athai than to their mother.

The servants too began to give more respect to the Delhi Amma than to the Amma of the house. If Lalita asked them to do something in a certain way, they would answer without compunction, 'But Delhi Amma has asked us to do it in a different way!'

Sundu had never paid any attention to Lalita's requests. But Sita had to merely ask once, and he ran pell-mell to do her bidding. In fact, he anticipated her needs before being told.

Lalita was content with this state of affairs. She was delighted that her dearest friend was treated with deference by everyone. Often, she would tell Sita, 'Athanga, who knows what magic philtre you possess! Everyone is mesmerized by you.'

10

ACCURSED ELECTIONS!

The victims of the flood ultimately came to benefit from the relief work. Each man, woman and child, got two sets of new clothes. They got huts – brand new and well built – in a better and healthier location. A small Ganesa temple was built at the centre of the colony, where group singing was conducted on Saturdays.

But those who worked on the relief project began to feel lost. With no more work to occupy him, Pattabhiraman became disheartened once again. Sita began to ruminate over her husband who was abroad and her child in Madras. The house became less animated. Every face looked downcast.

One evening, some of his friends came searching for Pattabhiraman. They said that the city council elections were to be held and that Pattabhiraman should put up his candidacy. They tempted him with the possibility of getting the municipal chairman's post if he were to win.

Pattabhiraman did not care too much for this proposal. He had the forewarning of his father's election experience and the adverse results that followed. But he did not reject it altogether. His friends assured him that since he had made sacrifices for the nation and gone to prison in the nationalist cause, no one would stand against him. Moreover, they told him that all of Devapattinam had been astounded by the service he had rendered for flood relief. His victory was a certainty. Should anyone dare to stand against him, the whole town would teach his opponent a sound lesson. 'I will think about it before I give you an answer,' was Pattabhi's reply.

That night, as they sat down to eat, Lalita enquired, 'So many visitors today! What did they say?'

'They asked me to stand for the municipal elections. What is your opinion?' Pattabhiraman asked Lalita – and looked at Sita.

Lalita said, 'No elections please! Did the people who came seeking you think you are a fool?'

Sita asked, 'Why do you reject it outright, Lalita? Aren't they your husband's friends? Will they deliberately make a bad suggestion?'

'Athanga, you don't know about the goings on in this town! Long ago, his father worked for someone in the elections. That put a stop to all connections between us and our neighbours in the opposite house. Years later, Surya came and resolved the conflict. Hadn't I written about it to you?' Lalita asked.

'There is a great deal of difference between then and now. His father had not done anything for the nation. But your husband has been in prison for two and a half years. Who can oppose him if he stands for the elections? Those who stand against him will be utterly routed,' Sita declared.

'It's not as easy as you think! I hear that a man who has amassed wealth in the black market is going to stand in this ward. The competition will be tough,' Pattabhiraman said.

'Should you be put off by fear? If you stand for the elections, I am ready to go from door to door to canvass for you,' Sita said.

'If you are ready to work for me with such zeal, I too am ready to stand for the elections,' Pattabhiraman announced.

'How good it is to hear you speak with such vigour! We will begin the work at once, from tomorrow,' Sita said.

'It seems to me that we should give it some thought before we get into it. Why not consult Damodaram Pillai in the opposite house? He is a man of age and experience, someone who can give us the right kind of advice,' Lalita suggested.

'Why should we consult him? Don't we know that he belongs to the Justice Party? He will certainly advise against standing for the elections,' Sita said.

'Contesting for elections would be an expensive undertaking. We have no income now,' Lalita said.

'I hate it when people crib about money all the time! Are we going to take it all with us? I will sell the chain I wear to cover the costs,' Sita said.

'You don't have to sell your necklace. We have not become paupers,' Lalita responded sharply.

'Stop! Stop this useless talk,' Pattabhiraman said, looking at Lalita in irritation.

'Whatever anyone might say, I am not happy about your standing for elections,' Lalita said.

'When did you like anything that I have done? You said "No!" when I joined the protest against the law in 1942. What good can come out of listening to you,' Pattabhiraman snapped.

Tears trembled in Lalita's eyes. Ashamed, she turned away to wipe them surreptitiously.

She resolved never to argue with her husband before the servants. Why servants alone? She must not discuss anything in Sita's presence. What loss of face!

The next day Pattabhiraman informed Damodaram Pillai that he was going to stand for elections and asked for his blessings.

'I will give you all the blessings you want. But tambi, who gave you this great idea?'

'All my friends were united in urging me to do this. I too thought it was a good idea.'

'Have you thought about the pluses and minuses of this venture? You will have to spend a lot of money. Moreover, this will give rise to needless enmities. You have a very good name in this town. Why do you want to spoil it?' Damodaram Pillai asked.

'Why should my reputation be affected? Can we waste our time on thoughts like these when we have entered the service of the nation? I was not afraid of going to prison. Why would I fear anything else?' Pattabhiraman said.

'Tambi, going to prison is different. No one gains or loses by it.

But elections are a different ball game altogether. You will have to face animosity from many quarters.'

'I have made my decision and told my friends. I cannot withdraw now.'

'All right then! You may win. I will help you as much as I can, for the sake of your father and Surya. But there is one thing more. Tambi, when is that girl from New Delhi going back? It would be good to send her away soon.'

'Why are you coming up with this all of a sudden? You used to praise Sita quite often.'

'I praised her as long as she was doing good work. I don't think instigating you in this matter is a good thing.'

'Sir, there is no connection at all between Sita and my decision. Nor did she instigate me. Don't I have a mind of my own?' Pattabhiraman asked.

From the day Pattabhiraman announced that he would stand for the municipal elections, the house was overrun by visitors who bustled in and out noisily. Volunteers and friends dropped in at any time of the day and night. Many of them had their meals, as well as coffee and snacks in Pattabhi's house. Money was getting spent like water. A new pack of playing cards was purchased every day. Foodstuffs and groceries stored for a whole year were used up in a single month.

Lalita loathed it all. Other matters added to her distress. Day by day, Sita became more and more ostentatious and dominating in her behaviour. Her modesty suffered a decline. She joined the men who came on election business, engaged in loud exchanges and arguments with them, and clapped her hands as she roared with laughter. Neighbours who had praised Sita's fine qualities now began to talk ill of her. They also began to talk about Pattabhiraman with some ridicule. These rumours reached Lalita's ears and made her feel pained and disturbed.

One day, Pattabhiraman, Sita and his election cronies were making a bit of a racket as they talked and laughed loudly in the front drawing room. As she listened, anger rose in Lalita's heart. She waited impatiently for the visitors to leave. When they left, Sita came in and mounted the stairs to her room. Then Pattabhiraman came in. He looked at Lalita and said, 'Is lunch ready? I have to go soon.'

'In a hurry? Don't know what great things you are going to accomplish by leaving soon! This accursed election is making you dance to its tune.'

'Stop blabbering! Shut up,' Pattabhiraman roared.

'I am not blabbering. Only telling you as it is. Not just the accursed election, but accursed Sita too has seized hold of you,' Lalita spoke in fury.

Pattabhiraman flamed in wrath. His face turned hideous. Trembling in rage, he bellowed, 'What did you say? Take care! I will kill you if you open your mouth.'

'Yes. Kill me! At once! After all, that is what your Mahatma Gandhi has taught you.'

Pattabhiraman calmed down a little. He stopped to think of an appropriate answer. Before he could speak Lalita said, 'Stop trying to frighten me. Listen to me. Drop out of this accursed election. If you cannot do that, at least refrain from asking Sita to canvass for you. The whole town is laughing at us. I am losing my respect!'

'Who cares? I don't intend to give up the elections. Nor issue any stop order to Sita. You need not get into this matter. Mind your own business,' Pattabhiraman said.

'Who will get into it if I don't? If this is what you are going to say, I will send Sita away.'

'Who are you to send Sita away? On whose authority?' Pattabhiraman hollered.

'I brought my athanga here. I will ask her to go.'

'Sita will not leave this house. If anyone must go, it will be you.'

'Why should I leave my own house? Leaving a bitch who has straggled in from somewhere?'

Once again Pattabhiraman shouted in fury as he approached Lalita. 'What did you say? Whom did you call "bitch"? I will kick you out right now before I do anything else. Arrogant donkey,' he cried. Placing his hand behind her neck he began to shove Lalita to the door.

Lalita screamed, 'Ayo! Ayo!'

Precisely at that moment, Surya entered as if on cue.

Seeing Surya, both Pattabhiraman and Lalita stood petrified.

From the top of the stairs, Sita had been watching the drama. Her face mirrored the turbulence in her heart.

11

PATTABHI'S CRAZE FOR OFFICE

Though momentarily stunned by Surya's arrival, Lalita pulled herself together in an instant and assumed a bright and cheerful expression.

'Surya? How's this? How come you have turned up so suddenly, so unexpectedly?' she asked, and continued with a backward glance at Pattabhiraman, 'See, I told you not to play these games! Since it is Surya, it doesn't matter. Anyone else would have thought it was all for real.'

Pattabhiraman said with a silly grin, 'Welcome, Surya! You have come at the right time. In the middle of a domestic drama.'

For a moment, Surya wondered if what he had seen was real or play acting. Deciding to let it go he said, 'I am not alone, I've brought Amma along to see your drama.'

This made both Lalita and Pattabhiraman wince. Pattabhiraman looked up, wondering if he should go upstairs. Seeing Sita standing there with a woebegone expression, he became angrier. He strode into his office room and banged the door shut.

Lalita approached Surya and said, 'Anna, he is really angry with me. Please pacify him.'

Then, seeing Sarasvati Ammal entering with her bags and bundles and a jar of pickle, she went forward to welcome her.

Surya looked up. Sita who had been standing there a minute ago had now gone into her room. He went to see Pattabhiraman in his office room.

'Surya, I don't want to deceive you. Your sister asked me to put up an act. It is impossible for me to maintain it. I will tell you the truth. When you entered, I was really shoving Lalita by the neck and throwing her out of the house. Your athanga Sita is the reason. From the day she stepped into this house, your sister's nature has undergone a sea change. I am unable to bear Lalita's nagging, spite and envy. Please take your athanga and get lost,' Pattabhiraman's words came gushing out.

'All right! I will do what you want. Even in my dreams I couldn't have imagined you and Lalita reaching this state. I am sorry to think that I was the cause for this,' Surya said.

'What can you do, Surya? How is it your fault? How could you have known that women can be so appalling? Even I, who has been married for so many years, had been unaware of it. Listen to this! I begged Lalita not to bring Sita here. She wouldn't listen. She was ready to sacrifice herself for her athanga. Now she doesn't like Sita. Sita's elegance and social skills arouse her jealousy. Who stops Lalita from adopting them? Here I am trapped in this wretched election. The work is exhausting. Only two weeks left before the day of voting. If I don't slog now, all the money and effort will go waste. In this critical situation, should I attend to work, or to these women's quarrels? Thank goodness you are here! Take Sita away. I will get on with my work in peace.' The silence following Pattabhiraman's tirade was like the aftermath of a huge downpour.

Surya began with 'Pattabhi sir! You could have avoided getting into this election trouble…'

Pattabhi interrupted him. 'I *knew* you would say this. You are a total renunciate, a confirmed bachelor. Can everyone hate the world as you do? I have some things left to achieve in this world, some goals in life, the ambition to do some public service in this town and earn a good name. I am not attached to money or to wealth. But a reputation! Who can be devoid of the desire for fame? My father had been an influential man in Devapattinam. As his son, I am not satisfied to remain a non-entity. What is the use of a life without some social status? Besides, you know nothing of the political situation in this town. Hoarding enormous wealth in the black market, the old chairman performs atrocious deeds unchecked. He thinks that Devapattinam is his own fort, his personal property! If he is not defeated this time, the word "Congress" can never again be mentioned here. The unilateral opinion of everyone here is that no one can defeat that scoundrel but myself. You have neither the right nor the qualifications to interfere in this matter. I can undergo no greater humiliation than to withdraw when there are only two weeks to go before the elections. If I do, I can never show my face again.'

When Pattabhiraman paused for breath, Surya interposed quickly, 'Pattabhi sir, I am not asking you to withdraw at this juncture. I also know that I have neither the right not the qualifications to do so. All I said was that it was a pity you had gotten into this election mess. Am I so crazy as to ask you to withdraw after having put in so much work? What I wanted to say was completely different. I have heard that Sita has been of great help in this election campaign. Sending her away at this time will not be the right thing to do. Let her stay for just two more weeks. After that…'

'Surya, I can no longer put up with the torment of being trapped between two women. My work is badly disrupted. If Sita stays here, you should take Lalita away. As if things are not bad enough, your mother has arrived. Siva! Siva! Now there will be nothing but mayhem in this house, day and night. Surya, I beg of you, please take your mother and Sita away. Understand? Lalita and I will manage our affairs somehow. Did I get into the elections relying on Sita's support?'

'Pattabhi sir, please hear me out! You had always respected my opinions. Please give me a day's time. I will talk to both Sita and Lalita and give you my final opinion. If I feel that things will not work out, I will take Sita away as you wish,' Surya said.

'All right! Let me see how clever you can be,' Pattabhiraman agreed.

Surya went to see Sita and said, 'Athanga, did you see the drama that took place when I entered the house?'

'Yes, Surya. It is my fate! I carry my sins and misfortunes with me wherever I go. Even if I want to do something good, it ends badly. I have decided to leave this house today.'

'And go where?' Surya asked.

'Where? Is there no place to go to? Well, pond, lake, sea, train tracks. I must go to Madras and see Vasanti once. After that I will find my own destination. You don't have to worry about it,' Sita said through a shower of tears.

'Athanga, all sufferings must end one day.'

'It would be all right if my bad times are confined to me alone. Surya, they follow me wherever I go. I went to Rajampettai. I sent my dear uncle to the world of death. I came here. I triggered a fight between my dear friend and her husband. In Delhi, my husband lost his job because of me. Surya, do you know why I did not bring Vasanti here from Madras? I left her with her grandmother thinking it was the safest thing to do.'

'Athanga, it is harebrained to think that one's problems can be transmitted to another. Are you the only person in the whole world to have faced hardships? Nation after nation has endured hardships. Sixty lakh people died in Bengal from the drought. When the Americans dropped the atom bomb on the Japanese town of Hiroshima, two and a half lakh people were wiped out in an instant! Eight crore Germans who had dreamed but yesterday of having conquered the world, are now being ground to a pulp by four different nations. Why does suffering occur at all? This is a divine secret beyond rational understanding. One cannot generate sufferings for another. One's misfortunes cannot infect another.'

'All right, Surya. Is it possible for me to argue with you? Tell me, what is it that you want me to do?'

Surya replied, 'We must do our duty in the situation in which God has placed us.'

'What is my duty now?'

'Athanga, your duty at this moment is to make sure Pattabhi wins. No one understands mapillai Pattabhi's mind as I do. He is totally uninterested in status and position. If someone had asked him to stand for elections six months ago, he would have split his sides with laughter. You inflamed him with the frenzy of electioneering. You have assisted him in this task until now. If you relinquish everything now and leave, things may end up at sixes and sevens. Therefore, your duty is to stay and finish the work you began,' Surya said.

'I don't agree. Even if I do, how can I continue to stay in this house? You don't know what transpired before you came in. Lalita told Pattabhiraman to kick me out of this house. Pattabhiraman told her, "Sita will not leave this house. If anyone must leave, it must be you!" I heard these words with my own ears. Is it right for me to stay here when things have taken such an ugly turn?'

'Athanga, they would not have said these things in their right minds. Lalita blabbered in rage. Pattabhi has also said things in fury. I will make Lalita request you to remain here until the elections are over.'

'Mami too is here. She is already angry with me. If she were to get an inkling of this situation, would she allow me to extend my stay in this house?'

'Amma is now bent on seeing her mapillai attain the chairman's post. She may even fall at your feet to beg for your help to achieve that goal. Do you know that Amma has come here to make sure that you continue to stay?'

Sita was astonished to hear this. Her face brightened a little. 'Surya, is this true? Or are you making fun of me?' she asked.

'No. It is true enough. Amma herself will tell you so in a short while. I believe Rajampettai Seemachu Iyer is working against Pattabhi in the elections?'

'Yes. What about it?'

'Seemachu Iyer came to the village and complained to Amma about you. He told her that it was you who had persuaded Pattabhi to stand for elections, and that Lalita was totally against it. But the result turned out to be the opposite of what Seemachu Iyer expected. Amma is disconsolate about Pattabhi's not getting into some high-ranking position. She is praying to a hundred gods for him to get the chairman's post now. She has come here only to reprimand Lalita and to enthuse you!'

Sita marvelled at this change. Then she said to Surya, 'In any case I was planning to make a trip to Madras. Surya, I received a letter from

Vasanti yesterday. Schools are closing in four days. Vasanti has asked me to come to Madras and take her with me.'

'Athanga, you go about your election work. I will go to Madras and bring Vasanti here,' Surya assured her.

Sarasvati Ammal looked at her daughter Lalita and said, 'Never have I seen a greater fool! It seems that girl Sita is sweating it out to make your husband win the elections. And you are finding fault all the time.'

'Amma, this election madness has infected you. You think that it is a trifling matter. But it sparks a number of enmities. Do you know how my father-in-law suffered because he interfered in the elections?' Lalita asked.

'Are you instructing me? Were you born before me? That old man worked for somebody else and bought trouble. But here, mapillai himself is the candidate!'

'Will no animosities be generated if mapillai himself stands for the elections?'

'Is there any endeavour which does not trigger some animosity or the other? Set up a kiosk and earn some cash, you invite rancour. Wear a nice saree and generate jealousy. Ride a bullock cart and make enemies. Drive a motor car and make more enemies. Is it possible to live in this world if you fear antagonism? Only if you want to become a down-and-out pauper! They are saying that if mapillai wins this election he may get the chairman's post…? Is it true?'

'What is the use of getting the chairman's post?'

'Don't be a nitwit! My mother's father was the chairman in this very town. His house was called the "Chairman's House". There were no motor cars in those days. He used to leave for his office on a curricle drawn by two horses. All the people on the street would come out to watch the spectacle. I remember how once I too rode on grandfather's two horse carriage.'

Lalita wanted to laugh. But she also felt happy. She was relieved that her mother had not heard the rumours, which would have made her insist on Sita's being driven away from the house.

'Amma, the chairman no longer has the power he did in the past.

And what about all the money being spent on the elections? And do you know that the chairman's position is an honorary one?'

'So what? In the past, a chairman's post brought nothing but dignity. Now there is an income as well. The man who was the chairman here has earned two lakh rupees during his tenure. Fifty thousand rupees for providing sugar permits to businessmen. Last year, he celebrated his child's first birthday. The gifts he received were worth over half a lakh of rupees. Your child too had a first birthday! What did you get? Nothing but thrashings from the police!'

Lalita chuckled. 'In a way what you say is true. Some people are able to make money even out of the chairman's job. But your mapillai will not accept bribes or gifts, nor will he ask anyone for money.'

'Why should he? Once he becomes chairman, won't things come to him unasked?'

Sita came into the kitchen hearing those words. Lalita looked at her with a smile. She did not know that Sita had seen the fight between her and Pattabhi. So, it was with merriment that she said to Sita, 'Athanga, Amma is totally with you. Your side has the majority. I have become the minority! Amma is so enthusiastic that it looks as if she herself will canvass for votes from house to house.'

12

VAINGLORY

'Sita, come in! I have heard that you are putting heart and soul into making mapillai win in the elections. I am delighted. This is what we expect from kinfolk! Don't we need our own people to help us at times like these?'

Though Surya had told her about her mami's changed attitude, Sita was overcome by Sarasvati Ammal's words of affection and support. But without letting on, she said, 'Mami, now that you are here, my responsibilities are over. I have to leave in two days.'

'Leaving? Bhesh! Are you saying this because I came here? Sita, I will go back tomorrow.'

'Mami, Mami, I swear I didn't mean anything like that. It is just that I want to go back to my place.'

'You can do that after mapillai's elections are over. Mapillai is standing for elections because you have persuaded him to do so. They say you speak and sing in public meetings. The whole *zillah* believes it is because of you that mapillai is going to become chairman. Who will help him if you go away so suddenly?'

Sita said, 'Your mapillai is so brilliant that he doesn't need anyone's assistance. But it will be a great help if your daughter Lalita stops carping about everything. The people of Devapattinam are delighted at your mapillai's standing for elections. Wherever he goes, they assure him that they will vote for him. Lalita alone is averse to the proceedings. She is constantly grumbling and moaning about it. She acts as though mapillai's standing for elections will bring nothing but ruin. Then he gets fed up. Now he has become so frustrated that he has begun to say, "I give up! I will go off on a pilgrimage." Why, even today, they have been fighting since morning!'

Casting an angry glance at Lalita, Sarasvati Ammal said, 'Lalita, Bhesh! Is this the way to behave? Have you gone crazy? Perhaps someone is influencing you to behave like this! Don't open your mouth again. If you can't do that, go to Rajampettai and stay there until the elections are over.'

'All right, Amma. I will go,' Lalita said, jokingly.

'Look, mami. She says she will go away! Tomorrow, when mapillai wins the elections, are they going to cheer her – or somebody else – as the chairman's wife? Are they going to garland someone else? Invite some other person to tea parties and dinners? Are they going to beg some other woman to attend weddings and housewarming ceremonies? Who is going to sit next to her husband in group photographs? Without giving a thought to any of this, she casts aspersions on everything nonstop! You must give her some advice.'

'Why *some*? I will give *lots* of advice! It is not just Lalita, her brother too goes on blubbering nonsense like this. Brother and sister are cast in the same mould. Both take after their father. Didn't their father say that all the fields he had inherited from his ancestors should be donated to the field workers? Now daughter and son say, "must not stand for elections, must not earn money"! But mind you, you must go to jail! Sita, why can't these two have at least a fraction of your intelligence?'

Sita experienced a physical thrill, an overwhelming sense of vainglory. Her mind was filled with vanity. She had never imagined that the day would come when the aunt who detested her, would praise her to the skies.

Lalita found her mother's words bittersweet. Sarasvati Ammal's overt selfishness was abhorrent, but her changed attitude towards her dear friend was welcome. Why, her husband's standing for elections had been worth it if only to bring about this positive result.

'Amma! I am happy that at last, you have recognized athanga's good nature and intelligence,' she said.

'What are you saying, Lalita? Have I ever said that your athanga was bad or stupid? Sita, why don't you say something? I did talk about your mother and father not having lived harmoniously together. But I spoke with concern, not rancour. Sita, don't say anything about leaving. You may hold me responsible if things in this household don't go according to your wishes,' Sarasvati Ammal said.

'Mami, I have had a letter from Vasanti. She says that schools are to be closed. Must I not go to see my child?'

'Surya can go and bring Vasanti here.'

'I will not go against your express wish, Mami. Ask Surya to go. But tell your daughter that she must not complain.'

'Don't worry. You may take me to task if Lalita opens her mouth again. I will slap her and lock her up in a room. Seemachu mama made all kinds of accusations against you. I dismissed him. He has made enormous profits in the business. Built two houses with two storeys. The present chairman got Seemachu mama the licence for selling textiles. Therefore, he is killing himself to slog for him. Friendship, kinship, all gone for a toss! These days, money is the only thing that counts. Sita, I have never seen anyone with family attachment like you. How patient you have been with this girl's nonsense. And for that alone, Lalita should be ready to do anything for you,' Sarasvati Ammal declared.

Sita forgot the pain she had felt just a little earlier and lost herself in exhilaration.

13

RAGHAVAN'S DAYDREAM

The steam ship was tearing through the blue sea. *SS Elizabeth* was making its way from England to India, with Saundara Raghavan among its passengers. It was with great difficulty that Raghavan managed to book his passage on that ship, as not even a year had passed since the end of the great world war.

Raghavan went to England a few months after the world war was over. His intention was to get reparation for having been unjustly dismissed from his post. Very quickly had he realized that a job in any company, however high the salary may be, was not equal to a government posting. Besides, why should there be a false accusation against him in the government records? He could have found some solace if Britain had lost the war with a concomitant change in the government in India. But Britain had won the war, and the British Raj was continuing in India. As things stood, how could he be indifferent to government employment?

The Englishman who had commended Raghavan's acumen in economics and given him a job in the government was in England at that time. Raghavan hoped he could tell him his side of the story, lodge his complaint and get the man's recommendation. The futility of that hope became apparent to him only upon reaching England.

During the war, much of England had been devastated by German Messerschmitts. After spending millions upon millions in the war, England was in dire straits, facing the threat of bankruptcy. The people were suffering without many of the necessities of life, including food and clothes. Under such circumstances, who was going to be moved by the unjust treatment meted out to Raghavan? Who was going to make the time to listen to his grievances?

Certainly, the Englishman who had given Raghavan his job and treated him like a favourite son did not. 'Mr Raghavan', he said. 'It has become extremely difficult for us to make ends meet. Even the richest of men now stand in daily queues to buy half a loaf of bread. And here you are, making a great big fuss about losing a job. If I take your grievance to anyone and make a recommendation for you, they will simply laugh at me. If I can get a job in the company where you are employed, I too will make my way there. Don't waste your time and efforts here. Go back to India and hold on to the job you have secured.'

Raghavan was startled by this counsel from the former chief of the Department of Revenue and Expenditure. The durai added another bit of information, 'Raghavan, in India, government posts will no longer enjoy the importance they once did. The ministers of the Labour Government here have decided to give India its independence. It is the right decision. Because we can no longer manage to rule over a country with a population of forty crores. We have neither the manpower nor the facilities. If India attains independence, the Congress will come to power. You will not want to work under the Congress government, will you?'

Raghavan became more muddled. He did not know how to answer his durai's question. But he lost the hope of regaining his government post. Thank goodness, he had not given up his company job. He had only taken leave for four months. He decided to return and rejoin the company.

It was extremely difficult to get into any ship bound for India. What he saw and heard as he waited to get his ticket home brought about a startling change in his mind. 'How amazing the English people are,' he thought. 'So valiant! What sufferings have they not borne to retain the freedom of their country? How they labour for the welfare of their land. But what was I doing in India? Sweated in slave labour under foreign domination. And travelled so far to beg to be allowed to return to that labour. What a shameful way of making a living! How despicably has English education affected my brain. To make up for the past I must do something astounding for India's freedom.'

These thoughts flew in and out of his mind as Raghavan sat musing on an easy chair on the upper deck in *SS Elizabeth*. When he let his mind wander freely, it found its way back to the voyage he made fifteen years ago from Karachi to Bombay. What a blissful trip that had been! An ordinary fourth rate cargo steamship, not even fractionally comparable in size, grandeur, beauty or facilities to the ship in which he was travelling now. And yet the voyage he made on that ship was as blissful as a trip on a celestial chariot surrounded by gods and goddesses! All because Dharini was travelling with him on the same ship. If only he had persisted in his determination to marry Dharini, how happy his life would have been.

From Dharini, his mind jumped to Sita. If it was wrong to have disregarded Dharini, it was a greater mistake to have married Sita. If he had married Kitta Iyer's daughter Lalita, at least his life would have been peaceful. But Sita crossed his path. The glance from her large eyes had enchanted him. It must be admitted that Sita had incomparable eyes, more beautiful than even Dharini's. But is it enough for a woman to have beauteous eyes? Why hadn't he had the power to penetrate through those eyes into her heart? Such a vacillating mind! Such a quarrelsome temperament! Such envy! Such rage! Brahma the creator must have shaped Sita with every nasty feminine trait. Rather than 'Sita', the name 'Surpanakha', would have been a perfect fit for her.

But was it all Sita's fault? He too was not free from blame. He had encouraged her to adopt a modern lifestyle in New Delhi. If he had kept her in her place right from the beginning, she would have listened to him and remained submissive. That idiot Surya was also responsible for Sita's nature getting vitiated. Hadn't she begun to value Surya's opinions more than his own? Finally, that scoundrel had pushed her into this quagmire.

Feminine nature is strange indeed! What did these women find in Surya that was so compelling, so marvellous? For Sita, at least he was the cousin to gush over. But what could make Dharini bond with Surya? What an act of derring-do Dharini had performed to whisk Surya away from police custody? What audacity! What guts! After disappearing on that day, they are yet to make an appearance. All the efforts of the central government's investigations have been in vain.

The most bizarre outcome was Sita's being arrested and imprisoned in Dharini's name. When he moved to Calcutta, only after a while did Raghavan come to know about this development. But he was unable to take any action in the matter. If he said that she was Sita, not Dharini, would the authorities not demand why she had not disclosed this fact at the time of arrest? And why she had come from Delhi to Calcutta? How could such questions be answered? He had decided to let her stay in prison. Let her learn her lesson. Let her come out when everyone is released. Then he would see! In any case, Sita must be given another chance.

There were important reasons for Raghavan's magnanimous decision. When Raghavan went to see Vasanti before going abroad, the child had looked at her father with her guileless eyes and asked, 'Appa, you didn't bring Amma with you?' He found it impossible to forget the yearning in her voice. He had decided that at least for the sake of the child, he had to try to make a home with Sita.

There was another and rather preposterous reason.

One day, before Raghavan left New Delhi, a woman came into his house at 10 p.m. Her appearance alarmed him.

'Do you know who I am?' she asked.

'No,' Raghavan said.

'I am your wife's mother,' the woman said.

Raghavan laughed as he asked, 'How many mothers does Sita have?'

'Don't laugh! Keep your cleverness to yourself! Sita *is* my daughter. Not born from my womb, but she means more to me than that. Your wife wore a ruby necklace. Do you still have it? Or have you sold it?' she asked.

Raghavan was surprised and scared. Without letting his

pusillanimity show, he asked menacingly, 'Why do you ask? Who are you? What is your name?'

'My name is Raziya Begum. It was I who gave Sita her ruby necklace. I know that you torment Sita. She has gone to prison, preferring incarceration to your oppression. One day she will come out. When she does, you must take care of her and treat her properly. If not, I will kill you with a single stab of this knife,' the woman said and showed him a knife.

Raghavan was now terrified out of his wits. He could not open his mouth. He remembered having heard about the 'madwoman of Rajnipur' who was said to be wandering in Delhi.

'You are Rajnipur's…' he began hesitantly when the woman cut in with, 'Yes. I am the Maharani of Rajnipur. Take proper care of my darling daughter. Otherwise, I will stab you to death!' Then she left.

Raghavan could not get this incident out of his mind. He was extremely eager to know the identity of the madwoman of Rajnipur and her connection to Sita. Though the panic induced by Raziya Begum's threats faded with the passage of time, Raghavan's desire to discover the truth became an added reason for wanting to bring Sita back and start their life together.

The sea breezes were blowing pleasantly against the droning resonance of the waves on the sea. Raghavan felt his eyes closing.

His siesta brought a dream. A vast palace. A central durbar hall. On a marble platform under a canopy of pearls, a queen was seated on a gem-studded throne. From somewhere afar he could hear cries of '*Rajnipur Maharni ki jai!*' Raghavan, who had been standing at a distance, now approached the throne. The queen looked at him, smiled, and asked, 'Do you know who I am?' Raghavan replied, 'The Queen of Rajnipur!' The queen said, 'Look again!' As Raghavan gazed at her, the queen's face began to appear like the face of someone who had stolen his heart. 'Ah! Dharini,' he cried. The woman on the throne told him, 'Look more carefully,' Raghavan looked. Now it appeared to be Sita's face. 'Ah, Sita! Is it you? When did you change yourself to resemble Dharini?' he asked. 'Your eyes have changed, not I,' Sita said. 'Forgive me for tormenting you!' Raghavan said. Sita said, 'The fact that we tormented each other has cancelled the need for forgiveness. Where is Vasanti?' Raghavan said, 'I will go and bring her at once.' Then he began running. He could not remember where he had left Vasanti. He ran on the riverbed where his feet sank into the sands, across a stream where he got drenched, in the wilderness and on the mountains, until he reached a balcony on the top of a huge palace. He ran on shrieking Vasanti's name again and again until his throat was choked, his feet stumbled, and his head began to spin. Making a huge effort he shouted again, 'Ayo, Vasanti!'

From the time he had that dream, Raghavan felt an overwhelming desire to see Vasanti. He told himself again and again that he would never allow himself to be separated from the child. The dream made him pray incessantly for Vasanti's safety.

Disembarking from the ship at the Bombay port, Raghavan took a flight to Madras. He reached his father Padmalochana Sastri's house in Padmapuram. A vehicle stood outside his house, waiting. Raghavan wondered, 'Is someone about to start on a journey?' His mother came out when she heard the taxi. She welcomed Raghavan eagerly and said, 'You didn't even write a letter to say that you were coming.' Disregarding her remark, Raghavan asked, 'Amma, is anyone leaving town?' 'Yes, my son. We didn't know you were coming. Surya is here to take Vasanti. Fortunately, you got here before that.'

'Where did he say he was taking the child?'

'To Devapattinam. Her mother is there, isn't she?'

'Is that so?' Raghavan bellowed.

'Since you are here now, the child will not be leaving today,' Kamakshi Ammal said.

'Not today! In fact, never!' Raghavan said as he went in.

Though she was ready to leave with Surya, as soon as Vasanti saw her father, she ran to hug him.

Raghavan pulled out a pistol from his trousers' pocket. Aiming it straight at Surya he roared, 'You rascal! There is absolutely nothing wrong in killing a scoundrel like you.'

Surya stood transfixed.

14

THE PRINCESS OF RAJNIPUR

Overcoming his astonishment, Surya said, 'Mapillai! Did you happen to see too many English movies? Is that why you want to gun me down for no reason at all? Don't waste the bullets! They may come in useful later.'

'I know that you are a clever braggart. Don't show off your impertinence to me. Didn't you take Sita and run away with her? Now you have come to kidnap Vasanti. I will hand you over to the police before I do anything else. Don't try to escape. I will shoot you if you make a run for it!' Raghavan threatened him.

Kamakshi Ammal who was standing behind Raghavan now said, 'Son, Raghava! Why create such a racket as soon as you have come? Surya is not someone who will do anything improper. It was I who asked him to take Vasanti to her mother. The child had been languishing for a long time without seeing her mother or her father.'

Here Vasanti intervened to say, 'Surya Mama, I will hold Appa tight. Run! Quick!'

The child's reaction made Raghavan calm down. He became slightly ashamed.

'Mister Surya, I know that the women will always be on your side. All right. This time, out of pity, I will let you go. Get out,' Raghavan said.

'Sir, I am going, for sure! But before I go, I want to erase the misconception in your mind. Just now you said that I had taken your wife Sita away. I don't know if you truly believe that. If you do, nothing can be more wrong. Sita was abducted by the minions of the Rajnipur kingdom. I followed them only to rescue Sita. That was when the police captured me. I swear it,' Surya said.

Kamakshi Ammal said, 'Son, Raghava! Surya narrated all this to me as well. I believe everything he told me. Sita too said the same thing.'

Vasanti added, 'Appa, it is amazing and terrifying to hear about all the sufferings Amma underwent. They sound as if they are out of the *Arabian Nights*.'

Dropping the revolver into his pocket, Raghavan said, 'Surya, in that case, tell me everything before you leave. You are in no hurry to leave, are you?'

'Yes, I will, mappilai, sir. No, I am in no hurry at all.'

Raghavan became eager to know all the details as soon as Surya mentioned the Rajnipur men. When bath and lunch were done, he took Surya to his old room upstairs.

'Surya! I had a terrible dream on board the ship. I dreamt that Vasanti was lost and I was running across the earth and sky, searching for her through fire, smoke and mist. I could hear the child's piteous cry of 'Appa, Appa!' But I could not find her. As soon as I awoke, I vowed to myself that I would never be separated from my child again. That is why I became infuriated when I saw you about to take Vasanti away. You may forget it,' Raghavan said.

Surya replied, 'Mapillai, sir, do you remember athanga telling us about her dream when we went to Agra? But in athanga's life, many incidents have occurred which are stranger than nightmares.'

'Surya, is it not odd that *you* know more about Sita than what *I* – her husband – do?'

'Odd it certainly is. I'm not denying it. But circumstances make it so. Besides, with all the unnecessary suspicions you harboured, you did not pay attention to athanga.'

'No need to debate whether my doubts were necessary or unnecessary. Did you not spin some kind of a story about the men from Rajnipur abducting your athanga?'

'Not a story, Mr Raghavan. But the truth.'

'Let it be as you say. Why did the Rajnipur minions carry Sita away? What did they do with her once they abducted her? If you can only prove what you say, I will destroy the entire principality of Rajnipur.'

'Mapillai, I cannot prove anything. How can I get a witness to prove that certain random acts had been performed by someone long ago? It is up to you to believe me.'

'In that case, let me see you telling the story in a way that would make me believe it.'

'Once again you are calling it a "story". What is the use of my going on?'

'Let us not quibble. First, tell me why the Rajnipur men abducted Sita. Perhaps they thought she was the lost princess of Rajnipur,' said Raghavan sardonically.

'Yes. So, you know all about it,' said Surya.

Surya's response fuelled Raghavan's curiosity.

'It was a blind shot. But you say it is the truth. I will not allow myself to drown in astonishment. I will stay afloat to hear your tale,' Raghavan said.

'You haven't stopped scoffing...! Mapillai, sir, have you ever thought that Sita and Dharini resemble each other?'

This gave Raghavan a sudden jolt. Doubts and suspicions came rushing to his mind. However, maintaining his outward composure, he said, 'No Surya. I don't take much notice of women or their appearances. Let us say that Dharini and Sita do have a resemblance to each other. So what?'

'Just that the Rajnipur henchmen abducted Sita mistaking her to be Dharini.'

'Ah! Does it mean that Dharini...' Raghavan began and stopped mid-sentence with a question mark.

'Yes. Dharini is the princess of Rajnipur.'

Raghavan remained transfixed. Then he said, 'Surya, how did you know this? I have known Dharini for a long time. She never told me this, nor did I suspect anything like this.'

'Dharini did not tell me. It was Sita athanga who did.'

'How did you guess that Sita had been abducted because she was mistaken for Dharini?'

'The day before Sita was abducted, Dharini and I were talking in the Gandhi Maidan behind Chandni Chowk.'

Bristling with jealousy Raghavan asked, 'What were you talking about?'

'We were talking about the revolutionary movement, and how to drive the white man away from India. When Dharini left, three men approached me. Their demeanour made me suspect that they were minions of some royal state. They told me that they would give me a lakh of rupees if I helped them to capture Dharini. I did not know their intentions then. I thought that they were motivated by the lecherous intentions of some ruler. I shouted at them and sent them away. The next day, at about the same time, Sita athanga and I were sitting and talking under the same tree in the same maidan.'

'So that's how it was! Your pure and chaste athanga left the house without anyone's knowledge to meet you. Why?'

'Mapillai, if you don't get angry, I will tell you the truth.'

'So, you will lie if I get angry?'

'All right. I will tell the truth anyway! A little while ago you threatened to hand me over to the police. No great loss if you *had* done so. But once before, you had arranged to hand me to the police. The secret police were hiding near your house and waiting for me. If I had been captured at that time, it would have been highly detrimental to the revolutionary movement. It was your wife Sita who prevented it. She came to the Gandhi Maidan to warn me not to come to your house.'

Surya disclosed only one of the reasons for Sita's having come to see him. But it was enough to make Raghavan livid. He was maddened by the thought, 'Ah, so that's what the lousy woman did! Why was she so concerned about saving this scoundrel?'

But what he said was, 'Surya, I did not think that you would so completely be taken in by a woman's words. She repeated what I had joked about, believing it to be true.'

'Perhaps, Mr Raghavan, we must not joke about nasty things. See how your jokes led to disaster!'

'It doesn't look as if you are going to tell me about those disasters. And here I am, dying to know,' Raghavan said.

'How can I tell you unless you let me talk?'

'Silence!' Raghavan jeered, as he covered his mouth with his hand.

Surya gave him a brief account of everything from the mistaken identity that led to Sita's abduction and to her arrest upon reaching Calcutta.

Surya concluded with, 'The Calcutta police made the same mistake that the Rajnipur fellows did. Believing her to be Dharini, they arrested her under the Defence of India Act and sent her to prison.'

15

GANGABAI'S STORY

Many doubts sprang to Raghavan's mind as he remembered the woman known as the madwoman of Rajnipur who threatened him. A mystery to be unravelled. Perhaps Sita was the true princess of Rajnipur! This rascal Surya and his lover Dharini were perhaps engaged in some conspiracy. If not, why had they not disclosed that Sita was not Dharini and got her released?

'Surya, how do you say with such certainty that Dharini is the princess of Rajnipur? Why can it not be Sita?' Raghavan asked.

A smile broke on Surya's face. 'How good it would be if Sita could turn out to be the princess of Rajnipur! Dharini detests the title of "princess". I feel the same. But athanga has a highly romantic temperament. She will be elated if such a thing came about. I can see that it will make you happy as well. Your happiness will make you forget all your anger towards athanga. But what to do? God does not give people what they want, he gives them what they don't want,' Surya remarked.

'Keep your philosophy for later. I will tell you about something that happened to me a few days after Sita left Delhi,' said Raghavan and told Surya all about the crazy woman who appeared one day out of nowhere, knife in hand, and warned him to treat Sita well. 'Who was she? Why should a north Indian woman be so concerned about Sita? Can you tell me?' Raghavan asked.

'Yes, I can!' Surya's reply startled Raghavan.

'Initially, her name was Ramamani Bai. Now her name is Raziya

Begum. There is a reason for her interest in Sita. Mapillai, sir, it is a long story. A story that began some thirty years ago. Only a few months ago did I learn about it. And only when Raziya Begum shared it with me. That unfortunate woman usually wanders around in a state of delirium. There are some rare intervals when her mind becomes unclouded. I got to know about her during a chance encounter in one of those saner moments. I have not even told Sita about it. I am telling you because it is necessary for you to know it.' With this preamble, Surya narrated Raziya Begum's strange history.

Thirty years ago, the maharaja who sat on the throne of Rajnipur was as dissolute as several other rulers of the royal states. Leaving his divan and the British Resident to take care of the government, he spent all his time in his own wanton pursuits. There were many foul ministers to arrange those games. The most important among them was Madhonkar.

Once a musician from Maharashtra came to sing in the maharaja's court. Her name was Ganga Bai. The maharaja liked her as well as her music. Her elder sister Ramamani had accompanied Ganga Bai. She was a woman of grit. She also imagined that no one could trump her in the ways of the world.

Concerts were held in the maharaja's presence on three consecutive days. Then, Madhonkar came to the guest house where the women were staying and said that the maharaja had liked Ganga Bai very much. 'In that case, the maharaja may marry my sister,' Ramamani retorted. 'That is the maharaja's intention,' Madhonkar assured her. Ramamani was fooled by the word 'marriage'. She persuaded her sister to agree to it, saying 'You saw what a great connoisseur the maharaja is! His kingdom enjoys great prestige. No end to his wealth. You must have performed penances in your previous birth to become the maharani in a palace such as this!'

A 'wedding' took place, though at that time, the women did not realize that it was no more than tomfoolery. It was only after a while that they learnt that the maharaja was already married thrice and had three maharanis in his palace.

Though Ramamani was stunned by this revelation, she did not

immediately lose hope or faith. She learnt that all three queens had no issue. One day, when the maharaja came to see Ganga Bai, Ramamani met him alone and threatened him with her knife. She got him to promise that if her sister had a male child, that child would be proclaimed the crown prince of Rajnipur. She made the maharaja sign a document to that effect.

Madhonkar came to know of this. He had his own ideas about whom the Rajnipur kingdom should go to. So, he made his own plot to defeat Ramamani's plot. He made arrangements with the midwife to kill Ganga Bai's baby as soon as it was born, if it turned out to a male child.

The third queen happened to hear Madhonkar conferring with the midwife. She was a woman with ethical principles and a generous nature. She had Ramamani brought to her and informed her about Madhonkar's plans for infanticide. She offered her assistance as she advised that the fourth maharani be taken to Bombay before the time of birth. Ramamani found enough evidence to believe what the third queen had said. The maharaja had gone to Europe at the time. Therefore, Ramamani followed the queen's advice. Taking her sister Ganga Bai with her, she travelled to Bombay without the knowledge of Madhonkar and his henchmen.

As per the customs of Rajasthan, Ganga Bai was heavily veiled. So, it was not all that difficult to spirit her away. But other problems occurred. On the way, their money and train tickets disappeared. The ticket collector made them get down from the train at a small railway station close to Bombay.

Two unescorted women, one of them nine months pregnant, with no cash on hand. But they had the jewels that Ganga Bai was wearing. Selling one of them would bring them money. But where and how could it be sold? Where could Ramamani leave her pregnant sister if she went to sell the jewel? Whom could she approach for assistance?

It was a very small station. At night, such stations near Bombay became totally deserted as soon as the trains departed.

Ramamani took her sister to the ladies' waiting room. Ganga Bai came to know about the situation. Sobs could be heard behind the purdah that covered her face. Ramamani tried to console her.

The station master came in to see where the sobs came from. He saw a woman in purdah and a woman without a purdah. Recognizing that they were Maharashtrians he asked them in Marathi, 'What is the matter?' The station master who made those inquiries was none other than Sita's father, Duraisami Iyer.

Ramamani came out of the waiting room and explained that they were in dire straits. She begged him for shelter for the night and assistance in admitting her sister to a nursing home the next morning.

'What will you give me if I help you?' the station master asked.

At that time, Duraisami was earning but little. His wife Rajam had been admitted to the hospital and expecting the birth of her first child. He did not have enough money for his expenses and needed additional resources. That is why he asked, 'What will you give me?' From their appearance he guessed that the two women had lots of money.

Ramamani said, 'If you help us at this time, we will give you anything we have that you may ask for. Why, I will give myself to you.'

Duraisami was startled and embarrassed. He did not expect such an answer. He thought to himself, 'Siva! Siva! What can I do with you when I am unable to support my own wife?' But his heart was moved by the women's plight.

'Don't say such things, Amma! I don't want anything in return. I will help you in whatever way I can,' he told her.

The next day, he admitted Ganga Bai in the same hospital where he had admitted his wife. But he did not say anything about it to his wife because he thought it might give rise to needless suspicions and arguments.

Every day, when he went to the hospital to see his wife, Duraisami also checked up on Ramamani. Ramamani expressed boundless gratitude to Duraisami. That gratitude soon developed into utmost trust and heartfelt love.

Rajam and Ganga Bai both gave birth to their children on the same night.

By this time, somehow, Madhonkar sniffed his way to the hospital.

Ramamani came to know this. She wanted to go into hiding in some secret place where Madhonkar would be unable to find them. Again, she begged Duraisami for help. Totally snared by his infatuation for Ramamani by then, Duraisami yielded to her request. He found a place that could not be easily located. Ramamani, her sister Ganga Bai, and the child Dharini began to live there.

Duraisami frequented Ramamani's quarters without his wife Rajam's knowledge.

The boy born to Rajam at the time of Dharini's birth, died soon. To forget his loss, more and more did Duraisami visit Ramamani's house to play with Dharini.

The days rolled on. The Maharaja of Rajnipur returned from Europe. It was extremely difficult for Ramamani to get an audience to see him where he was staying in Bombay. When she fought her way through to tell him about their plight, the maharaja simply denied knowing anything about the two women. Ramamani showed him the letter that he had signed.

At the maharaja's command his lackeys forcibly snatched the letter from Ramamani and drove her out.

It was with boundless grief and disappointment that Ramamani gave a detailed account of the whole affair to Ganga Bai. Ganga Bai swooned and fell to the ground. Her mental state worsened day by day. In a few months, Ganga Bai departed from the world.

16

RAMAMANI'S DEFEAT

When Raghavan thought about Dharini as a blue-blooded princess, his mind experienced all the turbulence of a storm-tossed ocean. Suddenly, several things he had not understood before became crystal clear. It was with gratification that he recalled how he had always thought that Dharini was no ordinary girl. He felt all the vanity of having claimed the love of a princess. He felt angry with himself for not having made the right use of that precious love. A greedy thought flashed in the recesses of mind – why, the entire kingdom of Rajnipur should have come to him. How unfair that it should have been lost! He was also astonished by Surya's having been able to learn the secret of Dharini's birth, which he had not been able to discover. Princess Dharini had revealed her secrets to Surya. His rage flamed against Dharini, Surya and Sita. He felt that the three of them had bonded together to destroy his life.

But there was more to be learned from Surya. With great difficulty, he swallowed his rage, resentment, envy and malevolence to say, 'Surya, your story of Ganga Bai is like an astounding tale of fiction outdoing the novels of Scott and Dumas!'

'Any number of incidents occurring in the royal principalities have been more astounding than works of fiction. But I don't find them interesting. They generate heartbreaking sorrow and rage in me. Who knows how many women have suffered the fate of Ganga Bai and Ramamani Bai? How amazing that the tears and curses of those women have not burnt the royal states to cinders,' Surya said.

'No surprise to me. After all, this is the age of Kali, the age of the blackguards! The power of chaste women's curses to reduce evildoers to cinders is all gone with the virtuous past. But go on with the story. What did Ramamani do after Ganga Bai's death? What did that lucky station master – my revered father-in-law – do?' Raghavan inquired.

'Not much left to tell. Perhaps you may know more about it than I do. Still, I will tell you what I know,' Surya said.

Ramamani was thoroughly shaken by Ganga Bai's death. Her mind became unhinged. Now it became Duraisami Iyer's responsibility to take care of the child Dharini. And this strengthened his love for the child.

When Ramamani got her wits back, she vowed to take revenge on the Maharaja of Rajnipur and his evil genius Madhonkar, who had caused the untimely death of her sister. This frenzy steeled her body and soul and gave her the strength to withstand sufferings.

Ramamani needed a man's support to fulfil her vow and to save the child Dharini from falling into Madhonkar's clutches. Therefore, deploying all the manipulative powers of feminine wiles, she firmed up her bond with Duraisami Iyer.

Duraisami Iyer's lot was unenviable. With his meagre salary, he was compelled to maintain two households in Bombay. His financial troubles increased. Moreover, unable as he was to confess the truth to his wife Rajam, he was forced to resort to falsehood. He kept on telling her that he was losing money in horse races.

The death of her first male child had sunk Rajam into grief. She was deeply distressed by the fact that the husband whom she had believed to be a man of upstanding traits had begun to frequent horse races. She began to suspect that he had also gotten into other bad habits. She did not have the courage to openly ask him about her suspicions. She kept her sorrows to herself. This made them fester within.

Meanwhile, two years after Dharini was born, Rajam gave birth to Sita. She became more dejected when this did not bring about any reform in her husband's behaviour as she had expected.

But for the children – Dharini and Sita – the years flew by on wings.

Hearing Ganga Bai's story turned Dharini's attention to the state of her motherland. It stimulated in her an ardent desire to get involved in social service and the freedom struggle. She participated in the salt satyagraha, which had captured the imagination of the public at that time. The news about the earthquake in Bihar made her go there to serve the victims of that disaster.

Around this time Ramamani came to know that Rajam was afflicted by a life-threatening illness. Ramamani had long wished to see Rajam and her daughter, who had suffered because of her. She went to see Rajam when Duraisami was away, taking with her the sum of ₹2000 and the sole remaining jewel from Rajnipur. She gifted them to Rajam for Sita's marriage.

After performing this crucial 'duty', Ramamani decided to focus on fulfilling her life's mission. When he was in Bombay, she attempted to stab the Maharaja of Rajnipur to death. She failed. She was imprisoned for attempted murder.

In prison, Ramamani's madness increased. She was sent to the lunatic asylum. Eventually, she obtained her release from the asylum.

The Maharaja of Rajnipur did not live very long after Ramamani's release. This led her to focus on Madhonkar, her next target for revenge. She wandered through the streets of Delhi, waiting for a chance to find Madhonkar alone. But Ramamani failed in that mission as well. After a long search for Madhonkar, when she thought that she finally had him in her grasp, she found that another man, who had long wanted to have his revenge on Madhonkar, had succeeded in achieving this goal.

17

LUCKY ESCAPE!

After narrating the tragic story of Ramamani and Ganga Bai, Surya looked at Saundara Raghavan and said, 'Mapillai, sir, did you not say that some north Indian woman came to threaten you about Sita? She must have been Raziya Begum, formerly known as Ramamani. Don't you see the reason for her interest in Sita now?'

'I do. But Surya, like a modern novelist, you have brought the story to an abrupt halt, without disclosing what happened to the heroes and the heroines thereafter!' Raghavan remarked.

'What more do you want to know?' Surya inquired.

'Why! I'm asking you about my precious father-in-law. Haven't seen him even once after the wedding. Where is he now? What is he doing?'

'I don't know. Nor do I know where Raziya Begum is to be found. Dharini and I have searched high and low for them. No luck!'

'Why did you search for them?' Raghavan asked.

'Dharini has a major doubt about her life. Only Duraisami Iyer or Ramamani can clear that doubt,' Surya said, and added with a smile, 'Mr Raghavan, moreover, we were motivated by the fact that we need their permission and blessings for another venture.'

Surya's tone and the glow on his face kindled a suspicion in Raghavan's mind. 'What venture?' he asked.

'Can't you guess? Dharini and I have decided to get married.'

Raghavan let out a shout of laughter and said, 'Hey Surya! I thought you had some brains.'

'And now you think you were mistaken?'

'Yes. Otherwise, after having been associated with her for so long, will you say that you are going to marry Dharini? Surya! There was a time when I too thought I would marry her. She played the role of being in love with me. I thought you knew all this.'

'Raghavan, don't say such things about Dharini. You don't know Dharini if you say that she was play acting.'

'You think you know her better than I do,' Raghavan said.

'Certainly. If you knew Dharini you will not say that she indulged in pretence, or enacted a role.'

'What about her marrying you after once declaring her love for me? One of the two facts has to be a lie!'

'Not at all. Doesn't everyone have the right to change their mind? It is true that at one time Dharini did love you. How can it be wrong if she changes her mind after realizing that it was not compatible with her life's goals?'

'Surya, you should have become a lawyer! If you had, you would have acquired a fine reputation. But this is a waste of time. I know Dharini far better than you do. I know just why she pretended to be in love with me. For the paltry sum of two thousand rupees. After all, she is the daughter of a singer who went to royal courts in search of patronage. What else can you expect from her?'

Jumping up in rage Surya said, 'Raghavan, Take care! If you say anything about Dharini's character…' His lips trembled. He could not say anything more.

'What will you do if I talk about it? Will you stab me to death? Like Raziya Begum?'

'All right, mapillai. There's no point in continuing this conversation,' Surya said and got up.

'Adedey! Don't leave in a rage, brother. At least not before telling me what your athanga, the darling daughter of Duraisami Iyer who is famous for his moral rectitude – is doing now, and where she is. But you may start fighting with me if I were to say anything about her! You may even claim to know Sita better than I do. After all, I am only her wedded husband. But *you* are her precious cousin!'

Surya stood, head bowed, eyes down. Two drops of tears fell from his eyes.

'Weeping like a woman! The moment your athanga's name is mentioned, you melt, body and soul! What is the nature of that intimate relationship between you?' Raghavan asked.

Surya wiped his eyes, looked at Raghavan and said, 'Say anything you like about me or Dharini. But any scoundrel who vilifies Sita's name will go straight to hell. His tongue will rot, the earth will open and swallow him!'

These harsh words made Raghavan feel apprehensive.

Surya went on. 'Why am I concerned about Sita? I will tell you. With her last breath Sita's mother, my athai, asked me to take care of Sita. That is not all. I will tell you what I have not told anybody else until now. The day before your wedding, a telegram sent in Duraisami Iyer's name came to my father saying "Stop Sita's wedding." I received it. I did not give it to my father. I did not mention it to anyone. Mapillai, when you first came to Rajampettai, it was to see my sister Lalita. But you met Sita by chance. Until then, I had believed that love belonged to the world of fantasy, not real life. But in *your* life, I was thrilled to see love at first sight. I thought that even Sita's father did not have the right to interfere in a marriage where two hearts came together in love. The wedding took place. Half an hour later, Duraisami Iyer arrived. "Did you get my telegram?" he asked. I told him what I had done. "What can we do when this is God's will?" he sighed. I remember all this as if it happened but yesterday.'

Raghavan's mind began to boil. He was infuriated by Surya's presumption. It had ruined his life. If Surya had not interfered, his life could have taken a different direction altogether. Why should he have taken it upon himself to suppress Duraisami Iyer's telegram?

And yet, to learn more, Raghavan suppressed his anger. 'All right! Let us postpone examining the rights and wrongs of your action. Why did Duraisami Iyer send such a telegram?' he asked.

'Dharini was in Bihar when Ramamani alias Raziya Begum was sentenced to imprisonment for the attempted murder of the Maharaja of Rajnipur. Duraisami Iyer went to Bihar to console

Dharini. Hearing about Raziya Begum's fate brought her incalculable grief and shame. A debate ensued about Dharini's future. Duraisami Iyer wanted Dharini to marry and live in peace. Having heard about you from Ramamani, he tried to understand Dharini's heart. But by then, Dharini had begun have doubts about her relationship with you. When she heard about her mother's imprisonment, she gave up all intentions of marrying you. But Duraisami Iyer felt differently. He wanted Dharini to marry you and live happily with you. That is why he sent that telegram.'

'Surya, do you realize your mistake in suppressing that telegram?' Raghavan asked.

'Mapillai, I don't think it was a mistake. It was God's will. Even now I can see how Sita and you are perfectly matched. There's no dovetailing of ideologies between you and Dharini. Your marriage with her would not have been successful.'

'So, you think that your athanga and I are leading a successful life together in a state of bliss?'

'Mapillai, I remember how true this was in the beginning. Even now it is not too late. Athanga is waiting to return to you, ready to forget whatever happened and accept you as her god. Write a note to her and see if she does not come running to you.'

'Surya, I will cut off my hand rather than write to Sita asking her to return. Let her go on happily canvassing votes for Pattabhiraman. She can marry him if she likes. I am ready to give her a divorce.'

'Ayo, don't say such things! Sita will kill herself if she comes to know! Please listen to me. Let bygones be bygones. Forget it all and try to resume your life with Sita. You are sure to be happy. Raghavan, nothing can give Dharini or me greater joy than to see Sita and you living together in harmony.'

Surya's words added fuel to the fire blazing in Raghavan's heart.

'Dei! Idiot, take care! Don't make me angry.' Raghavan bellowed and landed a tight slap on Surya's cheek.

Surya raised his hand and dropped it forthwith.

'Mapillai, in the past I would have returned one slap with nine. But recently, Dharini and I have reframed our ideologies. Seeing that violence is pointless, we have vowed to follow the Mahatma's path of ahimsa. You have posed the first test to that vow.'

'Oh, I see! You have gone over to the Mahatma's side? What is the Mahatma's doctrine but Jesus Christ's injunction to turn the other cheek? Take this too,' Raghavan said and struck Surya on the other cheek.

Surya felt excruciating pain. He felt the pain vibrating from head to toe. 'Satisfied? Has your mind calmed down? Then I will take your leave,' Surya said.

'No, I am not satisfied. My mind will not calm down so easily,' Raghavan said and gripped Surya's neck in a stranglehold.

'Look, Surya, swear that you will see neither Dharini nor Sita ever again! If you don't, I will kill you instantly.'

'Mapillai, that is not fair. Why should I swear that I will never meet Sita? My heart is free from guile. Nor can I make any promises about Dharini. If you like, you may shoot me dead. Sita athanga, Dharini, your mother and Vasanti will be delighted. The CID man waiting outside will be happy too.'

'Dei! You imbecile, do you think you can frighten me?' Raghavan snarled and shoved Surya with all his strength. Surya went tumbling down the steps until his fall was arrested by the intermediate landing on the staircase. He managed to sit up.

Hearing the crash, Vasanti and her grandmother came running.

'Surya mama, Ayo! Did you fall down the stairs?' Vasanti cried.

'Yes,' Surya answered her.

'Vasanti, Surya tripped and fell down. But thank God, a lucky escape for the staircase, the steps remain undamaged!' Raghavan said and guffawed loudly in appreciation of his own wit.

18

PATTABHI'S TRIUMPH

Devapattinam was in a state of tumult. From every nook and corner rose cries of 'Up! Up! Patthabiraman!' 'Down! Down! Black Market'. From young children to white-haired senior citizens, everyone talked about the miracle. The whole town knew how the old chairman had distributed ₹30,000, determined as he was to win this election as well. Rumour had it that his herculean efforts included a bribe of ₹100 per vote. And yet, it was the popular candidate Pattabhiraman who won the majority vote. Shouts of joy rose to the skies as soon as the results were announced. Within half an hour, all the garlands from all the flower shops in town landed on Pattabhiraman's neck. A spontaneous procession began. Pattabhiraman was pushed into a motor car. Nadaswaram pipes and a music band appeared from nowhere. The procession took its time to go round the streets of Devapattinam and dispersed only after depositing Pattabhiraman in front of his house.

A few close friends and dignitaries followed Pattabhiraman into the house. Everyone congratulated him, swearing that his becoming the chairman was a done deed. Some of the older men took the liberty of asking, 'Where is Mrs Pattabhiraman?' Overwhelmed by delight and diffidence, Lalita joined them. One by one, they congratulated Lalita. 'This victory is all due to your good fortune,' they said.

When Lalita left them, someone inquired, 'How is that lady?' Pattabhiraman winced as he replied, 'All right.'

Another said, 'You are inquiring about Sita madam, aren't you?'

'When it comes to public life, such things are bound to happen. We must not be cowed by the lies of gossipmongers, nor allow our determination to flag,' Damodaram Pillai said.

'Mr Pattabhiraman, it is you who must put heart into Sita Madam,' advocate Appa Rao said.

'How can anyone hurl such vicious abuse? My blood boils when I think of it,' Pattabhiraman said.

'Pattabhi! Don't get all heated up over this! Did I not warn you? This kind of filth is bound to surface in any election. No point in making a fuss over it,' Damodaram Pillai said.

'Sir! Such scoundrels must not be allowed to go scot free. The man who published the pamphlet must be dragged to court and subjected to public ridicule.'

'It would be wrong to go to court,' advocate Appa Rao said. 'Don't we all know how difficult it is to prove libel? Best to leave it as beneath contempt.'

'That's right sir! If a dog barks at the moon, what loss is it to the moon?' the pacifist shrugged.

'That's what *we* think. But what does the *moon* think about it, I wonder!' quipped the humourist.

Finally, everyone left, leaving Pattabhiraman to rejoice over his victory with his family.

Readers may be mystified by the sympathetic remarks about Sita in the preceding conversation. What had happened was this.

Pattabhiraman's final campaign meeting was held on election day eve. A five thousand strong crowd had gathered, numbers hitherto unknown in municipal election meetings in that town. Several men and women sat on the dais with Pattabhiraman, Sita among them. All the electioneering she had done for the past one and a half months had turned Sita into a powerful orator. Her speeches were charged with fervour, surged with patriotism, flamed in fearless abandon. They shattered the black market, demolished oppression and injustice. They endorsed Pattabhiraman with words of affection and support. The words she aimed at the opposing candidate zipped past like Rama's arrows to attack corruption.

Therefore, audiences had become habituated to enduring other speeches as they waited impatiently for valiant Sita's outpourings.

But on that last public meeting the audiences were in for a great disappointment. Sita made no speech on that day. It is true that she got up to speak as usual. But she did not get beyond three or four sentences. Overcome by a sudden bout of sobs, she stopped, and sat down.

What was the reason for Sita's anomalous behaviour?

During the meeting, someone distributed pamphlets at the fringes of the crowd. Those who read the pamphlet, at once began to stare at Sita. The pamphlets changed hands and went through the crowd. Soon, most people lost interest in the speeches and went on staring at Sita. Some of those glances expressed pity, others displayed anger or derision.

Sita was compelled to take note of the fact that the people in the crowd were alternating between reading the pamphlet and looking at her. She began to experience an inexplicable sense of dread. Finally, the boy tossed a few pamphlets on the stage and ran away.

As the pamphlets changed hands, Sita took one. The initial sentences were enough to puncture her heart. As she read on, her heart threatened to explode. When she finished, she felt as if a thousand scorpions were stinging her. With distress came an upsurge of indignation and wrath.

The pamphlet slandered Sita and maligned her character, declaring that she had left her husband to run away with her cousin Surya. She had not been sentenced for serving the nation but for stealing on a train. The pamphlet ended by roundly abusing the idiots who were mesmerized by the perfidious rhetoric of a vamp.

It was with fury stimulated by agony that Sita got up to speak. She began with all the delirious rage of exposing the fatuity of the man who had penned the pamphlet. But her intentions could not be fulfilled. She was barely able to mouth a few sentences, before she broke into sobs and was forced to stop and slump down on her seat.

For the next two days Sita did not emerge from her room. To those who inquired about her, Pattabhiraman was forced to say that she was unwell. The incident disturbed and enraged Pattabhiraman as well. It did not dishearten him, rather it strengthened his determination to win the elections.

Those who worked for Pattabhiraman were similarly motivated. They worked more feverishly, convinced that if they did not win this time, they would lose all respect, and never be able to show their faces in Devapattinam again.

The pamphlet had no impact at all on the voters. Can anyone get the people's support by calling them idiots? The public will put up with any abuse. But no one can expect to get the people's endorsement by calling them fools!

The people of Devapattinam came to a decision. 'We will prove that the real fool is not the common man but the man who wrote the pamphlet.' Moreover, the general opinion was that the old bandicoot who had minted money in the black market had launched offensive rumours about a woman to achieve his own goal. The votes reflected this public opinion. Pattabhiraman gained an overpowering victory.

But that victory did not bring him the happiness it should have done. His exhilaration was affected by the defamatory hype against Sita. The person who had instigated him to stand for the elections, whose stupendous efforts had brought him victory, who had cheered him whenever he felt dispirited, was now unable to participate in celebrating his success. She had confined herself to her room for the last two days. What was the use of a victory that could not be celebrated with Sita?

Pattabhiraman was feeling disheartened by these thoughts when Lalita came to his office room with her mother. No one was more delighted by Pattabhi's victory than his mother-in-law. For the first time, Sarasvati Ammal abandoned her diffidence and spoke to her son-in-law with enthusiasm.

'Whatever you may say, Amma has more affection for you than anybody else,' Lalita said.

'Who denies it? But your mother's great affection is a great problem for me,' Pattabhiraman replied.

Lalita went on, 'Sita has taken to bed for the past two days. You were totally engrossed by the elections. Let us go and console her now. Why don't you come with me?'

'Should one lie in bed and keep on crying because some passerby spouts random nonsense? All said and done, women cannot change. Such cowards must never enter public life,' he said.

'That's what Surya said the other day. He said that women must not get into election hassles.'

Swelling with arrogance Pattabhiraman said, 'What does it matter what Surya says? He told me not to stand for elections. Today the entire town is filled with acclamations and shouts of victory?'

'They are shouting, "Victory to Pattabhiraman!" Today is the day of your coronation!' Lalita said lovingly.

'Enough, enough! Don't start boasting. Today is merely the day of the flag hoisting. You can talk about coronation when I get the chairman's position.'

'That too will happen in due course. My words will come true. Wait and see!'

'Bhesh! So, you are convinced that my victory is due to the power of your predictions. You seem to have forgotten how you threw a tantrum over my standing for elections. If Sita had not taken my side...'

'Who's talking about it now? Can we ever forget how Sita athanga helped us in the elections?'

'Are you saying that but for her, I would not have won?'

'Of course not! You won because of your sacrifices and influence. But Sita athanga has also worked very hard. We must not forget that. Come, let us go up and see athanga. You will lose nothing by telling her "I won because of you!" And it will bring her some satisfaction.'

'Impossible. Was I born for the express purpose of bringing satisfaction to your athanga? The entire town got together to arrange a procession to acclaim me! And she couldn't even come down the stairs. I cannot go up and hold her by the chin and plead with her. Understand?'

As Pattabhiraman was speaking these angry words, footsteps were heard coming down the stairs. The couple stopped speaking. After a couple of minutes, Sita entered the room.

'Athanga, you will live for a hundred years! We were just talking about you,' Lalita exclaimed.

'Welcome, welcome! We were talking about coming upstairs to see you. How is your headache now?' Pattabhiraman asked.

'My headache vanished the moment I heard the news of your victory. I am very happy,' Sita replied.

'Everything is due to your encouragement and assistance. I owe you a great deal,' Pattabhiraman said.

'What did I do? Everything is because of Lalita's good fortune,' Sita said as she stroked Lalita's cheeks and made the gesture of getting rid of the evil eye.

Lalita was in ecstasy. She was delighted that Sita had come down with a bright face. And her husband who had spoken harshly about her just a minute ago, was now talking to her with respect. Lalita's joy in Pattabhiraman's victory was now complete. 'Athanga, look at this man's greed! Winning the election is not enough, he says. Satisfaction is guaranteed only after gaining the chairman's post.'

'Your good fortune will make it happen,' Sita said.

Pattabhiraman intervened, 'Don't believe her. She is trying to put the blame on me. It is she who wants everyone to cheer her as the chairman's wife.'

'What is wrong with Lalita's wish? I too want to see you as the chairman,' Sita said with warmth.

'If that wish is to be fulfilled, you must help me as you did before, not go upstairs and lie down.'

'I can be of no help to you anymore. In fact, I may bring you harm. For the past two days I have been thinking seriously and concluded that women must never intervene in public events. The general public can be abominable.'

'You are completely wrong. Everyone who came to congratulate me today enquired about you warmly. Not a single person had a bad word to say about you.'

'They will not say anything today, but they will, tomorrow.'

'I don't know why you mistrust people. Can the entire populace be blamed for the nonsense spouted by a single individual?'

'I don't know if you saw that pamphlet. If you had, your blood would have boiled like mine. You would have wanted to hack to pieces the man who wrote it.'

Lalita interrupted, 'Enough! Why should we talk about this when we are happy? Come, let us go and eat.'

Laughter and playful chatter prevailed as they lunched together.

After lunch, when Sita went upstairs and Pattabhiraman to the pyol outside, Sarasvati Ammal told Lalita, 'It won't be right for this girl to stay here for too long. It will be good if she goes away.'

'What are you saying Amma? If athanga had not come here, mapillai would not have stood for elections, or won them. You said this so many times. And now you say it will be good for Sita to go away.'

'Am I denying what she has accomplished? But in the end, she dropped a bomb.'

'Done blame her without cause. Poor thing, what did she do?'

'How do I know what she did or did not do? There's no smoke without fire. If she had an untarnished character, would anyone have dared to publish a pamphlet like that?'

'Amma! Don't slander athanga. It is a sin.'

'You can shut me up. But can you silence the whole world? There is a big task left to be achieved. I am very worried about mapillai's becoming the chairman. If Sita has good intentions, it would be only fair for her to depart quickly. She too has a husband. She has a child. If she continues to stay in someone else's house, what will happen to her own household? Will you go and stay in somebody else's house like her? Think about it!' Sarasvati Ammal said. Lalita began to feel that there was some truth in what her mother said.

19

FEEDING THE SNAKE

The mother-in-law's aspiration did not go unfulfilled. Pattabhiraman was elected to the municipal chairman's post. The victory was accompanied by thunder, lightning and torrential floods.

Sita's mental fatigue disappeared in two or three days. Ignoring Sarasvati Ammal's mutterings, Lalita and Pattabhiraman strove to kindle her enthusiasm. Unfailingly did they take her to all the celebratory meetings and dinners. Sita enhanced everyone's spirits with her bonhomie and savvy conversation. True, those who were jealous and contrary-minded did mutter among themselves. But this did not reach Pattabhi's ears.

As election day drew closer, Pattabhiraman, Lalita and Sita began to feel more and more elated as it became clear that Pattabhiraman would win the chairman's post. But two days before, something happened to make Lalita feel as if she was struck by a thunderbolt.

Pattabhiraman had gone out in the morning. Sita was in her room upstairs, writing a letter. Lalita brought the mails in and deposited them on Pattabhiraman's table. There was a letter for her. Generally, a glance at the address was enough for her to know who had written the letter. Not this time. She did not know why, but her heart was beating rather fast as she opened the envelope.

There was no letter. Instead, there was a paper clipping from a magazine. The heading in large letters drew her eyes, 'Pattabhiraman's Antics'. Lalita began to shake like a leaf as soon as she read the first few lines.

She knew that she should not read it in the office room. What if her husband walked in? Or Sita? This must not reach their eyes. Clipping in hand, she ran to her room and locked the door carefully. She stood near the window and continued to read. She could not read more than half of it. Drops of scalding hot tears flowed down from her eyes and blinded them. Something like hot smoke rose from the pit of her stomach, suffocating her lungs before rushing to her head. Her head began to spin dizzyingly. She was afraid that she was going to swoon.

And yet, with astonishing mental strength, Lalita managed to put the news clipping into her trunk and lock it. Then she crashed on the bed. Her tears flowed like a river. 'Chee Chee! Should I allow my mind to get out of control because some spiteful fellow has printed nonsense?' The thought steeled her mind. She got up, wiped her tears, stood in front of the mirror to freshen up, and came out of the room. She went to the kitchen and enquired, 'Amma, is lunch ready?' There was no sign on her face to indicate the excruciating anguish she had experienced just a moment ago.

What was it that made Lalita experience the torments of hell?

Under the guise of exposing corruption in the personal lives of the dignitaries in Devapattinam, a yellow journal released reports too obscene to be spoken or written about. Decent, upright persons were ashamed to buy or read the salacious journal circulated through secret channels. But in their heart of hearts, they were afraid that it may contain defamatory information about them. Some people bought it furtively, enjoyed seeing others slandered, suffered to see themselves defamed, hoped and prayed that no one read what had been written about them.

Pattabhiraman was among those who had not fallen into this cesspool. He had neither seen nor read that journal. If others mentioned it, his disgust shut them up. No surprise then that this yellow journal had never found its way into his house.

Lalita had heard rumours about the existence of such a journal. She had wondered how such a magazine could exist at all. But now, when she read a report from that journal, what she felt was not astonishment, but rage and grief and boundless acrimony.

Someone had taken enormous pains to send her a report announcing that Pattabhiraman and Sita were lovers; Lalita was a moron to shelter Sita in her house. The citizens of Devapattinam had obtained the 'good fortune' of getting a man as 'morally upright' as Pattabhiraman for their municipal chairman. These details occupied the first half of the story. Lalita could read no more. But why did she put that lewd piece of writing under lock and key, instead of chucking it into the fire? The reason was known only to her inmost self, and to God.

After the initial shock and agony, Lalita displayed greater exuberance in speech and behaviour. She was proud to be able to carry on as before. Others attributed her exhilaration to the approaching election day. But to anyone with a keen eye, it would have been obvious that something was eating at her heart.

The elections took place. Pattabhiraman achieved a magnificent victory. Once again Devapattinam broke into noisy celebrations. After the public celebrations were over, Pattabhi's close friends accompanied him home and stayed talking to him for a long time. Again, Sita did not participate in the celebrations. Lalita too did not join the group of friends. When a friend mentioned it, another placed a finger on his own lips and warned him, 'We must ignore the slanders of base creatures. If we don't, it will mean that we value the opinions of reprobates.' Another said, 'The women of the house too must be made to understand this.' When Pattabhiraman asked them to explain these remarks, someone hushed him, 'Why talk about unsavoury matters at this time of jubilation?'

When his friends left, Pattabhiraman called Lalita. When she came, her face looked as if she had hastily wiped her tears. Pattabhiraman asked heatedly, 'Why do you look so down in the dumps? Did you have a crying jag because I won?'

'Perhaps my face is fated to appear gloomy to you,' Lalita answered sharply.

'What has happened to all of you today?' Pattabhiraman asked.

'Whom do you mean by "all of you"? I can only answer for myself,' Lalita retorted.

'I'm asking about your dearest friend Sita.'

'She is not my dearest friend. Perhaps she's your...'

'Whoever her friend may be, what has happened to her? She vanished upstairs the day I came home after winning the elections. She is doing the same thing today,' Pattabhiraman said.

'I don't know. You will have to ask her.'

'You too appear unwell. Ask your mother if she knows anything. She may have hauled Sita over the coals.'

'Why are you dragging my mother into this? She did not say a single word to anyone today. I will ask her to leave tomorrow. If you like, I too will go away. Any stray dog that wants to stay may do so.'

Pattabhiraman looked at Lalita as if he would torch her. The next instant he decided that there was no point in letting the meaningless quarrel grow. A suspicion had been growing in his mind for a few days – that his mother-in-law has been bad-mouthing Sita. Lalita was letting her do it. That suspicion was now confirmed. Why else would the woman who had been happy till the day before, refuse to come down today? His mother-in-law must have condemned Sita within her hearing. Sita may have remonstrated to Lalita about it. Lalita may have taken her mother's side. Sita has been hurt. Lalita's harsh words about Sita confirmed it. His mother-in-law was a demon. Can the daughter of a demon be devoid of diabolical attributes?

Helpless Sita was trapped between the two of them. Her numskull of a husband was becoming notorious after abandoning his wife to struggle on, alone! And here, where she had sought shelter, should Sita meet with this fate? Considering how much she had done for him, should he allow her to endure anguish and humiliation in his own house?

Pondering thus, Pattabhiraman finished eating. Without saying a single word to Lalita, he went straight to the bedroom and stretched himself out on the bed.

Sometime later, Lalita joined him. Pattabhiraman acted as if he did not see her. After five minutes Lalita asked, 'Are you angry with me?'

'Angry? Why angry?' Pattabhiraman said.

'Then why do you snap at me?'

'What else can I do in a house full of idiots?'

After a pause, Lalita asked, 'How many votes did you get in today's elections? How many did your opponent get?'

'What is it to you?'

'Are you saying it is nothing to me?'

Pattabhiraman remained silent.

'Have I no claim in your victory? Look at me and tell me the truth.'

'Did you behave as if you had such a claim?'

'In what way did I not do so? Please tell me.'

'Today I obtained the chairman's post. For the next three years, I am virtually the king of this town. I came back to the house with a tremendous victory. How did you receive me? With a glum face.'

'My face appears as it always does. How can it suddenly become appealing?'

'Who talked about appeal? I asked you if you welcomed me happily.'

'I was happy. To you I may have appeared gloomy. You were angry that Sita did not welcome you. You directed that anger against me.'

'Take it as you will.'

'What can I do if the obstinate devil takes to her bed upstairs?'

'It was you who said that she was goddess Lakshmi and Saraswati incarnate. Now she has become the devil?'

'I am guileless. I believed that she was innocent, like me.'

'When did you discover that she is wily?'

Lalita remained silent.

Pattabhiraman asked again. 'Until yesterday she was in high spirits. What misery overcame her today?'

'How do I know? She didn't tell me.'

'Take a guess!'

'She too has a husband, a child and a family. She might have had thoughts of rejoining them.'

'Who prevents her from leaving?'

'How will she leave without some efforts made for her departure? That is what Amma says.'

Pattabhiraman became lost in his own reflections. His suspicions had proved true. It was his mother-in-law's work. She had poisoned her daughter's mind as well. How could he rectify this deplorable situation? What would be the fate of the hapless woman abandoned by her husband?

Pattabhiraman was startled when Lalita asked him, 'Have you seen the magazine called *Yamadutan*?' He remembered the hints dropped by friends who had accompanied him home. So that's what this change in behaviour is about. Some report in that rag. And someone has conveyed that information to Lalita and poisoned her mind.

'You have not answered my question,' Lalita pressed him.

'No. Nor am I going to read it.'

'You may not read it but the whole town reads it. The whole town is laughing at us.'

'The whole town is laughing at us? Why?'

'Because of what has appeared in *Yamadutan*. The ladies in the neighbouring houses told me about it. You are the only one who doesn't know what the whole town knows.'

'Is that so? What is that great big thing that has appeared in *Yamadutan*?'

'It is so obscene that it cannot be spoken about. It has to be read.'

A suspicion dawned in Pattabhi's mind. 'Do you have that magazine?' he asked.

'Yes,' Lalita replied.

Pattabhiraman was inflamed. Controlling his fury, he said, 'Let me see it. Show it to me!'

'It is right here,' Lalita said as she switched on the light, opened the trunk, picked out the clipping and gave it to Pattabhiraman.

Pattabhiraman stood up. His blood boiled as he read it. The first part of the lurid report was that Pattabhiraman and Sita were secret lovers, while Lalita remained an idiot. The second part described an earlier relationship between Sita and Surya, and Surya's being soundly thrashed by her husband when he went to negotiate with Raghavan on Sita's behalf.

Gnashing his teeth as he read through the whole, Pattabhiraman asked for a matchbox.

Lalita brought it to him. Pattabhiraman struck a match. Lalita cried, 'Don't burn it!' 'Why?'

'I have read only half of it. I must read the rest.'

'Is that so?' Pattabhiraman asked, reducing the paper to ashes.

'You don't care about what I said? So, it is true that a guilty heart is gnawed from within.'

Pattabhiraman approached Lalita and struck her hard on the cheek. 'How dare you buy it?'

Emerging from her stupefaction Lalita sobbed out, 'I didn't buy it. It came by post.'

'Who sent it?'

'I don't know.'

'Why didn't you tell me as soon as you got it? Why did you lock it up in the trunk? Is this a treasure for safekeeping?'

'I thought I would tell you later, at leisure.'

'Later, tell me later? You are an evil wretch! Your mind is drawn to filth. That is why you locked it inside the trunk.'

Lalita remained silent.

Pattabhiraman switched off the light and came to lie down again.

Lalita said, 'What I did was wrong. Please forgive me.'

'All right. Don't do anything without my knowledge again. Now lie down and go to sleep.'

Accordingly, Lalita did lie down. But she could not sleep. Instead came sobs and tears. She suppressed them with great difficulty.

After a while she asked, 'Will you have to go to the office everyday as chairman?'

'Yes. Yes. You can boast to all the ladies in the neighbourhood, "My husband too goes to work."'

'I only wanted to know what kind of work you would have to do.'

'I am feeling sleepy. Don't disturb me. I will tell you tomorrow.'

Lalita made every effort to fall asleep. But sleep evaded her. Finally, she pretended to fall asleep in order to avoid disturbing Pattabhi's slumber.

The clock struck twelve.

From somewhere came the sound of a whimper. A whimper of heartbreaking grief and anguish.

It reached Pattabhiraman's ears and startled him.

The whimper sounded again.

It came from the top floor. It was Sita who was whimpering. There was no doubt about it.

Sita was the only person in the world who had truly understood his heart. She had completely empathized with his wishes and desires. It was she who had kindled in him a new enthusiasm for life. It was she who had given him a goal to work for.

Such a woman was lying alone and weeping – shaken by heartbreaking agony. Unable to sleep even after midnight. How the harsh words from his wife and mother-in-law must have tormented her! Or, she may have received some sad news. What was the use of his being alive without offering her solace? How else could his gratitude be expressed for all the assistance she had given him?

Why not wake Lalita and take her along? No. Never. She has begun to see Sita as an enemy. Perhaps she is responsible for the grief that has now befallen Sita!

Quietly, Pattabhiraman got up from the bed. Noiselessly, he opened the door and went out. Silently, he began to go up the stairs.

Lalita who had been pretending to be asleep, got up from the bed. Walking out of the open door she went to the staircase. She stood transfixed by the sight of Pattabhiraman ascending the stairs.

Two minutes later, Lalita's mother came to stand behind Lalita.

Sarasvati Ammal whispered, 'Girl, see! Didn't I bang my head on the wall saying that even if you feed it milk, a snake will always disgorge poison? See what the wretch has done? She has ruined your life.'

Lalita placed a finger on her mouth and shushed her mother.

The sounds of footsteps on the stairs ceased. The creaking sound of opening the door was heard, and the 'click' of the light being switched on. Then came the sound of the door being shut.

'Go, girl! Go!' Sarasvati Ammal pushed her. But Lalita needed no pushing. She rushed up the stairs as one demented.

Walking across the corridor upstairs she half-opened the door to Sita's room. The scene she witnessed was something she had anticipated. And yet, for a moment, it immobilized her.

Pattabhiraman was holding Sita's chin in his hand. In the dim light of the electric lamp, the tears in Sita's eyes were gleaming like graded pearls.

Lalita was overwhelmed by the kind of fury she had never experienced in her life.

20

BLOW AFTER BLOW

Anguished as she was by the blow she had received when the pamphlet defaming her was distributed at the public meeting, Sita received another blow which followed close on its heels.

This was a letter from Surya. 'When I reached Madras, Saundara Raghavan too had returned unexpectedly from abroad.' On reading that sentence Sita felt that all her sorrows had come to an end. She felt the shock of surprise and delight, and an irrepressible yearning to take flight and reach Raghavan at once. But reading on was to feel the shock of disappointment and grief. Surya had summarized his experiences and ended the letter with these words:

Athanga,

I wanted to bring you and your husband together. I thought that I could clear all your misunderstandings. I was eager to make your bonds strong enough to prevent all future squabbles. All that has been reduced to a daydream.

I don't want to come back. I am going to Delhi. I will write to you from there. I request you to let me know at once should your husband change his mind and write to you after returning to Calcutta.

Finally, there is something I wish to tell you. Please forgive me if you don't like it. I did not like Pattabhiraman's getting into the election swamp. Nor your campaigning for him. It would be best for you to avoid going out as much as possible. The world is a deplorable and envious place. And Devapattinam is full of petty-minded people. I don't have to say more.

After reading this letter, the distress and fury she felt were incalculable. She was furious with the world and with God. Greater fury was provoked against her darling daughter Vasanti. Hadn't Vasanti gone to Calcutta with her father because she did not want her mother? Sita's rage became so unreasonable as to make her decide that Vasanti was no longer any daughter of hers.

Her thoughts ran on. 'And Surya! He wants to mediate between us! If my husband doesn't want me as his wife, I too want no husband! What is the point of returning to a husband filled with such arrogance and venom? How long will it be possible to live in amity with him? Even after this long separation, his heart has not undergone any change. Why should I go and surrender at his feet? Look at the way Surya's mind works. He disapproves of my getting into the election campaign. Who cares? Surya would like anything that Dharini did! Even if she were to roam around in a man's garb, he would say, "Adadaa! What splendid courage!" But he will not approve of anything I do. Why should he? Was I born on earth only to carry out the tasks which are met with his approval? It is not as if there is no one to acclaim my addresses on the public platform. That is more than enough for me!'

Sita swallowed her disappointment and shock to assume outward ebullience. Once again, she began to attend parties and public meetings with Pattabhiraman.

She did not show Surya's letter to anyone. But it became necessary to explain why Surya did not bring her child to Devapattinam. She told Lalita that Saundara Raghavan had returned from England and had taken Vasanti to Calcutta.

But Lalita's mother would not keep her mouth shut. Pattabhiraman's and Lalita's prohibitive injunctions could not gag her. She was always hinting about the necessity for women to go and live with their husbands under any circumstances. When Sita heard this, she became angry with Lalita. She thought that Lalita had brought her mother home only to humiliate her. 'Let Mami babble on,' she thought. 'Let Lalita think whatever she likes. What should I fear when Pattabhiraman treats me like a queen!'

As the day of the chairman's election approached. Sita was flabbergasted to receive more shocks.

There was a letter from Delhi. From Surya.

I consulted Dharini. Dharini feels any attempt to interfere between your husband and you will only end in disaster. She thinks that it would be best for you to go to Calcutta and have a heart-to-heart talk with him. Athanga, sometime earlier, you had resolved to do this. You wanted to go to your husband and tell him, 'Let bygones be bygones. Let us start a new life.' Why not carry out that resolution now? I too think it would be best for you to leave at once for Calcutta. Do you remember the two daughters of the former divan in Delhi? I understand that they have gone to Calcutta. This makes me more anxious. The situation being what it is, is it not best for you to go to Calcutta at once?

The letter served to rub salt on the wounds. 'Is that so?' Sita asked herself. 'Let him bond with those devils! When I stand on the public platform, thousands wait with awe and wonder to hear me speak. I am no longer the old naïve Sita of New Delhi. Nor is there any need for me to fall at anyone's feet to beg and plead.'

On the day of the chairman's election, Sita received two letters. One was from Chitra in Calcutta:

My dear friend,

I thought you were intelligent. What is this foolishness? Your husband lives upstairs in the house opposite to ours. I see him every morning and evening, sitting by the window, frozen in a stupor. With great difficulty, my husband has made friends with him. Once or twice, I too went to see your child. What a wonderful child she is! How can you bear to be separated from such a dear child?

One day, Vasanti came to our house. I could not stop myself from asking, 'When is your mother going to join you?' 'Never,' she replied. 'Why?' I inquired. She said, 'My mother doesn't like my father.' I asked, 'Whom do you like?' She said, 'Both.' Then I said to her, 'But you are with your father! Don't you want to see your mother?' She told me, 'Yes.

I do want to see her. But Appa is alone here. How can I leave him all by himself and go away?' Sita, are you not the mother who bore this child? Don't you have at least a fraction of the pity and compassion this child has?

Two days ago, my husband understood what your husband thinks of you. Two stylish girls have been visiting him for some time now. They talk to your husband for ages. My husband doesn't like it at all. One day he asked, 'Who are these girls?' Your husband explained that they were his acquaintances from Delhi. 'They seem to be very close friends,' my husband remarked. 'They want to get closer,' he replied. To know more about what your husband thought, my husband told him, 'How long can you live alone? Why not marry one of them?' Do you know what your husband said in reply? He said, 'Are you asking me to substitute a ghoul for a goddess?'

My dear friend! Your husband calls you a 'goddess'. And you are somewhere far away! Can anything be more appalling?

Vasanti had a fever since yesterday. 'Amma won't come!' she babbled in her sleep. If you have any pity left in your heart, make your way here and immediately.

No surprise that such a letter should have disconcerted Sita. She wondered, 'Could what Chitra says be true? Could he have really called me a goddess? In that case, why did he not write even a single line, asking me to come? Perhaps it is also untrue that the child has fever. But if it were to be true? O my God, save my child! I will accept any punishment for the sins I have committed. Whether what Chitra says is true or false, I must tell Pattabhiraman and Lalita and leave this very night.'

Sita opened the second letter. There was a clipping inside. Some good soul who did not want to deprive Sita of what Lalita had seen had taken the trouble to send it to her.

Sita felt her eyes burning as she read it. She could not bear the humiliation. Would the earth not crack open for her to fall in, as it did for the legendary Sita? But how could a great sinner like herself expect the same good fortune?

Dazed by the shame of it all, little by little, Sita began to regain her wits and her power of thinking. Was this the reason for the change in Lalita's behaviour for the last two days? Did she allow Sita to stay in her house even after reading this? If so, it was she who was indeed a goddess incarnate! Never again could Sita dare to look at her face. Nor could she look at Pattabhiraman. After everyone falls asleep, she must depart without taking leave of them.

If at all Sita had any doubts about the steps she should take, they were dispelled by the storm that raged downstairs. It was a small house. And the conversation between Lalita and Pattabhiraman was loud enough to make Sita undergo the torments of hell.

Sita waited impatiently for husband and wife to fall asleep. She thought she would leave an hour after the voices died down. She lay in bed face downwards, counting all the sufferings she had undergone from the time she was born. So many women in the world. Did anyone of them suffer as she did? Why was God testing her alone? A sob rose in her throat. Afraid that it might be heard by the people downstairs, she tried to suppress it. But all her efforts could not control it. She got up and prepared to leave.

That was when she heard footsteps coming up the stairs. Her heart began to pound as instinct warned her of approaching danger. The door opened. She realized that the man who entered had to be Pattabhiraman. Ayo, why was he here, at this time, all by himself? Was he coming to murder her? Or was he coming to crush her soul? How to make him go away? Perhaps, he would he go away if he believed her to be asleep?

Sita's hope was unfulfilled. Pattabhiraman came in. He came close to her. He touched her shoulder and said softly, 'Sita!'

Sita jumped up, pushed his hand away, and sat down.

'Sita, don't be afraid. It is I,' he said.

He went on speaking. At first, she could comprehend nothing. Then, little by little, comprehension returned. What had been written in that journal was coming true. He was expressing his love for her. He was saying that he was ready to make any sacrifice for her. He would give up his house, property, and the chairman's post, to go with her to Ceylon or Africa or the Andaman Islands. Her sobs broke his heart. He would make reparations for all the injustice meted out to her by his wife and mother-in-law. All Sita had to do was to open her mouth and say, 'Yes.'

Oh my God! Why did he have to lose his mind? How to send him back? What if Lalita heard his voice and came up? Would it not end in shame and disaster? Ayo, why was he touching her chin?

The door opened again. Lalita appeared on the threshold, flaming in rage. Sita was transfixed. Her mind and body were immobilized. But she could hear Lalita's harsh words raining like arrows of fire.

'Devil! Fiend! This is how you betray me. Didn't my mother say that I was feeding the snake? Her words have come true. Did I bring you here for this? You have brought nothing but ruin on my household. Back then you crossed my path to stop me from marrying the man who had come to see me. I accepted it happily. Not knowing how to live with him, you ran away and came to me. I had still not learnt my lesson. I brought you into my house again, made much of you, indulged you in every way. Now you hold a knife at my throat! Will anything good ever happen to you? But what is the use of cursing you? When this wretch has turned out to be a monster of deceit! I must blame those who searched high and low to find a bounder like him and thrust me into his arms.'

Pattabhiraman who had been shocked into speechlessness until then, jumped up to shout, 'Lalita, shut up!'

'After doing what you have done, how dare you shout at me! How long has this been going on? What a racket you made over that magazine report! How you raged at me for having touched that piece of paper. So, all that was true. Now, I will write to that magazine. I will go out of the house and rouse the whole town with my screams.'

For an instant all kinds of horrendous ideas appeared and disappeared in Pattabhiraman's mind.

'Lalita, will you shut up? If you don't, I will kill you,' Pattabhiraman said and took two steps to come close to Lalita.

Lalita shrieked, 'Kill me! By all means, kill me!' Pattabhiraman's face turned hideous as he raised his hands and placed them on Lalita's neck. The moment his hand touched her Lalita screeched in terror as she crashed to the floor, 'Ayo, Amma! Sita and your son-in-law are strangling me to death.' Her lips trembled; her limbs contorted. She rolled her eyes until only their whites could be seen. She foamed at the mouth. Adding to the horror, eerie sounds emanated from her throat.

Pattabhiraman lifted her up with both arms. His mother-in-law rushed to him and said, 'Don't touch my daughter. Put her down.'

'Devil, get out of my way!' Pattabhiraman bellowed as he shoved his mother-in-law aside and carried Lalita downstairs. Placing her on the bed he sprinkled water on her face and began to fan her gently.

21

THE VISIBLE GOD

The tears evaporated from Sita's eyes. Consternation was replaced by clarity. She came to a firm decision about what she was going to do. Lalita's tongue-lashing strengthened her determination and brought her the calmness she had not known in recent times.

Sita packed a change of clothes and took all the money she had. Opening the drawer in the desk, she removed all the letters and tore them to bits. She shredded the newspaper clipping to scraps. Ready to leave now, she waited for things to quieten down.

For a while commotion reigned below. The children's wails mingled with Pattabhiraman's admonitions and Sarasvati Ammal's angry voice. In a little while. Lalita's feeble voice could be heard. Little by little, the sounds died down. The lights were switched off. The house lapsed into silence.

Sita lingered for some time, troubled about departing without informing anyone in the house. But soon, she began to feel the terror of the four walls of the room closing in on her and suffocating her to death.

Trying to get rid of that fear, Sita stood up, found a piece of paper, and started writing to Lalita. She stopped after a couple of sentences and decided that letter writing was not feasible. She picked up her suitcase and clutch bag, switched off the lights and came down the stairs soundlessly.

A dim blue light was shining on the verandah downstairs enabling Sita to see the portrait of Mahatma Gandhi on the wall. His smiling face and look of grace instilled in Sita the unearthly feeling of the Mahatma's benevolent presence. A good omen. Her mother's frequent observations that 'the Mahatma is the living God in the age of kali' had been deeply entrenched in Sita's heart since childhood.

Sita put the suitcase on the floor and prostrated before the portrait. 'Father, bless me. Please make me remain steadfast in the new path I am taking,' she prayed. But the prayer did satisfy her. Then, in a flash, she knew the cure for her trouble 'Bapu, I am leaving this house to make my journey all alone. Whatever hurdles or hardships I may face on this path, I will never do anything that may displease you. I take this oath in your presence. I will take any step, in any situation, only after asking myself, "Will this be acceptable to Gandhiji?" It is you who must give me the strength to keep this oath.'

Sita folded her hands before the Mahatma, picked up her suitcase again, opened the front door and left the house, thinking, 'This house was filled with love and peace when I entered it. Let the disruptions that I caused end with my departure. May peace be restored. Every member of this household showed me great affection. May God forgive me for repaying love with wrongdoing.'

The railway station was half a mile away from Pattabhiraman's house. Having initially engaged herself in flood relief work and election campaigns, Sita was familiar with every street and lane, every nook and corner of Devapattinam. Now she took a short cut taking her directly to the station.

At 3 a.m., the streets and alleys were bare of human presence. It seemed to be the hour of the world's deepest slumbers. And the right time for burglars to play their tricks. What if someone were to turn up to hit her and grab what she had? After all, she had been born to endure grief and misfortune. And did it not seem as though someone was following her? Keeping a distance, hesitating to come too close? One or more? It was possible that they were also going to the railway station. Why should she panic? Who could harm her? But for all that, her heart was pounding, faster and louder than the footsteps she heard.

She had enemies in that town. They had printed pamphlets and written filth about her and Pattabhiraman. Had they engaged spies? Were they following her now? Would they cut her to pieces? If they did, she would no longer have to bear the burden of life. Or would they see her depart and publish a pack of horrible lies about her once again? Better to be killed outright!

She had covered half the distance to the railway station before suspecting that she was being followed. When she almost reached her destination, her fears gave way to courage. She stopped under a municipal lamp post and looked down the street.

A man turned the corner. He was Surya's brother, Sundu. Sita's fears vanished. But fear was replaced by anger. Why could he not have joined her? Why did he trail behind to frighten her? Silly fellow! Among Kitta Mama's sons only Surya had some brains.

Looking at Sundu who approached her with a daft smile, Sita asked, 'Why are you following me? Don't you have anything else to do? Or did your mother send you to make sure that I got into the train?'

'I followed you at Surya's bidding. And you damn my mother?' Sundu said.

'Sundu, did Surya write to you?' Sita asked eagerly. The thought that Surya showed concern for her gave Sita solace in this hour of grief.

'Surya wrote from Delhi. He said that you may go to Calcutta. If you did, I was to escort you at least up to Madras and put you on the train to Calcutta or accompany you all the way if you wish. But I did not expect you to leave in the middle of the night...'

'Sundu, where were you all these days? I never saw you! How did you appear all of a sudden today?'

'Where did you have the time to see me during the election racket? I was in Rajampettai all this time. I came to Devapattinam as soon as I got Surya's letter. I wanted to congratulate athimber if he won. But it seems that condolences – and not congratulations – need to be offered to athimber for securing the chairman's post.'

'Come, let us go to the station as we talk,' Sita said. The train was to arrive only at 4.30 a.m.

'Do you know what happened at night?' Sita asked. She thought that he may not know all the humiliating details.

'I was sleeping in Damodaram Pillai's house. He and I talked late into the night. We heard most of the quarrel. The rest we could imagine. I went to sleep when the racket ended. But poor Damodaram Pillai couldn't sleep at all! It was he who woke me up when he saw you leaving.'

'Damodaram Pillai is a good man. If we had listened to what he had said long ago, none of these things would have happened. What a mistake!'

'Athanga, the fundamental mistake you made happened twelve years ago in Rajampettai. You should not have married Saundara Raghavan. In all fairness, you should have married Surya. Then both of you would have led happy lives. Now, neither of you has found satisfaction.'

'You are wrong, Sundu! If I had married Surya, our lives would have never been happy.'

'Why do you say so? Don't you know how much Surya cares for you? He worships the ground you tread on! Even now he worries night and day thinking about your sufferings. If not, would he have written to me when I was studying for my examinations?'

'I know how much Surya cares for me. But affection is one thing, marriage is another. There are vast differences between his life's goals and mine. I need appreciation all the time. I don't like somebody else being praised when I am around. I feel ecstatic when bright faces watch me and applaud me as I deliver an address on the public platform. But for Surya, it is enough to help others and serve the nation. He is totally uninterested in fame or making a name. How can we be happy together?'

'There is some truth in what you say, athanga. But where on earth do you find couples who are perfectly compatible?'

'There is someone in New Delhi. Dharini. I have often thought that Surya and she were extremely well matched.'

'Surya has told me about Dharini. But I don't think anything will come of it. They are planning to get married after India attains independence. India? Freedom! Not in our lifetime! I don't mind admitting to you that my marriage is getting postponed because Surya is not getting married.'

Sita broke into involuntary laughter. 'Is it not enough that all of us are suffering because we got married?' she asked.

'Do you think I will make the same mistakes? If the man falls into a ditch, does it not warn the man standing behind him? Just joking! I have absolutely no intention of getting married,' Sundu said.

22

DIRECTOR SHYAMSUNDAR

At 3.30 a.m., even the railway station was devoid of its usual din. Here and there, people were lying asleep in clumsy heaps.

Sundu and Sita reached the platform and sat on a wooden bench.

Sundu said, 'Shall I tell you what I have wanted to say for a long time but never found the opportunity to say?'

'Sure, go ahead,' Sita said.

'Athanga, God has shaped a path for each person. Our sagacity lies in discovering that path. Forsake that path and you end up in misery. Athanga, my humble opinion is that you have not discovered why you were born.'

'Very true, Sundu!'

'You say this because you are embittered by sufferings. But I am saying that you have not discovered the sphere to which you belong in life. If you disbelieve me or mock me, I will not doubt myself, but only conclude that you are not lucky enough to recognize your strength.'

'I'm in no state to make fun of you, Sundu.'

'Athanga, my considered opinion is that you were born to be an actor. On the stage, you will be hailed as a national star. In the film world, you will achieve international renown like Greta Garbo, Rita Hayworth and Norma Shearer. God has chiseled your face for the film screen.'

Temptation sprouted in Sita's mind. Sundu's clever words fueled her vanity.

'No one has called me a beauty until now. And I am going to be twenty-eight.'

'I am not saying you are a beauty! Who wants beauty? Mostly it is fools who are beautiful. Beauty is one thing. A face glowing with intelligence is another. For the stage and the silver screen what is required is not beauty, but a chiseled face. You have it.'

'Sundu, nothing has been chipped off my face yet!'

'See, you *are* making fun of me.'

'Don't be angry. I shouldn't have teased you. Go on.'

'Your countenance is perfect for the silver screen. This is not only about the angles of your face, but your ability to reflect all that you feel in your heart on your face. You don't even have to speak – your eyes and eyebrows, the crease on your forehead, the quiver on your lips – they speak for you. And is that all? I don't know if anyone has told you about your graceful manner of walking. No Hollywood film star can equal it. After seeing you, I realized how right our ancient poets were when they compared a woman's walk to the gliding of a swan. Even today, I stayed behind you only to admire the way you walked. No Hollywood director would let go of a woman who can walk like that!'

'Sundu, if only you had been four years older and married me!'

'Athanga, haven't I told you that I don't believe in marriage? This is not only about the angles of your face, but your ability to reflect all your feelings in the heart on that face. Just as I know why you were born, I have discovered that I was born to uplift the art of film making in India. Until now, none of the many brilliant sons of south India has paid attention to the art of film making. Only idiots, lechers and good-for-nothing wastrels have entered the field of cinema. If you collaborate with me, together we will conquer not only India but the entire world! The first film made by director Shyamsundar is going to become an international blockbuster, and win the Hollywood academy award!'

'Sundu, who is director Shyamsundar?'

'Me, of course! I will be inexpressibly happy if you agree to star in my first film. Then you will see how fame and glory will come to you.'

Sita had been goaded by temptation. Now it was inflamed. Why should she suffer with a husband who did not care for her? Why not help someone who had as much faith in her as in the gods?

Sita remembered the face of Mahatma Gandhi in the portrait in Pattabhiraman's house. The face looked at her with eyes full of pity. 'Not even half an hour has gone by since you took the oath. And you succumb to temptation so soon!'

Sita looked up. Scattered thickly across the sky, the stars twinkled out their warning.

Ding-ding-ding! The bell rang to signal the train's having left the previous station.

Sita said, 'Shyamsundar, I greatly appreciate your affection and trust. Just twenty minutes ago, I vowed that for one last time, I would join my husband once again, and try to build all the rapport I can with him. If I fail, I will join you.'

'Athanga, listen to me. If your husband had a brain at all, he would not confine you to housework. He will surrender you to the art of cinema. Millions of women can run a household. But only one among them can become a star on the silver screen. But let things happen according to what fate has in store for you. What do you want me to do now? Shall I come with you to Calcutta? At least to Madras?'

'No need, Shyamsundar! If I go on talking to you, my fickle mind may yield to temptation. Get me a ticket and put me on the ladies' compartment.'

'Surya will surely scold me,' Sundu said.

'Why should he? When Surya returns to Rajampettai, please convey my thanks to him.'

'I doubt if he will return.'

'Why do you say that? Didn't Surya say that he was going to turn Rajampettai village into a heaven on earth?'

'Surya lost that battle. Postman Balakrishnan has quit his job and joined the Communist Party. He is working in our region. His main goal is to defeat Surya's efforts from bearing fruit. Paying our workers double as Surya is doing is of no use. They have started saying that the fields belong to the workers. Every field in the village has been harvested, but more than half of ours is lying barren. Surya's heart is broken.'

'I always had my suspicions about that Balakrishnan. He is a rogue. Perhaps all that rubbish written in the papers was his work.'

'Not at all, athanga! Balakrishnan did not slander you. He has spoken several times to me about his respect and regard for you. He is keen to induct you into the Communist Party. I know who vilified you in print. It is the work of Seemachu Iyer from our village.'

'Aiyyayyo, our Seemachu Mama! Unbelievable!'

'I know it for a fact. One day I am going to teach him a lesson!'

'No need, Sundu! Let him write what he wants. Why should you nurse a grievance against him when I don't?'

'Should I let him off the hook because you are not angry with him? Athanga, but for you, there was no chance at all of athimber becoming chairman. I am sorry that my mother and sister don't remember that. I don't know how Lalita became a monster overnight.'

'Don't say a word against her. Nowhere in the world can you find someone as noble as Lalita. My time is out of joint. That is why I had to leave the way I did.'

Puffing smoke and emitting screeches, the train finally arrived. Sita took her seat in the ladies' compartment and bid Sundu goodbye.

23

SITA'S PRAYER

Sita travelled on the Calcutta Mail for two days. The two days passed like two interminable epochs. A few other Madrasi women travelling to Calcutta had boarded the same compartment. One of them lived in Howrah. She became friends with Sita. Conversing with her helped pass the time.

The train took longer than usual to reach Howrah. But from the morning, people were found chattering in groups in every station they passed. The passengers on the train too were subject to some agitation. But no news reached the ladies' compartment.

In the station before Howrah, a south Indian gentleman from another compartment came to the ladies' coach and asked, 'Do all of you have some male escort? Or will your menfolk come to receive you in Howrah? Those who are travelling alone must be careful. There seems to be some trouble in Calcutta.' This raised no fear in Sita's mind. A great danger had threatened her on the very day she reached Calcutta on her previous trip. What could happen now that would be worse?

But Sita realized how wrong she was the moment she got down at Howrah station. On that day of 15 August 1946, ghouls from hell were visiting Calcutta where they cloned themselves a millionfold to perform acts of diabolical monstrosity. Making no distinctions between men, women and children, they ran howling through the city as they slaughtered and swallowed their prey. Thrusting a knife into women's bellies to pull out their intestines, kicking children and flinging them to death, grabbing people alive and feeding them to the fires – such demonic acts became commonplace in Calcutta on that day. At times, the slogan 'Pakistan Zindabad!' could be heard between the shrieks.

Those who disembarked from the trains in Howrah found themselves chilled to the marrow by a medley of sounds – the shrieks of lakhs of men, women and children, the caterwauling of thousands of ghouls, the crackling and sputtering of burning houses, the crashing of bricks and beams, the din of people running helter skelter, the fusillade of gunshots, and the tumult of the troops.

The people who had come to receive the woman Sita had made friends with on the train said that that no one could enter Calcutta as it was being ravaged by monstrous riots. They invited Sita to stay with them and go into Calcutta once the riots were quelled, and after locating her hosts there. Sita was bewildered, the world was spinning around her. But she told them, 'No, I will have to go now, nothing will happen to me.' 'Try,' the Howrah folks said. Sita managed to stumble along and reach the bridge outside the station. But a huge crowd surged in and swept Sita back to the station. The people who had waited until then, took her home with them.

Sita experienced indescribable agonies on those four days spent in Howrah. Sleep was impossible. If she fell into an exhausted doze, she was jerked awake by nightmares. She wished she had come a day earlier, before the riots broke out. Then she could have been with husband and child during the time of danger. When she thought that she may never see them again, she felt as if her heart was being gored by a dagger. The news that came from Calcutta at frequent intervals served to thrust a burning stake into the open wounds. She suffered unbearable grief as she heard of little children being flung to their death and being roasted live on fire. The thought of her child exposed to such dangers made her head feel as if it would explode. She vowed to herself a thousand times that whatever the provocation, she would never again be separated from her child, and never quarrel with her husband again. But would he accept her? Somehow, she would make her peace with him. Nothing should harm him or the child.

Not that the people in Howrah had no anxieties. The riot could cross the bridge and come to Howrah. Moreover, the offices where many of them were employed were in Calcutta. What was happening to those offices? Even if the riots ended, would it be possible to live in peace in a city ruled by Suhrawardy*?

Hope returned on day three, when the riots began to show some change of direction. On that day, the Sikhs, and the milk vendors who had moved to Calcutta from Bihar, began to show what they could do. Slogans of vengeance resounded everywhere. Suhrawardy and his colleagues who had watched the fun until then, made tremendous efforts to stop the riots and restore its reputation to Calcutta. Their efforts bore fruit on day five. The riots were quelled.

Sita reached Amarnath's house on the eighth day after reaching Howrah Station and enduring a week of indescribable anguish. Raghavan and Vasanti were no longer in the opposite house, but on the first floor of Amarnath's house. The house had become a sanctuary to over a hundred south Indians, including women and children, who had escaped from places affected by the riots. Sita's heart was filled with pride when she heard that it was her husband Raghavan who had brought most of them out of danger. She also regretted that she had not been lucky enough to be by his side to help him during that time.

Even in Howrah, Sita had learnt about Raghavan's deeds and how Amarnath's house had become a sanctuary to south Indians.

As soon as Chitra saw Sita she said, 'So madam, you are here. Good that you made it. Your husband is your responsibility. He is lying upstairs. Go and take care of him.'

With a thudding heart Sita asked, 'Why is he in bed?'

---

* Huseyn Shaheed Suhrawardy (1892–1963): Bengali barrister and politician, prime minister of Bengal (1946–1947) and prime minister of Pakistan (1956–1957). His tenure in Bengal saw the Great Calcutta Killings in 1946. The Muslim League called a strike to press its demand for the creation of Pakistan. The strike degenerated into brutal and widespread Hindu-Muslim riots in which thousands were killed on both sides.

'Fever, 105 degrees temperature, catalepsy, delirium, everything! No surprise after all that he has accomplished in the last seven days. Anyway, what does it matter if a man dies after having saved a hundred lives?' Chitra said, who found it natural to talk recklessly about death, after having lived through the mass killings.

'Chitra, please don't talk like this. There is no real danger? He will survive, won't he?' Sita asked.

'Depends on the nursing, that's what the doctor says. Your daughter Vasanti! Such a wonderful child. How helpful she was to me through these seven days. Totally unafraid! When everyone was shaking with fear, she energized them all with her indomitable spirit. Not a murmur or complaint whether it is serving the hundred people in this house, or taking care of her father. What on earth did you have to do in Devapattinam that made you abandon such a husband and child? Go and take care of him.' Chitra was still muttering as she walked away.

With anxiety propelling her forward and embarrassment drawing her back, Sita managed to go upstairs. It was noisy and crowded, but no one paid any attention to Sita.

One room alone seemed to be quiet. Sita gently pushed the door open. Raghavan was lying on the bed. His eyes were closed. He was moaning in a state of stupor. Vasanti was sitting next to him and placing the ice bag on his head and forehead by turns.

Vasanti raised her head and looked at Sita. Eagerness, amazement, love, indignation, pity and fury were mingled in that glance. Not a single word escaped her lips.

Very hesitantly, Sita made her way to the bed. Gently, she touched Raghavan's foot, and palm. They were cold. She went closer and placed her hand on his neck, and forehead. They were burning like an iron pan on fire. Sita had planned to say so many things to Vasanti when she met her. She had even thought of saying, 'So, you went off with your father without coming to see me? You are not my daughter!'

Now she said, 'Vasanti, give me the ice bag. Your hands must be aching.'

'No, Amma. You don't know how to place the ice bag over the entire forehead.'

'If I don't do it right, you can teach me.'

With Vasanti by her side, Sita began icing Raghavan's forehead. For some time, mother and daughter confined themselves to glancing at each other. Slowly, a smile bloomed on Vasanti's face.

'Amma, you will never leave Appa and me and go away again, will you?' she asked.

Sita's face brightened a little. 'Darling, I won't! Appa and you came here without bringing me along.'

'Let it be. Amma, you will never go away from us again?'

'No.'

'The riots raged for five or six days, and got worse day by day. They were saying that the entire population of Calcutta was going to die. Can you guess my thoughts at that time?'

'No, darling, you will have to tell me.'

'I thought that if I died without seeing you, I would return to see you as a spirit, at least once,' Vasanti said.

'Don't, Vasanti! Talk about good things,' Sita said.

'You feel uncomfortable when you hear about death. The subject has become commonplace for us.'

'Let it be, Vasanti. What did the doctors say about Appa's illness?'

'They say that it is due to shock, and he needs painstaking care. But I have this crazy faith that Appa will surely survive. Do you know how he has survived innumerable ordeals in the last eight days?'

'Everyone is talking about what Appa did. What *did* he actually do, Vasanti?'

'What Appa has done is the stuff of epics. I will give you an example. The rioters surrounded a house and threatened to set fire to it. Appa called the police and said that Hindus were attacking a Muslim's house. He knew that was the only way to get help from the authorities. The police did arrive. Appa took them to the house and personally rescued all the people in it. This made the rioters target him for killing. But for all their boasts, they couldn't succeed!'

At this moment Saundara Raghavan began to babble deliriously.

'If you come any closer, I will shoot you dead! Sword for sword, gun for gun, murder for murder, revenge for revenge! Don't think I am Mahatma Gandhi!' As he shrieked, Raghavan tried to sit up. Sita and Vasanti caught hold of him and made him lie down once again. Raghavan opened his eyes and saw Sita. But he did not recognize her. He simply closed his eyes.

Sita prayed, 'Lord, grant me this boon! Even if he dies of fever, let him see me at least once and recognize me, let him know that I am here nursing him.' But her fears proved to be false. Raghavan got better and his mind became clearer day by day.

24

MY HEAVEN

Sita's arrival seemed to have made Raghavan's condition improve. Sita's touch was enough to quell his wildest bouts of feverish, nonsensical outpourings. It calmed him at once, in body and mind. Noticing this Chitra said, 'You came at the right time to save your husband's life. You have atoned for all your sins.' Hearing this, Sita's eyes filled with tears.

At first, there was no recognition in Raghavan's glance. But two or three days later, when Raghavan saw Sita, his eyes showed surprise, his face brightened. Then, little by little, he began to talk to her. He inquired about when she came to Calcutta and where she had stayed in Howrah. He spoke with great appreciation about the people who had given her shelter there.

One day, Raghavan asked Sita the same question that Vasanti had asked. 'Are all your travels over? You don't need to go anywhere else, do you?'

Sita said, 'I didn't have to go anywhere before. Nor do I need to travel anywhere anymore.'

'If you have to go, don't leave Vasanti behind. Take her with you.'

'I am not leaving Vasanti. Nor do I have any intention of leaving you and going anywhere.'

'Why bother about me?' Raghavan asked.

Sita did not answer. She looked at him, her eyes brimming with sadness.

On another day Raghavan asked, 'Sita, Chitra told me that you liked Calcutta a lot. Is it true?'

Sita brightened as she said, 'Yes, I like Calcutta. I am totally content to live here.'

'Very good. Vasanti and you can stay here. You will have good protection. Nowhere can you find people as good as Chitra and Amarnath.'

Sita asked somewhat doubtfully, 'Vasanti and I…! Stay here…! What about you?'

'I don't like this city. I have come to hate it after seeing the terrible things that happened here. My brain will never recover if I stay here. I am thinking of leaving as soon as I get well.'

'Please don't dissociate yourself from me. I don't like this city if you don't. The place you like is the place I like. Where are you planning to go?'

'I intend to go to the Punjab.'

'If you are going to the Punjab. I will also come to the Punjab.'

'You might dislike it.'

'Why? Back in Delhi, I had always wanted to visit the Punjab. The magnificent Golden Temple of the Sikhs is in Amritsar. I believe that town has the largest mosque in India as well. We can see all those things!'

Raghavan winced. 'Sita, I am making a request. Talk about anything you please. But don't mention the word mosque when I'm around. I get the shivers.'

Old memories gushed forth in Sita's mind. She remembered all the ills that befell her because of her yearning to see Akbar's tomb and the Taj Mahal.

'I spoke without thinking. From now on, I don't need to see any place. It will be enough to go on looking at Vasanti and you.'

These words of Sita gave Raghavan ineffable joy, the kind of happiness he had not experienced in a very long time.

On another day, Raghavan asked Sita, 'Do you know why I decided to go to the Punjab?'

'No, but I don't need to know. The fact that you want to go to the Punjab is reason enough for me.'

'No, you must know the reason. As soon as I returned from abroad the people in the company where I work asked me, "Will you go to the Punjab? We will give you the post of manager." I did not give an answer at once. Since Punjab was close to Delhi I did not wish to go there at that time. But after seeing all the events that occurred here starting on 16 August, I decided that it was in the Punjab that I had to live. Many great men have established many religions in the world. I consider Guru Nanak who founded the Sikh faith to be the greatest of them all. He was the only leader who established not only a creed but a valiant society. Sikhs must be counted as first among the warriors of the world. Listen, Sita! Do you know what I thought during the first two days of this riot? I reckoned that in all of Calcutta and Bengal, there will be no man, woman, or child left to be called "Hindu". Do you know what happened on day three? They rose, the Sikhs did! Most of them were men who drove cars and cabs. It was only when they stood up, kirpan in hand, that we saw how Calcutta too had its brave men. The lives of thirty lakh Hindus were saved. Punjab is the homeland of those valiant heroes. I think that it is a blessing to dwell in their land. Perhaps you will not be able to understand the state of my mind.'

If truth be told, Sita could not understand Raghavan's stance. Her memories of the Punjabis were not all that satisfactory. She had known Punjabis in Delhi. Roughnecks, uncouth, she thought. The brief encounters she had had with the people in Calcutta had given her an excellent impression of the Bengalis. How cultured, educated and refined they were! The opinions of Amarnath and others bolstered her view.

In the old days, Sita would have countered every word of Raghavan with nine words of her own. But now, that had changed. Nor did Raghavan's state of health allow opposition.

Therefore, after listening to what Raghavan had to say, Sita replied, 'Why do you have to talk in circles? Haven't I already told you that I don't want reasons. The place you like is the place I like. That is what I thought in the past. That is how I think now. In between, fate made me stray. I am not going to part from you anymore. Wherever you may be, that is my heaven now.'

Chitra and Amarnath heard these words as they entered the room. Chitra said, 'Now I feel truly happy. There's something good to be found in everything that is bad. The riots have brought you together.'

'Should a catastrophic riot and the massacre of tens of thousands take place to bring us together?' Sita exclaimed.

Raghavan said banteringly, 'After a few days you may even say that it was the two of us who started this riot!'

Amarnath replied, 'You did not launch the riots. Your wife Sita did. Didn't the rioting start on the day she arrived at the Howrah railway station?'

25

THE FOLLOWING YEAR

As our story approaches its end, we too need to proceed with haste. Let us skip across a whole year, and reach 15 August 1947 when the great city of Delhi shone with resplendence as the capital of independent India.

August had become an important month for India since 1942. The freedom struggle reached its zenith in that year and month. Later, in 1946, it was in August that the Muslim League wished to launch the day of direct action, which led to communal riots lacerating Mother India.

In 1947, August attained matchless significance in Indian history. It was on 15 August that India ended its enslavement of over a thousand years and became an independent democracy. Forty crore Indians were endowed with freedom. Among them, thirty-four crore became citizens of the free Indian Union, while the rest became the citizens of free Pakistan.

People across the entire nation celebrated the attainment of independence. This was particularly true of the capital city, where India's independent government had been established. From the morning, Delhi – Old and New – were in a state of festive jubilations.

Not even in the days of Akbar, Jehangir and Shah Jahan could Delhi have witnessed the spectacular festivities showcased on the evening of its first Independence Day.

In particular, the historic Chandni Chowk, with its clock tower and Town Hall, and all the surrounding areas, was ornamented with lights of dazzling brilliance.

On that evening, Surya and Dharini were walking down the Silver Street, enjoying the illuminations and the celebrations. Their faces were as radiant as the refulgent city.

Dharini and Surya had walked on the same Silver Street a number of times, in disguises, hiding in the shadows, trying to escape from the police. But now there was nothing to fear. No qualms. No need for furtiveness or hiding. Surya wore a khadi cap and Dharini an orange saree. They were holding hands and chatting merrily as they strolled on with a blithe, self-forgetful exuberance. Though they were among thousands of people, they were supremely unconscious of the presence of anyone other than themselves.

'How fortunate to be able to witness India achieving independence in our lifetime! Can we ever attain greater good fortune?' Dharini exulted.

'As far as we are concerned there is something greater to be attained. Our wedding,' Surya responded.

'Today, we may be able to count the stars, but not the city lights! The lights of Delhi are competing with the stars in the sky!' Dharini exclaimed.

'I was referring to our impending marriage, but you are talking about something wholly different! Hadn't we decided that we would get married as soon as India became free? What about it? Please tell me.'

'Strange to remember how many times we walked on this same Silver Street, skulking, hesitant, fearing the police! I want to laugh when I remember our discussions back then! Didn't we decide that India would never attain independence through Gandhiji or the Congress leaders? Didn't we think we should drive them all off and launch a revolutionary movement of the masses which only the Socialist Party would be able to mastermind? Finally, it is that old man and those Moderate leaders of the Congress who achieved India's independence,' Dharini said.

'Why get into that debate now? As they say, "No need to quibble about the baking pan after the baking is done." Independence has been attained. All the barriers to our wedding have been removed,' Surya said.

'Do you say that India has really achieved freedom! Somehow, I cannot believe it.'

'Why not? How can there be any doubts left? There are cries all over the nation, "Gandhiji's soul power has won!" "India has attained independence!" "Hail Mountbatten!" Our next and most important programme is our wedding,' Surya said.

'Surya! You are singing the same refrain, again and again!'

'What else can I sing? Are they not continuously murdering "Jana gana mana" and "Vande mataram" on the radio? All right, let us fix the date of our wedding on this auspicious day.'

'If it is true that India is free, why should the nation be carved into two? Is this an act performed independently by independent India?'

'What have we lost by India being divided in two? Let both parts enjoy freedom, each on its own! Besides, does it mean that India was cut by an axe? Split by an earthquake like the one in Bihar? This sacred land mass of the subcontinent remains a single entity still,' Surya said.

'That is what I am sceptical about. I feel like a mother's arms have been ripped apart.'

'It is not so. From times immemorial our country has been divided into many kingdoms.'

'Those divisions were based on political motivations. But this division has taken place in the name of faith.'

'I don't buy that! How can religion be the cause of this split? Muslims are going to continue to live in India, and Hindus in Pakistan.'

'That remains in doubt. Surya, did you not see *Dawn* magazine today? The market street in Amritsar is burning!'

'What appeared in *Dawn* could be fake news. Even if it is true, let it go! We have worried more than enough about the nation. Let things take their own course. Now, let us talk about our wedding.'

'How is marriage possible for us? You are a Hindu. I am a Muslim.'

'Are you putting up a new hurdle? I am no Hindu. You are no Muslim. We don't subscribe to any creed. We have talked about this many times and arrived at a decision. Our credo is humanitarianism. Moreover, I don't believe that you belong to Islam. At times you have worn a Muslim woman's costume. That cannot make you a Muslim.'

'If one's mother and father are Muslims?'

'What does the Princess of Rajnipur care about anyone's parents being Muslim?'

Dharini broke into rollicking laughter.

'In some ways, the disguise of a Muslim woman turned out to be most convenient! If not, I could have never gotten out of the Rajnipur palace. The Maharaja of Rajnipur and his mother tried everything to make me stay there. They might have even given me half the kingdom! But they could not tolerate the fact that I was a Muslim. That is the reason they let me go. Even now, I have only to declare that I have not joined Islam. I will immediately become the queen of the Rajnipur palace!'

'Never, it is enough for you to be the queen of the kingdom of my heart. As soon as we are married…'

'Surya, don't you have any reticence? Should love and marriage be discussed in the middle of thousands of people? Can't you find a more secluded spot to talk about them?' Dharini asked.

26

THE MYSTERY OF THE TELEGRAM

Dharini and Surya went to the flower garden behind the Town Hall and seated themselves on a marble bench. Like the moon, the glittering lights on the Town Hall cast their glow everywhere. The boisterous celebrations of independence rose and fell from many parts of the city.

Groups of people were walking up and down on the paths, passing by their seat with merry chatter and much laughter. With all their attention focused on the day's celebrations, no one bothered to look at Surya and Dharini seated by themselves.

Surya spoke eagerly, 'No eavesdroppers here. We can surely speak openly. Honestly, I thought it would be very special to talk about our wedding and take a decision with thousands of witnesses around us. Once before we had sat by ourselves like this and decided that we would get married once India became free.'

Dharini intervened to say, 'You are not completely right. We decided that we would *think* about our marriage when India became free.'

From the Silver Street came loud cries of 'Victory to Mahatma Gandhi!' 'Victory to Mountbatten!'

Surya said, 'Hear that? So many people are rejoicing with the belief that India has attained independence. You alone continue to doubt it!'

'I do believe it. But, for some reason, my mind is not at peace.'

'Then it is not my fault. It is Mahatma Gandhi's fault. There is nothing that I can do to correct that fault. Dharini, is there anything else to block our wedding?'

'Yes, I don't want to get married before I know the truth about my parents. If I don't know who they are, by what rite can we get married?'

'Dharini the revolutionary leader, imbued with reformist frenzy, develops faith in orthodox rituals! Have we not talked any number of times about breaking out of blind superstitions and obsolete rituals to marry in the presence of the deity of love?'

'It seemed all right when we talked about it. But when it comes to action, I feel hesitant. Surya, I cannot be at peace until I know the identity of my parents. Until now, the nation's independence movement had claimed all my attention. That is no longer the case. My mind will be constantly plagued by this concern. And until it is resolved you will not get happiness or peace in married life from me.'

'That does not bother me. I will share your anxieties. Any distress I may face because of you will be nothing but pleasure to me. And yet, I do agree that it is extremely important for you to have peace of mind. For that I am willing to do everything I can. Dharini, have you never suspected or guessed who your parents may be?'

'Many times. But my suspicions turned out to be wrong. At first, I thought that Sita's father was my father and Raziya Begum, my mother. But it became clear that Raziya Begum was my foster mother. I tried to find out who my birth mother was. I learnt that Raziya Begum's sister Ganga Bai was my mother, and that unfortunate woman died young. After that I have been trying to discover the identity of my father. Until today this has not come to light.'

'Dharini, are you not the daughter of the Maharaja of Rajnipur?'

'How can I say? The senior queen of Rajnipur says that I am a princess. Raziya Begum who refuted it at first now says that it is true. She even wants me to ask for a share in the late Maharaja's wealth. But something tells me that I cannot be the daughter of the king of a royal principality.'

'Dharini, I feel as if a great burden has been removed from my heart. Your instincts have usually been correct. They must be right in this instance too.'

'But I want to get it confirmed. Surya, sometimes I get this strange feeling. The men of Rajnipur abducted Sita because they mistook her for me. At times I have wondered why. After your escape from the lock up, I went to Rajnipur to check on Sita. At the insistence of the queen mother and the prince I stayed there for a few days. They told me over and over again that Sita's face resembled mine and that was the reason for their mistake. Is this true? If so, what could be the reason? Can you make a guess?' Dharini asked.

Surya became immersed in thought. Why did the Rajnipur men make that mistake? Could there be something connected to Dharini's birth in that mistake? What could it be? Surya was nonplussed.

'I am not able to think of any reason. Dharini, is there no one who can unravel this riddle?'

'Why not? Raziya Begum and the maulvi saheb certainly can. One day I happened to overhear them arguing. The maulvi saheb insisted that I must be told the truth. Raziya Begum disagreed. In fact, they had a big fight over this. I acted as if I had heard nothing. Because my demanding would not bring out the truth. I am waiting for the right opportunity to ask them and discover the truth.'

'Whom do you refer to as the maulvi saheb? The man who was reading the Quran in that house on that lane where you were staying for a while?'

'Yes, Surya!'

'Who is he, Dharini? Who is the maulvi saheb?'

'What kind of a question is this? The maulvi saheb is Raziya Begum's husband.'

'I know that. I am asking you for the name of the maulvi saheb before he became Raziya Begum's husband.'

Dharini thought for a while and said, 'It is something you should know. I thought you would have guessed. No use in hiding it anymore. That maulvi saheb is none other than Sita's father, Duraisami Iyer.'

Surya remained silent. His mind was digesting what Dharini had disclosed.

'You seem to be lost in astonishment!' Dharini remarked.

'Not really. I reminded myself of a few things. Sita told me that a

Muslim had taken the witness stand in the Agra court and saved her with his testimony. I immediately thought of the maulvi I had seen in your house. I added two and two and arrived at four. Dharini, I wish to see the maulvi saheb at once.'

'Why? To pick a fight with him?'

'Yes.'

'For marrying Raziya Begum? For betraying the Hindu faith?'

'No, for his having forgotten you, his whole family! Dharini, I must go and see him immediately. If only I had stopped Sita's wedding after seeing his telegram! Sita's life would not have been so miserable. At times, the acts that we perform in good faith produce such negative results!'

'Nothing done with good intentions can end badly. You will be enchanted to see how happy Sita and Saundara Raghavan are at this moment.'

'How do you know they are happy? Dharini, you talk as if you have seen them in person.'

'Yes. I went to the Punjab and saw them in person.'

'Ah! When? When did you go to the Punjab? Is Sita truly happy?' Surya asked with unbridled eagerness.

'Such frantic eagerness the moment athanga's name is mentioned!'

'It is obvious that your concern for Sita is greater than mine. I did not go to see them. You did! And that, despite our vow of not interfering in their lives as we decided that it produced more harm than good.'

'I myself am not able to understand why I have such affection for Sita.'

'Dharini, was it really affection for *Sita* that made you go to the Punjab?'

'No. When I left for the Punjab I had no intention of seeing them. I resumed my historical research at the beginning of this year. My friend Nirupama and I went to Takshashila which is close to Rawalpindi. On the return journey, we had to pass through Haushangabad where Sita is living now. I didn't have the heart to not get down and see her. It was a good that I did. Do you know how happy Sita, Raghavan and

Vasanti are! Vasanti's cheeks are like Kashmir roses. That child's face refuses to leave my mind. Sita is also in good health.'

Dharini could not control her surprise when Surya said, 'Saundara Raghavan too is looking well. No indication at all to show that this time, last year, he was on the brink of going to the netherworld.'

'Did you see him? When? Where?' Dharini asked.

'Such frantic eagerness the moment Raghavan's name is mentioned!' Surya said.

'I have forgotten our history. He too has forgotten it completely. So has Sita. Looks as if *you* haven't,' Dharini said.

'Sorry. The old story came to mind since I saw Raghavan this morning.'

Dharini, hastily got up from her seat.

'This morning? Then you must have seen him in Delhi. Just Raghavan? Or was Sita with him?'

'I saw only Raghavan. He had not brought Sita with him. He is once again tantalized by the notion of regaining his job. Now that the government of independent India is going to be formed, he has come to see if he can get his old post back. He has been in Delhi for a week.'

'Ayo, what a calamity! Now I know why Sita has been so frequently in my thoughts for the past two days. Surya, where is Raghavan staying? I must see him at once.'

'You cannot see him at once. This morning he boarded the train to Calcutta. Some of his official records have been left behind there. He is going to recover them. He was thrilled to tell me that he was getting his old job back and would be returning to Delhi. Dharini, why should you get into a flap over it?'

'I don't know, Surya! You said that you believed in my intuition. My intuition tells me that Sita is going to face some danger. I must leave at once to go save her.'

'What madness is this?'

'I am not mad. I was in the Punjab during the riot in Rawalpindi. I tremble even now when I think of the horrors. People who come from there say that a thousand similar horrors are going to be unleashed all over the Punjab. Many of our party comrades have returned, not wanting to stay there.'

'If that is so, won't Saundara Raghavan know about it? Why would he come here, leaving Sita alone?'

'You called me mad. I am not mad. He is mad. He labours under the strong delusion that no one can do anything against the Sikhs of the Punjab. That is why he has rented a house in a colony of Sikhs. Surya, are you going to come with me? If not, I am going alone. It may be better for you to stay here.'

'Not at all, Dharini! I have said many times that with you I am ready to go even to hell. I will do it if it is necessary. But we must think again about whether it is necessary or appropriate. Every time we have intervened in Sita's life, she has landed in trouble.'

'Who knows? This could be the opportunity to atone for them all,' Dharini said as she got up and started walking in quick strides. Surya followed her.

27

A VOICE IN THE DARK

Midnight was approaching. The hands of the clock were getting close to number 12. Sita was holding the *Tribune* in her hands. She read the news, fell into a reverie, then looked at the clock, and went back to reading again. On the nights when sleep eluded her, Sita usually read a book or the newspaper. It invariably made her fall asleep. But on that night, despite spending a long time in reading, she simply could not make herself go to sleep. There were many reasons for her to feel disturbed. They were intensified by what she read in the newspaper.

Hers was a bungalow in a corner of Haushangabad city, surrounded by a small garden and compound wall. Sita was alone in the room upstairs. Not all alone. Her daughter Vasanti was asleep on the bed beside hers. But the child could not be counted as a companion. The Sikh watchman usually went home for dinner at 9 p.m. and was back by 9.30 p.m. For some reason he had not returned on that day. Could there be any connection between his absence and the newspaper reports?

Sita's glance fell on Vasanti on the adjacent bed. The child had apple cheeks now. Asleep, she looked charming. Her health had improved since their moving to the Punjab. She had grown so much in a single year! In the south, people would have urged the girl to start draping a 'half saree' over herself. But in the Punjab, women went about wearing a piece of cloth thrown over salwar and kameez. This was the traditional wear in the region. Why should Sita worry about it?

Sita looked at Vasanti's photograph on the wall. She was dressed in salwar, kameez and dupatta like the Punjabi girls. The costume suited Vasanti. But Sita wondered if it would appear suitable after a few years. If they continued to stay here, perhaps this is what Vasanti would wear even when she grew older.

What objections could there be to their remaining in Haushangabad? From every perspective, the Punjab state remained unequalled in prosperity. Two and a half *seers* of super thick milk for a single rupee! An abundance of apples, oranges, grapes, almonds, and just about everything else. Why wouldn't everyone enjoy good health? No wonder the people of this land grew tall and strong.

And the beauties of nature in the realm! People talked about spring in south India. But who knew anything about it there except in books? But here, in mid-February, one could see the birth of spring with one's own eyes. The trees stood bare until the day before. But on 15 February, tiny little red leaf buds appeared. First, the buds opened. Then the leaves unfurled themselves. Even on just the day before, the ground in front of the houses remained dry and parched. Exactly on the fifteenth, tiny yellow flowers appeared everywhere. How indescribable to see Mother Earth smiling in exhilaration! Why should they leave such a land of beauty?

It was true that the summer was incredibly hot. But Kashmir, Shimla and other hill stations were close by. Nothing to worry about the other months if May and June could be spent on the hills.

Sita's life had been a round of sheer bliss after moving to the Punjab some ten months ago. No friends, no enemies, no gossip, no envy, no rage, no jealousy, no resentment. It was just herself, her husband's love, and the child's ingenuous chatter. What else did she need in the whole wide world?

Who knew for how long such a life of bliss would last! Who knew whether there would be a return to dreadful Delhi! Why should her husband be once again obsessed about a government job? All said and done, the ways of men were strange indeed! It was not enough for them to have a house filled with peace and gladness. Life had to be packed with crowds, din, authority, pomp and spectacle. They could not be happy without clubs, parties and formal dinners. If not, why did Raghavan's initial enthusiasm gradually diminish?

Only ten days ago Raghavan had announced, 'Sita, India is going to attain independence on 15 August. Our own government is going to be formed. Did I not lose my job because I gave shelter to insurgents? On 15 August, I will get my job back.'

'Does this mean that we will have to leave this town and return to Delhi?' Sita asked. Sensing the anxiety in her voice Raghavan said reassuringly, 'It is not mandatory to return to Delhi. We can go if we want to. If not, we can opt for Pakistan and continue to work in the Punjab. All said and done, a company job cannot equal a government job. Even if I get a thousand rupees less, a government job has its own status.'

After that, Sita wanted to make no objections. She said, 'No doubt about it! Who will say no if one gets a government job back?'

'But the job will not come seeking us. I must go to Delhi and pave the way. Only if I go at once will it happen. It may take ten to fifteen days before I return. Sita, will you stay here or come with me?' Raghavan asked.

'Will my coming be a bother?'

'A little.'

Sita gave up the idea of accompanying Raghavan. This would be like one of the many work trips he undertook for the company. Why should she get worried about it? Perhaps he would have to stay longer if she accompanied him. So Sita composed herself and bid Raghavan goodbye.

Two days after Raghavan's departure, Bhama put in an unexpected appearance. Back in the past, Sita had been aggravated by her. But now, there was no room in Sita's mind for anger, resentment or jealousy. If at all any indignation made itself felt, she remembered the oath she had taken at midnight before the portrait of the Mahatma in Devapattinam. At once the resentment died down and tranquility prevailed. So, Sita welcomed Bhama with affection. She was happy to see that Bhama too had changed for the better. From Bhama, Sita learnt another reason for her husband's trip to Delhi.

The company where Raghavan worked was preparing to pack up and move out of the Punjab, because that region was going to join Pakistan. Therefore, they had asked Raghavan if he would like to go to Madras. Bhama suggested that Raghavan must have been frustrated by this and therefore gone to recover his government job. Bhama's father had gone to Lahore to wind up the company's affairs. Bhama, who accompanied him, had come to Haushangabad to know what Raghavan was going to do.

Sita was perplexed. She could not understand why the company had to be closed because Punjab was to join Pakistan. But she realized that it was natural for Raghavan not to want to go to Madras. She told herself that she should not object if he had to work in Delhi.

Bhama stayed with Sita for a few days more. She recounted all kinds of horrible tales about conditions in the Punjab. She blamed Raghavan for leaving Sita alone in such a situation. When Sita refuted her, she said, 'I will stay here until Raghavan returns.' But on 12 August she left announcing, 'My father will be worrying about me. I cannot stay any longer.'

After Bhama's departure, Sita began to feel her 'aloneness' even more. Her perturbations increased by the hour. She tried to steel herself by frequently repeating to herself, 'I have seen all the horrors there are to be seen in the world, gone through all the miseries that have to be experienced. What new sufferings will I have to bear?'

It was now four days since Bhama had left. No letter from Raghavan. Why had she not insisted on accompanying him? It was also a mistake to have not insisted that Bhama should stay on. The newspaper reports did scare her. They declared that it was impossible to make predictions about what would happen, or where and when they would happen. A volcano was rumbling all over the Punjab, they said.

Sita switched off the light and went to bed. The clock struck twelve. After the twelfth stroke, the silence surged in. But soon, from faraway came an unidentifiable sound – like waves on the ocean. Gradually, it grew louder and came nearer. Chee Chee! Nothing but hallucination! Was her old problem returning! For five or six months, her ears had been filled with something like the susurration of the waves. It began softly and increased in volume. Raghavan had suggested that it could be an ear infection. She must get a good ENT specialist to check her ears thoroughly. Didn't she have problems enough, what would she do if she became deaf as well?

The sound of the waves increased in volume. Sita got up from the bed in an attempt to dismiss the illusion. She made her way to the bedroom window and looked out.

The city lights were usually kept on all through the night. But how surprising! That night, she could see no lights at all. Was there a power failure? But lights were burning in her house until midnight. A shutdown after that? Should she check by switching the light on…?

From somewhere came the sound of a whistle being blown. Another whistle answered it. A dog howled. Boom! Boom! A drumming resounded hideously in the distance.

Sita shivered. Why this crazy fear! Was it surprising that the police should blow their whistles? What does a dog do but howl? The drum must be the beating of a tattoo in some gurudwara of the Sikhs. It may be the day of some festival. Why should all this make her nervous?

Suddenly, a new and sinister idea came to Sita's mind. Two eyes were staring intently at her. Where were they? Within the room? Outside? Did they belong to a man or a beast, to an owl or a fiery ghoul? At different times she thought the eyes were staring at her from behind, and from the sides. A tree loomed a little beyond the window. In the dark it appeared to be a gigantic black spectre. It was from that tree that two eyes peered at Sita. At first, they looked like ordinary eyes. Then they shone like burning pieces of coal.

Sita gave her head a shake. She glanced at the neighbouring house. Two eyes were peering at her from its rooftop. She looked inside the room. Two eyes were glaring at her from the wall. Again, she looked out. From all around the house pairs of eyes in their hundreds, glowing like fire, stared at her intently.

'My mind is unhinged. Who knows, pretty soon, I may become insane. I must keep my wits at least until my husband returns!' she thought she as she left the window and came to lie down on the bed once again. Her hands searched under the pillow and felt the torch and revolver. For the past ten months Raghavan had been in the habit of sleeping with a torch and the revolver beside him. He had asked Sita to do the same when he was away. Sita followed those orders. But of what use was the revolver! Her enemy was not outside! How could a revolver prevent her brain from getting addled? She could commit suicide. But what would happen to Vasanti if she did? Sita remembered how, once, long ago, she had intended to kill herself with the same revolver, and how Surya had come to stop her. What could Surya be doing now, and where would he be? When will he and Dharini get married? Would she get a wedding invitation?

Ah! What's this noise? A rippling sound from the tree close by. The sound of someone climbing the tree. Who can it be? A burglar? Perhaps the Sikh watchman? But why would a watchman scramble up the tree instead of sleeping in the front yard?

Whoever he was, the man who climbed the tree had now jumped onto the balcony. The sound of his landing was clearly audible. What would he do next? How would he enter the room?

A shadow appeared by the window on the balcony. A hideous black shape stood there, its limbs unidentifiable.

How dangerous it was for women to stay alone without their menfolk! If she managed to escape this time, never again would she make such a mistake. But how was she going to escape today?

It was impossible to gauge the rate of Sita's heartbeats. In her ears the sound of the waves was replaced by the heartbeats. The heartbeats began to sync with the ticking of the clock. She sweated and shivered from head to toe.

With a shaking hand, Sita managed to pick up the revolver. The moment she touched the revolver, the shaking stopped. All she had to do was to aim at the window and shoot. The man would fall dead.

But, as soon as she picked up the gun, Mahatma Gandhi's face emerged from the portrait on the wall. Looking at Sita with compassion, his eyes said to her, 'Sita, I do not approve of violence against any living being. You can take life. Can you give life?'

Sita pondered, 'Who knows why the man is here? He could be an impoverished old geezer, compelled to steal because he is unable to bear the agony of starvation. Why kill him? Why should I commit this sin? In any case, the man cannot enter through the window. Let me see what he will do!'

All these thoughts rushed into Sita's mind simultaneously. Through the tumult they caused, Sita heard a voice. 'Sita, Sita! Get up. Get up without making a sound.'

Ah! To whom did that voice in the dark belong? Why did it make her tremble?

Sita put the revolver down, picked up the torch and switched it on. It beamed on the figure standing on the balcony outside the window.

28

OPENING THE GATES OF HELL

The figure she saw by torchlight aroused no fear, only surprise. She had seen that bearded Muslim before. He had come to the court in Agra and saved her. The desire to know why a stranger had offered such great help had been dormant within her. Now it rose to the surface.

The figure spoke. 'Sita, switch off the light! Open the door. Quick! We don't have much time.'

Sita switched off the torch. The darkness that seeped in once again filled her with distress. She dismissed the fears and went to the window.

'Open the door, Sita! Open the door!' the voice in the dark said.

Sita was not ready to open the door so quickly.

'Who are you?' she said, and added, 'There are no men here.'

'I know. That is why I am here. Don't you know me?'

'In the court in Agra…'

'Yes. That was me. Nothing more? My voice…'

'… Appa…!'

'Yes, Sita. I am your father.'

'This disguise…?'

'Is this the time to ask such questions? Sita, in half an hour's time the gates of hell are going to open in this town. Bloodthirsty fiends are going to perform their gruesome dance.'

'Ayo, who is that?' Sita shrieked as a woman's form emerged from behind the wall nearby.

'Don't shout! Our attempt will fail. That is your stepmother. She too is here to save you.'

The woman spoke up, 'No. I did not come for her. She is an ungrateful fool! I came to save my darling Vasanti, my granddaughter. Keep your brainless daughter. Girl, will you open the door at once or shall I stab you to death?'

Sita knew who she was at once. No point in delaying anymore. Sita realized that they had come to save her from some great, imminent catastrophe. She unlatched the door with trembling hands. The next instant, both visitors opened the door and entered.

'Appa, should I see you at this time… in this guise?' Sita asked.

Raziya Begum intervened, 'When should you see him then? All fathers come to indulge and cosset their daughter when she is in a good place. But today, you are going to see the love your father bears you. Girl, do you know for how many days this old codger lost his sleep because of his anxieties about you? He dragged me to this lousy place and has been squatting here for a month now!'

'Don't believe her. Sita, it was she who dragged me here!'

'Let us save our quarrel for another day. Tell her what has to be told at once,' Raziya Begum said.

Sita's father said, 'Yes. We are wasting time. We wasted a whole month. But I did not think that the situation would get so bad. Sita, terrible incidents have been taking place all over the Punjab since yesterday. People are doing things that no human being should do. In half an hour, they are going to open the gates of hell in this town. Ghouls in their thousands and ten thousands are going to indulge in macabre sport. We cannot say what they will or will not do. It is doubtful whether any Hindus or Sikhs, including children and infants, are going to survive in this town. For your child and you there is only one way of escape. You must trust us. First, you must send your child with her. Then you must come with me.'

'Appa, I can send the child with you. But I cannot come. If he returns and searches for me…?'

'Crazy girl! Are you talking about your husband? He is a damn fool. See how he has left you alone and gone away at a time like this,' Raziya Begum snarled.

'Amma, I am happy that you have come to help me. But I cannot tolerate anyone finding fault with my husband.'

'All right. *All right*! You, your husband, and your father, can all get lost! You said that you would send your daughter with me. Wake her up, quick! There...!'

From afar came spine-chilling shrieks... and howls... Black forms holding burning torches could be seen running here and there...

'Oh my God! The gates of hell have opened,' the maulvi said. 'Sita, not an instant's delay! Wake Vasanti at once.'

Disturbed and dithering, Sita asked, 'How can I send the child? If he returns and asks...'

The maulvi cut in, 'Sita! I am the father who raised you. But Raziya Begum has greater love for you than I do. Entrust the child to her.'

'Even if both of you get killed, I will find your husband somehow and hand over the child to him,' Raziya Begum said.

Sita's eye fell upon the portrait of the Mahatma hanging on the wall. In the dim light it seemed to say, 'Trust her. Nothing bad will happen if you send the child with her.'

Sita ran to the bed and woke up the child with shaking hands. Vasanti sat up and stared at the people standing before her.

Having decided what to say to the child Sita began, 'Vasanti, Appa is unwell in Delhi. We must leave for Delhi at once.'

'Yes, Amma, I'm ready,' Vasanti said and jumped out of bed.

'My darling,' Raziya Begum said as she hugged her.

Vasanti exclaimed, 'I know this auntie! The other day in the marketplace, you gave me an apple and kissed my cheek.'

'Yes darling! So, you remember,' Raziya Begum said.

Sita said, 'Vasanti, are you not a good child who listens to her mother? You must leave at once with this grandma and go to the railway station. I will lock up the house and join you with this grandpa.'

'I am a good child who listens to her mother. But don't lie to me anymore,' Vasanti said.

All three were taken aback.

'I was only pretending to be asleep. I heard everything you said,' Vasanti explained.

Sita was both angry and amused. 'All right, what do you say? Will you go with this grandma?'

Vasanti replied, 'I will, Amma. All I'm saying is that you too should come. It was a big mistake for Appa to have gone, leaving us here. You will be making a bigger mistake if you stay here.'

Raziya Begum kissed Vasanti and said, 'Sita, you refused to listen to us. Will you at least listen to the child?'

'Let it be as God wills. I will come,' Sita agreed.

The sounds of the fearful rampage were now getting closer.

The maulvi saheb looked at Vasanti to say, 'You are a very good child. Vasanti, it will be dangerous for all of us to try to escape together. Grandma and you go first. In quarter of an hour, I will bring your mother with me.'

'All right,' Vasanti said.

The next instant saw Raziya Begum and Vasanti rushing down the stairs.

'Appa!'

'Sita!'

'A little while ago I was saved from committing a heinous sin. My husband has taught me to use a gun. I was about to shoot you when you were standing near the balcony window.'

'Why didn't you?'

'Gandhiji's face rose in my mind and stopped me from shooting. If I had, what a heinous sin I would have committed! My own father...'

'I may be your father, but it would have been fitting punishment for all the sins I have committed. But it wouldn't have stopped there. Many eyes are fixed on this house. The gunshot would have brought them running. You and the child...'

'Appa, what should we do now? Should we not leave?'

'No, Sita. We cannot leave at once. They have stationed sentinels around this town to prevent anyone from escaping. I am one of those people who has accepted guard duty. I will go to my appointed place and keep watch. The marauders will come to this house. I will lead them. You must not be surprised by anything I may do. Nor be afraid. Not even if I come to stab you with a knife. If possible, fall down and pretend to swoon. Don't ask questions. I will tell you everything once we escape. Now, survival depends on using our wits.'

The furore and tumult came closer. Houses had begun to burn. In the ghastly light of the burning houses, black forms with axes and scythes were silhouetted as they hurtled around shrieking horrendously.

'Sita, remember what I said. May God save you,' the maulvi said and went quickly down the stairs.

Sita waited. Every minute lengthened into an age of torment.

Tumult, shrieks, fire, smoke, wails and laments were all coming closer.

Sita recalled the happy days of her childhood in Bombay, when her father put her on his lap, and both mother and father cossetted her. Was it the same Duraisami Iyer who appeared today?

Suddenly, she remembered Rajampettai where Surya had come running to save her when their vehicle capsized on the road. He stood beside the rill into which she had fallen. Where was that Surya now? Was he in a state of stupor, intoxicated by Dharini's love? The word 'love'! Created by a dunderhead, used by fiction writers to fill book after book. Hogwash! Moonshine!

But can it be completely dismissed as hogwash and moonshine? Was Raghavan's coming to Rajampettai to 'see' Lalita and falling in love with her just a delusion?

What did a lifetime of suffering matter? What could equal the joy she had experienced for the past year in the beauteous land of the Punjab? It seemed as if that joy had come to an end…

Now… here… they have come close to the house…

Things happened quickly after that. Sita did not experience them as incidents in her own life, but as scenes in a movie shot in superfast tempo. An ear-splitting din was heard outside the house. Next came the sound of axes breaking everything, feet drumming in a stampede, the tattoo of footsteps ascending the stairs.

The maulvi led them. A knife flashed in his hand. With a great jump, he landed near Sita and threw her down. He planted his foot on her body and shrieked, 'She is mine! She is mine!' For a moment, the monsters who followed him hesitated. One laughed. Another said, 'Look at the old geezer!' A man pounced on the maulvi with an upraised knife. Somebody else stamped on Sita as he rushed to stop the man with the knife. Sita's father did not move an inch. Just then a voice screamed, 'Fire!' The maulvi saheb shouted, 'Run! Run!' A miasma of smoke came swirling from above. Those who had rushed into the room began to run out. One of them yanked out the picture of Gandhi from the wall and threw it to the ground. As the glass shattered explosively, a shard hit the maulvi saheb below the knee. Blood gushed out of the wound. Men ran noisily down the stairs. Outside, flames blazed through the smoke. Sita began to lose consciousness. Before she fainted, she could hear a loud noise reminding her of the waves on the sea.

The flames of hell were burning in every direction. Smoke billowed up like masses of clouds and spread everywhere. Ghouls, phantoms and devils howled as they ran amok. They grabbed old women and infants and threw them into the blaze. The strange guards of this inferno stood with guns in hand, shooting and felling those who tried to escape the fire.

In this pandemonium, a single benign spectre carried Sita through the dark lanes and alleys, intermittently stopping to check on all sides as it moved warily. It alternated between slow motion and high speed. Sometimes it stood glued to the walls, or disappeared behind the trees. The journey seemed never ending. But at last, the cries of horror faded. The billowing smoke and blazing fire did not scorch the face anymore. Instead, cool breezes blew. It seemed as if the gates of hell had been crossed.

Sita began to regain consciousness. With great difficulty, she forced her eyelids open. She caught sight of the endless silver stars passing in slow motion. Painful bumps and rattling wheels made Sita realize that she was travelling in a cart.

'Appa!'

'Sita, you are awake!'

'Did I sleep for very long?'

'The day is about to break.'

'Vasanti...?'

'The child will be safe, don't worry. Your stepmother has managed many situations like this.'

After remaining silent for a while Sita asked, 'What kind of a vehicle is this?'

'This is an ancient vehicle of the land of the Punjab. A mule drawn cart.'

'Who is driving it?'

'A boy who has been working for me for a month.'

'Can he be trusted?'

'How can we say who can be trusted in these times?'

'How did you get this cart?'

'Bought it. Thought it might come in handy at a time like this.'

A little later Sita asked, 'Do we to have ride on this cart for a very long time?'

'It must be extremely painful for you, especially after the way we stamped on you! I will ask the boy to stop the cart. There, see! We can park the vehicle behind that rock,' the maulvi saheb said.

Sita sat up and looked out. Both sides of the road were thick with short trees of wild date palm. Like a titanic monster, a bare rock stood a little ahead.

Sita looked at her father. Finally, she asked the question that she had kept suppressed for so long. 'Appa, why did you convert to Islam?'

Her father remained silent.

'Forgive me if it was wrong for me to ask this question. I asked only because I want to know if you have faith in God. If there is a God, why does he make people undergo such sufferings?'

'Everyone comes to doubt the existence of God in times like these. You will have to find the answers from the wise. But I will answer your first question. In fact, I was wondering how to begin! I will begin at the beginning and tell you everything. Sita, I am also going to share an important secret with you. If you ever get to see Dharini…'

'Appa, is there a relationship between Dharini and me?'

Sita's father said, 'That is what I am going to tell you.'

29

FIRST DAUGHTER

On both sides of the lane dwarf trees of wild date palm had grown into a forest. A rock, huge and tapering, stood on one side. The maulvi saheb spoke to the cart boy. The boy left the lane to find his way through the tangled shrubs and stopped the cart behind the rock.

Father and daughter dismounted. The maulvi saheb pulled out a rug from the cart and spread it on the ground.

'Sit down. We will have to spend the whole day here,' he said.

Sita sat down and asked, 'Why Appa? Can't we travel by day?'

'If we do, we may encounter two kinds of dangers. If Sikhs or Hindus see us, they will try to kill me thinking that I am abducting a Hindu woman. If Muslims see us, I don't know what they will do to you.'

As he spoke, the maulvi saheb sat down with a bag and a small box which he took out of the cart. 'This bag has some water. This box has some biscuits. I don't know for how long we will have to make do with them. Nor can we know just when we will be able to get out of this Punjab inferno.'

'You call it the Punjab inferno now! What a beauteous realm it was when we came here a year ago. How warm-hearted the people were. After witnessing the horrors in Bengal, your son-in-law and I thought this was heaven on earth. What happened in the last year to change it all?'

'The people have lost their minds, that's all. They took vengeance in Noakhali for what happened in Calcutta. Now they are taking revenge in west Punjab for Bihar. Only God knows what consequences will ensue from this. In the middle of all this grotesqueness, that good man is proclaiming the creed of love. Truly, he is a great soul.'

'Appa, do you have faith in Gandhiji?'

'After committing all the sins that should not have been committed, I have developed devotion for Mahatma Gandhi now. Your mother had devotion for the Mahatma right from the beginning. She would insist, "The Mahatma is none other than God." My life would not have turned out like this if I had only listened to her back then.'

'Appa, don't be angry with me. I am asking a question that has troubled me for a long time. Have you ever been loving to Amma?'

'I am not angry, in fact, I am happy that you did come out with this at last. I am going to get rid of the burden that has weighed me down for the last thirty years, a load that cannot be lifted unless I tell someone about it. I never had the courage to disclose it to your elder sister. That termagant Raziya Begum stood in the way. Fortunately, she is not here now. To confess one's crimes to one's own daughter is a hard thing to do. And yet, if this opportunity is missed, who knows if there might be another?'

With this preamble, Duraisami Iyer began to talk about incidents of thirty years ago.

When Duraisami married Rajam and began to run his household with her, their life was filled with happiness. Every day was filled with joy. Rajam became pregnant for the first time. The couple were on cloud nine.

The circle of life went round. The benevolent planets yielded to the influence of malefic planets. A tiny seed of sorrow was planted when Duraisami fell a prey to the game of poker. The seed began to sprout.

As a man with a small salary, Duraisami wanted to recover the money he lost in the poker game somehow. He went to the horse races with borrowed money. Once he began gambling, it became impossible to control the addiction. Profit and loss alternated. With wit and skill, he believed he could recover his losses and even make a profit. Once he made a decent sum, he would give up gambling.

Giving false reasons, he took the few jewels Rajam wore and mortgaged them to borrow more money. He went on getting mired in the sludge. It was time for Rajam's delivery when things reached a desperate stage. Unable to arrange for the child to be born at home, he left her in the hospital. There was no money even to pay for a vehicle to take her to the hospital.

He was on duty, agonizing over his lot when Ramamani arrived at the railway station with sister Ganga Bai. The tears in her eyes and the poignant tale of her sister's story melted his heart. He also felt that he might get out of his state of penury with their help. He had Ganga Bai admitted in the same hospital where he had left his wife.

Whenever Duraisami went to the hospital to see his wife, he visited Ramamani Bai as well. She cast her net of enchantment over the man who was already caught in the web of poverty. Duraisami thought of resigning his job and going back to settle in his native region once his wife safely delivered the child. But the next instant, his mental resolve would take wings and fly away. He would build castles in the air about leading a life of love with Ramamani. At times Duraisami was startled by the thought that should Rajam die in childbirth, he could marry Ramamani and live happily ever after.

Rajam and Ganga Bai gave birth on the same night. Duraisami was on duty at the railway station. He did call the hospital once to check things out. He was told that Rajam had a normal delivery, giving birth to a girl child. In the morning, as soon as his hours of duty ended, Duraisami went to the hospital to see Rajam. Though exhausted after undergoing great pain and suffering, Rajam's face shone with a proud smile. 'It was my prediction that came true,' Rajam told him. 'What do you mean?' Duraisami asked. 'You said that it would be a girl,' Rajam answered. 'Can my word prove to be untrue? After all, I am a scion of Sage Bharadwaja's line,' Duraisami said. 'But it did,' Rajam countered. 'Can you turn a girl into a boy?' Duraisami asked, thinking that Rajam was merely teasing him. 'You can check it out,' Rajam retorted. When Duraisami raised the mosquito net he saw that it was indeed a male child. He decided that those who gave him the information at night must have made a mistake.

But his mind was not wholly at peace. He was troubled by half-formed doubts. He met the nurse alone and asked her, 'Why did you say on the phone that it was a girl child?' She looked hard at him and said, 'I did not say that. Nor would anybody else have said it. You must have been mistaken.' When Duraisami insisted she said, 'Perhaps it might have happened when you enquired about Ganga Bai.' When Duraisami asked, 'Has Ganga Bai also given birth?' the nurse answered, 'Yes. She has had a girl child.' Duraisami confirmed this by going to see Ramamani. That helped him regain some equanimity.

He felt that it was natural that he should have been informed about Ganga Bai's giving birth to a girl because it was he who had admitted her into the hospital.

Duraisami took Rajam and the child home. A little later, the child died. There was no end to the couple's grief.

To get over his grief at losing his own child Duraisami often went to see Ganga Bai's child. Ganga Bai too passed away soon. Ramamani was taking care of her child. She was staying in the quarters that Duraisami had found for her. One day, when Duraisami went to Ramamani's flat, he heard her talking to someone inside. Hearing his name, he listened attentively and discovered the bizarre hoax. On the night of their birth, the children of Ganga Bai and Rajam had been exchanged. At first, he wanted to knock the door down and have a fight with Ramamani and the nurse. But he was worried about the consequences of such an act. He decided that he would wait to clear his mind and take proper action. He entered the house only after the nurse left it.

But the moment he saw Ramamani, his control snapped. He cursed and fought. Ramamani cried out and burst into tears. She thrust a knife into his hands. 'Kill me and take the child away,' she sobbed. 'I had given all my love to my sister. She died. I thought I could continue to live by looking at this child's face. If you take the child away, I have nothing left in the world.' Finally, she got her own way. She made Duraisami swear that he would not take the child away.

Duraisami asked her to explain why she exchanged the babies.

Ramamani had believed that if her sister had a male child, he would become the king of Rajnipur. For that reason, she was afraid that the maharaja's evil ministers would find the child and kill it. The danger would be averted if the child grew up elsewhere. When the time came, she could disclose the truth. But Ramamani did not expect Ganga Bai and the child to die. Most of all, she certainly did not expect that the child she had brought home in exchange would steal her heart.

Reflecting on the entire situation, it seemed to Duraisami that leaving the child with Ramamani was the best thing to do for the time being. If he took the child to Rajam and declared it was hers, would she believe him? She was suspicious by nature. What if she came to believe that the child was born to Duraisami's mistress? His whole life would be devastated. Duraisami returned home in confusion, pondering, 'There are lakhs of people in Bombay. Why should such an astounding, outlandish incident occur in my life alone?'

That astounding outlandish incident gave rise to more astounding, outlandish events.

Duraisami's love for his child growing in Ramamani's house grew day by day. This forced him to continue his relationship with Ramamani. He had to capitulate to all her demands. He was forced to prevaricate and lie to his wife Rajam about his comings and goings. And subject that innocent woman to endless mental trauma.

'Sita, Dharini is the girl who was born to Rajam and raised by Ramamani. It is she who is my first daughter. You are her younger sister. You cannot imagine the torments I underwent when you were both children. No one in the world would have experienced such miseries. Brutal kings of yore had a curious punishment to give. They had two elephants standing on either side of the victim, pulling his left and right hands in two different directions. Similarly, my love for Dharini and my love for you pulled me in two opposite directions. I was tortured by being caught in between. But there was a singular kind of happiness in that torment,' Duraisami Iyer said.

Sita came to understand many things about her life as never before. Many mysteries were resolved. She knew why the Rajnipur abductors had mistaken her for Dharini. More importantly, she knew why Raghavan was attracted to her from the very first moment he saw her in Rajampettai. Doubtless because he saw Sita's resemblance to Dharini. Sita also understood very well why Dharini had shown her so much love. It was the blood tie of having been born from the same womb. She too had felt an upsurge of affection for Dharini. But rank jealousy had suppressed that love. How mean she had been! How small minded, how envy-ridden! And what a generous nature Dharini had. How large-hearted she was. If she escaped from this disaster by God's grace and had the good fortune to meet that blessed woman again…?

'Appa, does Dharini Akka know all these details?'

'She knows some of them, not all.'

'Does she know that I am her own sister?'

'No. I am a coward at heart. Several times did I think of telling her but refrained for lack of gumption. Raziya Begum also insisted that I should not tell her.'

'Why?'

'Madness! She was afraid that if Dharini knew the truth, she would stop loving Raziya Begum. That was not all. Even now your stepmother nurses the hope of getting half the kingdom of Rajnipur for Dharini. She has not realized that the world is turning upside down and that royal principalities will cease to exist pretty soon.'

Sita reflected for some time and then asked, 'Appa, why did you not come to see me for so long after I got married?'

The maulvi saheb hesitated. He asked, 'Do you want me to tell you the truth?'

'As you will. Tell me if you feel you can.'

'I will have to tell the truth. Sita! I was angry with you. I thought you had married the man your sister loved, and therefore betrayed her. Later I understood that you had done her a great favour. Amma, I have shed tears on many, many days, ruminating on all the miseries you endured because you married Saundara Raghavan. All those miseries were to have been endured by Dharini! What a great favour you have done Dharini by marrying that scoundrel.'

'Appa, please don't say anything derogatory about my husband. I cannot bear it.'

'No. I will not. Forgive me,' the maulvi said.

'And what you said just now is not even true. If Akka had married him, she would not have suffered like me. They would have lived together ever so happily. Wretch that I am, unlucky as I am, I intruded in their life and ruined it.'

'Don't say that, Sita. To each and every person on this earth, everything happens according to his or her destiny. One cannot ruin another person's life.'

'I don't believe in destiny. Appa, everything is the result of karma. First, I betrayed Akka. Then I betrayed my dear friend, Lalita. How can I be redeemed if I don't atone for those betrayals?'

'You have not knowingly done anything wrong, Sita, everything was decided by destiny. Don't torment yourself needlessly.'

'Appa, you must grant me a boon.'

'Am I God to grant you boons?'

'To me you have appeared like a God now. Besides, isn't there an adage, "the mother and the father are the first gods"? My mother is gone. To me, you are the only god left. If something happens to me on this journey, if some danger overtakes me and I happen to die, you must meet Dharini Akka and pass on this message from me. You must tell her that I am asking with heartfelt sincerity to forgive me for my treachery.'

'What kind of talk is this?'

'In case I die along the way, you must tell Dharini Akka that my husband is unable to erase her from his mind. Akka must marry him. If I die, my soul will be at peace if Dharini Akka marries him and they live happily together.'

'What is this madness! It is my fault. I shouldn't have told you anything.'

'I will move from this place only if you swear to pass on what I said to Dharini Akka.'

'I will swear this to please you, Amma. But it will not be necessary.'

'Why?'

'We will see your sister on the way. Then you can tell her yourself.'

'Why do you say that we will see her on the way?'

'I know astrology. I will give you proof. See, the boy who drove our cart...'

'What about him?'

'There! He is singing.'

The boy was sitting behind the rock at a little distance and singing a talkie song, *chal chal re nau jawan!*

'The boy is humming some old song. What about it?'

'Keep looking. That boy is planning to cheat us and run away.'

Two minutes later the sounds of the mule being hitched to the cart could be heard.

'You are right. The boy intends to run away with the cart. What will happen to us then?'

'Don't worry, Sita! He will not be able to carry out his plan.'

'How do you say that?'

'I'm making a prediction. Keep watching.'

In a few minutes the sound of rolling wheels could be heard. The boy and the mule cart came into view.

The maulvi saheb grabbed the pistol from his lap and released a shot. The bullet leapt out with an explosive sound.

Sita could hear the faint sound of the waves now, whispering, 'Death, come to me!'

30

'DEATH, COME TO ME!'

The maulvi saheb's shot must have missed its mark. It did not stop the moving cart. The frightened mule ran on and dragged the cart along faster. The boy drove on, cursing loudly.

'Sita, my prediction turned out to be wrong. We cannot tarry here. Let us get going at once,' the maulvi said.

To Sita, the events of the next seven or eight days did not seem to belong to real life. They appeared to be incidents from a previous birth, from misty dreams, from accounts read in epics and sagas, or retellings heard long ago. Though she was a character in those situations, her spirit had left her body to stand aside and watch the macabre proceedings with detachment.

Apart from the scenes happening without, there were scenes that faded in and out within her mind. Sita fell at Lalita's feet and begged her forgiveness. She made Saundara Raghavan take an oath. She hugged Vasanti and blessed her. She bowed to her father-in-law and mother-in-law. She embraced Dharini and shed tears. She became angry with Surya and scolded him. She caught her father's hand in a firm grip and stroked him. She held Raziya Begum's chin and pleaded with her. She enthroned Mahatma Gandhi in her heart and prayed to him.

Intermittently her weakened heart cried out, 'Death, come to me!' The waves resounded in her ears.

During the day, Sita and her father hid themselves in the caves on the hills, shrubs in the woods and in dilapidated mosques. In the dark, they travelled warily, looking ahead and behind them. On the way they had to cross villages and towns that had been torched. The flames continuing to rise from those houses turned night into day. Dark and gruesome hounds of hell howled as they ran through the blaze, brandishing grisly weapons in their hands. Father and daughter took long and circuitous routes to keep themselves away from such places.

In the nights, they made their way with their hearts trembling and skipping several beats whenever they heard footsteps ahead or behind them. At times, the resounding uproar of huge rushing crowds made them run and hide in some adjacent wood. Herds of monsters came chasing those who were running in fear. Mingled with their yells and howls were the piteous wails of women and children. The sound of the waves continued to reverberate in Sita's ears long after all the wails were silenced. Her heart continued to call out, 'Death, come to me!'

The endless walking brought agonizing pain. Her legs turned black and blue and began to get swollen. She felt she could walk no more. 'Appa, shoot me with the gun and go away,' she begged her father. The maulvi saheb shook his head and said, 'No, Amma. No!' But Sita pleaded again, 'I am going to die anyway. Let it be at your hands. Why this torture?' But the father would not agree. So, Sita lurched on with her hand on her father's shoulder. Her mind called out, 'Death, come to me!' Her ears heard the roar of the waves increasing in volume.

One day, a huge cloud of dust rose behind them and covered the sky. Father and daughter left the road to hide themselves in a broken-down Gurdwara close by. A colossal crowd appeared. Sikh soldiers with guns strode along to protect the people. Human beings, about a lakh in number, went endlessly past in a mile long procession. Men, women, senior citizens, infants, children, sick people, pregnant women, vehicles drawn by camels, cattle and donkeys, a few lorries, bags, bundles, boxes, trunks…

'Shall we join them?' asked the maulvi saheb. 'No, Appa! I will go mad in the dust and din,' Sita said.

A ghastly stench arose with the crowd and poisoned the air in the sky. Sita and her father found another crossroad to follow.

They reached a small railway station. They sat in the waiting room, waiting for the train. Sita was terrified whenever anyone looked in. The waiting stretched endlessly. Sita dropped off to sleep in her seat. She was startled awake by the crashing waves. Then she realized it was the sound of the train arriving.

The train was impossibly packed. All the compartments were locked from inside. Sita did not want to get into that train. The maulvi insisted. They ran from compartment to compartment, pleading to be let in. Finally, they succeeded in getting one of the doors open and got in. The passengers were talking about the horrors they had witnessed along the way.

The train moved slowly. To Sita, the chugging of its wheels resounded like the waves of the sea. Her heart wailed, 'Death, come to me!'

The train halted at a station. It seemed as if it would not be easy to get it going again. As time passed, the passengers' anxiety increased. Commotion reigned within and without the train.

Suddenly the maulvi saheb exclaimed, 'There! Dharini!' Sita looked eagerly at where he pointed. Yes. Dharini and Surya were walking in the crowd at a distance. Their faces were visible for a split second before they vanished 'Sita, wait! I will find them,' her father said as he jumped down, ran, and was swallowed by the crowd.

Every instant stretched to an age. After the passing of many aeons came a blood curdling uproar. Hundreds of barbarians came leaping, knives in hand. They scythed through the people who had been standing on the platform. Blood, blood everywhere. The thugs jumped into the train. Five or six came running to Sita's compartment. Sita closed her eyes in terror and revulsion. Her last thought was, 'Finally, my prayers are answered. Death has come to me.' Four or five men got in. With closed eyes, Sita anticipated a knife plunging into her heart. But it did not. Nor would her eyes open. She felt movements around her. Someone threw her down. She fell flat with a thump. Someone stamped on her as he ran past.

'Sita, Sita!' a soft voice called out. Gentle hands raised her. Opening her eyes, Sita saw that they were Dharini's hands. She saw blood gushing from one of the hands that raised her. 'Akka!' she screamed.

The three days that followed were the happiest days in Sita's life. They were the days she was hidden upstairs in some unknown house with all the windows sealed. There might have been light and air on the street below. But not here. And yet, they were happy days for Sita because she was with Dharini, towards whom she had felt the rush of affection even before discovering that she was her own sister.

Dharini had brought her to that house. Sita mentioned their relationship and asked, 'Did you know this before?' Dharini answered, 'I had suspected it for a long time. But nothing could make that old man and woman reveal the truth.'

'How unfair! Hadn't I given my heart to you even without knowing that you were my own sister? How much greater my love would have been had I known this? How happy we could have been,' said Sita. Dharini recalled how Sita had tormented her out of jealousy. But she did not remind Sita about it. 'What's the use of regretting the past? Let us make the most of what we have now,' she said. Sita answered, 'Of course! My sorrows are all over. Why should I not be happy?'

And yet, it was not as though there were no fears and suspicions deep within their hearts.

Sita hung on Dharini's neck through all the waking hours and shared intimate thoughts. She slept with her arm on Dharini. Somewhere inside, Sita feared that Dharini may leave her and go away.

All too soon, Sita's fears came true. The time came for her to part from Dharini. When she knew this, Sita began to throw tantrums.

'I will not leave you. If you leave me, I will thrust a knife into myself and die,' she cried.

Dharini comforted her in many ways. 'I will join you in Delhi. My friend Nirupama is in Peshawar. I must bring her out.'

A long argument ensued between the sisters.

Finally, Sita said, 'Akka, I will agree to let you go if you make a promise.'

'Ask away,' said Dharini.

'If I die on my way to Delhi, you must marry my husband. I will let you go if you swear to do so.'

'What madness is this!' Dharini exclaimed and tried to change Sita's mind. But Sita would not listen. Dharini's refusal made Sita more and more adamant. Finally, Dharini declared, 'Listen, if you die and I live and your husband agrees, I will marry him.'

Dharini handed a burqa to Sita. It covered Sita from head to foot, leaving only a slit for the eyes. At midnight Sita and the maulvi saheb came down the stairs of that house. A jeep was standing in readiness outside. A police driver was waiting to drive it.

Sita hugged Dharini and said, 'Akka, don't forget your promise!'

Her father kissed Dharini on the top of her head and said, 'Amma, forgive me for my sins!'

Tears sparkled in Dharini's eyes under the dim light of the stars. She said, 'Appa, forgive me for all the troubles I have given you! I must serve you all my life to atone for them. But will I be lucky enough to do that?'

The jeep driven by the police constable raced at meteoric speed. It crossed all the hurdles along the way and kept going. It broke through the crowds. In some places, where trees had been felled to block the streets, the jeep got off the street and made its way ahead. Elsewhere... Ayo! The goriness of it... the jeep ran over the corpses littering the street. Life had departed from those bodies long ago. How did it matter if a jeep ran over them? Or even a road engine?

At first, when the jeep started going hell for leather, Sita felt that there were no more perils to encounter. But very soon it proved to be false. Another jeep seemed to be following them at a distance. But why should it be following them? Could it not belong to others who were also trying to escape? Somehow Sita could not get rid of the notion that it was following them. She believed that death was coming for her in that vehicle. Her mind chanted, 'Death, come to me!' The sound of the waves became clamorous.

Their jeep reached a river and made a halt. Thank goodness. No sound of any jeep following them. That must have been a hallucination. How amazing! Surya is standing here! How did he arrive before they did? And with a hired boat? There was no one like Surya! Her cousin was matchless!

Entrusting father and daughter to Surya, the policeman turned his jeep around. Surya and he spoke to each other in some sign language. There was no time to discover what it was about. But that could wait.

Surya guided them into the boat. Then he too got in. The boatman pushed the boat into the river.

When the boat began to move, Sita lost all her fears. She was filled with exhilaration. She learnt that she was on the Chenab, one of the rivers in the land of the five rivers. The river flowed on with billowing waves. Piercing winds blew. Sita removed her burqa and placed it on the boat. Looking at the maulvi saheb she said. 'Appa, how nice it would be if you too could remove your costume and look as you used to do in the old days!'

'Sita, don't criticize this costume. It saved you,' the maulvi saheb said.

'Well, all the saving is over and done with. Nothing to fear anymore,' Sita said.

'Don't be hasty. I will change when we reach Delhi,' the maulvi saheb answered.

But do things happen in the world the way people think they should? What they fear passes them by. But a thunderbolt falls just when they think that there is nothing more to fear.

The boat had covered some distance when a cloud of dust rose behind them on the road by which they had travelled. The jeep which raised that cloud came to a halt on the river's shore. Sita saw a man jumping down from the vehicle. He had a gun in his hand. He stared hard at the boat on the river. The next instant he lifted the gun, aimed at the boat and discharged a bullet. A shout rose beside the stupefied Sita, 'Ayo, I'm dead!' She saw blood dripping from her father's cheek as he began to fall. She jumped up to catch him and prevent him from falling into the waters. The boat rocked. Sita fell into the flooding river.

Sita sank down, down, down, endlessly. Then she felt herself rising without making any effort. Her face rose above the waters. Her eyes opened for an instant. She saw her wounded father struggling as he swam ahead. Surya was swimming further away. But neither saw Sita's face where it surfaced. The boat was faraway.

A wave came towards Sita. It was barely a foot high. But because it hid the boat and the other two from sight, Sita thought it was mountain high. The wave roared like the turbulent ocean and crashed over her. Sita's eyes closed in panic. She thought she was going to drown again. This time she would not be able to rise above the currents. 'Death, come to me!' This time her chants would be answered. This time death was a certainty.

As the wave hit her, and she began to drown, a visual flashed through her mind's eye. Saundara Raghavan and Dharini were holding hands. It was enough to bring peace to Sita's mind. 'They will be happy!' was the thought with which she sank into the waters. Vasanti's innocent face, Surya's eager face, the maulvi saheb's face, they rose one by one. From the photograph on the wall, the Mahatma's face appeared, and disappeared with a smile. After that, nothing but the roar of the waves. Consciousness faded. Peace. Unfathomable peace. Boundless darkness. Silence.

31
THE SURVIVOR

To be in Delhi in winter is to know just what it means to be cold. The freezing cold penetrates through thick woolen garments and stuffed quilts, seeps into skin, flesh and blood, pierces the bones, and turns the body into a block of ice. In January 1948, Delhi was colder than it had ever been before. Over two lakh refugees who had left their country, town, home, kinsmen and friends, were numbed by the extreme cold on the streets in and around Delhi. But their minds and hearts were flaming in rage. The fire spread to the hearts of Delhi's ten lakh citizens and continued to burn. A single noble soul was trying to put out that blaze and replace it with peace serene.

At seven in the evening a motor car tore through the fog on the Jantar Mantar Road. Vehicles were sparse and pedestrians few. But suddenly, the car was braked to lurch and wobble as it ground to a halt. A man who had been crossing the street, escaped death by a hair's breadth. Was he one of the refugees who came in droves from the Punjab? Was he making a deliberate attempt to commit suicide?

Saundara Raghavan and Bhama got out of the car to check if the fallen man had sustained injuries. But he got up before they reached him. In appearance and attire, he resembled any refugee from the Punjab. But his face disclosed his identity.

'Adey! Surya, how did you pop up here? I thought you were a Punjabi refugee attempting suicide,' Saundara Raghavan cried.

Surya stole hesitant glances at Bhama and Raghavan. Then his face showed that he had made up his mind about what he would say.

'You are not completely wrong, Mr Raghavan! I *am* a refugee. But I did not attempt suicide. It has become essential for me to stay alive for some time more. Thank you for refraining from driving your car over me.'

'Thank the brakes in this car, not me. Never mind. Surya, where are going? Do you have anything urgent to do? If not, you can come and talk to me for a while. I have many things to ask you, and to share with you,' Raghavan said.

'I do have some urgent work. But half an hour's delay will make no great difference,' Surya replied. He too had things to tell – and to ask – Raghavan.

The car reached Saundara Raghavan's old house. Bhama took her leave without getting out of the car. The other two got down. As he entered the house, Surya's mind became perturbed. Sita used to be there in that house to welcome him. It was here that once, Surya had saved Sita, when she was about to shoot herself with a revolver. All those memories rushed into his heart like floods breaking through the dam and caused a tumult within.

When Raghavan said, 'Surya, see how empty this house seems!' Surya was overcome by tears. He suppressed them with difficulty.

'Have you got your job back?' he asked.

'Yes. Otherwise, would I have got this house? Even after regaining the job, it was a herculean task to get this house back. A Punjabi had come to occupy it. I had to literally push him out by the neck. I have never seen such cowardly ruffians like the Punjabis. There was a time when I thought that all Punjabis were valiant. I was completely mistaken! If you had seen these blokes come running from west Punjab at full pelt in August last year…'

'Did you?' Surya asked.

'Yes, I did.'

'How? You had gone to Calcutta on the 15th of August!'

'I see! I remember now. You were here then, weren't you? And I told you about going to Calcutta. Surya, have you been staying in Delhi since then? What have you been doing?' Raghavan asked.

'What is there to do? I am knocking around,' Surya replied.

'What does knocking around mean?'

'I am trying to do what I can in the refugee camps.'

Immediately Saundara Raghavan burst out with, 'Surya, by any chance, have you seen anyone we know in any of the refugee camps?'

'What do you mean by people we know?'

'Dharini or Vasanti.'

'No, Raghavan. I was going to ask you about them.'

'Is that so?' Raghavan said and heaved a big sigh.

'Haven't you been able to get any information about them?' Surya asked.

'I can't say that. An amazing letter came two months ago, in Dharini's hand, saying that Vasanti and she were well and safe and would come to meet me as soon as possible. But the funny thing was that the letter had been addressed to Sita. So, I deduced that Dharini did not know about Sita's plight.'

'What is Sita's plight?' Surya asked, his face lengthening into a question mark.

'It is a big, tragic story. Surya, no one in the world has been afflicted by the kind of misfortune I have had. And no misfortune can compare with my finally losing Sita as I did. Ah, what a blissful life we had led together for a whole year in Haushangabad! God could not stand it.'

'Why do you drag God into this, Raghavan? What can God do? You know Kitta Iyer, my father, don't you? He raised his three sons and then let us go saying, "Lead your life as you will." I think God does the same thing. Having created the world and the people in it, he gives them total freedom to "make heaven or hell out of this planet as you will". It is not fair to make God responsible for the things that happen on the earth… Never mind! Tell me about Sita,' Surya said.

'Did I not meet you in New Delhi on 14 August last year, and say that I was going to Calcutta? Let me begin from there,' Raghavan said.

32

RAGHAVAN'S GRIEF

When he reached Calcutta, Raghavan saw India's Independence Day being celebrated with great exuberance. He saw Hindus and Muslims embracing each other and shouting slogans – Jai Hind! Vande Mataram! Hindu Muslim Ek Ho!

It was with astonishment that he wondered if such things were happening in the same Calcutta where Hindus and Muslims had massacred each other the previous year. He decided that lucky times had come to India. He left Calcutta after picking up the official documents he had left behind in Amarnath's house. When he returned to Delhi, he got the news of Punjab burning. Bhama sought him out and told him everything about happenings in the Punjab. She also told him about visiting Sita in Haushangabad and how Sita refused to yield to Bhama's plea that she should go back to Delhi with her. Raghavan became a little angry with Sita. 'How convenient it would have been if Sita had come back with Bhama,' he thought. But there was no point in continuing to indulge in such speculations. Sita and the child Vasanti had to be rescued, somehow. He had to enter the tiger's cave.

Bhama's courage, savviness and social skills proved to be of immense help to Raghavan. The revulsion that he had felt for her vanished. He came to think that all women had to be brave like her.

Both managed to find seats on an aircraft and reached Lahore. Fortunately, a branch of the company where he worked was continuing its operations there. As an official employee of that company, Raghavan could get a permit to enter Lahore.

A part of Lahore was in flames. The streets had become open graves for those who had been killed and stabbed to death. It was said that things were worse in the interior regions. Fortunately, from their apparel and manner, neither Raghavan or Bhama could be easily identified as Hindus. They could be taken for Parsis and Anglo Indians, which made it easier for them to travel into the interior towns.

With the help of the sympathetic English officers, they managed to hire a jeep. What they saw on their journey made them anxious and fearful about Sita's plight. Somehow, they finally did manage to reach Haushangabad.

When they did, they found that all those who had survived the massacre had been assembled in one spot. Those survivors were to begin their journey as soon as the Sikh soldiers arrived for their protection. With permission from the authorities, Raghavan and Bhama entered that throng and searched everywhere. Neither Sita nor the child could be found.

Then they dared to enter the town itself. They went towards the house where Saundara Raghavan had lived. All that was left of the house were a few broken, blackened walls, along with heaps of stones and ashes. Thin strands of smoke were still rising in some places. Raghavan crouched down and sobbed his heart out as he had never done in his life. Bhama burst into loud wails.

Meanwhile, a crowd began to gather to watch the spectacle. The police officer who had accompanied them urged them to leave at once. As they were leaving, a young boy sidled up to them. Raghavan remembered having seen him before with a mule cart at the railway station. The boy said, 'Saheb, I need to tell you something.' Raghavan asked him to get into the jeep. When the jeep started moving Raghavan asked him, 'What is it?' The boy told him that he did not know anything about the child, but that the woman of that house was not dead, she had been taken away by an old Muslim man. The boy added that he had taken them up in his cart. They had travelled through the night and rested behind a rock in the morning. He could take them that spot.

They took the boy with them to that place and saw cart tracks there. Moreover, one of the glass bangles that Sita wore lay broken on the ground. This heightened Raghavan's grief. He thought that it would have been far better for Sita to have died in the burning house than to have been abducted by an old Muslim man. What would he do to her? Would he sell her? Raghavan's fury became all the more intense when he thought of what could happen to Sita. His exploding rage wanted an eye for an eye.

They let the boy go and drove on. On the way, wherever Raghavan saw a lone Muslim male, he shot him down on the spot. Bhama's attempts to restrain him proved to be ineffectual. They had to make an overnight stop in some town, in a house that belonged to a famous Hindu advocate. Raghavan had been in touch with him through his company. Since the town had a large Hindu population it had not been endangered until then. But the people remained prepared and vigilant, expecting to be attacked at any moment. On that night, his host received the news that a Hindu woman was being taken away on a jeep by an old Muslim man. The news was brought by vigilante spies who had been appointed to keep track of all the happenings in the surrounding areas. When he heard this, Raghavan began to suspect that the woman could be Sita. What did it matter even if it were not so? What was the use of living without making an effort to forestall the danger threatening a Hindu woman? Raghavan remembered all that he had heard about valorous deeds performed by Rajput warriors to save the honour of the women of their clan.

Learning about the direction in which the jeep had gone, Raghavan took the same road. It was full of hurdles. But he did not give up his quest. At a certain point, it looked as if that jeep had escaped. Raghavan guessed that it must have left the highway and taken a short cut. He turned his vehicle into a lane crossing the road and soon reached the river Chenab. A boat was moving in mid river. But Raghavan saw a Muslim greybeard and a Hindu woman on it. In no way could that boat be reached or stopped. Where was the need for more speculation or investigation? Raghavan pulled out his revolver, aimed at the old man, and shot at him. The bullet did not miss its mark. The old man swayed sideways and toppled into the river.

What followed was something that Raghavan did not expect. The others on the boat, a woman and another man, also jumped into the water. Only the boatman remained on the boat. Raghavan was in a state of manic frenzy. He shot the boatman. The boat took the hit and capsized quickly.

This took the edge of Raghavan's frenzy. He was now assailed by misgivings. Had he done the right thing? He convinced himself that he had been just. And yet, a small, niggling doubt remained. Could the woman in the boat *not* be Sita after all? He comforted himself with the thought that it may not be Sita. Why would Sita jump into the water after the old man? Anyway, so what if it *had* been Sita? Was it not better that she should drown in the river than live as a slave in a Muslim household?

After that, Raghavan and Bhama crossed several perils and reached Delhi at last. But Raghavan was not at peace. He went to search not only in the refugee camps in Delhi but also those in Panipat, Karnaul and Kurukshetra. He could find no trace of Sita or Vasanti anywhere. He was forced to conclude that they were both dead. But two months later, he was once again traumatized by the arrival of the letter from Dharini, addressed to Sita.

'Surya, where are you staying now?' Saundara Raghavan asked.

'I don't have any permanent place of residence as yet. I will let you know as soon as I do. When you and Bhama get married, don't forget to send me an invitation,' Surya said. There was a cruel smile on his face, mingled with revulsion and amusement.

'Ah! How did you know this? Surya, we haven't told anyone yet,' Raghavan said.

'It is something to be inferred, not "told"! How long can you live in this empty house all by yourself?'

'True, at least you understand and sympathize with my plight. The world has become steeped in selfishness. There's no one left to notice the sufferings of others and sympathize with them. Do you know how selfish the Congressmen have become, particularly those who call themselves self-sacrificing *tyagis*? Why, in comparison, people like our former divan Adivarahachari appear better by far!'

'Yes. That is the way of the world. Good men become bad men, and bad men turn out to be good, tyagis become selfish, scrooges morph into philanthropists. Mahatma Gandhi alone remains unchangeable, for which he is paying the price!'

'You must be singular indeed to acclaim your Gandhi! I am unable to tolerate your Gandhi's unjustifiable actions! He makes me angry, ashamed. Why does he have to come to squat here in New Delhi! I cannot understand how he can have the heart to sympathize with Pakistan, even after seeing all these refugees and their miseries. Didn't he undertake a fast to compel Sardar Patel to hand over 60 crores to Pakistan? My tongue refuses to call him the "Mahatma"!'

'No loss to the Mahatma! Or to you! Some of us, crazy fellows that we are, think that everything the Mahatma says or does is right. Not that it matters to anyone. Let it be… When does your wedding take place?'

'I don't quite know. Surya, one thing is sure. I cannot go on like this. Nothing is known about Sita. Moreover, Dharini's letter has utterly befuddled me.'

'Why should Dharini's letter befuddle you?'

'Why should I not tell you, Surya? It is something you already know. Dharini is my first love! She alone can make me overcome my grief at losing Sita. You may have your objections in this matter. But it is best that you don't interfere.'

'I am sorry, Raghavan! I am not someone who interferes in other people's lives. It is more than enough for me to be still going through the consequences of having interfered in somebody else's life once! If Sita is dead, her soul may find happiness in seeing you and Dharini get married. She may even appear at your wedding in the form of a spirit and bless you,' Surya said.

33

RAGHAVAN'S RAGE

Suddenly, Raghavan became angry. He wondered if Surya was mocking him. He jumped up and shouted, 'Dei! You have not lost your arrogance or viciousness. Get up, get lost, at once!'

Surya got up saying, 'I was just waiting for you to say, "Get out".'

By that time Raghavan's anger had simmered down.

'No, Surya! Stay! Do you really think so? My marrying Dharini will make Sita…'

Surya continued to stand as he said, 'Why should you hesitate to spell it out? It will certainly bring satisfaction to Sita's soul. There is reason enough for that.'

'What reason?'

'Sita and Dharini are sisters. The daughters of the same father. Born from the womb of the same mother. What greater reason can there be?'

'What are you babbling about? Have you lost your marbles? Flipped out?' Raghavan asked.

'Take it as you will. I am leaving now,' Surya said and made to move.

'No, Surya, don't go! You drop a bombshell and then say you are leaving! Is it true, what you just said? Are Dharini and Sita siblings? Who told you? Where's the proof?' asked Raghavan in a state of agitation.

'The father who bore them told me. I heard it from his own lips.'

Then Surya narrated in detail all the amazing incidents that

Duraisami Iyer had gone through in the early years of his married life. Incredible as they were, Raghavan instinctively realized that they had to be true. The many incidents in his own life, which had been clouded in an impenetrable mystery, now became clear as crystal.

'Surya, where is he? Duraisami Iyer? Why did he suddenly disappear after Sita's wedding? Where did you see him?' he asked.

'Raghavan, why do you ask? If you know, you will be sorry.'

'Why should I be sorry? You speak in riddles.'

'You are a highborn brahmin of vedic lineage. Won't you be sorry to know that your father-in-law is a maulvi saheb? Your father Padmalochana Sastri's heart would simply stop.'

'Why do you drag my father into this! My fine father-in-law is after all, *your* uncle! Why should he become a maulvi saheb? Is it because Islam offers redemption sooner than the Hindu faith?'

'I don't know about his religious ideologies. My surmise is that he adopted that disguise to deceive the world. But the disguise did bring him redemption – quite suddenly – and in a manner he least expected.'

Raghavan's heart began to throb with an ominous and amorphous fear. He felt that a horrendous sin, hidden behind a black mask, loomed before him. He did not have the courage to tear the mask. He wanted to change the subject at once.

'This is offensive! Duraisami Iyer turning maulvi saheb! I am revolted even to think about it. Is there any other subject that we can talk about?'

'No,' Surya said as he got up once again.

'By any chance if you should see Sita again…'

'You mean, if I should see Sita's spirit?'

'You talk as if you are convinced that Sita is dead.'

'Can what one sees with one's own eyes be disbelieved?'

In a trembling voice, Raghavan asked, 'What did you see with your own eyes?'

Surya replied, 'With my own eyes I saw Sita drowning in the river's currents.'

'Ayo!'

'I too was in that boat. All three of us were in it. I had my suspicions about the person who shot at the boat from the shore. Today they are confirmed.'

'What are you saying, Surya? I am confused. What does "all three of us were in the boat" mean? Who was on the boat?'

'Sita, Sita's father and I were on the boat. We were escaping from the Punjab. Sita's father thought that his maulvi saheb disguise offered protection to his daughter. But his son-in-law thought differently.'

'Ayyayyo! Does it mean that the Muslim in the boat I shot at...?'

'Yes. You aimed at your father-in-law and shot him. Nor did you miss the target. Raghavan, the only person who knows about this unfortunate happening is myself. You know it now. I am not going to divulge this to anyone. Nor will you, I think.'

Raghavan sprang up. His veins stood out in rage. He flapped his arms up and down as he spouted fire. 'Adey, you blockhead! Are you a man? Did you watch a woman drowning in the flooding river without doing anything about it? You boast about being a warrior, a champion, a self-sacrificing hero! You brag about bending the sky like a bow! And you were unable to bring a drowning woman out of the river?'

Surya answered tranquilly, 'Raghavan, I could have saved Sita. I could have brought her to the shore. But I didn't. Do you know why? Because if she survived, she would have to continue to live with a blackguard like you. I had taken a vow to take revenge on you for pushing me down the stairs. I have done so. Goodbye!'

Surya walked away. Raghavan stood transfixed. Surya's final words pierced his heart like sharpened arrows. He did not have the strength to reflect on the consequences of the news that Surya had given him. The only fear he felt was that Dharini should not get to know about it.

As soon as he came out of the house, Surya quickened his pace. His haste indicated his mental stress as he reflected, 'What I said was not entirely untrue. After all, it is Sita's spirit that I am going to see now. And, as far as Saundara Raghavan is concerned, Sita is like one dead.'

34

SITA'S SPIRIT

Above her head the floods gushed, and gushed, and gushed on. Above her forehead the waves crashed, and crashed, and crashed on. The soughing resounded in her ears like the desolate wail of thousands of human voices, swelling into the stupendous roar of a titanic wave quashing all other sounds, as it boomed, and boomed, and boomed on. The weight of the torrents above, the blast of their ear-splitting clamour, the force of the waves lashing her forehead, remained unceasing, unbroken, as they stretched on and on.

No. It was not endless. Thank God! At last, the waters were getting calmer. The waves were not battering her forehead as before. There! The waters were subsiding. They receded below the neck. It was possible to breathe. The eye could see now. But the susurration in the ears put out all other sounds...

Sita's thoughts ran on. What is this? Where am I? What am I looking at? A dark cave! How did I get here? How did I get here after falling from the boat and drowning in the river? Is this the world of the dead? If so, it will be full of darkness, refuse and stench. This must be that other world. What other destination could be allotted to a sinner? What else can a woman who ran away from her husband expect? This fate – and worse – can be nothing but fitting for one who turned traitor to her dear friend. I have heard that those who commit only a few crimes stay in hell for a little while before going to heaven. But I need not aspire for paradise. I will have to suffer in hell forever.

Who is standing by me! The god of death? Or his messenger?

No... The face is familiar! A face seen before! What does he hold in his hand? No. Not a club! Nor any other kind of weapon. It is a jug. A jug of clay. It has a long, narrow beak sprinkling drops of water on my forehead. Why...? Ah...! How pleasant it is! Who is this man...?'

With a sudden movement, Sita sat up in bed. The bed was nothing but an old blanket spread on the floor. It felt prickly wherever it touched the skin. Unmindful of it, she turned to take a good look at the man who was sprinkling water on her forehead. A smile creased the man's gaunt and wrinkled face. Ah! This man was her father, wasn't he? Father Duraisami Iyer, as in the old days. Not the bearded maulvi saheb. He had lost weight, become thin and dark. The bones protruded on his cheek. His eyes were sunken. But it was the old Appa. Her true father who had saved her and brought her here. Perhaps all those grisly images on the journey were no more than dreams. She could ask her father to explain!

Sita tried to talk. She tried to talk to her father and clear her doubts. 'Aren't you my father Duraisami Iyer? Why are you sprinkling water on my head, drop by drop? Where are we? Why are we in this dark and filthy room? Where is Surya? Where is my child, Vasanti? Where is he – my husband?' All these questions raced through her mind. Her tongue trembled as it tried to ask them. Her lips opened and shut themselves. She tried again and again but no words emerged.

Her father was saying something to her. All she saw was that he was opening and closing his mouth. How could she hear him? All she heard was the interminable sound of the waves. It was driving her crazy. It made her wish that she had drowned once and for all.

All the events of the past few months flashed through her mind in an instant. Thousands of tents in the Kurukshetra refugee camp stretching as far as eye could see, lakhs of men, women and children with no more than a single garment to cover themselves, having to go without drinking water on some days, standing in knee deep rain water on certain other days, Surya and her father nursing her when she came down with high fever...

And then, there was the day she went to see why a crowd had gathered, and found Mahatma Gandhi standing among the people.

How unfortunate that she could not hear the golden words spoken by the *avatara purusha,* the living God! The crowds had blocked her when she tried to follow him out of the refugee camp...

Then came hard winter. Surya and her father thought that her life would be endangered if she remained in the tent during the cold foggy weather. With great difficulty, they took permission from the authorities in the Kurukshetra camp and went into Panipat town. Luckily, they found the deserted tomb of a Muslim fakir. They occupied it.

Sita had frequent bouts of fainting. At such times she became as stiff as a wooden slab. Consciousness returned if water was sprinkled gently on her forehead. That was what her father had been doing.

Surya had gone to Delhi to see if he could get a place for them to stay there, and to try to get news of Vasanti, Dharini and her husband. That was not all. He had also gone to get information about Mahatma Gandhi's whereabouts.

Sita believed that she did not have long to live. Nor did she want to do so. She had lost the ability to speak. Her jaws ached when she tried to speak. She had lost all her hearing. Her ears were constantly filled with the ghastly roar of the sea. It was certain that she was going to die, and soon. Before she did, she must see her darling Vasanti, give her a hug and a kiss. She must see the Mahatma once more, the personal God she had worshipped in moments – high and low, awake and asleep, in joy and sorrow, in times good and bad. She must touch his sacred form and place on her eyes the fingers that had touched him. This was all that her heart wished for.

As these thoughts were racing through Sita's mind at lightning speed, her father Duraisami Iyer brought her the hot tea he had made. Taking it from him, Sita drank it. Then she touched him to gain his attention and asked in gestures, 'Where is Surya?' Her father made signs to explain that Surya had not returned. Sita's face drooped even more. She had been told that the riots had not ended in Delhi. Was Surya in danger there? Ill-omened creature that she was, did anyone who came to her aid escape misfortune? So many people would be made happy if she left the world. And yet, her end was not in sight!

Millions died in the Punjab riots, but not she! She had survived every disaster!

Sita picked up the photograph of Mahatma Gandhi that she kept carefully beside her bed and gazed at it. She prayed humbly, 'Bapuji! Can't you take me into your fold? Will I not serve you as best I can?'

35

THE PANIPAT CAMP

Situated some thirty miles north of Delhi, the small town of Panipat enjoys great fame as the combat zone for the three great battles that changed the direction of Indian history.

Ibrahim Lodi, the last king of the Pathan race, was ruling Delhi when Babur, a descendant of Timur the Lame, invaded his kingdom with a huge army. Babur's ten thousand warriors and Lodi's hundred thousand met on the vast grounds beside Panipat town. Lodi's army was made up of mercenaries. Babur's ten thousand were disciplined soldiers. Moreover, Babur had a few cannons. Lodi's men met with a thumping defeat and fled precipitately. Babur founded the Mughal empire of historic fame in Delhi.

Later, the fourteen-year-old Akbar defeated Hemu's colossal army on the same grounds in the battle of Panipat, and reclaimed the empire that his father Humayun had lost.

Two hundred years later, the mighty king Ahmad Shah came from Persia to attack Delhi. The Maratha rulers who had captured power in central India gathered a huge army and marched to fight him in Panipat. The Maratha warriors were completely routed. From that day, the sun began to set on the Maratha kingdom.

In the historically renowned town of Panipat, on the same grounds where many battles had changed the destiny of India, thousands of tents had been put up now to shelter the refugees from the Punjab. Those tents housed people who had lost their sons, daughters, parents, husbands, and all the members of their families except themselves. Among them were those who had been millionaires six months ago, now in tattered garments, wondering when they would get dry rotis to assuage their hunger. Some of the refugees had lost their wits because they had seen gut-churning torments perpetrated upon their friends and family members.

Surya had been serving in the refugee camp as best he could. Therefore, as soon as he returned from Delhi, he was surrounded and bombarded with questions. 'What is happening in Delhi? Is it true that the Hindu-Muslim feuds are still raging? How can Mahatma Gandhi perpetuate such injustice? Why should he fast for the sake of Muslims? Is he really saying that all the houses that have been taken away from the Muslims in Delhi must be given back to them, and Muslims who had been driven away must be invited to take up residence in them once again? This is unwarranted! Will they return all the houses we left in Pakistan? Is it true that Gandhiji is asking for all the mosques in Delhi sheltering refugees to be vacated and returned to the Muslims? Is this fair? They torched the Hindu temples and Sikh gurdwaras to the ground. What's wrong with Hindu refugees occupying mosques for a little while? Why should they be driven away?' An agitated woman cleaved her way through the throng to confront Surya, 'They say that swaraj has been established in Delhi. Is this also true?' 'Yes, yes,' Surya assured her. The woman asked again, 'Then, will I get a change of clothes?' The saree she was wearing was threadbare. Surya wiped his moist eyes and said, 'Yes.' He answered all the queries as best he could, informed the camp manager that he had returned. Then he made his way into Panipat town.

Like most towns in north India, Panipat too was a town of narrow lanes and alleys. Vehicles had to struggle to clatter through the bumpy cobbled streets.

Six months earlier, half the population had been Muslim. They were in excellent terms with their Hindu neighbours. The Hindus enthusiastically joined the Muslims in the annual festivals honouring the Muslim saints entombed in Panipat.

But now, not a single Muslim – man, woman, or child – could be spied on the streets of Panipat town where, for hundreds of years,

Hindus and Muslims had lived like brothers. They had departed, leaving their town and country.

In east Punjab, the Hindus found their blood boiling when Hindu refugees who had been brutalized in west Punjab came in their thousands, recounting tragic stories, their faces reflecting the horrors they had endured. Many were roused to a maddened thirst for vengeance. But before that, the Muslims had begun to depart, bag and baggage. From Delhi to Amritsar, not a single Muslim was left anywhere in east Punjab. It was so in Panipat as well.

There was neither bustle nor brio inside the city. Hardly any movement on the streets. Those who straggled in by chance appeared lifeless.

Surya crossed streets long and narrow. From one of the alleys a footpath cut through to a high mound. Surya followed it. There was a mosque on top of the mound where women refugees were given shelter. Some of the women were plying the charkha. Others were making children's garments. A few were engaged in weaving ornamental flower baskets. Their sunken eyes were blind to the happenings around them, their ears deaf to all sounds. They were like corpses back from hell, spellbound to sit up and engage in work.

Casting a piteous look at them, Surya crossed the mosque and walked on. He entered a dark house in an extremely narrow lane. Sita and her father sheltered there.

Duraisami Iyer was sitting in the front room reading the newspaper.

'Come, Surya! Why so late? Why did you not come last night?' he asked.

Surya was silent.

'Why are you silent? Any news from Delhi?'

'Nothing but the usual. Hatred, rage, fear everywhere. No peace at all.'

'Did you not attend the Mahatma's prayer meeting this time? You always say that it brings you peace of mind.'

'I did. But this time, even there, I found no comfort. I feel that the Mahatma should not be in Delhi at this time. He should go elsewhere.'

'This is a new tack to take! Tambi, how does the Mahatma's staying in Delhi affect you?'

'Gandhiji is under fire from everywhere. No one in Delhi approves of anything he is doing. Officials, Congressmen, businessmen and the common people are all bitter about him, not to mention the rage of the refugees. Nor does it seem as if the Muslims for whom Gandhi expresses empathy feel any gratitude towards him.'

'Was it out of ignorance that the elders remarked, *yatharthvadi bahujana virodhi*? Those who are pragmatic will always be the enemies of the people. Whatever others may do, Gandhiji has a disciple of unquestioning faith. Yes, I'm talking about your athanga Sita. You must take her to see the Mahatma. It may cure her dementia. She swooned today. It became extremely difficult to revive her. Her screams as she regained consciousness made my hair stand on end. Only you and I can put up with this condition.'

'If Sita must have the darshan of the Mahatma, it must happen soon. With the situation being what it is, I don't think Gandhiji will stay in Delhi for long. Know about the bomb thrown at his prayer meeting?'

'It was all over the papers. But will Gandhi be scared away by such transgressions?'

'He is neither afraid, nor does he bother about them. I too thought it was a bit of a stunt when I read it in the papers. But I did not see it as mere divertissement when I went to the actual spot. The impact of the bomb has shattered a side wall.'

'The Mahatma may not be scared, but obviously, *you* are! Surya! Did you see anyone else in Delhi? Any news?' Duraisami Iyer asked.

'I saw your precious mapillai!' As soon as Surya said this, Duraisami Iyer's face showed signs of eager interest.

'Why? I had told you not to see him.'

'I did not go searching for him. It just happened. For the third time, your mapillai tried to kill me! He tried to run over a pedestrian walking on the street. I escaped by God's grace.'

'I can see that! What else? Did he talk to you? Did he ask you about anything?'

'Why not? He took me home in his motor car. He asked me if I knew anything about Sita.'

'What did you tell him?'

'I told him that Sita was dead.'

'Rascal! Why did you say that?'

'What else do you want me to say? On the one hand your daughter insists that he should never know that she is alive. On the other, he is desperate to marry again.'

'He wants to marry *again*? Who will marry the blackguard?'

'Athimber, what are you saying? You have an elder daughter, don't you? He is thinking of her.'

Duraisami Iyer who had been reclining all this time, sat up with a jerk and asked, 'Surya, did he say anything about Dharini?'

Telling him about Dharini's letter addressed to Sita, Surya said, 'Dharini and Vasanti have survived. That's good news as far as it goes.'

'Somehow Dharini must be found. Surya! We must prevent what you mentioned from happening,' said Duraisami Iyer in a perturbed tone.

'I must be in Delhi to find Dharini. She will certainly go searching for your mapillai's house.' Surya said.

'Let us do that. We can all go to Delhi.'

'Athimber, I have an idea. Will you please listen?' said Surya with a hint of devilry.

'What is this new idea? Go on. Let me hear it,' Duraisami Iyer said.

'Before that I must remind you about a few things. I encountered your daughter Sita for the very first time on the road to Rajampettai. The cart had toppled, and she had tumbled into the rill beside it. I ran to save her. But I was disappointed to see that the water was only knee-deep. So many things have happened since then. By hiding your telegram, I made it possible for Saundra Raghavan and Sita to get married.'

'I have cursed you innumerable times for that misdeed. But go on,' the old man said.

'Athimber, have I not made reparations many times over for that mistake? Did I not stop Sita from shooting herself and save her life?'

'You did. But what about the problems she had to face because of you? What would have happened to her if I had not kept an eye on your activities?'

'All right, let us overlook that! Did I not save her from drowning in the flooding Chenab? You nearly got me drowned in the waters when I came to save you after taking her to the shore. By God's grace – no, no, by Allah's grace, both of us survived. Believing you to be a Muslim, a Muslim boatman from the shore came to help you. After that, God knows how we managed to escape from him!'

'Surya, are you mad? Why are you recounting all those harrowing experiences?'

'Why? Only to establish my claim on Sita. You gave birth to her and raised her. I released her twice from the grip of death. Now, Sita's life is not her old life. It is the new life I have given her. Therefore, Raghavan has no claim on Sita now. If you agree, let us both go to Raghavan directly and ask him to release Sita from her marriage to him.'

'If he releases her…' Duraisami Iyer's face had turned red in fury.

'I thought you would be able to guess the rest. If I have to spell it out, I will do so. After the divorce I will marry Sita. I will marry her and take her to Kashmir. Or take her to Nepal. Her dementia will disappear if she goes to new places and meets new people. Athimber, I swear to you that I will take care of your daughter till the very end.'

There was a pistol beside Duraisami Iyer. He picked it up. Aiming it at Surya he said, 'Surya, once before this pistol missed its mark. This time it will not. If you talk about Sita in this manner ever again, I will certainly shoot to kill.'

Surya remained still, with his head bowed down. Then he looked up. 'Athimber, surely, I must be mad. Otherwise, I would not have spouted such nonsense.'

'You have realized that you have gone mad. That means you have some sanity left. Let it go! I will forget your nonsense. And you too should forget it. Get ready to go to Delhi.'

'I feel sad about leaving the refugees here. Athimber, for the last ten years, I had been screaming for independence. Independence has arrived. But not even in my dreams did I think that it would be such a bitter pill,' Surya said.

'Medicines are bound to be bitter. What's the use of being daunted by that?' the old man remarked.

Duraisami Iyer was still holding the pistol when Sita came in and saw it in his hand. She gazed at Duraisami Iyer sorrowfully, as her tears filled with tears.

The pistol slipped from Duraisami Iyer's hand and fell to the floor. He picked it up, gave it to Sita and gestured to her to throw it away. Then he looked at Surya and said, 'Surya, Surya! Tell your athanga that you are going to take her to Delhi to see the Mahatma. Hope she will not start fainting again.'

Surya pointed to the Mahatma's photograph and gestured that he was going to take Sita to see him.

Sita looked at her father's face. He made a sign confirming the statement.

Sita's tears stopped at once. Her face glowed. A new sparkle came to her eyes.

Silly woman! Will your last wish come true? Since suffering and loss have been ordained by your horoscope, how can you attain such extraordinary and singular good fortune?

36

31st JANUARY

Sita's misfortune did prevent her from achieving the dear wish of her heart. It had been arranged that the three of them would leave for Delhi in two or three days. But before that, on the evening of 30 January, the news came to Panipat like a bolt from the blue. Those who heard it on the radio suspected it to be a scam. They thought that Radio Pakistan was pretending to be All India Radio and spreading the rumour as a sinister stratagem. A few others suspected that Muslims in Delhi had 'captured' the Delhi radio to broadcast the lie. There were those who thought, 'Even if a scoundrel had shot at the Mahatma, would life have departed from him so quickly? A hasty announcement has been made by mistake. It will soon be followed by the news that he has survived.'

But at 8.30 p.m., all doubts ceased. How could any doubts remain after Jawaharlal Nehru and Sardar Patel announced the news of Mahatma Gandhi's assassination in their own voices, clear as crystal, though with choking throat and in whimpering tones?

Hearing that horrifying news in the refugee camp, Surya ran to his own quarters. Duraisami Iyer was trying to get Sita out of her swoon. He said that around 5 in the evening, Sita had let out a piercing shriek and fainted. Surya shared the appalling radio announcement. Apart from their own mental anguish over the news, the two men had to think about whether it should be shared with Sita at all. It could affect the condition of her heart. But was it possible to keep it from her? If they did, would she not feel perpetually betrayed? Would it not be better to take her to Delhi, and let her glimpse the Mahatma's mortal remains?

Sita regained consciousness, though with more bewilderment and exhaustion than usual. Communicating urgently through gestures, she said that she was not going to live for very long and therefore it was imperative that she should be taken to Delhi forthwith. This made the two men arrive at their decision. In the morning, Surya would take Sita to Delhi. On the way, he should use his wits to tell her about Gandhiji's demise, or leave her to discover it on her own.

Duraisami Iyer could not accompany them as he lacked the physical stamina to travel. He cautioned Surya a thousand times to take Sita safely and bring her back carefully.

In Sita's life, once again incidents took place as in dreams. She was preyed by apprehensions when she saw the crowds on the highway from Panipat to Delhi. Surya responded to her questions by merely shaking his head.

Finally, they reached Delhi. They saw a sea of people going from Old Delhi to the New. Sita walked with them in a dream. Surya followed her anxiously, mindful that he should not lose her in the crowd. A great weight was oppressing his heart. He could still not gather the courage to tell Sita the truth. There was no need for it anymore. Soon, Sita herself would learn the truth. What would happen to her when she did? She should not faint in the middle of the mammoth crowd.

Sita and Surya reached New Delhi when the Mahatma's final procession was about to start. Making a stupendous effort, they pushed and pummelled their way through the crowds to reach the spot from where they could glimpse his face. Sita made haste, with all the edginess of someone about to make a huge discovery.

When she saw the Mahatma's body lying in state on the flower-strung hearse in the funeral cortege, Sita came to understand what had happened. The great leaders were seated around him. The grief-stricken multitudes were racked by sobs and tears.

An ear-splitting roar rose from that mammoth crowd. The dull roar of the sea which had constantly filled Sita's ears, now mingled with the roar rising from the sea of humanity. Her heart swelled and rose to block her throat. Then, all of a sudden, above the neck and between the ears, a nerve snapped, like the breaking of a lute's bass string. The twang of that splitting nerve crashed through the sounds of the two seas and streaked into her head...

Stupefaction was replaced by mental clarity. Sita regained the ability to think. Ah! The opportunity to see the man sublime had occurred many times in her life, but missed due to many reasons. Should she have to see him at his funeral procession, after life had departed from his body? How many times had she thought of joining the Mahatma's ashram, to surrender her life in his service? How many times had she wanted to remove all the ornaments she wore and offer them to his cause? Now, none of those wishes were going to be fulfilled.

'Sita! Why were you born in this world? Were you born only to see every wish of your heart dissolve into nothingness? Were you born to bring troubles to your friends and kin? Hadn't the Mahatma declared that he would live to be a hundred and twenty! Was it to prevent you from seeing him that he chose to depart now?'

These thoughts chased each other as she followed the crowd. At times she was pushed far away from the flower-bedecked vehicle. But somehow, she would squeeze and butt her way towards it. She felt an irrepressible desire to touch the Mahatma's mortal remains and place those fingers on her eyes. It was this yearning which energized her to make a tremendous effort to propel herself close to the hearse.

Once she had seen the Mahatma, Sita forgot all about Surya. Separated from Sita in the melee and terrified at the thought of losing her, Surya pushed and shoved through the crowd, desperately trying to find her again.

Finally, around 4 in the afternoon, the procession reached the river Yamuna. The pyre was built. The final rites were performed. By then Sita had been pushed to the outer rim of the crowd. Despite her best efforts, she could not succeed in cleaving her way to get in again.

The pyre is torched! The flames leap to the sky. A huge wail rises from the vast multitudes as if all the seven seas were clamouring in unison.

Everything had ended. Her life had ended. The world had ended. All her wishes and dreams had burned and smouldered and smashed themselves to cinders. What was the use of standing there anymore?

Sita turned away. Without knowing where she was going, she followed her feet to wherever they took her. She had no thought to spare for Surya or anybody else. Gone was the flame, which gave light to the world. The world would be dark for ever more. The only thought uppermost in her mind was that the great man had departed. The man whom she, a woman steeped in sorrow, had wanted to serve; believing in the inmost recesses of her being that her life would find its purpose in that surrender. And now, how did it matter where she went or what she did? The God of death would follow anyway. Let him come! Why should she bother to worry about anyone anymore?

The child! Vasanti! What about her? Is she alive? And if she was, who would care for her? Why? God would take care of her...

God! If there was a God, why would he watch such sufferings and atrocities? If he did, would he be God? Can he be called the 'ocean of compassion'? Why did Gandhiji go on talking about a compassionate God? What was the basis for that great man's faith?

Sita walked, and walked, and walked on. She walked on knowing not where she was going. Finally, she began to totter. She had not eaten since morning. She became aware that her feet were in great pain. She halted outside a bungalow, holding on to the compound wall. A song came from within the house. A song on the radio. A song that melted the heart. A song that brought tears to the eyes. A song that moved body and soul.

Hari tum haro jan ki bheer! Lord, banish the sufferings of humanity!

'What is this...! *I can hear again*! I am able to hear the song! It flows into me like a flood of nectar! What happened to the sound of the waves roaring in my ears forever! How did that unceasing, harrowing din disappear? Gandhiji! You are the abode of compassion! In your death, did you give me life?'

Gandhi's favourite song of Meerabai was being broadcast on the radio at the time his body was being cremated. Sita continued to hear the song.

Lord! Banish the sufferings of humanity!
Did you not save Draupadi's honour?
Did you not show compassion to the child Prahlad and save him?
Did you not shower your grace on the old elephant king and banish his fears of death?
Are you not always present wherever there is suffering?
Lord, banish the sufferings of humanity.

Sita forgot herself as she listened to the song. Cars honked on all sides. There were other kinds of noises as well. It had become quite dark. Dew was drizzling down. People walked on the streets talking in many different languages about Gandhiji's demise.

As she looked around, Sita also noticed the wall that she was holding on to for support. Ah! What's this? Whose house was this? It looked like hers! The house where she had lived for many years, believing it to be her own. Who could be living in it now? Why! It had to be her husband. It was he who was listening to the radio. God himself had brought her here! Why not go in and see him? Why not say, 'Let bygones be bygones. Let us start a new life?' But… would she be able to say all those things to him? Surely, God who had restored her hearing must have also given her the power to speak!

Sita felt that her tongue had regained its flexibility. She felt that she could speak clearly. The gate was open. With trembling heart and stumbling feet, Sita entered the bungalow's garden.

37

RAGHAVAN AND DHARINI

Sita entered the garden and walked timidly, hesitantly, and came to a halt by the steps at the threshold. Inside, the song had stopped. She could hear someone speaking on the radio. It could be seen that the door was shut, but not locked from the inside. No watchman outside either.

It was her husband who was inside. No doubt about it. How would he react if she simply went in and stood before him? Would he be startled? Yes, she would be able to hear him speak. But would she have the guts to speak to him? Would her tongue have the power of speech? Wouldn't her throat get blocked?

As these misgivings made Sita waver at the front steps, she heard someone open the compound gate from the outside. Sita was surprised to find that her auditory sense had become so acute. But surprise was followed by trepidation. Who was approaching? Who knew how the newcomer would react to her? Sita slipped behind the wall of the house to remain unseen while observing with a keen eye.

The visitor was a woman who came in a burqa that covered her from head to toe, with two slits for the eyes. Ayo! Who is she? O God! It looked as if the house is occupied by Muslims. She had unknowingly wandered into it. She must escape as soon as the woman went in. But where could she go? To the shore of the Yamuna river? Would the Mahatma's body still be burning there? Would it have turned into ashes? Would the massive crowds have dispersed? Could she go there and find herself alone so that she could at least smear her forehead with the sacred ash of his remains?

The woman in the burqa came with noiseless steps to stand by the front steps. Like Sita, she too dithered for a while. Why should she stop and pause if she is the owner of that house?

The woman ascended the steps and stood on the verandah. Then she walked slowly to the front door and knocked.

A voice sounded from within. 'Come in!' When she heard it, a quiver ran through Sita's body. For more than twelve years, that voice had brought her boundless joy and boundless sorrow. There was a time when that voice aroused an inexpressible elation within her. There were also days when it had aroused endless loathing and outrage. It was he. The king of her heart who had held her hand and married her. The husband who had tied the sacred tali around her neck to make her his wife. It was he who was inside the house.

What did this burqa clad woman have to do with him? Who was she? Does he already know her? Was he expecting her arrival on that day? The hallowed day on which the Mahatma was cremated? Was it not her duty to stop the woman who might harm him...? Sita was preyed by a thousand doubts.

When Sita saw the woman in the burqa open the door and enter the house, she was infected by an irrepressible desire to follow her. She gritted her teeth to control herself and wondered what she should do. If she went in by the front door, her husband would see her at once. In which case she may not be able to learn what she wanted to know.

If the back door had been left open, she could get in and stand in the adjacent room and hear what they said. She could also see the woman and discover her identity. If the back door were to be locked, she could stand near the bedroom window and eavesdrop on their conversation.

Sita's feet took her to the backyard. The back door opened at her touch without a single creak. Sita walked in slowly, step by step. She entered the room next to the living room with the radio. The living room doors were slightly open. She could even spy through the gap at need. Sita's feet faltered. She sank into a sofa near the doorway.

Raghavan spoke in a harsh voice, 'Who are you? Why are you here? You must have mistaken this for some other house. Go away! I am alone here. No women in the house. Get going at once!' The harshness sounded sweet to Sita. She was delighted when he said, 'No women in the house!'

There was a moment's silence. Raghavan must have switched off the radio earlier.

Once again Raghavan spoke in a strident voice. 'What are you waiting for? Aren't you leaving? Shall I call the police? Those hulking servant boys have both gone off God knows where! Let them return and I'll let them have it! It was a mistake not to have locked the door. Some damned refugee woman fleeing from Pakistan has turned up here!'

Raghavan was cut short when a woman's voice said, 'Raghavan, forgive me. I have no intention of giving any trouble. I will leave soon.'

A quiver ran through Sita's body once again. It was Dharini's voice. Sita wanted to get up, run in, hug her and cry out, 'Akka!' With great difficulty she suppressed the urge. Suddenly she decided that her husband should never know that she was alive. She had to sustain her mental strength to hold on to that resolve.

'Dharini? *Dharini*! You! In this guise! Why this horrible veil? Take a seat, Dharini, take a seat! Will I ever ask you to leave? I have been aching for so long just to have a glimpse of you! Please do sit down,' Raghavan said.

'All right. I am feeling very tired. I will sit down and tell you what I came to say. I won't be here for long, just five minutes,' Dharini told him.

'Five minutes! Will I let you go in five minutes?' Raghavan exclaimed.

'You said I that there was no woman in the house, and I was to go away at once.'

'I thought you were some accursed refugee.'

'I too am an accursed refugee. I have to leave quickly. Otherwise, Vasanti will get worried.'

'Dharini, where is Vasanti? Why did you not bring her with you? Is she well?'

'She is well. I came only to tell you about her. I will bring her and leave her here whenever you ask me to do so.'

'Are you saying you will leave her here? All right. What does it matter that I will have to struggle to care for a motherless child in this empty house.'

'Why do you say a motherless child? Do you know anything about Sita for certain?'

'Yes, Dharini! No one can be more unfortunate than myself in this whole world. Sita was drowned in the River Chenab. It seems Surya saw this with his own eyes.'

Sita heard sobs. She did not know who was sobbing. It could have been Raghavan or Dharini. Why not rush in and let them know that she was alive? No. Never. With great determination Sita forced herself to remain in her seat.

'I would not have believed it if Surya had not told me that he had personally witnessed it. I would have been searching for her still. My heart breaks when I think of having left her and the child in Haushangabad to come running in search of this miserable job. But how could I know that the people in Pakistan would turn into fiends overnight?'

'Raghavan, don't go on thinking about the past with sorrow. Sita is lucky that she died in the flooding river. We who are alive are the unlucky ones. We have witnessed the assassination of the great soul who personified nobility to the world.'

'After getting this news last night, I have been thinking of Sita all the time. Sita had a special kind of devotion for the Mahatma. And during the year we spent in Haushangabad, she had come to worship him as a divinity. How bereaved she would have been!'

'Sita had good karma. I will take my leave now, Mr Raghavan. I will bring your daughter tomorrow and leave her with you.'

'What are you saying, Dharini? You are talking to me as if we are strangers! Where do you want to go? Where are you staying? Where have you left the child? You had written to Sita two months ago. I was expecting you. Where were you all this time?' Raghavan rained questions in perplexity.

'I came to this city as soon as I wrote that letter. I went to the house near the Jama Masjid where I had once stayed with my parents. Riots began in that area on that very day. For two months, I could not leave the house. I was scared to bring the child. That was the reason for this long delay. Today, all of Delhi has gone to the Mahatma's final procession. I too found the confidence to come here,' Dharini explained.

'I must be the only person in the whole city who did not get out of the house today. Even the servants have gone to the Mahatma's funeral procession. I stayed at home, listening to the commentary on the radio. It turned out to be a good thing that I did.'

'Yes. It was good that you were at home. I will leave now. Tomorrow...'

'Don't talk of tomorrow. I will take the car and come right now. Let us go and bring Vasanti. But don't think you can escape after dropping that motherless child with me. I cannot take up that responsibility unless you agree to take Sita's place in this house and raise Vasanti.'

'What are you saying? What do you mean when you say that I must take Sita's place? Haven't you gotten over that old madness yet?'

'No. As long as there is life in this body that madness will not leave me.'

'You are saying this because you don't know this truth. Sita is my sister. My blood sister.'

'It is not a secret unknown to me. Surya told me that you are Sita's elder sister. He also said that nothing would bring greater peace to Sita's soul than for you to marry me. Think about it, Dharini! Is there anyone more qualified to stay in this house and raise Vasanti? No. You will not want to talk about it today when all of us are in a state of trauma. Let us go and bring the child here. But you must remove your burqa, at once. I don't like you wearing this hateful costume.'

'All right! I will take off my burqa. But I don't want to postpone the talk of marriage. My mind will be at rest if we can finish that talk right now.'

'I have no objections, Dharini! But what is there to talk about? All that remains is for you to give your consent. As for me, I have been performing a penance for the last sixteen years for this boon.'

'Before I tell you about what I want, I must tell you that I have pledged my word to my sister Sita...'

'What pledge?'

'I swore to Sita that if you agreed to marry me, I would do so.'

'Do you intend to fulfil it? Or wash your hands off?'

'When Sita was alive, she endured many sufferings because of me. All my attempts to protect her failed. Shouldn't her soul find some peace at least now? I am not going to break my vow. If you consent to marry me, I will. But you must reconsider before you make that decision.'

Sita's conscience told her, 'Silly woman! Why are you still here? Go. Run! At once. Best to go when your mind is firm. Is it not possible for it to change?' Sita got up, left soundlessly by the back door, went round the house, crossed the compound gate, and began to walk exceptionally fast. Dusk fell all around her.

Sita, what have you done? Couldn't you have stayed in that room for five minutes more?

38

THE BELL RANG!

It is not easy to write this chapter. The hand trembles, the heart hangs back. But it must be done. After all, it is the writer's duty to finish his story.

The great problem in writing an account of this kind is that the readers recreate the story along with the novelist, developing their own ideas about the course of events and how they should end. Some insist that the heroine should die, others say that she should not. Some expect the hero to be punished, others want him to be coronated.

The novelist gets trapped in the horns of a dilemma. Should he tell the truth or change it to please the reader? Is it not the duty of the storyteller to narrate whatever happened in exactly the way it did, however bitter and painful that truth may be?

Readers may have guessed the reason for this long winded preamble. Nothing but the reluctance to go on. But how long can the writing be stalled or postponed?

When Dharini looked at Saundara Raghavan and said, 'You must reconsider before you consent', it was with vexation that Raghavan asked, 'You keep on asking me to reconsider. What is there to think about?'

'Think about what your parents, friends and relatives will say.'

'Madness! I have forgotten them since way back when. Presently my parents are living happily and contentedly with their elder son and daughter-in-law. They don't pay any attention to me. I too don't bother about them.'

'You may not bother about them now, but does it mean that you never will? Blood ties can never be broken. Nothing more is needed to prove this than my father.'

'A great father indeed! An enemy to both his daughters.'

'Forget your parents. You will have to work in New Delhi and live your life here. What will people think about your marriage to me?'

'They will think that I am an exceptionally lucky man. Is there anyone more beautiful than you in New Delhi? Anyone who can excel you in style, elegance and social skills? Can I feel any greater pride than in taking you with me to clubs and parties?'

There were suppressed sounds of laughter behind the burqa. For no reason at all Raghavan felt a chill, and with it a frisson of an inexplicable fear.

'Dharini, why are you laughing? Is this the time or the occasion for laughter?'

Dharini stood up.

'It was wrong of me to have laughed. Forgive me. Whatever you may say. I give you one more day – twenty-four hours – to reflect. I will bring the child here at the same time tomorrow,' she said.

'You are just as obstinate as ever. Never mind, Dharini. Do as you will. But before you go, please remove this ghastly burqa and show me your face, just once. Otherwise, I will not let you go. I will remove the veil by force,' he said.

As he was speaking, Raghavan remembered a song that Sita used to sing whenever they came across burqa clad women in Delhi. A song by the poet Subramania Bharati, about the custom of women covering their faces, introduced by Muslims in Delhi. Raghavan used to enjoy it and wander into a world of his own. But now, a shiver coursed through his flesh as he remembered the song.

'I will fulfill your wish right away. But don't blame me,' Dharini said, as she removed her burqa and let it drop to the floor.

Raghavan had been feeling all the euphoria of one who walks blithely by the mountain slope, enraptured by the beauties of nature. Now, out of the blue, a rock rolled down to smash his head, a burning torch was thrust into his eye, a thousand scorpions stung his feet, and a gruesome monster sprang up before him to strangle his neck.

The unveiled shape which appeared before him was not the enchanting figure that he had gazed at so many times, a form that was imprinted in his heart. It was not the embodiment of beauty that he yearned to see. The face was not that of Sita's own sister, glowing like the full moon.

What he saw was a grotesque configuration. A woman's figure with an arm chopped off. A form which had a hollow for an eye. A ghastly face slashed across from the right side of the forehead to the left cheek. An ethereal image crafted by a master sculptor now smashed to fragments by the frenzied attack of an invading iconoclast.

Raghavan stood in wild stupefaction engendered by terror, horror, pity and revulsion.

For some time, he stood staring with his eyes and mouth wide open. Then, as all his strength drained from him, he slumped onto the sofa.

The form opened its mouth to speak, the absence of two front teeth making its grotesqueness appear more deformed. 'Sir, forgive me. I thought that I should not give you pain. But you would not listen. You insisted that I should remove my burqa.'

Yes. It was Dharini's voice. No doubt about it. In all its mutilated misshapenness, it was still Dharini's face.

And yet it was not easy for Raghavan to trust that it was so. Hoping against hope he thought, could it not be somebody else? He even thought that it might be some conspiracy to bring grievous disappointment to him.

'I am leaving. Answer me after a day's reflection. Take a week if you like,' Dharini said.

A hundred little devils jumped into Saundara Raghavan's head and laughed loudly in derision.

'Don't go, Dharini! Don't go! Say something before you go! Otherwise, I will go completely mad,' he gasped.

Dharini sat down, 'Please don't be agitated. Don't distress yourself. What do you want me to say? Tell me and I will say it,' she said.

Raghavan subjected Dharini to his gaze once again from head to foot, dropped his head upon the desk and sobbed.

'Sir, you have studied philosophy. Please remind yourself of all the wise doctrines that you have studied. Who can conquer destiny? What is the use of crying over what has come to pass?'

Raghavan raised his head and howled. 'Dharini, why has fate kept me alive? To endure this gory sight? Couldn't I have died of fever in Calcutta?'

'God has not given us the power to conquer fate. But he has given us the power to conquer suffering and sorrow. Today the whole country laments the death of Mahatma Gandhi. After a month people are going to forget him. They are going to be engaged in their own daily activities. In this world, no joy or pleasure is permanent. Similarly, suffering and sorrow are not eternal. God has given us the power to get over grief.'

'Don't take the name of God! I swear that there is no God! How can I believe in God after seeing you in this state,' Raghavan groaned.

'Only after becoming what I am now has my faith in God become complete. Sir, I saved your child and the mother who raised me. God took me to them at the right time. It was in that attempt that I lost an arm. And an eye. And received this knife wound on my face. But I was able to save the mother who raised me. I was able to save my dearest sister's child. What is this but divine mercy?'

After that Dharini told him about the zealots attempting to torch the mosque in the Rajnipur kingdom, in which several women were impounded, and how, as she singlehandedly opposed them, the queen mother of Rajnipur came with an army to save her and all the others imprisoned in the mosque.

Saundara Raghavan had already read an account of these events in the newspapers. He had been furious with the queen mother for having saved the mosque. After listening to Dharini's account his mind was filled with indefinable bewilderment. O God! It was from that mosque that his child had been rescued. If the Maharani of Rajnipur had not arrived in time to save her...! If she had made it half an hour later? Was it indeed God's mercy...?

The telephone rang loudly.

39

GOD'S MERCY

The sages have defined human understanding as finite, and God's wisdom as infinite. The acts of God are beyond human understanding. If human beings can unravel the rationale behind God's actions, would they not rise above their humanness and claim divinity?

Many men go through their entire lives knowing nothing but suffering and oppression. They close their eyes forever without having experienced a single moment of joy. Infuriated by this unfairness, we wonder why God, if at all he exists, remains a passive onlooker as atrocities take place. We conclude that even if God does exist, hailing him as *deena bandhu*, the friend of the hapless, is a huge mistake.

In the same world, when we see some people always luxuriating on a bed of roses, we exclaim, 'Ah! If there is a God at all, how biased he must be.'

What does the sick child think? 'I am weak and need strengthening. But mother gives me only gruel. My three brothers are hefty fellows. She gives them sumptuous fare. How unfair she is, how biased!'

The child is unable to understand his mother's actions. He does know that his mother gives him gruel only out of concern, or that his mother is constantly worried about him, far more than about her other boys. If the sick child has total faith in the mother, there would be no need for him to lose heart. Even if he is sick in body, at least his mind would be at peace.

When we complain and find fault with God because we cannot comprehend God's compassion, or his actions based on that compassion, we merely inflate our sufferings. But faith gives us the ability to withstand all the sufferings that may befall us in life. It gives us the courage to maintain our mental composure even when we are surrounded by troubles.

Can a man pray for any greater boon in this world?

To Raghavan, who was completely dazed after listening to what Dharini had to say, the ring of the telephone came as a reprieve.

'Who is calling me at this hour?' he exclaimed in exasperation and picked up the receiver. 'Who is it?' he barked.

The information that he received must have been extraordinary. It transformed the expression on his face.

He put the receiver back, looked at Dharini and said, 'Listen, Dharini! I don't know why Surya lied about Sita drowning in the river. You know Bhama, the daughter of the former divan! Sita is in her house now. So is Surya. Bhama has asked me to come there at once. Will you…' Raghavan broke off in mid-sentence.

Dharini fully understood the reason for the elation in his voice. There was no need for him to think about marrying a monster without an eye and an arm. No need to answer Dharini's question about marriage.

'Yes, I will come with you,' Dharini said.

Dharini knew full well that Raghavan was not pleased to take her with him. But how could she not go to see Sita at once, after learning that she was alive?

Raghavan hastened to bring the car out. Dharini took the backseat. During the drive, Raghavan gave her a few more details about what he had learnt. 'It seems Sita and her father were in Panipat all these days. Surya brought Sita to Delhi to see Gandhiji's funeral. They got separated in the throng. Happening to spot Bhama as the crowds were getting dispersed, Surya told her about it. They went to Bhama's house to call the police and found Sita lying unconscious in front of the house. They have taken her inside and tried to revive her.

A doctor has arrived. I don't know why Surya told me such a big lie. What a scoundrel he is!'

Dharini interrupted, 'Why curse him? We will know the truth only if we ask him. Perhaps he did not know that Sita was alive when he met you?'

'Possible. But what a miracle, Dharini! Is it not a wonder that Sita was found today? This can only be attributed to God's mercy.'

The car came to a halt in front of Bhama's house. As soon as they heard the car, Surya and Bhama came to the threshold. Grabbing Raghavan's hand as soon as he got out from the car, Bhama said, 'Quick!' and took him inside. As he went in, Raghavan said to Surya, 'Surya, you duped me! Let it go. Dharini is in the car. Attend to her.' As he spoke, Raghavan speculated on Surya's reaction when he saw Dharini's grotesque form.

As Surya strode to the car, Dharini saw how perturbed he was and said, 'Surya, don't come near me. I am unclean.'

'Dharini, I will never agree that anything in the world can be purer than you.'

'We'll keep all this for later. How is Sita?' Dharini asked.

'The doctor says she will not survive. She has regained consciousness. The moment she did, she mentioned Vasanti and you,' Surya said.

'Ayo, the child must be brought here at once. She is in our old house. Will you come with me?'

Surya said, 'Certainly, I will. Poor man! Let Raghavan have some personal time with Sita in peace, at least in her last moments.'

40

'LUCKY SITA!'

The doctor was preparing the injection. Bhama was assisting him.

Raghavan had taken Sita's head on his lap. His sobs could be heard intermittently.

Sita struggled to speak as she said, 'Why should you cry? Like the noble Kasturba, I too had prayed that I should die on my husband's lap. Those prayers have been answered. Who can be luckier than me?'

Raghavan was torn between grief and embarrassment. He said, 'Sita, don't talk like this. There's nothing wrong with you. You will get well and be up and about in no time at all.'

'No, I am not going to live for long. I don't care. Please forgive me. I eavesdropped on you and Dharini Akka. With my own ears I heard Dharini Akka agreeing to marry you. I left at once. I want nothing more. Where is Akka? Ask her to come. I must thank her.'

'Dharini has gone to fetch Vasanti. And things will not happen the way you think. Even God cannot bear it if you leave me,' Raghavan said as he prayed with all his heart, 'Lord, please save Sita, just this once! After this I will remain morally upright. I will never do anything wrong again. I will never behave in a selfish manner.' He prayed to all the gods in all the temples from Kasi to Rameswaram. Never before had Raghavan been such a committed theist.

The doctor came with the syringe, ready to give the injection. That done, he said, 'I will take my leave now. Call me in the morning and tell me how things are going.'

After seeing the doctor off, Bhama said to Raghavan, 'It would be good to ask your wife if she wants to say anything to you, if she has any wish in her heart.'

Raghavan lost his temper. He retorted, 'What nonsense! It will be good if you keep your mouth shut.'

Sita interposed. 'Why are you getting angry with her? What she says is true. I do have a wish in my heart. You must marry Dharini Akka after I am gone. Akka has promised me. She will not break her vow.'

Soon, Dharini returned with Vasanti. Vasanti, who had seen innumerable tragedies, was left unmoved by her mother's condition. She came and sat down by her mother's side and asked, 'Amma, where were you hiding all these days?'

Sita tried to raise her feeble arms to bring the child's face close to her own. But her arms were not strong enough. Dharini brought the two faces close to each other. Sita looked up. Seeing the purdah clad woman she asked softly, 'Who is this?'

'Don't you know me, Sita?' Dharini asked.

'Akka, you are here! I heard you talking to him. I am happy, and at peace. But why have you veiled your face? Take it off, Akka! I must see your face before I die. I will carry that image with me as I go to the world above. On the way I will look at the full moon in the sky and see if it is really as beautiful as my sister's face...'

As she was speaking, Sita's eyes began to close.

Dharini checked Sita's pulse. It was very faint and very fast. Dharini realized that the time had come for the bird to leave its cage.

'Sita, I am taking off my veil. Open your eyes and look at me. Don't be frightened. This happened when I was trying to save Vasanti, your child. You need not feel sad about it, not in the least...'

Sita did not hear her words.

When the veil was lifted and she saw Dharini's face, Sita's face shone bright, like a lamp flaring up before it gets extinguished.

In a voice softer than ever, but brimming with joy and wonder, she whispered, 'Akka, Your face! How beautiful! I have never seen such loveliness in my life! If I do get to the world of the gods, I doubt if I will see any beauty there to equal you. No surprise that my husband was not able to love me after falling in love with you. I am lucky. Akka, I am going with no regrets, my mind at peace. No one should grieve for me. Surya will say that he is heartbroken. Tell him not to be sad.'

When Sita mentioned his name, Surya came forward to bend down and look at her. 'Sita, I am here,' he said. At that moment, even Saundara Raghavan did not try to stop him.

Sita said in a very faint voice, 'Write to Lalita. Ask her to forgive me.'

'Is that all, Sita? Anything else you want to say to me?'

'No, Surya. Nothing more. I am lucky. Get married, soon!' Sita said.

Sita was lucky indeed. Who could deny it? Surya sobbed. Raghavan howled. Dharini, Vasanti and even Bhama wept aloud. But nothing fell on Sita's ears. Nothing was felt by her senses.

Sita's life departed from the ephemeral body. Rising higher and higher, it floated in the spaces above, seeped itself in the colours of the rainbow, pierced through the bevy of silvery clouds, inhaled the fragrances borne by the gentle winds, experienced the sweetness of music, and moved to the highest plane of bliss.

Blossoms from the coral lily trees of paradise came down in a shower and swirled around her living spirit.

With their celestial forms gleaming in the colours of gold and rose and tender mango leaves, the gandharvas and kinnaras, the celestial musicians, stood at intervals to welcome her with their sweet strains.

Sita's spirit soared higher and higher.

Ethereal figures of exquisite beauty glinted in and out through translucent cloud curtains.

Ah, Sita knew some of the forms. Laila and Majnu sang and danced by. Satyavan and Savitri strolled with clasped hands. Romeo and Juliet sailed on the swan-shaped skiff. Nala and Damayanti took winged flight.

Ah, this radiance! This resplendence! An effulgence appearing from nowhere! There! It is right there! What are the assembled gandharvas and the kinnaras saying as they point to the streak of lightning, shining like a thousand suns, and whizzing by like the arrow from Rama's bow?

'We see it!' 'We see it!' 'The light of the Mahatma!'

All the fragrant flowers raining in the heavenly spheres, the gentle winds that blew, the celestial music floating by, the salute from the gods and goddesses – everything had appeared to hail the Mahatma. Sita had been blessed indeed to reach the astral spaces on the day the Mahatma's soul ascended to the heavens.

She must not leave him. She must not get separated from him. If she followed that shining light, she would be able to see Mother Kasturba. Where would Gandhiji's soul go but in search of Kasturba's soul?

Sita's spirit followed the light on its path. But soon, it disappeared to where it could not be followed.

But Sita did not lose heart. Her faith did not diminish. If she went on travelling through the spaces above, would she not find that light, somehow?

Sita's spirit traversed many worlds. It went circling through the starry galaxies. How many worlds! How many suns! How many moons! How many stars! Could she cross them all and transcend them all? Was there a space called beyond the Beyond?

Yes. It must be so. She had crossed all the spheres and the worlds and the suns and the moons and the endless galaxies of stars. Now there was nothing but space. Illimitable space. Endless blue. The flood of bliss without a beginning or an end.

No doubt about it. Sita was indeed fortunate.

41

SURYA'S HEART

Surya was in the habit of frequently subjecting himself to self-examination, analysing and reflecting on his overt mental processes, the promptings of his rational mind, and the hidden desires in the inmost recesses of his heart. If he found himself muddled, if he sensed any contradictions between mind, heart and reason, he would engage in profound contemplation. At times, he also wrote in his diary to banish confusions and clarify his feelings.

On 10 February, this is what Surya wrote in his diary:

Sita's tenth day death ritual was completed today. Her husband performed all the vedic rites with interest and commitment. It is amusing to see how Raghavan has developed this sudden faith in religious rites. More amusing was the interest that Bhama showed in them. She organized all the ceremonies in her own house, thus sparing Raghavan the demands of having to make the arrangements. Shameful! Couldn't the man who had just lost his wife wait for a decent interval before indulging in the kind of behaviour that invites ridicule?

Sita, you managed to free yourself from this heartless scoundrel and depart. How stupid it is to say that the god of death is pitiless? What could be a greater act of compassion than his taking you away…?

Did I perform my duty to Sita in the right and proper way? Did I fulfill the promise I gave my aunt? This thought will keep returning to me as long as I live. I have done my duty as best I could. I have disregarded the cost of my own life to save Sita. But what was the use? The help I rendered turned into injury. In fact, I am responsible for her life of misery. If only I had not hidden my uncle's telegram...

Duraisami Iyer's life too has come to an end. What a pity that he had not thrown his gun away as Sita asked him to do. But how could he have thrown it away when he was fated to die by it!

In a manner of speaking, it is a good end for him. One of his daughters is dead. Another has reached a state worse than death. Which father can endure this horror? He had come to believe that his own wrongdoings were responsible for these tragedies. That is why he shot himself. Poor man! Before I could go to Panipat, they cremated him as a homeless drifter. The man got lucky in death. The newspapers reported that he had shot himself out of excessive grief over the Mahatma's assassination.

Sita is dead.

Duraisami Iyer is gone.

But Dharini is alive.

We must forget the dead and think of the living.

In Dharini's case, am I ready to do my duty? Are my heart's feelings, my mind's desire, and my reason's promptings one and the same? Are the words I spoke to Dharini nothing but the truth? Words of truth rising from the heart? Or were they spoken in haste, out of obstinacy and swagger? Later in life, will I ever regret the words I spoke today...?

We met this evening in our old place in the Gandhi Maidan. We talked about our future. I will try to write down that conversation. Later, if I go over what I write, I will be able to judge if I am mistaken in my assessment.

At first, we talked about the pitiful deaths of Sita and Duraisami Iyer.

Dharini sobbed. I was eager to wipe the tears rolling down from her eyes. But I did not have the courage to do so. She had covered her face with a veil. Did I not know why? I had seen her face for a moment on the day Sita passed away. Ayo! I am terrified to recall it.

But then, did it make my mind change, even fractionally, towards Dharini? No! Never! What people may see as disfigurement does in fact enhance her beauty. That is how Sita saw it in her last moments.

And yet, I could not find the courage to remove Dharini's veil or wipe her eyes. After the sobs and tears ceased somewhat, I asked her, 'How long can we rue the past? Should we not think of the future? What do you intend to do?'

'I have no intentions. Not even the power to think. You must tell me. What is your plan for the future?' Dharini asked.

'How can I tell you about my plans? *My* plans will be made only after I know *your* intentions.' I replied.

'About what? I don't have my father's courage to give up my life, not yet.'

I said, 'We need courage to live, not to die.'

'I have courage enough for that. Moreover, don't I have a responsibility towards Vasanti?' Dharini said.

'Yes. The responsibility towards Vasanti and the promise given to Sita. Dharini, if you want to marry Raghavan to fulfil that promise, I will not stand in the way,' I told her.

Dharini laughed. I did not like her that laugh, not at that time.

'Why do you laugh?' I asked her.

'What is the use of *my* wanting? It is Saundara Raghavan who must want it,' she said.

'Why do you say that? Is there anyone in the world who is stupid enough to *not* want to marry you?'

'Surya, I am surprised that you should lie. Who will dare to marry me after lifting my veil and seeing my monstrous face?' Dharini said.

'Forgive me, Dharini. It was wrong of me to have expected this knowing Raghavan's nature as I do,' I said.

'Why single out Raghavan? No man born on earth would marry a woman with such a hideous face,' she said.

'Don't say that. Don't put everyone in Raghavan's category. Raghavan knows only the beauty of the face. He knows nothing of the beauty within. He knows nothing at all about true love. I have loved you from the time I saw you in Akbar's palace in the Agra Fort. It is not your *face* that I love. It is *you*,' I said passionately.

Dharini remained silent for a while. Then she said, 'Surya, I have never doubted your love. But love is one thing, marriage is another. On the wedding day, the groom must hold the wife's hand, mustn't he? What if the bride has no hand to be held?' she said.

I broke in to say, 'To Raghavan it may be a handicap. Not to me. He may think about the impossibility of holding hands and going to parties. To me, marriage is not a ceremony of holding hands. Marriage is about the mingling of minds. No other couple will have minds as compatible as ours. Dharini, all you have to do is to make the decision. We can fix the wedding date at once.'

Her throat choking with overwhelming emotions, her tongue slowing down in an excess of blissfulness, Dharini said, 'Surya, when I think that the world has in it someone as noble as you are, I too begin to feel the desire to live. I have understood your thoughts. And yet, please give me a few days to think about it.'

I have now gone through everything that I have written so far. I pondered whether the words I spoke to Dharini were genuine. I probed deep into my heart and examined it. No doubt about it. Every word I spoke to Dharini was true. My love for her has no beginning, no end, no decay. It is not about the flesh, or face, or the colour of the skin. It is the love of the mind for the mind. It is love – pure and heartfelt – generated when two souls meet. Our love has neither match nor metaphor.

It is true that I felt affection for Sita from the first day I saw her. But there is a great difference between that and my feelings for Dharini. I was willing to give my life towards Sita, but not my heart. There were times when my anger towards Saundara Raghavan made me think up odd plans for Sita's release. Once I even had the silly notion, 'Why not get her a divorce and marry Sita?' I told Duraisami Iyer about it. But never was my mind tainted by any dishonourable thought towards Sita. Saundara Raghavan too knew this very well. That is why he never became angry about my close relationship with Sita. He was enraged only by my friendship with Dharini.

By God's will he has been completely defeated. The selfish lecher who is interested only in the beauty of the flesh can no longer compete with me. His love has been proved to be false. That is what he deserves.

Now, Dharini belongs to me. No one can snatch her away from me.

Even though I mourn Sita's death and her father's suicide, I am exhilarated by the thought that from now onwards, Dharini belongs entirely to me.

42

LALITA'S SISTER-IN-LAW

No longer did any nameplate hang at the gate post on the two houses facing each other in one of the main streets of Devapattinam. Following advocate Atmanatha Iyer, his friend Damodaram Pillai too had departed, to continue his law practice in the courts of the realms divine.

For a short time, the nameplate proclaiming 'Atmanatha Iyer, BABL' had been replaced with the nameplate announcing, 'A. Pattabhiraman, Chairman, Municipal Council.' But it had to be removed in no time at all. The crooked businessman who had been Pattabhiraman's opponent, claimed that the elections had been fraudulent and lodged a case for its annulment. The power of money brought a judgement in favour of the black marketeer. Pattabhiraman lost the chairman's post.

Some people advised Pattabhiraman to make an appeal against it, and others said that he should enter the election fray again. Lalita alone declared, 'What we endured is more than enough.' Accepting her advice, Pattabhiraman firmly refused to stand for re-election.

Coming home at the time of Damodaram Pillai's death, Amarnath did not wish to return to Calcutta.

The two friends were discussing the launch of some business to increase independent India's economic prosperity, when they were shell-shocked by the news of Mahatma Gandhi's assassination.

Their angst was intensified by the news of Sita's death. Amarnath, who had saved Sita when he found her lying unconscious on a street in Calcutta, was filled with pity to hear about her end. Pattabhiraman remembered how life had been full of exuberance when Sita had been a guest in their home, and of all the sufferings she had to undergo because of a blunder he had made when he was emotionally overwrought. The two friends expressed and compared their opinions about Sita's good and bad qualities.

But their wives would not agree that Sita had any negative traits at all. Lalita took all the blame on herself and was overcome by penitence. She shed tears as she condemned herself repeatedly for having caused all the miseries that overtook Sita. Hadn't Saundara Raghavan seen Sita when he had come to see her, Lalita? By marrying him, hadn't Sita undergone all the sufferings that Lalita should have experienced? And yet, how cheerful Sita had been when she was with them, never revealing her mental stress? How animated their house had been when Sita was around. Life itself had acquired a new sheen and buoyancy. Lalita had vainly suspected and wrongly blamed Sita, forcing her to run away from the house in the middle of the night. How would God punish Lalita for that sin?

Chitra consoled her in various ways. 'What can you and I do? Everything happens according to the writings of destiny.'

'Very clever! If everything is decided by fate, does it mean that there is nothing good or bad in human actions? Was it fate that made Gandhiji die? Will you say that the rank sinner who shot him dead committed no crime?'

'Lalita! How can you compare these two things? If fate is responsible for Gandhiji's death, is it not fate again that brings punishment to the assassin? In our actions, we must discriminate between good and bad. But things will happen according to what is destined for each person.'

'Some people do discriminate between right and wrong and do right always. And yet they go on suffering, without experiencing even a moment of joy. Is this destiny? Act of God? I don't understand your philosophy.' Lalita said.

'You are completely wrong. It may seem as if some people die after a lifetime of unalloyed misery. But in fact, in every life, joy and sorrow are interspersed.'

'Not at all. Look at Sita. She suffered through her entire life until she died.'

'Lalita, I too have known Sita for a short time. Enough to know that the joy she experienced was excessive, so was the sorrow she underwent. There are some people in the world whose life remains insipid. I cannot agree that they are the lucky ones. Do you know what Tagore, the great poet of Bengal, said? This is the boon he craves, "Lord! I want nothing but the good fortune of being able to shed tears!" A real life is a life in which joy and sorrow are intermingled. Look at all the poems, epics and sagas. Is there any hero or heroine who does not suffer?'

'Sita's life too has ended like a story. Chitra, I think of the days when she and I passed the time in telling stories as we sat beside the pool in Rajampettai, with the moon shining bright in the early hours of the night. How many stories she could tell! Laila and Majnu, Romeo and Juliet, Anarkali and Salim, Damayanti and Nala, Shakuntala and Dushyantan… As she told those stories, she would imagine herself to be the heroine. How many dreams she had! And she is gone with none of her dreams fulfilled,' Lalita said and burst into loud sobs.

Chitra tried to pacify her. When kind words proved useless, she resorted to indignation. 'You weep for Sita. Can't you sympathize with her sister, a little? Is she not more to be pitied for having to live on after losing an arm and an eye?'

Lalita's sobs stopped. She said, 'I am overwhelmed by pity when I think of her. I have never seen my eldest cousin. Should I have to see her for the first time like this?'

'Why are you thinking of yourself even now? Lalita, look at your brother Surya. A man of true valour! Who will have the guts to marry a woman whose limbs have been mutilated? Your husband or mine would run far away! No need to say what Sita's husband would do!'

'True. Chitra, let them all be deemed abominable! But is Surya doing the right thing? I cannot bring myself to think so. Why go in for such a wedding at all? Marrying a woman without an eye and an arm! The whole world will ridicule him.'

'It will be a great humiliation for you as well. Won't you be ashamed to call a woman without an eye and an arm your sister-in-law? But Lalita! Surya will not shame you. He will never bring Dharini here. If he does, go to Rajampettai at once. I will give them an earful and send them packing. Why should those shameless creatures land up here?' Chitra said sarcastically, running Lalita down.

'I am not such a brute! And yet I feel sad about Surya getting into such a marriage. My mother would die if she came to know.'

'Let her die! So many people die in this world. Mahatma Gandhi himself is gone. What is the purpose of your mother's continuing to live? Your mother must have performed great good deeds to get a son like Surya! Whose fault is it if she does not recognize her good fortune? Why should you weep with her? If I had a brother like Surya, I would simply burst with pride. I will brag to the whole world about my matchless brother. Lalita, please read that part of Surya's letter aloud to me once again.'

Lalita picked up the letter and once again ran her eyes over the part where Surya said,

> *My dear sister, do you remember how Sita and you had a double wedding under the same canopy? This question came up when you, Sita and I were talking in the poolside bungalow two days before the wedding. As the couple go round the sacred fire, should the mapillai hold the bride's left hand with his right hand? If he does, how can they walk round the fire together? We had a long argument over this and came out with varying opinions. But during the actual ceremony, no one noticed how it was done.*
>
> *Lalita, this complicated problem will not crop up when I marry your athanga Dharini. She has but one hand. It is that hand I will have to hold. I am not sorry that she has no other. It is with pride and joy that I think again and again about how the lost hand saved two hundred women, how it saved Sita's child. I am a very lucky man. Waiting for so long to marry has not been in vain. From now onwards, all my life will be one of bliss.*
>
> *Lalita, I have spoken to you once or twice about Dharini's beauty.*

Before this, hers was the beauty of the earth. Now, in my eyes, she is suffused with divine beauty. What do I care about what others think? What is it to me if others gossip?

As she read the letter, Lalita felt a lump rising in her throat. Chitra had tears in her eyes. When they became less emotional, Chitra said, 'Lalita, the saints of our land have said that the world has no sorrow, for sorrow is nothing but an illusion. Some other great souls have even said that true joy inheres in sorrow. I never understood the significance of those words. Today, I do. There is no joy in this world, or the world above, to equal the joy of undergoing sufferings, to remove the sufferings of others. She who is to become your sister-in-law claims this joy. Your brother Surya is the lucky man who knows this. I am eager to see them both as a married couple.'

43

BHAMA'S VISIT

The road to Rajampettai village was shaded by trees growing thickly on both sides as before. The post office too looked as it did fifteen years ago, without any great alteration. Runner Thangavelu walked in a leisurely manner though, and he did not hurry as he used to do in the past. His bells too rang in a slow tempo.

Rajampettai agraharam too remained much the same. However, it was true that the village lacked its old liveliness. Pattamaniam Kitta Iyer was no longer there. His pattamaniam post had been taken over by Shyamsundar or 'Sundu'.

Sundu had given up his ambition to become a film director. He believed that if he made a film at all, it had to have Sita in the lead. If not, it was pointless to go on. He held on to that hope until the news of Sita's death dispelled it completely. After that he calmly devoted himself to the tasks of the village munsif.

The absence of 'What, oy?' Seemachu Iyer was another reason for the lack of bustle. He was undergoing two-years' rigorous imprisonment. In the 'black market' case, the scamster managed to escape by turning Seemachu Iyer in. But no one in the village had much sympathy for him. When Seemachu Iyer acquired wealth, he became arrogant and treated others with contempt. So, the villagers were now content merely to remark, 'Will "what oy" Seemachu come out of it alive?'

In Kitta Iyer's house, Lalita was sitting in the hall, braiding her daughter, Pattu's hair. Her son Balasubramanian was spelling out each letter loudly, as he read the story of Gandhi from a weekly. Sarasvati Ammal was seated on the swing.

When she heard the jingling of the runner's bells, Lalita's eyes became moist with old memories.

Sarasvati Ammal asked, 'Lalita, when you were Pattu's age, do you remember how you used to run when you heard the mailbag arriving in the post office?'

'How can I not remember? Even now I feel like going to the post office to see if there's a letter for me,' Lalita replied.

'You may do it too! Who can rival you in boldness?' her mother remarked.

Half an hour later, Lalita did get up and run to the front door when she heard the postman's call. She wondered idly if it could be Balakrishnan. And then she saw that it was indeed Balakrishnan himself!

'So you are here, Amma. Good to see you. I don't like town life. I came back once and for all,' he said.

'I was wondering why I hadn't seen you in Devapattinam for some time. Are your children doing well?'

'Yes, by the grace of God. But what is "doing well"? They have killed someone like Mahatma Gandhi. After this what does it matter who is well and who is not well?' Balakrishnan said as he delivered her letter.

Lalita opened it. It was from her husband. After enquiring about the children, the letter went on to say:

> *Don't faint! I am going to tell you something amazing. Your brother Surya is here. He has brought his wife. You may be disappointed when you see his wife. I don't want to write any more. You may see for yourself. All three of us are taking the train tonight and will be there.*

The letter threw her out of kilter. The most important reason for her visit to Rajampettai was to tell her mother about Surya's marriage. However, until then, she had been unable to gather the courage to do so. She could no longer postpone the disclosure.

Lalita first told her mother about the letter from her son-in-law. Then she told her that he was bringing Surya to Rajampettai. Finally, she told her that Surya was married and was bringing his wife with him.

Sarasvati Ammal was surprised, delighted, and startled. 'Marriage! Without informing any of us? Who knows who the girl may be?' she groaned.

'I don't know…! I did… hear something. Didn't think it could be true. This letter makes me feel that it must be true,' Lalita said.

'What is true? What did you hear?' her mother asked.

'I hear that the girl Surya has married has lost some limb or the other. Some say an eye is missing. Others say an arm is missing. Surya always does things like this! I don't know, Amma. I am extremely worried.'

'Nonsense! Why would a boy do such a thing? Can it be true? If it is, how will I be able to face anyone?' Sarasvati Ammal lamented.

Pattabhiraman, Surya and his wife came in a bullock cart with its bells ringing. Lalita went to the threshold in a state of agitation. The thought of meeting Dharini made her panic. Though she had steeled herself, when the moment arrived, she could not but be rattled. She dreaded the rumpus her mother would make when she saw Dharini.

Pattabhiraman and Surya got down first. Then a woman dismounted. What a surprise! The woman was holding a small case in each hand. No eye missing either! True, she seemed steeped in high fashion, but there was no disfigurement of any kind. Lalita waited to see if Dharini followed. But no other person got down. Lalita welcomed everyone and took them inside the house. 'Surya, who is this lady? In your letter you said…'

Surya said, 'What I had written was something different. But this is the woman who came forward to marry me. She is the daughter of Divan Adivarahachari. Her name is Bhama. We have been married for two weeks. We are here on our honeymoon.'

Lalita regained her composure. Lalita's mother too contented herself with the thought that though her daughter-in-law looked somewhat like a little devil with tousled hair, she was not mutilated as Lalita had told her.

Later, when Lalita met Surya alone and talked to him, he told her, 'You must have suffered a little disappointment. For me, it was a huge disappointment. But the person who disappointed me was not your athanga Dharini. It was Saundara Raghavan. He surprised everyone who knew his nature well. He swore that he would marry Dharini, and that he had not loved for her the beauty of her face. Moreover, he insisted that Dharini must not break her promise to Sita. He would not listen to Dharini's objections though she made many. When Dharini told him that it would be detrimental to his professional life in Delhi, he said that he had already decided to quit his job. Lalita, I realized that Dharini too had affection for Raghavan. Therefore, I gave her up, stayed with them in Delhi and conducted their wedding. Saundara Raghavan has indeed given up his job. They have both gone to Rajnipur, taking Vasanti with them. Though the kingdom of Rajnipur has been merged with India, the queen mother has enormous wealth and properties. She is extremely fond of Dharini. The Rajnipur queen told them that they should come to Rajnipur and try to get the refugees to settle down with their families, and that she was going to leave her property for their rehabilitation. I suggested that I should take Vasanti to Rajampettai. But the child refused to come.'

Sarasvati Ammal heard his last words as she came up to them. 'Very good! Is it not enough that her mother came here and created a racket? Should the daughter come and make more mischief?' As they knew their mother's nature very well, both Lalita and Surya remained silent.

Then Lalita asked, 'How did you catch hold of this woman?'

'At first, I had disliked her. I had completely misread her nature. It was Dharini who told me all about her and disclosed that Bhama had feelings for me from the first time she saw me. And that is not all. In 1942, Bhama had secretly helped our movement a great deal while appearing to be at home in government circles. It was she who had sheltered Dharini for a long time and prevented her from being captured by the police. Again, it was she who had helped to arrange my escape from police custody. Moreover, Bhama had tried to save

Sita by bringing her out of the Punjab. When I heard all this, my mind underwent a complete change. When we talked, I realized that our goals are more or less the same. Don't come to any conclusion based on her outward appearance. Get to know your sister-in-law and then tell me what you think.'

Shyamsundar was happy to see his brother and sister-in-law. Surya's marriage had cleared the way for his own.

'Anna, have you come here with a return ticket or are you planning to stay for some time?' he asked.

'Unless you drive us away, we intend to stay here for a very long time. The nation has attained independence. Mahatma Gandhi made the final sacrifice and has established peace in the land. Going on, we must work for our country's economic prosperity and agricultural development. I am planning to make a start in our village. We must enthuse those who plough the fields.'

'Nowadays, we don't have any kisan problems in these regions. The man who headed the revolt disappeared after stealing five thousand rupees from the labour association. The movement has slumped since then. Unless you revive it…'

'Sundu, it is meaningless to be satisfied because the kisan movement is no longer active. Those who work in the fields must feel satisfied and energized. They must feel that they are getting a fair share of what they produce. Otherwise, there will always be chaos and rebellion and that will impede food production. Therefore, I am going to settle with the workers first. Then, I am going to introduce exemplary modern methods of agriculture. My wife Bhama says that she will help me. Sundu, what do you say?'

'What is there to say? Anna, I will be content even if you divide all our lands and give them to the field workers. It will be enough if you stay put here, and not go wandering from place to place. I can go anywhere and find work,' Sundu said.

'The time will come for dividing and sharing the land. We must be ready for that too. We must learn to survive by training ourselves in various professions right now,' Surya said.

Sundu thought to himself, 'There is always film making to opt for.'

Their mother came to them and said, 'Do whatever you like. But wait until my eyes close.'

'We can wait, Amma. But will earthquake, cyclone, volcano and the deluge wait for us?' Surya exclaimed.

Lalita said, 'When you talk of earthquake and deluge, I remember how athai and Sita frequently talked about hearing the sound of the waves. Was it delusion or some kind of ear disorder?'

Surya said, 'I don't know whether it was delusion or auditory ailment. I don't even know if by some divine power the signs of the coming horrors prefigured in their minds. As she was escaping from the Punjab, Sita fell into the river and became totally deaf. All she could hear was the loud and fearful reverberation of the waves. But on the day Gandhiji's sacred body was cremated, she began to hear again. The first sound she heard was the song close to the Mahatma's heart, *Hari tum ho jan ki bheer.* I believe that it is a good omen. After the supreme sacrifice made by Mahatma Gandhi, never again will any devastating calamity appear in this great country of ours. From now on, our nation will see nothing but progress and prosperity.'

May that selfless patriot's desire be fulfilled!

GLOSSARY

Adadaa (Tamil): Exclamation of surprise, admiration, wonder, regret, etc.

Adey (Tamil): Calling a boy or a man in a familiar scornful or minatory way

Aei (Tamil): Calling a male or a female in a familiar haughty or scornful way

Aenna (Tamil): Literally 'What?' used by Tamil brahmin women to address their husbands whom they are forbidden to call by name

Agraharam (Sanskrit): Village street of brahmins

Aiyangar (Tamil): Subsect among south Indian brahmins

Akka (Tamil, Marathi): Elder sister

Angavastram (Sanskrit): Piece of cloth worn over the shoulder by men

Anna (Tamil, Marathi): Elder brother

Anna (Hindi): Currency unit formerly used in British India, equal to $\frac{1}{16}$ of a rupee

Appa (Tamil/Marathi): Father

Appappaa (Tamil): Exclamation of fatigue or wonder

Athai (Tamil): Aunt, or father's sister

Athanga (Tamil): Cousin, or daughter of father's sister

Atharva veda (Sanskrit): Last of the four ancient scriptures of Hinduism

Athimber (Tamil): Husband of paternal aunt or elder sister

Avatara purusha (Sanskrit): Masculine embodiment of mythic or divine elements

Ayyayyo (Tamil): Exclamation of fear, regret, ruefulness, apprehension

Bale! (Tamil): Exclamation of approval (real or satirical)

Bhadrakali (Sanskrit): Fierce goddess, term used to describe a termagant

Bhagavatam (Sanskrit): The legend of Lord Vishnu in Sanskrit

Bhavati bhikshaam dehi (Sanskrit): 'May you give me food/alms'

Bhesh (Tamil): Exclamation of approval (real or satirical)

Chaiwala (Hindi): Tea vendor

Chal chal re nau jawan (Hindi): The opening words of an old Hindi film meaning 'Get going, young man!'

Chamba rice: Rose rice

Champa (Sanskrit): Plumeria, a flower known for its fragrance

Chavukkandi (Tamil): A simple building in a village, often used as a public office

Chee! (Tamil): Exclamation of disgust or disapproval

Chinnamma (Tamil): Young mistress

Chinnayya (Tamil): Young master

Chittirai (Tamil): The first month of the Tamil calendar, usually commencing in April

Darshan (Sanskrit): The beholding of a deity, a revered person, or a sacred object

Dei (Tamil): A term used to hail or address a younger or socially inferior male person

Dhaka: City in West Bengal, now the capital of Bangladesh, where very fine muslin was manufactured

Dharma (Sanskrit): Law of righteousness, truth, ethics governing the universe

Diwan-i-Aam (Urdu): The hall of audience

Diwan-i-Khas (Urdu): The hall of private audiences

Durai (Tamil): Term of respect for a man, usually applied to the white man

Dwapara yuga (Sanskrit): The third and third best of the four yugas (world ages) in a Yuga Cycle, preceded by Treta Yuga and followed by Kali Yuga

Gopi (Sanskrit): Cowherdess in the mythical pastoral wood, playmates of the young god Krishna

Hatha yogi (Sanskrit): A master of the practice of hatha yoga, a branch of yoga using physical techniques to preserve and channel the vital force or energy

Inquilab zindabad (Urdu): Long live the revolution!

Jaldi (Hindi): Quick

Janab (Urdu): Term of respect for a Muslim elder

Jibba (Urdu): A long top worn by Muslim men

Kadamba (Sanskrit): Evergreen tropical tree with scented flowers in clusters, *neolamarckia cadamba*, burflower-tree

Kala Hazar (Urdu): *Visceral leishmaniasis,* also known as kala-azar ('black sickness' or 'black fever')

Kali purusha (Sanskrit): Male form personifying all the negative elements that characterize the Age of Kali

Kali yuga (Sanskrit): The age of deceit, brutality, suffering and sin, the last of the four world ages of Hindu mythology

Kalidasa (circa 4–5 CE): The greatest dramatist in classical Sanskrit

Kamban (1180–1250 CE): One of the greatest Tamil poets, with his *Ramayanam*, the Tamil version of the great Indian epic

Kameez (Urdu): Long tunic worn in the Indian subcontinent

Kasi yatra (Sanskrit): Pilgrimage to Kasi, the sacred city of the Hindus

Kolam: Daily ritualistic and instant art design, drawn with rice flour, at the entrance of the house and before the family deity indoors

Krishna: The dark god in the Hindu pantheon, an avatar of the god Vishnu, who appears in several legends and epics, as a cowherd, flautist, dancer, lover, prince, warrior and philosopher

Kumkumam (Sanskrit): Red turmeric powder used for making the distinctive Hindu mark on the forehead

Kuyil (Tamil): Indian cuckoo

Laddu (Hindi): Indian confection, typically made from flour, sugar, and shortening, that is shaped into a ball

Lalita Sahasranamam (Sanskrit): A hymn stringing the thousand names of the mother goddess

Maaf keejiye (Hindi): Excuse me

Maidan (Urdu): An open ground for games, recreational activities and public meetings

Mamava pattabhirama (Sanskrit): A song by Carnatic music composer Muthuswami Dikshitar

Mami (Tamil): Mother's brother's wife, or a term of respect used to refer to older woman

Mangalyam (Sanskrit): Talisman tied round the wife's neck by the husband as a symbol of their marriage, to be removed only when/if the husband dies before her

Manoranjitam (Sanskrit): The climbing ylang-ylang or tail grape shrub found in India, Burma, southern China and Taiwan, with flowers renowned for their exotic fragrance

Mapillai (Tamil): Son-in-law

Maro (Hindi): Beat him/them!

Marugelara (Telugu): Song by Carnatic music composer Tyagaraja

Masal vadai (Tamil): Spicy fried snack made with Bengal gram

Maulvi (Urdu): Learned teacher or doctor of Islamic law, a learned Muslim who ministers to the religious needs of others.

Mithai kadai (Tamil): A sweet stall

Munsif (Urdu): A petty judge in civil courts in British India, with jurisdiction over villages and rural regions

Muthuswami Dikshitar, Syama Sastri, Tyagaraja: The greatest composers of Carnatic music

Nagumomu (Telugu): A song composed by the Carnatic maestro Tyagaraja

Nahi, tum jao (Hindi): No, you may go!

Naidu 'garu' (Telugu): A suffix to a person's name in Telugu, denoting respect

Nalangu (Tamil): A playful ceremony during the wedding rituals

Namaste or Namaskaram (Sanskrit): Traditional greeting with folded hands

Nansei (Tamil): Fertile wetland for agriculture

Panchang (Sanskrit): Hindu calendar and almanac, following traditional units of Hindu timekeeping, presenting important dates and calculations

Paniwala (Hindi): Vendor of water

Pannir (Tamil): Rose water

Patnam Subramania Iyer: Carnatic music composer of lively songs

Pattamaniam (Tamil): Village officer, formerly appointed by the district revenue establishment to collect land revenue

Patti (Tamil): Grandmother

Periamma (Tamil): Mother's elder sister

Postal runner: Officials employed to carry mailbags, including through jungles, hills, deserts and places without any other means of transport, and who were armed for self-defence with spears, to which bells were attached

Pottu (Tamil): Ornamental dot on the forehead

Prem nagar mein banaongi ghar (Hindi): I will build my home in the city of love

Puris (Hindi): Deep-fried bread made from unleavened whole-wheat flour that originated in the Indian subcontinent

Pyol (Tamil): Raised platform on the front verandah on one or both sides of the entrance

Quaid-e-azam zindabad (Urdu): Long live the great leader!

Rabindranath Tagore (1861–1941): Indian polymath, poet, writer, composer, philosopher and painter from Bengal, the first non-European and first lyricist to win the Nobel Prize in Literature

Saami (Tamil): God

Saheb (Urdu): Term of respect used to address or as a suffix to the name of a respected Muslim male

Sakuntalam (Sanskrit): Iconic play by classic Indian dramatist Kalidasa

Salwar: Loose pajama-like Indian trousers worn by men and women

Sanyasa: Renunciation

Saroja dalanetri (Telugu): Song by Carnatic music composer Syama Sastri

Seemantam (Sanskrit): A ritual performed by a couple expecting their first child

Seer: A traditional unit of mass and volume used in large parts of Asia prior to the middle of the twentieth century – in India it was equal to 1.25 kg (2.755778 lb)

Seth (Hindi): A term used in south India for north Indian businessmen

Seva nagar: The city of service

Silapadikaram (Tamil): *Tale of the Anklet*, the earliest Tamil epic c.100-250 CE, a poem of 5,730 lines detailing a tragic love story of a couple – Kannaki and her husband Kovalan

Subramania Bharati (1882–1921): Modern Tamil poet, journalist, writer, revolutionary Indian independence activist, social reformer, one of the greatest Tamil literary figures of all time

Sumangali prarthanai (Tamil): Ritual performed by the women of the house to honour a chosen group of married women (with living husbands), and pre-pubescent girls, before an imminent family function, particularly a wedding

Swayamvara (Sanskrit): A method of marriage in which a woman chooses a man as her husband from a group of suitors by placing a garland round the neck of the man of her choice

Tai (Tamil): Tenth month in the Tamil tradition corresponding to January and February, an auspicious time for weddings

Tali (Tamil): Tamil name for mangalyam (Sanskrit)

Tambi (Tamil): Younger brother, and an informal way of addressing a boy or a younger man

Thehro (Hindi): Wait! Stop!

Tonga (Hindi): A curricle drawn by one horse

Tumbai (Tamil): *Leucas aspera*, a plant species found throughout India with tiny white flowers, most commonly known as *Tumbai* or *Tumba*

Valaikappu (Tamil): A ceremony of adorning women expecting their first child with bangles

Vanaprastha (Sanskrit): The third forest-dwelling stage of the four stages of the brahmanic scheme of life

Varnashrama (Sanskrit): The caste system in Hindu society dividing members into four varnas – brahmin, kshatriya, vaishya and shudra

Vellala (Tamil): Generic term used to refer to various castes traditionally pursuing agriculture as a profession in the Indian states ofTamil Nadu, Kerala and north-eastern Sri Lanka

Veshti (Sanskrit): A type of sarong, a lower garment forming part of the national or ethnic costume for men in south India

Vinaashakaale vipareeta buddhi (Sanskrit): Doomsday generates perversity

Yagna (Sanskrit): A ritual sacrifice in Hinduism

Zamindar (Urdu): Landowner, especially one who leases his land to tenant farmers

TRANSLATOR'S ACKNOWLEDGEMENTS

I wish to thank:

Swarnima Narayan, Priyanka Sarkar, Abhivyakti Singh, Anupama Manral and Parul Sharma, whose intellectual and empathetic response to the text, sagacious editing, and tireless support through the blood and sweat of translating a major work of fiction, got me through this daunting project.

Mini Krishnan – whose passion for getting Indian writings translated remains unequalled – for introducing the text to Hachette India.

The Tamil Nadu Textbook and Educational Services Corporation for its generous support to this work of translation.

My uncle K. Rajendran, Kalki Krishnamurthy's son, whose recollections of his father writing this novel enthused me to pursue this project.

My husband V. Ramnarayan and son Abhinav Ramnarayan for their handholding and trust.

My daughter Akhila Ramnarayan and sister Rukmini Ramachandran who heard me read aloud the original novel in Tamil, with insightful comments and the conviction that the novel does not only have an urgent contemporary relevance, but an appeal for readers beyond the Tamil horizon.

Fellow translators who inspire me to persevere by continuing in their labours – though mostly overlooked, unrecognized, ignored, forgotten.

And of course, the reader. Without you, there is no book, no publishing, no literature, no writing, no translation.

